THE
VEIL OF A
THOUSAND TEARS

Tor Books by Eric Van Lustbader

The Ring of Five Dragons
The Veil of a Thousand Tears

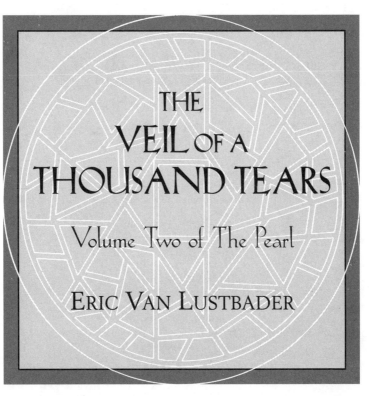

THE
VEIL OF A
THOUSAND TEARS

Volume Two of The Pearl

ERIC VAN LUSTBADER

TOR®
fantasy

A Tom Doherty Associates Book
New York

THE VEIL OF A THOUSAND TEARS

Copyright © 2002 Eric Van Lustbader

Map by Ellisa Mitchell

Edited by David G. Hartwell

A Tor Book
Published by Tom Doherty Associates, LLC
175 Fifth Avenue
New York, NY 10010

www.tor.com

Tor® is a registered trademark of Tom Doherty Associates, LLC.

Library of Congress Cataloging-in-Publication Data

Lustbader, Eric.
    Veil of a thousand tears / Eric Van Lustbader.—1st ed.
        p.   cm.—(The pearl ; v. 2)
    "A Tom Doherty Associates book."
    ISBN 0-312-87236-4 (alk. paper)
    I. Title.

PS3562.U752 V45 2002
813'.54—dc21

                                                                    2002019002

First Edition: July 2002

Printed in the United States of America

0 9 8 7 6 5 4 3 2 1

For David, Linda, and Tom

THE
VEIL OF A
THOUSAND TEARS

Unknown Territories

Djenn Marre Mts.

Great Rift

NORTH

Im-Thera   Site of Za-Hara-at

Bandichire   Agachire

Shelachire   Okkamchire

The Kornush

The Great Voorg

Kundala

The Northern Continent

2002 Ellis & Mitchell

Book One:

SUNKEN GATE

Of the fifteen Spirit Gates,
Sunken Gate is the one in which
the spirit lies, turning over leaves
of fortune and the future;
it is here that promise begins,
and dreaming ends.

—Utmost Source,
   The Five Sacred Books of Miina

1

Breach

Riane and Giyan were alone in the Library of the Abbey of Warm Current. It was midnight. A cold wind sighed through thorned sysal trees, and rhythmic pulses rippled through the dense bedrock beneath the abbey, where the power bourns wove themselves like strands of the Great Goddess Miina's ruddy hair.

The Library, columned, marble-clad, lay dreaming like a castle keep in the fastness of the fortresslike complex. The Ramahan abbey had been abandoned for many years before Riane and her friends—the Kundalan sorceress Giyan, the V'ornn Rhynnnon Rekkk Hacilar, the Kundalan Resistance leader Eleana, the Rappa named Thigpen—had made it their sanctuary some weeks before. Khagggun packs roamed the countryside searching for them. Once, they had swept through the abbey, and it was only Giyan's sorcery that had saved them. She had roused them from sleep and, gathering up all evidence of their stay, they had fled into the nearby forest, there to wait in stony silence for the enemy to depart.

The abbey itself, sacked decades before by the V'ornn invaders, was half-burned and crumbling when they had first come upon it. Gimnopedes nested in untidy eaves. Spiders turned shadowy corners into delicately veined cities. A beautiful sysal tree had, for decades, grown up through thick plaza paving to split the lintel of the east-facing temple. The hoary knuckles of its basal roots displaced the artful pattern of the stone, an ironic comment on how life reclaims the void and transforms it. The Library, alone, remained intact, having been protected by a powerful spell that Giyan had counteracted in order to gain entry.

Riane looked at Giyan, tall, slim, beautiful, golden, radiant, save for the blackened crusts of the sorcerous chrysalides that covered her hands and forearms. Even now, she could scarcely believe that they had been reunited. Giyan's presence gave her a sense of profound dislocation. She was not simply Riane, a sixteen-year-old orphaned Kundalan girl who could not remember her parents or where she came from. She was also the V'ornn Annon Ashera, eldest son of Eleusis Ashera. Eleusis had been regent of Kundala until a ruthless coup by his archenemy, Prime Factor Wennn Stogggul, and the head of Eleusis' own elite body-guard, Kinnnus Morcha.

Riane's searching gaze caught Giyan's whistleflower-blue eyes. "Every time you look at me I see surprise on your face."

Giyan's heart ached, for she heard the sentiment behind the formal words, the fragile sentence Riane could not bear to speak: Do you still love me? "It is a marvelous moment, to be here with you, alone, in private. To be able to call you Teyjattt." Teyj were the beautiful mul-ticolored four-winged birds the Gyrgon—the V'ornn technomage caste—bred and took with them wherever they went.

"Little Teyj. You loved calling me that when Annon was a child."

A sudden fear, a stab in Giyan's heart. "And Annon did not?"

A moment's pause. "Annon did not, I think, appreciate your love. He did not know what to do with it."

"It is odd the way you phrase it."

"I am no longer Annon." Riane spread her hands. "Annon is dead. All Kundala knows it."

"And we? What do we know?"

Riane looked up at the magnificent dome of the Library, encrusted with a mosaic of Kundala and the sinuous star constellations surround-ing it. Composed of millions of tiny colored glass tiles, fitted cunningly together as only the Kundalan artisans could, the dome produced an ethereal glow like a perpetual sunrise or sunset. Beneath this sheltering sky she felt safe from both Annon's enemies and those of the Dar Sala-at. For Annon was not simply the heir to the Ashera Consortium. He and the former Riane together—this unique fused entity—were the Dar Sala-at, the chosen one of Miina, prophesied to find The Pearl, the most powerful, mysterious, and ancient artifact of Kundala, to lead the Kun-dalan out of their one-hundred-and-one-year enslavement to the tech-nologically superior V'ornn.

"Here, alone, together," she said at length, "we can share a dead past. Like ghosts conjuring the root stew of life."

"Stirring the cauldron."

"Yes." Riane smiled a painful smile. "Making something special of it."

She saw movement out of the corner of her eye. The vigilant figure of Rekkk Hacilar passed before the high, leaded window to the east. His long, tapering, hairless skull was cloaked in a battle helm fashioned, it was said, from the skull of a fallen Krael, and he held his shock-sword at the ready. His purple armor glittered darkly. Once a Khaggun—the V'ornn military caste—he had declared himself Rhynnnon, turning his back on his caste, turning his efforts to a greater cause. In this case, he had dedicated himself to the service of the now dead Gyrgon, Nith Sahor. Because Nith Sahor wanted the Dar Sala-at found and kept safe, Rekkk had sworn himself to protect Riane. Now he was also Giyan's lover.

"We have been given a unique gift, haven't we?" Giyan said. "A second chance."

Rekkk, in the ruins of the courtyard outside, began a ritualistic set of thrusts and parries with Eleana. She was the same age as Riane. Her V'ornn shock-sword looked massive in her delicate white hands, but she swung the twin blades deftly through the night air. Under Rekkk's tutelage she was quickly becoming an expert in its use. They practiced endlessly. He said it took his mind off his wounds, physical and emotional.

Riane watched her for a moment, her heart in her throat. Annon and Eleana had fallen in love. Now, like everyone else, Eleana believed Annon was dead. As for Riane—this new Riane—she loved Eleana still, and did not know what to make of this love or what to do with it.

Giyan, attendant to Riane's gaze, said, "You long to tell her, I know."

"I love her so. I will always love her."

"And your love makes you want to confess everything." Riane's silence was as good as an answer. "But you cannot. If you tell her who you really are, you put her life—and yours—in grave jeopardy."

"She is Resistance. She is used to secrets."

"Not this kind. It will be too much. Like a mountain on her shoulders."

"Perhaps you underestimate her."

They all heard the sound at once and froze. Their eyes rose skyward as the drone of the Khaggun hoverpods, bristling with ion cannons, flattened the soughing of the wind, silenced the twitter of night birds. There ensued a period of heart-pounding terror, as if the breathable elements were being sucked from the atmosphere. They could see the pale ion trails, ephemeral as smoke, lighted by moonlight, making baleful runes beneath the tremulous clouds. Tense moments later, the drone drifted away, fading from an echo into a stillness that made their ears ache.

Riane and Giyan exchanged a look of relief, and Riane returned her gaze to Eleana, her eyes filled with the girl's lithe movements. Dark lashes. Moonlight on her cheekbones. Soft swell of her belly. "Or is it something else? You do not trust her."

"It isn't simply a matter of trust," Giyan said carefully.

"Isn't it?" Riane said this rather more sharply than she had intended.

"I have told you. It is written in Prophesy that of the Dar Sala-at's allies one will love her, one will betray her, one will try to destroy her."

"It could not mean Eleana. Not her."

"No." Giyan's voice was soft, gentling. "You would not think so, I know."

"She is carrying Kurgan's child." Kurgan was Wennn Stogggul's eldest son; he had once been Annon's best friend. "She will need our help and support in the days ahead."

"You are the Dar Sala-at. You have larger issues to contend with."

"She is still haunted by her rape at Kurgan's hands. What is larger than an individual's anguish?"

"The destiny of our people."

"The destiny of our people is built on anguish. You of all Kundalan would be the first to acknowledge that."

Giyan gazed in astonishment at Riane, golden-haired, sun-bronzed, firm-muscled from her beloved mountain climbing, and thought that this strong, beautiful girl might easily have sprung from her loins had she taken a Kundalan between her thighs. "You must forgive me, Teyjattt," she said. "I have lived my entire life with secrets. First, keeping hidden my Gift for Osoru sorcery, which has been daemonized by the Ramahan. Then, concealing my status as Lady from the V'ornn, who would have killed me had they known. Finally, keeping your true identity a secret, which, had it become known, would have gotten you killed. These have been the boundaries of my life."

Through the five arched windows set into the Library's thick walls, light from two of Kundala's five moons fired the glass tiles, lending them the depth of three dimensions. Giyan, caught in the moonsglow, seemed to throb with sorcerous energy. Her white robes were pale as the snow cloaking the jagged crests of the massive Djenn Marre mountain chain to the north. Her hands and forearms, dead black from the chrysalides covering them, were the only parts of her that did not shine like beacons. The chrysalides had formed after she had violated the sacred circle of the Nanthera, in a futile attempt to keep Annon alive. Well she might have, since he was her son. She had borne the son of the regent, Eleusis Ashera. This was a potentially dangerous fact she had told no one, not Rekkk, not Annon himself. From the beginning, Eleusis had impressed upon her the need for absolute secrecy. Periodically, the Gyrgon sent Khagggun packs to round up the children born to Kundalan females as a result of V'ornn rapes. These half-breeds, though outwardly looking like any other V'ornn, were taken by V'ornn Genomatekks to Receiving Spirit, the vast medical facility in Axis Tyr that had once been a Kundalan hospice. What experiments were perpetrated upon them there even Eleusis had not been able to discover.

Giyan shook her head. "Still, I will not tell you what to do. This must be your decision."

"Whatever decision I make," Riane said, "I promise you that it will not be a rash one."

"I cannot ask for more, Dar Sala-at."

She returned her attention to the book Giyan had given her to study. Giyan, like her twin, was a Ramahan priestess. But, unlike Bartta who had practiced Kyofu, the Black Dreaming sorcery, before her death in a sorcerous conflagration, she was a practitioner of Osoru, Five Moon sorcery. Riane, too, had the Gift; Giyan had passed it on to Annon. She was just beginning her Osoru studies, but she was impatient to become a sorceress-adept like Giyan. Though Stogggul and Morcha were dead, though she had defeated the powerful Kyofu sorceress Malistra, the Dar Sala-at's enemies were legion. And far more powerful than Malistra. They had worked their dark schemes and plots through her; when she had died, Riane was certain, they had moved on, enlisting others to battle for them. But there was another matter, more immediate, that needed explaining.

She set down the book full of complex Old Tongue runes, and approached Giyan. Dust motes hung suspended in the air, flaring as they hit the lamplight. One full moon, the palest green of new grass, hung suspended in a pane of glass, an insect caught in a spider's web.

"Have you so quickly finished your lesson, Teyjattt?" Thick hair of spun copper cascaded around Giyan's long neck, settled on her square shoulders like liquid light.

"In truth, my mind is too filled with questions to absorb any more." Riane put her hands on the long ammonwood refectory table that ran the length of the Library. "You must tell me if you know why I wasn't able to open the Storehouse Door."

For the longest time Giyan said nothing. Doubtless she was thinking, as Riane was, of the Storehouse Door set eons ago by Miina into the caverns beneath Middle Palace.

The Storehouse was where Miina had secreted The Pearl for the time when Prophesy said it would be needed. Kundalan lore held that it could only be reopened by the Dar Sala-at, using the Ring of Five Dragons. But the Door could only be opened by the Dar Sala-at. Defeating the Dark sorceress Malistra, Riane had tried to open the Door with the Ring, but it had stayed firmly shut. Why?

Giyan was about to speak when sudden pain clouded her features. She gasped, grabbed at the chrysalid on her right forearm.

"Giyan—"

"It is all right," she whispered. "Already the pain is passing." Beads of perspiration hung in her hairline.

"I want to help."

"Alas, wanting will not make it so." Tears trembled in the corners of her eyes. She was white-faced, and took a moment to compose herself before she went on. "There is only one reason the Ring of Five Dragons would not open the Door for you. Miina put one last safeguard in place when She built the Storehouse. Impossible as it sounds, the Portal between this realm and the Abyss has somehow been breached. There are daemons here where they have been banished for eons. As long as they are in this realm, the Door cannot be opened even by you."

Riane felt her heart turn over painfully in her chest. "The Tzelos—"

"Yes. You have seen the Tzelos twice, once as part of a spell cast on you, once as a sorcerous Avatar of Kyofu. But I must conclude that the Tzelos has manifested itself here. It is a daemon from the Abyss. It has crossed over into our world."

"But how?"

Giyan's eyes grew dark. "I fear it is my doing."

"Yours? I do not understand."

"Conjuring the Nanthera posed grave risks," Giyan said. "Not the least of which was opening the Portal to the Abyss." In a last-ditch effort to save Annon from his enemies, Giyan and Bartta had conjured the Nanthera, temporarily opening a forbidden Portal to the Abyss. Thus, Annon's essence, all that made him unique, had been transmigrated into the body of Riane, a Kundalan girl dying of duur fever. He was saved while his V'ornn body was delivered up to his enemies. Thus had he joined with Riane to become the Dar Sala-at, the chosen of Miina. Upon this new Riane rested the future of Kundala.

"But you told me that the Nanthera does so under a number of careful and powerful safeguards."

"True. But I violated one of them. I reached back through the sorcerous circle to try to get you. I couldn't help myself. I . . ." She put a hand to her head.

Riane encircled her with her arm. "Even if you are right, even if that is what has happened, what's done is done. It doesn't matter how the Portal seal was violated. What matters is sealing it again."

Giyan shook her head. "It is more complicated than that, Dar Sala-at. When Miina created the Abyss to imprison the daemons and archdaemons, She seeded it with seven Portals, each of which She provided with a different sorcerous lock. This was a safeguard. Even if an archdaemon—Pyphoros or one of his three offspring—somehow managed to slip through one Portal, the other locks should protect us. For only when all seven Portals are opened simultaneously can all the daemons escape into our realm." Giyan walked back and forth in a tight anxious orbit. "The real problem is not the Tzelos but the archdaemon who brought it through."

Riane stared at her. "An archdaemon in this realm?"

"The consequences will be catastrophic," Giyan said. "Unless we can find the archdaemon and somehow neutralize him, the damage he can do is incalculable."

"But surely if he is here someone would have seen this . . . archdaemon by now."

"On the contrary. Archdaemons cannot appear for long in their own form until all the seven Portals are open. They must take hosts—possess them, work through them. Their infiltration is more difficult to detect and therefore more insidious. Legend tells us that their control of their hosts is imprecise. The hosts' actions may, from time to time, appear out of character because the archdaemon does not have immediate access to all their knowledge. However, that can change over time."

"We must either destroy them both or return them to the Abyss," Riane said. "Otherwise, I will never be able to open the Storehouse Door. I will never find The Pearl."

Giyan, flexing her fingers inside their eerie shells, smiled grimly. "We must speed up your sorcerous training. Thigpen and I can only do so much. Miina's Sacred Texts, *Utmost Source* and *The Book of Recantation*, both of which you have read, require interpretation so that you may understand the inner workings of language as science, science as sorcery. The interpretations require the precise mixtures, constructs of phrases, incantations, theories, ideas, whispers, shadows, and light. Once you have absorbed these lessons, you must practice those interpretations over and over until they are ingrained in you, until they become part of you."

A shadow passed across Riane's face. "Mother could have taught me," she whispered. "But Mother is dead." She was wearing turquoise silk robes made from Mother's garments after a terrible Kyofu spell had caused Riane mistakenly to kill her. The murder had been foretold in Prophesy, but that did not make it any easier to live with.

Giyan stirred. When she gazed at her child, transformed, she saw great promise, but never without the pain of regret. Regret that she could never tell Annon that he was her son, regret that she had been forced to hide him inside Riane, to leave Riane with Bartta, who had abused Riane terribly. Claws in the lining of her stomach.

"Mother would have been the first to tell you that no one teacher will suffice." She vibrated with her child's sorrow, wished she could take it all upon herself. "Your journey is long, Dar Sala-at, arduous and complex. There is someone who I must get you to as quickly as possible. She will commence your studies. Her name is Jonnqa. She is an imari at Nimbus, a kashiggen in the Northern Quarter of Axis Tyr."

"What could a mistress of pleasure at a salamuuun palace have to teach me?"

A small smile played across Giyan's lips. "Again you sound like a V'ornn. I know you are impatient, Teyjattt, but you must get it through your head that you have much to learn. There are no shortcuts, sorcerous or otherwise. As I said, the Dar Sala-at's path is a most difficult one. Up to now your life has been as a male V'ornn of high privilege or as a Ramahan cloistered in the Abbey of Floating White. In both instances you were protected from the everyday world. Both these lives are now at an end."

"I do not understand."

Giyan turned around the book she had been reading so Riane could see the Old Tongue text. "You see here, in the days before the V'ornn, when lightning played across the sky, when all of Miina's magical beasts—the Rappa, the narbuck, the perwillon, even the Ja-Gaar and the Five Sacred Dragons—roamed the land and the skies, all Kundalan were in harmony." She turned the page. "Females and males alike shared everything, including power. The Ramahan, too, included priests and priestesses."

"But then a cabal of male Ramahan wrested control from Mother," Riane said. "They held her captive for more than a century."

"Until you found her and freed her." Giyan, sensing Riane's disquiet, continued. "But here is the important thing. Nowadays, male Kundalan treat our females as inferiors, just as the male V'ornn do their own females. This is what you will be up against when you venture out into the world." She closed the book with a snap. "It makes my blood run cold. It is a manifestation of the worst thing the V'ornn have done to us. Do you know what that is, Riane?"

"That they have taken away our freedom."

"That is evil, but it is not the worst."

"That they have killed and tortured tens of thousands of us."

"Terrible, yes." She shook her head. "But the worst is being done now, systematically. The V'ornn use time, ideas, the masses against us. Why do you think the youngest Kundalan males treat their female counterparts with contempt? Because it is all they know. Each day brings new converts to the new Goddessless religion of Kara. Where did Kara begin, do you think? With the V'ornn, of course."

Riane was startled. "Are you certain? Annon did not know this."

"I daresay most V'ornn do not. It is a device of Gyrgon origin. And yet it continues to win converts. With every generation the great Kundalan narrative that Miina labored so hard and long to teach Her children is being eaten away by V'ornn acid. You saw as much when you were at the Abbey of Floating White. Osoru is no longer taught, Sacred Scripture has been distorted beyond recognition. And the worst part is that those distortions are being accepted by the acolytes. They cannot see the truth because the morality inside the abbey has been murdered, and without morality truth has no dominion."

Tears stood in the corners of Giyan's eyes. Riane felt her pain as if it were her own. The V'ornn-ness inside her recoiled at the words, at the emotions, at the implication of what the V'ornn had perpetrated. This disconnect made her feel weak and dizzy, so that she was obliged to grab the table edge lest she pitch over onto the gleaming floor.

"Understand this, Riane," Giyan whispered. "Time is the great ally of the liar because when lies are repeated long enough, the truth fades and is forgotten. Then the lies become the truth. History is remade, and all is lost."

Riane thought of how Bartta, who had run the abbey, had murdered her friend Asta and pretended it was an accident. She recalled how Bartta had tortured her and almost killed her. Bartta was wicked, but Bartta had come to believe the distortions and lies she herself had made up. She was perpetrator and victim rolled into one.

"And yet . . ."

Giyan's whistleflower-blue eyes regarded her levelly, and a kind of current passed between them, a language of their own design begun with Annon's first memory. What a powerful thing such a language can be, for it flows in the blood, informs the bone with unshakable knowledge.

"And yet, what mystery beats within the V'ornn heart," Giyan whispered. "There was Eleusis, brave, compassionate Eleusis; there is Rekkk, brave, compassionate Rekkk. And most mysterious of all, perhaps, there was the Gyrgon Nith Sahor, who gave his life for us."

"And yet, what mystery beats within the Kundalan heart," Riane answered her, "for you to raise Annon and not hate him as a mortal enemy, for you to love him as if he were your own flesh and blood, for you to save him from the enemies of the Ashera at risk to your own life."

"The enemies of the Ashera are my enemies," Giyan said simply.

When she spoke thus her power was undeniable, defeating even that last bastion of V'ornn maleness that still beat within Riane's soul.

"I love you, Giyan," Riane said. "I find it miraculous that you of all Kundalan are the Lady destined to guide the Dar Sala-at."

"I love you more than life itself, Teyjattt." A tear slid down Giyan's cheeks. She reached out for her child, but could feel nothing through the inconstant electrical jolts delivered by the chrysalides.

"Together we will labor to bring back Miina's sacred narrative in all its glory," Riane said with a resolved heart.

"I fear we will labor greatly."

Riane felt something inside her quail. She knew from experience that there was something oracular about Giyan. Then Annon's V'ornn-ness took over, and she said: "If this is our destiny, then so be it."

Giyan smiled through her tears. "When you speak thus I am re-minded of Nith Sahor. I miss him. His death was a terrible loss to our cause."

"I only met the Gyrgon once." Riane said. "But without his help I would not have reached the Storehouse Door in time to stop the Tym-nos device from destroying Kundala."

"You would have appreciated his wisdom, might very well have come to like him. It is a great pity he was an anomaly among Gyrgon."

For the first time, Riane saw the title of the book Giyan had been reading: *Darkness and Its Constituents*. She gestured with a sun-bronzed hand. "Is the Tzelos described in there?"

Giyan smiled grimly and reopened the book. Riane saw a line draw-ing, filling up an entire page, precise as an architectural blueprint, of the horrific beast she had seen in Otherwhere. The drawing was fas-cinating and repellent at the same time.

"A profane experiment of Pyphoros' gone terribly wrong," Giyan said. "Like all his experiments."

"What was he trying to do?"

"Create life, something only the Maker can do."

"The Great Goddess Miina?"

"Can give life, so it is written. But that is not the same. Even Miina is not the Maker. She cannot create a new life out of the elemental components of the Cosmos."

"But She created Kundala."

"Ah, no. She bade the Sacred Dragons to create Kundala, and they did so with the help of The Pearl. They caused matter to cleave to matter. They brought fire and air, water and earth. Metal from dark distant stars. When Kundala was born, in the Time before the Imag-ining, the hand of the Maker moved and the Kundalan appeared."

Riane stood for a time absorbing her words. The weight of history lay upon the shelves ringing the Library, voices of Kundalan ancestors disturbed from their long slumber by the discussion of Creation. The faintest stirring seemed to play against her cheek, a liquification of the light reflected off the mosaic sky, the exhalations of generations past. Hopes, fears, dreams alive here in the twinkling mosaic stars, the burnished continents, the rakkis-dark seas. She felt all over again her deep and abiding love for this woman who had raised Annon, who had saved him from certain death, who had been willing to sacrifice everything, including her life, to save the V'ornn child she had raised. Part of her would never understand that miracle; another part felt only gratitude.

Typical. The V'ornn searched for answers to everything—this is, doubtless, what led the species to continue its long lonely quest through the Cosmos. This is doubtless what drove the Gyrgon to continue their mysterious experiments. Looking for the answers: who are we, where did we come from, where are we going. It was said that the Gyrgon lusted after immortality, that they wished for nothing less grand than to be like the god, Enlil, they had rejected. Was it the truth? No one knew. The Gyrgon were masters of secrecy, subterfuge, misdirection. They were already demigods in their way, powerful, manipulative, remote. Except for Nith Sahor.

"And where was Miina?" Riane asked with a teenager's directness. "Did She see the Maker?"

"She slept," Giyan said with the simple power of faith. "And when She woke, we were here, Her name already on our lips."

She would have continued. Her mouth was partly open, the next words about to be released, when she felt a dreadful hammerblow of pain. With a moan, she slid to her knees, hugging her arms close to her slender waist. Riane knelt beside her, held her as tenderly as once Giyan had held Annon when his young body had trembled with ague.

At that moment, a shadow fell between them, and they looked out the window to see a crowned owl crossing before the full moon on huge silent brindled wings. An omen, Giyan thought, her heart constricting. Miina has sent us a sign.

And then it seemed as if the crowned owl had crashed through the window, or perhaps it was the moonslight itself that had been transmogrified to a solid column of energy. The books flew off the table, their pages ruffling like the feathers of angry birds. Others exploded off the shelves, great ranks rising in unison in response to the disturbance.

Riane herself was flung backward, skidding across the floor, trying to right herself, being shoved sideways by the unknown force. She fetched up against a heavy ammonwood chair, which had crashed over onto its side. A leg struck her rib cage painfully.

She saw Giyan, her back arched, her arms stretched upward, pulled as if by invisible cords. Drafts of air, cold as death, circled the Library, howling, so that when Riane tried to call out to Giyan her voice was swept away. Riane's heart turned over. As she watched with mounting horror, Giyan rose into the air.

An eerie glow was emanating from the chrysalides that covered Giyan's hands and forearms. They were black no longer, but had begun to turn an ash grey. As their color lightened, thin layers peeled off and, like plates of armor, whirled around and around in the vortex. Upon reaching the periphery, they were hurled like ice-white missiles, slicing through books, furniture. They lodged in the fluted columns, in the carved lintels above the doors, in the walls themselves. Riane ducked as one passed centimeters from her head. It made a sinister whistling sound as it spun away like the beveled blades of a fan.

She tried to stand and fell back in a heap. All the heat was being sucked out of the Library. A chill entered her bones, sheathing them in pearly frost, making of their marrow a dry white ash. Breath caught in her lungs, painful as a sandstorm, as if the air itself were being torn asunder, remade into something dark, dense with menace, wicked as sin.

At last, the chrysalides had let go of Giyan, the sheaths had come off, and her hands and forearms stood revealed, thick with sinuous red veins and ropey yellow arteries, standing out in convolute profusion.

Her eyes were wide and staring, their blue turned an eerie opalescent white, and in their center pinprick black pupils. Her mouth was drawn back in the rictus normally associated with death. Through her long, thickly flowing hair was now wound shards of a dark metallic substance that at once cradled the back of her head, curling up into cork-screwed points, a kind of thorned crown, living things that shifted and shimmered in the lamplight, glimmered and glistened as they wove themselves into a pattern of hideous design.

The moonlight, flooding through the rent window, was pale, insubstantial. The dust motes held in its columns shivered. Riane felt herself caught as if in a deep dream, her limbs felt like deadweights, her thoughts slow as frozen sap. As in a nightmare, she felt both terrified and helpless. She had the presence of mind to understand that her very helplessness compounded the terror, and yet that knowledge was of little use to her. Her mind was filled with an awful martial drumbeat that foretold her losing Giyan once again. She did not think that she could bear it.

But now there was no more time for thought. Giyan fixed her with her bizarre and frightening white eyes and her left arm came down, describing a shallow arc that brought her hand to point directly at Riane. Riane could see in the center of each palm a corkscrewed spike similar to the elements of the thorned crown piercing her flesh right through, though there was no blood or even any semblance of a wound. Rather, the spike seemed part of her, as, indeed, the crown seemed to have grown from the bones of her skull.

She saw the vein-wrapped forefinger unfurl, the black nail, long and gleaming, extending from it. Riane felt displaced, separated from the world around her. Her Third Eye opened in response to the horror and saw blood all around her, buckets of blood, cauldronsful, a veritable ocean of blood, life draining away down an ancient stone drain clogged with eons of blackened moss and decay, the slimy debris of time. Here was a moment she would remember all her life, a moment that would haunt her waking hours and stalk her dreams, Giyan is dead, long live . . . What? What foul beast had the Lady become?

As best she could, she cast about for a counterspell to the sorcerous transformation the chrysalides had worked on Giyan, but she knew so few spells, and none of them seemed right. *You are untrained. Even with a power as great as yours you are at a grave disadvantage against your enemies without the knowledge of the ancients*, Mother had told her. *This is why you must exercise extreme caution. This is why you must keep your identity hidden as much as you can until your schooling in the sorcerous arts is complete.*

Oh, yes, Mother was right. And so was Giyan. Her enemies had wasted no time in mounting another attack. In desperation, she spoke the words of the Old Tongue, conjuring Earth Granary, the most potent of Osoru healing spells.

At almost the same instant, she heard the quick sizzle, as of frying flesh. It made her skin crawl, her heart beat fast. And then all the breath was knocked out of her as the sorcerous spell hit her dead on. It was well that she had cast Earth Granary, for it afforded her a measure of protection, the difference between life and death.

She flickered between consciousness and unconsciousness as she crawled painfully across the Library floor, and she set all her reserves of energy into redoubling the spell, holding it close around her, so that it would not fly apart in a thousands shreds, exposing her entirely to the ferocious attack.

And, then, there it was, leaking from the suppurating ends of Giyan's fingertips: the Tzelos, writhing in its noncorporeal state as the thing that had been Giyan gave birth to the daemon from the Abyss.

The rotting cor-meat stink of the Tzelos assaulted her. It was black as steaming pitch, its twelve-legged body segmented like an insect's, its bloated thorax protected by a hard carapace. Its long flat ugly head, brown-black, shiny as obsidian, was guarded by monstrous serrated mandibles. Twelve faceted eyes, burning like garnets, fixed on her.

Riane struggled to rise as the spell dissipated, drew her dagger, preparing to defend herself. Giyan was moving, but Riane's attention was wholly taken up with the advancing Tzelos. And then she saw something out of the corner of her eye, a furry, six-limbed creature with triangular ears, a long, striped, puffy tail, and dark, intelligent eyes. Thigpen was Rappa.

"Thigpen, get back!" Riane cried.

The creature ignored her. Shaking off her dizziness, she grabbed an upended lamp, hurled it in a sidearm motion. It struck the Tzelos and passed right through it. An illusion, just like the one that had appeared when she had mistakenly killed Mother. The Tzelos rushed at her, and she instinctively steeled herself.

"Ignore it," Thigpen said. "Use your Third Eye to distinguish what is real and what is not."

Riane felt a brief chill, like ice sliding down the back of her neck. Giyan began to rise off the ground. Her arms were spread wide, her head thrust slightly back, her jaw clenched and set. Employing the sorcerous sight from her Third Eye, Riane detected another presence inside Giyan. It coiled inside her like a gigantic serpent, spiraling up her spine. With a sickening shock, Riane realized that it had entered her brain. The presence was levitating her.

Riane watched, stunned, as Giyan, her long hair writhing like a nest of bloodworms, flew toward the broken window and passed through it.

"We must not allow her to escape," Thigpen cried.

"Something has taken possession of her! I can feel it!" Riane said. "What is happening?"

"It is Malasocca," Thigpen whispered. "It means 'Dark Night of the Soul.' I do not know the way of it; I'm not sure anyone alive does. But I understand this much: piece by piece, her spirit is being replaced by that of a daemon. If we cannot stop her, if she heeds the call, if she vanishes, she will be lost to us, Riane. Lost for all time." Thigpen was scampering across the floor, ignoring the shards of glass that stuck to the pads of her slender handlike paws. "Worse, she will be replaced by our most implacable enemy."

"How do we stop that from happening?"

"If the host body is destroyed, the daemon is returned to the Abyss," Thigpen said.

"I will not kill her."

"It is the way of the Malasocca," Thigpen replied.

"There must be another way."

"I do not know of any. The daemon is still vulnerable now, but not for much longer."

"Still. I will not harm her."

Thigpen's whiskers were twitching, a sure sign of her acute distress. "I love Giyan as much as you do, Dar Sala-at, but terrible forces have been unleashed. Before this is over, you may very well wish you had killed her while you had the chance."

Riane, gaining the windowsill, balanced precariously for a moment, gathering equilibrium and momentum before launching herself upward with outstretched arms, grabbing Giyan around the ankles. Thigpen, just behind her, shrieked a warning as she leapt to the ground.

Giyan glared down, her unholy eyes alight, and cold fire sprang from her fingertips. Riane cried out and released her grip, falling two meters into the sere grass just outside the shattered window. Above, the pale fire traveled across her back until it reached the image of the Tzelos. There, it seemed to be sucked up into the daemon's outline, filling it out, causing it to pulse and glow. A nasty rustling arose, as of an army of insects ominously on the march.

The Tzelos swiveled its flat triangular head. A kind of crusty substance bubbled out of a series of palpitating apertures behind its faceted eyes. Its wicked-looking mandibles clicked together. Riane could see

Rekkk and Eleana, weapons raised, approaching the daemon. But surely it was the sight of Giyan so hideously transformed that caused the look of consternation on their faces.

"Lady—" Eleana began before she choked on her words.

"Giyan, what the N'Luuura has befallen you?" Rekkk's face was white and strained.

"The chrysalides have broken open," Riane said.

"We must help her." Thigpen regarded them each in turn with her dark intelligent eyes. "Mercy, yes, we must help her now or all is lost."

Rekkk leapt over the wreckage of the broken window. Fearless, Eleana was just behind him. The Tzelos reared up on three sets of hind legs. Its upper appendages lashed out, trailing glistening cilia behind them. A wedge of mouth opened just as Rekkk swung his shock-sword and the Tzelos vomited up a gout of a yellow sticky substance that clung to the blades. The pitch of their vibration altered, causing a blow-back pulse that sent a wave of agonizing pain up Rekkk's arm.

Eleana was following in his wake, her shock-sword drawn back. Riane could see the tension in her arm, saw her concentrated completely on the daemon, saw what she failed to see, Giyan's right arm sweeping downward and, with it, a shower of crystalline sparks. A terrified gimnopede, frightened out of its nest, launched upward. Caught in the spiral band of the sparks, it turned black and rigid, plummeting like a rock to the ground.

The spirals were almost at Eleana's height when Riane threw herself forward. Eleana skittered, her booted foot slipping, and, as she toppled over, the scythes of crystalline sparks passed centimeters above her. Riane caught her, cradled her, aware in one all-encompassing instant that Eleana's heat and warmth, her scent, wound around her, binding her.

Just above where they lay, the air was sizzling, momentarily drained of heat. Then Eleana, the entire world, dropped away down a well. Riane felt the dislocation that came when she shed her corporeal body, crossed over into Ayame, the deep trance-state of Osoru.

In Otherwhere, she confronted a horrible sight: the great bird Ras Shamra, Giyan's sorcerous Avatar, was caged, its powerful wings pinioned at its side. The image of the real Giyan was imprisoned by some unknown wicked force. Ras Shamra saw her, uttered a soul-shattering cry that shook the very foundations of the sorcerous realm. When Riane tried to approach the cage, Ras Shamra became frantic, shrieking over and over, throwing its body against the bars until it bled in many places.

"Stop! Stop!" Riane cried. *"I only want to help you!"*

But Ras Shamra would not stop. If anything, as Riane approached, the Avatar become even more frantic.

Riane began the ritual for the Star of Evermore, the spell she had used to free Mother, to try to break the bars of the sorcerous cage. But as she did so, a shadow fell over Otherwhere. She looked up, the incantation frozen in her throat. A great Eye was opening, the Eye of Ajbal, and now she knew why Ras Shamra was shrieking. It was trying to warn her. She knew she was no match for this powerful spell. Indeed, it had once almost undone Giyan herself.

"Don't give up," she said to the image of Giyan. *"I will come back for you, no matter how long it takes."*

Giving Ras Shamra one last look of longing, she abandoned Otherwhere, only to hear Thigpen's sorrowful cry:

"Gone."

Eleana and Rekkk turned at the hollow sound emanating from deep inside Thigpen.

The Rappa was weeping, crystalline tears rolling freely down her furred cheeks, dripping off her muzzle. "She's gone."

And they saw she was right. The daemon Tzelos had vanished into the night sky and, with her, their beloved Giyan.

2

Rescendance

The V'ornn regent's palace in Axis Tyr, once the Ramahan Middle Palace, was a seething hive of activity. Lines of functionaries, ministers, petitioners from all castes snaked through the long, columned, light-strewn antechambers, overflowed the vast and magnificent public rooms like surf at high tide. All were clamoring for a fragment of the new regent's attention.

Kurgan, ignoring them, ignoring the duties of his office, went up a staircase where he was sure to avoid being seen and walked quickly and silently through his quarters. These private chambers were much changed. In the days when Eleusis Ashera had ruled the space they exhibited the sober orderliness of the career diplomat. Intimate groupings of chairs where Eleusis met with ministers and brokered deals were surrounded by mementos of a career built upon judicious compromise. It was, at bedrock, a working residence. After Kurgan's father, Wennn Stogggul, had Eleusis Ashera assassinated and briefly attained the office of regent, he had employed a host of Mesagggun and Tuskugggun to transform the residence. The result was a kind of opulence rarely seen save among an elite cadre of Bashkir lords. Over his family's protestations, Kurgan had immediately auctioned off his father's vast collection of artwork, a deliberate act of cruelty and disrespect that had pleased him immensely. Nowadays, the chambers had about them the spare, masculine functionality of a Khagggun Line-General's quarters. Racks of war trophies—weapons stripped from the alien dead on far-flung battlefields light-years distant—hung upon the walls in precisely aligned rows, gleaming with oil and wax, cataloged, arrayed in alphabetical order.

But he often felt stifled here. Worse, bored and disgusted, surrounded as he was by ministers, court Bashkir, aides, flunkies, and the like. Having mastered the art of appearing busy while doing nothing at all, they were worse than contemptible; they were deadly dull. He discovered that they expended astonishing effort defending their tiny slice of the fiefdom, to the ruination of those around them. They were like wyr-hounds, sun-dazed by the dazzle of the regent's court. They barked and bit each other mercilessly. These efforts had with an alarming swiftness begun to emit the foul odor of inertia. And yet, as Star-Admiral Olnnn Rydddlin had pointed out, he was powerless to dismiss them because of their intimate knowledge of the day-to-day functioning of the regent's office, whose complexities were staggering. As far as he could see, the weight of protocol kept the functioning to the bare minimum. Quite un-V'ornnlike, in his opinion, and it made him wonder whether this situation had been created by the Gyrgon to keep the regent from making any changes at all. This stasis he meant to crack wide open, whether or not the Gyrgon approved.

Axis Tyr was the center of life on Kundala. But in a way only he could comprehend this was beside the point. Axis Tyr was a city tainted by ignominious defeat, a place that in Kundalan lore had been holy and now was desecrated by the V'ornn occupation. In fact, the V'ornn were headquartered in the city's two most sacred structures. As regent, he lived and worked here, the former Middle Palace, while the Gyrgon had transformed the Abbey of Listening Bone into their Temple of Mnemonics.

Truth to tell, what he liked best was to see for himself these humiliations, to see these open wounds in the hollow-eyed stares of the Kundalan who were allowed into the city. Their diminished status enlarged him all the more. Due to V'ornn innovation and technology, Axis Tyr was a humming metropolis beneath the sadness and despair. Kundalan plots were everywhere—in fact, to Olnnn's dismay Kurgan encouraged them. He could sense the desperation that accompanied the formation of ragged cadres, misaligned alliances, jury-rigged governments-in-exile. Snatches of seemingly innocent conversations overheard down this alley or along the edge of that plaza harbored secrets that made the air tremble like the rising of heat currents. It was a game—ferreting out the collusion, identifying the conspirators, apprehending them just when it appeared to them that they were on the verge of success. Then he had the pleasure of meting out the punishment for their transgressions.

Beyond the regent's quarters lay a vast labyrinth of rooms, corridors, loggias largely unexplored since the time the Ramahan who had ruled from this place were slaughtered. He walked through the chambers, ornate in the fevered Kundalan style, whose purposes were long forgotten. Now they were littered with goblets and plates, furry with cobwebs and dust. Vestiges of unknown celebrations or rites. Through skylights, oculi, open loggias were patinaed by the melancholy autumnal light. Frescoes frowned down at him. Sculptures were rendered irrelevant by the long occupation. Fueled by his hatred for his father, he had spent a great deal of time and effort in the meticulous planning of his ascension to the regency but none at all in the contemplation of the office itself.

How hollow rang the silence in the aftermath of his victory! He had burned to become regent. Aided by Olnnn Rydddlin, he had concocted an intricate scheme whereby his father and his mentor, once allies, had destroyed each other. But now that he had achieved his dream the seemingly self-reproducing minutiae of running a planet were plowing him under. How had Eleusis Ashera had the patience to deal with this host of jabbering sycophants? No wonder his own father had been a failure at it. He hated Eleusis all the more for excelling at something for which he himself clearly lacked all aptitude.

A sickly-sweet odor was everywhere absorbed into the furniture, the carpets, even, he was convinced, the marble-clad walls which, when he came near, seemed to exude the must of death. Unable to bear the weight of melancholy a moment longer, he stepped out onto an unfamiliar balcony with braided porphyry columns and darkly gleaming tilework balustrade. Leaning over the edge, he looked out over the city, the bright splashes of color, the insectlike droning from crisscrossing hoverpods, the crunch of fallen leaves underfoot, the skein of clogged streets rippling away in all directions, the bobbing heads of passersby, the V'ornn gleaming bald and coppery, the Kundalan with their hair, thick and loose, the babble of voices, the smells of spices and oils and broiling meat and burning metal. A young Kundalan female, laden with packages, passed below him. Her long, lustrous hair hung down to her buttocks. She paused long enough to switch her burden from one shoulder to the next. In the process, her hip canted out, her hair swung from one shoulder blade to the other and back. He felt a stirring in his tender parts. He had a definite thing for Kundalan females of a certain type, the single trait he had inherited from his father. V'ornn, who were utterly hairless, often found the luxuriant growth on Kundalan females an exotic and powerful aphrodisiac. Her face moved from shadow to light and unbidden a memory surfaced of spying on just such a female when he and Annon had been out hunting, the female he had taken by force, the female he and Annon had almost come to blows over.

He and Annon had been best friends, sharing everything despite the rivalry between their families. Or perhaps they had bonded so closely *because* of that rivalry, because defiance ran strong in both their bloodstreams. Up until that moment, he had considered Annon to be more or less mild-mannered. The wild look in his eye that day was something to behold. If was as if he had let his guard down and showed a side of himself that Kurgan had never seen before. He sighed, leaning on the balustrade, watching the Kundalan female vanish in the current of the thronged street. Thinking of the female and of Annon he was reminded of the life he had left behind and, again, the melancholy welled up inside him. Times like these he missed Annon with a fierceness he could not have imagined when Annon had been alive. To be best friends with an Ashera was ironic in the extreme. That friendship had vexed his father no end. He began to smile, his melancholy lifting somewhat. Only he of all the Stogggul siblings had provoked in his father that certain choleric look. And Marethyn, of course, but that was different. She was Tuskugggun, a female.

He heard his name being called, but he neither moved nor responded. He waited for the Gyrgon Nith Batoxxx to approach him through the dimly lighted rooms. Even with his back turned, he could feel the Gyrgon's presence, the slow atomic crawl along the skin of his arms that would have stirred his hair had he any to stir. He could see what the two of them had in common. Besides their ambition and the agendas they kept hidden from one another, they were conquerors in the center of things living off the fruit of their conquest. All about them were the remains of the Kundalan beasts who had fallen beneath the ion sizzle of their shock-swords, and with the merest flick of their hands they could cause this wounded mass to move this way or that, to do or say anything that on a whim they might think of.

Having a Gyrgon around the palace had its benefits. For one thing, it made those around him anxious; he fed off the slow shredding of their nerves. For another, Gyrgon had about them the distinct aroma of power, of secrets being carried just beneath the glittering alloy skin of their exomatrices.

It was a great pity that he could not abide this particular Gyrgon, who, in his disguise as the Old V'ornn, had been his teacher and mentor. He had been forced to pledge himself to Nith Batoxxx, a noxious state of affairs he detested and would not long tolerate. Now that he had become regent his goal was to find the weakness in the Gyrgon Comradeship and exploit it to gain access to the treasure trove of new technology they created and zealously kept under lock and key. They were all—V'ornn and Kundalan alike—under the Gyrgon's ion-mailed thumb, and this hegemony he fervently wished to overthrow.

Not that it would be easy. Not with this particular Gyrgon riding such close herd on him. Nith Batoxxx in his guise as the Old V'ornn had trained Kurgan to become regent. Why? And what else did this Gyrgon want from him? It irked him to think that without the Gyrgon's help and guidance he would be just another sixteen-year-old Bashkir scion, learning how to run his family's Consortium.

"You cannot hide from me," Nith Batoxxx said from the edge of the shadowed interior. "You know this very well." Light spun off the black alloy of his exomatrix. Protected within it, he looked vaguely insectoid. "And yet here you are, alone." His mailed hand moved along the wall, a constant threat. "Shirking your office."

He was unlike any other Gyrgon in the Comradeship, Kurgan at least knew that much. Though what precisely made him different was a perplexing mystery.

His long gaunt face was a pale amber. A complex spiderweb of tertium and germanium circuitry ran across the taut skin starting from the crown of his skull down the back and along the sides of his neck. Ruby pupils studded obsidian-black eyes. At the point of each cheekbone was implanted a tertium neural-net stud that pulsed to the beating of his hearts.

"What is it you want of me?" Kurgan said curtly.

In two long strides, the Gyrgon closed the space between them. With a lazy, almost contemptuous gesture, the tip of his mailed forefinger touched Kurgan on his breastbone. Kurgan fell to his knees, his legs turned to water. But even in his pain he would not cry out; the Old V'ornn had trained him better than that.

"It is not for you, not for any V'ornn, to ask questions of me, Stogggul Kurgan."

Nith Batoxxx towered over him. Kurgan had the good sense not to

move, not even to look up. A crackling of hyperexcited ions had commenced, bringing with it the unmistakable whiff of death. Nith Batoxxx
held his hand just above Kurgan's bent head.

"You believe you can get the better of me. A bitter misapprehension,
you will find." The Gyrgon said this softly, his voice drifting, it seemed,
on the burnished late-afternoon sunshine. "You have the arrogance of
youth. You are fearless. You can outwit a Gyrgon. This is what you
believe."

Staring down, Kurgan could only see the Gyrgon's tertium-studded
boots. A vertical row of glittering black metallic talons marched up the
center of each boot. He felt his hearts beating fast. As always, he paid
very close attention not only to what Nith Batoxxx was saying but also
how he said it.

"Fear is my currency, Stogggul Kurgan. Never forget that. I can sniff
out the fear in even the staunchest spirit." Of a sudden, Nith Batoxxx
knelt and, with his forefinger beneath Kurgan's chin, lifted his head.
There was no pain this time at the contact. The ion fire sizzled, quiescent for the moment. "The truth is you hold your fear close inside
you where no one can see. But I will get it out of you."

No one knows me, Kurgan thought. But Annon had, reluctant though
he was to admit this.

"Your only danger, Stogggul Kurgan, will come from forgetting that
I know you."

He put his long, lupine face so close to Kurgan's that Kurgan could
smell the mingled scent of clove oil and burnt musk coming off him in
waves. It was so strong it made him momentarily dizzy.

"That night in the caverns, the night of the Ring of Five Dragons,
did you come across the Dar Sala-at? This is what I need to know."
Nith Batoxxx's voice had changed slightly, darkening in timbre and
seeming disconnected from his body.

"No," Kurgan replied, carefully monitoring this change.

"That is a very great pity. I know the Dar Sala-at exists," Nith Batoxxx continued in this same eerie voice. "He was there that night,
lured by the promise of the Ring. I could feel his power; he engaged
Malistra in sorcerous battle. But you tell me you never saw him."

"That's right."

"Even though I sent you to find him."

"It was chaos down there. Rekkk Hacilar was hiding in Haaar-kyut armor. He was causing havoc everywhere. I was diverted."

"It is imperative that I know the Dar Sala-at's identity, do you understand me?"

"Not in the least." The lies in among the truth had sprung surprisingly easily to his lips. He had, indeed, met the Dar Sala-at that night in the caverns below the regent's palace. To his consternation the Dar Sala-at was a young female. He did not know her name, but he was absolutely certain that he could pick her out of a crowd at fifty meters. This was his secret, hoarded for a time when its use would be of most value to him. He would never tell Nith Batoxxx, nor anyone else until it served his purpose.

"The Dar Sala-at is one of the few who is destined to know the location of the seven Portals."

"What are they?"

"You simply cannot manage not to ask questions, can you?" Nith Batoxxx looked at him out of glittering eyes. "The Portals are important because they lead to . . . a land of riches."

Why had the Gyrgon hesitated? Kurgan asked himself. Was he lying? And, if so, why?

"I know the location of three of them, but not the other four."

"Why do you need to know the location of all seven?"

Nith Batoxxx threw him an evil smile. "None can be fully opened unless all are opened simultaneously. This is a fiendishly difficult process. The first step is to locate all seven Portals. Then we will move on to the next stage of our assault."

"I noticed you said *our*."

The Gyrgon abruptly rose and strode to the balustrade. The silence stretched to a kind of breaking point, forcing Kurgan to turn and look. It seemed to him—and not for the first time—that Nith Batoxxx's posture had altered subtly from his normal very erect carriage. Was it his imagination, or were the Gyrgon's shoulders twisted slightly, one higher than the other? He rose and obediently followed Nith Batoxxx outside.

"This is why I have named you regent, Stogggul Kurgan. You are of such tender years to rule Kundala, but if I am any judge, you are the right one to rule."

"These Portals—"

"All you need know is that whoever brings me their location will be handsomely rewarded. Pray that it is you, Stogggul Kurgan."

Kurgan said nothing. He felt somehow as if he and the Gyrgon were doing a balancing act on a high wire in the dark. One false step, one word spoken out of place and he would fall into utter blackness.

Nith Batoxxx's gloved hand gripped the balustrade. "Hear me now, Stogggul Kurgan. I wish the construction of Za Hara-at to resume. This you will order posthaste. You will resurrect from its tomb the ancient city of the Korrush."

The voice sent a small shiver down Kurgan's spine.

"Yes, Nith Batoxxx." He knew when to acquiesce. Was there something here for him, a long-buried secret, a glimmer of the lever by which he would unlock the mysteries of the technomages' power?

"Cement your business relationship with SaTrryn Sornnn."

"I know he is the other major partner in the proposed construction," Kurgan said. "I know that my father agreed to move Bronnn Pallln aside, the leading candidate for Prime Factor, in order to name this young scion of the SaTrryn Consortium to this important office." He liked the initiative Sornnn SaTrryn had taken, liked that he hadn't been intimidated by the powerful Pallln Consortium. But what he liked best of all about Sornnn SaTrryn was ambition, a trait he could relate to without reservation. His own ambition was, after all, what had impelled him into an alliance with Olnnn Rydddlin. "Other than that I know very little about him."

"He is on familiar terms with the Korrush," Nith Batoxxx went on in his eerily disembodied voice. "He has been to Za Hara-at many times. These are vital assets."

To me or to you? Kurgan wondered. To the Gyrgon, he said, "May I ask why you have changed your mind? Up until now you have been the most vehement opponent of Za Hara-at being rebuilt."

"That was because of Ashera Eleusis." Nith Batoxxx's voice abruptly snapped back to normal. He turned to impale Kurgan's with his lambent crimson stare. "Ashera Eleusis was a dangerous heretic. He wished for an equality between V'ornn and Kundalan. That is why he is dead."

Why was Eleusis Ashera dangerous? Kurgan asked himself. *How could any V'ornn be dangerous to a Gyrgon?* Then something clicked inside his head. "It was not my father who engineered the coup that felled Eleusis Ashera. You did."

"I manipulated your father," Nith Batoxxx said. "Does that come as a surprise to you?"

"Not really, no. My father was weak-willed."

"Unlike you."

Was he being ironic? Kurgan wondered. Behind his back, his fist clenched white and trembling.

"Go now," Nith Batoxxx said with a dismissive gesture. "There is much for you to accomplish before darkness falls and the Rescendance begins."

W hat would you have me say, regent?"
"First," Kurgan said, "get down on your knees."

He saw the brief flare in Jerrlyn's eyes before he acquiesced. He looked over the top of the bowed back of the Kundalan to scan the crowds lining the great hall. They were packed in between the immense gold-jade and green-porphyry columns. The columns were fluted. Their capitals were carved into the faces of fantastic creatures.

Jerrlyn was the head of the Fourth Agrarian Commune District. As such, he was a highly respected Kundalan among his race. This, of course, meant little to Kurgan other than arousing his curiosity as to just how deeply involved Jerrlyn was in the Resistance.

"Now," he nodded, "you may continue."

"What would you have me tell you?" Jerrlyn began again. "There have been thirteen deaths among my Commune this month alone. Last month there were only five. Have we displeased you in some way, regent?"

Kurgan sat forward. "Are you implying that I am in any way responsible for these deaths?"

"Not at all," Jerrlyn said hastily. "But the deaths are all unexplained, all from unnatural causes. It does seem likely that they were perpetrated by the Khagggun."

"What proof have you of this allegation?"

"My Commune is in terror."

"You have no proof. Just as likely the individuals were killed by your own Resistance forces. These extremists view you as collaborators."

"We have discovered ion-fire wounds on many of the dead."

"All the more reason to suspect your own Resistance. There has been over the past year an escalation in the theft of Khagggun weaponry from secured depots in and around the city." He smiled. "To date, we have not apprehended the perpetrators, but your pleas give me an idea.

If you would be so cooperative as to supply the names of those involved in the thievery, I would speak to my Star-Admiral. I am certain that I could convince him to guarantee the safety of your Commune."

"Then we *would* be collaborators."

Kurgan sighed as he sat back. "Jerrlyn, I grow weary of your whining. I have given you a solution to your problem."

"An unacceptable solution! I am the leader of the largest Commune on the north continent. We supply you with seventy percent of your foodstuffs."

"I know full well the percentages harvested from each of the seven Communes, Jerrlyn. After all, it is we V'ornn who carved up the territories and created the Commune system. It is so much more efficient than the helter-skelter structure you had in place. Each Commune has now tripled its output since inception. An impressive advance, even you must admit."

"Yes, but the bulk of the increase goes to feed the V'ornn populace, leaving us less than we had before. And then there is the matter of our tithes—"

"Ah, the tithes you pay us. Now we come to the heart of the matter."

"Your father increased the tithes just before he died. They are killing us."

"No," Kurgan corrected. "As I have pointed out, your own Resistance is killing you. Do what I ask and in addition to keeping your Commune safe I will consider rolling back the tithes."

Jerrlyn shook his head. "Even if I did know, I would not betray—"

Kurgan jumped up. "Then the tithes are doubled."

"What?" Jerrlyn was aghast. "Regent, I beg you—!"

"This outcome is a direct result of your own truculence. Do you think you are playing with an ill-informed dolt? I am nothing like my father. We shall now see what breaks your back. Do not return here with your piteous plaints until you are prepared to meet my terms."

At the imperious wave of his hand, a pair of Haaar-kyut detached themselves from their positions and took Jerrlyn away.

As soon as the Kundalan had been hauled from his sight, he gestured to the Star-Admiral to come to his side. Olnnn Rydddlin was tall and thin to the point of emaciation, with an unnaturally pale, pinched face, whose occasional baleful smile turned his eyes into fusion lamps. His formidable countenance was embraced by those who served under him, but there were many Bashkir who distrusted a V'ornn marked by Kundalan sorcery. Never mind that he was a brave warrior, had sacrificed his leg in single-minded pursuit of their enemies, Rekkk Hacilar and his Kundalan skcettta, Giyan. It was Giyan whose loathsome spell had stripped the skin, flesh, and sinew from that leg, leaving only bare bones. It was another Kundalan sorceress, Malistra, who had saved him. Now the Star-Admiral kept that leg unarmored. Through sheer force of will he had transformed the ensorceled bones from a source of embarrassment into his hallmark, a symbol of his bravery. And so the rank-and-file Khagggun loved him, this strange, ambitious, deeply bitter Khagggun not many years Kurgan's elder. But what of the high command, those upper-echelon generals and admirals far older and more experienced than he? How could they not hate him and envy him at least a little for his breathtakingly swift advancement over them? Kurgan had determined to keep a close eye on the Star-Admiral. Olnnn Rydddlin was the only other V'ornn who knew that he had plotted his own father's demise. To ensure that remained a secret he would kill even an ally because he knew better than most V'ornn the bitter choices ambition forced upon you.

To win is everything, the Old V'ornn had taught him. *To win at everything is to be alone.*

For the moment, then, he would treat Olnnn Rydddlin as a trusted compatriot, so that when the time came, before his power could become a threat, he could slip a knife between his ribs. Toward that end, he had already formulated a plan that fit in with his overall scheme to find some form of leverage he could use against the Gyrgon. What did the Gyrgon prize most? Stasis. It followed, then, that what they feared most was change, change from within. If that happened and if he could present them with a solution, he would have his leverage with them.

"It seems that you have been quite effective in terrorizing this Commune," he said with just the right amount of praise in his voice.

"Those were your orders, regent," Olnnn Rydddlin replied.

"I am simply following one of the basic precepts of armed occupation, Star-Admiral. One that I have no doubt is familiar to you. Namely, keeping the populace in a constant state of terror ensures that they cannot think, plan, or organize competently. Perpetual disorientation is the order of the day for these Kundalan."

"Absolutely, regent. This is one of the reasons their Resistance is virtually ineffective. You cannot have a properly functioning military without support from a viable political system. The adults are too busy wondering who the next victim will be to produce a leader with real vision, and because we have ensured that their children are systematically losing touch with their religion and their past, because we have left them with nothing, they have lost the ability to fight for what is theirs."

Kurgan, seeing the self-satisfied expression on Olnnn Rydddlin's face, immediately felt an urge to wipe it off.

"What good is all that when these thefts continue?" he said shortly. "Disturbing enough that you are losing ion cannons to the Kundalan Resistance but your inability to apprehend the criminals is undermining our air of invincibility."

Olnnn Rydddlin stiffened at the rebuke. "Regent, I have studied the reports of these thefts at length and have come to the inescapable conclusion that the Kundalan Resistance is being aided by a V'ornn traitor. There is simply no other plausible explanation for the continued success of these thefts. On their own, the Kundalan are incapable of circumventing the increasing levels of security Line-General Lokck Werrrent and I have put in place."

"We are both but newly placed in high office," Kurgan said. "We need to show the Gyrgon that he was correct in putting his faith in us. We need results, not excuses."

"Yes, regent."

Kurgan rose from the regent's chair, beckoned Olnnn to come closer still. "There is a matter about which you must be informed," he said softly. He knew he had to word this in just the right way. "The Gyrgon Comradeship has been closely monitoring the embedding of okummmon in Khaggun, due them on their ascendance to Great Caste status and, to be honest, they are troubled."

"What by, regent?"

"There appears to be a greater degree of difficulty among your caste in adjusting to the implant." This was an outright lie, part of his plan to keep the Khaggun—and especially Olnnn Rydddlin himself—from gaining too much power.

"I confess that I had not heard this, regent."

"Of course not. It is Comradeship business."

"But it directly affects us!" Olnnn said.

"That is why you must trust in the wisdom of the Comradeship, Star-Admiral," he went on soothingly. "Of course they have your best interests at hearts. All officers of the rank of General and higher have already received the okummmon. That being the case, the Comradeship has decided to suspend further implantation. But the Gyrgon assure me that will be only until they can assess the ramifications of the period of adjustment."

"This sounds suspiciously like discrimination to me."

"Keep your voice down." The conversation was not going the way Kurgan had planned it. He had meant for Olnnn Rydddlin to believe he was being taken into the regent's confidence. Instead, he had become defensive. "Star-Admiral, there is Nith Batoxxx not ten paces away," Kurgan said with what he felt was just the right amount of persuasion. "If he even suspected that I had confided this to you, I guarantee you he would be thoroughly displeased."

"You do not subscribe to this point of view, regent, do you?" Olnnn said, somewhat alarmed.

"Certainly not," Kurgan lied. "Have you forgotten that it was I who sponsored you as my Star-Admiral? Rest assured that at the Summonings I am your greatest advocate. But even I cannot gainsay the Comradeship. And besides, according to the Genomatekks at Receiving Spirit, there is cause for concern. You would not want to put your Khaggon in any precipitate danger, would you?"

"I will be candid, regent. I do not like this sudden turn of events."

"Nor do I, my friend. I counsel you to be patient. Their concern will pass; I myself will see to it. In any event, one thing you must learn. It never pays to second-guess the Gyrgon."

The Ancestor Tent was huge, covering one square hectare in the center of Axis Tyr. It was made of a neural-net monofilament the color of dried V'ornn blood, indigo, the color of mourning. Inside, at its center, on a draped tertium podium, floating in a stasis field of hyperexcited ions, were the two hearts—one large, one small—of the dead regent, Wennn Stogggul. Before that, the body had been prepared by a sect of Genomatekks known as Deirus. By Gyrgon decree, the dead regent lay in state in the forecourt of the regent's palace so that all V'ornn could pay their respect. The mourning period lasted six weeks, after which the preparations for the Rescendance could begin. Tonight, nine weeks after his death, the hearts of Wennn Stogggul would be transmuted in the rite of Rescendance.

All around the perimeter of the tent—in the light of many fusion lamps—the new regent's Haaar-kyut, his personal bodyguards clad in horned battle armor, ranged at regular intervals. They scrutinized the somber crowds with a restless energy, an inbred contempt, as if wishing for some unexplained or unruly behavior so they could tear someone limb from limb. As Sornnn SaTrryn watched, he was reminded of the lymmnals, the furred, six-legged animals used as guards by the tribes of the Korrush, the Great Northern Plain of Kundala's north continent. The lymmnals were pulled prematurely from their mother's teats, fed warm blood until their lust for it was all-consuming, and then were half-starved. They were trained as attack animals. As such, they were fiercely loyal, and when they were loosed their aggression was complete, terrible to behold. Like the lymmnals, these Haaar-kyut, in their distinctive purple armor, were edgy, itching for combat.

"Ten days I have been at this," one Haaar-Kyut whispered to another.

"Bashkir custom," said the other out of the side of his mouth. "We performed the rite of Rescendance on Star-Admiral Kinnnus Morcha within an hour of his death."

"We Khagggun have no time to waste on prolonged mourning rituals," the first one rejoined.

"We live for battle," acknowledged the second. "But all we are given is *this*."

Sornnn SaTrryn, smiling, continued past more Khagggun arrogantly shouldering their way through the throng. Their sudden proliferation, like poisonous mushrooms after a prolonged rain, was an evil sign, one of many he had observed as he had made his way into the capital city. He entered the tent now, wearing his wariness like a mantle of subdued sorrow and respect, and made his way toward the new regent.

Kurgan was standing near the baein, the hearts receptacle. Sornnn was somewhat taken aback to see a particularly sinister-looking Gyrgon standing not too far away. There was a zone of emptiness around the Gyrgon. He was being given a wide berth even by the Haaar-kyut, who averted their gazes, glaring even more darkly at the assembled mourners the better to cover their fear. Every V'ornn, it seemed, whether Great Caste or Lesser Caste, was frightened of the Gyrgon.

They were V'ornn of another hue—reclusive technomages who spent their time in their vast laboratories trying to unlock the mysteries of the Cosmos. All V'ornn technology flowed from them. They guarded their discoveries with a zeal that bordered on obsession, and they were the sole pipeline, feeding the new technologies to the others only when and where they saw fit. Though the regent ruled Kundala, he served at the pleasure of the Gyrgon. He, like every other Great Caste V'ornn, had an okummmon, a quasi-organic neural net designed by the Gyrgon, implanted into the inside of his left forearm. Using the okummmon, the Gyrgon would periodically Summon the regent to their presence, there to feed him his own worst fears, the better to bend him to their will, there to order him to carry out their edicts, continuing their rule by proxy.

Sornnn lifted a slender goblet of fire-grade numaaadis from the tray of a passing Mesagggun and slowly sipped it, using the gesture to cover his scrutiny of the new players with whom he was sharing this fresh playing field. Kurgan Stogggul, scion of the powerful but troubled Sto-gggul Consortium, took up most of his attention. He was no more than a child, and yet he had with breathtaking swiftness ascended to a heady office. There were among the ranks of Bashkir those who were prone to dismiss the new regent as a temporary aberration who would sooner rather than later be swept away on the tide of history. Seeing him now, Sornnn disagreed. There were arrogance and ambition in abundance here, no doubt of that, but in the sharp, angular features Sornnn recognized a keen intelligence. Besides, he could not have been named regent without the consent of the Gyrgon. Obviously, they saw in him something the Bashkir naysayers did not.

As he continued to approach the new regent, he observed that the Gyrgon's black eyes had pupils the color of rubies. They met his for a moment, then passed on. He felt a chill sweep through him, as if he had been stripped not only of his robes but his skin and flesh as well. With an inward shudder, he turned his attention back to the young regent. In truth, he had been preparing himself for this encounter for some time, hoping, on the one hand, that this day would not come for many years, suspecting, on the other hand, that it would come sooner than anyone imagined. As a direct consequence of his foresight, he had spent weeks analyzing the intelligence his Consortium had compiled on Kurgan. He had known almost instantly that he would have a far more difficult time with the son than he had with the father. It could not be helped. *Koura,* as they said in the Korrush. *It is written.*

Kurgan saw Sornnn SaTrryn when he was still a few meters away. Sornnn SaTrryn was tall, lean, with a vaguely dangerous air. He had pale blue eyes that, like all the SaTrryn, were almost almond in shape, and the agile, long-fingered hands of a professional conjurer. Kurgan saw with ill-concealed distaste that he was wearing a wide-striped robe of the kind worn by the tribes of the Korrush. The bright colors were dull with the dust of hard travel.

"Forgive my appearance on the night of your father's Rescendance, Kurgan Stogggul," Sornnn said in his deep, commanding voice. "As you can plainly see, I hastened here directly from the Korrush so that I could pay my respects." He appeared to have absorbed the absolute stillness of the wild and primitive Korrush tribes from whom his Consortium bought the spices they sold.

Kurgan inclined his head, his night-black eyes ever avid, ever watchful, a pair of midnight pillagers. He was dressed in a formal robe of deepest indigo. He disliked the color, was uncomfortable wearing it now. He burned to don the regent's royal purple. "At a time like this, it is good to have my Prime Factor close at hand once more."

"I have heard that Wennn Stogggul's death was sudden and tragic," Sornnn SaTrryn said, breaking into Kurgan's thoughts. "You and I have something in common, regent."

"Indeed. Your own father died some months ago, yes?"

Sornnn inclined his head in sad assent.

Kurgan glanced fleetingly to his left, saw Star-Admiral Olnnn Rydddlin sizing up the young Prime Factor, compiling a mental list as one does with an enemy, trying to divine his strengths and his weaknesses.

He turned back and to cover his brief inattention signed to one of the nearby servants to bring them drinks. They were delivered a moment later on a chased-copper tray. Sornnn SaTrryn exchanged his empty goblet for a full one. When the Soul Departure Toast had been gravely made, the fire-grade numaaadis consumed, Kurgan asked, "Where in the Korrush have your travels taken you?"

"I was for the past weeks in the area of Okkamchire."

"Those names sound alike to me," he said. "By all reports the Korrush is a primitive place, so I hear. Dust, kuomeshal dung. An altogether unpleasant way, it seems to me, to make a living."

"Exquisitely woven rugs, a drink that makes even fire-grade numaaadis taste like water." Sornnn SaTrryn's smile was gentle, disarming. "An enchanting village of tents that moves about at the will of the chieftain, or on a whim of the weather." He paused. "Then, again, the spice trade has proved enormously lucrative."

Kurgan grinned, on firm ground again. "Well worth the buzz of bloodflies and the stink of kuomeshal dung, I imagine."

"Absolutely, regent."

"Well, then, I daresay I won't admonish you for spending so much time there. On the other hand . . ." He paused, having seen his sister Marethyn making her way through the throng. She was certain to make a scene as she had done on the day of his father's death; it remained only to discover what sort of scene.

"Yes, regent," Sornnn SaTrryn said expectantly. "On the other hand?"

Kurgan returned his attention to his Prime Factor. "On the other hand, it is my wish to resurrect Eleusis Ashera's plan to rebuild Za Hara-at."

Sornnn's smile was a kilometer wide. "Why this is magnificent news, regent! Truly magnificent!"

"The ruins are currently being excavated, are they not?"

"Yes. For years now, the Beyy Das, one of the Five Tribes of the Korrush, have been carefully unearthing the bones of the ancient city. But the work is both difficult and dangerous. There have been a number of cave-ins because of old silicate mines that were buried for centuries as well as devastating raids by the Jeni Cerii, a rival tribe."

"I shall have to assign a detachment of Khagggun to stand guard over our Mesagggun."

"That might be wise, regent," Sornnn SaTrryn said. "But I would caution them to keep well away from the site itself, as it is a holy place."

"Only for the primitives of the Korrush. But in these matters I understand you are the expert, so I shall heed your advice." He nodded. "Excellent, Sornnn SaTrryn. I am pleased that we have begun on such a productive note."

"It is my hope that you will allow me to accompany you on your first trip to the Korrush."

"But I have no such trek planned."

"The SaTrryn are partners with the Stogggul Consortium in the building of Za Hara-at, the so-called City of One Million Jewels. I think it would be wise for the regent to make a tour of the site."

Kurgan considered for a moment. "Well, one thing is clear, you were taught well how to speak." He showed his teeth. "Very well. I will leave it to you to make all the arrangements. But for now, Prime Factor, I must excuse myself. The Rescendance will begin shortly, and I must prepare myself."

"Of course. Thank you for this interview, regent. Again, my respects to you and to your late father."

"As you have said, you came quickly and from a distance. I will not soon forget your loyalty."

With a nod, Sornnn SaTrryn bade the regent a formal farewell, and was gone in a swirl of Korrush-woven fabric.

Kurgan stood looking after him for a moment or two, lost in contemplation. Olnnn Rydddlin, finished with the last-minute instructions to the Haaar-kyut guards, crossed the tent to stand beside him.

"What news of the fugitives we seek?"

"We are closing in, regent."

"Careful, Star-Admiral. We have been down this road before"

"This time is different."

Kurgan's eyes cut to Olnnn Rydddlin's face, a book with so many hidden passages, an ally and a danger. "Then shortly they shall be in custody, is that correct, Star-Admiral?"

Olnnn inclined his head.

Marethyn Stogggul waited until she saw the Star-Admiral take his leave of her brother before she attempted to approach him. She was a tall, willowy Tuskugggun with a beautiful, regal face, intelligent, wide-apart eyes, and sensual lips. Whether she was aware of it or not, she possessed some of Kurgan's swagger, unusual in a V'ornn female. Hers was the kind of body that V'ornn males dreamed of, yet in her dress and her movements she was wholly unself-conscious about her attractiveness.

She had been standing with all the other females, in a roped-off section of the tent beyond whose periphery they were enjoined from roaming. By now, she had had her fill of small talk and gossip, discussions of the relative tensile strength of tertium versus tritanium, the warp and weft of textiles. From across the rope barrier she caught snippets of male conversations that had at their root the angling for deals, the ferreting out of negotiating weaknesses, business rivalries, grudges, envy, ambition. The stuff of life!

She put a smile on her face even though she was dreading this encounter. As a Tuskugggun who believed, quite heretically, that her gender should be the equal of males, she held no especial feeling for the male members of her family who, because of her views, were prone to give her even shorter shrift than her sister or her mother. She had learned early in life how to be independent. Unlike her ambitious brother, Kurgan, and her spoiled sister, Oratttony, she did not trade on the reputation or power of the Stogggul Consortium, even after her father had become regent. Wennn Stogggul had despised her, and she had seen no reason not to return the emotion. In fact, it had given her no small pleasure to be openly contemptuous of him, to berate him for all but abandoning his firstborn son, Terrettt, to the suspect therapies dispensed by cold and strange Deirus at Receiving Spirit. She alone, of all the family, visited Terrettt in his awful sterile quarters among the lunatics, and she went without fail three times a week. How many times had she begged her mother, cajoled her, then tongue-lashed her for cruelty.

"He is your son!" Marethyn had shouted at her mother.

"I have never thought of him that way," her mother had said in a voice drained of emotion. "And I never will."

Shaken, Marethyn had said, "Then I am no longer your daughter."

Somewhere inside Terrettt's skewed brain, she knew, he was grateful for each visit, even though he rarely expressed it. He acted differently when she was with him, she didn't need Deirus to tell her that, though they often did.

As Kurgan turned toward her, she was acutely aware of her mother, of Oratttony and her brood, the other females of the family obediently standing behind the indigo silken cord, removed from the place of honor where only the Stogggul males were allowed. For all Oratttony's sharp tongue she lacked the courage to emerge from the pen to which tradition had unfairly consigned her, but her eyes grew dark and turbulent at the sight of Marethyn doing just that.

"Are you mad?" Kurgan said into her face.

Those were the first words her brother had uttered to her since the day of their father's death.

"I bring Terrettt's good wishes to you, as well as his regrets at not being able to attend the Rescendance."

A twisted smile flared across Kurgan's face for a moment before dying out. "You *are* mad, sister. My *brother* is capable only of drooling out of the side of his mouth. Anything more difficult would likely split his head asunder."

"I knew it." Though she had promised herself she would remain calm, her rage overcame her. "You deliberately blocked my attempts to bring him here."

"Of course I did. I could not have him embarrassing the entire family in front of all of Axis Tyr."

"He is your brother, the firstborn son. Wennn Stogggul was his father, too. He has a right—"

"Let me tell you something," Kurgan hissed. "My *brother* has as much right to be here today as you do confronting me like this. He is a dangerous mad V'ornn and nothing more. *I* am my father's only true heir, never forget that." He glared at her as if daring her to gainsay him. "If you do not leave this instant, I will order my Haaar-kyut to escort you to your proper place behind the—"

"And embarrass the Consortium in front of all of Axis Tyr? I think not." She lifted her hands against the gathering darkness of his expression. "Keep your animals to their tight leash. I have said all that I came to say."

He stiffened his spine. "And had it fall on deaf ears."

She inclined her head. "As always, brother." Her eyes were cold as the jagged tips of the Djenn Marre. "You do not disappoint me."

In urgent need of flexing his sorcerous leg, Star-Admiral Olnnn Ry-dddlin stalked in a scimitar-shaped arc through V'ornn decked out in their best finery. All castes showed their grief in the appropriate manner: Khagggun had replaced the left arm of their battle armor with one of an indigo color; the Bashkir wore wide indigo sashes, Mesagggun had painted their faces indigo; Genomatekks and Deirus wore indigo bands around their skulls; Tuskugggun, cordoned off to their own sections to either side, wore indigo sifeyn.

Olnnn ate little, slept even less. And when he did finally drift off, his dreams were rife with eerie and disturbing images, harsh cries and insistent murmurings that jolted him awake, sweating, his hearts thundering in his chest. He was never without pain in his leg, needles in his marrow, a shocking sensation to a V'ornn inured to most pain. And when it didn't pain him it was stiff. *Keeping still is a liability*. This Khaggggun saying had become quite literal for him.

The Haaar-kyut he passed bowed to him as they sought his approval. It was more than they had done for Kinnnus Morcha, the previous Star-Admiral. As he moved in his rather awkward gait, he kept the regent as the fulcrum of his arc. He meant to give the impression of wanting to get a better sense of those who had power, longed for power, would never have the power and thus were envious of those who did. But, in fact, he was searching for Line-General Lokck Werrrent.

Olnnn was a Khaggggun born of parents he hardly knew, the youngest of four brothers, all of whom, it often seemed, lived to humiliate him, a self-made officer unlike so many of his acquaintance who had traded on their family name. He had no family name; no family at all, abandoned by brothers both alive and dead. Alone in the world, he had grown strong of his own accord. As a child, his life had promised nothing; now he had almost everything he had ever dreamed of, everything others who had assumed themselves his better desired and, now that he was here at the pinnacle, would never have.

And yet he was on edge. In the short time since Kurgan had become regent Olnnn had noticed a certain tension arising between them. The regent asked unreasonable things of him, and when he failed to achieve them, blamed him. Then there was the matter of the baffling thefts from Khaggggun storehouses. Despite the regent's opinions, Olnnn was convinced that the SaTrryn Consortium was behind the collaboration. They had a history of alliances with the Korrush tribes. Consequently, it was possible to suspect that Sornnn SaTrryn had "gone native." On the other hand, the regent clearly liked Sornnn SaTrryn, so Olnnn knew that he had to tread lightly or not at all. That meant somehow discrediting Sornnn SaTrryn without implicating himself in any way. He needed plausible deniability, and for this he required a stalking-horse.

"Star-Admiral."

He turned to see the face of Bronnn Pallln, round as a Kundalan moon, glistening with a faint sheen of sweat. "I have been here four hours, long before most Bashkir, and I still have not been able to gain an audience with Kurgan Stogggul."

"The official mourning period is not yet over, Bronnn Pallln," Olnnn said, craning his neck for a glimpse of Line-General Lokck Werrrent. "And he is preoccupied with the vicissitudes of his office."

"His father and my father were—"

"I think it would be best to put off any audiences for the time being."

"I have been patient for nine long weeks, should that not count for something?" Bronnn Pallln whined. "I was hoping that I could at last show Kurgan Stogggul what a mistake his father made in naming Sornnn SaTrryn as Prime Factor over me."

All at once, the conversation was of extreme interest to Olnnn. It was as if his wish to find a stalking-horse had been heard and granted by some mysterious force. One more reason to keep this Bashkir from talking to the regent. "On the eve of Wennn Stogggul's Rescendance I hardly think it prudent to tell the regent that his father made a mistake, do you?"

"Possibly not. But by rights the office of Prime Factor should be mine. Wennn Stogggul had all but promised it to me when Sornnn SaTrryn—"

"Kurgan Stogggul's temper is as legendary as it is volatile. But I imagine, Bronnn Pallln, that I need hardly remind you of that."

"Indeed, no, Star-Admiral."

Olnnn put his forefinger to his lips, tapped lightly in a show of contemplation that was entirely false. "However, your words have moved me."

"They have?" Bronnn Pallln appeared stunned.

"Indeed." He put a hand on Bronnn Pallln's meaty shoulder and steered him away from the regent. That was when he caught sight of the Line-General in question. "Let us speak of this matter in a day or two when the sorrow of the Rescendance has settled."

"Certainly, Star-Admiral." Bronnn Pallln appeared to be trembling slightly as he allowed himself to be led back to his Consortium. "It would be my greatest pleasure."

Olnnn left him quickly behind, striding over to the towering figure of Line-General Lokck Werrrent. He was the commander of the Khagggun forces for the Sudden Lakes quadrant and, as such, wielded the most power among the general ranks. He was an intimidating-looking

V'ornn, even among Khagggun. His large, square head seemed almost all jutting jaw and beetling brow. His eyes, sunk deeply beneath that brow, smoldered with what he liked to call the passion of discipline. He was old enough to be Olnnn's father yet he had no offspring of his own. Because, he said, he was married to his service to the V'ornn.

"Star-Admiral, good to see you once again!" he said in a deep resonant voice that could seemingly shake the rafters of the largest hall or gallery.

"And you as well, Line-General." Olnnn gripped Lokck Werrrent's wrist. "It seems to me that these days we do not see one another often enough."

"I am at your disposal, Star-Admiral. I will arrive at your quarters first thing tomorrow morning."

"No, you won't. And you will not make any sudden changes in your official schedule."

Lokck Werrrent's mighty brows knit tightly together. They knew each other so well that he did not ask questions that could not now be answered. "I am off to Dobbro Mannx's for my weekly dinner and a spirited round of hobbnixx tomorrow at the twenty-first hour. Shall we meet for a drink beforehand?"

"Do you have a venue in mind?" Olnnn was not a social animal; save for the raucous Blood Tide on the Promenade at Harborside, he was not conversant with Axis Tyr's many taverns.

"Judging by the gravity of your mood we should meet someplace unfrequented by Khagggun. Do you know Spice Jaxx's?"

"I am afraid I do not."

"It is in the center of the spice market. It is marked by a red-and-orange awning. You cannot miss it."

"Tomorrow at twenty hours, then."

Ah, the scion of the SaTrryn Consortium. I see you have brought a little of the Korrush back to Axis Tyr."

Sornnn turned at the sound of the female voice.

"Marethyn Stogggul." His face was utterly neutral as he turned to face her. "I have not seen you since, hmm, when was it exactly?"

"Two days after your father's death," she said. "Do you not remember?"

"A thousand pardons." There was a quizzical expression on his face. "As a matter of fact I do not."

"I was there. Representing the Stogggul family. Members of the Consortium attended as well."

"Ah, yes. Well, there were so many attendees during the two weeks of mourning."

"And you in shock."

"Yes."

"I trust you have recovered from the tragic loss."

"One never fully recovers from such a shock," Sornnn said. "How can one ever replace one's father?"

"How, indeed."

"Ah, that was thoughtless of me. This is, after all, your father's Rescendance."

"Save your condolences for someone who needs them," she said shortly.

"How have you been?" he said, piercing the awkward silence.

"My own work goes well, though business at the atelier is somewhat static."

"But your brother's work."

"Ah, yes. Terrettt's paintings always sell."

"And he is?"

"The same."

"Such a pity."

"I thank you for your concern, Sornnn SaTrryn." She turned her head slightly, as if watching for a moment someone or something behind his left shoulder. "Look there," she said softly. "A Deirus comes."

Sornnn turned to see a solemn figure clad in the ash-grey tunic of the Deirus.

"Look how those around him wrinkle their noses and step aside when he comes near," Marethyn said.

"It is true enough," Sornnn said. "Deirus are not well liked."

"Well, that is an understatement. They are considered sexual deviants and, as such, pariahs."

"Another of your causes, Marethyn? Don't you have enough already?" Sornnn was acutely aware of Olnnn Rydddlin's movements. It seemed clear that he was shadowing them.

"Considering the criminal experiments the Genomatekks at Receiving Spirit perform on the unfortunate children of V'ornn-Kundalan origin, their contempt for Deirus is hypocritical." Marethyn made a face. "And why should any difference—the Deirus' especially—mean that they are fit only to serve the dying and the insane?"

"That way no one of importance will catch their 'disease,' as the Gyrgon put it," Sornnn said dryly.

"As if it actually *were* a disease. As if there was anything wrong in males loving males. I daresay they are more loving in their relationships than you males are with us females."

"What's the matter, Marethyn," he said mockingly, "don't you believe in true love?"

"Should I?"

"I thought all Tuskugggun did."

"I thought no males did."

"The Deirus included? Poor fools! Save for their aberration they could take their place among the highly regarded Genomatekks instead of toiling on their own among the dead, the dying, and the insane."

"It is disgusting how they are abused. The periodic raids—"

"It is the Gyrgon way of ensuring that the aberrant behavior does not spread outside the Deirus caste," Sornnn said.

"On such barbarism turns the Modality!" Marethyn lifted a goblet of numaaadis off the tray of a passing servant. "What news of the Korrush?"

"The Korrush abides. It is almost entirely the same, despite the ravages of our occupation."

Marethyn took a sip of the liquor. It burned her throat like fire. "The Gyrgon feel the tribes are beneath their notice."

"Like blood-fleas on a hindemuth's backside. Apparently so."

"But you know better."

"My Consortium makes its living from their spices."

"I have wondered." She cocked her head. "Why do you bother trading with them? Why not simply go in with a wing of Khagggun and take the spices? We have taken everything of value from the Kundalan."

"Not yet everything, I warrant. But that is another story." He pursed his lips meditatively. Having all this time kept Olnnn Rydddlin in the corner of his eye, he became convinced that the Star-Admiral was subtly following him like the mysterious dark mote on the Kundalan sun. "To answer your question, let me see, how best to put it? There is no answer."

"By which you mean that the Gyrgon are planning something in the Korrush."

"Did I say that?"

"Not in so many words."

He frowned. "I think it would be best not to put words in my mouth."

"How could you accuse me of such a thing? I am but a lowly Tus-kugggun, after all. I doubt I have the intelligence to put words in your mouth."

"You are as barbed as a sysal tree."

"And twice as obdurate, so it is said."

"Which is no lie, I see." He could see Olnnn Rydddlin smiling slightly as he passed close by.

"The only thing I can see is that you are as dull and stupid as every other Bashkir."

"Now I *am* offended."

"Try not to take it personally," Marethyn said as she turned away. "According to some, I have amassed quite a reputation for offensive behavior."

As Nith Batoxxx watched Kurgan begin the rite of Rescendance, his mind was elsewhere. How could it be otherwise? What Gyrgon would concern himself with day-to-day V'ornn affairs? Death was of interest to Nith Batoxxx only inasmuch as it was a path not to be taken. In truth, it was deeply disturbing being here in a public spot, amid the swirl, glitter, and constant movement of a gigantic throng, exposed to life outside the Temple of Mnemonics, where he had his laboratory. The cacophony of voices alone made him slightly uneasy, as if sunk within the crowd's incessant rustling, its restless energy, he had difficulty hearing himself think. Even filtered through the neural nets of his biosuit the acuity of sensation made him feel as if he was being rubbed raw. He gritted his teeth against it, the muscles at the side of his jaw bunched and spasmed.

Possibly, however, his agitation had something to do with the bronze neural-net serpent that had been his link to his pawn, the Kundalan sorceress Malistra. Though Malistra had been killed by the Dar Sala-at, the serpent that had been with her had escaped, returning back to its master. But when Nith Batoxxx had fed it into his okummmon, returning to its original ionic state, he had discovered that it had somehow been damaged. While he could access the record of the battle, he could not see the identity of the Dar Sala-at. This seemed impossible to him, and thus the defeat was bitterer still, and had made him grind his teeth in fury and frustration.

As these unpleasant thoughts whirled through him, he swiveled his head this way and that. He saw a clutter of Bashkir drinking and talking under their breath, Mesagggun ripe from the mines, the power plants, the underground conduits, Tuskugggun, their heads covered in sifeyn, the traditional cowls all decent females wore over their heads. He could feel their fear of him, basked in it, allowed it to calm his jittery nerves. V'ornn and Kundalan alike, they were of no consequence to him save in all the ways he could conjure for them to wipe his tender parts. They were nothing more than extra pairs of hands and feet, there to do his bidding before being lopped off as they outlived their usefulness.

Which line of thought led him straight back to Kurgan Stogggul. In exchange for Nith Batoxxx's help in gaining swift ascendancy to the regent's office, Kurgan had pledged himself into Nith Batoxxx's service. Forever. He was an ambitious lad. And highly motivated. He was far more clever than his father ever was. And just as ruthless. He was not averse to getting his hands wet with another's blood. Perhaps he even reveled in it. But was he up to the task in store for him? This was a question Nith Batoxxx intended to answer without undue delay.

But not this day. This day he was required to stand quietly and observe the world around him, feeling the constant ion fire of his neural nets as they compiled detailed notes, a library of minutiae, transmitted not to the main cluster of Gyrgon data crystals, but to a lone crystal, throbbing blue-white in a secret compartment of his laboratory, a place hidden even from the supposedly omniscient eyes of the Comradeship. It was a task he loathed; it reduced him to the role of messenger, data-processor, librarian. It was demeaning and obnoxious, yet he performed these seemingly unending tasks flawlessly and without a word of protest. Protest was impossible in these circumstances.

*   *   *

O, *I am in a foul and bitter mood,* he silently cried. *And why is that?* But he knew. He knew as surely as he knew that the blighted sun of Kundala with its purple spot would rise in precisely three hours, twenty-three minutes, 17.973 seconds. He felt the lack, the lack of a worthy adversary. He had done battle with his nemesis, Nith Sahor, wounded him grievously, wounding him unto death. And now that Nith Sahor was gone, Nith Batoxxx felt the void in his world, felt, in fact, the warp and weft of reality somehow flat and dulled. Without Nith Sahor to oppose him, he was bored. And sad. Imagine that! Mourning the death of one's bitterest enemy. At another time, he might have laughed at the absurdity of the notion.

He had despised Nith Sahor and all he had stood for. Nith Sahor had deserved his fate, had deserved the execution Nith Batoxxx had delivered upon him. He had been seduced by Kundalan lore, Kundalan history, Kundalan sorcery. He had seen merit where there was only swill. He had confused a conjurer's trick with true insight, had mistaken myth for knowledge. Worse still, he had wanted to rock the very foundations of the Comradeship. He had begun to doubt the basic Precepts that all Gyrgon know are true and right from the moment their cortical nets are hardwired into their brains, the Precepts from which the main data crystal bank had been programmed Precepts that had been downloaded into the V'ornn databank just before their homeworld was destroyed. Nith Sahor believed the Precepts were suspect. It was his contention that noxious emissions from that unimaginable conflagration had interfered with the data transfer, so that what came through was either corrupted or highly fragmented. He had blasphemed against the Comradeship—against the V'ornn race itself. He was a traitor of the most virulent kind, for he sought not only betrayal but subversion. In the end, his delusions had led him to conspire with the enemy, first Eleusis Ashera, the former regent, then the sorceress Giyan and her turncoat consort, the Rhynnnon Rekkk Hacilar.

Nith Batoxxx's blood seethed when he thought of Nith Sahor and his vile treachery, and this only made him feel the void all the more, for it was true that his own power rose most keenly, most vividly against a powerful enemy. And now that enemy was gone, consigned to the frozen wastes of N'Luuura, if there was any justice in the world.

Greenish moonslight slanted through the open sides of the Ancestor

Tent, the combined energy of the throng sizzled, heating the tent like a photon reactor. The air tasted musty to him, crowded as it was with V'ornndom, the huge line of mourners snaking into the tent on one side, out the other, an unending serpent. He wished only to be back in his laboratory, to lose himself in his experiments. He watched from slitted eyes the crowd eating and drinking and talking in hushed tones, heaving like a mass of foolish cattle, and he hated them all. What concerned them? The insignificant events of their petty lives, the minute quotidian dance that he—that all Gyrgon save Nith Sahor—had long ago foresworn. For the Gyrgon had looked into the face of eternity, and after that sight nothing could ever be the same again. It was a magnificent, towering, orgiastic feeling to hold the stuff of the Cosmos in the neural net of one's gloved hand, to manipulate it, to catch the shimmer of its remaining mysteries, to be held spellbound by the microscopic orbits of the energy that composed all life.

Yes, his experiments made his contempt for the inferior castes universal—almost universal. There was one here who did interest him somewhat. He let his ruby eyes alight for a moment upon Kurgan Stogggul, who was looking imperious, proud, dangerous—all the things that Nith Batoxxx, in his guise as the Old V'ornn, had taught Kurgan from a very early age. Kurgan Stogggul was a conundrum worthy of Nith Batoxxx's superior intellect and scientific curiosity. Some special fate had touched Kurgan at the moment of his birth, some destiny far beyond most V'ornn's imagining.

And in a very real sense Nith Batoxxx had brokered that special fate.

Nith Batoxxx moved to Kurgan's side, and a pinwheel of space and silence formed around them. V'ornn and Kundalan alike averted their gaze. Their fear was palpable, but it did nothing to dispel this discontent that covered him like a mourner's veil.

"It is the appointed hour," he said softly, eerily. "The Rescendance must commence."

Kurgan approached the baein. Nith Batoxxx watched as he turned a knob on the baein. The hearts of the dead regent pulsed and, in the simulation of the return to life, commenced to melt, dissolving into a thick blue-black liquid that drained into the Soul Chalice.

Silence passed through the vast crowd like a photonic wave. Nith Batoxxx could hear them quietly breathing, a beast at bay. Not a word was spoken. All eyes were on Kurgan as he lifted the chalice, which was made of crystal, so all could see the liquefied hearts within. Kurgan faced the assembled throng, intoned the Prayer for Rescendance, which ended with the familiar phrase, "Life is death, death is life."

Then Kurgan drained all the liquid from the chalice.

3

Conundrums

"Whatever are we to do," Eleana said, "now that Giyan is gone?"

They were all huddled together under the light of the three moons, Riane, Rekkk, Eleana and the six-legged Rappa, Thigpen.

"Rescue her," Rekkk said with a warrior's straightforward logic.

"That will be anything but simple," Thigpen warned.

Riane told them of Giyan's suspicions about the origins of the chrysalides.

"But Giyan is such a powerful sorceress," Eleana said. "How could she be imprisoned?"

"This is Malasocca, dread sorcery of the highest order."

Riane recognized the word as being Venca, the root language of the Ramahan Old Tongue; the language of the Druuge, the nomadic tribes who inhabited the trackless wastes of the Great Voorg, who were said to be the descendants of the first Ramahan.

Thigpen's whiskers twitched in anxiety. "I warrant its like has not been seen on Kundala for many centuries. It is ancient, from the Time before the Imagining. Only the death of the host will counteract it." The creature looked from face to face. "We may have to accept that the Lady is lost to us."

"There must be a way," Riane said.

"We will go after her," Rekkk said firmly. "Surely all of us together—"

"That is precisely what we will *not* do." Thigpen, her triangular ears laid flat against the ruddy fur of her head, stood up on her two sets of sturdy hind legs. "If we do, she will kill us all, of that there can be no doubt. And even if by some miracle one of us remains alive, what then? Which one of us will plunge a blade through her heart to free her?"

"Then what do you propose?" Eleana put her hands on her hips. "I, for one, am unwilling to sit idly by while some daemon from the Abyss steals Lady Giyan's soul from her."

Thigpen's whiskers were twitching madly. "Your loyalty to Lady Giyan is touching, dear. I am not questioning what is in your heart, merely how the volatile emotion of love is played out." She steepled her slender fingers, tapping the long nails together rhythmically. "The plight of the Lady Giyan aside, I cannot impress upon you the extreme danger the Malasocca poses for all of us, for it presages the dread return of the daemons to our realm."

"You don't know—" Rekkk began.

"Ah, but I do know." Thigpen opened her jaws. Her slender yellow tongue rolled from the back of her mouth a small spherical object. She plucked it from between her teeth, held it aloft for them to see. In its depths clouds seemed to form and dissipate in a never-ending pattern. "This tells me there is a future—not *the* future, mind—but certainly *one possible future* in which you and Riane go after Giyan and die by her hand."

"More Kundalan mumbo jumbo!" said Rekkk. "I don't believe a word of it!" He scabbarded his shock-sword. "I am going after her and, somehow, I will find a way to free her." It was clear that he wasn't really listening, wasn't thinking straight.

"You're not going anywhere yet," Riane said. Thigpen's words had chilled her to the marrow. "For a start, you don't even know where Giyan went," Riane pointed out.

"She is right, Rekkk." Eleana sighed. "I want to go after Lady Giyan as much as you do. But for the moment, at least, it seems we have little choice but to listen to what Thigpen has to say."

The night was growing cold, and they had already been chilled by the horror they had all witnessed. Following Riane's suggestion, they climbed through the shattered window, returning to the Library, pulling up heavy ammonwood chairs in a rough circle beside the long refectory table.

"Before I listen to any more of this," Rekkk growled, "I want an explanation as to how you could possibly know the future."

Thigpen, curling her furry body in the chair seat, sighed. "As I said, it is only one possible future out of many."

"How many?" Eleana asked.

"A great many, my dear. An infinite number."

Rekkk was far too agitated to sit still. He sprang up almost immediately and, crossing the tiled floor, busied himself with piling split logs into the huge blackened fireplace and starting a fire.

"The explanation," he said.

"Patience, warrior."

He turned from his work. "What little I possessed went with Giyan. Proceed with all due haste."

The Rappa showed them the tiny sphere again. "As Riane can attest, those of us who can Thrip have residing within us a wormlike creature known as a mononculus."

Eleana made a sound. Her face showed her disgust.

"Is this true, Riane?" Rekkk asked, brushing soot from his hands. "Do you carry one of these creatures inside you?"

"Yes. It is essential in order to continue Thripping. As you move through the Realms you pick up all sorts of energies, some of them quite noxious. The mononculus acts as a kind of filter, metabolizing the energies, purging our systems."

"What Riane does not yet know," Thigpen said, "is that the mononculus absorbs all sorts of radiation as one Thrips. The Realms are infinite. They exist side by side, as well as layered upon one another. When one Thrips there is no time or space—at least not as we understand it. All the Realms exist at once. Therefore, it is not surprising that many oddments are inadvertently picked up along the way." She rolled the sphere between her fingers. "Slivers of the past, or the future become embedded in our beings. They are harmful to us so the mononculus takes charge of them. Unlike the radiation, it cannot metabolize these slivers so it does the next best thing. It binds them together, around and around."

Riane took the sphere from Thigpen, peered at it intently. "Until it makes this."

"Precisely." Thigpen appeared pleased. "Then it expels the object."

Having successfully started the fire, Rekkk came and stood beside Riane. "But the future? The past?"

"How shall I say it?" Thigpen used a forefinger to scratch behind one ear. "Think of sunlight glancing off water, or lamplight reflecting off a pane of crystal. Think of these glimmers caught in the corner of your eye, seen but not seen. This is what the sphere is made up of."

Eleana, too, drew close, to better inspect the object of curiosity. "And you saw the future—a future—in there."

Thigpen nodded solemnly. "Somewhere, someplace, sometime, it happened just as I have said. Riane and Rekkk perish at the hands of the daemon that Lady Giyan is becoming."

"N'Luuura take it!" Rekkk cursed.

Eleana looked shrewdly at the Rappa. "Then we must ensure that that particular future never happens."

Thigpen sat up. "My dear, you have grasped the essential nature of the matter." She looked at Rekkk. "Do you understand this, impetuous warrior?"

"She is my true love, Rappa. Do *you* understand *that?*"

She gently laid a paw on his arm. "Better than you could ever imagine, brave one."

"Well, then, give me an alternative to finding Giyan and battling the daemon that possesses her. This talk of prophecy gives me a headache."

"We will find Giyan," Riane said. "But first we must find the way to displace the daemon without killing her." She saw Thigpen watching her with glittering eyes. "A strong arm and a brave heart are not enough to defeat daemons. We must use knowledge."

Scowling, Rekkk said, "I do not understand, Dar Sala-at."

"One thing I have learned about daemons," Riane continued, "is that they are made of fire. Battle them in a straightforward manner with might and main and they simply grow stronger. Think of it this way, they are like bloodthirsty reavers—the harder you push them, the harder they push back. But like reavers they are limited—clever in their own way—but with no deep understanding."

"The Dar Sala-at is quite correct," Thigpen said. "Evil repeats itself over and over in an unending pattern. Evil is powerful, implacable, a deadly force, certainly so, but it has no free will. It is programmed, shall we say, to achieve its goal. Therefore, its actions are—what is the best way to put it? Its actions are mechanical, predictable."

"At last we come to it," Rekkk cried. "The chink in the enemy's armor!"

"But this is pure evil we are speaking of now; therefore, nothing is quite what it appears to be."

Eleana frowned. "What do you mean?"

"What I tell you now is vital to our survival." Thigpen looked into each of their faces in turn. "The nature of evil, the very thing that is the chink in its armor, as Rekkk so colorfully put it, is often its greatest strength. For its mechanical, predictable methods can prove all too hypnotic to the likes of us."

"That's preposterous!" Rekkk blurted out. "Surely all of us have proved time and again that we know good from evil."

"Of course you have," Thigpen said. "But consider, Rekkk. Malistra was able to crawl inside you, to take you over so completely that you tried to kidnap the Dar Sala-at. And would have succeeded, mind you, had Riane not been so resourceful and quick of wit."

"That will never happen again," Rekkk said darkly. It was clear he did not care to remember that incident.

"Rekkk, I know you believe that. I am absolutely sure your intentions are good." Thigpen tapped her nails together. "However, inside all of us is a dark place. You know it, Rekkk, because you have been there. The Ramahan call it White Bone Gate. There resides all the rage, despair, envy, greed, all the negative emotions we harbor. Unlike Rekkk, most of us are not even aware this place exists. In fact, we'd likely deny it. The point is that daemons instinctively know how to open White Bone Gate, how to manipulate us so that the emotions pent up in that dark place inside us come swarming out. The closer we get to evil, the more time spent in its company, the more likely White Bone Gate will be breached, the more likely that dark place will be opened and all the sewage will spill out, polluting us, dazzling us, leading us astray. That is why Riane is correct when she says that we must have knowledge. We must know precisely what we are doing before we confront the daemon that is taking over Giyan."

"Then tell us!" Rekkk thundered.

"Alas, I cannot. I don't know enough about the Malasocca."

"Who does, then?" Eleana asked with a quick warning look at Rekkk's strangled cry.

"No one I know of." Thigpen spread her arms. "But look around you. We have the collected wisdom of the blessed Ramahan here at our fingertips."

"I can't read Old Tongue Kundalan and neither can Rekkk," Eleana pointed out.

Thigpen clucked her yellow tongue against the roof of her mouth. "But Riane and I—"

"I have another idea," Riane broke in. "Giyan told me who I needed to see for the next stage of my sorcerous training. Jonnqa, an imari at the Nimbus kashiggen in Axis Tyr. I think we should go there. I would wager she can help us."

Thigpen shook her head. "That is precisely what we will *not* do."

"I vote we go," Rekkk said shortly. "I have been to Nimbus. I know where it is, and I am familiar with its interior layout. Right now it's our best chance."

Thigpen thumped her thick, striped tail loudly against the chair back. "Listen to me for a moment. We must assume the worst, that the daemon already has possession of Giyan's most recent memories. That being the case, it is a good bet that Giyan—and the Tzelos—will be looking for Riane there." She held up the tiny sphere. "Nimbus is the place where it happens, Rekkk, where you and Riane die. You must avoid that future. You cannot go there."

There was a small silence into which the whistle of the wind intruded, causing the branches of the trees to dip and wave. They scratched against the side of the Library. An owl hooted mournfully.

Rekkk grunted, stalking out through the ruined window.

"I guess you and Riane had better start your research right away," Eleana said, before following Rekkk outside.

For some time, they stood together looking at the gathering sunrise. A chill wind, the first taste of autumn, fluttered their garments, crept up their arms and legs.

"This inaction is intolerable," Rekkk said at length. "Somewhere out there she's imprisoned, in pain, fighting for her life."

"You can't think about that now," Eleana said softly.

He threw his head back, shouted into the dawn. "That's all I *can* think about since it happened. It's all I *will* think about until she is safe at my side."

"Then you are in serious danger of driving yourself mad."

"Good. I deserve nothing less."

"What are you talking about?"

"I should have protected her."

"That's absurd. Giyan herself, with all her powerful sorcery, couldn't protect herself. You could not have helped her, Rekkk. You know that."

When he did not reply, she reached up and tugged at him. "Rekkk, look at me." Reluctantly, he turned. "This isn't about not being able to protect Giyan, is it?"

He glared at her, then could not continue to meet her gaze. When he tried to turn his head away, she guided it back with hands on his cheeks. "Talk to me, Rekkk."

He broke away, went stumbling down along one of the abbey paths. Eleana followed him, and when at length he stopped she came up to him. He had his hand curled around the bole of the sysal tree that had grown up through the lintel of the east-facing temple, splitting it asunder.

Eleana put a hand gently on the small of his back.

"Funny," he said in a hoarse whisper, "how something as innocuous as a tree can break through stone and mortar." He shook his head. "I mean, half the time you don't even notice trees, do you? They live at the periphery of your vision, there but not there. You take them for granted."

"Rekkk," she whispered, "what is it?"

He looked up into the rustling branches. "This tree is like . . ." He closed his eyes for a moment. "Like that place inside me—what did Thigpen call it?"

"White Bone Gate."

He nodded. "The place Malistra touched inside of me, twining like a serpent in the darkness. The place I never knew was there, the place that lived at the periphery of my consciousness. She took possession of it, made me into . . ." He snatched his hand from the sysal tree as if it had caught fire.

"Rekkk, please—"

"Don't you see?" He turned to her. "The same thing is happening to Giyan now—only it's worse for her, far worse. She's being taken over body and soul, remade into something . . . horrific, unholy, evil."

"We'll find her, Rekkk, we'll save her. Have faith."

"Faith." He laughed harshly. "You don't know what it's like to have something of pure evil crawling around inside you, boring into your brain, imprisoning you. The horror of it!" He took her hand in his. "Pray it never happens to you, Eleana. Pray to your Great Goddess Miina to spare you from that fate."

Eleana led him over to a stone bench. "You're exhausted, Rekkk. Let's sit for a while and speak of other things. Or not speak at all." She took his hand in hers. "Together, we will watch the sun come up and marvel at its beauty. We will count the colors in the clouds and free our minds. We will let our hearts rest from our pain."

W e have set ourselves a difficult task," Thigpen said as she took down a stack of books from the Library shelves.

"Tell me something I do not already know."

Thigpen took note of Riane's tone of voice as she watched her thumb through *The Origins of Darkness*. "On the other hand, we have a great advantage. You are able to read and absorb text at an astonishing pace."

Riane was aware of the weakness of the thrumming beneath her feet, Each abbey was built atop a major nexus point on the sorcerous grid of power bourns that enmeshed Kundala. Each nexus was different. The meaning of both these facts had been lost for more than a century. All night, she had felt the bourns stuttering, like the belabored breath of a patient.

Riane voiced a suspicion that had been forming. "You persuaded us not to go after Giyan because you are trying to protect me."

"That is one reason, yes. But if you think I lied to you—"

"The time for protecting me is past, don't you think?"

"Not at all," Thigpen said sharply. "You know so little about your fate. You are the Dar Sala-at and yet . . ."

Riane watched her carefully.

"You are young. Your Gift is raw, only partially trained. You are only in the first flower of your ascendancy. Plus, you are female. You do not yet fully appreciate the difficulty this will present. We have been awaiting the advent of the Dar Sala-at, yes, because you will lead us out of our time of bondage. But even the Ramahan who believe in you most fervently have been expecting a male savior. This will come as a great shock to them when you reveal yourself, and there will be the inevitable cabal of naysayers. It is written that you will have a holy protector at your side."

"The Prophesies again. How is it that I have not been told about this holy protector before?"

"The Prophesies are written down now, but they came down to the Ramahan orally, through numerous generations. There are thousands of them, intertwining like tropical vines. Many intersect, others overlap or even are contradictory. There is a Prophesy that has been interpreted by some to indicate that the Dar Sala-at will be a male. But if, as we believe, these Prophesies have their origins in Miina, the complexities, the entanglements, even the paradoxes make sense. Miina never viewed us as Her slaves. We have free will in most matters. This is why the Prophesies must be interpreted; this is why some of them will be proved true and others false. Our lives are complex, even at times seemingly paradoxical. In any case, the future is unknown. What, otherwise, would be the point of living? Still, the Prophesies exist and so the Seers interpret, but, as you know, the Seers soon go mad, and die."

"You must be this holy protector, then."

"I?" Thigpen laughed. "He is known as the Nawatir, a fierce and relentless warrior. He springs into being through sorcerous transformation. His coming marks the next step in your evolution, Dar Sala-at. As for me, I am and always will be a Rappa, a member of a race close to Miina, once companions to the first Ramahan until we were falsely accused of killing Mother and forced into hiding."

Riane looked down. Who would be her Nawatir? How could she know? She put aside for the moment her questions and began to read. The pages of the tome flip-flip-flipped past her eyes. After a time, she became lost in the text, and then, suddenly, the text began to dissolve. Her head felt light, and she knew another memory of Riane's former life, before the dying husk had been joined with Annon, had broken off from the glacier buried deep in their mind . . .

She was walking along an ice-encrusted ridge. A blue wind scoured her with frozen snow. At the top of the world high amid the ragged peaks of the Djenn Marre she moved with slow deliberate strides. She kept the air, so thin it barely existed, deep in her lungs. Her heart beat fast as her breathing slowed. She was tired but, somehow, at the same time exhilarated. A sudden cry caused her to turn, and she saw the bird winging in on a thermal current, its snow-white wings and black-and-white-speckled body hurtling toward her. It was huge, larger than any bird Annon had ever seen or read about. It was three times her size. She held her ground as it approached. It studied her with piercing blue eyes, and feelings of comfort and of love enveloped her. She spoke to it in a language—

With a start Riane sat up straight. She had spoken to the giant bird in Venca! What had she said? But the memory stopped there, as if it were a storybook whose pages had been maliciously ripped out. She massaged her head, trying to will the memory to continue. She could never do it. The memories surfaced, presented themselves, isolated fragments of the original Riane's life, in their own time, in their own mysterious way. There was simply no controlling them. It was like working on a vast and unknowable puzzle. She had a number of pieces now, but so far she could not see where they fit together.

Riane looked over at Thigpen, who had opened the first book on the stack. She sat, reading, her tail curled around her, on the refectory table, humming a little to herself. This sight served to jolt Riane back into reality, and she grew angry.

"Don't you care?" she said.

"What?" Thigpen looked up, blinking.

"Don't you care at all that Giyan is being slowly destroyed?"

Thigpen sat up straight. "My dear Riane, of course I care. I care a great deal. But panicking about it isn't going to do anyone any good, least of all Giyan."

"But you seem so frightfully calm!"

"A state of being I have spent centuries cultivating." She padded down the table toward Riane. "Rappa tend to have high blood pressure, you know. Comes from eons of being the favorite food of the Ja-Gaar. See one coming, we keel right over, like as not. Shocking lapse in the survival instinct, let me tell you. Still, such a deficiency makes the smart of the species smarter, eh? If you've got a brain in your cranium, you're forced to figure out ways to keep the old pressure under control, aren't you? Otherwise, you're dead meat. So, yes, I am calm, and you should be, too. Promotes clarity of thought, which is what is required of us now."

"Of course you're right, but . . ." All at once, a memory surfaced and her heart contracted. "Thigpen, Giyan told me that in order for the Tzelos to be in our Realm it had to be carried here by an archdaemon."

The Rappa's eyes opened wide. "Then we have another enemy to deal with. Oh, dear!"

Riane's eyes grew fierce. "I lost her once, Thigpen. By some miracle I got her back. And now, now . . ." Her hands balled into fists. "I swear to you that I will move the stars to save her." Her voice shook and tears stood in the corners of her eyes. "But how? How?"

"Patience, Dar-Sala-at, we have only just begun to—"

"To N'Luuura with patience!" Riane swept books off the table. The two looked at each other for several trembling moments. "I need a sign,

Thigpen." Riane was almost pleading. "Something to tell us that we have a chance to get her back."

Thigpen leapt lightly onto the floor. "This is a time of great testing." She began to gather the scattered books one by one. "You must find that sign inside yourself, Dar Sala-at." She scrambled under the table to get the last book. "This is a time—" Silence.

"Thigpen?"

The Rappa backed out from under the table. "Riane, look there!"

Riane got down on her hands and knees, ducked under the refectory table overhang. And that is when she saw it, lying innocently deep in the shadows. She glanced upward, saw where it had been affixed to the underside of the table. Doubtless, the coming of the Malasocca had dislodged it.

Thigpen sniffed at it, her snout quivering nervously. "V'ornn technology. What is it?"

It was about the size and shape of a seedpod, but it was made of tertium and germanium, dull as an overcast day. "It is a duscaant, a Khagggun recording device."

Thigpen sat back. "That cannot be good. What on Kundala is it doing here?"

Riane held it up to direct light and it vanished. "An object of stealth, of clandestine watching. It is a stealer of secrets, a repository of information."

Thigpen regarded it as if it were a packet of V'ornn explosives. "We should destroy the dread thing. Now."

"No."

Thigpen shuddered. "But—"

"As you know, no V'ornn can penetrate the Library now, not even a Gyrgon. The logical conclusion is that the duscaant was secreted here before the spell was cast." Riane turned the thing over, pressed a hidden stud with her fingernail. "Here is the date on which it was placed here and activated."

Thigpen bent closer, read with rising alarm the V'ornn numbers. "That is five years before the abbey was invaded, its members dragged away to V'ornn interrogation chambers some ninety years ago." Her eyes flickered up to Riane's face like flames. "How? How could a Gyrgon listening device be planted inside these walls? How could such a thing be?"

"You know," Riane said slowly and deliberately, "because there can be only one answer."

Thigpen's eyes were wide and staring. "A Ramahan collaborator."

Riane nodded. "Someone very powerful. Doubtless a sorceress." For they both knew that the Gyrgon dealt only with individuals who, in their own ways, wielded great power. "That is why we will not destroy it. In here, perhaps, resides a clue to the identity of that collaborator."

"Or fooling with a Gyrgon object will get us killed." Thigpen rubbed her cheek with the back of a forepaw. "We will discuss this no further, and certainly not mention it to the others. There is already far too much anxiety floating around for my liking. Let us resume our reading, and leave this conundrum for another day."

A while later, Eleana appeared, bearing plates of cold food and tankards of water, which she placed before them, her eyes asking the question she was afraid to voice. Neither of them said a word, and she retreated, ashen-faced. Riane briefly rested her bleary eyes on Eleana's form before returning to her reading. The books in this Library were maddening. They assumed knowledge that she did not possess even though she had memorized both of Miina's Sacred Volumes. The result was somewhat akin to looking at the pictures in a book while not being able to read the accompanying text. Some references were simply incomprehensible. For others, she could extrapolate some things, infer others, but without a clear understanding of the overarching principles and theories under which everything operated she could not be certain her conclusions were correct. Perhaps, she surmised, the problem stemmed from the fact that the books predated both *Utmost Source* and *The Book of Recantation*. What came before these two holy pillars of Miina's rule? Riane did not know and clearly Thigpen didn't either. She felt like an infant invading an adult domain. There was so much she longed to know, so much sitting right here at her fingertips. It was maddening. If only she could understand what she was reading! Giyan was right. She needed more training, that much was indisputable.

Toward evening, she said, "I may have found something. The Malasocca is transformational, it says here."

"Now we are getting somewhere."

"Apparently, daemons possess only knowledge of Kyofu sorcery, not Osoru. If they knew both they would be able to conjure Eye Window spells, which are much more powerful."

"But Giyan is an Osoru sorceress."

"Yes," Riane said, "and that is the point of her possession. Once the Malasocca is complete the daemon will have access to all her knowledge, including Osoru."

Thigpen's whiskers were twitching fearfully. "And then it will know—"

Riane nodded. "Everything. Yes."

"But in the distant past before Miina cast the daemons into the Abyss there were incidents of Malasocca."

"The daemons gain possession of the knowledge only while they are in the host body. Once they are cast out, they cannot retain it."

"Well, that is something, at least. But . . ." Thigpen's eyes were dark with foreboding as she voiced the question they had both been afraid to ask. "How long do we have before Lady Giyan is completely taken over by the daemon?"

"It doesn't say; this is only a passing reference." Riane continued to read. "It does say that after the halfway point it becomes increasingly more difficult to reverse the transmogrification."

"By what means can we effect the reversal?"

Riane shook her head. "But there is a word here. *Maasra*." She frowned. "It is neither Old Tongue nor, to my knowledge, Venca."

"Cross-references?"

"None that I can find."

"Then this mysterious word is the only clue we have." Thigpen stretched and yawned, her yellow tongue curling up. "What we need is a first-class dialectician."

"Where on Kundala are we going to find that?"

Thigpen took up a piece of meat, sniffed it. "As it happens I know one." She wrinkled her nose as she popped the morsel into her mouth. "Unfortunately, he's dead."

4

Madness Is As Madness Does

The Sea of Blood was choppy in the following southwest wind, dark as ludd-wine, dark as its namesake. Small fishing boats bobbed in the slips at the wharf and, farther out, the tall-masted ships of the Sarakkon, the wild seafaring race of Kundala's southern continent, rode uneasily at anchor. The Sarakkon believed in many gods, female and male. The great, arcing prows of their trading ships were carved into their brooding visages—part Sarakkon, part fearsome beast.

From the south-facing window high up in Receiving Spirit, Marethyn Stogggul had a splendid view of the Sarakkonian vessels currently loading and unloading their cargo. The Kundalan especially prized kingga, a decorative hardwood with magnificent striations, as well as foodstuffs of an exotic nature that could not be grown in the harsher climate here on the northern continent. In exchange, the Kundalan sold their fanciful dry goods, bolts of handmade cloth and casks of thick, sweet mead the Sarakkon coveted. But Marethyn also knew there was other Sarakkon cargo, not openly spoken of—laaga, for instance, the dried, ground leaf which, when smoked or chewed, produced a pronounced narcotic effect that was highly addictive. It was a crude and dangerous drug, especially when compared to salamuuun. On the other hand, while salamuuun was not addictive, laaga was far cheaper, and readily available in the city's back alleys. The Ashera Consortium kept tight control on salamuuun, allowing it to be sold only in licensed kashiggen.

With a sigh, Marethyn turned back into the stark white interior of the madness ward and smiled into her brother's blank face.

"I saw your brother, Kurgan," she said without leaking a trace of the anger she felt in her hearts. "I told him how aggrieved you were not to be at the Rescendance. I gave him your respects, and he asked me to give you his. You were greatly missed at the rite."

Terrettt did not respond or give any indication that he had heard her. He sat in a chair, his torso bent forward and tense, his robes hanging loosely on his too-thin frame. His black eyes, sunk deep in their sockets, burned too brightly, as with a high fever. Before him was a drawing table with an angled top. On it was a huge sheet of paper, along with an array of precisely aligned drawing implements. He was drawing with quick, jerky movements of his hand and forearm. His artistic accomplishments were undeniable but also quite unfathomable. No matter. Marethyn spent much of her time in her Divination Street atelier selling the fruits of his labor alongside her own. He drew constantly or he slept. This was his life.

His black eyes watched her briefly as she moved, then flicked downward to his current work in progress. She wondered what he was thinking. On the wall in front of him was a huge topographical map of the northern continent, which she had put up after he had clawed down three different paintings. He never had a reason for destroying the artwork she had brought, at least none that she could determine, and it could be said without fear of contradiction that she knew Terrettt better than anyone, including his own mother.

She had come upon the map, rolled up and dusty, in a small curio shop on the Street of Dreams and had seized upon it immediately as a replacement for the ripped paintings. His room was just too depressing without *something* on the walls. So far, he had not marred it, though the only way she could be sure he was aware of it was that its colors were slowly creeping into his newest paintings. This seemed huge to her, an important victory for him as well as for her.

Terrettt began to drool. She came away from the window at once to wipe his red lips. Oblivious, he continued to draw. For a moment she studied his face. While Kurgan was all harsh angles, cunning eyes, and an avaricious nature, Terrettt possessed a certain serenity that was so profound the frightening seizures that violated it were all the more heartbreaking. Every time she looked at him she hated her family all the more. They were too busy being embarrassed by him even to acknowledge his existence.

"What are you working on today?" she asked as she came around to his side of the table. "Is this the sea, the sky, the land?" She pointed. "And what are these circles? Stars in the sky? A constellation, perhaps?" These seven circles had begun to appear in his work in one form or another starting several weeks ago. That's when she had bought him the huge sheets of paper he obviously needed. He had never before created a repeating motif—in fact, that was one of the major elements that had separated him from other artists who, like writers, tended to revisit the same themes, tackling them from different angles and aspects.

"Terrettt," she said, giving up on the drawing, "will you talk to me today?" She sat on a chair beside him and tenderly wiped more drool off his lips. "I would so like it if you would talk to me." She took the brush from his fingers, engaged his eyes with the animation of her lovely face. "Won't you try? For me?"

Terrettt sat frozen for some time. At last his mouth opened, the lower jaw flapping up and down.

"That's right," she said excitedly. It was all she could do not to hug him, but she had learned the hard way that he could not tolerate physical contact. "Speak to me. I know you want to."

"Water," he enunciated slowly and painfully. "Blue."

Marethyn's hearts leapt. "Yes!" she cried. "The water is blue. You can see it from the window." She pointed. "There!"

"Water," Terrettt said. "Black."

Marethyn frowned. "The water is black? Well, it's black at night, I guess. Is that what you mean? Is this a drawing of the sea at night?"

Terrettt's eyes seemed to be trying to tell her more than his mouth could. An agony of emotion contorted his face for a moment. His mouth worked convulsively, but all that came out were unintelligible sounds, followed by a fresh spurt of drool.

"Water," he repeated, as Marethyn moved to clean his chin. "Black." He pointed to the drawing he was making, his trembling forefinger stabbing out at the circles he had drawn.

"Terrettt, what are you trying to tell me?"

His mouth worked spasmodically as he tried desperately to express himself. All that emerged was a series of heavy grunts. Tears stood out in his eyes, and he pounded his balled fists against his temples.

"No, Terrettt!" She tried to pull his hands away. "No!"

His face filled with blood, his eyes rolled up in his head. She backed away just in time. He struck out at her, missed, tried again and, instead, off-balance, fell to the floor, where he began to thrash and foam. His eyes were as opaque as a corpse's.

Marethyn shouted, and a Deirus appeared in the doorway. "You will have to leave now," he said as he glided up. He was tall, stoop-shouldered, thin to the point of emaciation. His deep-set eyes were pale and watery, as if he had been staring at the sun for too long. The hollows beneath his cheekbones had an almost painful depth. His hands were long and thin, their fingers stained mahogany by the curious fluids he worked with daily. She had seen him several times before. His name was Kirlll Qandda.

Terrettt was very quick, but he was no match for the Deirus, who was surprisingly powerful. Unfortunately, the Deirus locked Terrettt's wrists behind his back. The intolerable touch made him all the wilder, his eyes rolling madly in his head, spittle flying from his snarling lips.

"It is too dangerous for you when he is like this," Kirlll Qandda said as he struggled to subdue Terrettt.

"His name is Terrettt. And do not talk as if he isn't here." If her tone was sharp she felt she had just cause. Too often the Deirus' suppressed rage at being separate from and unequal to the Genomatekks of their caste took the form of small but galling discourtesies to those who most depended on them. Perhaps their intensive five-year training with the Gyrgon contributed to this superciliousness. But though they irked Marethyn, it had never occurred to her to complain to her father. In-deed, save for her monthly reports on Terrettt's progress, or rather his lack of it, she had avoided him at all costs.

"I apologize," Kirlll Qandda said as he scrambled after Terrettt. "But your brother—er, Terrettt—does not like to take his medicine."

The Deirus had Terrettt in position, and he applied the transdermal spray directly to her brother's eyes. Apparently, the retinas were the most efficient pathway to the brain. Marethyn had heard stories of desperate laaga addicts spraying their eyes with a mist distilled from the dried and cured leaves. Slowly, the eerie, soulless look faded from Terrettt's eyes, and his breathing returned to normal.

"Why does this happen to him?" Marethyn asked as she wiped the spittle and flecks of blood off his face. In his frenzy, he had bitten his lower lip.

"You must let him rest now," Kirlll Qandda said not unkindly. "We can talk as I walk you out."

She looked up at him. Seeing her brother in such agony exhausted her. "Tell me, Kirlll Qandda," she said, "how long have you been on Terrettt's case?"

"I was recently transferred on, mistress."

"Please do not address me in that manner."

Kirlll Qandda appeared startled. "I do not understand. Mistress is a term of respect."

"Mistress is a term created by males. It is demeaning. It is meant to keep females in their place." She stood up. "I am ready to leave now."

The hallway was bright, startling in its starkness, as starkness was not the Kundalan way. The walls were sheets of pale featureless gypsum fastened together with copper-headed pins. There was a beauty in their smoothness, in the way they had been quarried and cut so that the subtle sedimentary grain flowed in one direction. Marethyn saw this with her practiced artist's eye. Overhead, oval skylights let in the day-light. They passed doorways into wards similar to the one in which Terrettt lived. In some she could see beautiful clouds of sparkles in the air, sure indications of ion-force-field barriers. Occupants shuffled about their quarters or stared fixedly at her as she passed by. Their empty gazes seemed to suck the life out of her.

Kirlll Qandda smiled with his pale, watery eyes. "Terrettt's painting gets better all the time, don't you think?"

"I would prefer you talk to me about my brother."

He sighed, as if they had come to a point in the conversation he had been dreading. "I wish I had good news for you." There were other Deirus in the hall now, along with several armed Khaggun. They were passing the violent ward, and he kept her at a brisk pace. "I wish I had any news at all." He spread his hands. "Unfortunately, I do not. Your brother is as he was when he was brought in here ten years ago. No therapy we have tried has had the least effect on his condition. The seizures appear randomly. They seem to have no apparent trigger, though stress and exhaustion are certainly major factors."

"I understand," Marethyn said with heavy hearts. This was old news, but at least it had been delivered by a Deirus unlike the others who had spoken to her. "Is it really necessary to drug him so often?"

"I am afraid that without the periodic transdermal sprays your brother's seizures would become uncontrollable. He would injure him-self, as he did when your family first brought him here. Then there are the other inmates to consider."

"I am grateful that he hasn't been transferred to the violent ward."

"To be perfectly honest it's been a constant struggle. Some in the administration are . . . uncomfortable with him in his current surroundings."

"And where do you stand on this matter, Kirlll Qandda?"

"I have two of Terrettt's paintings hanging in my residence."

They had reached the staircase, a typically wide, florid Kundalan work of art in honey-and-black onyx illuminated from above by a light-well in the shape of an eye.

Marethyn glanced back down the hallway. It was always a jarring moment when she left him, knowing she was free to go wherever she chose while he was locked away in here. "Is there no hope for him at all?"

The Deirus was silent.

"I am well aware that the Gyrgon forbid you to give out any information on your patients. But he is my brother, and I love him. Nobody else does."

Kirlll Qandda shook his head. "I am Deirus. If I was found out, I would be subject to—"

"But, dear, Kirlll Qandda, you are the only one who can help me." Marethyn paused to lick her lips. "As you say, you are Deirus. Perhaps one day you will need my help as I now need yours."

She reached out and touched him on the arm, and Kirlll Qandda's eyes followed the movement of her hand.

"You are not afraid to touch me."

"Why should I be?"

Kirlll Qandda gave a little laugh. Quickly stifled. He nodded to her, led her out of the crowded corridor and into a small, dimly lighted cubicle lined with locked metal cabinets. It was deserted. He closed the door softly behind them.

"The condition your brother has," Kirlll Qandda whispered, "well, it defies all conventional gene therapy. Tests show that his DNA is undamaged. His brain chemistry is, of course, abnormal, but each time we try to rebalance him we fail." He looked at the door for a moment, as if fearful a Khagggun or, worse, a Gyrgon would barge in. "It is almost as if his condition continually mutates to actively resist our best efforts." He tried to smile. "It is something of a mystery, I am afraid, one that we have been unable to solve. It is why Terrettt's Deirus keeps getting reassigned. The case defeats them."

"But, surely there must be—" Marethyn shook her head. "I mean, he is a Stogggul, after all. A great artist."

Just then Kirlll Qandda's wrist-communicator buzzed and a Genomatekk called his name in a sharp, imperious tone. He gave her a quick, sad smile. "I am sorry, but now I really must be going. Good afternoon to you, Marethyn Stogggul." He turned on his heel and quickly went out of the cubicle.

Marethyn, gaining the door, craned her neck, briefly glimpsed a pack of Khagggun. Some held babies roughly in their arms. Others herded a group of small children—mixed breed, V'ornn and Kundalan. A Gyrgon came into the hall, lifted a beckoning hand. Kirlll Qandda and the imperious Genomatekk took charge of the group as they filed through the doorway in which the Gyrgon stood. *What are they doing with those children?* she wondered. Just then, a Khagggun noticed her and came striding down the corridor toward her.

"This area is off-limits," he said sternly.

She took a quick step backward. It angered her that she was so easily intimidated.

"You are ordered to leave, immediately."

What choice did she have? As she turned and descended the main staircase she noticed a speck of Terrettt's blood like a tattoo on the back of her hand.

The SaTrryn Consortium long-range grav-carriage, sleek and glimmering with impeccably harnessed power, waited just outside the grounds of the regent's palace. Kurgan could see Sornnn SaTrryn with two of his orderlies making the last of the preparations for their overnight trip to the Korrush. He stopped, and so did his heavily armed Haaar-kyut escort. As he watched Sornnn go about his small routine tasks Kurgan was once again reminded of how apart he remained from the mainstream of V'ornn life. Oddly, deep inside he found a desire to insert himself into the bits of overheard colloquy, but owing to his office he could not. Ministers, Bashkir and Khagggun alike, fell silent at his approach, their conversation cut off in midsentence. The spell of fear he had so ruthlessly cast had worked too well, and now here, in the

very center of this glimmery web, he found himself isolate, deprived
of friends his own age, of the breath of life essential to a still-young
and growing V'ornn. By his own machinations he had arrived prematurely at the stage of eminence normally granted to those of advanced
age who had had the advantage of years to gain experience in how to
cope.

Then, with a silent *N'Luuura take it!* he shrugged off his lingering
melancholy and strode to the side of the grav-carriage. It was a gleaming
copper color, perhaps ten meters long, with a smallish cockpit up front
for the pilot-captain and the navigator. Behind was another cockpit,
spacious and luxuriously appointed, for the passengers. In the rear was
space for provisions and supplies and the like.

Sornnn SaTrryn greeted the regent as he clambered aboard. He said
not a word of protest as the pair of Haaar-kyut guards sat on either
side of him. Three hours later, deep in the Kundalan countryside, with
bales of dried wrygrass, glennan, and oatgrass neatly stacked in the yellow fields on either side of them, Sornnn broke out the food, and they
had a midday meal. They saw folk gathering for one of the many Kundalan festivals.

At first, they spoke of inconsequential matters, then, at Kurgan's
request, Sornnn talked at length about the Korrush.

"I cannot pretend that spending so much time among the Five Tribes
has not changed me," Sornnn said finally.

"It seems to me that Kundala had changed us all," Kurgan said, wiping his lips.

"In what way has it changed you, regent?"

The farmers had erected a multicolored pole; they wore horned
masks and danced around a bonfire, their implements placed in a larger
circle around them. They stopped, however, as soon as they spied the
oncoming hoverpod. Quickly, they hurled their masks into the fire.
With a fearful look, they gathered up their tools and returned to their
labor.

"I think of us, of our long stay on Kundala, of being idle, of being in
one place too long, of being deprived of both home and of the forward
momentum impelling us to find another home."

"Did it ever occur to you, regent, that we may at last have found a
home?"

"What, here? Kundala?"

"That's right." Sornnn nodded. "It seems to me that we V'ornn have passed through the stage when we can continue to labor under the delusion that there is a certain romanticism in being wanderers. I look around me at my fellow V'ornn, and this is what I see. I see a race that finds its wandering enervating. And being the eternal outsider seems to be at the heart of our motivation for the destruction we wreak on every civilization we encounter."

Sornnn said, "The one emotion, I think, that we cannot allow ourselves is self-pity, and so we annihilate those who might harbor like the plague that selfsame pity."

"There are those who would consider your words treasonous."

"Why? I have said nothing against the V'ornn Modality, only that I find our creeping ennui disturbing. Surely, these are the words of a patriot." He laughed easily. "Besides, I have little regard for the opinions of others. I have found, regent, that even the cleverest assault on a closed mind is a waste of time."

Now it was Kurgan's turn to laugh. "I take your meaning, Sornnn SaTrryn, and mark it well. I suspect that there may already be unexpected benefits to this sojourn to primitive lands."

They traveled on, north by northeast. The high haze of late summer had been swiftly overtaken by the clear, crisp air of autumn, which was with every day deepening into the profound cold of the Kundalan winter. The smell of fallen leaves and kuello-fir needles, turned to mulch by the autumnal rains, perfumed the air. Here and there a patch of ice could be seen glistening, a harbinger of winter.

The neat geometric patterns of agriculture were rapidly replaced by long bleak scars in the denuded hillsides, evidence of the extensive V'ornn program of strip-mining for lortan. This lucrative operation marched into the west like the tines of a mammoth rake, and with it the temporary villages supporting the ragged Kundalan slaves who worked the mines directed by their Mesagggun and Khagggun overseers. Lortan was a dense substance that lay in thick arteries beneath the topsoil of the hillsides. It was this homely black clay that the V'ornn Mesagggun refined into veradium.

The oblate sun passed behind their left shoulders. Its cool, brittle light flared against the ice-blue crags of the Djenn Marre. With the changing of the seasons, the snow line had markedly advanced. They could clearly mark the higher elevations, where the Abbey of Floating

White and its many-tiered town of Stone Border were to be found farther to their northwest. Ahead stretched the Great Northern Plain known by its inhabitants as the Korrush.

All at once, they were engulfed in eerie twilight. Clouds massed on the western horizon, lit up, utterly still. The sky was orange. The entire world seemed to be on fire. Nearing the village of Im-Thera, the vastness of the Korrush became overwhelming, the sheer immensity of the space a kind of crushing weight. Kurgan could not explain it, had not believed Sornnn SaTrryn when he had warned him of this initial effect, and yet this crepuscular steppe engendered in him a kind of existential dread.

They overflew Im-Thera, a tiny, mean-looking village of tents and not much more. The place looked filthy to Kurgan. Probably insect-infested, too, he thought. Nothing moved save the tent flaps, but in a small, dusty, open space a cooking fire blazed unattended.

Beside him, Sornnn rose and, bent over, whispered something he could not hear to the SaTrryn pilot-captain. The moment Sornnn regained his seat the grav-carriage went into a long, swooping dive.

"Regent, I do not wish to alarm you, and I most certainly do not want your Haaar-kyut to act precipitously," Sornnn said calmly but authoritatively, "but I fear something is amiss."

Kurgan peered ahead of them.

"No, regent, look low the sky."

Kurgan saw a coven of large blue-black birds, circling on enormously long wings. As he watched, one dipped down to earth, only to rise again with something in its beak.

"Cshey'in. Carrion birds of the Korrush," Sornnn said. "They will eat anything that is dead, but what they prefer is the flesh of tribesmen."

Kurgan lowered his gaze to the spot above which the cshey'in were circling. "I don't see anything."

"When we land," Sornnn continued, "it is imperative that you remain inside the grav-carriage no matter what happens. Your guard will keep you safe."

"What is it?" Kurgan said. "What has happened?" Far from being frightened, he itched to feel the weight of an ion cannon in his arms.

Im-Thera, the pathetic village of nomads, was just under a kilometer behind them.

"See there?" Sornnn pointed. As they crested a low ridge, a warren of earth mounds became immediately visible, below which could be seen a subterranean gridwork of ancient walls, crumbled, clotted with fibrous roots. To one side, a scattered rune of red, its edges fluttering in the fitful gritty breeze. "Do you mark the pale red robes? Those are bodies of Beyy Das, the tribe that oversees the archaeological dig of Za Hara-at."

The SaTrryn navigator turned his hatchet face to them briefly. "Killed only hours ago," he said in his laconic manner. "The corpses are not yet picked clean."

Sornnn took out an ion cannon and, with admirable precision, knocked the birds out of the sky. Their screams echoed through the emptiness.

"I take it you have a permit for that weapon," Kurgan said to cover his admiration of Sornnn's accuracy from a swiftly moving vehicle.

The navigator reached into a forward compartment, offered an official Khagggun yellow-red data-crystal for his inspection. He waved it away.

A moment later, they had landed. Sornnn jumped out, his pilot-captain, similarly armed, just behind him. The navigator took over the grav-carriage's controls, the engine ready to lift off at the least provocation. Kurgan's Haaar-kyut were standing on either side of him, weapons at the ready.

Warily, Sornnn and the pilot-captain reconnoitered the site. At one end was a long tamped-dirt ramp, which they eventually took down into the remains of Za Hara-at itself. They were gone for some time. Kurgan kept a keen eye out, but he saw nothing moving. The wind stuttered and keened through the ruins, creating snatches of a mournful melody that hinted at mysterious death and long-ago destruction. His guard were at once vigilant and serene; they were used to off-world missions. Kurgan had no doubt that they would give their lives in order to save his.

At length, Sornnn and his companion reappeared. They had between them a Beyy Das tribesman. He was clearly injured. Blood streamed from a gash in his skull, and halfway up the ramp they were obliged to half support him back to the grav-carriage.

As they hoisted him aboard, the navigator broke out a first-aid kit.

They began to examine the Beyy Das as he slumped heavily against a bulkhead.

"A raid, he tells us," Sornnn said, plunking himself down next to Kurgan. "Jeni Cerii reavers. The Jeni Cerii are the most warlike of the Five Tribes. The other tribes are subject to periodic raids. Especially here."

"Why is that?" Kurgan asked.

"Come with me and I will show you." Sornnn stood up. "The Jeni Cerii are long gone. It is perfectly safe now."

Nevertheless, his Haaar-kyut insisted on accompanying them down into the bowels of Kundala. As they descended the earthen ramp, Kurgan was astonished at how extensive the excavations were.

When he mentioned this, Sornnn replied, "Za Hara-at was a citadel of enormous proportions. By many accounts, it was far larger than Axis Tyr. And the excavations here are bearing that out. Already three layers of the city have been uncovered, but only partially, even though almost a square kilometer has been dug out. Not all of what has been unburied has been explored."

Where the ramp ended the long-dead streets of Za Hara-at began. They appeared to be constructed quite improbably of beaten bronze that glowed in the gathering dusk. There were walls and windows, doors and trestles, crossroads and corners, all unfinished or, more accurately, frozen in the midst of their death throes, still standing, partially decomposed. The inquisitive Korrush wind pushed through these dead spaces with a vigor altogether lacking in the rest of the landscape.

"This is what I wanted to show you." Sornnn was kneeling in the dust. As Kurgan watched, he ran his fingertips over runes carved from lapis and emperor carnelian. "You see these ancient symbols? You see how they have been desecrated with excrement? And here. This pile of burnt bones. Bones of the ancestors of Za Hara-at, painstakingly and reverently exhumed by the Beyy Das. The Jeni Cerii have no religion. Za Hara-at was a Holy City, and yet they deny such a thing. But, you see, it draws them like a magnet, though they do not know why and, not knowing, they beat at it, defile it with an unreasoning hatred that masks their own ignorance."

Kurgan recalled the conversation they had had over the midday meal. "According to your unscientific theory," he said somewhat sardonically, "they are not dissimilar to us V'ornn."

"Admittedly, philosophical theories are not provable by scientific methodology," Sornnn said as he regained his feet. "Nevertheless, they are often useful in provoking spirited debate among thoughtful individuals." He turned to Kurgan. "What do you think, regent? Is there a similarity?"

"I will admit that rage is a major component of the V'ornn psyche," Kurgan said despite himself.

"The next question to ask is, why? I think you will agree that the answer is a vital one."

Kurgan's attention was directed to a shard of a vessel clattering through the dust devils on the bronze street. Like everything in the grave of Za Hara-at, the shard was infused with unknown meaning. It reminded him that there was an uneasiness here, a certain restiveness as if the long sleep of death had never been fully accepted or had been irrevocably disturbed by N'Luuura knew what numinous force. Kurgan, not normally attuned to necromantic nuances, nevertheless had the creeping sensation that something still abided here, ancient and unknowable. He said as much to Sornnn.

"I must say that I am impressed, regent," Sornnn replied. "I do not pretend to know the truth of it, but the Beyy Das believe that such a thing as you speak of—whatever it may be—does exist. They also claim that it periodically emerges from its ancient home and kills one of their own."

"Have you seen the body of any of these so-called victims?"

"As a matter of fact, I have. It may be that he was murdered by a Jeni Cerii raiding party, but if so they have rituals far stranger than any of the other tribes. This corpse the Beyy Das showed me was without either bones or blood."

"That seems impossible!"

"I certainly would have said so, regent, had I not seen the victim with my own eyes. It was as if something had sucked the life right out of him. All that was left was a sack of skin and desiccated flesh."

Kurgan looked around again, not with any degree of fear, but rather with renewed interest. He wondered once again why Nith Batoxxx was now so intent on rebuilding Za Hara-at. "Resurrecting" it, as he had put it. What was lurking in these ancient ruins? What power did Nith Batoxxx hope to unearth here? Kurgan was now doubly pleased that Sornnn SaTrryn had suggested this journey, for standing in these vast and eerie ruins, he felt the spell of Za Hara-at enfolding him, and he knew he was one step closer to unlocking the secrets of the Gyrgon's mind.

It was a busy night at Nimbus, and Mittelwin's attention was required in many places at once. The old V'ornn seer who worked the plush entry chamber, amusing clients on their way in and out of the kashiggen, was ill again. The local Genomatekk said it was chronic Kraelian cytosis, but Mittelwin knew better. She knew the signs of advanced salamuuun addiction. No one spoke about this noxious aspect of the drug. In fact, it was vehemently denied. Yet she knew salamuuun was addictive, having seen the results of it too many times.

One of her imari had the night off because of a death in the family, another had been beaten by a particularly aggressive Khaggun. By Gyrgon decree, there were strict laws against such behavior in the kashiggen. Which was not to say that it didn't happen. Mittelwin had her own way of handling such disturbing matters. When she arrived at the chamber, Jonnqa appeared as if she had been run down by a hoverpod. She signed for Lace, the massive Mesagggun who worked for her, to bind the offending client. It mattered not to her what caste he was, when he was in her kashiggen he abided by the rules set down by the Gyrgon or suffered the consequences. Every client was advised of this upon entering for the first time.

In her time as dzuoko she had learned a thing or two about punishment—and about the mechanisms of terror. She approached the Khagggun, whom Lacc had pushed down onto a chair. His arms were bound behind his back, his ankles lashed together. Standing before him, she spread her long legs. Slowly, she raised her floor-length gown until it was clear to the Khagggun that she was naked underneath. His eyes drank her in, his nostrils dilated slightly as he scented her. She sat athwart his powerful thighs, took his head in her hands, and kissed him hard. As she did so, she ground her hips down on him. His tender parts began to swell, rising up to meet hers.

Males are so predictable, she thought. *They think with their brains only so long as their tender parts are dry.*

When she felt him in full flower, she raised herself up, reached down with her hand, and did something very nasty indeed. The Khagggun's eyes opened wide. He made a sound of guttural pain that rose in pitch and intensity. It gave her a measure of satisfaction to be able to elicit pain from a caste bred to be inured to it. It was an exquisite example of the completeness of her training, a long, arduous process that broke many of those who sought to be imari, sending them off to easier, more appropriate careers.

" 'Whosoever harms an imari shall suffer compensatory damages and banishment from all kashiggen,' " she recited. " 'Whosoever kills an imari shall himself be killed.' "

Tears stood out in the corners of the Khagggun's eyes, trembling as he shook with agony. She had brought him not only great pain but terrible humiliation. She saw as much in his eyes.

"You are henceforth banned from this kashiggen—from *any* kashiggen," she said softly, almost gently. "You will pay to repair the damage you have done to Jonnqa. If you cannot pay or if you cannot pay fully, your family is liable. If you violate any or all of these dictates, I will personally see your head on a pike."

She stood up and took Jonnqa's hand, brought her close, kissed the blood off her face and shoulders and back. Then she took her out of there, leaving Lacc to see to the Khagggun's final disposition.

Mittelwin loved all her imari as if they were her daughters. This, too, had been part of her training. She took Jonnqa down the dimly lighted hallway. In the bath, she gently stripped Jonnqa, then stepped out of her own clothes. They showered together, like two young girls. Mittelwin used all her talents to minister to Jonnqa's contusions, which were starting to puff up and discolor. The girl moaned a little, and once she started to cry. Mittelwin held her tenderly until her sobbing subsided.

After the shower she applied soothing unguents to her body and examined more carefully the damage to her face. From her preliminary probing she determined that nothing was broken, but Jonnqa suddenly started to tremble as shock set in, and Mittelwin sat her down in a warm, shadowed corner of the bath. She wrapped her tight with a thick towel, stroked her hair, then went to the opposite end of the bath where the fresh robes and gowns were kept in a low cupboard that ran the entire length of the bath chamber. Kneeling, she opened the doors, searching the neat stacks of folded clothes for just the right outfit. She wanted something lively and gay that would help lift Jonnqa's mood.

Behind her, Jonnqa sat very still as if afraid that any movement would further fracture her fragile equilibrium. Gradually, so subtly that she was not even aware of it, the shadows around her deepened, stirring as if with an ethereal life. A rippling commenced in the gathering darkness, out of which appeared six pairs of ruby-red eyes, then a triangular head, the segmented body of a gigantic insect. Thin, ciliated appendages wrapped around Jonnqa's mouth, neck, chest, waist. There was for Jonnqa a moment of terror, of searing pain, vanishing as quickly as the corpus of the Tzelos, which had been absorbed into her body.

The struggle for control was intense but fearfully brief. By the time Mittelwin had turned back, clothes for both of them in her arms, Jonnqa's essence, bound and gagged inside her own mind, had disappeared altogether.

5

Aura

Rekkk waited until he was certain Thigpen was asleep, curled into a furry ball on a chair in the Library before he shook Riane awake. Riane had dropped off in the middle of a complex passage in a book called *The Gathering of Signs*. She had fought sleep for as long as she could, but the third time through the long, meandering paragraph of dense Old Tongue prose had put her under.

Morning filled with metallic light streamed through the windows. Dull glints of broken glass, the chirruping of insects, the ominous drone of hoverpods crisscrossing the countryside.

"Walk with me," Rekkk whispered, as soon as Riane's eyes opened. "I have a proposition to discuss with you."

"I'll wake Thigpen. She ought to be—"

Rekkk was shaking his head. "Just you and me, Dar Sala-at. No one else."

Riane nodded and got up. Her eyes felt gritty, and her body was still sore from her encounter with the daemons. She did not have long to wonder what Rekkk wanted. As soon as they were outside, he began.

"Of all of us here I am the closest to Giyan."

Riane said nothing. Dew flecked their boots as they moved off the stone path.

Rekkk went on, "I think I should have the last word when it comes to how we're going to rescue her. I don't know about you, but I still think our best and only option is to go to Nimbus and ask Jonnqa for help."

"You heard about the future Thigpen saw if we do that."

"I do not believe she saw anything worth talking about, but let us for a moment set my skepticism aside. Let us assume she did, in fact, see the future. By her own admission what she saw is *one possible* future, one of an infinite number, she said. That being the case, there must be many futures that result in us going to Nimbus, not just the one she saw."

Every hour that passed, Riane was growing more impatient. She could see Rekkk fraying at the edges, and Eleana was clearly terrified. The toll on them from Giyan's transformation was enormous and would only get worse. "What are you proposing?" But she already knew.

"You Thrip to Nimbus," Rekkk said. "You take me with you."

"And if it is a trap? If the Tzelos is already there waiting for us?"

"Then we deal with that when it happens."

"That is hardly a solution."

"Perhaps not. But the way I figure it we've got two extra things going for us." Rekkk's face was set and grim. "First, remember that a trap is only effective when it is a surprise. Second, that Tzelos daemon sticks out like a Kraelian sundog in the regent's palace."

Riane kept trying to find another, less risky solution, but the fact was there simply wasn't any. It was this or inaction. "When do you want to go?"

Rekkk grinned. "How about right now?"

Eleana felt them go. In her dream, she had been walking side by side with Riane, only Riane wasn't Riane at all but someone else, someone hauntingly familiar. She felt completely at ease. In the peculiar manner of dreams, she could see herself laughing in response to something Riane said even while wondering how she could feel so at ease with the Dar Sala-at, how she could be laughing knowing that Lady Giyan was in pain. But Lady Giyan was not part of this dream, and so the dream-Eleana banished her to another realm while she walked with Riane or whoever Riane had become. As she took Riane's hand, her face wreathed in a smile. Sunlight struck her in a dazzle. They were walking in forests known to her, the haunts of her childhood amid the foothills of the Djenn Marre. A kind of aura emanating from the sun or from the forest itself bathed them, and everything was perfect. For just a moment. And then it was gone, the aura winked out, and she awoke with a start. Her heart was pounding, and her breath was coming fast.

She scrambled up, running through the abbey, knowing Riane was not there. Neither was Rekkk. She burst into the Library, breathed a sigh of relief to see the Rappa safely asleep in her chair.

"Thigpen!" she called. "Wake up! Wake up! They're gone!"

"Who's gone?" Thigpen said as she stretched.

"Riane and Rekkk! I checked all over. They're not here."

Thigpen froze in midyawn. Her snout lifted, and her nostrils dilated. "I smell a Thrip." She growled low in her throat. "By Pyphoros' five heads!" She leapt off her chair, bounded across the floor and out the broken window. She put her snout to the ground and inhaled deeply. Her whiskers were twitching madly. "They have gone to Axis Tyr, to Nimbus," she said in a disgusted voice. "Those idiots!"

"Idiots?" Eleana echoed, taken aback.

"Yes, idiots! I told them clearly enough the likely consequences of such foolhardy action! Which part of the warning did they not understand?" She shook her head, her thick fur bristling, making her look twice her normal size. "I swear I do not know what gets into these normally thoughtful bipeds. Is it a fever of fools that suddenly comes over them, a swoon of stupidity, an illness of illogic? What in Miina's name is it?"

"Oh, that's simple enough," the girl said easily. "It's love."

"Love?" Thigpen's nose wrinkled up as if she had smelled something deeply distasteful. "Well, in that case I am doubly glad I am not prone to that pernicious affliction."

"Why, Thigpen, I do not believe you." Eleana crouched, wrists on her knees. "You do not care what happens to Riane?"

"Of course I care! She is the Dar Sala-at, and I am duty-bound to—"

"That's not what I mean."

Thigpen snorted. "You are wasting my time."

"Am I?" Eleana reached out and stroked the Rappa's fur. "Even you would not deny that you have established a bond with Riane."

Thigpen eyed her suspiciously. "Well, of course I have. But I fail to see what—"

"She loves you. She counts on your advice. You are like a parent to her."

"Then why did she ignore my advice?" Thigpen said crossly. "Why did she take Rekkk and Thrip into what is most certainly a trap?"

"You mean why did she put herself in danger." Eleana kissed Thigpen on each furry cheek. "When we catch up with them you must ask her that yourself."

*   *   *

Olnn Rydddlin leaned back, pulled his nondescript traveling cloak close around him, and said, "I understand you used to bounce Kurgan Stogggul on your knee."

"That was a long time ago," Bronnn Pallln said sourly. "A lot of numaaadis has passed through the gullet since then." He craned his thick, veiny neck, peering darkly at the reeking room in which they sat. "This is the heart of surly Harborside, a place I make it a strict point to avoid. Why are we meeting here in this noisome Sarakkon tavern, what is it called?"

"Blood Tide."

"Blood Tide, indeed," Bronnn Pallln said with a trace of petulance. "Had I been meeting with the regent, I daresay it would have been in the opulence of the regent's palace."

"Allow me to say bluntly that you would not be meeting with the regent."

To which reply, Bronnn Pallln glowered glumly. "Indeed not. And why? I am the head of a powerful and well-respected Consortium with a long history of alliances with the Stogggul. All right, I will tell you why not. Ever since that young interloper stuck his nose into Wennn Stogggul's tender parts as far as the new regent is concerned I have been relegated to second-Bashkir status."

"Sornnn SaTrryn was clever enough to make his deal with the Stogggul, and you were not," Olnnn said, twisting the knife into the fresh wound he had caught sight of. He leaned forward conspiratorially. "I will tell you a secret, Bronnn Pallln. I dislike Sornnn SaTrryn as much as you do."

The tavern was low-ceilinged, purposely dim. Filigreed lanterns hung from the ceiling, but they were turned down low. The heartwood walls were stained and grimy, hung with portraits of Kundalan harbormasters dating back hundreds of years. There was a copper-topped bar along one wall and a small raised platform along the other where the occasional itinerant musician or comedian foolhardy enough to brave this raucous crowd held forth. It was also the space where nightly the Kallistotos champion was crowned to a serenade of bawdy songs sung by a chorus of the challengers he had defeated.

Olnnn sat with his back against the wall at this rear corner table. From this vantage point he could see everyone who came and went through the front door. He also could clandestinely watch Rada, the owner of Blood Tide, whom he often dreamed about at night. She was a Tuskugggun of dark good looks possessed of a long tapering skull gleaming with spiced oil, who dared wear her sifeyn folded at her neck, leaving her head uncovered. But not bare. She had on a thin tertium and veradium diadem. Others had foolishly judged her to be a Looorm on the side, for the whores were the only Tuskugggun brazen enough to bare their skulls in public.

Opposite him, the air of defeat had left Bronnn Pallln's meaty shoulders and he sat up a little. Distant glimmers danced behind his eyes. "Does that mean I have an ally?"

He is so terribly anxious, Olnnn thought. He drank the sweet mead, but what he was tasting was the other's desperation. He could see in Bronnn Pallln's corlike eyes all his weaknesses, as if reading again the list his staff had compiled for him. Yes, he thought now, Bronnn Pallln was just the sort of V'ornn he needed for his stalking-horse—weak, docile, malleable. He was interested only in prestige and preening. Yes, indeed. He would do whatever Olnnn told him to do. He had had the great good fortune to be the only son of Koun Pallln, a very savvy Bashkir. When the old patriarch had died, Bronnn Pallln found himself in charge of a first-rate Consortium with not the slightest idea of how to run it successfully. Perhaps that is what Wennn Stogggul recognized because, in allying himself with Bronnn Pallln, Kurgan's father had reaped a host of lucrative deals, raking in unconscionable profits off the top of Pallln business in return for rendering advice on such projects as building the spice market and renovating Receiving Spirit. Rich percentages he was apparently willing to forgo for the Ring of Five Dragons Sornnn SaTrryn traded in return for having Wennn Stogggul name him Prime Factor.

"Sornnn SaTrryn was the regent's father's choice as Prime Factor," Olnnn said. "The regent prefers you, but he cannot be seen to move precipitately." He gained immense enjoyment from spinning this fanciful tale. "The SaTrryn Consortium is very powerful, and the regent has just attained his office. I think you understand."

"Of course, Star-Admiral. His power base is at a delicate juncture."

"Precisely so."

"But these unfortunate circumstances, you see, are the problem."

"Then we must find a way to solve the problem."

"Truly, Star-Admiral? But how? Have you formulated a plan?"

It was all Olnnn could do not to laugh in the fool's face. Bronnn Pallln was pathetically easy to manipulate. "Well, now, that all depends."

A trio of Sarakkon burst through the door, trailed by a gust of the chilly autumnal night. They stamped on the worn wooden floorboards with their high shagreen boots, setting the copper and brass and jade runes in their thick beards to jingling. Their boisterous voices added to the general din of the place.

Bronnn Pallln's muddy eyes were alight with avarice. "On what would it depend, Star-Admiral?" He noisily guzzled his sweet mead, a solitary toast to his growing good fortune. "Please. I am all ears."

"That is good, for you see my plan relies solely upon you."

"Me, Star-Admiral? I am not certain that I . . ."

Olnnn stitched a smile to his face. "Ambition is a virtue in V'ornn like us, don't you agree?"

Bronnn Pallln brightened a little. "Oh, yes, indeed, yes, Star-Admiral. Ambition was my father's watchword. Therefore, I have made it mine."

"That is good. Ambition is what is required. Along with a healthy portion of resourcefulness."

"You have but to ask," Bronnn Pallln said.

Olnnn signed for another round and, as he did so, absorbed the length of Rada's legs as she bent over to gather a pair of empty goblets off the floor where a couple of drunken Sarakkon had dropped them.

Just as the waitress was approaching their table, Olnnn hissed to Bronnn Pallln, "Find the means to discredit Sornnn SaTrryn."

"Star-Admiral?"

Olnnn waited while the fresh goblets of mead were placed onto the smeary tabletop. Then he turned back to the waiting Bronnn Pallln and, despite the rising din around them, lowered his voice even further. "Listen to me, for I will say it but once." He kept his face impassive, though Bronnn Pallln had all but crawled across the tabletop in his gluttonous zeal. "As I have said, the regent cannot be seen to touch Sornnn SaTrryn. If, however, it were to become known that the SaTrryn scion was involved in some illegal activity, well then . . ."

"But the SaTrryn's reputation is unimpeachable."

Olnnn rubbed his temple where a vein beat beneath his skin. He considered strangling Bronnn Pallln right then and there. Then he reined in his temper, took several deep breaths, and smiled. "As Star-

Admiral of all the Khagggun I am privy to many things unknown to the general populace. One in particular interests me greatly." Olnnn watched Bronnn Pallln swallow the hook whole. "The Khagggun high command suspects a high-ranking Bashkir is involved in supplying the Kundalan Resistance with stolen ion cannons."

"Star-Admiral?"

"Oh, do not look so shocked, Bronnn Pallln. As it was with Eleusis Ashera there are V'ornn who have foolishly fallen under the malign spell of Kundala. N'Luuura only knows why! In any event, we have been looking for this traitor for years."

Bronnn Pallln rubbed his hands together. "Are you telling me it is the SaTrryn, Star-Admiral?"

Slowly and carefully, Olnnn said, "That is precisely what I am saying."

He spread his damp, chubby hands. "But what would you need me for?"

Strangling would be too good a death for him, Olnnn decided. "Sornnn SaTrryn is exceedingly clever. To date, he has eluded being implicated in all official investigations." He waited for the light to come on. "But you, Bronnn Pallln, are as unofficial as it gets. When I ran into you at the Rescendance it occurred to me that as the head of a first-tier Bashkir Consortium you would have contacts unavailable even to me."

"I suppose that might be true enough."

"All that is required is for you to bring me the evidence."

The big Bashkir tapped his thick lips with a spatulate forefinger. "And when Sornnn SaTrryn is removed from office . . . ?"

"Pack your bags," Olnnn lied smoothly. "I have it from the regent himself, it will be moving day."

Rekkk Hacilar had returned to Nimbus and, to be honest, he liked it not. It was here that he had encountered the Gyrgon Nith Sahor, first in his guise as Mastress Kannna, later as the embodiment of Giyan herself. While he was grateful for Nith Sahor's assistance, he could not quite say that he missed him. Gyrgon had always made him uneasy, but it wasn't until he had met one in person that his flesh had truly begun to creep. There was something distinctly disconcerting about being with a V'ornn who could change his shape at will. You never knew whom you were talking to, what intimate knowledge you were inadvertently giving away. No, he decided, they were better off now that Nith Sahor was dead.

He stood in the opulent Cloud Chamber of the kashiggen and tried not to recall the salamuuun flight he had taken with Nith Sahor. While under the influence of the drug he had spoken with his dead mother and been shaken to his core. As always, he was deeply uneasy with emotion of any kind, and never more so than now. His Khagggun training had not only submerged his emotions but had made it supremely difficult to bring them back into the light. With good reason: emotion was the last thing you wanted when you went into battle. It impaired reasoning, clouded judgment. That salamuuun flight had opened the door to the vault, so to speak. It had allowed him to express his love for Giyan and, now, that love had brought him here to take the first step in finding her, in saving her from the most powerful forces of darkness. But he worried that his love for her would cause him to make a fatal mistake that could end his life and Riane's.

He saw Mittelwin enter the Cloud Chamber, so-called because of its domed ceiling, exquisitely enameled in the lush Kundalan style.

"I remember you," the dzuoko said. "You were here in a season previous with Mastress Kannna."

Rekkk gave a little nod.

"I daresay you look a lot better than you did that afternoon." She offered him her professional smile. "Bloody but not bowed, wasn't that it?"

"This is Riane," he said, wanting desperately to change the subject.

Mittelwin eyed Riane appreciatively. "An exceptionally handsome girl—on the cusp of becoming a young woman." Her smile widened. "In what way may we please you?" she said in the formal kashiggen greeting.

"We seek an hour's time with an imari."

"But of course. We have many—"

"One particular imari," Rekkk said.

Now he had caught Mittelwin's attention. "Ah, well, here at Nimbus we are ready to satisfy all desires." She laced her long fingers together. "Which imari do you require?"

"Jonnqa."

"Now that will be something of a problem. Jonnqa is unwell at the moment." She smiled her best professional smile. "I can offer any number of other imari, all of the Third Rank."

"It is Jonnqa we must see," Rekkk said.

Mittelwin shook her head. "I'm afraid I cannot—"

"Please," Riane said quietly. "It is a matter of the utmost urgency."

Mittelwin turned her attention to the Kundalan girl. There was a curious intensity about her, an unusual strength of purpose.

"We will not tax her unduly," Riane continued. "I give you my word."

Mittelwin stared straight into the girl's light eyes and liked what she saw. "All right. But it may take some time to make her presentable. You understand."

"Yes," Riane said quickly. "Thank you, dzuoko."

Mittelwin nodded. "It is my pleasure." She indicated the ornately carved settees. "Please make yourselves comfortable. I will have food and drink brought to you while you wait."

As she walked down the narrow, circuitous hallway, Mittelwin wondered what the Khagggun and the Kundalan girl could possibly want with Jonnqa. How did they even know about her? Her clients were nothing if not discreet.

Mittelwin frowned as she followed the corridor to her left. The beautiful old filigreed lanterns washed the walls in long warm ellipses of light, transforming her shadow into a tail. She made it a strict habit not to speculate about her clients' motives, but in the case of this Khagggun she could not help herself. For one thing, it had been made known that he had turned Rhynnnon, that any sighting should without delay be reported to the Khagggun or the regent's staff. Mittelwin felt it was a sure bet that Kurgan Stogggul and Star-Admiral Olnnn Rydddlin were bent on planting his skull atop a pike outside the regent's palace. If that were so, she would doubtless be rewarded handsomely for traducing them. Not that she would do anything of the kind. She liked not the Stogggul scion, liked even less the thought of a callow youth in such a position of power. Nothing good could come of it. Either he would prove incompetent or exceedingly dangerous.

For another thing, the Khagggun was now in the company of this Kundalan girl with an uncanny strength and prescient eyes. He was treating her not as a member of an inferior race but as an equal. This interested her. In fact, as she thought about it she would have to say that Rekkk Hacilar interested her greatly.

She came at length to the end of the corridor, knocked quickly on a door, and went in. To her surprise, she found Jonnqa already awake, already bathed, already coifed and clothed. Her face seemed astonishingly free of bruises and puffiness.

"You have come to inform me that I have clients," Jonnqa said with uncharacteristic bluntness.

"How did you know?" Mittelwin asked. Was there a preternatural glow to her eyes or was it merely the lighting? The glow vanished.

"I . . . Why, I don't know," Jonnqa said. She seemed all at once confused. "I was roused out of sleep by a feeling of urgency. Thinking it a result of a full bladder I went to the bath and relieved myself. The urgency remained. I came back here."

"You bathed."

"I do not remember."

"Fixed your hair and dressed in your finest robes."

"I did. I mean, I must have."

Mittelwin peered more closely at Jonnqa. "Your bruises looked healed. How is that possible?"

Jonnqa said nothing. Now Mittelwin was certain something was amiss. A muddiness had invaded the girl's eyes. Perhaps she was ill. "I think it would be best if we put this off until another time."

"No!" Jonnqa grabbed Mittelwin's arm then, as if abruptly becoming aware of the breach in strict protocol between imari and dzuoko, she released her, dropped her gaze and her voice. "Please forgive me, dzuoko. I meant no offense." Her voice had returned to its normal tone. "But these clients asked for me by name, did they not?"

Mittelwin said nothing, stood contemplating the girl. An unnamed fear massed in her belly. "The clients can come back another time."

"But I wish to see them now," Jonnqa said, in that other blunter voice.

"Why?"

Jonnqa looked startled. "What?"

"Why do you want to see them now? What difference could it make?"

Something moved across the imari's face, quick and sure, a powerful eddy of emotion like the formation of a resolve. "No difference," she said stonily. "Tell them to return another time if that is your decision."

"It is," Mittelwin said firmly, as confounded as she was angry at Jonnqa's insolent, inexplicable behavior. What was wrong? Perhaps internal injuries had occurred during the beating she had sustained. If so, she vowed she would make that Khaggun pay compensatory damages beyond anything he could imagine. "Wait here until I return," she said shortly. "I want you examined by a Genomatekk." She had turned, her hand already on the door when she was whirled around, assaulted by something extruding itself through Jonnqa's nostrils, ears, open mouth, the very pores of her skin.

Mittelwin's mind was paralyzed with disbelief, frozen with shock, gripped by terror. The huge insectlike creature inserted the ends of its mandibles into the side of her neck. A burning commenced, as if she had been set on fire. Blood began to spurt, and the last thing she saw was a flat, triangular head shooting forward to catch every drop in its lipless mouth.

Olnnn Rydddlin whistled while he slowly peeled back a strip of skin from the Kundalan's side. This Kundalan was one of more than a hundred rounded up by his Khagggun during the latest sweep in his stepped-up efforts to find Rekkk Hacilar and Giyan. He did not hear the screams, the entreaties, did not smell the stench of terror.

"Have you seen them?" he said to the Kundalan. "If you have, tell me precisely where."

He paused, observing politely the time of reply. When none was forthcoming, he recommenced his peeling. Another strip. More screams. Blood dripping from the interrogation chamber bench in the caverns beneath the regent's palace, like moments of time running backward, memories he had tried unsuccessfully to bury . . .

First came the aura of opalescent light, then the image of Malistra bending over him. She was crooning in a language Olnnn Rydddlin had never heard before, or, perhaps he was so painracked from his leg he was hallucinating. When the sorceress Giyan had turned Malistra's own weapon against him, his world had dissolved in a web of agony so excruciating he could scarcely recall it. To have the skin, muscle, tendons, ligaments, nerves eaten away from a part of your body—well, that was something for which even a Khagggun was unprepared . . .

"Where are they?" he said in a rather mechanical voice. "The Rhynnnon traitor, Rekkk Hacilar, the Kundalan sorceress Giyan, they have not vanished off the face of Kundala, they are not ghosts. They must find food to eat, a place of shelter, at the very least. You must have heard something of them or know someone who has. This is the only possibility."

A small silence, the blood traversing the width of the bench, dripping off the edge, setting up a rhythm not unlike a heartbeat. With some difficulty, he worked another strip off the fatty layer of flesh. This was the seventh Kundalan he had interrogated today. In the cells all around him, his Khaggun were interrogating others. A warren of pain and blood and fear . . .

Still, the aura of opalescent light lingered in his mind, sweeping him inward, backward in time. He would have died without Malistra's sorcerous intervention, he knew that much. As she remade him, a bond had grown between them, and when she was killed another piece of him had been flayed off. He felt her absence with every breath he took, a pain in his side he was glad would not go away. He cherished that pain, deep and abiding, as assurance that Malistra had not abandoned him totally. Nights, while his swollen eyes scanned the ceiling of his bedroom in a vain search for sleep, he felt her moving in him, sweeping through his viscera, turning his marrow into a river down which she sluiced. Always, she pooled in the gleaming bones of his stripped leg. He could feel them pulsing with knowledge of her, imagined them a quick-breathing animal beneath the covers . . .

Olnnn turned the horizontal spit he had erected just above the Kundalan's eyes. Even if the Kundalan turned his head to the left or to the right he could not fail to see the strips of his own bloody skin hanging there as if ready to be roasted. He had devised this particular form of interrogation, the only one he would himself perform, not long after he had become Star-Admiral. It had come to him in a dream, even though his nights were largely sleepless, as they had been since Malistra had brought him back from the dead. An aura of opalescent light and the image of her bending over him, crooning. Her hands were moving upon him or just above him, stirring the dark viscous air as if it were a pot of stew. What was she doing?

The Kundalan gasped, and his red-rimmed eyes at last met Olnnn's. This particular form of interrogation always worked, Olnnn had found. It was only a matter of time. And now that time had come.

"The Northern Quarter," the Kundalan gasped through his swollen, bloody mouth. He had bitten his tongue and lips many times. "The Rhynnnon and a Kundalan female. I heard they were seen earlier on Dayblossom Street."

There is a thing I do not understand," Riane said to Rekkk as they waited for Mittelwin to return. "The kashiggen are Kundalan—they are, essentially, pleasure palaces, are they not?"

"To the best of my knowledge, yes." Rekkk was standing in the Cloud Chamber so that he had a view of the corridor down which the dzuoko had disappeared. Periodically, he glanced that way, his hand on the hilt of his shock-sword. He seemed preoccupied, as if listening to Riane with one ear while the other was calibrated for trouble.

"When the V'ornn took them over for salamuuun flights they installed V'ornn dzuoko but kept the Kundalan imari."

"Uh-huh."

"*Dzuoko* is derived from the Old Tongue *dezeke*, which means 'she who provides.' "

"So what?" Clearly Rekkk was in no mood for a lesson in comparative linguistics.

"It is a Kundalan word." She waited for a reaction that did not come. "Used by Tuskugggun." She waited again. "Rekkk, are you listening to me?"

He turned, a scowl on his face. "What is your point?"

"The kashiggen seems to be a place where V'ornn and Kundalan peacefully coexist."

"It's a female thing," Rekkk said. "Why don't you ask Mittelwin when she returns." His head swiveled and he peered long and hard down the corridor. "*If* she ever returns."

"But doesn't it seem odd to you that on all of Kundala, here is the only—"

"What seems odd is how long she is taking."

"I know, but will you answer my question?"

"I imagine it's the Gyrgon's doing," he said. "It's well-known that they frequent the kashiggen, though what they do here is any V'ornn's guess."

"You said you were here with a Gyrgon."

"Ah, that was Nith Sahor." Rekkk had taken several steps toward the corridor. "That was different. He brought me here for a specific purpose. I have no more idea than you do of how Gyrgon take their pleasures."

Hearing soft footfalls, they turned. Someone was coming down the corridor. Riane was aware of Rekkk's rising tension, and she found herself gripping the hilt of her dagger.

Rekkk relaxed a little when he saw Mittelwin coming toward them.

"Everything is in readiness," the dzuoko said, beckoning them forward.

They went single file, Mittelwin leading, followed by Rekkk, with Riane taking up the rear. The farther they went the more certain Riane was that something serious was amiss. From the moment they had entered Nimbus, she had been using her limited knowledge of Osoru to cast a Net of Cognition. This spell was used to identify Caa, the energy auras thrown off by sorcerous Avatars like the Tzelos and whatever kind of daemon it was that had invaded Giyan. However, the Net of Cognition was so finely tuned that it could also identify the comparatively weak auras thrown off by nonsorcerous beings. The spell had shown her, in passing, Mittelwin's aura, and now as she walked more and more slowly she realized that it was coming from a spot abreast of her, then just behind her.

She stopped, retracing her steps to a left-hand branch in the corridor. She peered down its short length. It looked like a utility hall. Mittelwin's aura was weakening, and she hurried into the dingy narrow space, silently opened the second door on her right, and entered the tiny darkened chamber.

Something dripped somberly, water from a broken tap. In that instant, Mittelwin's already weakened aura winked out. Riane fumbled for a fusion lamp, lighted it. She saw a utility chamber. Buckets, mops, jars of enamel, slabs of marble were neatly stacked on the floor. To their right was a cart piled with soiled linen and robes beside a chute to the basement where the washing was done at an appropriate remove from the kashiggen's clients. Floor-to-ceiling cupboards lined the wall to her left. Something caught her eye, a dark stain pooling beneath the crack between cupboard doors.

With a sense of foreboding, she yanked open the doors, and Mittelwin, naked, waxy in death, hollow as a shell, mummified as if she had been dead for decades, pitched out at her.

*   *   *

Riane ran down the utility hall, turned into the main corridor and picked up her pace. Where had they gone, Rekkk and Mittelwin—or, more accurately, the thing that had taken Mittelwin's place? She cursed herself for not saying something to Rekkk, but everything happened too quickly, she had been going purely on sorcerous instinct, and, anyway, what could she have possibly said that would have not alerted the daemon?

"Rekkk!" she cried. "Rekkk, where are you?"

The sliding door at the end of the corridor burst outward off its tracks, and there was the Tzelos. Tatters of Mittelwin's robes fluttered off its segmented body. It held Rekkk aloft by two of its skeletal forelegs. As it charged her, Riane was horrified to see that it had skewered Rekkk with one of its wicked-looking mandibles.

For an instant, all she could think was that the future Thigpen saw was coming true. That was all the time the daemon needed. It was stupefyingly quick, scuttling down the corridor straight at her. Knowing brute force was useless against it, she conjured spell after spell in her limited repertory, but none seemed to affect the Tzelos in the least.

It grabbed at her with a pair of waving appendages, and she ducked away, twisting, reaching for Rekkk. She had no thought for herself now. She had to get Rekkk away from the thing. Wrapping her arms around Rekkk's midsection, she hauled on his weight. But the Tzelos, clever daemon that it was, lifted its blunt, triangular head, raking its mandible through Rekkk's flesh. He screamed, and Riane immediately let go.

The Tzelos made a vicious lunge for her. She used the honed edge of her dagger to hack off the end of the closest appendage. Immediately, it grew back. The Tzelos began to shake its head, and Rekkk screamed again in pain. This served to focus Riane on her immediate mission. The Tzelos was attacking again, relentless. There was precious little room to maneuver, and so far that was working to the daemon's favor. Time to reverse that.

As the Tzelos darted at her again, Riane leapt upon it. Using the segments of its body, she climbed upward. One appendage, then another whipped around her. She reversed her grip on her dagger, plunging it point first into one after another of the daemon's ruby-red eyes. What damage she was inflicting she could not say, and she did not wait around to find out, but turned and slid Rekkk off the mandible's spear-points. As he fell to the floor, she tried to jump after him, but she was held suspended by the appendages, the mandibles searching to impale her. Then she twisted free and, as she gained her feet, began to drag Rekkk backward down the corridor.

The daemon shook itself and, as it recovered from her attack, began to pursue. Riane looked up from her efforts. She was out of ideas. In a moment, the thing would be on them.

At that moment, she heard a commotion behind her. In a blur of motion, she saw a burly Mesagggun, ion cannon drawn, pounding toward them. She shouted, trying to warn him not to fire, but it was too late. A thin, wavering stream of pale blue light shot from the blunt muzzle of the weapon directly at the head of the Tzelos. For a moment, the V'ornn energy blast wreathed the daemon's head. Then the Tzelos opened its mouth, sucking it inside it. When it emerged it was black as death. The Tzelos spewed it out so quickly the Mesagggun had no time to react. The instant the black stream struck him he began to sizzle. The Mesagggun shrieked. The nauseating stench of burning flesh filled up the corridor, making Riane gag. Still, sweating like a cor in heat, she managed to keep hauling on Rekkk, putting more distance between them and the Tzelos.

Then the Mesagggun was gone. Only a pile of cinders and ash remained. The Tzelos returned its attention to Riane and Rekkk. It rushed them again, faster than before. Riane wondered how anything so ungainly in appearance could move so fast.

In desperation, she conjured the Spell of Forever. It was one of only two hybrid spells she had learned. Part Osoru, part Kyofu, it was Eye Window, most ancient of sorceries, virtually unknown among present-day Kundalan sorceresses. Instinct had come to the fore. She did not consciously know why she had conjured that particular spell until it showed her what she needed to know. The Spell of Forever was a divination spell, and like all Eye Window spells it was exceptionally potent. It opened secret doorways. It could find things deeply hidden, people who were lost, it could re-create past events.

But because she was inexpert, she could not immediately focus the spell's lens. Instead of the Tzelos, she saw a flash of dark light, saw Giyan's face, a rictus of pain, saw behind her the ragged line of a mountain chain which, though grown grim, was nevertheless oddly familiar, saw her wrists and ankles pinioned, to what?

The vision faded as swiftly as it had appeared, and now the lens was focusing on the Tzelos. Almost immediately, Riane saw its vulnerable spot.

But now the daemon was upon her and it was too late. Then, as the Tzelos grabbed her, she heard her name being called. Thigpen! Thigpen was here!

"Quickly," she cried. "There is a—" She gagged as something putrid gushed out of the daemon's mouth, covering her in an increasingly viscous and sticky web. "Look to the—" The web had spread over her face. She could not take air into her lungs. She struggled, then on instinct again fell back on her mountain climbing training. She was used to high altitudes, where the air was gossamer thin. She had learned how to store what she needed in her lungs until she could take the next breath. The web was thickening, tightening, hardening. She tore it away from her mouth long enough to shout, "Thigpen, the bottom of the thorax, left side! There is a pale spot!"

"Hang on, Dar Sala-at!" Thigpen cried as she shot past Riane's left ear.

Her razor-sharp teeth were bared. They sank unerringly into the tiny pale spot on the Tzelos' thorax. She raked it with her extruded talons. The Tzelos reared back, an eerie sound emanating from it that made Riane want to scream.

At the same time, she felt hands upon her, felt fingers pulling the hardening goo off her.

"Dar Sala-at, are you all right?"

It was Eleana.

"I am fine," Riane gasped. She saw the outline of the Tzelos wavering, the center of it growing blurred, insubstantial. Thigpen leapt back as the daemon vanished. "Look to Rekkk!" Riane said. "I fear he has been grievously injured!"

"Miina protect him!" Eleana crouched by Rekkk's side, put her hand on his bloody neck. Her face was white as she looked at Riane and Thigpen. Tears were streaming down her face. "He is dying."

6

Orange Sweet

When Sornnn SaTrryn stopped beneath the gaily striped awning of the stand on Momentum Boulevard he was being watched. When he bought a small bag of orange-sweet he was being watched. When he ambled through the crowd munching on the delicious fruit he was being watched. As he stopped to let a trio of Khagggun strut by he was being watched. And when he passed the intersection of Divination Street he was being watched most carefully.

A darkness at noon as clouds gathered thickly overhead. At precisely the striking of the fifteenth hour, Marethyn Stogggul had emerged from her atelier, locking the door behind her. She allowed Sornnn SaTrryn a twenty-pace lead before she began to follow him down Divination Street. He walked neither quickly nor slowly so that it was impossible for any interested observer to judge whether there was a purpose to his direction.

Perhaps a half mile farther on he paused before the russet-and-black awning of Gamut, an excellent but out-of-the-way cafe. As if making up his mind on the spur of the moment, he turned and passed between the shanstone columns into the dimly lighted interior. Wide beaten-bronze braziers at each corner of the cafe held flickering flames. He chose a table in the darkest corner and sat down. A server in crimson robes arrived, and he ordered.

Marethyn observed this ritual as she stood in the surf of the crowd making its way up and down Divination Street. She looked around, as if unsure where to go or what to do next. She studied the faces of Bashkir hurrying by, of Tuskugggun, arms laden with packages of spice, bolts of cloth, thin titanium and germanium sheeting rolled up and tucked under their arms. She watched the practiced movements of Khagggun as they threaded the throng, searching for mischief-makers, black marketeers, Kundalan Resistance. A hoverpod passed overhead, lifting the hair on Kundalan heads, stirring robes and tunics, whipping up tiny spirals of grit. She heard the raised voices from the nearby meat market; she turned away from a Tuskugggun of her acquaintance before she could be recognized. A fistful of children whirled by her at a run, laughing, pelting Kundalan servants with stones as they went. The river of life flowed on, the details blurring now as she wended her way between the outdoor tables of the cafe and stepped into Gamut's grottolike interior.

She walked straight back to the bath, stood inside the small closed chamber for some time. She listened to the throb of the kitchen seeping through the wall, the heavy *clip-clop* of water buttren pulling a dray as they passed on a side street, the beating of her own hearts. An older Tuskugggun entered, and Marethyn washed her hands though they were clean enough. Then she went out, slipped into the seat beside Sornnn SaTrryn. He had a drink waiting for her—a marsh queen, her favorite. He had placed a segment of orangesweet in it, which she plucked out with her fingertips and ate with enormous pleasure, the pleasure she felt being here with him. She smiled and looked into his rugged, sun- and windburned face, trying to memorize every square centimeter of it as if she would never see him again.

As a waiter hovered expectantly, Sornnn said, "We should order. I have much to accomplish today."

"We have, at least, a little time for ourselves."

When they had ordered, and the waiter had departed, Sornnn's eyes grew dark and serious. "Marethyn, I need to be certain. You are not growing tired of this?"

"What, of you?"

He laughed. "Now that would, indeed, be a tragedy. No, I was speaking of the clandestine nature of our meetings, the coldness of our exchanges where we by chance are thrown together in public."

She knew he was thinking of the Rescendance. "On the contrary. It amuses me to playact."

"You are so good at it."

"Growing up in my family, I learned how to be devious." She drank him in over the rim of her pale blue glass. "Besides, I adore watching you move through a crowd. I love standing shielded, anonymous in throngs while you sit alone. You are apart from everyone and everything, and I know this because you are waiting for me. You are a magnetic current pulling me while I hold back just long enough for the anticipation to build toward the moment when I feel the brush of your arm against my breast."

"You missed your calling." The skin around his eyes crinkled up when he smiled. "You should have been an actor."

"Except there are no female actors allowed."

He took her hands in his. "That very much depends on the venue."

Their lunch came: roasted gimnopedes, stuffed with clemetts, along with wrygrass salads.

"This is another thing I love about you," she said softly. "What other male would say that to me? What other male would treat me as an equal? My father did not; certainly my brother—"

"It is because of Kurgan that we have kept our liaison an absolute secret. Have we failed?"

"No. I spoke to him at the Rescendance. He has no idea."

"And yet I know the regent's spies are everywhere."

She took his hand. "What is it then?"

Sornnn bit his lip, deep in thought. "I have told you about the finbat, have I not, one of those nocturnal creatures of the Korrush. By what means does it fly in total darkness?" He touched the tip of his finger to the center of his forehead, pushed the finger outward. "Like a finbat, I sense the wall before I see it."

"Are you speaking now of Kurgan?"

"He has gone out of his way to treat me as an ally, a friend, even. But I do not trust him."

"A wise decision, I am certain. If he has marked you as clever as well as powerful, all the worse. I know him, Sornnn. He will brook no rivals."

"I? I have no wish to be his rival."

"I very much doubt that you could convince him of that. He is as paranoid as our father was."

"In that case, I will have to vigorously defend myself."

"Oh, do not say that so lightly, my love!" She squeezed his hand hard. "The worst thing you could do would be to underestimate him. He may be sixteen, but he has the mind of a V'ornn decades older. He is far smarter, far more clever and ambitious than my father ever was. There is something different about him, something dangerous. This has been so for as long as I can remember. My father was obsessed with taking revenge on the Ashera. Kurgan is obsessed with taking revenge on everyone."

"There is an ancient saying passed among the tribes of the Korrush. It is said that the ambitious fall from a great height, and when they do nothing is left of them but their sins."

Marethyn put her hand against his cheek. "Ah, Sornnn, please do take my warning seriously."

"I assure you that I take it very seriously, indeed."

"Being a Stogggul embarrasses me more than you could know, Sornnn. The entire family could use a lesson in manners."

"You know very well why they shun you, Marethyn. Tuskugggun are—"

"Caged, powerless, made impotent. We are treated as little better than the Kundalan."

"Now you are being melodramatic."

"Then I am obliged to do so in order to make my point." She tossed her head. "All my life I have been treated by males as if I am a mental defective, as if my opinions are laughable or, worse, subversive."

"But your opinions *are* subversive," he said with a small smile. "You are pushing for equal status for Tuskugggun. Ours is a caste-bound system, Marethyn. Never forget that."

"Your mind is not caste-bound."

Sornnn settled himself more comfortably beside her. "From the time I was young my father took me with him on his treks into the Korrush. I quickly became used to the long, arduous travel, the dust, the windstorms, the lack of V'ornn amenities that we take for granted. I not only got used to living without them, I grew to love the rough tribal life. I fell in love with the Korrush. I saw the majesty there, the magic of the landscape, the enormous sky, the pleasure in reading the weather, in training lymmnals, in riding between the humps of a kuomeshal. I learned to weave rugs, to excavate through the dry red soil, to cherish a lost past, to fall asleep beneath a blanket of stars." He took her hand. "Now the Korrush is inside me, it has changed me forever, and I would not have it any other way."

"Nor would I," she said. "It has made you a better V'ornn."

"Remember when we met?"

"At the consortia congress last spring." she nodded. "My art installation was being used as decoration."

"I saw you from across the hall, in the midst of a huge throng. You were wearing that sky-blue—"

"The male-style robes, yes."

"You caused quite a sensation."

"It was a statement."

"Of course it was. That was why they told you to leave."

"The Stogggul name only goes so far when you are Tuskugggun."

"I saw you and said to myself that I must meet this singular Tuskugggun, not having any idea who you were."

"And when you found out that I was a Stogggul . . . ?"

"I came after you, didn't I?"

"That you did."

"The truth is I never thought of you as a Stogggul."

She looked at him skeptically. "Now that seems unlikely."

"I was too taken with you to care what family you were from."

She let out an involuntary laugh. "You must be joking."

"I love you, Marethyn."

She stared into his beautiful eyes.

"My love sees a way for you to use the power you have inside you, a way in which you can don your male-style robes again and not be so easily cast from the arms of society."

Marethyn felt a clutch in her stomachs. There was something about him, some secret that both fascinated and frightened her. The longer she knew him, the more desperately she wanted to know this secret. And yet . . . Her blood ran cold with the thought of it.

"And that is what happened to me that night," her beloved was saying. "That is what drew me to you. That is why you have become *wa tarabibi*."

"What does that mean?" she breathed, though her hearts already knew.

"My beloved."

Ion-cannon fire found them as soon as they exited Nimbus. The narrow alley in the Northern Quarter of Axis Tyr was burning with phosphorescent tracers.

"Khagggun pack!" Eleana cried.

Riane, who was helping Eleana carry Rekkk out of the kashiggen, was still surrounded by the Spell of Forever. "It is Olnnn Rydddlin's pack," she said. "I can sense him."

"What can we do?" Eleana said, as they ducked, scrambling for the cover of an inset doorway. "Carrying Rekkk, we cannot outrun them or even hide for very long."

"No problem. We will all Thrip back to the abbey."

"Absolutely not," Thigpen said. "Thripping is devised for moving through Realms, not within a Realm. To do so is unsafe. The effects are cumulative—very soon it begins to permanently impair your ability to Thrip at all. As for those without mononculi, the effects rapidly become lethal. Rekkk is near death, and Eleana is with child. I cannot sanction Thripping. We all stay."

An ion-cannon burst exploded the window beside the doorway in which they were huddled, raining glass, stone chips, and plaster down on them.

"Olnnn Rydddlin has given us no other viable choice," Riane said urgently. "If you do not get Rekkk out of here now, he will surely die."

"What about you, Dar Sala-at?"

"For the past nine weeks we have been hounded night and day by Khagggun. For the past nine weeks we have done nothing but hole up and lick our wounds." Riane said this with no little intensity, and Thigpen, who had been about to argue, shut her snout. "With Olnnn Rydddlin here, I believe we have an opportunity to strike back hard, to throw our V'ornn enemies off-balance, at least temporarily."

Thigpen eyed her with undisguised suspicion. "I cannot imagine what you have in mind, Dar Sala-at, but I know it carries with it too much risk."

"More than anything else we need breathing room," Riane said. "You must agree that we cannot remain cloistered in the Abbey of Warm Current indefinitely."

"Even so," Thigpen said grudgingly, "I cannot abandon you, you know that. I am bound to you."

"Which is why you will do as I say, when I say it," Riane said. Another explosion collapsed part of the building's roof. Groaning load-bearing timbers made it all too clear that they had little time left in their temporary sanctuary. "Now is not a time for stubbornness. Eleana and I are best suited to handle what must be done here. Without Rekkk holding us back we're mobile. I have Osoru, and since Eleana has fought him before, she knows Olnnn Rydddlin's tactical mind. It is an ideal opportunity, one which may not be repeated anytime soon. Take Rekkk and go. Now."

Thigpen gazed down into Rekkk's bloody face, carefully lifted first one eyelid then the other. "The Thripping will kill him for sure."

Riane threw her head back, reached down her throat with two fingers. In her mind, she sang a song she had learned in *Realms of Thripping*, one of the books in the Library, ancient as Time.

Alarmed, Thigpen said, "What on Kundala do you think you're doing?"

"Giving Rekkk my mononculus." Riane drew the wormlike symbiont out of her mouth.

"Dar Sala-at, I told you that each mononculus is meant for a single individual."

"Wipe that shocked look off your face," Riane said. She opened Rekkk's mouth, dropped the mononculus into it, closed it with the heel of her hand on his chin. "The mononculus will protect him from whatever harmful emanations you may pass through, and his body will temporarily keep it alive and well until I join you."

"*If* you join us," Thigpen said darkly. "Have a care, Dar Sala-at. Youth is rash with its life—"

Of a sudden, the Rappa's stern admonition was drowned out by an ominous thrumming. "N'Luuura take it! A hoverpod!" Riane cried. "We're out of time. Go! Go!"

She turned away, feeling the telltale ripple in her psyche, the soft internal breeze aimed at the back of her neck, that told of a Thrip.

"What are we going to do?" Eleana said breathlessly. "They have both ends of the alley blocked and there's a hoverpod overhead, so forget the rooftops."

With a terrible groan, the doorway in which they were crouched began to splinter.

"Follow me and don't look back," Riane shouted. Between tracer rounds, they zigzagged back across the rubble- and fire-strewn alley, banging through Nimbus' copper-and-bronze door, dented and heavily discolored by the ion fire. Riane took a moment to lock and bolt it behind them.

"Do you think this is such a smart idea?" Eleana asked, as they ran through the Cloud Chamber. "Chances are high Olnnn Rydddlin will trap us in here, and that's the good news. The bad news is we'll encounter the Tzelos again. Either way it'll be carnage."

"Khagggun have a saying when they go into battle," Riane said, with a tight grin. " 'Carnage is another name for victory.' "

"Will you at least tell me your plan?"

"What plan?"

Eleana registered shock. "You told Thigpen—"

"I had to convince her to get Rekkk to safety. I am making this up as I go along."

"Miina preserve us!"

They were racing down the now deserted corridor. Everyone in the kashiggen was either dead or had evacuated the premises. Behind them, they could hear ion fire muffled by the door. It was only a matter of time before it gave way and Olnnn Rydddlin's Khagggun charged in.

"Tell me about the Star-Admiral," Riane said.

"He is clever, ruthless, dogged. He will never give up. He does not think in a straightforward tactical manner. If he can find a new stratagem, he will try it without thought to the risk it might pose to his own pack."

"In other words, he is impulsive and bloodthirsty."

Eleana nodded. "Rekkk was able to use this against him."

Riane found the narrow branch off the main corridor, took the hard left, kicked open the door to the utility room. Mittelwin's corpse lay in mummified paralysis where Riane had pushed it.

"Over here!" she called as she headed for the wash chute. She grabbed the upper lip of the chute, swung her legs and lower body into it. "Let's go!"

Without a word, Eleana followed her.

It was dark in the basement, but not in the least musty. Obviously, Mittelwin had been as fastidious about the service areas of the kashiggen as she had been about the public parts.

Riane conjured Flowering Wand, a cloaking spell.

"Now they won't be able to see the chute," she whispered to Eleana. "It's only temporary, but it should hold long enough."

"Long enough for what?" Eleana whispered back.

She followed behind Riane, as Riane lit one fusion lamp after another. They were in what amounted to a long tunnel-like chamber. One end was solid bedrock, the other held an old iron door shut with a rusted lock. Eleana severed the lock with one sweep of her shock-sword, but the door's immense hinges were corroded, and it took all their combined effort to move it. But what they found behind it made Eleana's heart sink. The chamber beyond had suffered a cave-in. Tons of rock had cascaded down, filling it completely. No escape there.

As they retraced their steps, Riane stopped suddenly.

"Do you smell it?" she asked.

"What?"

"The dampness." Riane put the flat of her hand on the rock wall to their left. "Odd. As you can see Mittelwin was a meticulous Tusku-gggun. She would never allow her basement to be come dank. Un-less . . ." She felt a sudden tingling in her mind, and was all at once aware of the sound of the power bourns running deep beneath the foundations.

"Dar Sala-at, what is it?"

Now she crouched, her palms feeling the minute vibrations. She moved them slowly until she came to a specific spot. The power bourns seemed quite strong, as if something was drawing them toward the surface. When she put her ear to the wall she could hear a gurgling. "There's an underground spring just behind here."

"I don't understand." Eleana shook her head. "How will that help us?"

The Tzelos, Riane thought. *Where have I read about daemonology? Not in* Utmost Source, *surely. But what about in its sister volume* The Book of Recantation? She closed her eyes, her eidetic memory reviewing page after page until she came to a particular passage.

All at once, her eyes snapped open. "Ah, yes, we have a chance, after all."

Grimly, she signaled that Eleana should sit down just where the wall was the dampest, then she paced off the steps from where they had landed at the base of the laundry chute to where Eleana sat.

"What are you doing?" Eleana asked.

"Trying to judge how long it will take the Khaggggun to get to us."

"You're joking, aren't you?" Eleana's eyes were big around. "You're *not* joking."

"I am sorry," Riane said. "I should never have allowed Rekkk to talk me into this. Now we have put you and your baby at risk."

"Dar Sala-at, in a time when we are held hostage on our own world, there is always risk."

"But this—"

She put a hand on Riane's wrist. "If it means freeing Kundala from the V'ornn, I believe any risk is acceptable."

Riane sighed. "How is the baby?"

Eleana put her hand on her lower belly. "I can feel it kicking. Sometimes I sing to it."

"Would you like to know whether it's a male or a female?"

"I don't know. I—Can you really tell?"

"With Osoru, yes, I can."

"The sorcery won't hurt the baby, will it?"

"Not in the least." Riane smiled. "Promise."

Eleana nodded. "All right then." She scrutinized Riane's face. "Dar Sala-at, why are you doing this? Why should you care?"

Once again, Riane felt the powerful urge to confess everything, to tell Eleana who she really was. But a combination of Giyan's admonitions and her own heightened sense of duty kept her silent. Still, it was torturous. With her hand on the small swell of belly, she was filled with Eleana's scent, the scent Annon remembered so well, the scent that had followed him down into dreams, haunting him. The sensation of Eleana's warmth pressed up against her was pure intoxication. She imagined Eleana's tongue flicking out and— She shut her eyes tight and wondered why she was torturing herself. Even if she eventually did tell Eleana the truth, she had no real expectation that Eleana would feel the same way. Annon was dead and gone. Why should she love Riane as she had loved Annon? With an effort, Riane pushed these thoughts aside.

"It is a male," she said. "Definitely male."

She felt Eleana's hair brush her cheek, felt her warm, fragrant breath as she whispered in Riane's ear, "Thank you, Dar Sala-at, for not judging me, for not wanting me to abort a baby who is part V'ornn. I am so grate—" Eleana froze in midsentence.

The sudden creaking of floorboards above their heads signaled that the Khaggun had forced their way into Nimbus.

*   *   *

There is something about the smell of orangesweet in the morning that turns my stomach," Nith Batoxxx said. "I drink it just the same, every day without fail."

"Why?" said Nith Isstal. "Clearly you don't like it."

"In fact, I detest it."

The laboratory was almost obsessively neat. It was a windowless, lozenge-shaped chamber deep within the heart of the Temple of Mnemonics. The sprawling, organic-looking structure that, up until the V'ornn occupation, had been the center of Kundalan religious and cultural life, crouched upon the city's only hill, in the Western Quarter of Axis Tyr. As such, it seemed a lonely place, never more so since the Gyrgon had made it their home.

Light was provided by thirteen tear-shaped fusion lamps spinning in an oval orbit, which emitted the cold purple-blue illumination of a walk-in freezer. Centuries before, the stone walls had been carefully plastered over by Kundalan artists, who then drew vast murals that covered every square centimeter of the large chamber. The murals were obscured now by vines, which for some reason grew in profusion beneath the chill light.

Nith Isstal lay, naked, in the center of the laboratory, suspended by countervailing ion fluxes directly below an enormous array of complex instruments and armatures that depended like stalactites from the concave ceiling. Holoscreens flickered readouts of every system in his body, transmitted from the semiorganic sensor net draped over him. His utterly smooth face was androgynous. He looked male or female depending upon the angle from which he was seen.

Nith Batoxxx began to walk around his laboratory. "Do you see all these green shoots and leaves, these woody vines that twine about my laboratory."

"I admit I have been curious about them, yes." Throughout Nith Isstal's utterly hairless body ran a neural network, fine as spider's silk, connected up the back of his neck to the grids in his skull. "Is it all right if I get up now?"

"Oh, yes." Nith Batoxxx drew an equation of blue ion fire in the air and the sensor net vanished. Nith Isstal's physiognomy pulsed, switching from male to female and back again. "I have finished adjusting the last germanium and tertium latticework in your skull. As soon as I activate the array . . ." He touched a number of holobuttons on the left side of one of the screens.

"Ah," Nith Isstal sighed. "Yes, I see." By which he meant, *I see everything*. Because he was now fully integrated into the Comradeship. "I can feel the male and female parts aligning themselves, balancing."

"That is in the nature of reaching maturity, a definition of our sexual harmony—the stasis of life." Nith Batoxxx gazed down upon the other. "Pity those V'ornn of other castes who must live their lives as either male or female." He gave Nith Isstal a hand, helping him to sit up. "Imagine that."

"In truth, I cannot. It is a fate too horrific to contemplate." Nith Isstal looked again at the greenery. "Nith Batoxxx, if we may return. The orangesweet that twines about your laboratory, the orangesweet you drink every day though the odor turns your stomachs. Would you explain?"

Nith Batoxxx plucked two leaves from the vines and, bringing them back to Nith Isstal, placed them in the palm of his hand.

"What do you see?"

Nith Isstal suddenly looked worried. "I know this is a test I will fail."

"You are justifiably nervous," Nith Batoxxx said. "Think of it not as a test, but as a lesson."

Nith Isstal nodded and took a deep breath. "I see, well . . ." He shrugged. "Two orangesweet leaves."

"But they are so much more." Nith Batoxxx went over to the vines. "They are the very embodiment of K'yonnno." He was speaking of the central Gyrgon theory of Chaos and Order. "Do you see these leaves?" He plucked handfuls, dropping them into Nith Isstal's lap. "A veritable blizzard of leaves, so many that you and I together could spend months counting them. And look, look! Every one has precisely five lobes. That is what is called Order. And yet, look again, each leaf has a different reticulated pattern to its veins, unique unto itself. The Chaos of individuality. Here, right under our noses, we have the living proof of K'yonnno. That is why my laboratory is filled with orangesweet; that is why I drink of its juice every day. To remind me of the rightness of our path, the righteousness of our belief in the essential stasis of things. Stasis and Harmony are synonymous, never forget the First Rule of K'yonnno."

He clapped his gloved hands together, sending tiny fountains of ion fire into the air. "Now come, clothe yourself. I hear the tolling. It is the time for the convocation."

It was almost time. She struggled to keep her mind clear for what she had to do.

The creaking drew closer and, straining, she could hear the sounds of clipped V'ornn conversation. Khagggun battle-speak. Riane summoned Osoru. The atmosphere began to congeal.

"What's going on?" Eleana whispered hoarsely.

"There are Khagggun searching the utility room. I am countering the spell I put on the chute. In a moment, they will see it."

"You're *what?*" Eleana shook her. "Are you crazy?" She began to draw her shock-sword.

"No!" Riane said sharply. She could feel the telltale shift of jihe as part of her moved into Otherwhere. "Whatever happens, keep your weapon scabbarded. Just follow my lead, all right?"

"No, it's not all right. I don't intend to—"

With a shout, a Khagggun slid down the chute.

"Got them!" he cried in triumph.

Another and another followed him, until six of Olnnn Rydddlin's pack were in the underground laundry.

"Well, well, well, what have we here?" one said, waving his shock-sword in their direction.

"Two delicate prizes," said another with a big grin on his face. "An added bonus. Rape and killing."

A third Khagggun leveled an ion cannon at them. "You two, get up," he growled.

Eleana did nothing, glaring defiantly at them.

"Oh, ho, look at this," said the first Khagggun. "I will doubly enjoy bloodying her tenderest parts."

The third Khagggun took a step toward them. "I said, 'Get up!' Now!"

"Do as he says," Riane murmured. The architecture of Otherwhere was all around her, and she turned, at once confused, because her Third Eye had registered the difference, some subtle change, a soft susurrus just at the threshold of awareness, a restless indefinable quality that disturbed the deep sacred silence of the Otherscape. She had no time to think of this now as she cast a sorcerous beacon into the pure white sky as she had seen Giyan do. Would it be sufficient? It had to be!

"But—"

"Remember what I told you," Riane said, pulling Eleana to her feet. The sorcerous beacon arced, streaking though Otherwhere.

"Now what?" Eleana was watching the leering grin on the Khagggun's faces. "Just wait for them to rape us?" Her hands clenched. "At least let me draw my shock-sword so I can take a few of these animals with me."

"No. Do not give them any cause to fire their weapons."

There was a disturbance in Otherwhere, a Darkness stained the white horizon. Riane took Eleana's hand. "As soon as I give you the signal I want you to run toward the door."

"Why? We can't get out there. It's sealed tighter than a—"

"Shut up, you two!" barked the Khagggun with the ion cannon trained on them. "No talking."

The Darkness irised open. Riane left just enough time to see six pairs of ruby-red eyes before she popped fully back into the corporeal world. She felt it coming, the dimness behind the six Khagggun deepening, fulminating, coalescing into—

"Miina preserve us!" Eleana cried in fright. "The Tzelos has found us again!"

Either the Khagggun didn't hear her or didn't believe her.

"Run!" Riane shouted. "Run!"

As they raced back down the chamber, the Khagggun leveling the ion cannon at them took aim, but another forced his arm down.

"Our orders are to bring them to the Star-Admiral alive," he said. "In any event, we have them trapped." Following his reasoned lead, the Khagggun pack advanced methodically in pursuit.

This was what Riane was betting on. She counted off the seconds as she had counted off the paces from the chute landing to the damp patch on the wall. When she judged the Khagggun to be in the right position, she sent a spell hurtling toward the Tzelos. The daemon reared up, bellowing. The Khagggun turned, stunned and horrified at what their disbelieving eyes saw. One of the Khagggun fired his ion cannon without effect. The others drew theirs and fired in unison.

For a moment, the Tzelos was completely enveloped in pale blue ion fire. Then, its hideous jaws swung open and it swallowed the energy whole. An instant later, black fire spewed out. It slammed the six Khagggun against the wall with such force that the ancient mortar literally disintegrated. Instantly, a flood of water gushed into the chamber.

"Let's go!" Riane cried, dragging Eleana toward the flood.

"What—?"

"How good is your swimming?" She shoved Eleana into the hole, then leapt in after her.

The water hit her like a shanstone wall. It was freezing, its flow trying to push her back into the underground laundry where the Tzelos still lurked.

Eleana, having an even harder time with the torrent, slipped in the muck oozing at the bottom of the spring. She fell back heavily against Riane, and Riane felt a vicious tugging, saw first one, then another hairy appendage wrap itself around her, dragging her inexorably back to the underground lair where the Tzelos crouched.

7

Teyj

The Comradeship of Gyrgon met in formal convocation once a day in the great listening hall of the Temple of Mnemonics. Once, it had been the central temple where the Ramahan prayed to their Goddess, Miina. There, upon the scarred and stained porphyry altar, they had made their barbaric sacrifices to that imagined divine being. Here, amid the onyx seats of the shell-like amphitheater, the priests had listened to their leader, Mother, blather to them the myths she made up as she went along. At least, that is how Nith Batoxxx imagined it had been before the time of the V'ornn.

He escorted Nith Isstal to his seat in the tiered half round before drifting away to take his own place halfway around the great listening hall. One thing you had to give the Kundalan—possibly the only thing, he thought—they knew how to construct with acoustics in mind. How their music could sound like the caterwauling of a razor-raptor in its death throes was a complete mystery.

As other Gyrgon filed into the amphitheater he felt the stirring inside him, an autumnal wind scurrying the death of summer before it, scouring his interior landscape of superfluous thought. A beacon of black light struck him from out of his interior, blinding him momentarily, then, as he grew used to it, settling him in single purpose. He felt a premonitory ruffling, then the cool energy surged through him, making him tremble slightly until synapses and nerve endings alike adjusted to the heightened load. Each time, he had recovered more quickly. Each time, he felt himself longing more deeply for the exquisite sensation. He felt different, renewed.

Eternal.

But that had been the promise, hadn't it? Yes, it most assuredly was. And now eternal life was his, and his alone.

His head swiveled and his ruby irises scanned the hall until he found

Nith Settt. Lifting a forefinger, he beckoned the other Gyrgon over.

"What news?" he whispered.

Nith Settt inclined his head. "Nothing good. These tribes with their strict fundamentalist views!"

"Their very fundamentalism should make them that much more susceptible to manipulation."

"And so it does," Nith Settt whispered. "But as for Perrnodt. She is forcing our hand. In order to get to her, we will have to destabilize the entire region."

"No!"

Several Gyrgon around them turned their heads at Nith Batoxxx's raised voice. He ignored their stares, leaned in, lowered his voice. "You are under strict orders not to destabilize the region. You understand this?"

"I most certainly do not." Nith Settt's voice was distorted by frustration. "We are Gyrgon. We own Kundala and everything on it. I simply do not see the problem. We want information from this dzuoko, we should take her and break her bones one by one until she tells us."

"She will *never* tell us," Nith Batoxxx hissed. "Not by coercion, certainly. That has been tried once."

"Not by me."

"You really are a rather bestial thing," Nith Batoxxx said in an echoey tone whose oddity was lost in the cavernous acoustics. He studied the other for a moment before he went on slowly and carefully as if explaining a complex lesson to a particularly thick student. "We must be more clever than that." He smiled until all his teeth showed. "We must give her a reason for wanting to find the *Maasra* rather than protect it. Then she will lead us right to it without even knowing she is doing so."

Nith Settt blinked. "And how do you propose we do that?"

"Fortunately for you the triggering mechanism has already been set in motion. After the convocation return swiftly to Agachire. Keep a sharp eye on Perrnodt and follow events as they transpire."

"Yes, Nith Batoxxx. It will be done."

"As I have outlined."

"Precisely."

He smiled, touched Nith Settt on the gleaming veradium point on the crown of his skull. When he took his seat, he saw across the amphitheater the imperious Nith Nassam, who caught his eye for a moment, before the other rose and descended to the center space that held the Kundalan altar. It was Nith Nassam who had joined him in his final, lethal assault on Nith Sahor.

At this signal, two other Gyrgon separated themselves from the crowd and took their place flanking him. Bizarre to see them grouped around such a primitive bloodstained artifact, he thought. Yet less so now that the cool energy blew through him. With his new perspective, he saw the rightness in the juxtaposition, just as he was now able to recognize the hidden power locked within that solid block of porphyry.

The trio of Gyrgon were known as the facilitators. Representing Order, Chaos, and K'yonnno, they changed with each convocation. They brought the assembled to silence by beginning the Creation Chant, which manifested a gigantic atom and the twenty subatomic particles from which all matter in the Cosmos was composed.

And then the assembled spoke as one: "Deliver us from darkness, from ignorance, from false theorem." A short pause while they stared at the spinning atom their collective energies had created. "Deliver us from the Centophennni, deliver us home."

The convocation was invoked.

Came the stillness, the deepening silence before the discussion began to flow. Naturally enough, this took the form of equations, lit across the firmament of the great listening hall, bursting like ion-cannon fire, question equations, followed by answer equations, positive and negative theorems batted back and forth among the assembled Comradeship.

It was the job of the three Gyrgon standing by the altar to keep the dialogue moving, to break up equation jams of those Gyrgon trying to voice their opinions at the same time. Nith Batoxxx watched them as it became more difficult to maintain a disciplined equation flow, as arguments became more and more rancorous, as factions banded together, further fracturing the already sundered whole. And as he witnessed the growing pandemonium, an elation took hold of him, a cold fire in his lowest belly, a conviction—as if he needed any!—of the rightness and righteousness of the path that had chosen him.

In the old days, it was always Nith Sahor's theorems that quieted the bickering, that soothed the antagonists, that formed the compromises. But Nith Batoxxx, working in the shadows, saw to it that those

compromises were temporary, that the rifts re-formed, the old antag-
onisms resurfaced. It was accurate to say that at night he undid the
good Nith Sahor did during the day.

Stasis.

And yet, not really. Each convocation brought the Comradeship
closer to pitched battle. Each convocation took Nith Sahor further into
the retreat of his studies. Until fear, uncertainty, and consternation
strode through the dim passageways of the Temple of Mnemonics, fracturing the Comradeship's once steadfast solidarity. Now there was a
lack of purpose, rooms filled to overflowing with doubt. The last ob-
stacle to the growing weakness about the Comradeship was Nith Sahor.
Nith Sahor, who had the will and the intelligence to unite them again.
Now he was dead, by Nith Batoxxx's hand. The black beacon that had
formed inside Nith Batoxxx had shown him that the rifts had gone
deep enough for him to come to the fore. For the others to acknowledge his leadership without question.

Enough!

Nith Batoxxx used an equation that stilled all the others just long
enough for him to rise from his seat and stride down the tiers to take
his place at the porphyry altar. He gestured and theorems ringed the
amphitheater.

This petty bickering has gone on long enough, he told the assembled
through equations. *Days, weeks, months, years have dissolved in enmity
and squabbles. What have we become now—Bashkir?* He heard the stirring of the silence, a good sign. *First we fought over how to treat the Kundalan, for there were those of us who believed them special of all the races we
have conquered. Then we fought over the continuation of the House of Ashera
as regent. There were those who were infected by Ashera Eleusis' belief that
we had come to Kundala now, at this moment in time, for a specific reason,
a higher purpose, that Kundala was an inextricable part of our future, that
we could learn from the Kundalan. What equation do I see posited? Learn
from an inferior species? How could this be so? How could such anathema
exist? And yet, as I look around me, I recognize those who, at first, believed
in this foolishness.*

*Then the dissension morphed again to the change in leadership among
the other castes. There were those of you who raised equations against
installing the House of Stogggul in the regent's chair. Even a theory or two*

was mounted to that effect. And that dissension continues now that the son, Stogggul Kurgan, has succeeded his father. Kurgan is young, some say. Kurgan is untested, others decry. But not long, and certainly not loudly. Because the spark of dissension is gone. Our brother, Nith Sahor, is dead. Without fear of contradiction, I say that Nith Sahor was a great Gyrgon, a brilliant theorist, yes. But he was terribly misguided. He believed, as Ashera Eleusis did, that the Kundalan are our equals, that we must res-urrect Za Hara-at, the so-called City of One Million Jewels in order that V'ornn and Kundalan live side by side. Za Hara-at is important but not in the way the Asher heretic imagined. Beneath the ragged tents and ku-omeshal dung lies a treasure trove of Kundala's past. One we are now free to plunder without interference. Or are we? The bickering remains, the seeds of doubt Nith Sahor planted about the rightness of our path, the righteous-ness of our belief in Stasis grow and grow. The heretical theorem he wrought lives on after he himself is dead.

I will no longer sit here and listen to you fight like the brattish children of the other castes. If that is your wish, be gone from here, your use to the Comradeship has come to an end. From this moment forward, we will tolerate only one vision, one theory, one single note sounded over and over in Stasis.

Nith Isstal stood up. *The convocation has always been about many voices.* Right on cue. *Perhaps it is wiser to allow all voices to be heard.*

You are young, Nith Isstal. Nith Batoxxx wrote this equation large upon the firmament above the amphitheater. *This is your first convo-cation, is it not?*

It is, Nith Isstal wrote. *But my family has a long history in the con-vocation. All my life I have been steeped in its strict and sacred protocol.* He looked around at the assembled. *And after all, isn't this protocol further proof of the Law of Stasis?*

His logic is impeccable, wrote Nith Nassam, and there came a chorus of like-minded equations.

And from elsewhere in the amphitheater, *He may be young, but his thesis has merit.*

Emboldened by the courage of a Gyrgon so young voicing his opin-ion, those who had but a moment ago held this same view in secrecy emerged full-blown into the convocation.

There is another theory that must be resurrected. Nith Recctor had risen, was writing ion fire in his typical elegant hand. No one ignored his equations or his theories. Other equations died away, awaiting the continuation of his theory.

Nith Batoxxx looked at him with a neutral expression on his face. Nith Recctor was one of the silent ones, one of the elder ones. One of Nith Sahor's suspected allies. Thus far definitive proof of this treachery had eluded him. This carefully choreographed dance he had devised using Nith Isstal as his stalking beast was working. Toxins must be drawn slowly to the surface, where they can be burned off. The most virulent toxins were the ones buried most deeply in the corpus.

We know from our studies that Kundala's atmosphere once possessed a strong electric charge. In fact, gravship records marked in detail the intensity of this charge as we approached Kundala. And yet, when we arrived the charge had vanished. Where once lightning ringed the skies none now exists, even during the most violent of meteorological disturbances.

Yes, yes, Nith Batoxxx wrote. *The Comradeship is well aware of Nith Sahor's theory that in some way our arrival dispersed Kundala's electrical charge.*

Not dispersed, Nith Recctor wrote in the lecturing style that set Nith Batoxxx's teeth on edge. *In one of his most elegant theories, Nith Sahor postulated that our presence on Kundala caused its electrical charge to retreat into stasis. As you are well aware, electrical charges are in constant flux; they abhor stasis. There is in known space no instance of a species affecting the electrical charge of a planet's atmosphere simply by its presence. Thus, Nith Sahor's conclusion that the V'ornn presence on Kundala was significant—no, I miswrote. Not simply significant. It is nothing short of revolutionary. He extrapolated a series of theorems that projected a different course for us, that in coming to Kundala we must recognize that our path has been irrevocably diverted. That the secrets lying buried here have the power to change us all.*

Dangerous, heretical theorems that this very convocation repudiated, Nith Batoxxx wrote with some asperity.

If memory serves, this body repudiated nothing. Nith Recctor went on, relentless. *To this day, Nith Sahor's theorems have yet to be disproved.*

Or proved.

He was never given the chance of proof. He was hounded from the Comradeship in the most repugnant display of partisanship and close-mindedness it has been my misfortune to have witnessed.

At that time, who stood up for him? Nith Batoxxx wrote. *You, Nith Recctor? Or you, Nith Hwelle? Or you, Nith Immmon?*

His death is a tragedy for the Comradeship, for all V'ornn, Nith Recctor wrote.

Easy to mourn a heretic after he is gone, Nith Nassam fired back.

I seek no expiation for my own shameful behavior, Nith Recctor wrote. *But the simple, inescapable fact remains. Since we arrived here one hundred two years ago there has been no evidence whatsoever of electrical activity in the atmosphere, and nothing we have tried has been able to revive it. I take this as—*

Listen to Nith Recctor wagging his finger at us, telling us that he is smarter than we are, telling us that we should believe in unproved heresy, that we should go on—what did Nith Sahor call it—faith? Yes, faith! That we should have faith that heresy would someday prove correct.

We have only your opinion as to what is heresy, Nith Batoxxx.

Would you have us repudiate K'yonnno, the very bedrock of our understanding of the Cosmos? Look! Look at this! He writes that we have been on Kundala for one hundred two years. Whose years, I ask you now? V'ornn years? No. He speaks in Kundalan terminology. He has been corrupted by this accursed place just as surely as Nith Sahor was.

I believe this body has heard enough from you, Nith Batoxxx.

On the contrary, it has not heard nearly enough! Nith Batoxxx felt the black beacon turning its exhilarating energy in one direction. His entire being vibrated as it concentrated its beam through his raised arm, his pointing finger. *We have had enough of secret studies, clandestine experiments. We have had enough of the corruption of our body of theorems, the corruption of our very ideals.*

We should hold a vote. Nith Recctor's equation hung in the air for a moment.

Just a smattering minority of equations. From the rest of the convocation, Nith Batoxxx noted only silence.

On this matter that option is inadequate, he wrote. *It is hereby terminated.*

A small disturbance in back quashed immediately by the baleful gaze of Nith Nassam. Thenceforth, a pool of silence, spreading, without the hint of a ripple.

A horrified expression appeared on Nith Recctor's face as he, at last, understood the nature of the trap that had been set for him.

Black fire erupted from the end of Nith Batoxxx's finger. Ion-fire contrails arcing into the firmament as the dark energy that infused him long ago speared Nith Recctor, spun him full around, took him off his feet, slammed him facefirst into the back wall of the great listening hall. For a moment, he hung there, quivering. Then a second fork of the energy beam took him quickly apart.

Whether the absolute silence that followed was approbation or fear Nith Batoxxx did not know. Nor did he much care. Either was acceptable. Both was preferred.

The water level was rising and with each minute that passed the heavy spray was making it more difficult to breathe. Desperately, Riane hacked with her dagger and heard the Tzelos scream with each cut she made. This was significant since it had shown no evidence of pain when she had hacked off the end of its appendage during its attack at the abbey. Heartened that the passage she had summoned up from *The Book of Recantation* was correct, she hacked some more, heard it scream again. The end of the appendage hung by a thread, water gushing over it, laced with the emanations of the power bourns for beneath, and a deep shudder went through the Tzelos.

"Riane! Watch out!"

She twisted her head up at Eleana's shout, saw the evil triangular head with its wicked mandibles coming toward her. The mouth was opening and—

"Throw water in its mouth," Riane shouted.

"Water? But why?"

"Do as I say!" she commanded.

The daemon's head was so close a mandible brushed against her cheek as she squirmed and fought to free herself. The stink of its foul breath made her want to gag. Then Eleana had scooped up the water and was flinging it into the Tzelos' open mouth.

The daemon gave a bellow. It began to shake as with an ague as the ineluctable energy from the power bourns began to eat at it like acid. Quickly, Riane cut her way out of its embrace. That was what the passage had told her, that the energy from the power bourns could burn through daemon flesh. The Tzelos appeared to be shrinking. In fact, it was being eaten from the inside out. The daemon screamed, took one last lunge at them before its husk was washed away on the tide of bourn-laced water.

Riane and Eleana plunged into the spring. Like fish wriggling upstream, they fought against the current, holding their breaths as they kicked upward with powerful strokes. After the first hundred meters, they were swept up in the current. Utter blackness surrounded them, and the cold was slowly seeping into their muscles, making them stiff, tiring them prematurely. But there was another, more urgent problem. Both of them had taken deep breaths, but the air in their lungs would only go so far. With her Gift, she sought out the bourn-lines, sensed them twisting and turning, and followed them as they rose from the depths.

But already she could see Eleana taken out of the swift current stream, slowing down. She swam up behind her, took her around the waist, and pressed on, pushing her long, powerful legs to flutter faster. Eleana's eyes were closing. Riane sensed that she was on the verge of passing out. Once that happened, Riane knew, water would seep into her nose and throat. She felt her own lungs begin to burn.

A sudden wave of dizziness sent her mind reeling, and at once she was in the midst of a snowstorm. She saw, now and again, the dark vertical ridges of the Djenn Marre. High up, she saw a cave. Flickering firelight illuminated the mouth, and then a tall, slender figure strode out into the storm. At first, she assumed this was another memory shard of Riane's resurfacing, but then she saw that the figure was a V'ornn male, judging by his size and hairless head. This V'ornn went to the lip of the ledge into which the cave was formed and spread wide his arms. Through the fierce snow gusts she caught a clear glimpse of his face and recognized him.

It was Rekkk!

Where was his armor?

This was a vision, no question about it. What was she seeing, the present or the future?

His lips moved, but she could not hear his words. All at once, he seemed to tilt his body forward, falling off the ledge into the heart of the storm. Riane wanted to cry out, but, of course, she could not make a sound. She wanted to catch him but, of course, she could not move.

All she could do was watch, horrified, as he plunged to his death . . .

In the blink of an eye, the vision vanished. Pushing the panic down, she reestablished contact with the bourn-lines, and ran right into a granite outcropping. The current swirled them away again, and Riane, half-stunned, fought to regain her equilibrium. It was as they were being whirled around that she saw a patch of light. Or at least she thought she saw it. And then, yes, there it was—dim, flickering, far off. She tried to orient herself, noted that the spot was almost directly above the granite outcropping.

Using every last ounce of strength, she pulled them both out of the current's grip. Once, Riane almost passed out, but the pain in her shoulder where she had collided with the rock kept her focused on what she had to do.

At last, she was able to reach out to the outcropping, launch them upward toward the light. It seemed to take forever. She kept shaking Eleana, keeping her conscious. She could feel every fiber of her being straining to push them faster. Up they went, the patch of light spreading out, rippling, becoming more detailed.

Pockmarks and pinpricks, tiny ripples spreading outward in a kind of hallucinogenic pattern not unlike a vastly complex weaving. Maybe she was going under . . . Maybe they wouldn't make it after all. . . . Maybe there were already drowning, water filling her lungs, black tide seeping the life out of them. Maybe . . .

With a gasp, she broke the surface of the water, splashing, pulling Eleana up, as she took huge draughts of air into her. She coughed up some water, turned her head, saw with terror Eleana's pale, bluish face. Her eyes were closed, she wasn't breathing. Desperately, Riane looked around. They had surfaced in the center of a huge stone cistern somewhere in a run-down section of the city. She called out but heard no response. Deserted. They were alone, Eleana was unconscious, and she herself was near exhaustion.

Olnnn Rydddlin was standing knee deep in water, hands on hips, when Kurgan slid down the chute into the underground laundry at Nimbus. The Star-Admiral was directing a team of forensic Deirus who were poking and prodding the pile of six Khagggun corpses.

"They have been cindered," Kurgan said, peering at the dead. "Burned to a crisp."

There were echoes in the underground space, echoes upon echoes, technical jargon droned into data-decagons, opinions and speculation being batted back and forth, the ebb and flow of a team hard at work.

Kurgan, listening hard to the echoes, said at length, "What happened here, Star-Admiral? One moment I get a report you have them trapped down here, the next I hear six of my Khagggun are dead, and the Rhynnnon Rekkk Hacilar and his Kundalan skcettta have vanished."

"The preliminary report from the Deirus is that ion-cannon fire was employed against the pack."

"Ion-cannon fire?" Kurgan went over to the hole in the wall, peered at the blackened perimeter where it was visible above the waterline. "It looks to me like a fusion bomb went off down here."

"A stolen fusion bomb or a homemade Kundalan explosive such as the Resistance uses leaves energy signatures," Olnnn said crisply. "The Deirus assure me they have found none."

Kurgan turned to face his Star-Admiral. "This setback is troubling. Neither of us can afford to allow this Rhynnnon to remain free and unpunished." He took a step closer, lowered his voice. "N'Luuura take it, Rekkk Hacilar was one of our own. He turned against us. Now he flaunts his treachery in our faces. This cannot be tolerated."

"We will find him, regent. This I swear to you."

Kurgan stood very close to the Star-Admiral. "Find the Rhynnnon and his skcettta and do it now. We are both just beginning to build our power bases. I want a total news eclipse on this incident. All we need is for knowledge of these deaths to ripple through the ranks. This . . . massacre could be construed as a sign of weakness on our part; it cannot be tolerated."

"I understand, regent." Olnnn Rydddlin nodded to the Deirus swarming over the corpses. "I have put our best team on it."

"No, you do not understand." Kurgan hissed. "I do not care an ice-hare's ass about your pack; I do not care an ice-hare's ass about your best team of Deirus. *You* take care of this mess personally, Olnnn Rydddlin. I will not have this kind of humiliation stand for long." His grip tightened. "And if it does, I assure you there will be a scapegoat. Some V'ornn well-known so the populace will recognize instantly his head on the end of the regent's pike."

Olnnn Rydddlin's voice was icy calm. "I am Star-Admiral."

"You would do well to remember who named you to that post."

Olnnn Rydddlin regarded the regent from out of a face closed tight as any fortress. "I have never for an instant forgotten it, regent."

Kurgan stood silent for a moment, then he smiled abruptly. "Of course, you're right, my friend. It is only that this . . . setback so soon after becoming regent has unsettled me somewhat. You understand."

"Perfectly, regent."

The smile widened. "Come, come, Olnnn. We have fought together, schemed together, killed together. I am always Kurgan to you."

Olnnn Rydddlin nodded rather stiffly.

"Good. Time and power, Olnnn, are both of the essence."

Olnnn Rydddlin was about to make a reply when Kurgan's okummmon activated.

"I am being Summoned," Kurgan said. He stepped away a moment to receive his mysterious communication from the Gyrgon Comradeship. A moment later, he looked up. "Star-Admiral," he said in clipped tones, "you and your contingent will vacate this space now."

"Regent?"

"Do as I order!"

When the basement was clear even of his Haaar-kyut, he spoke softly into his okummmon.

"All right, Nith Batoxxx. I am alone."

"I want to get a closer look at the bodies," the Gyrgon said, his voice emanating from Kurgan's okummmon.

Kurgan approached the pile of cindered corpses.

"Hold out your arm," Nith Batoxxx said.

As Kurgan did so, he felt a small tingling, and the okummmon emitted a kind of mist. A moment later, a holographic image of the Gyrgon appeared. It stooped down, peering closely at the bodies. It went so absolutely still that for an instant Kurgan thought something had gone amiss with the connection. Of a sudden, the image whirled and with a frightening countenance stalked over to the hole in the wall.

"Water," the image of Nith Batoxxx said as if reporting back to the Gyrgon Comradeship. "So much water." It lifted a finger, beckoned Kurgan over. "Regent, I want you to reach into this hole."

"What am I looking for?"

The hologram turned its lambent ruby-irised eyes on him. "Just do it. Now."

"Yes, Nith Batoxxx." Kurgan walked through the hologram on his way to the rent in the wall. Bending over slightly, he extended his arms up to the shoulder into the breach, felt around. To his surprise, he felt something hard, almost brittle floating up against the back side of the wall, directed by the water's current. Straining a little, he pulled it out.

"Ahhhh!" The image of Nith Batoxxx let out a sigh that was almost a wail.

Kurgan had no idea of what he was looking at, but it was clear the Gyrgon did. It was as black and sere as the cindered Khagggun, about five times their size but light as a sheaf of glennan. It appeared to be curled into a kind of fetal ball. Its head, if that is what it was, looked to be about three times too big for the sticklike body.

"How could this happen?" Nith Batoxxx asked himself.

Another thing Kurgan noticed. Whatever it was wasn't a biped. He knew better than to ask the Gyrgon what it was. What was clear was that it was neither V'ornn nor Kundalan. That left what?

Beside him, the image of Nith Batoxxx clenched its fists tightly. "There is only one way," it whispered just as if Kurgan was not there. "The Dar Sala-at!"

The cistern was set in the center of an octagon-shaped courtyard piled with rubble. High shanstone walls rose all around, featureless, grim, topped by scowling granite gargoyles that faced inward, crouched, sculpted muscles bunched and corded as if about to leap upon any who dared invade their territory. An arched, roofed walkway ran around all sides. Not a tree, not a blade of wrygrass could be seen in the packed-down dirt.

All this Riane absorbed in the split second before she began pumping rhythmically on Eleana's sternum. Water gushed out of Eleana's mouth, dribbling down each corner, but still she did not stir. Riane blinked rain out of her eyes, tried to purge her mind of the horrible vision of Rekkk's death. Uttering a prayer in Venca, she bent over Eleana, pinched her nose, opened her mouth wide, and began to force breath into her. She worked steadily, tirelessly, her mind half-frozen by fear and despair.

This cistern, on whose broad slimy rim Eleana lay, was where they had fetched up after their harrowing trek underwater.

Riane was listening carefully. The baby was still alive, she felt its aura, the strength of it, and something more, a sliver of the future, perhaps, or an imagined future in which the boy battled the personal daemons of his heritage. The blood of the Stogggul beat powerfully within him, singing its own imperative, but there was a singular oddity about his physical form that Riane could not quite define—he would be distinctly different from those Stogggul who had come before him. More clearly, she saw through the lens of Osoru the potential in the boy for great good and great evil. In any case, the sign under which he would be born, the sign that would rule his entire life, was Transformation. All this passed before her in the blink of an eye, then it abruptly vanished as Eleana went into a quick series of convulsions.

Opening her Third Eye, Riane could feel the thin and fragile membrane between life and death against which the baby lay. The fetus was uncoupling itself from its life-sustaining connections to its mother. The trauma that Eleana had just endured had shocked her system enough for the pregnancy to come undone. In an instant, Riane knew that if she did nothing, the fetus would abort, it would be gone in a matter of brief bloody seconds and all trace of Kurgan Stogggul would have vanished from Eleana's body and from Riane's life. Annon's V'ornn anger at what Kurgan had done to Eleana flared briefly like a white-hot coal, burning away logic and reason.

Then Riane gathered herself, felt stirring in her depths essential fragments of the original Riane personality, a logical, deeply committed core, and she conjured up Earth Granary, the most potent healing spell in her limited sorcerous vocabulary. She had no idea of all of its properties or whether it was the correct spell for what ailed Eleana, but she had to believe that it was better than nothing. She instructed the spell to enfold Eleana, felt it take her up in its cradling embrace.

At once, the convulsions subsided, the fetus quieted, its functions returning to normal.

Still, Eleana had not recovered consciousness. Drawing a deep, shuddering breath, Riane put her lips beside Eleana's ear. "Come on," she whispered fiercely. "Come on!"

No response. Eleana's breathing was shallow and rapid, her pulse was erratic.

Riane honed the focus of the healing spell, drawing it tighter around Eleana. Her own exhaustion fell away, her terror, as well, as she concentrated her entire being on Eleana.

"I won't let you give up, Eleana. I love you too much to let you die. I will follow you all the way to the gates of N'Luuura if—"

Eleana took a deep, shuddering breath. She coughed. Riane turned

Eleana's head to the side, and she expelled the last of the water. Her chest rose and fell.

"That's it! That's it!"

Riane listened for the heartbeats, strong now and steady, the Kundalan beat in concert with the V'ornn rhythm. She got up, ran through the abandoned courtyard, scrabbling through piles of rubble and ancient dustbins until she found a length of sailcloth. It was stiff and stained, but it would do. Returning to the cistern, she wrapped Eleana in the sailcloth and carried her beneath an archway where it was dry. She set her down, kneeling beside her. She could feel Earth Granary working its way deeper still, easing Eleana's respiratory distress, slowly returning her breathing to normal. She brushed Eleana's hair out of her eyes, wiped the rain off her face.

Again, Riane's training at high altitudes had proved crucial. This sixteen-year-old Kundalan girl into whom Annon had been sorcerously transferred had amnesia. She could not remember her parents or the village where she had been born. But she was convinced that it must have been somewhere high up in the Djenn Marre because of her skills in mountain climbing and her acclimatization to extremely high altitudes, as well as the occasional bursts of memory she had of ice-encrusted mountainscapes.

As she watched Eleana breathing, Riane was once again caught up in the strangeness and dislocation of being Kundalan and female. The odd thing was that while she felt Riane's biological urges, Annon's love for Eleana had neither changed nor diminished one iota. She did not know what to make of that. She marveled at the deep and abiding power of love that could transcend gender, species, and death. Not even the Gyrgon technomancy was its equal.

She was so beautiful. Riane could not help herself. She felt a powerful force drawing her down until she pressed her mouth against Eleana's slightly parted lips. She felt her warmth, tasted her cinnamon and chamomile breath, and for a moment she laid her head in the damp crook of her neck. A scent drifted off Eleana's skin and hair, indefinable, intoxicating.

For a long moment they lay that way, together, in what seemed to Riane to be a perfect kind of symmetry. She thought she heard the Cosmos humming all around them. At length, she sat up. She took Eleana's hands, warmed them between her own.

The rain dripped dolefully off the slanted tiled roof of the walkway. Birds fluttered in the eaves, peered solemnly down at them. She rose and walked a little way under the eaves, wondering where they were. It seemed likely that they were still within the Northern Quarter of Axis Tyr, but, if so, it was a section Annon had never seen before.

What was this building? It was huge and forbidding. The grotesques atop the crenellated walls were so exquisitely wrought they could only have been made by the hands of Kundalan sculptors, but for sure the creatures did not look Kundalan at all. They had the oddest faces, as if animal features had been stretched over a Kundalan skull.

"Unsettling, aren't they?"

Riane started. A very short, very wide individual had emerged from a doorway hidden behind a jumbled pile of crates. Even for a Kundalan, he was exceptionally hairy.

"I called out before," Riane said. "Why didn't you answer? We needed help."

The Kundalan squinted, which made him look not unlike one of the parapet gargoyles. He had a high prominent forehead like the prow of a Sarakkon ship, massive eyebrows, a small, veined, bulbous nose, and lips as red as a winter sunset. He had a bushy forked beard shot through with red. Thick hair stood up wildly from the top of his head as if in response to hyperexcited ions. His moss-green robes seemed too large for him; he was continually pushing up the sleeves, which ended at his gnarled knuckles. "Need help now?"

"No, I managed on my own."

"So what is the problem?" He walked with a decided limp. One leg was shorter than the other and as bandy as a bow. "What are you doing here?" he asked suspiciously. "The museum is closed."

"Museum? Is that what this is?"

The bandy-legged Kundalan nodded. "It has been closed, more or less, for years."

"Then what are you doing here?"

"Why, I am the curator," he said. "Not that it's any of your business."

"My name's Riane. That's Eleana."

"You almost drowned in my cistern, you did." He squinted at them through the rain. "How is it you ended up here?"

Riane bit her lip, not knowing whether to trust the curator with the truth. "We had to get away fast. Khagggun were after us."

"Ah-ha!" A smile wreathed the curator's face, and it instantly transformed him. He extended a pawlike hand. "Minnum's the name, tending to the past is my game. Such as it is." The back of his hand, Riane felt, was furred. "No business, these days. As you can see." He squinted again. "Not that there ever was much to begin with."

"The V'ornn shut you down."

"The V'ornn!" Laughter exploded out of Minnum's mouth. "Goddess take me, the V'ornn are the reason the museum still exists. Well, two V'ornn had a hand in it, really."

"Who?" Now Riane's curiosity had been pricked.

"Well, I shouldn't say, really. They are keeping it a secret, is what they told me." Minnum's face fell. "Though one of them is dead now. Tragic, really. Killed before his time, murdered most foully. And the other—" He heaved another sigh. "Goddess take me, I have not seen the other in over a month. Passing strange, that, as I was used to seeing him almost every day." He squinted hard at Riane. "How did you say you came to be in my cistern?"

"We were escaping a pack of Khagggun."

Minnum looked at her shrewdly. "You are no friend of the new regent, I warrant."

"He's trying his best to capture us."

Minnum nodded. "I despise him, that Stogggul. A pretender is what he is, just like his despicable father. It was the father, you know, who ordered Eleusis Ashera killed. Yes, it was." He paused a moment to see what effect this name might have on Riane. "You have heard of Eleusis Ashera, haven't you? Was the true regent, once upon a time."

Riane nodded, for the moment unable to speak.

"Well, Eleusis Ashera was one of the V'ornn who kept this place alive and safe from the scavengers and toughs hereabouts. He loved to wander through the exhibits. He was a very decent sort, for a V'ornn, listened to every word of my commentary, too. It's my opinion he had a distinct affinity for Kundalan history."

Eleusis had never told Annon anything about this place. "How could he slip away from his duties so often?"

Minnum grinned. "I asked him that myself." He touched the side of his nose while he rummaged around inside his robes. "You know, he gave me a present. A memento, so to speak. After he was killed I was doubly happy I had it." He finally produced a piece of alloy, the size and shape of a teardrop. "It is just a trinket, really. But."

He spun it in the palm of his hand and Riane gasped, for there standing in front of her, was Annon's father Eleusis Ashera, tall and slender, garbed as Annon remembered him best in white form-fitting trousers, gold metallic-mesh blouse beneath his pure white waist-length jacket, piped and braided in gold. In his piercing eyes Riane saw once again the reflection of Annon's own face as it had been once upon a time. She felt a little shiver run through her, and her heart ached to see him again, standing so noble and proud, the icon of the Ashera Consortium.

"You would swear it was him, wouldn't you?" Minnum said. He spun the teardrop faster, and Eleusis began to walk. "It's as if he is alive and breathing right beside you. It's a holoimage—Gyrgon technomagic. It's anyone's guess how Eleusis got this, but he would use this in the palace while he came here." He cocked his head appraisingly. "Still, good as it is, it's not perfect. There's a flaw, you see. Generic to these V'ornnish holoimages. I will not tell you what it is. You have to find it yourself."

Riane forced herself to concentrate as she walked all around the holoimage.

"Mayhap I should have him walk some more."

And as the holoimage of Eleusis Ashera began again to move, Riane saw it. "His feet don't quite reach the floor."

"Yes. That's it precisely." Minnum appeared pleased. "Asked him about this, and he said it had something to do with the Kundalan atmosphere interfering with the ion bursts. The Gyrgon had tinkered with it, of course, but they could not solve the problem."

Minnum snapped off the holoimage, pocketed the alloy teardrop. "In any event, Eleusis Ashera was not the only V'ornn who had an abiding interest in Kundala, no indeed. There was a Gyrgon who came. Nith Sahor. But I suppose a little snippet like you wouldn't know about—"

"I've met Nith Sahor," Riane said. "He died a month ago. That's why—"

"Nith Sahor dead?" Minnum's eyebrows gathered like storm clouds. "Well, that's the most scurrilous lie I have ever heard. I would know if that Gyrgon was dead, I have the gift, and I'm telling you he is alive."

"You have the Gift?" Riane asked excitedly. "Are you a sorceress?"

"There are no more males of that nature, you should know that. Unless you count the V'ornn technomages, which I certainly do not."

He squinted hard at Riane. "If there were, though, they would be called sefiror."

"*Sefirum* is a Venca word," Riane said at once. "It means 'mystical community.' "

Minnum scratched his hairy cheek. "Now how would a little bitty thing like you know that?"

"She wouldn't," Riane said.

Minnum looked hard and long at Riane, then chuckled under his breath. "Let's forget all about fairy tales of sefiror and preternaturally gifted girls, hmm? The fact is, I must prepare for Nith Sahor's next visit."

"I told you, Nith Sahor is dead."

Minnum scowled darkly. "Why do you keep saying that?"

"My friends were there when he was killed. They buried the body."

"And that is your evidence?" Minnum scoffed. "What is a body to a Gyrgon, eh, tell me that? Bodies are meaningless to them. Do you know I never saw Nith Sahor in the same one twice. Now how many bodies do you think he used when he came here?" He held up his stubby, stained fingers and began to count. "Ah, let me see—"

"He was already gravely injured when he came to us."

Minnum appeared unfazed. "All the same, he is not dead. I would know it."

"How?"

"How do you know it's daylight now?"

"That's a stupid question," Riane said.

"So is yours," Minnum retorted. He pointed up at the gargoyles. "So tell me, what is your impression?"

Riane looked again. "They're . . . creepy."

"That they are," Minnum acknowledged.

"Who are they supposed to be?"

"Nightmares? A reminder of the evil that lurks inside all of us?"

"I don't believe that."

"That's because you're too young to believe it. But the fact is we all have good and evil impulses inside us. It is simply a matter of which we decide to act on." Minnum spat into the rain. "I will tell you one thing, though, those statues are not made of any stone native to Kundala."

"It looks like some kind of granite."

"Except that it is twice as hard and three times as heavy. There are veins of undefined metal in it, as well as pockets of some kind of crystal fused from very high heat." He squinted. "Meteorites, I expect. Goddess knows what tools the crafters used."

"They're horrible, anyway."

"Funny, they were a particular favorite of Nith Sahor's." He chuckled. "They used to scare the Goddess out of whoever wandered in here in the old days before the V'ornn."

"That doesn't make sense," Riane said. "This is a museum, right?"

"The Museum of False Memory," Minnum said. "Over the years, though, I have come to believe that it is better that most folk don't see everything that is in here."

"What does that mean?" Riane asked, but just then she heard Eleana calling her name. She turned, saw Eleana sitting up, and when she turned back, Minnum had vanished.

"I'm here! I'm coming!"

As she hurried back to Eleana she could have sworn she heard Minnum's voice drifting through the rain, "You will come back sometime, won't you?"

"Where are we?" Eleana said. Her face was drawn and pale. "Are we dead?"

"No, Eleana. We are alive."

"This place looks so awful. I thought—Perhaps it was a dream . . ." She swallowed. "I was sure I had drowned."

"You nearly did. How do you feel?"

"Exhausted and cold—but safe." Eleana sighed. "You saved my baby's life." She cupped her lower belly. "I can feel him. Oh—!" She laughed, color flooding back into her cheeks. Taking Riane's hand in her own, she placed it on her stomach. "Feel him?"

Riane thought she might pass out with longing.

"He's swimming, kicking out as hard as he can. He must have known I was swimming, too. He is still trying to help." She laced her fingers with Riane's, kissed the back of her hand. "Thank you, Dar Sala-at."

Even the dismal stormlight brought Eleana's cheeks into prominence. The memory of Annon's first glimpse of her, as he and Kurgan spied on her from a dense copse of sysal trees as she bathed in the creek near Axis Tyr, remained undiminished in Riane's memory. The sight of her thick, dark hair cascading down her shapely back remained a physical presence, stirring Riane's depths. She looked quickly away, deeply ashamed of the stolen kiss she had placed on Eleana's tender lips.

"As long as my baby's safe, as long as my baby's safe." Eleana's whispered words were like a prayer.

Rain pelted the roof, sluiced over the eaves, blurring the view of the courtyard, drove serpentine rivulets across the packed earth. The wind had picked up, and now it whistled dissonantly across the courtyard in angry gusts.

All at once, the shock of their brush with death set in. Riane shivered so hard her teeth began to chatter. A strong gust of wind brought her a renewed drenching.

"Come here," Eleana said. "Don't you know enough to come in out of the rain?"

She opened the filthy sailcloth as she drew Riane close to her, then wrapped it around both of them. "You're freezing," she murmured. "Put your arms around me, you'll warm up faster." Their bodies were now pressed tightly together. Eleana rested her head against Riane's shoulder. "The oddest thing happened just as I was coming to. I thought I heard Annon's voice. It was as if he was standing right beside me. Isn't that strange? But maybe not. I mean, I know he's dead, but part of me . . ." She stopped for a minute as if groping for a way to proceed. "Maybe it's all down to faith. I had faith in Annon—he proved to me more than once what a good and kind heart he had, and we are taught, aren't we, that when you put your faith in someone, you commit a part of your own energy—your divine spark—to that someone. That's how it was with Annon. Dar Sala-at, do not think me foolish, but sometimes I am absolutely certain that he isn't dead at all, that he is stranded somewhere on a distant shore, all alone, and that one day he will return to me."

Riane was trembling. "I could not think you foolish, Eleana," she managed to get out in a somewhat strangled voice. She could scarcely breathe for the vise that clamped her chest.

"Oh, my love for him burns like fire!"

Riane's lips ached with desire. She could feel the words of her confession assembling in her throat, clamoring to get out. Instead, she untangled herself, backing away. With an enormous effort, she clamped down on her treacherous emotions and squeezed the intimacy out of her eyes.

"What is it?" Eleana asked. "Dar Sala-at, have I done something to offend you?"

"No, of course not. I—"

A sudden stirring at the top of the wall made Eleana start, for at first it appeared as if one of the more horrible gargoyles had come to life. Then, she and Riane saw the blurring of wings, the dart of brilliant color swooping toward them.

"Look!" Eleana cried. "A Teyj!"

Indeed, one of the four-winged multicolored birds bred and raised by Gyrgon was coming their way. It seemed unlikely that the Teyj would have taken much notice of them under the walkway, improbable that it would want anything to do with them. Nevertheless, it swooped beneath the eaves.

Now Riane could see that it carried something in its mouth. As it drew abreast of them, it let go of a small, tightly wrapped packet, made a little warbling song, and darted away over the courtyard wall.

The packet bounced once, then rolled to within a few centimeters of Riane's boots. For a moment, she looked at it blankly, then she picked it up. It weighed next to nothing. She turned it over. Its surface was a uniform matte black, and there was a curious silver cord, thin as a hair, holding it together.

"What do you think it is?" Eleana asked, instantly on the alert.

"I have no idea," Riane said. "What I want to know is what this Teyj—?"

"It is a Gyrgon thing," Eleana warned. "Remember that Nith Sahor had many enemies. Perhaps they have found us."

Riane shook her head. "If they knew where we were, doubtless we would be prisoners in the Temple of Mnemonics now." She plucked at the silver hair. "I'm going to open it."

"Dar Sala-at, I don't think that would be—"

Too late. Riane had pulled the hair. They heard nothing, but felt a slight percussion as the packet rapidly unrolled. But it did far more than unroll—it immediately began to expand exponentially.

"Goddess!" Eleana breathed.

What else was there to say? There, lying before them in all its mysterious splendor, was Nith Sahor's voluminous greatcoat.

8

Ashes

Courion had once shown Kurgan a seashell. It looked like nothing at all from the outside, merely a hard, curved surface, whorled and warty, of an indeterminate greyish hue. But when turned over, its inside was a perfect corkscrew, pink as a delicate spring sunrise, silken and opalescent, refracting the light into minuscule rainbows.

This is what greeted Kurgan now as he walked through the Portal of the Temple of Mnemonics. Just a few steps ago he had been in an angulate anteroom guarded by Khaggun in the distinctive black-and-chromium uniforms of the packs serving the Gyrgon stronghold. Rain had been falling outside; the long, narrow crystal windows were streaked with it. Now he was somewhere else, inside that very same seashell, for all he knew, but in any event wholly in the realm of the Gyrgon. For this was the meaning of the Summoning.

His okummmon, a semisentient bionic implant, alerted him the moment the Gyrgon required his presence. That was true of every regent on every planet. The difference here was that Kurgan's original okummmon had been replaced by one specially made by Nith Batoxxx.

As he proceeded down the corridor or whatever it was—this space without specific shape or obvious light source—he had cause to recall a conversation he had had with Annon Ashera, once his best friend, the boy he had betrayed to Star-Admiral Kinnnus Morcha, who had been returned to Axis Tyr with his head separated from his body to be presented to Kurgan's own father, who was then regent.

The two boys had been out hunting gimnopedes. Annon had said he hated wearing the okummmon because it tied him to another caste. Kurgan had argued that Annon should be proud he had been implanted with the symbol of the Great Caste, for the alternative—to toil in lesser-class anonymity—was unthinkable. But ever since he had discovered

that Nith Batoxxx was the Old V'ornn, the trusted mentor who had secretly trained him, ever since Nith Batoxxx had forced him to pledge
himself to the Gyrgon, ever since he had been implanted with this special okummmon he realized that Annon was right. Wearing the Gyrgon
neural net felt to him like slavery.

Every night he awoke into the utter darkness before dawn, the inside
of his left forearm afire with an itch he could not assuage. Many times
he would sit up, swing his legs over the edge of the bed, and, taking
up the triangular-bladed dagger given to him by the Old V'ornn, promise himself that he would cut the vile thing out of him. But he never
did, though the tip of the blade had dimpled his skin more than once.
It was prudence, not cowardice, that stayed his hand. He wished to
give Nith Batoxxx no cause to become suspicious of him, for in his
heart he wished not only to destroy this particular Gyrgon who had
betrayed his trust, but to find some way to put the entire Comradeship
under his thumb as they had kept all of V'ornndom under theirs.

And yet he knew he had to find some way to keep such thoughts
out of his conscious mind, for a Summoning was a serious matter. It
was a time of testing as well as of questions that would surely be difficult to answer. For the Gyrgon were masters of fear. Somehow—Kurgan would have given his left arm to know the secret—they were able
to dig down into the mind of the regent and extract that one thing he
feared the most. Then they would confront him with it, in order, perhaps, to see how he would react and, therefore, discover of what stout
material he was made, how easy it would be to manipulate him, how
far he might be pushed.

As he continued down the featureless space he smiled to himself.
Nith Batoxxx was in for a surprise, because as far as Kurgan knew there
was nothing he was really afraid of, not even the Gyrgon themselves.

He heard a sound, no, a soft soughing as of the wind through the
tops of sysal trees, but, no, it was subtly different, more rhythmic, like
water slapping against the side of a ship. And the moment he had the
thought, he found himself on the rolling deck of a ship. He looked
around. He was at sea; there was not a speck of land to be seen in any
direction. The sky was a deep cerulean blue, the sun beating down,
turning the wavetops to brilliant scimitars. Above him, he heard the
creaking of wooden masts and spars, the soft, wet slap of rigging, the
sharp crack of sails full out.

"Good afternoon."

He turned to see the Sarakkon captain Courion grinning at him, his shagreen-booted feet planted firmly on the deck. He had met Courion at the Kalllistotos. Ever since Courion had forced Kurgan into fighting in the Kalllistotos they had become wary friends.

"Where is the crew?" Kurgan asked.

"There is no crew. There is only the two of us," Courion said. "It is good to see you, friend. We had meant to ask you why you did not invite us to the Rescendance. Could it be that you are ashamed of befriending a Sarakkon?"

Kurgan spent a moment taking this in. Then he said, "All right, Nith Batoxxx, I will admit the simulation is impressive, but don't expect me to play your game. I simply won't—"

All at once, a ferocious gust of wind caught the sail, the ship heeled over, and Kurgan, taken completely off guard, lurched backward, lost his footing and toppled over the rail. He plunged down four meters into the ocean. It all happened so fast he had no time to react. And then cold seawater struck him like a hundred fists. Stinging salt water rushed into his nose and mouth, and he began to choke. He told himself that this was an elaborate illusion, that nothing was real, not even his sensation of drowning, but somehow his lung refused to be convinced. He *was* drowning, there was no mistaking it. Simulation it might be, but what if he could die here just as if it was reality?

He forced himself to kick, pushing himself toward the surface far above. As he looked up into the refracted and distorted disc of the sun, he saw a splash. Something was being lowered down toward him. A rope!

He kicked more vigorously and soon reached out to grasp the end of it. He gave it several hard tugs and was rewarded by its being hauled upward, and him with it.

"Like a fish in a net," Courion said as Kurgan broke the surface, gasping and coughing. "Just hold on."

The Sarakkon turned the winch, and Kurgan, soaked, bedraggled, and panting, rose up the side of the ship. When he came abreast of the toprail, Courion grabbed him around the waist and maneuvered him onto the deck. Kurgan sat with his arms on his drawn-up knees, snorting the last of the seawater out of his nose.

He wiped his face with the heels of his hands as Courion squatted down in front of him. "Real enough for you?"

"Tell me one thing." Kurgan looked into his light eyes. "Would I really have drowned?"

"Eventually." Courion shrugged. He fingered the lapis lazuli and jade runes in his full beard. "We all drown eventually, don't we?"

"Except, apparently, you Gyrgon."

Courion frowned. "Surely you mistake us, friend."

"Come off it," Kurgan said shortly. In the back of his mind, he knew this was all a stunningly conceived Gyrgon illusion, and yet it all seemed so real. Fighting this, he said, "You are supposed to show me the face of my own fear, Nith Batoxxx. I am unafraid of drowning, so I have proved you wrong. I have beaten you at your own game of illusions."

Courion wavered and vanished. In his place stood Nith Batoxxx. "While it is true that this construct is caused by the manipulation of hyperexcited ions, this isn't my world. It is *yours*. It is pulled from inside your own mind."

"What? Another Gyrgon falsehood? I do not believe you can read my thoughts."

"Not your thoughts, precisely. But the okummmon is a link of our own design. Through it you are Summoned at our pleasure. The particular communication link allows us this access. All regents are Summoned and, in the Summoning, are shown their deepest fear. Even those"—he smiled frostily—"who believe themselves free of fear."

"This is what you call my fear? I told you. I am not afraid of drowning."

"There is another thing here for you to fear," Nith Batoxxx said. "I find it interesting that you cannot yet identify it."

"I grow weary of this Gyrgon mind game."

"Your mind is a most curious realm, regent. Truly, I have never encountered its like before." Nith Batoxxx held out his gloved hand, and Kurgan's eyes watered. When they had cleared he was back in a simple windowless sparely furnished chamber in the Temple of Mnemonics.

"You are ambitious, yes, very much so. It is part of your special usefulness." He smiled, an unpleasant thing that unfurled like the banner of a reaver. "It is why I supported your petition to be made regent, why I disposed of all Gyrgon who opposed you."

"What do you mean?" Kurgan felt his hearts skip a beat. "You *killed* other Gyrgon?"

"I am powerful beyond your imagination." Once again, the Gyrgon's voice had taken on that eerie, disembodied timbre that made Kurgan shudder despite himself.

Kurgan said nothing; he could think of nothing to say. He wondered whether Nith Batoxxx was telling the truth or whether he was mad. It was becoming clearer to him that Nith Batoxxx was acting as if he had two different personalities.

Nith Batoxxx's teeth clacked together. "Understand this, *regent*: my continued support is crucial to you remaining in office. And that support very much depends upon your absolute understanding of who calls and who answers." The smile was a cold, calculating thing. "For a Stogggul that cannot be an easy thing, and I find myself wondering whether it is even possible. But I have staked more than you can know on you, Stogggul Kurgan, so it is something that you *will* learn. Believe me when I tell you that I will see to it." He lifted a finger. "Gyrgon are not in the habit of giving advice, but I find I have developed a disease. Its symptom is a curious affection for you. Therefore, heed well what next I tell you. Ambition is a tricky trait. If it gets the better of you." He reached out and snatched Kurgan's arm. Tapping the embedded okummmon, he said, "Here is what you must consider. If you exceed the authority granted you by the Comradeship, I will know. And I will be waiting to devour you."

Kurgan stared at Nith Batoxxx. The Gyrgon was bluffing. He could not know that Kurgan meant to control the Comradeship. He willed himself to keep calm, to be the Gyrgon's obedient servant while in his presence.

He ducked his head. "I will be diligent, Nith Batoxxx, in keeping my ambition in check."

Not many V'ornn could say they had heard a Gyrgon laugh. It was a sound that affected Kurgan in a peculiar way, making him feel as if grit were being rubbed into an open wound. He felt briefly sick to his stomachs.

"We are bonded, you and I, in ways you cannot possibly imagine," Nith Batoxxx was saying. "This world we have come to know, this Kundala, *will* come undone, but not in the way you think. Because it will be you and I who accomplish its undoing."

*   *   *

As it had once brought them into the city, Nith Sahor's voluminous greatcoat now whisked Riane and Eleana back to the Abbey of Warm Current. Riane knew that the greatcoat was a semiorganic web of neural nets, but how it actually functioned she could not say. Just as she did not know how it knew where to transport them. She had not spoken to it or in any way communicated with it. She had simply wrapped it around the two of them as Nith Sahor had instructed on that fateful night when she had made her desperate run to find the Ring of Five Dragons in the Storehouse Door in the caverns beneath the regent's palace. The instant the cloak closed completely over them, Riane felt the slight sensation of dislocation, a touch of free fall. And when she had unwound it, there they were in the infirmary of the abbey.

She held Eleana in her arms and, immediately upon their arrival, set her down upon one of the ancient cushioned shanstone cots. She was still weak and occasionally dizzy. Riane fetched her water to drink.

It was not until Eleana had drunk her fill that both of them realized that they were not alone. Across the infirmary, Rekkk Hacilar lay upon another cushioned slab of shanstone. Thigpen crouched over him, the upper set of her forepaws holding his head steady while a Teyj hovered over the horrific wound in his chest where he had been speared by the Tzelos' mandible. Its four wings were beating so fast they were a mere blur.

"Is Eleana—?" Thigpen began.

"With rest, she will be fine," Riane said wearily, and then, to forestall more questions, she added: "It's a long story."

"I am gratified to see you both back in one piece," Thigpen said shortly. "Dar Sala-at, I have something for you. It could no longer tolerate being inside such a damaged body. Please take it."

Riane extracted the mononculus from Thigpen's throat, transferred it to her own.

The beating of the Teyj's wings had set up a kind of harmonic in the infirmary. Like the clearest of notes sent forth when a tuning fork is struck, it kept doubling upon itself, strengthening until it had created what Riane could only describe as a wave. She could not see the wave, but she could hear it. And more than that, she could feel it, sense it from inside her, as if it was causing her very bones to vibrate at its perfect pitch. She experienced a sensation of extreme well-being, knew as she glanced at Eleana's face that Eleana was feeling the same thing.

All at once, she felt Eleana's fingers digging into her arm, and she saw something blacker than black appear directly beneath the beating of the Teyj's wings. It was a circle, then a lozenge, then an oval, then a trapezoid. A soft percussion, and it expanded just as the greatcoat had expanded at the Museum of False Memory, fitting itself like a second skin over Rekkk's bloody wound. And like a second skin it changed color, from deepest black to palest white before blushing to the coppery hue of Rekkk's hairless flesh.

"You might as well get comfortable," Thigpen told them, looking somewhat relieved. "I believe this may take some time."

Riane drew up a chair, insisted Eleana remain lying down. At first, Eleana did not want to. She had a warrior's heart, and seeing how badly Rekkk was wounded caused her considerable agitation. But in the end her utter exhaustion and her fear for the baby's welfare kept her on the shanstone cot.

The Teyj, abruptly ceasing its rapid wing beats, settled upon the "new skin" and with its beak began to peck away, quickly, precisely, drawing tiny bits of it up and redepositing it elsewhere. It was not long before Riane realized what it was doing. It was realigning the neural net it had spread over the wound to match Rekkk's energy pattern. Annon's father, Eleusis, had told him tales of Gyrgon healing. He had, of course, been fascinated. What boy wouldn't have been? On the other hand, they had seemed so fantastic, so miraculous that he had often wondered whether his father had been making them up. Now Riane was seeing one of these astonishing tales unfold with her own eyes, and she knew Eleusis had not been exaggerating.

Now the neural net began to pulse, just as if it was alive, a machine inflating and collapsing Rekkk's lung. The Teyj twittered, singing a heartrendingly beautiful song, and pockmarks began to appear in the skin of the neural net. They extended downward into the wound. And here was the most astonishing part, the Teyj itself appeared to be manipulating the probes or instruments or whatever they were.

On their short journey back to the abbey, the greatcoat had somehow managed to simultaneously warm them and dry their clothes. Riane still felt grimy and uncomfortable, but she knew she would not leave the infirmary until she was absolutely certain Rekkk was out of danger.

As she sat beside Eleana, Riane could not help but steal a glance. There now arose in her mind an air of awkwardness, a silence of un-spoken questions, an interrupted flux that felt distinctly uncomfortable. Her thoughts ran in agonized circles. How to act with Eleana? How could she hide her love and her desire which, like a living thing, was growing stronger every day.

"Do you think it's the same?"

"What?" Riane blinked as Eleana's voice broke through the veil of her anxiety.

"The Teyj." Eleana turned her head to look at Riane. "Do you think it's the same one that brought us Nith Sahor's greatcoat?"

"That it is," Thigpen said.

"But how?" Eleana asked.

"It's a Teyj, my dear." Thigpen was following the ministrations most carefully. The Teyj's song changed both in melody and in pitch. Thigpen leaned over Rekkk, using her middle paws to keep his head still, while placing her forepaws on his chest.

With a start, Riane realized that Thigpen was responding to the Teyj's song. Somehow they were in communication. She came around to stand by the Rappa's side.

"Careful," Thigpen warned.

Riane could feel a pressure—a kind of flux ebbing and flowing around Rekkk's body.

"Since when are Rappa experts on four-winged Gyrgon birds?" she asked.

"You see how it is with the Dar Sala-at, Eleana," Thigpen said. "She will not allow me to get away with anything."

"But she's right," Eleana said softly. "How do you know anything about Teyj?"

"The simple answer is I don't." There was a decidedly odd glint in Thigpen's eyes. "But over the last month I have come to know a great deal about this one."

"Wait a moment." Eleana rose on one elbow. "I remember seeing a streak of bright color—red, green, blue, gold—in the treetops during Nith Sahor's funeral." Abruptly dizzy, she lay back down. "Was it a Teyj, Thigpen? Was it *this* Teyj?"

Thigpen nodded distractedly.

"Then am I correct in thinking it is a very special Teyj?"

The Rappa lifted her head, her eyes alight. "Powerful enemies abound," she said softly, "making some knowledge for the time being too dangerous to pass on."

The strange bird twittered urgently.

"Yes, yes, but we must be quiet now and concentrate absolutely," Thigpen admonished. "We are at the critical juncture. Rekkk's life hangs in the balance."

Eleana's eyes were wide and staring. "Can it save him?"

"Rest now," the Rappa said quietly but firmly. "Let the Teyj—"

"No!" Eleana's voice was low but just as forceful. "I will not sleep until I know he is out of danger."

The Teyj looked up. It pierced her with its cool, enigmatic gaze. She could see the gold flecks in its black eyes. It twittered briefly.

"I'm here, Rekkk," Eleana whispered. "I won't leave you." Her eyes filled up with tears. "Promise you won't leave me, all right? Promise me, Rekkk. Promise me."

Riane recalled standing in the moonslight, watching Eleana and Rekkk practice with their shock-swords, and she was ashamed to admit a feeling of jealousy had crept over her. Annon, the male V'ornn, had longed to be the one Eleana looked at with such intensity, the one she looked up to, the one she learned from. Odd to see a Kundalan Resistance leader bonding so intimately with a Khagggun. Hurtful as well. Riane might as well admit that, too. She knew that if Annon had been alive everything would be different. It would be Annon who received Eleana's undivided attention, she had told Riane so herself.

Riane gritted her teeth. She hated herself. How could she be jealous of Rekkk Hacilar when he was lying there near death? Disgusted, she turned away. She felt undeserving of being the Dar Sala-at. Maybe it was all a mistake, maybe she was nothing more than a nomad, a displaced V'ornn imprisoned in a female Kundalan body, atoning for all the V'ornn's murderous sins. She felt tears welling in her eyes and despised herself all the more.

And then, in the midst of her own private agony, there commenced a clamoring in her head, the cacophony of voices so dense, so extreme the tumbled words fell upon her like hail. She rose and staggered to the door.

"Riane," Eleana called after her, "where are you going?"

Riane could not reply. She was being hammered by an onslaught so painful, so unexpected, that she cried out. In the deserted corridor, she fell to her knees, got up, staggered drunkenly along, swinging blindly through doorways, through rooms great and small, until she half tumbled down the steps into the courtyard.

The rain had abated, but the mossy stones were slick, puddles everywhere, and she fell into one and did not get up, but crawled to the cold, damp foundation stones of the building, where she crouched, wretched and shivering uncontrollably.

And then, through the awful pain in her mind, she heard a voice calling as if from a great distance, a voice struggling to reach her as if from twenty thousand fathoms beneath the Sea of Blood, a voice so familiar it stirred her blood and made her weep.

"Giyan!"

She was unaware that she spoke the name aloud, for she was instinctively conjuring Osoru, opening the Portal into Otherwhere, beginning her search for Giyan.

Otherwhere was filled to overflowing with shadowy presences. Riane had never seen it so, and she grew afraid. She recalled the subtle shift she had noted during her last visit to Ayame. So swiftly the susurrus had become a roar. What had caused it and what did it portend? The cacophony of voices was like a raging river against which she was obliged to force herself. Wriggling like a sea-asp, she knifed her way through the horde. It was easier than she had imagined, for they were, in fact, merely shadows, their voices leaking into Otherwhere, the massed sound manifesting shadows of these unknown spirits from some unknown realm.

By what sorcery had their voices been raised in Otherwhere? Riane asked herself as she searched for Giyan. And then, with a shock that sent a heavy shiver down her spine, she saw the distinct outlines of individuals moving within the shadow-mass and knew that these were not Kundalan spirits. They were misshapen, some with broad flat heads, others with hunched meaty shoulders, multiple limbs, and great sprouting ears. They were freakish—at once horribly grotesque and eerily familiar.

And then she uttered a little cry as she realized that these shadow-creatures matched the shapes of the gargoyles that crouched on the parapet of the Museum of False Memory. At first, she thought she must be dreaming, but then her training took firmer hold, and she knew that one did not dream of Otherwhere. So this was no nightmare. This was real.

But as quickly as the questions flooded her mind she put them aside, for she heard Giyan's voice, thin and quavery, calling her. She blotted out everything, casting the Net of Cognition, a spell designed to identify Caa, the energy auras thrown off by sorcerous Avatars. For no sorceress appeared in Otherwhere as herself. She was searching for the energy signature of Giyan's Avatar, the great and awesome bird, Ras Shamra. Strange to say, she did not yet know what her own Avatar looked like. Giyan had told her that would come in a ceremony inside Otherwhere when she had become a true sorceress. In the meantime, her presence took the form of a golden cube spinning widdershins on one of its corners.

Like a fisher, she drew the Net of Cognition tighter, felt herself traversing ever more swiftly the heaving mass of howling grotesques. All at once, the shadows parted, and she found herself racing across a flat, featureless plain.

In the far distance, she could see what appeared to be a mountainscape thrusting violently up toward the white, featureless sky. With dismay, she saw through a gap in the mountains the sky stained the color of blood. The presence of color was an indication of the use of powerful Kyofu spells in Otherwhere.

Her stomach contracted painfully, for she saw something horrible rising from the center of the plain—Ras Shamra, Giyan's sorcerous Avatar, her presence in Otherwhere, pinioned upside down onto an inverted equilateral triangle, black and scaly as the hide of a razor-raptor, whose point had been buried in the plain.

"Giyan!"

Riane's cry resounded, setting up a new geometry.

She hurried even more swiftly across the plain, lofted in the atmosphere where sound traveled queerly, like muffled drumbeats, and never, it seemed, in a straight line.

"Giyan!"

The Ras Shamra's head turned slowly and, it seemed, painfully. "Ah, Riane, at last. You have found me."

"I am here, Giyan. I will—"

"No!" The Ras Shamra twitched, its desperate shout bringing Riane to an abrupt halt. And now she could see that an odd kind of web, glowing and seething like strands of boiling lava, had grown over the Avatar's left leg and wingtip. "You cannot free me. Not yet, at least."

"Let me try. I know I can—"

"Listen to me, Riane! This is the archdaemon Horolaggia's doing, and you lack the necessary skills to counteract it."

Riane's stomach congealed. Giyan was possessed by an archdaemon!

"You must have patience," the Rad Shamra was saying. "You must gain the knowledge to defeat him."

"But how? Jonnqa is dead. I do not know where to turn."

"I cannot tell you."

Riane grew frantic. "But why not?"

"You see what happened the last time I tried that. Horolaggia found out—I know not how—and sent his minion to destroy you and Rekkk." The Ras Shamra shook its head. "You must find your way on your own."

"It sounds an impossible task."

"Have faith. You are who you are."

Riane knew what Giyan was trying to tell her: she was the Dar Sala-at.

"Now listen," the Ras Shamra hurried on. "Because of the Ring of Five Dragons the archdaemons know you exist, but they do not yet know who you are. Horolaggia will do everything he can to change that. Be extremely careful. If you act rashly, he will destroy you."

"But your life—"

"I am sworn to protect you, Dar Sala-at. That is my life, nothing more or less."

"I know that for a lie, Giyan. Your life is so much more. I swear I will not let you die!"

"Oh, please, swear no such vow, Riane, for it may prove your undoing—and thus the undoing of us all. You are the once and future hope of Kundala; nothing is more important than the resurrection of our race from the abyss into which it has basely fallen."

Riane shook her head, her heart and her mind adamant. "You have protected me in the past, Giyan. You have saved my life. Now I must save yours."

"Have a care, Dar Sala-at! Do not let Annon's fierce warrior spirit overwhelm you!"

"How can you expect me to stand here and do nothing?"

"No matter what you may think, you are not strong enough to stand against this prince of archdaemons." The Ras Shamra's head whipped around. "Miina protect us, no!" There was sheer terror in her voice.

"What is it?" Riane said breathlessly. "What is happening?"

The stain upon the sorcerous mountains was widening, as if they themselves were bleeding.

"Horolaggia comes! For the love of Miina, go, Dar Sala-at! Now!"

"Not until you tell me what is happening to you."

"The web binds me, transforming me slowly into Horolaggia or him into me, I do not know which, nor does it matter. What matters is there is still time before the winter solstice, before the web covers me completely."

Riane's breath was unnaturally hot in her throat. "What happens then?"

"Oh, do not ask me that."

"But I am. You must tell me. I will not leave until—"

"I will cease to exist as you know me," she said in a gasp. "Horolaggia will have my skills, my memories, everything that I am. Even my Gift." The Ras Shamra was weeping, though it tried valiantly not to. "It is part of the archdaemon's plan to escape the Abyss, to invade our Realm and enslave us forever."

"But this is monstrous. How can I stop them, Giyan?"

The Ras Shamra spoke more quickly now, the words tumbling out, running together. "But there is another part to their plan. They know that you are a threat to them, and they are doing everything in their power to delay your learning process while they plot and gather strength."

The sky was abruptly overrun by billowing crimson clouds, the sound of evil thunder was everywhere at once.

"Ah, great Miina—! The *Maasra*. Find it, Dar Sala-at. It will help you, and it will free me! Now go! Quickly, before—"

But it was too late. Out of the billowing bloody clouds Riane saw streaking an Avatar so shocking she felt paralyzed, for it was a dragon— a dragon out of some terrifying nightmare. It was as white as the ice atop the Djenn Marre, slender as a serpent with enormous, ragged wings and filthy yellowed talons as long as Riane's torso. Ash-white horns rose from its long, flat skull above evil red eyes, and a double line of the same color spikes projected along its spine and underbelly. As it dived toward her, Riane could see that its scales were rough, irregular and curled, possibly sickly and dying, for they flaked off in its wake, cracking open the plain of Otherwhere as they fell.

Riane was stunned. The only existing dragons she had ever heard of were the Five Dragons associated with Miina who, through The Pearl, had created Kundala out of sorcery and cosmic dust. Because these Dragons were sacred, it was impossible to choose one as a sorcerous Avatar.

There was no time to ponder this conundrum. The dragon's scream, when it saw her, turned her bones to water. Still, ignoring Giyan's warnings, she conjured the Star of Evermore, the most powerful spell she knew, an Eye Window spell, a potent mixture of Osoru and Kyofu, and projected it toward the beast.

The eerie ice-white dragon opened wide its jaws, emitting a gale of sulphurous ash and grit that rent the Star of Evermore into ten thousand dimming pinpoints. An instant later, it sucked all the energy out of Riane. It was sorcery on a level she had never experienced before.

Caught squarely in the vortex, her Avatar cube spun more and more slowly. It lost its golden glow. Gasping and disoriented, Riane hung helpless, watching the dragon rush toward her, talons extended. She tried to summon another spell, but could not.

Dimly, she heard Giyan's voice in her head, orienting her. Somehow it cleared a path behind her free of the debilitating sulphurous cloud. Riane no longer hesitated, but stumbled backward until she was clear of the horrific spell Horolaggia had cast.

The ice-white dragon roared, its red eyes filled with malicious intent. It swiveled its head on its long, sinuous neck. Up came one foreleg, and the huge talon arced, pointing at the Ras Shamra, which cried out in agony.

She lunged forward, but heard Giyan's dreadful shout in her head: "No! Go! Now!"

Terrified and heartbroken, Riane stifled her warrior impulse and forced herself to conjure the spell that opened and closed the Portal. There was a moment's familiar disconnect, then all at once, she was back on Kundala, in her wet and shivering body, crouched against the foundation stones of the abbey, sobbing inconsolably.

"What is this place?" Marethyn asked. "You have never brought me here before."

"I have never brought anyone here," Sornnn said.

They were in a wedge-shaped chamber lost amid a warren of corridors and enormous somnolent spiritless spaces in one of the many warehouses that hulked along the northern fringe of the Southern Quarter of Axis Tyr known as Harborside. The air was faintly yellow, thick and redolent with the commingled scents of a hundred spices. The incessant throb of the twilit city beat a tattoo against the small, square, smeary windowpanes, but here inside the warehouse all was still save for the homey creak of a floorboard.

The chamber itself was altogether nondescript, unpainted, unplastered, not a residence at all, it was clear, just a set of crude shelves climbing one inner wall, some low chairs, and, in its center, a carpet so magnificent that Marethyn was obliged to get down on her hands and knees to run her fingers through its thick pile, to lay her cheek lovingly against the hypnotic pattern of its glistering harmonious colors.

And one other thing, poking up from a slender crystal vase atop a tiny circular ash-grey table. A spray of fresh orangesweet, its colors positively violent against the washed-out background. By which she knew that her presence here was neither spontaneous nor insignificant.

He set down the long, dully gleaming alloy box he had been carrying on his shoulder and placed it in a corner on top of an identical one. Then he poured them tumblers of a jade-green liquid while Marethyn sat, cross-legged, delighted as a child. Downstairs, as they had passed through the main warehouse, she had idly run a forefinger through the dust on a container. He had taken her hand, rubbed off the dust with the pad of this thumb, and kissed each fingertip in a way that had sent shivers down her spine.

"Here it is only us," he said now, sitting down beside her. "In this place we are sorcerers and conjurers, we are artists and poets, warriors and thieves. It is possible to make of our lives whatever we wish."

They drank in silent and solemn approval of that sentiment.

"*Naeffita,*" he said, "from the Korrush. It means, 'to breathe.' "

It was rich and tasted of clove, cinnamon, and burnt orange.

"I love it," she said, her voice smoky with the aftertaste.

He watched her looking around the chamber. "The tribes weave—"

"Magnificent."

"Yes, magnificent magical carpets." He refilled their tumblers, and they drank again, more slowly this time.

Surrounded by the deep silence, they gazed into each other's eyes. She put aside her tumbler, slipped off her cloak. He rose and went to the shelves on which were placed souvenirs, things fashioned from glass, painted ceramic, striped stone, beaten bronze, perhaps, old and darkly reflective that he had bought, bartered for, or had been given by tribesmen, heads of tribes, all prized in their own way, and all most beautiful. Arrayed carefully, lovingly, almost religiously to remind him of the Korrush, to keep its intense flame burning inside him when he was here in dull seething political Axis Tyr. He told Marethyn about each one in turn, in a soft, introspective voice he reserved for their time alone together. Marethyn marveled at this voice, a singer's voice, really, rich, well modulated, a voice that was careful to pronounce every syllable completely, possessing the ability to catch you unawares and take you out of yourself. And then, thrillingly, he did sing, softly, almost shyly, a touching thing in itself, a folksong from the steppes, and though she did not understand a word, the gorgeous melancholy melody nevertheless held her rapt.

Then he had returned to the center of the chamber and was holding out his hand. Marethyn took it, and he pulled her to her feet.

She sipped the naeffita slowly, her eyes on him as he unfastened her robes and slowly unwound the fabric. As if she were a disembodied observer, she saw her own body revealed in stages, diagonal arcs that produced long swaths of luminous flesh, and she saw herself reflected in his eyes, the involuntary reaction of his own body, and a tingling heat stole through her, sunlight on bare flesh.

She smelled the curious spices of the Korrush, and through her artist's eye and her love for him imagined herself there, inside the unknown, far away from beetling oppressive strangulating Axis Tyr. She felt as real the fantasy of him gathering her up in his strong sunbrowned arms and whisking her off to the Korrush, never to return to the responsibilities she bore—for her work, her art, her poor brother, her convictions, which might one day bring her glory or bring her death. Conjuring up another life without connections, cares, or worries, with only him to fill her eyes and hearts. An evanescent moment, for though she could enjoy the grand and ecstatic sweep of fantasy, she was nevertheless firmly grounded in her reality.

Naked, she raised her arms.

"Yes. Just that way," he whispered.

He reached for her, and she came into his embrace. Her empty tumbler fell to the carpet, rolling back and forth. Sornnn's untouched tumbler sat on a shelf with the decanter of naeffita.

Instead, he was touching her, he was feeling her fingertips plucking off his clothes with mysterious ease, he was sinking into her moist, luscious lips on him, all over him, her throat humming, until he could no longer bear the waiting. They lay for a moment upon the lush, dazzling carpet, but he was far too excited to lie down for long. So, he saw with quickening pulses, was she.

Dusty light seeped through the windows. It was the deep deceptive enclosing light of dusk when, as a child, she had become briefly free of her hingatta obligations to pursue her passion for painting. It quickly became her private world, firing her rich imagination. And so she worked in twilight, and her early paintings were born out of this numinous matrix of animistic shadows. High in the wedge-shaped warehouse chamber, the soft dying autumnal glow, a small flame, red-yellow-red, passed like a conjurer's hand across the old bare wall, painting upon it their shadows in movement.

He backed her up until she was pressed between him and the cool, irregular stone. He took her like that with his eyes wide open, stared into hers, watching her pupils dilate and contract with every thrust and release. He heard her moaning, heard his own panting. His blood surged like the Korrush wind over the rolling sea of grasses, boiled like water over a crackling fire.

When she cried out, clutching him frantically to her, her thighs squeezing and relaxing, he reversed their positions. Now his back was pressed against the rough wall. He was still deep inside her. Her eyes were closed, her forehead pressed against the muscled ridge of his shoulder. She licked the sweat off him. Then her head came up, her eyes once again locked with his, and now it was she who began to thrust, to hurl him back against the stone as he had done to her. And he filled up with fluids, his tender parts heavy and swollen beyond anything he had ever known before. He felt her power, felt her power strong upon him, and he was startled and a little bit afraid. Afraid for her and of what he was getting her into.

Then all his thoughts dissolved in a heady rush of pleasure. He surrendered to it and to her because he had no other choice, because this had become his universe, and he wanted it, just like he wanted everything else.

Everything . . .

He brought his tumbler back to the center of the carpet, where he and Marethyn took turns drinking from it. For a time, they listened to the floorboards creak, small, expressive sounds that defined their isolation from the city, from the normal screech-and-hum of their lives.

"I want to go with you," she said when the tumbler had been drained. "To the Korrush." She was reclining in the crook of his shoulder. "I want to experience that beauty you see, that resides in you like this." She turned his hand over, scored a thin line of red dust from beneath the scimitar of his nail. She took the dust onto the tip of her tongue. "There. Now the Korrush is inside me, too."

"It is dangerous there, Marethyn."

"I do not care." She had the distinct sense that he was speaking of something else. A secret long hidden that had burst open inside him. "You know that."

In fact, he did, and his hearts quickened at the thought. Still, his guilt impelled him to add: "I would not willingly place you in any danger."

He said this so gravely that she was forced to laugh. "Nor I you. But it seems to me that there is a danger inherent in our seeing one another. And, in any case, there is a certain danger you live with every day, that you need, that you hold dear and sacred. That you cannot live without. That is your calling." She did not say this critically or with blame, only with the knowing intimacy that is an alchemical product of love.

"I chose this danger. But you—"

"Shall I put it in the bluntest terms, Sornnn? I welcome whatever it is you have in mind for me."

"Without knowing."

She ran a finger around the inside of the tumbler, put the wet spiced tip between his lips. "Like you, I am certain of my calling."

So she said. But Sornnn wondered whether he could believe her. What it boiled down to was a matter of trust. Could he trust her? With everything he was. He wanted to, he knew that much, but was that enough? There was so much danger, so much at risk. And hadn't his father died because of . . . ? But he had to start somewhere. He had to know and, in knowing, continue or end it. But slowly, ever so slowly, for trust was a delicate and often bloody thing, his father had taught him. *Trust can be a means to a bitter end, isn't that right, Father?*

He rose, went to the shelf, and plucked an item. As he returned to her, she admired anew his sleek, hard-muscled body. He opened his palm and displayed to her an old, worn, dun-colored stone carving of a bird. "This is a fulkaan," he said. "It is the mythical bird that sat upon the shoulder of Jiharre, the Prophet of the Gazi Qhan, one of the five tribes that dominate the Korrush. The fulkaan was Jiharre's companion, his protector and his messenger."

"It's strangely powerful," she said, running the tip of her forefinger over its rough surface.

"It is very old. It was given to my father by Makktuub, the kapudaan—the head—of the Gazi Qhan. My father believed that this bird, this fulkaan actually exists. He caught the notion from Makktuub, who swore it was true." Sornnn sat back on his haunches. "It seems to me that my father's life was one great search for hidden myths. He had that in common with Eleusis Ashera. That is how they became friends." He hesitated, staring down at the fulkaan as if willing it into life. "Eleusis Ashera had a deep and abiding interest in the Korrush."

"Za Hara-at," Marethyn said in a hushed voice. Her hearts were beating fast in her breast.

He nodded. "Earth Five Meetings, as it's known in the Kundalan Old Tongue."

"The building of Za Hara-at was Eleusis Ashera's dream, a city where V'ornn and Kundalan could live side by side."

"Za Hara-at is far more. It was my father who first took Eleusis Ashera into the Korrush and showed him the archaeological dig where the ruins of an ancient city had been discovered. My father was convinced that it was the legendary city of Za Hara-at, that it is a sacred place. And he convinced Eleusis Ashera of it."

"And you?" The edge of the ancient fulkaan's wing dug into her palm. "What is it you believe?"

"This carving is from the dig." He stroked the fulkaan's head just as if it were alive. Then he looked at her. "Like my father, I believe the ruins are the original Za Hara-at. I believe we have discovered a sacred place, a place of lasting power and influence."

"I believe you." Marethyn looked at him with shining eyes, and she smiled a secret smile that was for him alone, and as she smiled, she whispered, "Sorcerers and conjurers, artists and poets, warriors and thieves. I wonder which of these you and I will turn out to be."

Four furry, small yet powerful legs wrapped her in Nith Sahor's great-coat, and at once Riane felt warmed inside and out.

"Dar Sala-at, what has happened?" Thigpen asked. "One minute you're in the infirmary, the next minute you're gone."

Riane closed her eyes for a moment, but the afterimage of what she had just witnessed made her shiver again, and her eyes flew open. "I heard Giyan calling me from Otherwhere." Her voice was a reedy whisper; she began to speak faster and faster. "I saw her; she is partially covered in a sorcerous web. She—"

"Calm yourself, Dar Sala-at." Thigpen licked her face free of tears. "Leave this communication for when you can recall it all without so much fear."

"But Giyan—"

"Listen to what I am saying, little dumpling."

Riane sighed. It had been a long time since Thigpen had called her that; it brought back a time before she had been revealed as the Dar Sala-at.

Riane nodded at last. "How is Rekkk?"

"There seems to be a problem. The Teyj needs you."

The wound made by the Tzelos apparently left a toxic residue," Thigpen said, as they returned to the infirmary. "The Teyj has had no luck in counteracting it."

"What does it think—?"

"I told it you might be able to help." Thigpen jumped onto the shanstone slab upon which Rekkk was lying. "Please approach, Dar Sala-at."

Riane could see Eleana sitting up, watching her for some sign as to why she had fled the infirmary so suddenly. She turned her mind away, focusing fully on Rekkk.

"Forget Osoru," Thigpen was saying, "and concentrate on what you know of Kyofu."

"I don't know much," Riane admitted. "Even though I've read *The*

Book of Recantation, I have precious little experience with Black Dreaming sorcery spells."

"Right now anything will be of help."

Thigpen was adept at keeping her emotions hidden, but Riane thought she detected the smallest amount of desperation creep into the Rappa's voice. Were things so dire? Riane wondered. Was Rekkk at the brink of death?

She closed her eyes, using her eidetic memory to go through the Sacred Book of Kyofu page by page. The trouble was she had no idea how to translate the passages into spells. In the case of sorcery, academic knowledge was all but useless without training in practical application. Still, she plowed through her prodigious memory, and where she thought she detected spells, she tried to conjure them up. Once or twice, she was more or less successful, but nothing she conjured was of use.

"Dar Sala-at," Thigpen whispered, "Rekkk is running out of time."

"I'm doing the best I can," she said.

"You must do better."

And with just those few words the Rappa managed to convey her dismay and fury at Riane taking Rekkk into the jaws of a trap Thigpen had clearly warned them about. Riane's thoughts became scattered and cloudy, just as they had when Malistra had tangled her in Fly's Eye. *Rekkk is dying because of me*, Riane thought. *Miina help me.*

"Thigpen, I don't know what to do."

All at once, Eleana rose and came to stand behind her. She put her hands on Riane's shoulders, spreading warmth through them. "I have faith in you. My heart tells me the Dar Sala-at will find a way to save him."

And just like that, Riane's thoughts cleared. *Perhaps*, she thought, *I'm approaching the healing from the wrong direction.*

"Thigpen," she said, "ask the Teyj to collapse the ion field around Rekkk."

The Teyj began to twitter nervously.

"The Teyj says that if it does that, Rekkk will surely die."

"I need access to what is killing him," Riane said tensely. It all seemed so clear now. "I cannot do that with V'ornn technology in place."

"It will not allow you to—"

"How long will he last?" Riane said. Her mind was afire now.

"Five minutes, perhaps ten. No more. The venom is exceptionally virulent."

Was it enough time? Riane had no idea.

"Tell the Teyj I cannot help him with the field in place."

"It knows that." A terrible sadness informed Thigpen's voice. "It has collapsed the field."

Riane could sense that it was so, and she began work immediately.

"The Teyj will monitor Rekkk's life signs," Thigpen said. "If he starts to fail, it will reinstate the ion field."

Riane barely heard her. She was casting Penetrating Inside, a simple but effective spell to begin gaining knowledge of the chemical makeup of the venom the Tzelos had left behind. Because the daemon had a propensity for transmogrification, the venom was a dark, complex skein, difficult to parse into its individual components. She had to work out what the constituents had been before they had been deformed by the daemon's system.

"Three minutes gone, Dar Sala-at," Thigpen informed her.

Riane redoubled her concentration. Sweat formed on her brow, her upper lip, rolled tingling down her spine. There was no room for error, no room to fail. *Forget about all that*, she told herself. *Concentrate on defining the toxin.*

"Nearly five minutes." Thigpen's voice seemed to be coming from a great distance.

Halfway through decoding the toxin and already she was running out of time. She began to recite the Venca alphabet. Her knowledge of this sorcerous language was a memory of the original Riane. Where or how she had learned was still a mystery she would very much like to solve, because nowadays Venca was used only by the Druuge, the enigmatic nomads said to be the first Ramahan. They had left before the evil had invaded the abbeys, migrating to the Great Voorg, the vast trackless desert to the east of the Korrush, where they now lived in almost total isolation. On her way to find the Ring of Five Dragons Riane had come across the Druuge and had, firsthand, seen them chant it. She had used it once before, in desperation, to conjure the Star of Evermore. Now she knew she needed to use it again. The problem was that the process was a complete enigma to her.

"Dar Sala-at." Thigpen's voice broke ominously into her thoughts. "Rekkk's life signs are fluctuating radically."

She continued reciting the alphabet. The sorcery of Venca lay not in the individual letters, but in how those letters were used. It was all in the combining, the sorcery of language. Three-quarters finished decoding the venom.

"The Teyj is becoming agitated. A moment more, and it will reactivate the field."

Riane could not spare the time to answer. The decoding was not yet complete, but she had run out of time. She chanted the Venca alphabet into the warp and weft of the toxin's known constituents.

"Rekkk is failing, Dar Sala-at."

Just a moment more. She could see it forming and, as happened before when she conjured the Star of Forever, Riane felt the intuitive tug in her mind, and she used this intuition to choose the Venca letters she chanted. Words formed in the air like clouds chased by a following wind, like vapor steaming on a dewy morning, like smoke from a brush fire. Either she or the spell that was forming reconstituted the entire structure of the toxin, inserting itself between it and Rekkk, creating first a protective sheath and then a morphed antitoxin that spread through the wound like surf.

"He's stabilizing," Thigpen said, excitement tingeing her voice.

Dimly, Riane could hear the Teyj singing a beautiful song, a new melody.

"The wound is healing."

Riane finished the chanted spell, feeling the weariness seeping through her. She staggered, and Eleana caught her, hugged her tightly.

"You did it! I knew you would!" Eleana said excitedly.

Thigpen jumped down, letting the twittering Teyj tend to Rekkk. Silently, she padded over to Riane, jumped into her lap, curling up there.

"Dar Sala-at," she whispered. "What spell did you use?"

Riane did not know, but then, unbidden came into her mind the name. "Well of Unknowing," she said. "It is ancient."

"It is an Eye Window spell, is it not?" Thigpen said cannily.

Perhaps it was, Riane thought. Eye Window was the sorcery of the original Ramahan. A potent fusion of Osoru and Kyofu, it had been banned many, many centuries ago as being far too dangerous, too ripe for misuse. Even Mother had not been an Eye Window adept.

Thigpen twisted her head, staring up at Riane. "You may pet me if you like."

Riane regarded the Rappa. Her large triangular ears were flat to her furry, ruddy-and-black head, and her whiskers twitched spasmodically. Could it be that she was nervous?

"I didn't think you would want me to," Riane said softly.

Now the worry had invaded Thigpen's eyes. "I like it when you stroke my fur."

"I should not have disobeyed you, Thigpen."

The whiskers twitched more convulsively. "It isn't so much the disobeying that matters. It's the *disbelieving*." Her striped bottlebrush tail curled upward to touch Riane on the back of her hand. "It is natural for Rekkk to disbelieve in matters Kundalan, but you allowed his skepticism to infect you."

"That was a mistake. I'm sorry."

Thigpen's dark, liquid eyes searched Riane's face. "Dear Dar Sala-at, there is no need for you to be sorry. I merely want to be certain you have learned from your mistake."

"But when you spoke to me, you were so angry—"

Riane, guided by the bottlebrush tail, allowed her hand to be brought to the thickly furred back. Thigpen's voice was gentle. "I feared for your life. Dar Sala-at, you still have no conception of who you are or what you will become, nor should you yet. But I do."

Riane stroked the soft thick fur, and Thigpen started to purr.

The Teyj twittered, and Thigpen sat up. "Yes, that's right." She jumped down and said to both Riane and Eleana, "Rekkk needs time to heal, as do you both. Let us repair to the kitchen, where I will prepare you a meal you will not soon forget." She led the way down the stone corridor. "You must be famished after your activities, and you must tell me everything."

Sometime later, they were sitting at the small utility table in the scullery, sated and calmer. Riane and Eleana had recounted the events of the day after Thigpen had Thripped back to the abbey with Rekkk.

"That was a close call all around," Thigpen said. "A bold strategy, Dar Sala-at, but a dangerous one. Luring the Tzelos—"

"But Riane discovered that the power bourns that run beneath the surface can destroy a daemon," Eleana said, trying to catch Riane's eyes with her own, trying, doubtless, to make sense of Riane's sudden coolness.

"How valuable this will prove to be is anyone's guess. Bourn energy cannot be easily harnessed. You were fortunate the water provided the proper medium." Thigpen's expression told that she knew what Eleana was up to. "Nevertheless, an interesting piece of intelligence."

"Intelligence," Eleana said. "You sound as if we are in a war."

"Indeed we are," Thigpen said gravely. "A Portal to the thrice-damned Abyss has been opened. There are daemons in this realm now. The Tzelos is far from the most deadly."

"I know." Riane nodded. "I saw Giyan in Otherwhere. She is being held captive by the archdaemon Horolaggia."

"I beg your pardon?" Thigpen blinked repeatedly.

Riane told them why she had left the infirmary so abruptly, how Otherwhere had been invaded by an army of eerie shadows with raised voices. She was shaking as she told them how she had come upon Giyan's Avatar nailed to the inverted triangle, and of Giyan's warning about the archdaemon.

"So," she finished, "what can you tell me about Horolaggia?"

"Oh, this is bad. Far worse than I had imagined. Far, *far* worse." Thigpen had hopped down off the table and, in her intense agitation, was turning in a circle, biting the end of her tail.

"For Miina's sake, Thigpen," Riane said, exasperated. "Will you answer my question?"

"What? Oh yes. Yes, of course." Thigpen stopped her pacing, but her whiskers twitched incessantly. "Pyphoros, it is written, had three children. The two males, Horolaggia and Myggorra, are bastards. The female, Sepseriis, is a half sister." By this time, her expression was way past bleak. "If the archdaemon Horolaggia has taken possession of Giyan, well, then . . ." Her voice drifted off with her expression, and she began again to pace in a circle, chewing on her tail.

"Then what?" Riane and Eleana said almost at the same time.

Thigpen wiped her cheeks with her tail. "Then, my dear, we must consider her already dead. Worse than dead."

"No!" Riane shouted. "I will do nothing of the kind."

"But you must. She will become our most implacable enemy."

"She told me I must find the *Maasra*. What is that?"

Thigpen blinked again. "Why, I have no idea."

"Great," Riane fumed. "Just great."

"There must be someone who knows," Eleana said, looking directly at Riane and again attempting to engage her attention.

"Two or three centuries ago we would doubtless have had our pick of tutors," Thigpen said. "But in these dark days . . ." Again her voice trailed off.

"All right, let's backtrack," Riane said, her mind working furiously. She knew there had to be a solution, it was simply a matter of finding it. Then, in her mind's eye, appeared the piteous vision of Giyan nailed to that inverted triangle, and the terror that strangled her at Horolaggia's coming. *There may be no solution at all*. Riane thought in horror. *In which case, we are all lost*. She shook her head violently to rid it of these despairing thoughts. Despair, she had learned, was a self-defeating spiral into inaction and surrender, two things that were anathema to her. *Think, Riane, think!*

"The one clue we have is the word I found in *The Origins of Darkness*. This word, *Maasra*, is associated with the Malasocca. It may be the way to effect a reversal. The problem is we have no idea of the word's meaning. It is neither Old Tongue nor Venca." Riane snapped her fingers. "Thigpen, didn't you say that what we needed was a first-class dialectician?"

The Rappa nodded. "I also said I knew one, the only trouble was he was dead."

"Then let's resurrect him."

Thigpen fairly jumped. "I beg your pardon?"

"I read about such a thing in *Unbinding the Forms*. The rite is called Ephemeral Reconstitution."

"Oh yes, that." Thigpen waved a forepaw. "You can forget that particular avenue. Only sefiror were taught that rite, and there are no more male sorcerers left on Kundala."

"There you're wrong," Riane said, a spark of hope igniting in her breast. "I believe I met one this afternoon."

R eady," Nith Isstal said.
"Nervous?" Nith Batoxxx asked.

"Not at all. I know it is a controlled experiment. I trust you."

That was the problem with youth, Nith Batoxxx thought as he began his last-minute preparations. They had altogether too much trust that the Cosmos was essentially benign.

He stood at the far west end of his laboratory. Before him was the wave chamber, a device he had been constructing for five V'ornn years. It disgusted him that most V'ornn—even his fellow Gyrgon—had begun to think in terms of the Kundalan calendar, where thirty hours made up a day and seven hundred seventy-seven days made up a year, rather than the eighteen hundred ninety that made up a V'ornn year. A certain corruption had set in, a jungle rot he sometimes saw on particularly virulent off-world colonies where V'ornn had overstayed their welcome.

The wave chamber looked like nothing more than a giant-sized egg. It was pale with a cloud sheen of ephemeral colors, utterly seamless save for the round hatch that screwed in and out. It was very thick, however, more than three meters, and the composite material out of which Nith Batoxxx had constructed it was incredibly dense. Inside was a faint purple-blue glow from three ion tubes, just enough to allow Nith Isstal to see his way into the seat, set at a gentle recline, and strap himself in. This he was doing now.

Nith Batoxxx nodded to him and began the complicated procedure that screwed the hatch into place. There were one hundred thirty-seven separate procedures to ensure the hatch was properly sealed, because if it wasn't properly sealed . . .

What he was dealing with scared the equations out of him, and very properly so.

The goron wave.

A goron was the largest atomic particle, the rogue particle, the untamable particle, the death particle. It was astonishingly difficult to understand and, therefore, to control. So far, the particles had resisted every effort the Comradeship had made in trying to cluster them into a wave that could deflect a goron particle beam.

The Centophennni had used a goron-particle weapon to decimate the V'ornn at Hellespennn. A moment burned into Nith Batoxxx's memory, the implacable empire catching up with them, punishing them for what had happened three centuries before. The defeat had been devastating enough, but coupled with that was the withering realization that the Centophennni possessed a technology beyond even the Gyrgon's capability. The humiliation of it gnawed at Nith Batoxxx like a razor-raptor. That had been two hundred fifty V'ornn years ago. Two hundred fifty years spent fearful and fleeing; two hundred fifty years spent fruitlessly trying to perfect a defense. And for the last forty-odd years, they had been holed up on this grimy backwater world while the rest of the V'ornn fleet passed on, to continue exploring or fleeing, depending on which version of reality you subscribed to.

He and Nith Sahor had volunteered to head up the mission to explore Kundala because long-range sensors showed a remarkable goron flux at its core. In fact, the reason the V'ornn technology could not penetrate the ferocious perpetual storms over the Unknown Territories was because of a dense goron layer. This was why V'ornn telemetry had failed to pierce the opaque barrier to map the three hundred thousand square kilometers on the northern side of the Djenn Marre mountains. None of the off-world Khagggun teams that had been sent into the Unknown Territories had ever returned. Their sophisticated photonic-wave communications systems had failed the moment they had vanished into the ice and snowstorms, and that, as far as any V'ornn knew, was the end of them. Despite countless experiments, the Gyrgon still lacked the ability to manipulate gorons. It was widely believed among the Comradeship that only gorons could defend against a goron-beam attack.

Though he had vehemently argued against Nith Sahor's involvement, he had been overruled. The results had been predictable. While he had spearheaded the work on the first several generations of goron wave chambers, Nith Sahor had betrayed him and the entire Comradeship by distancing himself from the goron-wave experiments. Instead, he became obsessed with chasing Kundalan myth, with befriending the slaves. The other Gyrgon had proved too slow to grasp Nith Batoxxx's radical principles, and he had left them to bicker and orate themselves into a standstill while he threw himself into conceiving the new generation of wave chambers.

Now, on the verge of his greatest triumph, he felt conflicted, knowing that the blackness inside him had guided him to this point. Where would he be without it? It was impossible to say; he had been living with it for so long he no longer remembered what the old Nith Batoxxx was like.

He reached out, touched the curved, gleaming side. This was the fifth one. Its predecessors had failed. The chamber was so thick for good reason. It was divided into two layers. The outer layer generated random instances of goron exhibitions, the inner layer deployed the latest version of the device Nith Batoxxx had engineered, which would hopefully generate the goron wave.

Of course, Nith Isstal had no idea what he was volunteering for. That was because Nith Batoxxx hadn't told him the truth. Why bother? Nith Isstal only wanted to please him.

Nith Batoxxx double-checked all one hundred thirty-seven safety procedures. Then, and only then, did he begin the exhibition protocol. He was concentrated wholly on his task. When he did this, he accessed the world through his cranial neural nets. The world around him became particulate. He was aware of ions, photons, gravitons—particles, waves, fields, all overlapping, all impacting one another. His fingers, enclosed in his gloves, were plugged into the semiorganic chip-matrix from which all Gyrgon clothing was constructed. In this phase, he was part machine or, perhaps you could say that the machine was part sentient. It all depended on which layer of reality you subscribed to.

The goron wave was activated. All the readings looked as he had calculated when he had composed the equations. His hearts leapt in elation. Perhaps it would happen this time.

The goron bursts began, a random attack he could not control. This part was the worst, seeing a form of energy with immense power manifest itself without having the key to controlling it. Even after he damped the goron excitation, the bursts continued at a low level for several moments.

He waited.

When he was certain the chamber was clear, he began the protocol that would spiral open the hatch. Inside, the ion tubes had fused. Nith Isstal lay back in his chair. The air sizzled and sparked with residual radiation. There was a curious smell, as of the sweet-salt scent of Kundalan blood.

Nith Batoxxx played a fusion light over the body. Nith Isstal's eyes were open. The lids had been burned off, his eyeballs were completely white. No pupil, no iris. His mouth was half-open. His teeth had disintegrated into a nasty yellowish powder that filled his throat. Half of his flesh had become transparent, so that Nith Batoxxx could see his bones, which appeared to be in the process of disintegrating in the same manner as his teeth.

Nith Batoxxx uttered a guttural curse. According to his instrumentation, Nith Isstal was far too toxic to handle, and it was clear that within minutes he would be nothing more than a pile of waterless waste.

It was like watching the aftermath of Hellespennn all over again.

9

That Which Remains

So you have returned," Minnum said. "And brought the Rappa with you." The curator crouched to Thigpen's level. "It is marvelous to see one of your kind again. Deeply and truly marvelous."

Thigpen sniffed the air suspiciously, and Riane could not help but laugh. They were standing under the eaves in the museum courtyard. Torches flared all around, illuminating the cistern and its dark, fulminating water. No ion-fusion lamps were anywhere in evidence, no V'ornn technology whatsoever.

"Minnum, meet Thigpen," Riane said.

The curator smiled. "Welcome to the Museum of False Memory."

Thigpen cocked her head. "What did you do to give Riane the notion that you were sefiror?"

"Why, nothing," Minnum said as he stood up. "Nothing I can think of."

"I suppose you are aware that it is a major transgression to impersonate a sefiror," Thigpen said shortly.

"Let me assure you I leave the impersonations to Gyrgon." Minnum grinned at Thigpen and spread his hands wide. "Anyway, who is left to prosecute me?"

"There are konara," Thigpen said, speaking of the high priestesses of Ramahan.

"Oh, I daresay. Power-hungry fiends like Bartta."

"Bartta is dead," Riane broke in.

"Is she now?" Minnum raised a bushy eyebrow. "I would be careful, if I were you, about jumping to conclusions concerning Bartta."

"First you tell me Nith Sahor is alive," Riane said hotly, "now you tell me that Bartta is, too."

"That's enough, the two of you!"

Startled to silence, Riane and Minnum both looked at Thigpen. She was up on her hind legs, her teeth bared. Riane had seen her react this way only once before, when she was about to attack a huge perwillon, a sorcerous cave predator.

"I will hear no more about the Gyrgon; that's a warning you had best take to heart," Thigpen growled.

"Sensitive little thing," Minnum said. Then he shrugged. "No matter. This is a museum. We aim to please around here."

"Hold on," Riane said. "You told me it was best if most didn't see your exhibits."

"Oh, well, that." Minnum waved a hand. "Perhaps I should have said we aim to please *you* here, Dar Sala-at."

Thigpen came down on all sixes. "She didn't—?"

Minnum squinted. "No, she didn't tell me."

"Then how did you—?"

"Same as you, I expect." The curator hitched up his sleeves. "I think it best if we go inside now." He glanced at the sky filled with V'ornn light. "It is getting a mite cold for me." He began to walk off with his heavy limp. "You can catch your death with a chill like this, and that's the truth of it."

He led them around a dustbin piled high with debris, and Riane could see that there were several doors cleverly hidden, accessed by pressure-sensitive panels, one of which Minnum touched.

The interior of the museum was warm and cozy. Fires flared in mammoth basalt fireplaces. Seeing the black rock gave Riane a momentary start; it brought back the image of the inverted triangle, Giyan's prison in Ayame.

"This is the Great Hall," Minnum said, walking them to the center of the domed pentagonal space. "All exhibits can be accessed from this central location."

Shadow-grids lay across the sea-green jasper floor. Odd, eerie-looking furniture—seemingly composed of carved runes—crouched against the shanstone walls. Cream-and-black onyx columns spiraled up into the dimness of heavy beams, encrusted with soot. Copper censers emitted tiny drifts of a musky incense, which mingled with the scent of aromatic oil burning in the squat, filigreed, bronze lamps. There was a sense of deep silence, of isolation from the frenetic noise and hustle of the city.

Minnum turned abruptly and stared hard at Riane. "I said you would come back, didn't I?" He nodded. "I expect you did because you saw them."

"What is he babbling about?" Thigpen snapped. She was clearly still upset.

"Tell her, Dar Sala-at," Minnum said. It seemed a kind of dare.

"The carved gargoyles on the parapet are daemons," Riane said to Thigpen. "I saw their shadow-outlines in Otherwhere."

"At least one of them has figured out how to get out of his prison," Minnum said. "No longer any doubt about it."

"What do you know about it?" Thigpen snapped.

With that, Minnum made a complex figure in the air with the tips of his thumb and forefinger touching. There came the sound of a marc-beetle being put to a flame, and where Thigpen had crouched was now a very horrible-looking lizardlike creature. It had eight short but powerful legs, oily blue-black scales, a long, flat head with a flicking, purple tongue, and a thin, ridged tail studded with hooked barbs. Its lambent yellow eyes were alight with a malevolent intelligence. It hissed and emitted caustic orange fumes from its eight slitted nostrils.

"N'Luuura!" Riane cried, coughing. "A razor-raptor!"

"Ah, I see your knowledge extends to V'ornn xenobiology." Minnum nodded. "Impressive, I must say." He made another figure in the air, this time touching the tips of his thumb and pinky together, and Thigpen reappeared. She looked around, for a moment bewildered.

"Feeling all right after your little, er, sojourn?" Minnum asked.

"That was . . . I must say it was by *far* the most disgusting experience I have ever . . ." Thigpen drew herself up. "My apologies. I could not have imagined."

"That one of my kind could still exist?" Minnum smiled. "Thankfully you are not alone. I have survived this long by, uhm, how would you say it, keeping a flat outline."

"A low profile," Riane said.

"Precisely."

"But why do you have to hide?" she asked.

"We have no time for history lessons," Thigpen said briskly. She had recovered her aplomb with admirable alacrity. "Now that you have proved your credentials, Minnum, what can you tell us about the Malasocca?"

"No easy questions from you folk, I see. Well, I expected that. The Malasocca, eh? Now let me see." Minnum squinched up his eyes, staring at the smoke-dark ceiling high overhead. "A *very* nasty spell, that. It used to be invoked before Miina consigned the daemons to the Abyss. Power is their game. Power at any cost. The lust for it is built in them, really. Part of their essential makeup. But we could not have daemons transmogrifying themselves into sorceresses now could we? Very dangerous, that. It was one of the reasons they needed to be locked away. You cannot trust a daemon, not for an instant."

"Then why weren't they locked away from the beginning?"

"An excellent question. We thought we could change them. Well, that's part of *our* nature, ever optimistic, always seeking to make things better, that's *our* game." He squinted at Riane. "It is our greatest strength, Dar Sala-at."

"But it's also what caused needless suffering and death."

"Well, it surely caused that, suffering and death," Minnum said thoughtfully. "But I don't agree about the needless part. You see, we judge all creatures as good and worthy of life until proved otherwise. If we abandoned that philosophy, well, think of it, we would be as arrogant as, well, as V'ornn, wouldn't we? We have a lot of power, and with that goes responsibility. We cannot set ourselves above others, judging them before we give them a chance to show their true nature. Even if they prove to be evil, even then, we give them a chance to change. How can we do less?"

Thigpen shook her head. "We appreciate the history lesson, Minnum, but could we get back to the Malasocca?"

Minnum clucked his tongue against the roof of his mouth. "Malasocca is a difficult and complex spell. Why do you ask about it?"

"A sorceress has been attacked," Riane said.

"By the daemon that has managed to escape. Well, it would have to be an archdaemon to get through, wouldn't it?" Minnum shook his head. "But I wonder how?"

Riane could not tell him that in breaking the sorcerous circle of the Nanthera Giyan had violated Miina's law and inadvertently opened a Portal. Too many questions would be raised about why she had invoked the Nanthera in the first place, and that could jeopardize Annon's secret.

The curator eyed them both. "Which archdaemon has her?"

"Horolaggia."

Minnum frowned. "Sorry, my hearing must be going. I thought you said Horolaggia."

"I did."

"Ah, no!" Minnum sat down abruptly on a burnished heartwood chair. "Miina protect us all!"

A cold, clammy terror gripped Riane's heart as she saw the stricken expression on the sorcerer's face.

"What is it?" She was almost afraid to ask.

"I have no counter to this . . . abomination, a Malasocca invoked by one of Pyphoros' bastard get."

"How long can she last?"

Minnum squinted. "When was she taken?"

"Just days ago."

"Depends on how powerful she is, but I would say at the outside the dead of winter."

"Dear Miina! That is only six weeks away."

"Minnum, you must help us," Thigpen said. "Does the word *Maasra* mean anything to you?"

Minnum shook his head mutely. His eyes seemed far away.

"It is somehow associated with the Malasocca," Riane said urgently.

"Can't be," Minnum said bleakly. "Would know it or, anyway, have heard of it."

Thigpen put her forepaws on Minnum's knees. "*Maasra* is not Old Tongue, nor is it Venca. Our best guess is it's an obscure dialect of some sort. I know someone who might be able to help us. A dialectician. The problem is he's dead." As Minnum's eyes rose to lock with hers, she said, "We need you to conjure the Ephemeral Reconstitution."

Spice Jaxx's was an octagon-shaped cafe in the center of Axis Tyr's vast and seething spice market, which never closed. Neither did Spice Jaxx's. Line-General Lokck Werrrent had arrived for his appointment with Star-Admiral Olnnn Rydddlin with fifteen minutes to spare. This was deliberate. He wanted to sit alone with a flute of fire-grade numaaadis and gather his thoughts before Olnnn delivered whatever bad news he had.

Line-General Werrrent had for many years been close to Olnnn Rydddlin. They had what Werrrent privately thought of as a father-son relationship. Werrrent was proud of Olnnn's accomplishments, especially considering his background, and of how tough the younger Khagggun had proved himself to be. Still, there remained a thorn in the blood-rose of Werrrent's affection—the fact that Olnnn, so young and relatively inexperienced, had jumped over him and every other Line-General to be named the new Star-Admiral.

Not that Werrrent envied Olnnn's daily encounters with Kurgan Stogggul. The father, erratic and paranoid, had been difficult enough to deal with, but the son—well, in Werrrent's considered opinion Kurgan Stogggul was a dangerous egomaniac. Worse, Werrrent agreed with a number of the other Line-Generals that Kurgan Stogggul had a secret agenda that would benefit just one V'ornn: Kurgan Stogggul.

Why was it, he asked himself, that just when things looked as if they could not get worse, they did?

Before he could think of an answer, Olnnn Rydddlin appeared and sat down opposite him.

He waited until Olnnn was served his drink. "So. What news?"

When Olnnn had told him of the Gyrgon's decision to suspend the implantation of the okummmon among the Khagggun ranks, Lokck Werrrent sat still and silent.

At length, Olnnn said, "Don't you have any comment?"

The Line-General shrugged his shoulders. "What is there to say? It is a Gyrgon decision. We obey Gyrgon decisions. I, for one, am grateful that they have the best interests of my Khagggun in mind."

"In other words, you believe them."

Lokck Werrrent's dark eyes scanned the younger Khagggun. "I have no reason not to. I cannot claim to understand the decisions of the Comradeship, and neither can you." He took a swig of his numaaadis. "You have always harbored a dark and gloomy bent. I myself see nothing dire in this news. On the contrary—"

"They will never resume the program," Olnnn said softly, "I do not care what the regent claims."

"This is treasonous talk!" the Line-General said in great agitation. "We Khagggun were promised Great Caste status. To renege would be an intolerable dishonor."

"This is what I am saying."

Lokck Werrrent heaved a great sigh. "You are like a son to me, Star-Admiral. You know this well. And now you are my superior. But I am not so much a fool not to advise you to keep such radical thoughts to yourself. Any other general hearing these words—"

"Which is precisely why I have come to you. I trust you with my life. You do not know the current regent as I do." And then he did something he had sworn to himself he would not do. He told Lokck Werrrent how he and Kurgan had murdered the former Star-Admiral's concubine and had blamed Wennn Stogggul for it. "It was all part of Kurgan Stogggul's plan to pit his father against the Star-Admiral. As he had foreseen, they caused each other's death. Kurgan ascended to regent, and I became Star-Admiral."

Lokck Werrrent grasped Olnnn's wrists. "Your hands are covered in blood. You have already committed treason once."

"That is not the way I see it. I helped rid us all of Wennn Stogggul. That skcettta was born a razor-raptor. And as for his son—"

"Keep your voice down, Star-Admiral," Lokck Werrrent said with a pained expression.

"Lokck, I am uncomfortable with you addressing me by my rank when we are alone together. After all—"

"But you are my Star-Admiral. It is impossible to address you any other way."

Olnnn gave a wan smile. "This is you through and through, Line-General."

"Protocol must be observed. Without this discipline we would soon descend into a pack of wild animals."

"Perhaps you are right," Olnnn mused.

Lokck Werrrent studied him for some time. "But there are moments—brief and infrequent—when extraordinary circumstances allow a . . . bending . . . of protocol." He inclined his square head. "So tell me, Olnnn. What black thoughts have invaded that dour mind of yours?"

Olnnn rubbed his forehead. "The truth is, being so close to the new regent I grow ever more suspicious. This elevation to Great Caste status was his father's idea. It was how Wennn Stogggul was able to forge his alliance with the former Star-Admiral. But that alliance proved false. Why should this elevation to Great Caste status be anything else?"

"The Gyrgon gave it their blessing. The okummmon is a Gyrgon bioinstrument."

Olnnn Rydddlin's hand gripping his silenced him. Olnnn slowly turned his arm over, revealing the newly implanted okummmon.

"I have little use for this *bioinstrument*. And I am wondering whether the high command was implanted simply so that the regent could keep closer tabs on us."

"The regent?"

"Think about it. For centuries the castes have remained the same. Until Wennn Stogggul. How could he possibly convince the Comradeship—"

"Again, I would point out that none of us can claim to know a Gyrgon's mind."

"Gyrgon abhor change. That is indisputable."

"Yes, but you know as well as I do that the okummmon can only be implanted on Gyrgon orders."

"Perhaps the regent is in league with that Gyrgon, Nith Batoxxx, who skulks around the regent's palace as if it is his own. I do not claim to have all the answers, Line-General. But like it or not change is in the air and I grow fearful for us—for all Khagggun. I believe the son is building on the father's lie."

"Why would he do that?"

"To keep us under control; to deprive us of power."

"You are describing a decidedly paranoid individual."

"That is just my point," Olnnn said grimly. "He is a V'ornn who plotted his own father's assassination."

"You yourself pointed out that getting rid of Wennn Stogggul should be viewed as a virtuous act. You cannot have it both ways."

"You are blind, Lokck."

"Because of our long friendship I choose to ignore the insult. Kurgan Stogggul is my regent. You would do well to remember that."

"I believe he poses a grave danger to us."

"You enjoy the loyalty of every Khagggun. So long as this is true there is no danger." Lokck Werrrent shook his head. "Olnnn, when was the last time you had any fun?"

This was not a question to which Olnnn could respond.

"Even before your . . ." Lokck Werrrent could not stop himself from glancing at the bare bones of Olnnn's sorcerous leg. "Even before your misfortune you were a dour sort. How many times have I tried to spice up your life? Remember that time—"

"The four females you brought."

"Two were for you."

Olnnn crossed his arms over his chest, looked away.

"All death and no fun is no way to live your life."

Olnnn swung his head around. His eyes were baleful. "We are Kha-gggun."

Lokck Werrrent sighed deeply. "Even Khagggun must take their plea-sure. But there is no pleasure for you, is there, Olnnn?" He shrugged. "I thought perhaps coming back from the dead might have had a sa-lubrious effect on you."

"I no longer sleep at night. I dream without the benefit of sleep. I have nightmares whose meaning I do not understand."

"Perhaps a Genomatekk—"

"No Genomatekk can cure me."

"Then be kind to yourself. Come with me to Dobbro Mannx's dinner party. Do you know him? He is a well-respected solicitor-Bashkir. A very amusing fellow."

"Thank you. No." Olnnn placed some coins on the table. "I see this has been a waste of time."

"I never forget a conversation." Lokck Werrrent held him in his steady gaze. "Olnnn, you know me better than any other V'ornn. You know that given just cause I will defend my Khagggun to the death."

Olnnn returned the look. "Then I will bring you your just cause, Line-General." He inclined his head stiffly. "Enjoy yourself tonight."

"I wish you the same, Star-Admiral," Lokck Werrrent said as he rose. "But I very much fear my words fall on deaf ears."

The operative word here is 'ephemeral,' " Minnum said as he gathered oddments into a rough circle.

He had taken them into a smallish gallery in the north wing of the museum. Here were displayed a surprisingly small number of exhibits. These were all in superbly wrought cases of carved heartwood or etched bronze. Unlike the mess of the courtyard, everything here was neat and sparkling clean.

"Once this dialectician is cantated—that's what it's called, by the way—into this realm you will have three minutes, no more, is that understood? Humph!" He seemed to be muttering to himself. "Three minutes! Hardly a successful incantation at all. What *were* they think-ing?"

With the sefiror bustling about, Riane peered into one case after another, able to make sense of nothing she saw. The interiors seemed filled with a swirling mist. She might have thought the cases were un-used save for the fact that they had been lovingly hand-rubbed to a deep luster. There were no printed captions anywhere in evidence. And, in any case, what could a caption tell you about something you could not see? No wonder this museum attracted so few visitors.

"All right, then." Minnum stood in the center of the gallery, his strange and exotic paraphernalia piled around him. "Please stand there, Dar Sala-at. Yes, right. And you, Thigpen, just there across from—right, then, what is the name of this dialectician of your acquaintance?"

"Cushsneil," Thigpen said at once.

Minnum nodded, pushed up his sleeves, and conjured what looked like a stick of ice-blue chalk. On the stone floor of the gallery he drew an equilateral triangle.

This was the most ancient symbol of original Ramahan power, Riane knew. Which was, she supposed, what made Giyan's Otherwhere prison so terrifying on an elemental level. It was the inversion of the symbol, the sigil of Evil made manifest. But now what Minnum was drawing caught her attention fully. It was the inverted triangle super-imposed upon the first, creating a kind of six-pointed star.

"Pheregonnen," the sefiror said, beginning the rite. "Behold the De-sign whose Center is everywhere, whose Points are nowhere." Into a small fire-blackened brazier he sifted a succession of powders taken from uncapped phials, then grated a bit of odd-looking horn, along with what looked like shanin and latua. At length, he conjured a fire-red substance. It drooled thick as gelatin into the brazier, producing a dense, billowing cloud of yellowish smoke, which swirled around the gallery in similar fashion to the mist inside the exhibit cases.

Riane tried to hold her breath, but finally even her hardened lungs gave out. She inhaled the smoke and staggered, feeling light-headed and dizzy. The air seemed to sizzle and dance with little sparks that twinkled at the edges of her vision. But every time she tried to look at them directly they disappeared.

Then her attention was redirected to the center of the Pheregonnen, for the twinkling sparks were coalescing into a sphere, which elongated, slowly changing shape into that of a Kundalan male. From his robes it was clear that he was a konara, a high priest of Ramahan.

"Cushsneil!" Thigpen cried happily. "I thought I would never see you again!"

"Nor I you," the Ramahan said gravely. He had long grey hair that rose from a pronounced widow's peak in winglike waves, a blade-thin nose, and dark, hooded eyes. His was an ascetic's face, the face of a scholar, a Ramahan of unwavering dedication and service. "What has caused you to rouse me in this manner?"

"Mind the time," Minnum warned them. "There won't be a second chance."

"Right." Thigpen nodded. "Cushsneil, this is Riane, the Dar Sala-at."

"The Dar Sala-at?" The wise eyes opened wide, blinking several times as Cushsneil looked around. "If you are the Dar Sala-at, then where is your Nawatir?"

"I do not know," Riane said. "I have no Nawatir."

"Oh, dear. Oh, dear." The deceased dialectician clucked his tongue. "You are most vulnerable without your Nawatir!"

"We don't have time for this," Minnum muttered darkly. "For Miina's sake, get on with it."

"We need your help," Riane said urgently. "Can you tell us the meaning of the word *Maasra*?"

Cushsneil frowned. "If you ask about the *Maasra* then the Portal must have come unsealed. Horolaggia has been sighted?"

"Yes," Riane said. "A beloved sorceress has been taken by this archdaemon and is being transmogrified through the Malasocca. We have until winter solstice before the possession becomes irreversible."

"Evil times, indeed," the dialectician rumbled. "You must exercise extreme caution. I cannot emphasize this enough. Intensive training in the sorcerous arts is essential before you seek to engage Horolaggia, and even then, there is no assurance . . ." He shuddered. "Oh, dear, oh, dear."

"What about the *Maasra*?" Riane asked.

"Ah, that." Cushsneil rocked from his heels to his toes. "It is a colloquial word—a holy word, the Gazi Qhan would doubtless say, for it is of their dialect. The *Maasra* is another name for the Veil—the Veil of a Thousand Tears."

Riane almost jumped out of her skin in excitement. "The Veil of a Thousand Tears is what Giyan told me I had to find. Why? What is it?"

"It is written that when the Five Sacred Dragons of Miina used The Pearl to create Kundala the resulting cataclysm shattered The Pearl's outer layer. The largest piece of this survived the creation. It was used to catch the tears the Five Dragons shed at the birth of Kundala, and their tears turned the hard shell into flowing fabric of fantastic colors and incomparable sheen."

"Why did they weep?"

"Because they foresaw the death and destruction that would accompany the decline of the Kundalan race."

"So we were doomed even before any of us were born."

"Nothing is set in stone, least of all the subject of a sacred Dragon's second sight."

"Dear Cushsneil," Thigpen broke in, "can you tell us where to find the Veil of a Thousand Tears?"

"I cannot even tell you whether it exists. Though many warring factions have made obsessive lifelong searches for it, have murdered for its secret, have died in exile and madness, the Veil remains hidden, a legend only."

"But it does exist! Giyan told me I must find it. It is the only way to free her. If I do not, she will die."

"The Malasocca is worse than death—far worse. If the web is completed, she will be trapped, subservient to the archdaemon's will for all time." The dialectician's image began to sparkle, and they could see the far wall through his body.

"He is going," Minnum said. "I warned you."

"Please," Riane said desperately. "You must be able to tell us something more."

"I have already told you what I can." Cushsneil's voice was growing faint, indistinct. "The rest you must discover on your own."

"Wait," Riane cried.

"If you are truly the Dar Sala-at, it is written."

"Explain yourself!"

It was too late. The dialectician had vanished altogether.

Cursing mightily, Riane turned to the sefìror. "Who are the Gazi Qhan? Where are they?"

"Ah, at last an easy question." Minnum rubbed his hands together as he led the way out of the gallery. The yellow smoke had vanished along with the chalk-mark Pheregonnen. "The Gazi Qhan are one of the Five

Tribes of the Korrush. If you are determined to find the Veil of a Thousand Tears I suggest you start there."

"Doubtless we should begin our journey north as soon as possible," Thigpen said with a curious glance at Riane.

What was she playing at? Riane wondered. She would have expected Thigpen to raise another caution flag, especially in light of . . . Then she got it. She pulled at Minnum's sleeve so forcefully that the sefiror stopped in midstep. "Cushsneil was looking right at me when he warned of taking on Horolaggia without the proper training. I may be the Dar Sala-at, but I am not even an ordained sorceress. Giyan was right. I must be patient. I must spend the time allotted to me in learning."

"And?" Minnum inquired.

"Well, I was thinking that I could apprentice with you, that I could . . ." Her voice trailed off when she saw the dark look Minnum shot Thigpen. "What is it?"

"Will you tell her, dear Rappa, or shall I?"

"It is your right," Thigpen said. "And your duty."

Minnum nodded, sighing. "Much as I am pleased by your request, Dar Sala-at, I cannot honor it."

"But why not?" Riane asked. "You are sefiror, maybe the last of your kind. Like Mother, you are a connection with the time before the V'ornn. Who better to teach me sorcery?"

Minnum's expression softened. "Dear Dar Sala-at, it is precisely because of all this that I am forbidden to teach you or anyone the sorcerous arts." He lifted an arm. "But come, let us not speak of this in cold corridors."

He took them back through the glittering Great Hall into a narrow gallery filled with the sculpture of serpents. Riane, who automatically took in details, noted the similarity between these serpents and the citrine image of Miina's sacred snake that she had come across in the Kells below the Abbey of Floating White.

Minnum poured them flagons of a warm, crisp, highly spiced wine that Riane had never tasted before. They sat on upholstered chairs whose elongated backs reclined at odd angles, before a crackling fire in a stone hearth.

Minnum drained his flagon, then wiped his red lips. He sat forward, elbows on knees, and when he spoke his voice was scarcely above a whisper. "I suppose you have some knowledge of the uprising that usurped power from Mother."

Riane nodded. "It happened on the day the V'ornn arrived, the day The Pearl was lost."

"Ah, not lost, no." Minnum shook his shaggy head. "The Pearl was cast out from Kundala by the Great Goddess Herself. After the cabal of sefiror Ramahan took Mother's power and gained control of The Pearl, after they peered into its depths and saw not Truth but what they wanted to see, Miina in Her fury took up The Pearl and carried it far, far away. She had made The Pearl for Kundala—it was our birthright. But when we abused its power, we abrogated that right and She abandoned us.

"The consequences of this were many. We lost what power The Pearl might have given us to resist the V'ornn invasion. Miina stood by, mute, Her heart hardened against Her people while the sefiror cabal used the Rappa as scapegoats and had them slaughtered. She stood by, mute, Her heart hardened when the priestesses took back their power. The konara could have driven the sefiror out of the abbeys, but they could not strip them of their sorcery. So what did they do?" Minnum sighed. "They killed the sefiror. Every last one of them—save me. I survived by fleeing to a place where they would never think to look for a sefiror—the Korrush. For two decades I lived there among the Jeni Cerii, the fierce warlords of the steppes, in complete anonymity, learning the many ways in which to kill an enemy. That was where I got this." He slapped his bandy leg. "Chasing raiders, I fell from a kuomeshal going full gallop, took one nasty fall. We were a hundred fifty kilometers from nowhere, and they slung me across my mount and took me back to Bandichire, and I never made a sound. They set my leg as best they could, but the damage was already done."

Thinking of how Giyan had reset Annon's leg, Riane said, "Why didn't you use sorcery?"

"I was in hiding, wasn't I? I was among the Jeni Cerii; everything had to appear normal." He grinned. " 'Sides, they told stories about my bravery for months afterward." He resettled himself. "Now where was I? Oh, yes. Capsule history. I became an apt pupil because I had no other choice, then I became an adept. When I realized I was admired and feared I left straightaway. Returning to Axis Tyr, I discovered this place, abandoned and falling into disrepair, and decided I would become its curator. Then, on one of his long walks, Eleusis Ashera wandered in and stayed to view all the exhibits."

"But none of this explains why you can't teach me," Riane said. "I must save Giyan from Horolaggia. I will not allow her to be transmogrified. You must help me."

Minnum shook his head, and his eyes were suddenly sunken and sad. "However much I want to, Dar Sala-at, I cannot. This is my punishment, you see. Miina's punishment."

"What do you mean?"

"For allowing The Pearl to stray into evil hands, the Great Goddess stripped Mother of much of her power."

This was true, Riane knew, for Mother had told her as much when she, Riane, had freed her from her imprisonment.

"For being the only sefiror clever enough to survive our genocide, Miina meted out another form of punishment. I have knowledge, Dar Sala-at, so much knowledge. And yet I am unable to convey it in any form."

Riane's heart broke for Minnum. "But you did nothing wrong. In fact, you alone survived. Why should you be punished? How could Miina be so cruel?"

"Is it cruelty, Dar Sala-at? Do not be so quick to judge the Great Goddess. Through greed, envy, arrogance we lost the greatest gift. Could it have been because we had become complacent, because we no longer put much value on an object that is beyond value? Because we had become corrupted by the power we wielded? If that be so— and I, for one, fervently believe that it is—then what remains for us after the ruin we have been brought to? Another day, and another, all of which must be fought for with the blood and the death of loved ones. Suffering burns away arrogance, greed, envy. Only through this crucible of fire can we learn what we have forgotten. Only then will we come to know who we really are and where we belong in the Cosmos."

Riane hung her head. "You say you are enjoined from teaching, Minnum, but truly you have taught me something vital this night."

He smiled. "Then mayhap I have proved my worth to Miina, for I do not think that you arrived at my doorstep by simple chance."

"Then help me further," Riane pleaded. "I did not need Cushsneil to tell me I am unprepared to face Horolaggia. There is no use in trying to save Giyan only to die in the process."

Out of the corner of her eye she could see Thigpen beaming at her. She had learned this last lesson well.

Minnum was scratching his hairy cheek. "Mayhap you can learn what you need in the Korrush. Look here." He gestured with his right hand, and a map appeared on the floor. Riane and Thigpen hunkered around it.

"Behold the Korrush," he said. "The Five Tribes inhabit the wild steppe in a kind of uneasy truce, but there are always squabbles among the kapudaan—the chieftains—and skirmishes along the borders. Each tribe is centered around its own area, which is known as a chire. There is a central village in each chire with the same name." His stubby finger stabbed out. "The warlord Jeni Cerii are here in Bandichire." And again, moving southwest. "The Rasan Sul are the spice merchants the SaTrryn trade with; they are located here, in Okkamchire." His finger moved west. "The Han Jod are artisans here in Shelachire. Because the Bey Das are historians and archaeologists they have special dispensation to cross chire borders safely. They are essentially nomads, spread out all across the Korrush. Their main site is here in the barely visible village of Im-Thera. There lies Za Hara-at, the fabled and ancient Earth Five Meetings."

Firelight played across Minnum's face, highlighting the reddish hairs in his forked beard. A log gave way, crashing softly into the pillowy white bed of ash. Minnum rose, limped over to the hearth to put another log on. When he came back, he pointed again to the sorcerous map he had conjured.

"Here in Agachire, on the eastern section of the Korrush, near the border to the northwestern corner of the Great Voorg, dwell the Gazi Qhan, the tribe Cushsneil mentioned from whose dialect *Maasra* comes. They are the mystics of the Korrush, the Gazi Qhan, and I confess I know little about them save this. There is a district in the village of Agachire known as Giyossun. Here is a kashiggen called Mrashruth, which means, I believe, Tender Willow. It is run by a dzuoko named Perrnodt, who I think may be able to assist you."

Riane was shocked. "What does a Tuskugggun know of Osoru or Kyofu?"

Minnum cocked an eyebrow. "Who said she was V'ornn?"

"She must be. Every Kundalan dzuoko was replaced by a Tuskugggun when the V'ornn took possession of the kashiggen."

"Apparently not *every* dzuoko," Minnum said dryly, then he addressed Thigpen. "Is she always so sure of herself?"

"I would venture to say it works to her advantage as well as to her disadvantage," Thigpen said just as dryly.

Minnum grunted, turning back to Riane. "Be that as it may, Perrnodt is not V'ornn."

"She is Gazi Qhan then," Riane said, determined to listen more closely.

"Of that I have no knowledge," Minnum said softly, his eyes afire. "What is of interest to all of us, however, is that she is Ramahan."

"It is settled then," Thigpen said. "The Dar Sala-at and I will journey to the Korrush there to find this Perrnodt."

Minnum shook his head. "Where the Dar Sala-at now ventures she must do so alone."

"Impossible! This Korrush is far too alien and dangerous for me to allow—"

"You will not go, Thigpen." Minnum's voice was soft but commanding. "It is written in the Prophesies of the Druuge." He planted his feet firmly on the floor. "Moreover, she cannot go with her sorcery intact."

Thigpen's chest expanded, and she stood up warningly on her four hind legs. "Now you go too far. Without her spells, she will be vulnerable—"

"As you have doubtless discovered of late, she is vulnerable with the pitifully small bits of knowledge she has. Moreover, without proper training I warrant she could do more harm than good with what she does know."

"How dare you talk about the Dar Sala-at in that way!"

"I speak only the truth, Thigpen. Riane *must* be properly trained, and for that she must travel to the Korrush."

"There has to be another way. She—"

"I've heard enough out of the two of you!" Riane cried. "Stop talking about me as if I wasn't in the chamber." She took a breath. "Now, Minnum, tell me why I cannot use my sorcery in the Korrush."

"I said that you cannot go with it intact, Dar Sala-at. The two are not the same."

"How do they differ?" Riane said.

"I need to extract all your sorcerous knowledge. You will not remember one iota of it."

"Then how will I introduce myself to Perrnodt?" Riane said. "How will she teach me?"

"Excellent questions," Minnum replied. He went to a desk, pulled open one drawer after another. "Now where did I stash that blasted thing?" he mumbled as he rummaged through the jumbled contents of the desk. "Ah, here it is." He brought back a highly polished heartwood box entirely graven with unfamiliar runes, and opened it in front of them. It appeared filled with the same opalescent mist Riane had noticed in some of the museum's exhibit cases. But the mist did not dissipate with the box's opening; in fact, if anything it seemed to thicken. A certain chill had entered the chamber. It took Riane but a moment to realize that it came from the box, or rather its mysterious contents. Minnum dipped his hand into the mist and pulled it out. His hand appeared empty.

He seemed to be enjoying their consternation. "Look at the tip of my forefinger."

"I see only a black speck," Riane said.

"Quite so," Minnum replied. "And properly placed in plain sight such an item will go unnoticed by even the most discerning eye." He reached out, planted the speck beneath Riane's right ear. "Nothing more than a mole, eh?" He wagged a finger. "In actuality, what is it? The repository of all your sorcerous knowledge."

"What?"

"That's right." He was grinning. "You will carry your knowledge with you in a safe place, in a receptacle only Perrnodt will be able to recognize and access."

"But why all this secrecy?" Thigpen was frowning deeply, her whiskers twitching so violently Riane knew that she was highly agitated.

"Perhaps it will never be needed. But just in case . . . in the event of . . ." Minnum sighed. "I may be the only sefiror left alive, but there are forces in the Korrush, corrupting forces, dark forces that are lacking only sufficient knowledge to extend their power." He folded his arms over his chest. "They are known as sauromicians. They are necromancers. They study the dead, dismembering them in order to foretell the future."

Riane glanced over at Thigpen. The Rappa's whiskers were twitching in anxiety.

"They are that which remains," Minnum continued. "The end result of the sorcerers whose memories were burned beyond recognition."

"I thought you said the Ramahan killed all the sefiror save yourself," Riane said.

"True enough." Minnum nodded. "But before that happened, Miina, in Her rage, took Nedhu as well as several of his intimates in the cabal that rose up to appropriate The Pearl, and did this to them."

"She left them to wander the Korrush, and now they are a danger?" Riane shook her head. "Truly the Great Goddess moves in mysterious ways."

"So it is written," Minnum said. "So it has come to pass." He touched the black speck beneath Riane's right ear. "The chances of your encountering a sauromician are slim, but should the worst occur they will be unable to steal your knowledge."

Riane nodded. "I understand."

"But Dar Sala-at," Thigpen protested. "You cannot—"

"She must," Minnum said.

"If the worst should happen, she will be helpless to defend herself without her sorcery."

"I think you underestimate her resourcefulness," Minnum said. "However, I have no intention of allowing her to travel to the Korrush unprotected." He returned to the desk, pressed a hidden button, and a door popped open. "In the unlikely event you come across a sauromician, you will know him by two things: first, he will be dressed in black, hooded robes. Second, he will have the stigma the Great Goddess in Her wisdom has given him: on his left hand is a sixth finger, black and ugly as death."

Unlocking the lowest of four drawers, he produced a hexagonal box made of a dull grey metal alloy. It was protected by a lock, which he unsealed with a series of rhythmic darting motions of his forefinger. The top spiraled open, and he drew out a cylinder a bit over ten centimeters long of a milk-white color, smooth as silk. "You will hide this, Dar Sala-at," he said, as he pressed it into her palm. "And you will activate it just here, near this end, by pressing the gold disc that lies flush with the surface. Press it again to deactivate it."

Thigpen sniffed at it suspiciously. "What is that? It's not of Kundalan manufacture."

"And I warrant it's not V'ornnish either."

Riane turned it over and over. "Then where does it come from?"

Minnum shrugged. "I found it here, in the Museum of False Memory."

"What will it do?" Riane asked.

"This is an infinity-blade wand. Using a highly compressed beam of goron particles, it will repel the enemy—any enemy." He took it from her, lifted her thick hair, and placed it flat against her scalp just above the nape of her neck, where he affixed it. "But use it sparingly. You will only be able to activate it twice."

"But you must be able to tell me more."

"Would that I could." He laid a finger alongside his bulbous nose. "Remember what Miina has done to me. I have told you all I can."

Thigpen looked up. "So much danger, little dumpling." Crystalline tears stood in the corners of her eyes. "Of a sudden, I feel inadequate to protecting you."

"Dear Thigpen," Riane said as she stroked the soft, luxuriant fur, "I have come to realize that no one—not Giyan, not you—can long protect me from my enemies. This I must do myself, and I will fail unless my schooling continues. I know full well that the time when the Dar Sala-at may safely reveal herself is not yet here."

"And yet."

"I know what you wish for me." She kissed the Rappa. "Giyan once told me the Dar Sala-at's path was long and arduous and fraught with peril. I have been called, Thigpen. I can do ought but follow my path. It directs me into the heart of the Korrush."

It was almost midnight by the time Nith Batoxxx had recovered sufficiently from the failure. He had taken his daily salamuuun flight, using a dose a touch higher than usual. Still, afterward, he could not bear the sight of himself, and so he transformed his body into the one Kurgan knew as the Old V'ornn—skull copper-dark, aged as mortewood, hands crinkled like tissue. Thus cloaked, he ventured into the throbbing heart of Axis Tyr via a secret underground exit he had discovered in the Kundalan structure the Comradeship had renamed the Temple of Mnemonics. He had told no other Gyrgon of his discovery.

There were many reasons for this, not the least being that he was a hoarder of secrets. It was his opinion that the weight of the secrets he kept would crush most V'ornn like a qwawd-egg shell.

It was an invigorating walk of perhaps fifty minutes to the villa in which the Old V'ornn was known to live. He could have taken a hov-erpod, of course, but in the guise of the Old V'ornn he preferred to go on foot. The succession of salamuuun flights made everything look crys-tal clear, hard-edged, filled with wonder.

The recent storm had scrubbed the city clean. Freshets of rainwater still swirled down storm drains, and the packed streets were pock-marked with puddles. He passed vast striped-canopied markets selling everything from produce to dry goods to useless gewgaws to off-world gemstones to artless clothing to precious spices, bright-colored Bashkir auction houses where deals were struck every hour of the day and night, light-drenched Tuskugggun ateliers filled with crafts and artwork of every description. He passed the vast market where fish, fresh-caught from the turbid depths of the Sea of Blood, were laid out in precise ranks, their opaque eyes looking like those of the Kundalan who en-dured interrogation in the chambers below the regent's palace. A one-armed Kundalan merchant tried to sell him fresh clemetts still on the branch from the back of his buttren-driven dray. Another with a hid-eously scarred face watched him expressionlessly as he passed up his pathetic display of metalware. The aftermath of decades of interroga-tion were everywhere in Axis Tyr, sown at his direction like seedpods to sprout their bitter fruit, living proof of the futility of resistance.

Still, despite everything he had done, the Resistance abided.

He came upon his favorite shop, which sold one-of-a-kind artifacts plundered from the many civilizations the V'ornn had conquered. On impulse he went in, bought an Argggedian prayer wheel. The shop-keeper, who was knowledgeable about such matters, explained that the prayer wheel spun in three dimensions when exposed to moonlight because the Argggedians worshiped their cephalopod god at the time of the full moon. Or they had, until the coming of the V'ornn. Nith Batoxxx, who was hearing more about Argggedian religion than he wanted to know, cut the shopkeeper short by paying for the prayer wheel and exiting the shop.

From the outset of his walk, he had noticed that the streets were filled with Khagggun, much more so under this young regime than there had been even under the paranoid regent, Wennn Stogggul. The city seemed to be on war footing, an especially intimidating state of affairs for the Kundalan. Which was just the way Kurgan wanted it. And, Nith Batoxxx knew, Kurgan wanted it because he himself had told Kurgan to want it.

Nith Batoxxx considered his altogether intimate relationship with Kurgan Stogggul. Which had thrived ever since he, in the guise of the Old V'ornn, had years ago seduced the child away from his family in order to train him both in physical prowess and mental toughness. It had been an experiment, like many of Nith Batoxxx's endeavors. He was, after all, a technomage. He sought the answers to questions beyond the ken of the other castes. As the designated Ascensor, he had presided over Kurgan's Channeling in the Sanctuary of Ascension. Once, the ocular-lighted chamber had been a shrine to the Kundalan Goddess, Miina. Now it was used to remove the birth caul from Great Caste males, to implant them with the quasi-organic okummmon, welcoming them into adulthood. The okummmon was then attuned—or channeled—to the Gyrgon frequencies. Nith Batoxxx still had Kurgan's birth caul, having palmed it during the ceremony, replacing it with the birth caul of a Bashkir boy who had died during his own coming of age ceremony. Employing the proper theorem, the birth caul could be made to provide all sorts of interesting data about not only the individual from which it had come, but also about the bloodlines of his family. Nith Batoxxx had been studying Kurgan's birth caul since the evening of his Channeling. It was the main reason why he was so certain of Kurgan's fate.

But, again, what was fate, really? As a Gyrgon, he was used to manipulating the lives of those beneath him, of treating them as if they were experiments in his lab, exposing them to different reagents to see how quickly they were pulled apart. He was, in a very real sense, Old Man Fate himself. In Kurgan's case, he had stepped in, reshaping his very reality. He had turned Kurgan against his family, against his father, in particular. He had taught him how to hate, and had stood back, pleased and, yes, a little proud, as he watched his pupil plot with his particular cold-blooded single-mindedness the elder Stogggul's death. Kurgan's likes, dislikes, the choices he made, the very demons that drove him were solely of Nith Batoxxx's creation. It was like painting a perfect portrait of death. He had given Destruction a V'ornn name and a face, had given it false memories and, therefore, a manufactured purpose. He had set it in motion and was watching in a kind of vertiginous fascination the havoc it was wreaking.

Gimnopede Boulevard was ablaze with light, sound, noise, and jostling bodies. Three Tuskugggun artisans at an outdoor cafe were discussing their metalwork trade, exchanging samples of new alloys they had created. A young Bashkir boy ran through the crowd, cleverly swiping a trinket as he passed a shop. His exasperated mother ran after him, unaware, as was the shopkeeper, of what her son had done. Nith Batoxxx in the guise of the Old V'ornn smiled a secret smile, thinking of the child Kurgan, the cunning mind he had helped shape.

When he contemplated Kurgan's Channeling, he was struck by the knowledge that he had been an outsider in Stogggul family affairs who nevertheless knew more about Kurgan than anyone in Kurgan's own family. Save for the boy's best friend, Annon Ashera. Annon had been possessed of an intuition that was positively uncanny. For this reason, Nith Batoxxx had hated Annon as much as he had hated his traitor of a father. In a way, he wished Annon was not dead, so that he could have the exquisite pleasure of having him killed all over again.

Now Kurgan was bound to Nith Batoxxx in an even more intimate way. Nith Batoxxx had coerced him into service, the better to keep an eye on him. But there was something else. The boy was young, yes, but Nith Batoxxx had not chosen him randomly so many years ago. He had run his equations and recognized in Kurgan the seeds of greatness. If they were correct, Kurgan was destined to wield more power than any Bashkir before him. That being the case, he had wanted to ensure that Kurgan would have the proper philosophy because as Nith Batoxxx knew only too well having the power was a wild ride, one that could all too easily lead to ruin.

He turned off Gimnopede Boulevard, onto narrow, quiet Cinnabar Street.

The villa he had procured for himself had once belonged to a Kundalan artist of some repute, who had died owing to the repeated interrogations to which Nith Batoxxx had ordered him subjected. The artist's family, who had tried to claim ownership of the villa, were soon silenced in much the same manner as the artist. In any event, the villa became vacant, which was the whole point of the exercise. It was evident from the outset that the artist and his family never knew anything of strategic value.

The villa was pleasant enough, filled with light and space, but it was of only minimal interest to him. The courtyard in back was what had drawn him here, what had caused him to murder the villa's former owner and his family, and to spend long hours painstakingly constructing the courtyard garden. He had done it even though he had exhibited no former interest in gardening; he did it almost unconsciously, as if guided by a voice or a presence. Which was, of course, precisely what happened.

As Nith Batoxxx walked through the villa now, past the living room, into the huge atelier he had converted into a gymnasium for his lessons with Kurgan, he could feel the dark beacon rising both inside him and all around him. It inhabited this villa more wholly than he ever would.

At the far end of the gymnasium he touched a padded panel and it swiveled open. Before him stretched the courtyard. Using equations of fire and water, he had filled it with rocks, stones, boulders of every conceivable size and shape. The sound of water gurgling drifted to him, but its source, the pool he and Kurgan had built together, remained invisible unless you stood right next to it in the center of the garden. This was where the pool had to be placed, on the site of the ancient spring he knew would be there even before it had been dug up. *To stand at the center*, the presence said in his mind, *is to see everything*. He had taught this to Kurgan, as well.

He carefully placed the Argggedian prayer wheel on a flat black stone beside the pool, an offering, the kind of primitive act, full of ritual and respect, required of such a solemn and, yes, holy occasion. In this somewhat altered state, he gazed into the pool like a priest looking into the face of his god.

The water was pitch-black, unimaginably deep. He lifted his gaze, spun very slowly in a complete circle, taking in every detail of the courtyard garden, remembering as he did so the placement and planting of every rock, boulder, plant, and tree. It seemed to him in that last moment before he slipped into the pool that this garden was a living calendar of his days on Kundala. He had been elated to have the chance to become a hero—the Gyrgon who finally harnessed the death particle, the Gyrgon responsible for defending his race from the Divine

Horde of Destruction, as the Centophennni called themselves.

That was before the presence made itself felt, before the dark beacon rose, before the voice manifested itself, bypassing his neural nets to take possession of the cortex of his brain, periodically taking up residence there. At first, it had been able to come only infrequently and, at times, as he proceeded with his normal life, he had managed to convince himself that it was just a dream. But then, inevitably, he would be drawn back to the villa and would feel the presence rising again. It was patient, ever so patient, and over the decades it grew its black light like the gardener he himself would become.

The water was cold, but he did not mind. The sides of the pool were slimy with moss and algae, but he did not mind. Why should he? This was home, the darkness, the cold calling him, a prison whose lock must be broken no matter the cost.

He hung upside down in the darkness, waiting.

It was quiet, so quiet the beating of his hearts, the pulse of the blood in his veins was all that existed.

It was coming, rising up to merge with him fully, or as fully as it was able considering the awful chains that bound it. How long had it been imprisoned? Even his Gyrgon mind quailed at the intimation of the length of time. It was impossible. His supremely logical brain calmly informed him that it simply could not be.

And yet it was.

Here came the living proof, entering him with the familiar words, *Tremble all before me, for I am that which remains.*

Misty Mountaintop 1

*Y*ou said it was to be a small thing.

It is a small thing, and it is done.

The two huge Dragons crouched in the dense sorcerous mist atop Heavenly Rushing, Miina's sacred waterfall.

You said no one would know—no one but us.

And who knows but us?

The Portal locks Miina had us fashion out of fire, earth, air, water and wood—

—We five contributed to the Portal locks before Miina ensorceled them—

The point is they have been breached—

—as foretold—

The point is that now they have been breached there are daemons abroad.

There have always been daemons abroad.

These are archdaemons. We have not seen their faces for aeons.

One of the Dragons, ruddy as a sunset, stirred. *If they bring the lightning back—*

My dear—this Dragon was slightly smaller, black as pitch, black as ebonwood—*you cannot mean to give these archdaemons your blessing?*

I have no blessing to bestow upon them. Have you forgotten? None of us have. Not for eons. Not since the lightning ringed the sky, not since the narbuck vanished into the ice mists atop the Djenn Marre, not since the fire burned like molten magma in my veins.

Now the Dar Sala-at comes with our hope of redemption. You see, the Wheel is turning, one by one the Holy Prophesies are coming true.

Patience is not a virtue for fire.

The daemons—My point is, have a care how you transgress, for if our enemies should become aware of—

They will not. The red Dragon grinned, showing luminous fangs the size of a cthauros' foreleg.

The black Dragon's great tufted head swung around. *Whatever have you done?*

I am clever, I am.

My dear, do not boast. It ill becomes you.

A sound arose through the constant roaring of the waterfall that shook the ground and raked the sky. Clouds of terrified birds rose from their limbed sanctuary, wheeling in all directions at once.

Is laughter necessary? The black Dragon shook her head, annoyed. *What is so funny?*

When you told me that you did not want to know, I made a wager with myself, and now I have won that wager.

All right then. Tell me.

As you wish. The red Dragon looked smug. *I have brought Minnum into play.*

You haven't!

Oh, but I have!

This is what you call a little thing?

Well, you must admit, Minnum is not big.

You are insufferable, you know that, don't you?

The red Dragon sidled over to rub up against his mate.

Are you angry? Tell me you are not angry with me.

I am not one to bend the Laws.

Nor am I, but I had to do something. You see what Horolaggia has done, usurped the Malasocca.

I agree that was quite wicked of him, slaying the Cerrn and taking its place.

And Pyphoros. I have had enough of them flouting the Laws in our faces.

Minnum is, in himself, dangerous because he is so unpredictable.

A survivor, above all else.

Yes. And surviving inevitably means sacrificing others.

You are too dour.

But he will lie to them.

Of course he will lie. Miina saw to that. But that does not make him any less trustworthy.

And then there are the others. Surely they will be stirred out of their century's slumber by Minnum's machinations . . .

You heard him. Minnum believes they are already awake.

Yes, and if they are . . .

Have you no faith in the Dar Sala-at?

She is too young and raw yet.

But you, Miina knows, are not. Put your faith in her as I have done.

The black Dragon shook her craggy head. *Too much stands in her way.*

Then here she will be tried, as it is foretold in Prophesy. Here she will begin to earn your faith.

The black Dragon grew even more pensive. Her eyes were both beautiful and expressive, the color and luminosity of moonstones. *There is something else. Have you considered that Horolaggia's preemptive strike might have had another, more sinister motive?*

The red Dragon's crystal claws extruded as he stamped in anger. *More sinister than transmogrifying into Lady Giyan? What could be?*

It is possible that he sought the very response you have given, that he wants to draw us into the battle before our time, as was done to our sister, now imprisoned by the enemy.

Oh, yes, I forgot. There was a sneer on the red Dragon's face and fire danced in his nostrils. *We all have our time.*

Exactly. It is not like the old days, my dear.

But we are eternal. Our responsibility is to see the return of the old ways.

The black Dragon sighed. *True enough. But we must be mindful of our enemies and where we all are on Asa'ara.*

The Great Wheel of Fate.

There was a strange bitter tang to the red Dragon's tone that tugged mightily at his mate's heart. *Yes. If we move precipitously, we are vulnerable.* She let her spiked tail twine with his. *Let us pray to Miina that your little intervention does not cause the Dar Sala-at's undoing.*

Book Two:
GATE OF
FORBEARANCE

Of all the mistakes a sorceress may commit, impatience is, perhaps, the most egregious. With power comes the ability to act, and with the ability to act comes the gnawing desire to do so, even when inaction is clearly the most prudent course. Be now forewarned, o you eager disciples of Osoru! Learn forbearance, learn it well, else suffer for your imprudence all the rest of your days."

—Utmost Source,
  The Five Books of Miina

10

Ess

The lymmnal crouched in the shadows, waiting. The world around it was reflected in the curve of its three smoke-blue eyes. There was about the steppe, in the scoured pleats and folds, the gnarled islets of trees, beaches of pale lichen, and oceans of lavender grass, the sheer rumbling wrinkled breadth of it, a staggering sense of age, but also, something beyond age, a kind of unspeakable *aloneness* that arose, spectral and shivering, from its rigorous beauty. Newcomers found its vastness vertiginous, but by the time they had become coated by its fine ruddy dust, they were already intoxicated.

The night was moonless, chill, the air above the flat grasslands of the great steppe utterly without weight, magnifying the ghostly crenellated ice-pale peaks of the Djenn Marre. The grass, thigh high, had been thickened by the darkness into a mass with heft and presence, a world unto itself. Within that world, the lymmnal sensed something just below the threshold of movement, the small heat, perhaps, generated by a body similarly crouched, or again, possibly, the shallow anxious breathing, the accelerated pulse of someone coiled, someone about to spring into sudden action.

The lymmnal, lying low at the perimeter of the Gazi Qhan camp, had been trained to sense these ephemera. Its nostrils dilated, quivering, and its three eyes scanned the darkness for the trace of an outline that was out of place. A marmalon poked its head above ground for a moment, but the lymmnal, hungry as it was, ignored the rodent. The marmalon vanished at the soft swish of the finbats' flight. A formation of them dived and swooped toward the tops of the wild grass, skimming for supper. Then, they, too, were gone. High clouds scudded, a presence, darker than dark, and these, too, the lymmnal noted.

The scent came a split second before the movement, for it had learned that under extreme tension these biped interlopers exuded a scent. And so, it was already in midleap when the body began its run inside the perimeter.

Utterly silent, the lymmnal buried its triple set of teeth into the interloper's shoulder. Then its full weight struck the interloper, knocking him off his feet. The lymmnal dodged the one swipe of the interloper's blade, then snapped its powerful jaws, crushing his shoulder socket. The interloper passed out, and the lymmnal, well satisfied, dragged the body back into the circle of firelight that surrounded the tree.

The sixteen Gazi Qhan sat or stood around the tree, which rose, winged and proud, from the red soil. A fire cracked and sparked, a stewpot, crusty with soot, sat on ashes nearby. On the far side of the tree, but very close to it, a female lay on her back. Her belly was a mountain stroked by a male as he said the Ber-Bnadem, the birth prayer cycle. Another female knelt between the pregnant female's legs, speaking slowly and softly as if to the newborn about to arrive.

Othnam made a sign to the lymmnal, and it obediently released the interloper. Mehmmer, Othnam's younger sister, joined him in dragging the interloper to the tree.

"Jeni Cerii," Othnam said as he scruffled the thick fur behind the lymmnal's muscle-ridged neck.

Using the heel of his hand, he brought the Jeni Cerii back to consciousness. For a half hour they interrogated him without receiving a single answer.

Mehmmer spat onto the spy's face.

Someone threw a hunk of raw meat to the lymmnal, who immediately gulped it down with a brief snuffling sound. Lymmnals made little or no noise unless they were in extreme distress.

Othnam looked up at the thornbeam tree, gnarled, gray-black, old as Time itself, and utterly magnificent. He and his sister had tended this tree from the moment they were old enough to walk; their parents and grandparents were buried here, protected by its roots. It belonged to Othnam and Mehmmer now, a legacy of hope and transcendence. It would be their children's long after they themselves were turned to dust. When they returned from their long treks into the wilds, this tree was their anchor, their succor, the sight of which informed them that they were home.

Using the killing limb, the strongest branch of the tree, Othnam and

Mehmmer strung the Jeni Cerii up by his neck, letting him strangle slowly and painfully as was the custom. His kicking brought down a shower of small, hard fruit. No prayers were said at his death. This, too, was the custom.

Mehmmer's dark glittering eyes watched the death throes with a good measure of satisfaction. She was tall, as broad-shouldered as her brother. Her hair was blue-black, a mane of intricate braids strewn with tiny, spotted ghryea shell, discs of dark-striped amber, teardrops of emperor carnelian. She wore tight leather breeches that came to just below the knee, a loose-sleeved wraparound shirt of undyed muslin and yellow, thin-soled shoes with curled-up silver tips. A simple belt cinched her waist, from which hung a narrow-bladed sword, a scimitar, and a jewel-hilted dirk she had made herself.

In fact, she had forged her brother's push-dagger, which was most useful both in stealth and in hand-to-hand combat. The beautifully weighted ball hilt was held in the fist, the slender ovoid blade protruding from between the index and middle fingers. It was a stabbing weapon, rather than a slashing one, and so ideal in cramped quarters. It had saved Othnam's life more than once.

"Less than a day's trek from Agachire, and we are shadowed by the Jeni Cerii," Mehmmer said. "What should we do?"

"We shall bring this proof of Jeni Cerii perfidy to Makktuub," Othnam said.

"What if Makktuub asks." A look of alarm crossed Mehmmer's face. "What if he wants to know what we were doing?"

"We are simple merchants, pious and peaceful."

Mehmmer looked uneasily at the dead spy swinging from the noose they had fashioned. "It is the pious part that concerns me."

"The Ghorvish prayer sites are secret from both Jeni Cerii and Makktuub." Othnam looked away. "Rest assured, sister, that they shall remain that way."

"But going to Makktuub."

"I am well acquainted with the dangers," he said, more sharply, perhaps, than he had intended.

"Yes, of course, we both are. Our parents."

"Let us not speak now of their suffering," Othnam said softly. "We have spent the last three days singing the whole *Khendren* prayer cycle on the anniversary of their death in order to honor their lives."

"Yes, brother."

"We will not make the same mistake they did," he whispered. "We will be Makktuub's friends; we will do his will. And in return he will leave us to our beliefs and our faith."

While Mehmmer was dark, Othnam was not. He had golden hair, which he wore, as all the males did, in a thick, twisted knot, shiny with oils, on top of his head. His face, creased by sun, wind and, once only, an enemy's blade, was strong and finely sculpted. He possessed the eyes of the true mystic, seeing what others could not. These eyes, blue as the sky, were shot through with vivid emerald flecks—Ghorvish whorls, as they were called, proof that he was among the chosen of the Ghor, the wise men of ancient times who had received the *Mokakaddir*, the ecstatic prayer cycle the Gazi Qhan chanted, from Jiharre himself.

The lymmnal broke from Othnam's side, trotting over to the newborn and began to lick off its amniotic fluids. The mother beamed, touching with her fingertips the baby's tiny moist toes.

Brother and sister followed the lymmnal, firelight and the webbed shadows cast by the twisted thornbeam branches playing over them. Mehmmer took the female baby into the crook of her strong, sun-bronzed arm, wiping it down as custom dictated with her soft woven sinschal, the long scarf wound around the head and neck, protection from sun, wind, rain, and dust. Then she kissed the child in the center of her forehead. Othnam stood beside her, his curved dirk held before him. While Mehmmer chanted, he made the three small ritual cuts over the sternum with the tip of the blade. The child screamed, the blood flowed from her tender flesh, dripping onto the mother's bare belly. Then Mehmmer stanched the flow, using an ointment. The baby ceased to cry. Her unfocused eyes stared into infinity, and she took a firm grip on Mehmmer's finger. Smiling, Mehmmer passed her over to Othnam, who lifted the babe up to the night sky and recited the ritual prayer: "Life's first wound has been given and received. The tribe has received blood as proof of lifelong allegiance and devotion. The first blessing is now given and received. Little one, may you grow large, powerful of limb and mind. May all the Korrush be your pasture and your battlefield. May you live one hundred years, long enough to see unity and the face of the Prophet."

When the rite was over, Othnam returned the newborn, whose name was Jeene, to her parents, and he and Mehmmer set about cutting down the Jeni Cerii. They stripped off the clothes, took the weapons as booty, which they gave to the newborn's parents since the Jeni Cerii was killed on the night of their daughter's birth.

While the red dust of the Korrush skittered through the campsite, they squatted over the corpse, slowly and methodically stripping the skull of skin and flesh. They knew little of the Jeni Cerii—or of any of the other tribes, for that matter—save to fear them. The grisly work they did now served as a kind of balm to soothe this primitive fear. Not far away, the loyal lymmnal lay curled contentedly by the fire, watching them incuriously out of the eye that was set between its ears in the back of its head.

The lymmnal rose out of a shallow sleep, for lymmnal did not sleep as it is commonly understood. Opening its eyes one by one, it rose soundlessly, trotting away from the sleeping figures ranged around the thornbeam tree, crowned now by a new white skull, drying in the first ruddy rays of sunlight slanting across the Korrush.

The lymmnal kept its nose to the ground, its haunches semicontracted. The scent was wholly unfamiliar. Its long furred head wagged back and forth like the point of a compass. Though it crept forward in its standard attack stance, it was curious as well as wary.

The scent at length led it to an unfamiliar female creature who sat, a voluminous greatcoat swept tight around her. She was hunched over, possibly asleep, but at the lymmnal's approach her head came up very slowly. Her eyes opened and gazed upon the lymmnal.

The tension went out of the animal's frame, and it crouched, its forepaws stretched out in front of it. It gave a little sound and, after a short silence, the creature responded in kind. A murmured conversation ensued as the other creature crept a little closer, until finally their snouts touched, their noses twitched as they scented each other, then licked each other.

The lymmnal was thus surprised at the expressions on its masters' faces when it brought the new creature into camp. It could not understand why Othnam drew his sword and Mehmmer glowered at the hooded figure.

"What is this trick, stranger, that you have used to gull our lymmnal?" Mehmmer growled as the rest of the camp began to stir. Other weapons were unsheathed, lifted pointfirst toward the intruder. "If the Jeni Cerii sent you to plead for their spy's life, it is too late." She gestured to the skull whitening in the early sunlight.

Riane pushed the hood of Nith Sahor's greatcoat off her head with one hand while she stroked the ridged back of the docile lymmnal with the other. "As you can see, I am not Jeni Cerii nor a member of any of the Five Tribes. I come from the southern city of Axis Tyr. My name is Riane."

Mehmmer said, "That cannot be your real name."

"To that, I can only say that Riane is the only name known to me. I have no memory of my early years high in the Djenn Marre; I can recall neither parents nor whether I have any siblings."

An unreadable expression flickered briefly across Mehmmer's face before Othnam introduced himself and his sister.

"If you are Gazi Qhan, then I have not lost my way." Riane smiled. "To answer your question, I seem to have a way with animals. Also, I believe this creature knew I was no threat to you." She looked around at every face, marked Othnam and Mehmmer most closely.

"Assuming you speak truthfully, why have you journeyed so far from Axis Tyr?" Mehmmer said shortly.

"I wish only safe passage to Agachire. I seek an audience with the dzuoko of—"

"We know you not. You are mad if you think we will give safe passage into the heart of our territory." Mehmmer took a menacing step toward Riane, lifting the edge of her sword, but Othnam stayed her.

"My sister is still unsettled by the discovery of the Jeni Cerii spy," he said. "My apologies."

"I thank you," Riane replied, "but none are needed. I do not blame you for your suspicions. It seems you live in a precarious balance."

"Yes. There is continual war between the tribes, raid and counterraid, death and vengeance, which begets more vengeance and more death." Othnam pointed with his chin. "I see you carrying a dagger of an unusual manufacture. Would you allow me to see it?"

"Certainly." Riane handed over the dagger Eleana had given Annon. It was her most prized possession.

Othnam took it and, in one swift motion, put the edge of its blade to her throat. "Are you not afraid that I will cut you open from ear to ear?"

"I am afraid, yes, that your hand will slip and inadvertently draw blood," Riane said. "But as to your meaning, if I were afraid of you, I never would have given you my dagger."

Othnam grunted, reversed the dagger, holding it out to Riane.

Mehmmer again grew agitated. "Othnam, don't—"

"Hold it, if you wish," Riane said to Othnam. "While I am under your protection I can't think why I would need it."

Othnam nodded, seemingly pleased. "We will give you safe passage to Agachire."

Mehmmer rounded on him, her eyes blazing. "Brother, are you mad? You cannot mean what you say, this one came from the same direction as the Jeni Cerii spy we hung scant hours ago."

"I walked all night," Riane said. "I saw no one."

Othnam was about to answer her when a cry from the other side of the camp caught their attention. Paddii, the newborn's father was running toward them, gesticulating. "It is Jeene," he said. His face was a mask of anxiety. "She has stopped breathing. We have tried everything—We don't know—"

"Let me look at her," Riane said at once.

"Take one step . . ." Mehmmer warned.

"Please," Paddii said. "Someone do something. My daughter is dying."

Riane said, "Your guardian has saved your lives many times. It knows I mean you no harm. Why do you doubt its judgment now?"

"What if you have bewitched it with sorcery?" Mehmmer said.

"We have heard of sorcerers, evil beings known as sauromicians," Othnam said. "They blaspheme against the Prophet Jiharre."

"I am no sauromician," Riane said truthfully. "I have given you my weapon. Please let me help."

Othnam hesitated, then nodded. With Paddii jogging at their side, he led Riane to where Paddii's tiny daughter lay blue and unmoving atop her mother's belly. The mother was weeping, chanting prayers through her sobbing.

Riane knelt. She opened the newborn's mouth, stuck her finger down the tiny throat. "The baby has something in her windpipe. If you do not attend to her immediately, she will be dead within minutes."

The mother moaned, and Paddii rolled his eyes.

Mehmmer brushed Riane aside, stuck her own finger into the infant's mouth. "There is an impediment," she said. She hunched over, her face filling with blood an she concentrated. "I cannot . . . It will not come out."

"I can save the child."

"You will not touch her," Mehmmer said shortly.

"Will you deprive the newest member of your tribe the chance to live simply out of anger and suspicion?"

"Mehmmer," Othnam said gently, "as Riane said, our loyal Haqqa trusts her. We will watch her closely. Let her help."

Mehmmer scowled, then she rose, nodded curtly, and stepped aside to make room for Riane. "If the baby dies . . ." She waggled the tip of her sword.

Riane ignored her as best she could. On her knees, she took the little girl up in her arms, pried open her mouth. The cause of the obstruction, she soon discovered, was a tiny undeveloped fruit from the tree that had blown into her open mouth while she slept. It was lodged in the tiny throat.

"It must be true," Mehmmer said fretfully. "The fruit fall at the beginning of winter."

Riane tried to gauge the grave expressions on the others' faces. She was worrying that winter had already begun, and she seemed no closer to finding the Veil of a Thousand Tears. Clearly, these folk did not trust her. What if she could not get to Perrnodt? What if Perrnodt did not know where it was? Calming her mind, she put all her doubts aside and concentrated on the task at hand. "Do either of you have a narrow-bladed weapon?"

Mehmmer reacted as if Riane had struck her. "What would you—?"

Othnam handed over his push-dagger, and his sister glowered at him. "I pray to Jiharre you know what you are doing, stranger."

Riane kept the thumb and forefinger of her left hand at the hinges of the baby's mouth, while she lowered the narrow blade down the infant's throat.

The mother gave a stifled scream, and Mehmmer's prayers rose all the louder.

The point reached the level of the fruit. Riane knew she had only one shot at this. If she missed spearing the thorn, or even overshot the mark by a fraction, the blade had every possibility of piercing the infant's neck right at the spot where the main artery pulsed. But if she did nothing, the newborn was dead anyway.

Saying a silent prayer to Miina to guide her hand, she struck downward with the slight angle she had calculated in her mind. The tip pierced the fruit cleanly, and Riane drew it up and out of the infant's mouth.

Riane handed the push-dagger back to Othnam while she forced air into the baby's starving lungs. When the baby was breathing on her own again, she handed her back to her mother, who was weeping openly with relief and gratitude.

"Thank you," Othnam said.

Riane nodded and stood. "May I have something to drink?"

Someone started to comply, but with a gesture Mehmmer stopped them. She went herself and poured water from a crescent bladder hanging on a wooden peg into a copper cup, gave it to Riane. Briefly, their hands touched, they looked into each other's eyes.

"It would be an honor to give you safe passage to Agachire," Mehmmer said. She took the drained cup from Riane's hand, and said very softly, "Perhaps my anger and suspicion comes from stripping the flesh from too many of our enemy's skulls."

Riane said, "It would, I think, be wise to suggest to the mother that she move from beneath the tree. It was one of its thorns that almost killed the babe."

Mehmmer hesitated a moment. "You could have told her that yourself."

Riane smiled. "Mehmmer, would it not be better if it came from you?"

Mehmmer's dark eyes searched Riane's face. Then she nodded briefly and went to talk to the father about moving the family.

While she did so, Othnam gave Riane a look, and she followed him a little way from the campsite. Haqqa trotted after them, sat panting, leaning against their calves.

"You said something before about needing to find the dzuoko Perrnodt."

"I did not mention her name."

He laughed softly. "You did not have to. There is only one kashiggen in the Korrush: therefore, only one dzuoko."

"Could you make the introduction?"

His odd intense eyes seemed to scour the flesh from her. "Why are you seeking her?"

"I wish to be her student."

Mehmmer returned from her errand, and grunted. "You do not look like imari material."

Of course, she wasn't imari material. She had come to the Korrush to be taught by Perrnodt and to beg her to show her where the *Maasra* was hidden. It would be foolhardy to confess that to tribesmen she barely knew and who were already suspicious of her. "Nevertheless," she said as forthrightly as she could, "this is what I desire above all else."

Othnam nodded gravely. "Then I shall see to it myself. But first, of course, you will have to meet Makktuub."

Makktuub lived in a palace of silence. It was actually three structures in one, like three concentric circles. In the outermost part, the public part, all the quotidian official business of the tribe was transacted. There was a certain bustle, everyone moving at double time across carpet-strewn floors, the hubbub diffused only slightly by the latticework of fragrant lyssomwood screens. Beneath the tent fabric, wood, and stone the palace was composed of a formalism and geometry that spoke of the kapudaan's absolute power.

Beyond, in the middle section, was a smaller space, more comfortable perhaps, but rather less grand than the one surrounding it. Here, Makktuub met once a day to confer with the Djura, his inner council, composed of seven venerable religious judges. With voices no louder than the burble of water in a pond, soothing and controlled, the Djura hammered out laws, interpreted intelligence from the far-flung edges of the chire, sought remedies for problems both fiscal and military. The Djura sometimes met without Makktuub. The judges, long beards shot with grey, reclined on gold-appliquéd pillows, drawing sustenance from low, lacquered tables piled with dried fruits, boiled grains, and spiced sweetmeats.

There was an exquisite screen behind them, incised by the finest hands in Agachire, a lattice of the most fragrant lysommwood that had taken three artisans a year to carve into the shapes of branches, leaves, birds, animals, and fish. From behind this pierced barrier, Makktuub often sat in dappled shadow, listening in complete silence to the earnest arguments and bright ideas when the Djura thought he was away on other business. In this way he not only kept his finger on the pulse of his tribe, but also gained invaluable knowledge of his advisors, for, often enough, they were more apt to reveal their true feelings out of his presence. They, like every member of the Gazi Qhan, feared the ferocious acts that had brought him to power, and kept him firmly in place.

But it was in the center of the palace, a dizzying labyrinth of corridors, garden-courtyards, high-ceilinged chambers, light-strewn baths, and cushion-festooned salons where the kapudaan shed all his many public personas. Here, silence reigned supreme. No one spoke unless expressly directed to by Makktuub himself. The staff that served him by day, the females from his haanjhala who attended him at night, communicated through a form of sign language Makktuub himself had devised.

In the presence of this profound silence many small, subtle pleasures could be identified, isolated, and savored: the breeze rustling the leaves of the perfumed limoniq and lyssomwood trees, the sunlight on the blooms of the magnificent blood-rose bushes, the complex melodies of the golden laerq, hopping from bar to bar within their ornate copper cages, the pattern of clouds as they passed across the kapudaan's field of vision. It was Makktuub's firm and abiding belief that such moments of bliss allowed him to return refreshed and restored to the frantic swirl of motion, opinion, argument, intrigue and, ultimately, decision that was his life. For it was never easy commanding one of the Five Tribes, and most often it was profoundly difficult.

And so, it was to this trifurcated place that Othnam and Mehmmer brought Riane once the party had returned to Agachire. By blazing daylight, the setting was magnificent, so vast it made Riane's eyes water—a low-lying tree-strewn quadrant abutting a somnolent river that wound more or less northwest all the way into the jagged Djenn Marre, whose magnificent purplish silver massifs fulminated like storm clouds against the northern horizon. The peaks here seemed even taller and more forbidding than they were farther west—all save the Great Rift, that mysterious and deadly fissured rent in the mountain range that had swallowed whole the ill-fated V'ornn expeditions to the Unknown Territories. Though Annon had heard many stories about it, Riane had never actually seen the Great Rift before. That massive black slash, tempest-struck and impassable, seemed to draw her like a lodestone. For a moment, the longing to know what was on the other side was like a pain in her chest. Then, her more immediate surroundings seized all her attention.

To begin with, she was taken aback by Agachire itself for, truth be known, it was more of a city than the village of common Axis Tyr gossip. Her first impression was of a violent swirl of colors, a veritable rainbow of finely woven fabrics, all in a pattern of wide diagonal stripes. When she commented upon this, Othnam told her the fineness of the cloth was strictly a matter of utility—the more finely a fabric was woven, the better it would keep out the omnipresent dust of the Korrush, borne upon the incessant, sweeping winds endemic to the steppe. That proved a key piece of information, for, as she looked more closely, she noticed that the city was made up of highly imaginative and elaborate tents. To be sure, there were walls of some kiln-dried material, white-washed to a sheen that blazed beneath the sun, but the majority were of the gaily striped fabrics.

She passed numerous caravans of beasts of burden known as ku-omeshals, which she had first noticed in Mehmmer and Othnam's camp. They were six-legged, short-haired beasts of an orangey dun color about one-third again as large as a male cthauros. Everything about them save for their stunted ears seemed unnaturally elongated: their bulbous snouts, buck-toothed jaws, massive, muscled necks, and ungainly-looking legs. But their oddest feature, as far as Riane was concerned, was their ridged backs. Between these natural separators were crates, barrels, and iron-banded boxes lashed inside thick netting.

"They may have a comical appearance," Othnam had told her, "but they are able to carry at least three times the load of even the most powerful cthauros. Also, they require almost no water and a minimum of food, storing nutrients in their humps, making them ideal for long treks over even the most daunting terrain."

A vast panoply of smells and voices assaulted her. From behind rolling carts, street vendors were hawking everything from freshly baked flat bread to sweet paste candies made of what appeared to be ground seeds and amber honey. Naturally enough, the mingled aromas of spices rose everywhere from open stalls, enormous sacks, and groaning barrels. Cubes of skewered meats and vegetables sizzled on open flames, mounds of perfumed grains studded with nuts and sweetmeats were being ladled into bowls. Voices rose in singsong melodies as the merchants sought to entice passersby with their wares.

A vendor behind a black-and-white stand gestured to them and raised his oddly high voice, "You have the unmistakable look of weary travelers."

He was pouring a thick brown liquid with a most tantalizing aroma from a squat, swoop-necked copper pot into tiny cups without handles. "Come dust off your clothes and slake your thirst with a cup of my ba'du, made from the finest beans." His features were all but lost within the wild beard that climbed his cheeks like dense vines. His thick-fingered hands gestured almost as if he were dancing. "Come, come, now step this way. I go to the far ends of Agachire to gather my beans; I know how travels can take their toll. What better restorative than a cup of strong ba'du?" He placed a cup in Othnam's hand, then one in Mehmmer's. He cocked an eye at Riane and, nodding and grinning, gave her one, as well. "Drink up, my friends. Enjoy the best ba'du in all Agachire!" He snorted and shook his head. "What am I saying? The best in all the Korrush!" His eyes sparked and his hands danced. "If you do not agree, why, then you pay nothing. What could be fairer than that?"

Othnam and Mehmmer sipped at their cups. Riane tried to follow their lead, but she was unused to the small cup, and she swallowed too much. The sweet, strong liquid burned her throat, and she immediately coughed it up.

"Drink more," the vendor urged. "Drink more."

Riane cleared her throat and tried again, this time more circumspectly. After only a couple of sips her head began to buzz.

"Is this alcoholic?" she asked.

The vendor roared. "Oh, no, no. Ba'du has its own tonic—enzymes and such—brought out by exquisitely slow and careful roasting." He gestured toward the skull of the Jeni Cerii Othnam was carrying. "Feed it to that one, and I swear he has a chance to rise and live again!" He laughed and laughed, refilling their cups. "No charge for the refill," he said.

As Othnam was paying him, the merchant said, "Is that skull a trophy of victorious combat?" As Othnam transferred the skull from one arm to the other, the merchant continued. "Come, come, you cannot be ashamed of your prowess." His eyebrows raised. "Unless, of course, this is no trophy at all but the blessed remains of one of your kin."

Othnam shook his head. "It is the skull of a Jeni Cerii who came upon us not a full day's trek from Agachire."

"So close to the city. A deeply disturbing incident, to be sure," the vendor said. "Should this not be reported to the authorities?"

"As it happens we are on our way to see the kapudaan," Mehmmer said. "Your piteous importuning has delayed us."

"Only temporarily, I assure you," the ba'du vendor said. Then he fixed his black eyes upon Riane. "This is your first time in the Korrush, yes?"

Riane nodded.

"And what is your impression?"

"I am struck," she said, "by how complex and alive everything is."

"Indeed?" The vendor raised his eyebrows.

"The majority of the population of Axis Tyr is convinced that you are a primitive lot with nothing of interest to offer."

"And why have you come all the way from Axis Tyr?" the vendor asked. "For centuries the Kundalan have ignored us. As you yourself admit, you consider us savages."

"I have come to see for myself," Riane said. "And to find the dzuoko Perrnodt."

The ba'du vendor scratched his beard ruminatively. "Have you a vital message for her?"

"I seek to become her student," Riane said.

"You are to become an imari, then. Who was your dzuoko in your homeland?"

"I have no training as an imari."

"No one sent you, then?"

"I came entirely on my own. Since I have come all this way I hope I will find her at her kashiggen."

"Oh, there is no doubt of that," the vendor said. "Perrnodt never leaves Mrashruth, not even for a moment."

"Now that seems passing strange."

But the vendor apparently had lost interest in this topic, for he raised the copper pot, and said, "May I inquire, how do you like your first taste of ba'du?"

"I think it needs some getting used to."

"There will be no charge, then." He accepted the empty cup, smiling, his red lips just visible through the thicket of his beard. "I wish you luck on your mission, youngling."

"Thank you," Riane said, as they took their leave.

As she passed through the crowded, market-lined boulevard, flanked by Othnam and Mehmmer, she was given only cursory glances from the passersby. They wore a variety of clothing. Some were clad in the tight leather breeches Mehmmer favored, others in striped robes with sinschals over their head. All, however, wore the curious slipperlike shoes with the curling tips.

"They're exceedingly comfortable and well suited for the terrain," Othnam said with a glance at Riane's high boots when she asked about them.

Riane took time to study the faces of the Gazi Qhan, which were stained and deeply etched by the harsh elements of the steppe. These were fierce, proud faces with clear, intelligent eyes. If they appeared worn as desert stones, there was at least no fat around their necks, no slackness about their jaws.

The kapudaan's palace lay at the heart of Agachire, at the confluence of all the major boulevards, even though those thoroughfares were composed of little more than the tightly packed reddish soil of the Korrush itself. As they came within sight of it, Othnam delivered a warning to Riane to hold her tongue unless directly asked a question. Mehmmer gave her several hand signals to use if she wished to communicate with either of them.

There were no doors within the palace, rather a multitude of gates. These gates were made of fragrant wood, striated stone, cunningly worked copper, even, in one instance, tightly woven vines dotted with a profusion of tiny blushing flowers. Beyond this last gate, Riane glimpsed a bevy of giggling females before she and her group were swept onward, conveyed with the breathless alacrity of palace life by Sawakaq, one of the kapudaan's advisors. Each gate was flanked by a pair of burly armed guards, who regarded her with a scrutiny so absolute it was almost frightening.

And so they passed from the cacophonous outer section where rough justice was meted out by a member of the Djura, to the murmurous middle court where the Djura met. Riane was led past highly polished wooden latticework screens through which she glimpsed a small group of males—she went by too quickly to be certain of their number—who lounged on what looked like pillows of gold. They ate and spoke with a languor that was at odds with the speed with which everyone raced through the palace.

With a sweep of his arm, Sawakaq gestured them onward, into a large tented chamber where they were bade to wait. Sawakaq vanished without so much as offering them a swallow of water. There was no furniture whatsoever, no place to sit or take one's leisure.

They stood alone and silent in the center of this strange and eerie tented hall. Strange and eerie because the striped-fabric walls were lined with row upon row of bare-chested guards, who stood shoulder to shoulder, absolutely immobile, seemingly oblivious to the guests.

For over an hour Riane stood thus with Othnam and Mehmmer who, by their expressions, appeared to think nothing of this odd state of affairs. At no time did Riane notice one of the guards move so much as a muscle. Save for their steady, shallow breathing, they might have been statues most cleverly sculpted into simulacra of the real thing.

Thus Riane was witness to Makktuub's adamantine will long before she arrived at the heart of the palace.

At last, Sawakaq reappeared, looking shining and refreshed. Without a word, he signed for them to follow him out of the hall of guards, through a corridor, and into a tiny entry. He gestured at the plainest of wooden gates through which he himself appeared forbidden to go.

Again, the guards flanking the gates scrutinized Riane, but this time she gazed back at them with a kuomeshal-like placidity.

Through the gates, they found themselves in a formal garden dominated by a tiled hexagonal pond. Amber-and-black fish of several varieties, none of which were familiar to Riane, swam serenely among the floating blue-green pedda-pads. Birds trilled from their perches in thorny fire bushes.

Riane hurried after Othnam and Mehmmer, who were striding through this fantasy land as if it were a hectare of barren featureless steppe. Down a corridor with billowing diagonal-striped walls they went, their thin-soled slipper-shoes making no sound whatsoever on the wooden floor. Riane was instantly aware of the noise, however small, her boots were making. She became more and more self-conscious until, with a sign to Othnam and Mehmmer, she stopped, pulled off her boots, and thenceforth carried them under her arm.

The short corridor gave out onto a chamber strewn with so many cushions Riane could not see the floor. All were studded with gold circles, incised with a curious birdlike sigil. Low graven copper tables were here and there scattered about, and filigreed oil lamps gave off a warm and comforting light. But it was the walls that took her attention. They were made of a matte black fabric, densely woven and completely covered in a blizzard of arcane silver lacquer lettering, all shallow arcs, bright dots, quick slashes, scimitared streaks.

Riane opened her mouth to ask about the writing, but Mehmmer quickly put a finger to her lips, cautioning her to remain silent.

The chamber was deserted, but apparently Mehmmer and Othnam were expecting this, for they stood just inside the doorway, still and waiting. When dealing with the kapudaan, they had informed her on their journey here, strict form, custom, and courtesies were of paramount importance.

Riane felt as if the world had been steeped in silence. She felt waves of it rolling across the chamber, felt the coolness of it against her cheeks, and when, at last, her ears were filled to overflowing with it, Makktuub made his appearance.

He was not tall as Gazi Qhan went, but he was unquestionably imposing. He had a rather large head, and it was squarish, as if he had come into the world unfinished. This lent him the appearance of someone feral, unpredictable, and, therefore, dangerous. His cheeks were very red, as if scrubbed raw by the wind, and he was dressed in indigo from curly-haired head to curly-tipped slipper-shoe. He wore loose trousers and blouse under a floor-length sleeveless outer garment worked in an intricate geometric pattern of jeweled beads and iridescent thread. Around his waist was a wide belt of suede, dyed indigo. A matched pair of ceremonial dirks rode at his hips, the sapphires embedded in the butts flashing like winking eyes. Each of his thick fingers was banded by a jeweled ring.

He smiled when he saw Othnam and Mehmmer, and held out his hands, took one of theirs in each of his.

"Othnam. Mehmmer," he said in a booming voice. "You have not been in my house for many years."

They did not say a word because he had not yet asked them to speak.

His canny black eyes swept across Riane for a moment before returning to the brother and sister. "I understand that you have brought me a gift of the enemy."

Again, not a word in reply was uttered.

Makktuub lifted his left hand and as if from out of nowhere a bare-chested servant appeared with an enormous ceramic jar on his shoulder. As the servant came up, Othnam held out the bleached skull of the Jeni Cerii. As the servant took the jar off his shoulder, Othnam turned the skull upside down. The servant slowly poured the clear liquid into the receptacle of the skull. First, Makktuub drank from the skull, then Othnam and Mehmmer. Riane had the distinct impression that she was witnessing a solemn and important ritual.

"All guests drink from the *hadaqq*." Makktuub nodded, and Othnam turned to Riane, tilting the skull toward her mouth.

Riane's eyes watered as the fiery spiced liquid coursed down her throat.

Makktuub threw his head back and laughed from deep in the pit of his belly. "At least it did not come back up." He slapped Riane hard between her shoulder blades. "That shows me fortitude. I am well pleased." He said this last in the odd high voice of the ba'du vendor.

As Riane stared at him, he produced a thick black mat of hair, which he placed over the lower half of his face. "My cheeks get so chapped from the glue," he said, throwing his head back and laughing again. His voice had returned to its normal booming pitch. "Do not be shocked. I gain immeasurable pleasure and knowledge from my periodic incognito forays into the city." He threw the fake beard to the side, where it was deftly caught by one of his servants.

He made another discreet sign, and another servant took the skull from Othnam, washed and dried it, wiped it down with a fragrant oil, and set it carefully on one of the copper tables.

"Now that the formalities have been dealt with, we will take our leisure." Makktuub gestured to the cushions, but they did not sit until he did.

By lifting a hand, he caused yet another servant to hurry in with a beaten brass tray holding a large bottle and blue glassware laced with gold.

As the servant filled the glasses and served them, Makktuub pointed a ringed finger at the gleaming skull. "I am most eager to learn the details of the circumstances by which this came into your possession." He looked expectantly at them.

Othnam and Mehmmer took turns describing how the Jeni Cerii had been taken by one of their lymmnals as he tried to creep into their encampment.

"And this not a day's march from here?"

"Yes, kapudaan," Mehmmer told him.

His face darkened, and he jumped up with such fury he almost over-turned the brass tray, which the servant whisked away from him with-out, astonishingly, overturning a cup or spilling a drop. "Did you interrogate the spy?"

Othnam nodded. "We did our best, kapudaan."

Mehmmer spread her hands. "But we are not ourselves spies and so—"

"He remained mute," Othnam said.

"No matter." Makktuub whirled, the skirts of his floor-length coat rising upward in a spiral. "His presence in such close proximity to Aga-chire confirms the warning I have been given of renewed aggression by our neighbors," he said in a lowered, almost guarded, tone.

"Is there in truth no hope, kapudaan?" Mehmmer said. "Is there never to be peace among the Five Tribes? Are we to be continually at one another's throats?"

"This time, one way or another, there will be an end," Makktuub said "There is total war brewing, so my spies inform me, and my bones reverberate with the voices of my ancestors, who cry out as one for us to defend our land from those who wish to take it from us."

Of a sudden, he paused and, as if another thought possessed him entirely, he swung back around, plunked himself upon a mound of cushions close to Riane. He stared deep into her eyes. "And now, at this very moment, a stranger appears amongst us. Tell me how this came to be."

Riane opened her mouth, Makktuub's face broke into a thin smile, and she saw out of the corner of her eye Mehmmer put a finger across her lips.

Othnam then told a precise and accurate account of Riane's appear-ance, the curious connection between her and the lymmnal Haqqa, and how their initial suspicion was melted by her offer to help the newborn girlchild. "It is a surety that Jeene would have died without Riane's intervention," he concluded.

Makktuub's tongue pushed out one cheek, then the other, working overtime, as it seemed to do when he was lost in thought. At length, he said, "The ba'du vendor asked you about your impressions of Agachire. Now I ask you about your impressions of my court."

Riane thought but a moment before speaking, for she had already discerned that Makktuub admired forthright answers above all others. "My impression is this, kapudaan. Your court is like an egg. First comes the shell, which is hard and seamless and protects the whole. Inside the shell is the protein, deceptively clear because it is also viscous enough to entrap anything that might somehow penetrate the shell. At the center, protected by all that lies around it, is the yolk, richest in nutrients, the source of both sustenance and perpetuation."

There was a small silence, by which Riane was able to deduce that she had surprised Makktuub, though nothing of this appeared in his face.

He looked for a moment, not at her, but at Mehmmer and Othnam, addressing them when he spoke. "Mayhap you have brought me a prize beyond your knowing."

They did not answer because they intuited that Makktuub required none.

His eyes lowered, taking in, as if for the first time, Riane's feet. His red lips pursed. "What is this? We cannot have you go barefoot in Agachire." Seeing Riane hold up her boots, he shook his head. "Those simply will not do, not in my court." He raised a hand and a servant miraculously appeared with a pair of maroon shoe-slippers in his hand.

The servant knelt on one knee, took Riane's right foot behind the heel, and slipped on the thin-soled shoe, then did the same with the left one. Riane all but gasped. Othnam had been telling the truth: the shoes were exceptionally comfortable.

Makktuub cocked his head. "Do your new shoes please you?"

"Yes, kapudaan, most assuredly they do."

"Good. Then I, too, am pleased."

A clear tone of finality caused Othnam and Mehmmer to stop drinking. A servant took their empty glasses, then they rose and Riane with them.

Makktuub watched his obedient followers beneath hooded eyes. "You did well," he said languidly, "by bringing me evidence of the Jeni Cerii treachery that I can parade before our people. You will be amply rewarded for your loyalty before your feet cross the outer threshold to my court."

As they turned to go, he raised his hand. "Hold. Riane will stay here."

"As you wish, kapudaan," Mehmmer said, bowing. "You have only to tell us when we may return for her."

"As I said, Riane will stay here."

The briefest glance passed between brother and sister. "A thousand pardons, kapudaan," Othnam said, "I have promised to myself convey her to the kashiggen Mrashruth. It is her desire to be introduced to Perrnodt."

The dark expression on Makktuub's face was terrible to behold. "Would you repeat the misstep of your mother and father?"

"No, kapudaan," Othnam said hastily.

"They may obey you," Riane said, "but I will not." Her eyes flashed. "I did not come to the Korrush to become your prisoner."

Makktuub gestured and, at once, the chamber was ringed by armed guards. Two of them stepped behind Othnam and Mehmmer, the sound of metal rang out, and scimitars were placed against their throats.

"If you attempt to defy me, youngling, I will have their throats slit. Here. At once." Marking the defiance in her eyes, he continued: "Heed me well. On the day my father died, I murdered my three brothers so that I would become kapudaan. I have absolutely no abhorrence of blood or killing."

Riane, looking deep into Makktuub's eyes, knew he was telling the truth. She could not allow Othnam and Mehmmer to be killed on her account. She came and stood beside him. He laughed raucously as he cuffed her on the side of her head. Riane felt a sharp, swift pain that took her breath away. Makktuub's face, those of Othnam and Mehmmer began to swim, doubling, tripling.

Then she pitched forward, plunged into the bottomless abyss of unconsciousness.

11

Haan Jhala

You were going to leave, once again vanish into thin air, and this
time for who knows how long." Eleana stands accusingly before
her. "Without a word said to me about what has or has not
passed between us."

"You were sleeping," Riane says calmly, though not calmly enough
to keep her heart from fluttering into her throat. "You need your rest.
I did not want to disturb you."

"Liar! Coward!" There are tears in Eleana's eyes. "You simply didn't
want to answer any questions."

"Questions?" Riane says as they stand just outside the Abbey of
Warm Current on a cool starless night just moments before she will
wrap herself in Nith Sahor's neural-net greatcoat and imagine herself
into the Korrush. "What questions?"

"About why you're suddenly acting like I am contagious."

"You are imagining that."

"Like I have thoroughly disappointed you. What have I done that
you should push me away?"

"You've done nothing—" Riane says. "You see the impossibility of
this."

"I see only an enigma."

A sadness weighing Eleana down that Riane finds unbearable, even
though she knows she must accept it.

"I thought I knew you, but you have shut me out."

For an instant, Riane, torn by the madness of her love, feels the truth
bubbling in her mouth. But she knows Eleana would be horrified if she
ever discovered the truth, and that is something Riane knows she cannot live with. So she says, "Nothing has changed. We are still friends."

"Friends do not leave in the dead of night without so much as a
good-bye."

"If a good-bye is what you want, then you have it."

Eleana slaps Riane hard. Then, her face abruptly pale, she turns and flees down the cracked stone path.

"N'Luuura take it," Riane says under her breath. She catches up with Eleana on the far side of the western temple and, taking her by the elbow, whirls her around. Tears are streaming down Eleana's face.

"Now you do hate me," Eleana cries. "How could I have struck the Dar Sala-at? I beg you, please forgive me."

Her heart breaking, Riane says kindly, "There is no need."

"But I *should* be punished."

"For what?"

Eleana shakes her head, the tears streaming down her face. She breaks free and walks some distance away.

"Go," Eleana says. "It's what you have to do, I understand that."

"Eleana—"

"No, really. I do."

Riane opens her mouth to reply, shakes her head mutely, begins to turn away.

"Why is this happening?" she hears Eleana say, and turns back. "Rekkk is lying near death. Lady Giyan promised to take care of me through the birth of my child. She was helping me through—Miina forgive me for my selfishness, but she is gone now, and in a moment, you will be, too."

So that is it, Riane realizes. Eleana believes she has been abandoned by everyone. For the first time, she experiences Eleana's inner fear at bearing and rearing a child alone, a child who is half-V'ornn.

And then, through the attenuated lens of her dream, she hears Eleana saying, "That dagger you wear, I know it well. I gave it to Annon months ago. How did you acquire it?"

And Riane had to think fast, angered that she had forgotten all about hiding it from Eleana. "Giyan gave it to me on the afternoon when we first met. She said she wanted me to have it. Does that go against your wishes?"

"No, I . . ." Eleana shakes her head wildly as the tears begin to stream from her eyes.

"Oh, do not cry, beloved," Riane says as her heart breaks, "for it is your own Annon who stands before you. Can you not see him inside my eyes?"

But Eleana has already vanished. . . .

Arising from her dream, a heady mix of wish fulfillment and the recent past, Riane found herself facing an intricately worked lattice screen. As she focused, she saw that the highly detailed central carving was of a male and female locked in an intimate and vividly sexual embrace. It was so lifelike, she started.

"Exquisite, isn't it?"

She turned at the soft, melodious voice. A beautiful young woman lounged on the same huge bejeweled cushions upon which she herself lay. Riane licked her lips; her tongue felt swollen and her mouth was unnaturally dry. All at once, she remembered her interview with Makktuub and the way he had drugged her.

As she put a hand to her temple, the beautiful young woman said, "Oh, don't fret, the needle hasn't left a mark." She smiled oddly, almost coldly. "It never does."

Making a quick inventory, Riane saw that Nith Sahor's greatcoat was gone.

"You had better get used to it," the beautiful young woman said with a smirk. "You own nothing now, and you never will again."

Her name, she said, was Tezziq, and she was small, dusky-skinned and dark-haired like Mehmmer, with long, pale, almond-shaped eyes that curled like slipper-tips at their outer corners. With her flat cheekbones and pouty lips she resembled the female on the latticework screen. Her hair, unlike Mehmmer's, fell in a waterfall down her back, the high gloss of oil on it. Near the very end it was gathered in a gold oval fillet incised with the same sigil carved into the stud that pierced her left nostril.

She saw where Riane was looking, and said, "That is the sign of the fulkaan. It is Makktuub's mark." She cocked her head. "Do you even know what a fulkaan is, outlander? No?" There it was again, that odd, cold smile. "It is the mighty bird of legend that sat atop Jiharre's shoulder and served as his personal messenger." She made a moue. "But, oh, I forget, an outlander like you does not know who Jiharre is."

"Jiharre is the Prophet of the Gazi Qhan," Riane said, "is he not?"

"He came to the Korrush from the Djenn Marre, an orphan seeking asylum," Tezziq said.

"And initially met with distrust, just as I have."

Tezziq's lip curled in contempt. "Comparing yourself to the Great

Prophet is an efficient method of getting yourself killed in some quarters."

"I will keep that in mind," Riane said.

A small unpleasant smile played across Tezziq's mouth. "If you would know, he lived in the small town of Im-Thera, where he employed his remarkable skills at negotiation first to settle disputes between individuals, then, as his reputation grew, between families and, eventually between Tribes."

"It was Jiharre who united the Five Tribes, was it not?"

"Through him they were bound by faith rather than by blood."

"But now the Tribes are in a perpetual state of war."

"When Jiharre died, the faith holding us together factionalized. Disputes arose among the holy ones as to the meaning of Jiharre's words." Tezziq's eyes narrowed and became canny again. "But you are not here for a lesson in religious history. Do you have any idea where you are, outlander? No? You are in the kapudaan's haanjhala, the silken womb of his palace, the very organ of his pleasure and desire." Her upper lip curled into her serpent of a smile. "Do you know why you are here? No?" She slowly spread her shapely legs. "Do you see these diaphanous clothes I wear? Through them you can see my flesh and yet you cannot. One moment I appear all but naked, the other it seems I am as demurely clothed as a crone whose once-potent sex has been shriveled by time."

Her long, slender fingers danced in the air. "There are many beautiful females in the haanjhala, and all—all, that is, save you, outlander—have been trained to give Makktuub nights of optimum pleasure."

"You are nothing more than Looorm—whores."

Tezziq's dark eyes flashed. "We are ajjan!" she said proudly. "We live to serve the kapudaan. What he asks of us we accomplish in the most artful ways imaginable. In this we are no different than those who fight for him, scheme for him, plow and sow for him."

"It is shameful what you do."

A baleful expression momentarily disfigured Tezziq's beautiful face. "Another reason to despise you, outlander, you who drags your own shame like stinking offal into our sanctuary."

"If you hate me so much," Riane said, "why are you bothering to talk to me?"

"I have no other choice," Tezziq spat. "As Makktuub's first ajjan I am ordered to train you in the nocturnal arts of most interest to him."

Riane felt her stomach double-clutch. "You don't mean that the ka-pudaan . . . that Makktuub means to . . ."

"In every orifice he can find."

There was no mistaking the pleasure Tezziq gained from Riane's dis-comfort and consternation.

"Whatever he has in mind," Riane said softly, "I will not comply."

"Of course you will." Tezziq, thoroughly enjoying herself now, grasped a hand mirror that lay beside her. "In fact, you have already begun to do so."

She held up the hand mirror in front of Riane's face, and Riane gasped.

"Exactly," Tezziq said acidly.

Riane gingerly touched the gold sigil-stamped stud that now pierced her left nostril.

Tezziq's grinning face appeared around the side of the hand mirror as she leaned forward. "Is the truth beginning to penetrate that thick skull of yours, outlander? Oh, yes. Yes, I think it has." Her long, green-tipped fingernail rimmed the mirror, then tap-tap-tapped its center. "In here is the truth. What do you see reflected, hmm? I will tell you then, outlander. It is your own future."

Divination Street ran on a more or less east–west line through Axis Tyr, and it was as wide as any of the city's boulevards, so that those buildings on its north side were blessed with abundant light even during autumn and winter. This was, primarily, why Marethyn had chosen the location for her atelier. She was an artist, and light was the one com-modity she could not do without.

Early in the morning, when the light was thin and crisp as a wafer, Sornnn watched Marethyn at her easel. The easel was set up in the center of the atelier's light-flooded atrium, a huge and complicated contraption, pigment-spattered and oil-stained, that looked, to him, like the beginning of the construction of a suspension bridge. The notion of a bridge did not come idly to his mind, for it seemed to him that it was the easel, rather than the canvas or the paints, that was the midwife to giving life to Marethyn's ideas. Judging by her expression, it was her home, the place where she dwelled most deeply and completely. It was both a passionate and a compassionate world.

As he watched, Marethyn turned her head a little, the better to assess how the light fell upon her subject. For her part, the old Tuskugggun standing proudly in her crookedness seemed well at ease, despite the carved heartwood cane on which she was obliged to lean. By her right elbow was a small paint-smeared table on which were sitting a cup and pot, both filled with star-rose tea.

"You're certain you're all right?" Marethyn said without breaking her rhythm. "You're sure you're not tired, Tettsie." Tettsie is what she called her grandmother Neyyore. It was a loving name, speaking of giggling fun, damp kisses, and tiny treats, a survivor from Marethyn's childhood.

"I am perfectly wonderful, darling," Tettsie said, trying for a moment to crane her neck to get a look at the painting. "Glowing like a mother with her first child."

This made Marethyn laugh, a sound so pure and rich and full that it pierced Sornnn's hearts clear through. That night they had made love at the warehouse, he had been on the verge of telling her everything. He had felt it rising up inside him, a pithy warmth, not at all an urge to confess, but a desire to share. But, in the end, something had made him pause, an innate caution at the lack of a clear and uncompromised sign that would make him certain he was right about her. Divulging anything of a personal nature did not come easy to him; in this, he was like his father.

"Do you remember," Marethyn said, talking to Tettsie, "when you would take me down to the deep pools in the woods?"

"On the hottest days of summer," Tettsie said, taking a brief sip of her beloved tea, careful to return to her pose. "Your father would have been very cross had he ever found out I had exposed you to the world outside the city walls."

"That didn't stop you."

"No, it certainly didn't," Tettsie said. "In fact, I kept pushing the boundaries."

Her eyes had sunk inward, recalling that moment in glowing detail, the past on occasion more vivid to her than the present. She had a regal head with tissue-thin skin. She had lived long, though it was clear she had not emerged unscathed from time's assault. She seemed to cherish her age, a precious commodity that made her special. And, indeed, she was special, and not only in Marethyn's eyes.

Marethyn switched brushes and laid on the new pigment thickly with the side of the brush, a brief deft stroke, learned technique refined by instinct. "No one could ever make you flinch, Tettsie. You were not like Mother."

"Do you remember the cthauros holding pen I used to take you to?" Tettsie was not comfortable talking about her daughter.

Marethyn smiled. "Of course. We went practically every week. You taught me how to ride. I felt so wickedly delicious, and I thought you looked so amazing sitting with your back straight, your head held high, galloping across the countryside."

"Form is most important in riding, yes, darling? That is why it is a metaphor for life." Tettsie took a another sip, quick and dainty, of her star-rose tea, and this time Marethyn noted the increased tremor in her hand. "But I am thinking of one time. It was late in the year, just around this time, I believe, yes." The past was so close she could feel it brush up against her shoulder. "The scent of baled glennan and fertilizer, the cthauros' slow wheezy exhalations." She took a deep breath, let it slowly out. "The weather was so filthy we turned around and went back."

"I remember."

"That was the first time you held an ion pistol."

"I felt *really* wicked. I felt as if when I was with you I was leading another life."

Tettsie laughed, a little girl's laugh, much as Marethyn's, lovely and musical. "Oh, my dear, you made *such* a fuss that day!"

"I hit the qwawd's-eye." Marethyn stopped painting for a moment. "Three times."

"That was me. You didn't hit it until your third lesson."

"Oh yes. But after that I never missed."

"You were a natural sharpshooter. It was your artist's eye for nuance and detail." Tettsie pursed her lips. "Do you remember that Khagggun who used to come to the stables now and again? It was his ion pistol. Our little secret."

"Good thing, too." Marethyn washed her brush free of green, dipped it into a pool of indigo. "Mother would have confined me to the hingatta forever."

"I made sure she knew nothing about it!"

"That is just the way she still likes things, isn't it? When I complained to her about Kurgan keeping Terrettt away from the Rescendance she professed perfect ignorance."

At the mention of Terrettt's name, Tettsie's face darkened. "Sadly, your mother is content in her ignorance," she said in an uncharacteristic bout of candor. "Well, she is in all ways a conventional Tuskugggun."

"My father saw to that."

Tettsie's eyes rose briefly to meet Sornnn's, flashing him an enigmatic look. "He did what all V'ornn males do."

Marethyn's brush shot across the canvas.

Tettsie said mildly, "When can I see the painting?"

"We're almost finished for today. Don't you want to sit down?"

"No. I do not. This is a standing portrait, not a sitting one. This was my wish."

The many lines radiating out to the corners of her face, furrowed now by the freshet of anger the conversation had caused made her seem like a temple to the dead god Enlil, crumbling and empty but still potent enough to disturb long-forgotten childhood memories.

Sornnn had no good memories of his own mother. Like all V'ornn families, his was dominated by the males, the more so because his mother was often missing from the hingatta where she was supposed to have raised him. Wives of Great Caste V'ornn lived their lives in hingatta after they had given birth. The hingatta were communal residences, where groups of Tuskugggun fulfilled their duties raising their children and, if they were lucky and did not need much sleep, plied their arts—weaving, painting, sculpting, composing music, forging armor, and the like—in the small hours after their children were safely tucked in bed. With his mother gone so often he would content himself with playing with the Phareseian colorsphere she had given him for his sixth birthday. It was a small, hard, cool ball, he remembered, containing three gases found on Phareseius Prime. The gases were incompatible and therefore shifted constantly inside the sphere in an effort to get away from each other. The resulting chemical reaction caused endlessly varied displays of violent color. And, if you held it long enough, you felt a rhythmic pulsing not unlike the beating of V'ornn hearts. He hadn't thought about the colorsphere in many years. What had become of it? he wondered. Gone, doubtless, along with all his other childhood toys.

But he had loved that toy until, one day, something quite inexplicable happened. His mother returned to the hingatta, as abruptly as she had left, and she had changed. She exhibited a distinct aloofness toward him, and he was sure he had disappointed her in some way that she could never forgive. And no matter what he did that coldness just grew worse, until he gave up and she became a stranger in his eyes. In direct consequence, he cleaved ever more closely to his father, eager to absorb everything that Hadinnn SaTrryn taught him.

When Hadinnn had died some months ago, his mother came to see him. She should not have. She was not wearing indigo, the color of mourning, and she did not stay long. Outside, Sornnn had spied a stylish two-seat hoverpod with a tall, slim, handsome Bashkir behind the controls. This individual sat slouched slightly down, his bootheels on the polished titanium trim, arms crossed easily over his chest.

Sornnn should have been calm, but he was not. The lessons he had learned in the Korrush momentarily deserted him. His father, the one V'ornn he idolized, was suddenly, shockingly, tragically dead, and here came his mother, without an ounce of respect, in the company of another V'ornn. He couldn't even remember what she said to him because he had exploded, hitting her so hard across the face that she had cried out.

"Just like him," she had said with her hand to her stinging cheek. "Well. I suppose I should not be surprised." There was no anger in her eyes, only a distant sadness just beyond her reach.

The tall, slim, handsome Bashkir had come running in response to her cry, at once advancing on Sornnn but, surprisingly, Sornnn's mother had gripped him hard before he could utter the irrevocable challenge, spinning him around, guiding him out of the residence without a backward glance. The ion hum of their hoverpod had slashed through the thick mourning silence.

"What would I have done without you?" Marethyn was saying now to her grandmother.

"You would have found a way to survive," Tettsie said matter-of-factly. "Just as I did."

Marethyn washed the wide fan-head brush she had been using. The smell of the paints was very strong. "How *did* you survive, Tettsie? How is it Grandfather never treated you like my father did my mother?"

"It wasn't for lack of trying, my darling. No, indeed. But I fought back in the only manner he would understand. I became a font of knowledge about his rivals. I became an invaluable ally."

Marethyn looked up, startled. "So there was no love—?"

"Love is not possible without respect." Tettsie shrugged. "You, of all people, should know that."

Marethyn could not help but steal a glance at Sornnn, who stood still and silent and grave. "But you said you became his ally." From the first, he had been at ease with Tettsie, and this had made Marethyn very happy.

"True enough. But I think your grandfather soon came to despise what I did because when I came to him . . . what I proposed . . . To him it was a kind of coercion that Tuskugggun ought not to know anything about. I not only knew about it, I was singularly proficient in it. I gained in power, yes, but I became anathema to him."

"Why didn't you stop?"

"It was already too late. For me. I could not go back to the way I had been, the way all the Tuskugggun around me lived. Ground down by their mates. I found that reduced form of life unacceptable."

"But you loved Grandfather!" Marethyn cried. "You told me so yourself."

"Well, yes." A rueful smile played around Tettsie's mouth. "But the loss of that love . . . It was the price I paid for living life the way it *should* be lived."

Marethyn came around the side of the painting. "What about Grandfather?"

"What about him?"

"Didn't he love you?"

"Once. So he said. But male V'ornn—" Tettsie broke off, and with another quick glance at Sornnn, smiled. "Let us now speak of other, less weighty matters."

"No," Marethyn said stubbornly. "I want to know what you meant to say."

"All right, if you wish it." Tettsie's fingers gripped her cane more tightly. "I am of the opinion that V'ornn males are incapable of romantic love. Most have no conception of what it is. The ones, like your grandfather, who claim they do"—she shrugged—"are simply deluding themselves."

Marethyn turned to Sornnn. "And what is your opinion?"

He held up his hands. "This is strictly a family matter."

Tettsie said very calmly, "A family into which you intend to enter, if my intuition is right."

"Grandmother!" Marethyn cried in shock.

Tettsie's eyes were riveted on him. "Tell me if I am wrong, Sornnn SaTrryn."

"I see that I am going to be dragged into this whether I like it or not," he said in an attempt to make a joke of it.

Her eyes never left his. "For me this is a matter of the utmost import."

"Very well, then."

Marethyn liked that he respected Tettsie's wishes as she herself did.

He nodded. "It seems to me that Tuskugggun are just as incapable of love as males."

"I do hope you have a specific example in mind," Tettsie said dryly.

"As it happens, I do. My own mother. She shirked her duty at the hingatta; she was cold and unfeeling. I think she despised me, possibly because I was a male and not a female with whom she could share her feelings."

"*As it happens.*" Tettsie repeated the phrase. "*As it happens*, I know your mother, Sornnn SaTrryn. We have been friends for many years now."

"What?"

"Oh yes, it's true. It was to me she came when your father beat her."

"Why did you—What are you saying?" Sornnn's head was spinning. "My father would never—"

"Why do you think she was absent from the hingatta so often?" Tettsie limped toward him. "She was in hospital, and then, when she was released, she stayed with me because she did not want you to see the bruises, did not want you asking questions, did not want you to know the truth about how your father was with her."

Sornnn was reeling. "My father was a good V'ornn." His throat was so tight he could scarcely force the words out.

"We both know he *was* a good V'ornn in many ways," Tettsie said with a kind of gentle pity. "But he was many things. My intent is not to denounce or demean him, it is simply to show you the entire individual."

"I do not understand any of this," he said almost wildly.

Tettsie put a surprisingly strong hand on him. "Whatever you thought of your father, however he was with you, it wasn't how he was with *her*."

And then he remembered what his mother had said to him that horrible day of his father's death just after he had struck her. *Just like him. Well. I suppose I should not be surprised.*

Sornnn felt sick to his stomachs. "But he couldn't possibly . . . I mean, how *could* he?"

"Because he was paranoid and fearful and jealous." She looked deep into his eyes. "Do you understand me, Sornnn SaTrryn?"

And then, at last, he remembered what it was his mother had said to him the moment before he had struck her: *I'm not here because of him. I came to see you.* So many fragments of memories swirling around his mind. He shook his head, confused and unnerved.

"Let me then ask you a simple question." Tettsie smelled faintly of flowers and powder, a confluence of scents he recalled from his childhood, from the hingatta when his mother was at his side. "This life— the life you have chosen for yourself—is it possible that it could make you paranoid and fearful and jealous?"

"I am not that sort of V'ornn."

"And yet you do not live your life entirely in the open. I am speaking now of your relationship with Marethyn." She paused a moment. "I say this because I am protective of my granddaughter. Extremely protective."

He nodded, swallowing hard. He knew this, of course, knew this must be coming.

"If you continue in your pursuit of her, be mindful of her, not simply of yourself. Be mindful of what you will be taking her away from. Be most especially mindful of what she will be left with if you forsake her."

"I would never—"

"I charge you with this, Sornnn SaTrryn!"

She said this so fiercely that he nodded like a little boy, and said, "Yes, of course, I—"

Then something outside his ken came into her eyes, and she said, most softly, "I believe I would like to sit down now."

Of a sudden, her eyes rolled up and she staggered. Her cane skidded, then cracked in two and she fell away from him, fell heavily and awkwardly against the easel, capsizing it so that she and it crashed to the floor together. The painting spun on its corner like a mobile, muted colors and masterly brushstrokes blurred, then slowly came to rest in a thick stripe of shadow. Sornnn knelt beside her, the tips of his fingers cool against her pale, dry, crepey skin. He was mindful of Marethyn screaming her grandmother's name, he was mindful of searching for Tettsie's nonexistent pulse, he was mindful of his hearts swelling as he held grandmother and granddaughter both while Marethyn, a little girl once more, wailed in shock and grief.

Riane had slept through the night and the whole of the following day. When she awoke, the first thing Tezziq taught her was how to eat properly in the Gazi Qhan fashion. Of course, she waited until the platters of food were set down before them. Gauging the extreme hunger in Riane's expression, Tezziq invited her to dig in.

"There are no utensils," Riane pointed out.

"We do not use utensils."

Riane shrugged. She was so famished her stomach had turned painful. Eagerly, she reached toward the platters, only to receive a stinging slap on her hands. She started. One eye on the guards lining the walls, she restrained herself.

"Start again," Tezziq said coldly, without so much as a word of explanation.

When Riane again reached for the food, Tezziq slapped her, harder this time. Despite herself, Riane cocked her arm in retaliation, but in the blink of an eye two guards had scimitar-shaped dirks at her throat.

Riane lowered her hand, and Tezziq nodded silently to the guards, who reluctantly retreated to their former positions. They seemed disappointed not to have been able to draw blood.

"Now," Tezziq ordered. "Again."

The third time Riane picked up the food, Tezziq slapped her so hard across the face it flew out of her hands.

Riane's eyes blazed. "You command me to eat, then punish me for it," she cried. "What do you want from me?"

"Will you weep now, outlander, at the injustice of it all?" Tezziq sneered. "Forget justice. You are in the Korrush now. You will learn to be civilized or be struck down like a rabid slingbok." Her chin jutted out. "Now eat."

Riane sat with her hands folded in her lap.

"Are you deaf?" Tezziq shouted, her face flushing. "Eat when I tell you to eat!"

Riane sat immobile in the ringing silence.

Tezziq nodded. "Good. It appears that you may be trainable after all." She lifted an arm. "Even when we are in the wild we wash the dust from our hands before we eat."

Riane saw a large woven basket in which were two wet towels. She took one, washing her hands with it.

"You may eat," Tezziq said.

Riane reached for the food and had her hands slapped so hard it turned their backs ruddy. She wiped the defiance off her face, silently commanded herself to sit placidly. "What am I doing wrong?" she asked.

"Impudent outlander." Tezziq slapped her across the face.

Riane took a breath. "Please, Tezziq, teach me the proper way to eat."

The serpent smile crawled across Tezziq's lips, but it did not reach her eyes which continued to regard Riane with their implacable stare. "We eat with first two fingers and thumb of one hand, those fingers only. Do you understand, outlander?"

"Yes."

Tezziq slapped her across the face.

"Yes, Tezziq."

"Now eat, as a Gazi Qhan eats."

Keeping one hand in her lap, Riane reached out with two fingers and her thumb for a morsel of food, put it in her mouth. No punishment was forthcoming.

She reached for another and promptly got her hand slapped. She said nothing, but sat unmoving, both hands in her lap, staring at Tezziq, careful to keep her expression neutral.

"Chew your food and swallow completely before reaching for more," Tezziq said. "It is both polite and allows you to savor completely the flavor of each dish. This behavior honors your host and yourself."

Riane chewed her food and tried not to enjoy it. But by the time she had taken her third mouthful she knew that Tezziq was right. By sitting quietly and chewing each tender morsel she was able to concentrate fully on its flavor, texture, and aroma. It made for an uncommonly serene and enjoyable meal.

When she had eaten her fill, Tezziq pointed her chin toward the large woven basket. This time Riane needed no explanation. She wiped her right hand clean with the remaining towel.

"Well, outlander," Tezziq said, rising, "perhaps there is hope for you yet."

It did not take Riane long to feel lost in the maze of the innermost palace as she followed Tezziq from one tented chamber to another. At length, they came to a small antechamber, unadorned save for the ubiquitous guards.

"Stand just there," Tezziq ordered. She walked around Riane, sniffing. "These robes are ripe besides being ugly. Remove them."

As Riane glanced uncertainly at the guards, Tezziq's laughter trilled through the tent. "Pay them no heed," she said. "Look!" She went over to one and bared her breasts. Holding them in her hands, she rubbed them against his massive chest. The guard's expression did not change. Tezziq reached between his legs, massaging him.

"You see? Nothing." She turned to regard Riane over her shoulder. "All the guards of the inner court are *saddda*; they have been altered. They are without a sex organ." Mistaking the look on Riane's face, she added, "Do you think Makktuub would otherwise trust them among us? The temptation would be too great."

The sight of Tezziq's naked breasts, her lascivious behavior had had their predictable effect on Annon's powerful male psyche. Riane's heartbeat quickened, and she could feel all the telltale signs of arousal on her flesh.

Tezziq returned to Riane and flicked her hand. "Enough talk. Disrobe."

Riane stood immobile for a moment. She was terrified that Tezziq would recognize her erotic excitement and become suspicious.

"Do as you are told, or I will do it for you!" Tezziq barked.

Riane took off her clothes. She did not even look at the guards, so acutely aware of Tezziq's scrutiny was she.

"Well, well," Tezziq said thoughtfully, "what a beauty you are." She circled around and around. "Your legs are powerful, as are your shoulders. Your buttocks are strong. And your breasts—magnificent! The nipples so hard!"

Riane swallowed hard, her face on fire.

"Luck is with you. You have the kind of body Makktuub covets."

Something in her voice caused Riane to forget her extreme discomfort. Was it envy she heard, curling like a bile-worm inside an overripe clemett?

"Yes, he will be all too eager to welcome you to his bedchamber."

No, Riane thought. It was sadness. And then, looking into Tezziq's eyes, she thought she understood why. For the first time, she felt something other than hostility toward this beautiful young female. Wasn't she as much a prisoner of the haanjhala as Riane was? Riane felt her defiance tempered, her rage dissolved.

"I would not go," she said softly, "had I the choice."

"Then you are a fool," Tezziq said shortly. "For sex is a kind of power." She came and stood close to Riane. "The only kind you and I have."

"And what has this power availed you?"

"I am Makktuub's first ajjan, his favorite. I am most blessed he has chosen me to pleasure him above all other ajjan."

"And when his fancy is taken by another?"

Tezziq averted her eyes. "That is none of your concern."

"You—your entire being is defined by him. If this is so, when he finds another, you are annihilated."

Tezziq whirled, slapping Riane across the face.

"Striking me will not make it less so."

Now she struck Riane with her balled fists until Riane grabbed her wrists, held her immobile. The guards at once advanced, but with a sharp command, Tezziq froze them in their tracks. They watched the two girls with jaundiced eyes, thinking their unknowable *saddda* thoughts.

Riane and Tezziq, locked together, strength against strength, will against will, stared nakedly at each other until one lone tear emerged from Tezziq's eye and began to roll down her cheek. With a stifled cry, she wrenched herself free and turned her back on Riane and the guards alike.

Riane took a step toward her. "Despite what you may think, I do not covet him nor the kind of power you believe his pleasure brings," she whispered to Tezziq's back. "For males like him are never truly sated no matter how drunk they become on your wiles. Their sights are always set on what lies unknown just beyond their fingertips." She took another step closer. "You know this well, Tezziq. You know this is why he wants me. And, in truth, what power could possibly lie in that?"

From the fastness of the Abbey of Warm Current, Eleana leaned against cool stone blocks, looking out at columns of smoke rising from the foothills of the Djenn Marre. So absorbed was she in her own thoughts that she did not stir when the tall armored figure came up behind her.

"You should be resting," Rekkk Hacilar said.

"How can I rest?" She pointed to the smoke, rich and dark, which seemed to hang motionless, blotting out the mountains behind it. "You see what is happening? The Khagggun have found Resistance cells and are burning our warriors to ash."

Rekkk still moved gingerly. His wound, though all but fully healed outwardly, still pained him now and again, deep inside. And yet, it was healing at an astonishing rate. He put this down to the changes Nith Sahor had made in him when he had implanted the special okummmon on the inside of his left wrist.

Eleana looked so melancholy, his heart ached for her. "Where is Thigpen?" he asked, looking around.

"Gone," she said. "She was called back to the Ice Caves on urgent business, she told me."

"That sounds mysterious."

"Ominous, more like."

He sighed as he sat beside her. "I cannot believe I am saying this, but I miss her."

Eleana nodded. "I do, too." But he could see her eyes were fixed on the lazy columns of smoke hovering balefully over the mountainside. She shook her head. "When Wennn Stogggul had Eleusis Ashera murdered and became regent, I thought it could not get worse for us." She cupped a hand beneath her distended belly. "I was wrong. Under Kurgan Stogggul and Olnnn Rydddlin, the Khagggun have stepped up their patrols, their killing sorties. It is like the first days of the invasion. They are brutal, relentless. I should be there with my compatriots."

"To meet your death?"

"I'd like to think I'd make a difference," she said bitterly. "Instead, I hide away here in this sanctuary."

"Have you so quickly forgotten that the Star-Admiral himself searches high and low for us?"

"I forget nothing," she said shortly. The columns of smoke were lightening now as a slight wind broke across the forested hilltops. "But I feel so utterly useless."

"Come away from this." He touched her shoulder. "It does no good to rend your heart so."

She allowed him to turn her around. "What shall we do, then, Rekkk?"

"You will do nothing at all. You must think of the baby now. You cannot put him in jeopardy."

"That is no answer, at least not for me." She shook her head. "If I sit idle much longer, I shall go out of my mind." She took his hand, squeezed it. "Lady Giyan has been captured, the Dar Sala-at is in the Korrush, perhaps already in danger, Thigpen is on her mysterious mission, and here we are, sitting around mourning lost friends." The smile she offered was bleak and despairing. "I am already fighting the nesting instinct inside me."

He regarded her levelly. "That nesting instinct, perhaps it shouldn't be trifled with."

"I would die of shame if I could no longer contribute."

Then, without warning, she burst into tears. He took her by the elbow and led her down the abbey paths into the central atrium of the largest of the temples. Clemett trees rose at the four corners, and bloodrose bushes, their leaves still green and glossy, massed along the perimeter, in desperate need of pruning. The garwood maze in the center was barely distinguishable, a tangled mass with the odd gap here and there.

"A sad end, isn't it?" Eleana wiped her eyes. And then she turned to him, "I fought with Riane just before she left."

"About what?"

"Now that you ask, I do not know exactly." She drew a stray lock of hair off her forehead. "You see, I was angry that she going away, that she was abandoning me."

"Don't be so hard on yourself. With the baby coming—"

She looked up into his face. "But now, I think maybe I was angry about something else entirely."

"What, exactly?"

"Maybe it's . . . I mean, when I'm near her, there's something that goes right through me . . . an electric . . . a premonition . . ."

"That's hardly surprising. She is the Dar Sala-at, after all."

Eleana nodded her head. "Of course. She is. But she is also Riane and she's carrying the dagger I gave to Annon and when I am with her he seems so close . . . Oh, it's suddenly all so confusing!"

Rekkk sighed. "Clearly you're overwrought. You need to rest."

He led her over to a bench, where they sat for a time, Eleana idly scraping moss off the clawed stone feet with the heel of her boot. The wind scouring the bare-branched trees sounded to her like a death rattle. In her mind's eye, she saw Riane's face just after she had struck her, a sudden explosion of emotion and then, almost immediately, a door slamming shut. She closed her eyes against the image, saw instead the charred and twisted bodies of her former compatriots with only the columns of black oily smoke to mark their passing. Her eyes burned with sudden tears, and she began again to sob.

Rekkk put an arm around her, and said, "How beautiful this time of day. How the low sunlight streaks the grey stone with gold." He sighed. "It isn't hopeless, you know. You can't allow yourself to think that."

"But that's exactly what I *do* think!" she cried. "The Resistance is being methodically wiped out. You only have to look to the north to see the evidence."

Then she raised her head at the sound of beating wings, and she saw the Teyj with its magnificent red-blue-green plumage arise from the dense thicket of garwood with something in its beak. It alighted on the bench and cocked its head, its glossy eyes regarding them both. Then it ducked its head and dropped into her lap a small oval object.

"It looks like a seedpod," she said, turning it over. "But it's metallic."

"Tertium and germanium," Rekkk said.

She blinked away her tears. "V'ornnish."

He nodded. "It's called a duscaant. It's a Khaggggun recording device. A sophisticated instrument of espionage."

She glanced at the Teyj, but Rekkk shook his head.

He plucked it from her hand. "Thigpen and Riane found it in the Library."

"But that's impossible," Eleana said. "The Library was sealed with an

Osoru spell before the V'ornn entered the abbey complex."

"So it only could have been placed in there *before* the V'ornn arrived."

Her mouth opened. "A Kundalan spy?"

"Ramahan. This is what Thigpen related to me just before she left."

"A Ramahan working with the V'ornn." Eleana shuddered. "But what would make a priestess of Miina betray her own kind?"

"Here is a better question to ask. How is it that the Khagggun are having so much success searching out and destroying Resistance cells in this quadrant of the northern continent?"

"What do you mean?"

"There was a time when I was assigned to the western quadrant, beyond the Borobodur forest. When I linked in with the other Pack-Commanders there I discovered that they were far less successful at rooting out Resistance cells than were the packs here, along the Land of Sudden Lakes corridor."

"The Ramahan spy?"

He nodded. "It is a logical assumption. The intelligence has to come from somewhere."

All Eleana's formidable faculties were fully engaged now, her lethargy and despair forgotten. "When you were a Khagggun Pack-Commander where did your information come from?"

"From the office of Line-General Lokck Werrrent." He cocked his head. "What are you thinking?"

"I was wondering who inside Werrrent's office is the control for the Ramahan spy."

Rekkk held up the duscaant. "Perhaps this will give us a clue."

"Do you know how to activate it?"

The Teyj fluttered its top wings and began to sing.

"No," Rekkk said, "but I believe the Teyj does."

Steam rose almost straight up, a column as ephemeral as the city of tents that surrounded it. And yet it possessed an unmistakable strength. The steam was pungent with dried limoniq leaves, and this powerful scent gave the column a weight like alabaster.

It was raining a little when Tezziq led Riane into the bathtent; the center of the steaming pool, where the tent was open to the elements,

was puckered with it. It beat upon Riane's head as, naked, she luxuri-
ated in the melting heat.

"Look, look here," Tezziq said, taking one of Riane's hands in her
own. "Already the dust is under your nails. That is one reason we paint
them."

Tezziq had a beautiful body, small, sleek, gently muscled, virtually
flawless. Her dusky skin shone with natural oils. Her breasts hung like
limoniq ready to be plucked. The patch between her legs was tiny, dark
as shadowed twilight. Riane was all at once reminded of the baths at
the Abbey of Floating White, of the long months it took her to become
accustomed to her new female body, of having it scrutinized by other
females, of the confusion of continuing to feel Annon's powerful male
pleasure in the naked female form, of dealing with her reawakening
desire. Unlike the Ramahan acolytes of the abbey with whom Riane
had bathed, Tezziq knew what she possessed and used it accordingly.
Every movement, every gesture no matter how small or trivial was in
the service of her body. Either she had been born a sexual creature or
in the haanjhala had been trained to be one. Her stiff nipples scraped
against Riane's back as she ran a soft-bristled brush down Riane's spine.
Riane could not help but shiver.

Doubtless, Tezziq marked this, for she pressed her breasts hard
against Riane's back as she leaned in and whispered in her ear, "*Wa
tarabibi*. That is a special phrase used only among intimates. It means
'my beloved.' " Her tongue flicked out, running the shell of Riane's ear.
"I may spread my thighs for the kapudaan whenever it pleases him, but
as for myself my taste runs to somewhat more . . . delicate flesh." Her
small white teeth captured Riane's earlobe for just an instant, taking
the merest nip before she resumed her scouring.

Steam continued to rise about them, and the gentle rain obscured
all behind an hallucinatory wall. The heat, the pungent aroma of the
limoniq leaves, the cleansing with its distinctly erotic overtones made
Riane drowsy and excited all at once. She used her fright and her intense desire to be free to combat these feelings. Except it wasn't as
simple as that. Much to her chagrin, she found herself mired in the
frustration and guilt that was a direct result of her oblique relationship
with Eleana. Nothing she felt or yearned for could ever be shared with
the female she loved best and most deeply. Had she been asked, she

would have denied most vociferously having any intention of straying from that love. And yet, a love as wild and strong as hers, cruelly thwarted, will inevitably seek an outlet elsewhere, making her vulnerable to temptation. Her longing for Eleana had only become more acute with distance. Eleana she could not have, but the longing remained, festering like a wound that resists conventional treatment. A temporary balm might be just that, might even be perceived to contain an element of danger, and yet in certain circumstances it seemed preferable to continuing the pain unabated.

She leaned her head back onto Tezziq's bare shoulder. "Tell me about Makktuub," she said. "What does he whisper to you after a night of lovemaking?"

The slightest ripple of tension informed Tezziq's body. "A spy would wish to know these things, would she not?"

Riane took Tezziq's free hand and placed it just beneath her breast. "So would a novice ajjan who must be aware of all the things that will please her new lover."

"Which are you?" Tezziq trembled a little. "Spy or novice ajjan?"

Riane's hand covered Tezziq's, moved it slightly so that it cupped the lower half of her breast. She heard Tezziq's tiny indrawn breath in her ear and thought she had her.

Slowly, Tezziq's hand squeezed inward until it was Riane who gasped. "Do not mistake me for a fool, outlander," Tezziq hissed. "I am not so easily seduced. You have shown me your defiance and your contempt." She had dropped the brush, and she reached roughly between Riane's thighs. "I could take you with the brutal finality of a male taking a female. I could—"

But Riane had whipped around, surprising her, pulling her tight, stroking her as gently as if Tezziq was being fanned by a gimnopede's wings, for she sensed in this girl a burning need to be gentled as her master, the kapudaan, would never think to do. Did she, as well, acknowledge her own need to be held, gentled, wanted?

"If I showed defiance," she whispered, "it was because I was frightened. If I showed contempt, it was in defense of your clear hatred of me." Light lay along the water, glimmering, reflecting their intermingled bodies so that it was impossible to tell where one left off and the other began. Tezziq's flesh rose in a field of tiny bumps as Riane continued to stroke her in long, sinuous passes. "But as you see, that can change in the single beat of a heart." Across the sheened hills, the shadowed valleys, her fingertips traced every curve and quivering nuance of Tezziq's body. "In truth, I have no taste at all for males. The savagery they take to bed sickens me wholly."

Tezziq's eyes fluttered closed, and when she opened them the irises had darkened somewhat. "Whatever you may be," she said huskily, "you are surpassingly clever."

She took Riane's head between her hands and hungrily kissed her.

When she was finished, her eyes locked with Riane's. "Whatever you are, it may be I have been waiting for you." Her tongue came out in a brief flick as Riane's fingers passed between her thighs. She grabbed Riane's wrist and held it tight. "But mark me, outlander. If you lie to me, if you play me false even once, I swear on the holy words of the Prophet I will carve out your heart and feed it to you."

Kurgan began to notice that when Nith Batoxxx was at the regent's palace he went out of his way to avoid mirrors.

He was in his private quarters, affixing his hold-signature to a stultifying pile of official documents when he heard the whisper of a voice. His first thought was to summon his Haaarkyut guard. But some deep-seated instinct made him hesitate. He sat very still for a moment. From the balcony outside came the shrill cry of a blackcrow. After a moment's silence the voice began again. He put aside his dreary work and cocked an ear, listening more closely. The voice was familiar and yet it was not. Its tone danced on the periphery of his memory, tantalizing him. He silently pushed back his chair and rose.

He walked this way and that about the chamber until he had located the direction of the voice. Without making a sound, he moved to an open doorway. There he waited a moment, listening intently. The voice was so low he still could not make out individual words. He moved slightly, insinuating himself into the open doorway. Luckily, it was late in the day. The windows in his chamber faced east, and, thus, he cast no shadow into the chamber from which the voice was emanating. He moved again, and now he could hear more clearly. Unfortunately, he was listening to a language wholly unfamiliar to him.

Filled now with an unbearable curiosity, he craned his neck. Peering around the doorframe, he spied Nith Batoxxx. The Gyrgon was standing in front of a small mirror—one of the very few in the residence.

Improbable as it might seem, it appeared as if he was speaking into the mirror. In a language other than V'ornn. An unknown language, in fact. Kurgan stared. Judging by the periodic pauses, it appeared to him as if Nith Batoxxx were having a conversation with the mirror. So he *was* mad, after all!

Or was there another explanation?

He remembered when he himself had been in this room. Nith Batoxxx had come to the side doorway, the one directly opposite where he was now standing, and instead of coming into the chamber, had beckoned for Kurgan to come to him in the adjacent room. Kurgan still felt the quick flush of anger he had felt at the time. Then there was the time that he and the Gyrgon had been walking into the Great Hall. Kurgan had ordered an octagonal mirror for the chamber in which he housed his small-arms collection, and some V'ornn had left it propped against the hallway wall. Instead of walking past it, the Gyrgon had abruptly excused himself, appearing in the Great Hall, through a different door, sometime later. At the time, Kurgan had not connected Nith Batoxxx's behavior with the mirror, but now he had to wonder.

He had to wonder whom the Gyrgon was talking to in that mirror. Perhaps these mirrors were a new form of Gyrgon spying device. But then why would Nith Batoxxx seek to avoid them?

Determined to get an answer to his questions, he pulled himself back from the doorway, went through the chamber he had been in and out into the hallway. There was a doorway to the adjacent room that faced the mirror. When he came upon it, it was closed. He grasped the knob and, taking a deep breath, carefully opened it a crack.

He saw a thin wedge of the room, the Gyrgon's shoulder. He opened the door wider until the edge of the mirror came into view. He moved his head so that he could see Nith Batoxxx's reflection in the mirror, and it was all he could do not to scream.

It was Tezziq who dismissed the serving girls; she had decided to plait Riane's hair herself. It was a long, slow, languorous dance, even, in a way, a loving one the way Tezziq choreographed it. Unseen, clasped in Riane's fist, was the infinity-blade wand that Minnum had affixed to the nape of her neck.

They reclined on silken cushions, while she told Riane all about the kapudaan. "Makktuub is an exceedingly proud male," she said softly.

"He comes from a long line of kapudaan. He was born to lead. This means he is ruthless, brutal, pious, relentless. He is a great kapudaan, perhaps the greatest in a century."

Riane could tell that Tezziq believed this wholeheartedly. "Is he also fair?"

"Fair?" Tezziq paused in her plaiting. "Piety precludes fairness. But then fairness is a weakness, isn't it? And Makktuub has no weaknesses."

Everyone has a weakness, Riane thought. *Perhaps Makktuub's piety is his.* But these musings she kept to herself. This much, at least, he had already taught her. All she said was, "Tell me everything I need to know about him."

Tezziq recommenced her plaiting, her fingers working deftly on the complex pattern. "Makktuub has plucked one saying from the *Mokakaddir*, which he faithfully adheres to," she continued. " 'One sin leads to all others.' "

His piety again, Riane thought. "Does Makktuub come from a pious family?"

"Not at all. But every day Makktuub is in residence at the palace a certain religious scholar comes precisely at midnight and for the next two hours instructs the kapudaan in the *Mokakaddir*."

"How do you know this?"

"This scholar comes by the provisions gate, on the west side of the palace. It is near the haanjhala baths. I saw him, once. An ancient, bearded Ghor."

"A Ghor?"

"The Ghor are a fanatical, ultrareligious sect. They claim to be direct blood descendants of Jiharre's disciples, the guardians of the *Mokakaddir*. Being a Ghor is strictly hereditary; the privileges and responsibilities are handed down from one generation to the next. They take these responsibilities—the Burdens of Jiharre, as they call them—most seriously. Even the kapudaan is wary of gainsaying their will—*azmiirha*—the Path of the Righteous."

"Is this your belief also?" Riane asked.

Tezziq hesitated, but that instant spoke volumes to one listening as intently as Riane was.

"I have no beliefs," Tezziq said softly. "I have only my desire to serve."

"You have more than that, don't you? You have your will to survive."

"Yes. I have that."

Riane turned slowly in the embrace of Tezziq's arms, until Tezziq released her plaits. "The will cannot long survive malnourished," she whispered. "This I know from bitter experience, for I am an orphan without even a memory of home and hearth to sustain me." Her hands alighted on Tezziq's shoulders like the kiss of a thrice-banded flutterfly. "If I know anything, it is this: if your will survives, it is only because of belief."

Tezziq's eyes, darkening still, stared into Riane's. "Belief in what?"

"Are you asking for me, or for yourself?"

"For you. What do you believe in, outlander?"

"A better world."

There was a moment's hesitation before Tezziq burst into laughter. It was far from a happy sound, possessing as it did a decidedly caustic edge to its bitterness. "For a moment you had me going. But I know you cannot be serious."

"I am perfectly serious," Riane told her.

Tezziq shook her head, her waterfall hair swaying against her shoulder blades. "But how could you be? Look around you. You are a prisoner in a strange world, with no hope of escape."

"All the more reason to believe in something better," Riane said simply.

Tezziq drew back. "Now surely you mock me."

Riane took her head in her hands and kissed her, as Tezziq had before kissed her.

"Riane . . ."

It was the first time Tezziq had used her name, and Riane was a little surprised it had meaning for her. It was because she heard Eleana's voice. She closed her eyes and thought of Eleana, wished Tezziq was Eleana, but was afraid of that, too, as if even imagining herself and Eleana together was dangerous. Without her sorcerous Third Eye she felt blind, crippled, cut off from the auras of those she loved. She existed now in a featureless chamber without even the hint of an echo to remind her that she was not altogether alone. Tezziq had somehow slipped into this prison, and the exile in which both girls found themselves made each irresistible to the other.

"It is my unwavering belief that keeps me strong." Riane ran a finger down the side of the girl's face. "What belief keeps you strong, Tezziq?"

Tezziq shook her head. Her eyes were liquid; she seemed on the verge of tears. "In truth, I do not know."

"Then we shall strike a deal," Riane said. "You will teach me about the secrets of love, and I will teach you to unearth the belief inside you."

Tezziq searched her face. "Is that all you want?"

Riane recognized that look. Tezziq needed the truth, so she gave it to her. "No," she whispered. "If I am to escape, I will need help."

Tezziq bit her lip. "What you ask is strictly forbidden."

"I believe in a better world."

What better reasoning could Riane give her?

Olnnn Rydddlin led sixteen handpicked Khagggun officers through the densely wooded hillsides at the foot of the Djenn Marre. The recruits were made up of the most promising First-Captains and First-Majors. Olnnn had them put through a grueling test that he himself had devised. To accrue their long-term loyalty, he had taken the test with them, cutting no corners, giving himself no slack. He had pushed his sorcerous leg to its limit, ignoring the fiery pain flickering in the marrow of his exposed bones. They had spent two weeks in the high Djenn Marre wilderness without alloy armor or photon communications. He force-marched them fourteen hours a day, most of that on steep upgrades. They were blinded by sun, drenched by freezing rain, scoured by knife-edged winds. They carried no rations with them, were required to feed themselves with what they were able to catch. In the beginning, the recruits used ion fire, but that obliterated their prey, so they took to building snares out of bark-stripped wood and short lengths of vine. Hunger sparked their ingenuity. Similarly, they carried no portable sonic showers. They grew used to the smell of each other between bouts of bathing in the deep, crystal-clear pools that dotted the Land of Hidden Lakes corridor along which they roamed.

They grew used to the cold, and then, inured to it, took to trekking stripped to the waist. They grew to like their armorless torsos. The sun and the wind deepened the color of their skin.

On this moonless night, Olnnn took them along a perilously narrow path that snaked down a steep ridge into a narrow gorge. Far below them, a black river faintly glittered in starlight.

This was the site of their final exam. Those who survived would attain the rank of Attack-Commandant, a new officer rank that Olnnn had decided on. After his fateful meeting with Line-General Lokck Werrrent at Spice Jaxx's he had decided to interpret the regent's orders in his own way.

Olnnn led his unit, silent within the small sounds of a wilderness night, down into the gorge. He could feel the heightened tension of his recruits. They knew what was about to ensue. They knew it was possible that some of them would not survive.

He had decided to construct a unit of commanders, as ruthless as they were absolutely loyal to him, insurance against the day he felt certain was coming, when Kurgan Stogggul would try to usurp his power base. *You enjoy the loyalty of every Khagggun. So long as this is true there is no danger,* Lokck Werrrent had told him. Not knowing Kurgan Stogggul as Olnnn did, he had missed the point entirely. It was this very loyalty that threatened the regent's power.

Just before entering the gorge, the path widened somewhat, and the way became less steep. Olnnn held them up. They crouched there in the night, listening. He heard the insects buzzing, the wind soughing through the kuello-firs. He smelled the thick carpet of needles beneath their feet, the rich dampness of newly turned silt mounded at the edge of the riverbank. He wrapped a photon lens around his skull. Now, able to see in the dark, he could clearly make out the encampment on the other side of the river. There was no movement, but he saw the sentry posted at the perimeter. His back was to the river, believing that to be an impregnable barrier to attack.

Olnnn made a hand sign, and one of his unit ran in a crouch to the riverbank and slithered in. Through the oculus of the photon lens Olnnn followed his progress. Just the top of his head showed above the waterline. Within moments, he had emerged from the water and, making an utterly silent run, had efficiently slit the sentry's throat with his ion blade. Now the rest of the Resistance cell was theirs to take at will.

Final exam.

Olnnn ordered them forward. They hit the water as a unit, swam as a unit. They did not like the water. Like all V'ornn they were uncomfortable without solid terrain under their feet. But their training was holding; they moved grimly forward.

Through his oculus, Olnnn saw the point Khagggun crouched and ready, waiting for them. Behind him, the Resistance encampment slept on, oblivious. This was not the first Resistance cell they had taken on. Over the course of the past two weeks, they had slain many Kundalan as they learned the lessons Olnnn was teaching them.

The unit had just passed the midway point. Olnnn, swimming hard, had momentarily lost track of the point Khagggun. When he swung his oculus back around, the saw the Khagggun slumped over, an arrow sticking out of his side. He was crawling, his mouth opened to utter a warning shout, and an arrow filled it. He spasmed like a fish caught on a hook. Olnnn whirled. Tracing the arrow's trajectory, he saw three bark canoes bearing silently down on them. The canoes were filled with Kundalan Resistance. That is when he knew that the encampment was empty.

The unit responded with admirable discipline to his cry of "Ambush!" But by then the attack had already commenced. The black water ran with blood, and he saw his recruits flailing around him. The water churned, familiar heads sank from view. He redoubled his efforts, but even he was growing tired. Prudently, he ordered a retreat back across the river. In the water, they were no match for the weapons-laden war canoes.

Melting back into the high stands of kuello-firs, he assessed the damage. Three recruits killed, double that severely wounded. How much damage they had done in return was impossible to say. Still, a number of valuable lessons had been learned, the most important of which was that Resistance fighters were clever and not without their own resources.

But what was of most interest to him was that the attack had its positive side, for it cemented the determination of the survivors to remain together, to give their lives for one another, to gain revenge for their fallen comrades.

For the first time, they plotted together—one unit, one mind—and just before dawn they reengaged the Resistance cell. One of Olnnn's group was mortally wounded in the assault, but all twenty of the Resistance cell members were slaughtered. Olnnn watched with glittering eyes the feral savagery with which his group fell upon the enemy. It seemed to him that in finding this connection to each other their appetite for destruction had been unleashed.

There was one in the unit—soon to become Attack-Commandant

Accton Blled—whose appetite for destruction outstripped the others.
His sleek dark-skinned head was shaped like a finned ion missile. His
slablike cheeks and slash of a mouth seemed fashioned by some de-
mented sculptor, his jutting chin was the butt end of a particularly
lethal-looking weapon. Utterly fearless, he reveled in bloodletting, and
claimed he felt a kinship with death that would be the envy of any
Deirus.

It did not take long for Blled to become something of a legend in
the unit. During their first encounter with the Resistance, he killed two
before ripping the throat out of a third with a horrific snap of his jaws.
In the aftermath, he decapitated his victims, stuffed their own tender
parts into their mouths, and mounted the bloody heads on stakes as an
example, so he said, as well as a warning that he was here and would
take more life whenever and wherever he chose.

Olnnn had observed these grisly antics with a mixture of amusement
and approval. Bloodletting was something he could respect. He knew
instinctively that Accton Blled would make Attack-Commandant. Unless the final exam killed him. Therefore, he marked Blled, making
plans for him following his inevitable field promotion.

Following the slaughter, the unit took a vote on Blled's suggestion
not to burn the Kundalan bodies, but to tumble them into a mass grave,
an open pit that would serve as a warning to the Resistance. By this
time the bloody sun had risen above the eastern mountain peaks. A
rime of hoarfrost lay upon the dead like a shroud. They roasted ice-
hare, rending the beasts as they stared at the results of their final exam.
Their faces grew shiny with grease, and they laughed at coarse jokes.
Occasionally, one of them would kick a carcass or spit into a glazed
Kundalan eye. It seemed clear they wanted more Resistance to kill. Like
predators, they had scented blood, and their hearts pounded for the
rush of battle to the death.

After the meal, they turned the encampment into the mass grave.
They thought that fitting. Flies were collecting, and large black birds
circled overhead, calling plaintively. They dragged the bodies to the
edge of the pit they had dug and kicked them in.

In a short ceremony, witnessed only by the dead Kundalan, Olnnn
promoted them to the rank of Attack-Commandant. Each one, he told
them, would get his own pack to lead. They would leapfrog the chain

of command. They would be answerable only to him. They were silent, and in their silence, content.

Olnnn walked a little away from the unit and motioned to Accton Blled. The two of them walked beside the river. It had been much on his mind lately as to why Kurgan should be so insistent that he track down the traitors himself. Unconsciously, he reached down and stroked the sorcerous bones of his leg. Yes, he still burned for revenge. But he was also acutely aware of how his search was taking him far from Kurgan and Axis Tyr, and he had begun to ask himself whether his absence from the center of power was wise. On that score, he had come to a decision.

He said, "Attack-Commandant, during these past two weeks you have acquitted yourself with the highest honors. Therefore, you will be first to gain your own command."

"I appreciate your confidence in me, Star-Admiral."

"You are also the first to get an assignment."

"Rest assured, Star-Admiral, whatever you ask of me it will be done."

"I am pleased to hear it," Olnnn nodded, "because I am entrusting you with a most important mission. You are to find the Rhynnnon, Rekkk Hacilar, and his skcettta, Giyan."

"I am honored, Star-Admiral. I consider it my personal mission to find them and bring them to you."

"Alive or dead," Olnnn added. "It matters not to me."

"Ah, death." A slow smile wreathed Attack-Commandant Blled's face. "All the better for me." His sharp teeth shone in the morning sun.

The following night Riane saw someone come for Tezziq, a tall slim-hipped male with a huge black animal's tooth through his topknot. His hair was lighter than Othnam's, so light, in fact, it seemed altogether without color. She got but a glimpse of him as he silently entered the haanjhala. He had only to glance in Tezziq's direction and she rose, following him out with not even a glance behind her.

After Tezziq had gone, Riane rolled over and closed her eyes, but sleep seemed nowhere near, and she rolled again, staring up at the high, tented ceiling, wishing she could see the stars and the moonslight. She thought of Eleana, and her heart contracted; she thought of Giyan in the grip of the Malasocca, the dark night of the soul, and her blood ran cold. It was winter already. Time was ticking away, time during which the daemon Horolaggia was spinning its web around her, transmogrifying her. Time when the solstice was coming ever closer.

She must have fallen into an uneasy slumber, for she dreamed of odd wailings and rhythmic thumpings that shook the very cushions on which she tossed and turned.

How many hours passed she could not have said, but at length a shadow passed over her and, opening her eyes, she saw that Tezziq was returning to the haanjhala. Riane rose on one elbow but, to her surprise, Tezziq did not lie down on her cushions, but instead went immediately to the bathtent. Riane rose and silently followed her.

Standing in the shadows of the polished limoniq-wood gateway, she watched as Tezziq ripped off her gauzy garments with breathless grunting sounds. Naked, she slid into the water, which reflected the moonslight in tiny shimmering crescents.

Tezziq waded into the center of the pool, lifted her head, and made an eerie keening sound. All at once, her shoulders heaved, and she gave a deep sob. She ground the heels of her hands against her eyes as if to scrub away an horrific sight.

Without thinking, Riane disrobed and entered the pool. She moved slowly toward the center, but she was brought up short when Tezziq's eyes snapped open.

"What are you doing here?" Tezziq whispered fiercely. "You should be asleep."

"I saw you come in," Riane said. "Why are you weeping?"

"I'm not weeping." Tezziq wiped her eyes. "What made you think that?" She tossed her head. "Go back to sleep."

"I had a nightmare," Riane said. "I heard an odd wailing, and the cushions shook as if with an earth tremor. Do you have tremors here?"

The serpent smile reappeared on Tezziq's face, sending an unpleasant chill through Riane. "Oh, we have tremors," Tezziq said softly, "but hardly the kind you mean."

"I don't understand."

"As long as you're here . . ." Tezziq turned and handed her the soft bristled brush. "I feel dirty."

"But you bathed just before—"

"Do as I say," Tezziq snapped.

Riane lifted Tezziq's long hair out of the way.

"What is this?" Her fingertips ran over the reddish rune tattooed at the base of her spine.

"Brush me hard," Tezziq commanded.

Riane did as she was bade.

"The *tew* is a family crest," Tezziq said softly.

"I have not seen it on the other girls."

"That is because they are all Gazi Qhan."

Riane paused in her brushing. "And you are not?"

"Continue," Tezziq snapped. She shivered a little as Riane resumed scrubbing her down. "I am Jeni Cerii." Her voice was a whisper. "I was brought here as part of a peace initiative between kapudaan. It was Makktuub's idea for the two kapudaan to exchange first ajjan. As a sign of good faith. Jasim, my kapudaan, cheerfully lopped off the head of Makktuub's gift. Knowing him as I do, I am sure he laughed while doing it. He sent the head back to Makktuub in a common wine sack."

"He did not care what happened to you?"

"I rather think he entertained himself imagining the possible consequences to me."

"And yet Makktuub did not retaliate in kind."

Tezziq shivered.

"What *did* he do?" Riane asked.

"For an entire year, nothing. Then, early on the anniversary morning of his first ajjan's murder, he sent a raiding party into Jeni Cerii territory. They butchered one hundred children."

"Miina protect us." Riane felt her throat constrict. "But you are alive. And you have become his favorite."

"Harder," Tezziq whispered in an odd, strangled voice. "Harder."

Riane applied more pressure than she knew was necessary. Tezziq's flesh began to redden.

"Did you not hear me? I said harder!"

And then, in the soft moonlight, Riane saw something that made her gasp. The water around Tezziq was stained dark. She dropped the brush, took Tezziq by the shoulders, and turned her around. "I've hurt you," she said.

"No, it is coming from between my thighs." Tezziq's eyelids fluttered closed, and she let out a long-held breath. "That was no nightmare you had," she whispered.

"What do you mean?"

"The truth is . . ." Tezziq's pale eyes regarded her levelly. "Here lies the other part of Makktuub's revenge. He makes me call him *wa tarabibi,* and then his prodigious rutting makes me bleed each time I lie with him."

12

Very Black Things

"She is a monster."

"Worse even than Konara Bartta, if that is possible."

"It is, and she is."

Two konara, best friends and compatriots, sat in a small, slightly creepy, barely furnished chamber in a disused part of the Abbey of Floating White. They sat on dusty uncomfortable chairs with stiff backs and unforgiving seats. Save for cobwebs, in the entire chamber there was nothing to look at but each other. An old oil lamp threw rickety light over them.

"It took but an instant for Konara Urdma to don Konara Bartta's mantle of power," Konara Inggres said.

"She snuffed out our investigation into Konara Bartta's death the moment she got wind of it," Konara Lyystra said.

Konara Inggres was prompted to nod. "The anger rolled off her in waves." She was brown-eyed and red-cheeked, with square shoulders and a bow of a mouth, a healthy-looking specimen who, thanks to her athletic bent, was in charge of making sure the acolytes got their thrice-weekly exercise. "Well, what can you expect? She's never liked me; she thinks I spend far too much time in the back rooms of the Library researching my History of Sorcery class. She's always telling me what to keep in the curriculum and what to omit without the slightest regard for historical accuracy."

"Doubtless that is because there are many dangers in the Osoru sorcery of decades ago. Isn't that why those books were relegated to the back rooms, where only konara have access to them?"

"So she claims."

"Besides, of what possible use is research on Osoru? All those Ramahan with the Gift were expelled from the abbeys years ago."

"True enough. But there is value in knowing the gnarled pathways of our roots." Not for the first time, Konara Inggres contemplated confiding in her friend the fact that she had discovered a latent talent inside herself—the Gift for Osoru. But the idea that she was using a good portion of her time in the Library to teach herself Osoru was such anathema she could not yet bring herself to tell anyone, even Konara Lyystra. "After all, those who are ignorant of history are doomed to repeat its follies."

"This word *history*," Konara Lyystra said. "I sometimes find myself wondering. Does it pertain to us Ramahan?" She was dough-faced, slightly round-shouldered owing to her height. A large mole marinated like a piece of dried fruit in the crevasse between her lower lip and her chin. "What I mean is this. We continue to worship Miina without having the slightest notion of whether She existed at all."

"Is that not the definition of faith?"

"I am speaking of fact, of *history*." Konara Lyystra shrugged off this argument. "Once upon a time Miina was as real as you or I, so the sacred texts tell us. But what if that isn't true? What if Miina never existed, what if She was a figment of the imagination of the Druuge?"

"Surely you are not saying that you believe our religion is built on a lie?"

"Not exactly." The most womanly parts of Konara Lyystra had atrophied from lack of use, or possibly they had never fully developed. In any event, this gave her the aspect of a child who would never know the full flower of womanhood. "But we know that Venca was both the Druuge's language and their sorcery. If this is true. If all the power in the Cosmos lies within the seven hundred seventy-seven letters of Venca, is there not justification for claiming that the language *is* the Goddess, that Miina is created every time it is spoken?"

"This is science—possibly an aberrant form of semantics—not religion." Konara Inggres may have looked shocked, but she wasn't. The very best part of having a close friend was disagreeing with her and learning something important from it.

"Tell me the difference."

"Religion brings comfort to those who have none. Science—what does science do? It asks questions that cannot—and probably should not—be answered. It says that the Goddess is dead. It says that She never, in fact, existed. You have only to observe the V'ornn to see the truth of this. And then the storm comes, as it must to every life, and science provides no shelter, no comfort whatsoever."

"The day you cease to ask questions," Konara Lyystra said, "is the day you die. In any event, look at what our religion has done for us. It codified language, advanced agrarian techniques, stimulated social intercourse through the many festivals, provided a governmental structure under which we thrived. Strictly speaking, is that religion?"

"What you fail to take into consideration is that all of this civilization you speak of would not have been possible without our faith in Miina. What would happen, do you think, if you in fact were able to prove that the Great Goddess was a figment of the Druuge? Faith is all we have left holding us together in the face of annihilation from the V'ornn."

"Possibly you are right," Konara Lyystra acknowledged. "But I am saying that what the Druuge did was good, irrespective of Miina's existence. Our belief in Her brought us out of the darkness of anarchy; it delivered us into the hands of civilization. Even more, it gave us a foundation for an understanding that the Cosmos contains more than what can be encompassed by our five normal senses. In the face of that revelation don't you agree that what the Goddess says or doesn't say is mostly irrelevant?"

"I most certainly do not," Konara Inggres said hotly. She was enjoying this debate immensely. It kept her from dwelling on the depressing state of the abbey. "It seems to me that the word of Miina is more important than ever. You forget that the evil we sense invaded the abbeys the moment we began straying from Her scripture. And the more we stray the more of a stranglehold evil has on the Dea Cretan."

"You see evil everywhere, and I wish to study Venca," Konara Lyystra replied. "Well, one thing is for certain. Konara Urdma finds novel ways to punish us for our rebelliousness, this unending night duty being just the latest. And yet I do not for an instant regret questioning the official explanation for Konara Bartta's death."

"Neither do I," Konara Inggres said. "I still would like to know what happened to Konara Bartta."

"Good riddance to her, I say. Konara Urdma is simply aping her mentor. She lacks Bartta's evil imagination. In time, I believe we can find a way to handle her."

Periodically, the priestesses fell silent and cocked their heads, listening to the tiny nighttime sounds the abbey gave off like perfume. The wind whistling as it worked its way through cracks, the soft grinding of the foundation stones as the abbey continued to settle into the mountainside, the small insistent scurry of rodents that nightly scavenged for food, soft footfalls now and again, the sound of water running briefly, then the silence once more coming down like a heavy curtain at the end of a show. They were familiar with the full gamut of noises. They had been here so long that the sounds gave them a small comfort they took to bed, a companion of sorts, a sleeping draught to ease their troubled minds.

"It was as if Konara Urdma knew what was going to happen to Konara Bartta," Konara Inggres nodded. "Waiting for her chance to grab power."

"Hush now." Tension lent Konara Lyystra's body a certain dissonance. "Konara Urdma is our leader."

Konara Inggres leaned forward. "Every day the scripture changes more and more radically." She was somewhat younger than her friend, but no less shrewd. She daily wetted her finger, metaphorically speaking, the better to gauge the direction of the political wind. Konara Lyystra had taught her to faithfully follow the flow so as not to be blown off her feet, but it was difficult stifling her opinions. "You see it yourself. Miina's teachings—the teachings I learned as a child—have been twisted and deformed. The result serves one end: the agglomeration of power for the ruling konara."

Konara Lyystra shook her head in sharp warning.

"I must spill my heart to someone, for it is breaking. We are no longer doing Miina's sacred work. We do not serve Her as we were meant to do. We are no longer in grace. We have become willing political pawns, reduced to base marionettes dancing at the end of a string. We are helpless, living in fear, perpetuating a lie greater than we can imagine."

"Keep still, I tell you!"

"It is well past midnight. Who can overhear us? No one comes to this part of the abbey."

"Konara Bartta came," Konara Lyystra said, her eyes darting this way and that as if expecting Konara Bartta's ghost to materialize, "though we know not why."

"Konara Bartta is dead. Vaporized in the conflagration that incinerated the interior of the chamber not ten meters distant from where we now sit."

"The very same chamber Konara Urdma barred us from entering."

"The likelihood of a dangerous residue, she claimed." Abruptly Konara Inggres rose, her eyes alight. "Come on," she whispered. "Let's do it."

"Do what?" Konara Lyystra said, though she knew very well what her friend had in mind.

Without another word, Konara Inggres leaned over, pulled Konara Lyystra to her feet, shoved the oil lamp into her hand.

At the door, Konara Lyystra said, rather weakly, "This is foolhardy."

Her friend gave her a silent laugh. "You sound just like Konara Urdma."

They crept down the cramped, dank, cobwebbed corridor, listening breathlessly with each step for even the smallest sound that might seem out of the ordinary. They heard none, and so advanced to the door of the chamber in which the mysterious fire had arisen.

"The curious thing," Konara Inggres said, "is that for all its ferocity, the fire remained completely inside the chamber." She pointed. "Look here. Not a mark or bit of soot in the corridor. Is that the way fire acts?"

"Fire is the other side of water," Konara Lyystra replied. "Water runs, seeking its own level. Fire spreads through air drafts made by cracks and imperfections."

"It should have whooshed out here into the corridor or spread to adjacent chambers is what you're saying." Konara Inggres knelt before the door, pointing out the space between the bottom of the door and the sill. A span of two fingerwidths. "Why didn't it do that?"

Konara Lyystra squinted at the door and sighed. "There is a blocking spell. Konara Urdma, in a typical fit of paranoia, has sealed it tight."

Konara Inggres rose, her arms spread out, her hands slightly cupped.

Konara Lyystra's face blanched. "What are you doing?"

"We want to see what's inside, don't we?"

"But if we—"

"Don't worry. I'll put the blocking spell back in place after we're done. Konara Urdma will never know the difference."

"But how—" Konara Lyystra shut her mouth because she could sense that the spell was gone. *How did she do that?* she wondered. *What spell did she use?*

Konara Inggres gripped the handle and the door creaked inward. It was black as death inside, and a sharp pungent aroma of burned pitch arose and something else, less well defined, like the slightly sweet air around a grave.

Konara Lyystra held the oil lamp high as they crossed the threshold. Something about the chamber made her stomach tighten, and she heard herself emit a tiny whimper. Part of her wanted to turn around and run out. A shiver ran through her, rattling her teeth.

"What is that smell? Fear?"

"Fear, yes," Konara Inggres whispered. "But what else?"

The stone walls, ceiling, underfloor were black and gritty with the fire's aftermath. Whole lines of the rock walls had been deeply scored, where veins of metallic ore had been liquefied by the inferno, making it appear as if they had entered a cage that had recently held a raging monster.

They gingerly approached the center of the chamber, where a small pile of ash lay heaped. Lifting the hem of her robes, Konara Inggres hunkered down as Konara Lyystra lowered the lamp.

"Someone has been in here," Konara Inggres said. "You can see the finger marks combing through the center of the ashes."

"Looking for something," Konara Lyystra affirmed. "But what?"

"I will bet you Konara Urdma knows." Konara Inggres rose. "It was she who sealed this chamber. It's a surety she performed her own private investigation."

"You were right. She must have suspected Konara Bartta was coming here." Konara Lyystra licked her lips nervously. "Could we think about leaving now? There's something in here that makes my stomach crawl."

"Pray to Miina."

"I have. The Goddess seems to be absent from this chamber."

Konara Inggres was too engrossed to respond. She was studying the underlying pattern of the pile of ash. Her eyes followed the longest finger of ash into a shadowed corner of the blasted chamber. "Let me have that." She took the lantern from her friend, advancing into the corner, Konara Lyystra just behind her. The shadows reluctantly retreated before the lamp's flame.

"Ah, what have we here?" Konara Inggres bent and retrieved something small that had been thrown into the very deepest corner. Using the hem of her robe, she rubbed the brittle charcoal crust off it. A small bit of etched bronze was revealed, gleaming dully in the lamp-light. She cleaned it completely and held it up, turning it slowly be-tween her fingertips. "What do you make of this?"

With a deep and abiding trepidation, Konara Lyystra took it from her, examined it closely. "It is old, hand-forged. It looks . . . If I didn't know better . . ." She bit her lip.

"What? What do you think it is?"

"I have seen pictures. In a book. Diagrams." Konara Lyystra's eyes met her friend's and held them. "It's a trigger for a *had-atta*."

"What? The Flute is illegal." The *had-atta* was an ancient instrument, used, it was said, to test for infiltration of heretics. A slender crystal cylinder was slowly lowered down the suspect's throat, hence the name. It was used to discover if a Ramahan was a heretic, had become un-bound in her ties to Miina. "They were destroyed more than a century ago."

"Obviously not all of them."

Now they understood the rank smell of fear infesting the place.

Konara Inggres nodded. "Konara Bartta came here regularly—"

"Leyna Astar, Konara Laudenum, the acolyte Riane. Those missing Ramahan—"

"Died of accidents."

"So it was reported."

"Tortured instead. Dear sweet Miina!"

The visitor's bell sounded deep, muffled, faraway, but it made them start all the same.

"At this time of night?" Konara Inggres said, annoyed.

"It is my turn." Konara Lyystra, who seemed relieved to get away from this chamber of horrors, gave her back the trigger. "Guard this well." As she hurried through the charred door, she added, "Don't stay here alone. Seal it back up as quickly as you can."

Konara Inggres, who was staring intently at the trigger, nodded ab-sently.

The Lady Giyan stood by the leaded-glass window of Konara Urdma's office in the Abbey of Floating White, drinking in the black night. Below her, balanced on its many-tiered mountain ledge, Stone Border lay dark and brooding. She stared down at the place of her birth with otherworldly eyes as if with that one baleful look she could incinerate every inhabitant, as if she could wipe the entire excrescence from the mountainside.

That would come, she knew, in time.

Wrapped in her long black cloak, she had arrived at the front entrance to Floating White, and had rung the bellchain, announcing her arrival. Beneath closed lids, her eyeballs had commenced a furious movement. By the time the mammoth door creaked inward, her eyes, which had been transformed by the beginnings of the Malasocca, had resumed their perfectly normal appearance.

She had smiled into the acolyte's face. Riane would not have recognized that smile, for it bore no resemblance to Giyan's natural expression. With good reason. Beneath the shell of Giyan's Kundalan self lurked the very black thing, the seepage from the Abyss, the archdaemon Horolaggia. He was not completely inside her. But he gained enough control to manipulate her. What she did and said came from him.

In truth, that smile was a horrifying thing, but the acolyte saw only what she was meant to see, and she returned the smile, standing back, allowing Giyan and the very black thing entrance to the abbey and all that dwelled there in evil and in ignorance.

It had been Bartta who had continued and expanded upon the alterations of the teachings of the Great Goddess Miina, begun by Konara Mossa during her iron-willed reign in the abbey. Now it was Konara Urdma's turn. The evil that had begun to infiltrate the abbey in the form of Konara Mossa had continued to thrive under Bartta, and Konara Urdma, who was nothing if not an apt pupil and a quick study, was in the process of taking it to full flower.

Giyan had followed the acolyte through the gardens, the atria, into the interior of the abbey, where she asked another acolyte to ring for the konara on duty. The acolyte was small, fine-featured, slender as a reed. Too young to remember Giyan or even to have heard her name mentioned. In blissful ignorance, then, she had delivered Giyan here, where, after asking if she could bring the visitor food or drink, she had departed.

Giyan turned away from the window and her grim contemplation. Bronze filigreed lamps burned oil laced with incense. Small spirals of smoke curled from the tip of the lamplights, disappearing into the heavy wood beams of the ceiling. In the five minutes or so while she was alone, Giyan conjured a black serpentskin satchel from beneath her cloak. This she placed on one corner of the desk, arranging it just so. Then she turned, stared at her reflection in the mirror that hung on the wall. The thorned crown atop her head was plainly visible, as were the spikes corkscrewed through the palms of her hands. They were the physical manifestations of the psychic war being waged inside her for the prize of her spirit. In this realm, they were only visible in mirrors. Horolaggia now suspected that it had been a mistake to have moved against Giyan while the girl was with her, because the thorns were visible to a sorceress's penetrating gaze at the moment the Malasocca was initiated. The girl had doubtless seen them, and though he had discerned that she was but a novice, and therefore would not understand what she had seen, nevertheless she might someday come to use this knowledge against him.

Giyan raised her left arm, her fingers moved in a rhythm and pattern familiar to Horolaggia and the silvered glass of the mirror melted into a puddle on the floor, leaving a deaf, dumb, and blind space within the frame. She extracted from the serpentskin satchel a length of tightly rolled film that shimmered and glistered. This she unfurled on the spot where the mirror had been. A new thornless reflection appeared, answerable only to her own command. She turned from admiring her handiwork as she heard someone enter the office.

"Good evening, Konara Lyystra, or should I say good morning," she said in her most winning voice. "I do apologize for the inconvenient hour of my arrival, but I was late enough that no inn in Stone Border was open to take me in."

"The Abbey of Floating White is always open to—" All the blood drained from Konara Lyystra's doughy face, "Merciful Miina! Giyan? Is that you?"

"It is, indeed."

"Are you passing through—?"

"I have returned to the abbey, I have come home," Giyan said, and held out her arms just in time for Konara Lyystra to hurl herself into them.

"Oh, it has been so long, Giyan!" Konara Lyystra felt herself fairly overcome with emotion. "We had never dared hope."

"I know, I know. And yet I am here." Giyan stroked the back of her head. "And you have been elevated from shima to konara." She held the other at arm's length, beaming. "No less than you deserve, I am sure."

Konara Lyystra ducked her head in mute delight.

"Now pour me a drink of sweet icewine, konara, that I may offer a toast to suit this occasion."

"*Konara*, indeed. We were always more intimate than that." Konara Lyystra went to the sideboard, where a decanter and the slim, stemmed glasses that had once belonged to Konara Mossa clustered on a chased-copper tray. "You must call me as you always did. I insist."

Giyan laughed gently and sweetly. "In that event." She accepted the filled glass. The icewine had a slight reddish tinge, a sure sign that it was of the highest quality. Poorer grades were yellowish or greenish. She lifted her glass. "To you, Lyystra, and your spiritual elevation."

The rims came together and the crystal sang. But there was no joy in Konara Lyystra's face. "Konara I may be, but alas, as to my spiritual elevation . . ." She let her words gutter in the lamplight of the office.

Giyan frowned. "I do not mark your meaning."

"This is Konara Urdma's domain, and before her it was your sister's."

"This office."

"No," Konara Lyystra said. "The abbey itself."

Giyan's frown deepened. "But the Dea Cretan."

"Exists in name only." Konara Lyystra sighed. "It pains me to be the bearer of heavy tidings, but Konara Bartta lost her spiritual way."

"She—"

"And now she is dead, incinerated in curious and mysterious circumstances, and we forbidden to investigate."

Giyan put her icewine down on the desk almost untouched. "Who forbids it?" she said darkly.

"Konara Urdma, who has set herself up in your sister's place, moved into Bartta's quarters on the very day of her demise. Tell me. In your opinion is this seemly?"

Giyan shook her head.

"Worse still, Miina's teachings have been lost. Worse than lost. Perverted. You were exiled because you possessed the Gift of Osoru. All those similarly gifted have been purged. Only Kyofu is taught here now, and daily the lists of taboo words grow. We are forbidden, for instance, to speak of the Ja-Gaar, Miina's sacred beasts, and their likeness has been struck down or defaced wherever they are found."

"This is outrageous behavior. Unthinkable!" Giyan was opening the serpentskin satchel. With her back to Konara Lyystra, she daubed something onto the tip of her tongue. When she turned back, she lifted a forefinger. "You did well to forewarn me. And though my heart mourns for my twin sister, so long absent from my side, from what you tell me there is a great deal of work to be done."

A look of relief flooded Konara Lyystra's face. "I could not agree more. You are the one we have been waiting for to lift us out of the comfortable bed evil has made in our beloved abbey."

"Then come, brave Lyystra," Giyan said, putting her arm around the other. "Together we will right the wrongs that have been visited upon Miina's children."

As they neared the door, she swung Konara Lyystra around, grabbed her by the shoulders and kissed her. Before the startled Ramahan could react, Giyan's mouth opened and her tongue pushed through the other set of lips.

Konara Lyystra gasped and tried to wrest herself from Giyan's grip. She was strong, but not nearly strong enough.

And she abruptly lost strength. Something black and squirmy had taken up residence in her mouth. She bent over, gagging, trying to vomit up the thing. But it was tenacious and would not budge. Then she felt a searing pain in the roof of her mouth, as if a sword of fire was slicing through her, and she went down on her knees.

Giyan cradled Konara Lyystra's sweaty head, crooning a daemon-song, while she shuddered and shook and moaned every now and again.

And then it was done. Konara Lyystra gave a little gasp and Giyan took her under her arms, lifted her up, looked into her eyes, which were completely white now, white as Giyan's. Giyan passed a hand over her face, the lids fluttered closed, and the eyeballs commenced to roll this way and that. When they were still again, Giyan removed her hand. Konara Lyystra's eyes were the same as they ever had been.

"I am charging you with the removal of the mirrors," Giyan said. "All mirrors in the abbey must be destroyed. Completely."

Konara Lyystra nodded her head obediently. "Yes, Mother."

"If someone should inquire, you are to tell her that the evil that has infested the abbey sleeps within the mirrors. Is that clear?"

"Yes, Mother."

Konara Lyystra began to leave, but Giyan stopped her momentarily.

"It's all right now," she said softly. "Everything will be fine."

And Konara Lyystra smiled, a dead, wooden, soulless thing. "Yes," she said. "It is perfect."

Ever since he had seen the face—or whatever it was—in the mirror, Kurgan was prone to a particular nightmare. Not that he ever saw that face—or whatever it was—in this nightmare. Not that he would ever wish to again. He had thought himself fearless, but this *thing* he had seen in the mirror had brought a metallic taste to his mouth. He hadn't been able to eat for the rest of the day, and he had avoided Nith Batoxxx for as long as he was able. Now, when he was obliged to speak with the Gyrgon he could feel his blood run cold.

What he had seen in that mirror defied description. Each time he tried to recall it a shiver raced down his spine. That night, after the palace was asleep, he had stolen into that chamber and smashed the mirror to smithereens. So now, whether it be a communication device or, as he most feared, the repository of the Gyrgon's true reflection, it was gone.

The nightmare plagued him, but it had its positive side for it served to remind him of how much he did not know. That was something his father, Wennn Stogggul, never came to realize. Eventually, it caused his downfall. He had cut himself off from events around him both by his office and by his arrogance. An ignorant V'ornn—and an arrogant one, to boot—is ripe to be sucked into a snare. This Kurgan had cleverly done. This he vowed would never happen to him. He would never repeat the mistakes of his father.

To this end, he had determined that he required a trustworthy pipeline to the quotidian events of the city. Some V'ornn who heard and could report on both rumors and facts secreted away in hurried whispers and furtive conversations. His knowledge of the constantly shifting tide of crosscurrents would keep him one step ahead. He needed just the right individual. And at last he determined who that individual should be, and that night he gave orders for her to be brought to his private quarters at the palace.

By the time she arrived, night was in full flower. The Promenade would be jumping with the effusive eruption from the nearby Kalllis-totos, whose raucous discourse would surely drown out the voices of the fishers who would soon be taken away on the rising tide. Blood

Tide would be packed, hot with steaming bodies and volatile conversations. Secrets folded into every shadowed cornice and corner.

"Regent, it is good to see you again," Rada said when she was escorted into his presence by a pair of Haaar-kyut. "But may I ask the occasion for this summons?"

He had been lounging by the fireplace, keenly anticipating her arrival. The fire was behind him, a kind of imperial corona. He could see that she was not happy. This hour was the height of her business, and she was here in the regent's palace instead of tending to her customers. He was pleased. It was the proper reaction. He had established his power over her.

"Sit down," he said. "We shall share a drink together."

Her sifeyn was pulled over her fragrantly oiled skull, but he could see gleaming the tips of her diadem. The firelight threw her beauty into stark prominence, not that it mattered to him. For he was seeing not Rada but the Kundalan female whom he and Annon had come upon in the woods. She had been bathing in the creek; she had pulled a filigreed pin from her hair and it had cascaded down her back. The sight had filled his eyes, his mind, his loins, and he could do ought but act.

"You have something of import to say to me, regent?"

Her voice snapped him back to the present. But the afterimage of that Kundalan female caused the breath to catch in his throat.

"I wish to avail myself of your talents."

"This is surprising to me. I think you know nothing of them, regent."

"In that you are wrong." He came away from the blaze and sprawled on a sofa. "Please do sit down." When she had complied, perching herself on the edge of a chair facing him, he poured them both fire-grade numaaadis from a decanter sitting on a Khagggun beaten-bronze camp table. He handed her a goblet, took up the other. "Many times I have seen you at work in Blood Tide. I have seen you handle Mesagggun and Sarakkon three times your size. There isn't a patron who comes through your door who does not respect you. I want to tap into that."

"This bluntness comes, I suppose, from the rapid elevation of your status," she said.

"In truth, I have spent more time taking orders than giving them."

She pursed her lips. "Am I meant to feel sorry for you, regent?"

"This was no order."

"Better for both of us, I warrant."

She sipped her drink.

"What's the matter?" he asked. "Is the numaaadis not to your liking?"

"It's quite good," she said. "But this palace . . . it strikes me as a melancholy place."

"Personally, I like it. Dark, empty, serene. I have time to sort through my thoughts."

"What thoughts might those be, regent?"

"Lately, I am plagued by a nightmare."

"I am distressed to hear it."

"You do not know me well enough to mean that."

He looked into the fire. Often, he found those flames hypnotic, and he would fall into a brief reverie, a kind of waking dreamscape where his overweening ambition ran rampant. Since seeing that face in the mirror though . . .

"It is always the same, this nightmare. I am submerged in black water. The odd thing is that I have no trouble breathing. Odder still, is the face before me. It is female, and beautiful, but it is pale as death—ash-white with a bluish tinge—and eyes that seem to see right through me."

"A V'ornn goddess, a concubine of the dead god Enlil, perhaps."

"Not V'ornn. Kundalan," he said softly. "She has hair, thick as a copse of trees, long as a sea-snake. It, too, is white as ash."

Rada seemed amused. "Does she talk to you, this Kundalan female?"

"That is the oddest part. She is begging me for help."

Rada put down her goblet. "Regent, if I may ask. Why are you telling me this?"

"I suppose because there is no one else to tell."

"That seems terribly sad."

He rose and held out his hand, she took it wordlessly and he pulled her to her feet. She was standing very close to him. "I do not want you to leave," he said softly. "Not just yet."

He led her into his bedchamber and disrobed her. He could not wait, and took her against the wall. At the end, he thought she cried out, though there was an echo in his mind, sunlight off the skin of the creek, the thick hair entangling him, the lush Kundalan body, the thrusting. He wished Rada had hair, long dark thick. Entwining him.

But, after all, she was only a Tuskugggun.

While she dressed, he sat on the edge of the unrumpled bed, and said, "What if you no longer needed your business to live?"

She looked at him. He could read nothing in her expression. It was as if nothing had happened between them. For him, it seemed, nothing had.

"Running Blood Tide is all I can do," she said. "When my mother died . . ." She shrugged. "She was a gambler. There is a mountain of debt."

"A mountain to you. Not to me, I warrant."

"Dear regent." She cocked her head. "What do you have in mind?"

"You are proprietress of a casteless tavern. As such, it is a nexus point for a broad cross section of the city's populace. This is of great interest to me."

He produced a laaga stick, lighted it. After inhaling deeply, he passed it over to her. While she smoked, he said, "What I propose is a simple exchange. I pay off your debt." He watched her moist lips, half-parted, the dregs of the smoke drifting between them. "In return, you provide me with all the news, gossip, rumors, and secrets that nightly float through Blood Tide."

"A simple exchange. Regent, nothing about you is simple." She handed the laaga stick back to him. "Tell me. What am I missing?"

There came at that moment a discreet knock on the door. A look of annoyance, though fleeting, passed across Kurgan's face. When the knock came again he pushed himself off the bed, wrapped himself in a robe, and went to the door.

Nith Batoxxx stood just outside.

"I did not mean to intrude upon your privacy," the Gyrgon said.

Kurgan knew that was just what he had meant to do, and he despised him all the more for the pettiness of his action. But he showed none of this as he stepped across the threshold, pulled the door to behind him. Being so near the Gyrgon, he tried not to shudder.

"You have ordered the Khagggun to discontinue their ascendance to Great Caste status," Nith Batoxxx said. "This is as it should be. But the change in the status quo never should have begun in the first place."

"That was my father's doing," Kurgan said. "It had nothing to do with me."

"On the contrary." Nith Batoxxx's ruby-irised eyes blazed. "You are Stogggul. You are responsible. If there is any unrest among the Khagggun, you must deal with it decisively. I will not tolerate one breath of rebellion among any of the castes. Is that clear?"

"Eminently," Kurgan said.

Nith Batoxxx stood absolutely still for a moment. "And I will not tolerate insolence from you." He took a step closer to Kurgan. "You think you are invincible." There was a crackle of hyperexcited ions sparking. "I am here to tell you that you are wrong."

With that, the Gyrgon turned and walked away. It was not until he disappeared around a corner that Kurgan realized he was trembling. He spent a moment restoring himself to a semblance of equanimity before returning to his bedroom.

Rada, fully clothed, was out on the balcony. She had thrown the window-doors wide open, and the room was cold. He stood looking at her for a moment. Then he crossed the room and joined her.

She turned when she heard him. The end of the laaga stick was between her fingers. "You will pay off my debt?"

"First thing in the morning. If . . ."

Now she smiled. "Courage and fortitude, as the Sarakkon say. If what, regent?"

"If you will tell me what connection the Sarakkonian captain Courion has with Nith Batoxxx." He saw her expression, and now it was his turn to smile. "I have seen Courion and the Gyrgon together in your office." That was how, a little more than six weeks ago, he had discovered that the Old V'ornn was Nith Batoxxx. "They could not possibly have been in there without your knowledge and consent."

"The transactions between Courion and Nith Batoxxx take place regularly. The Gyrgon has taken a liking to my tavern. It is rough and raucous, and my clientele are only too happy to keep themselves to themselves." She put her hands together, laced her fingers. "A lot of coins cross my palms. For my own protection, I had a neural memory net installed."

"Neural memory nets are illegal."

"Really? I had no idea." She chuckled deep in her throat. "Well, then, I really must get around to ripping mine out one of these days."

"I should report you."

"Go ahead. I have friends in high places."

He laughed.

"The *illegal* memory net recorded some discussions between Nith Batoxxx and Courion of a highly *illegal* nature."

"And the gist of those discussions?"

"Nith Batoxxx has a particular interest in salamuuun."

"So do I. The drug is the sole province of the Ashera Consortium. Only they know where it is manufactured. My father believed that the Ashera murdered my grandfather to keep that secret safe. But why would Nith Batoxxx hold secret meetings with a Sarakkonian captain about salamuuun?"

"Courion is a smuggler like all captains, is he not?"

"True enough. He does a healthy business in laaga. But not salamuuun. It is simply not possible. The Ashera who took control of the Consortium here on Kundala after Eleusis and his family were killed are even more hard-nosed about salamuuun distribution than their predecessor."

"Nevertheless, the memory net makes it clear that salamuuun is the basis of their relationship."

Kurgan stared into the enigmatic eyes. He was pleased with her. She had provided the first tangible lead to a Gyrgon secret. If he could discover the basis of Nith Batoxxx's clandestine activity with the Sarakkon, he would have some badly needed leverage over the Gyrgon. For that, he would have to spend some time with Courion.

"You have done well," he told her. "But from now on I want us to have no direct contact. I do not wish to arouse the suspicions of anyone who frequents Blood Tide. But I will require periodic intelligence. Is this understood?"

"Yes, regent."

"Use data-decagons." He directed her with his raised arm. "Come. On the way out I will introduce you to one of my most trusted Haaar-Kyut. He will be at Blood Tide once a week. You will serve him. You will place the data-decagon at the bottom of his goblet. This will ensure your intelligence reaches me undetected."

She nodded. As she turned to go, he held her back a moment.

"Rada, tell me what you know of the seven Portals."

"I know nothing of them. What are they?"

Kurgan shrugged, betraying nothing of the extreme import of his question. Nith Batoxxx was desperate to find the location of those Portals, he had said that he would reward handsomely whoever provided the information.

"Keep your ears open. Ask around. Let me know what you come up with."

He closed the door softly after her.

Terrettt had begun to remember his dreams—or at least one, in particular. This dream recurred often, night or day, he no longer knew which, leaving a scar upon whatever part of his brain functioned normally. So he remembered, whether he chose to or not. He'd had the dream now for some time—so long, in fact, that when he entered his dream it almost seemed like coming home. Except this home was a scary place—an exceptionally scary place.

It was dark, for one thing; and for another, it was cold. So cold that he began to shiver the moment he felt the icy black water envelop him. Then, he did nothing, it seemed, but hang upside down in this water that was cold and clear and oddly slippery. It was this slippery quality that scared Terrettt most, scared him more than the cold, more even than the darkness, which he did not like at all. He didn't like the darkness because he was convinced that the voices he heard, the relentless clamor, the chaos of sound and fury that inhabited his head like a rabid horde, emerged from this darkness. It was a very special darkness, you see, not the indigo darkness of twilight—as he recalled it in his memory and resurrected in his frantically drawn paintings—not the velvet darkness of a moonslit evening, or even the bitter blackness of a storm-tossed midnight. No, it was something more, something deeper, darker, its absoluteness born of sinister mutterings and evil incantations, mid-wifed by envy, hatred, vengeance, and a perverse desire to take life and snuff it out like a pitiable candleflame.

And in his dream, he was immersed in this darkness, in this water that tasted of bitterroot and bile. He was peculiarly aware of someone else, hanging as he hung, and he was aware that this other was . . . well, waiting. A sizzle of anticipation, edged by elation and, yes, fear made ripples, so the water slipped and slithered over his bare flesh like cruel-eyed serpents, making his flesh shrink and crawl. He abhorred serpents with their legless movement, their silent spying, their black unknowable thoughts. And that is why he hated the slippery water so. But he could not move. As much as he wanted to climb out of the water, as much as the fear flooded through him, making tears stream from his eyes, he remained paralyzed. Utterly helpless.

Feeling it rise up from the depths below him. What was it? He never knew; he always woke up just as it approached. But he knew things about it just the same, oh, yes he did. The evil of it was so strong, so intense that it came to him as a burnt smell as of ravaged homes and spent dreams, a taste that made him want to gag and scream all at once.

More than once he grew terrified that he would choke on his own vomit, but his mouth never opened, and so nothing ever came out. That did not stop his stomachs from feeling as if they wanted to rise up into his throat and turn themselves inside out. It did not stop his hearts from pounding so hard he felt they must surely burst through the wall of his chest to flood his entire being with their rapid-fire pulse. It did not stop his nerves from screeching until he longed only for the sweet oblivion of unconsciousness.

And so, he sensed this thing of depthless evil—whatever it was—rising toward him, and he sensed, too, the opened maw of its horrifying embrace, implacable as the poisonous, taloned gates of N'Luuura.

It came. It came.

Just before it was about to devour him whole, he opened his eyes, sobbing . . .

And here came Kirlll Qandda at the run, responding to the guttural howls, the ghastly caterwauling he set up, to the thrashing of his body, to the heavy rhythmic thumps as he threw himself against the wall, screaming inside his head *get it out, get it out, getitout!*

He knew Kirlll Qandda's touch, knew the Deirus would not hurt him, and yet the part of his brain that was melted, that dreamed the nightmarish dreams, quailed and shivered, shuddered and shook at the touch. He tried to bite Kirlll Qandda, and he could not say why save that the liquid part of his brain, soaked in the black water of the well inside his head, made it an imperative. Because—and when he tried to think about it, it was not clear—what if this wasn't Kirlll Qandda at all, this thing with arms and long tapering fingers and breath like rotting clemetts, what if this room in Receiving Spirit was the dream, the illusion, the nightmare, what if he was hanging upside down in the well, waiting, and this was—

He screamed and thrashed, and he lashed out, drawing blood—his or someone else's, he could not be sure. The terror was like a living thing squirming inside him, the implications of the well and where it went, what lurked at its deep bottom, made his brain want to explode, made him want to rend his skin with his nails, made him want to hurl himself from the window across the room, plummeting through the soft air, to smash to the stone pavement far below, free at last.

And then his eyes were being pulled open and he arched back, knowing what was coming, hating it, fearing it, tasting it, somehow, as the spray coated his eyes, the potent chemicals absorbed into his system in the space of one ragged breath. Like air being let out of an overfilled balloon, Terrettt gave one long shuddering exhale, and the terror left him, life fled him—at least life as he could define it—and he felt a thick mask forming over his face, a mask of lassitude if not serenity. All at once, he forgot the well, the awful cold empty blackness, and what he had glimpsed swimming up toward him. All at once, he could not connect one thought with another, and did not really want to.

Dimly, he was aware of Kirlll Qandda carrying him back to bed, of his sister Marethyn, her face pale and drawn with worry, pulling the linens up around his chin, wishing him pleasant dreams. Which he had in great multitudes. What he regretted most was the concern he caused her. He loved Marethyn with both his hearts. He would gladly have sacrificed himself to make her happy. In fact, he would welcome such a circumstance, for it would prove to him that he had a purpose, that his own life had been worth something after all.

Much later, he arose and peed heavily into the sink where he dutifully and lovingly washed his brushes. Using his extreme hunger and parched mouth as goads, he grabbed his paints. He cut the pigments with his own sweat, in which he was drenched, and set to slashing and swirling, trying to express in an altogether different manner his horror and fear, everything he had seen and felt, everything the dream meant to him or might ever mean. But no matter how hard he tried it wasn't what he had seen or what he wanted to express. As usual, his memory was shot, the drugs in the spray altering the chemical makeup of the memories so that what he conjured up were copies of the originals, reflections, ghosts, softened, edited, riddled with gaps that always defeated him. He grunted as he worked, hunched over his palette, looking more like an animal than a V'ornn, and a Stogggul at that.

No wonder his family never came to see him. Save Marethyn, who could look beyond his nonresponsiveness, his violent outbursts. She listened when he spoke or, more accurately, listened when he tried to speak. But it was as if he was still trapped in his dream. He could hear the words in his head, even form them into phrases and sentences before he ever opened his mouth. But, then, what would come out? Madness. The cusp of madness, all his well-thought-out sentences drowned in the line of spittle spurting between his bared teeth.

For the thousandth time, he glanced up, working for want of a clearer memory with the topographical map Marethyn had put up on the wall. He returned to his painting and, almost instantly, his brush flashed across the paper. Nothing was more important than exorcising the terror that gripped him out of sleep, that ravaged his brain day and night with its bedlam of voices, its multitude of hands grabbing greedily for a piece of his mind. But he would not let them, oh no. He turned violent, hit out at them, screaming at them, and, for a time, they faded away. Then the dream would recur, he would be under the black water, hanging by his heels, staring down into the depths, waiting for *him* to appear . . .

He shook his head, grunting, drooling, painfully and painstakingly making himself put the end of one thought against the beginning of another, until he had a stream that he could render in color and texture on canvas. These were his paintings, his precious paintings, and as long as Marethyn had them he was confident that one day she would see them for what they were, she would understand that they were messages meant for her. Because she was the only one who came, who spent time with him, who did not believe him mad. And he was sure that sooner or later she would catch on, she would see what it was he was painting, and know it for what it really was.

Then he forgot what it was he had been thinking, forgot that he could think at all. He was screaming and screaming and screaming and eventually his screams were punctuated by the rhythm of pounding feet.

He is all right," Kirlll Qandda said, "for now."

Marethyn smoothed her hand over Terrettt's damp forehead. "How long will he sleep?"

"Long enough," Kirlll Qandda said, "to get his strength back."

Marethyn sat down by Terrettt's bedside. She was close to tears. She had been here ever since Kirlll Qandda had contacted her, all night, it seemed, and into this dreary, enervating morning. She missed Sornnn desperately, wished he was here beside her, but for a couple of hours at least she had stopped thinking about Tettsie's death. "And still there is no improvement."

Kirlll Qandda clasped his hands in front of him. "I wish I could be more encouraging, but nothing I have tried has had the slightest effect on his condition, which continues to defy diagnosis. Without the proper diagnosis, as you must know, there is virtually no hope of finding a cure."

All at once, Marethyn burst into tears.

"Ah, my dear, please ignore me," the Deirus said, wringing his hands. "I always say the wrong thing."

"It is all too much, you see," she sobbed.

"But, oh, how could I be so thickheaded?" he said. "I was honored you asked me to preside over your grandmother's remains."

Tettsie's final arrangements had been brief and without fanfare. Tuskugggun—even Great Caste Tuskugggun like Tettsie—were not entitled to the Rescendance. After Kirlll Qandda had examined her, she had been summarily cremated.

"It was clear that you and she were very close." He clucked his tongue against the roof of his mouth. "But as far as Terrettt is concerned you must not give up hope. I haven't."

She looked up at him. "No?"

"Absolutely not. Even now I have a number of radically new approaches I am devising." He raised a slender, bony finger. "You just stay here a moment and take deep, even breaths."

He went out of Terrettt's room for a moment. When he returned, he was carrying a small goblet. He knelt beside her, put her fingers around the stem. "You must restore yourself, Marethyn Stogggul."

She drank the fire-grade numaaadis gratefully. "I thought liquor was forbidden here."

The Deirus gave her a small smile. "Every V'ornn needs a bit of restoration, now and then."

"Thank you," she said, handing him back the empty goblet. "You were very kind and understanding with Tettsie, and now you are again."

"It is nothing."

"No. It is most assuredly not 'nothing.' You are the first one in here to show the slightest kindness toward my brother."

He spread his hands. "How could I do any less?"

"That sounds very Kundalan."

Kirlll Qandda looked at her for what seemed a long time. "Are you a sympathizer?"

"I beg your pardon?"

"No, no." He waved his hands. "It is nothing."

"I heard what you said. I will not forget it."

He blanched.

"No, you misunderstand. I would never betray your trust. In fact, I myself have been thinking . . ."

"There are quite a few of us, you know."

"No," she said, her hearts suddenly beating faster. "I did not."

"Well, it's true," he whispered, and giggled a little, possibly from an excess of nerves.

She lowered her voice as well. "It's odd you should say that. I was recently in a space within a warehouse, filled with artifacts from the Korrush and other Kundalan lands."

"What is odd about that?"

"It is owned by a Bashkir."

"Indeed?"

"And there were some boxes, Khagggun-looking because of the sigils, and I got the feeling . . . you know, it was just a feeling."

"Was it Sornnn SaTrryn's warehouse?" When she looked at him, he hastened to add, "I could not help noticing him with you while I examined your grandmother."

"Tettsie was his mother's best friend."

"The boxes were Khagggun, you say?"

As if suddenly becoming aware of the perilous turn the conversation had taken, she rose abruptly, and there ensued a small but thoroughly awkward silence, which had the effect of making the skin at the back of her neck crawl.

"Thank you again, Kirlll Qandda," she said at last. "For everything."

"I wish I had better news." The Deirus escorted her to the door. "Have faith. Perhaps next time I will."

Does it have to be so dark in here?" Eleana asked.

"The Teyj says yes," Rekkk told her.

"It's pitch-black." She could feel his presence, but she could not see him. And where was the Gyrgon-bred bird? "Not even one oil lamp?"

"Not even one photon of light, the Teyj says."

They had descended a precipitous staircase, a black-timbered upper portion followed by a stone flight, smooth and hollowed by wear. At its bottom was a warren of narrow cellar passageways and low-ceilinged chambers underneath the abbey. There was about the place a dank and decidedly forbidding air, as if they were approaching the repository for the bones of disgraced Ramahan. The sense of abandonment and regret was everywhere evident in the piles of icons, dusty and diademed, animal carvings, cracked and cobwebbed, altars and fonts, chipped and timeworn, in which vermin had made their nests. The dregs of a once-limber civilization in decline, lost now, mysterious even to itself.

"How do you know what the Teyj says?" she asked him as she stood in the dark.

"Something happened when he worked on me."

"It slipped a Gyrgon device into you, you mean."

"I don't think so," Rekkk said. "I'm already part Gyrgon. Nith Sahor altered me when he implanted this prototype okummmon in my arm. It's of his own manufacture."

"That doesn't explain why—"

"When the Teyj was repairing me he established a connection, possibly through the okummmon. It is a communication device."

"Yours is much more," she said. "I've seen how you can transmogrify matter from one state to another by feeding it into the okummmon's slot."

The Teyj gave a brief, fluted call, and Rekkk said, "Hush now, he's about to activate the duscaant."

"Why do you insist on calling the bird a 'he' when it's just an animal?"

The Teyj's shrill warning cry silenced her.

A brilliant cone of light pierced the darkness. It seemed to emanate from everywhere at once. Then, abruptly, it coalesced into a sphere that bubbled and pulsed with milky life. The milkiness turned transparent, revealing the inside of the abbey's Library where the duscaant had been secreted. And then, as if a set of doors had been thrown open, Eleana and Rekkk found themselves inside the Library, observing history, random moments from the past that the duscaant had recorded for its Gyrgon masters.

Ramahan passed to and fro, oblivious to its existence. There was talk of spells and lessons, there was small gossip and inconsequential asides, there was a somber airiness. A Ramahan wondered if she was getting too fat, another sitting at the long refectory table they had come to know so well confided to her neighbor that she had taken a book from the Library to study from overnight and had forgotten to return it. Bells chimed deeply and melodiously, and there was silence, and then the prayers began. And it was these quotidian stitches dropped out of the warp and weft of a history so recently written that made Eleana particularly uneasy, for she felt keenly the particular damage inflicted by the voyeur, the invasion of something that was meant to be inviolate. And she put her hands across her ballooning belly in an instinctual effort to protect her baby because this seemed to her to be an act of violence more heinous, even, than the slaughter that had sent the plumes of black smoke into the dying light of a foreshortened autumn afternoon. Because it crept in the shadows, gobbling up lives, hidden from view.

As a former leader of a Resistance cell she knew better than most Kundalan the value of clandestine intelligence gathering, and of course part of her would have given an arm for a single duscaant to plant in the headquarters of Line-General Lokck Werrrent. But with the baby growing inside her that life seemed distant and dim. She put a hand to her head. What was happening to her? She had been raised a child of the war against the V'ornn. Her parents had been murdered by Khagggun, her friends and compatriots, as well. She had always been defined in terms of her warrior's heart. And now here she was harboring these feelings, pulling back from violence. She could feel herself refocusing her energies from rage to protection. The baby inside her living, swimming, kicking, breathing when she breathed, his twin V'ornn hearts double-beating in counterpoint to her own. He was so unknowing, helpless, vulnerable, just like these long-dead Ramahan walking and speaking and praying all around her in the dusklight of the duscaant's irradiated theater. She would do anything to protect him from the savage beast ravaging the world.

The light changed abruptly, the Library, surrounded by the citadel of the night, lit with deeply incised bronze oil lamps, their orange flames reflected in the huge windowpanes. A whorl of violet V'ornnish letters and numbers was briefly superimposed in a corner of shadows and then vanished. A new entry in another time period.

Two Ramahan sat side by side in the otherwise deserted Library, their persimmon-colored robes marking them as highest-ranking konara. There was a thick book open between them on the refectory table, but neither was consulting it. Their upper bodies were curled slightly, bent forward as if responding to a powerful magnetic force flowing between them.

"—all you need or will ever need to know," said the konara with a nose keen as a knife blade.

"You cannot expect me to agree," the other konara said. She had wide-apart eyes that made her look surprised even when she was not. "What are you thinking?"

"I am offering you a way—the only way—to save yourself and your Ramahan." The knife-nosed konara had a very high, domed forehead that shone in the lamplight.

"Konara Mossa, no. It is out of the question."

"Listen, listen." Konara Mossa took the other's hand in hers. "This is the third time in three months I have come to see you. I speak to you now out of the depths of our long-standing friendship. I have traveled far, as you know. And why? In the hopes that you will see reason."

"But the bargain you must have made. What you are proposing I must do."

"For the sake of every Ramahan here."

"There must be another way."

"There is not, Konara Yasttur. I would have found it, otherwise."

"I wonder whether this is so," Konara Yasttur said. "Haven't you taken the expedient path, acquiesced to the only alternative they have presented?"

"Your acolytes are how young?" Konara Mossa asked sharply.

"They are my charges, my precious children."

"Yes. For them, Konara Yasttur. For the sake of their lives. For the sake of our order." She leaned in farther. "If not, there will be genocide. This the V'ornn have promised."

"I cannot believe that you have sealed the bargain," Konara Yasttur hissed between bared teeth. "With the enemy."

"Better the enemy you know," Konara Mossa said softly.

"You are deluded," Konara Yasttur said shortly. "Our culture, our daily lives, our history, all that we are, all that makes us unique is being systematically stripped from us by these evil—" She broke off, buried her face in handfuls of her persimmon robes.

"My dear, I come to you tonight as I have always come."

"Carrying a dread secret."

"As a friend."

Konara Yasttur looked up quickly. "Ah, Miina protect us from our enemies and our friends."

A window seemed to close in Konara Mossa's face as she slapped her thighs and rose. Looking down at Konara Yasttur, she said, "Then I cannot make you see reason."

Konara Yasttur said, "The reasoning of the damned."

"They will come, then, and they will destroy you all." Konara Mossa looked abruptly sad. "I haven't the power to stop them."

"Would you, if you could?"

"But, of course. What do you think—?"

"You have sunk to their level, you have accepted their violence, the inevitability of their victory. You have been infected by their evil, and you are cut off from the divine light of the Goddess. That is what I know."

Konara Mossa frowned. "It is you who are deluded, my old friend. I will be remembered as a hero of the order, I am doing what needs to be done so that the Ramahan may survive this final onslaught."

Konara Yasttur rose and faced her friend. "And have you considered that your decision, the very act of betraying your kind, will be the very instrument of our order's destruction." She held out a hand. "You are a servant of Miina, you are holy as the Great Goddess is holy. If goodness does not illuminate the abbeys, then this is, truly, the fall of everlasting night." Konara Mossa turned her face away, and Konara Yasttur's harsh, almost hysterical laugh ended in a sob. "Ah, don't you see? What need the V'ornn of direct atrocities when they have bent such as you to do their evil bidding?"

Light flared, a morning sun spilling white gold through the high windows. In the same shadowy corner, the whorl of V'ornnish letters marking a new time and new scene spiraled and vanished. The Library was utterly deserted, in the way that comes only at the very end of things. Through the windows a pack of Khagggun in full battle armor could be seen, their shock-swords out and swinging in a silent harvest as they slaughtered the Ramahan on the spot.

Just before the entry—the last one—ended, Konara Yasttur appeared, yanked by her hair. The last of her tattered robes was stripped off her, and the pack fell upon her, the ranking officers first, unhinging their bloody armor, then the lower-echelon warriors, licking their lips, their callused hands clawing and pulling at bare flesh. Her mouth was open. She must have been screaming, but in the sunny glow of the duscaant's photonic recording all was silence.

13

Beam

Kirlll Qandda was reading the latest holoscan of Terrettt's brain activity he had made when Jesst Vebbn poked his head into the cubicle, and said, "You are needed."

Though he had been engrossed in the anomalous readings, Kirlll rose without protest. He had no choice. Jesst Vebbn was the Genomatekk to whom he was assigned, whose orders he must fulfill without question or protest.

"What is it?" he said as he strode side by side with the Genomatekk.

"A new shipment has arrived," Jesst Vebbn said shortly. "One of them is dying."

Jesst Vebbn was walking so quickly that Kirlll had to hurry to keep up, but then Jesst did everything in triple time, including talking. He was a tall, clemett-shaped individual with shortish arms and legs that were almost comical. He possessed the clinician's typical face, closed and calculating. If he possessed any emotion, Kirlll had yet to see it.

Up ahead, Kirlll could see the knot of Khagggun sentinels. He despised Khagggun with all his being, just as he despised the ongoing program of which Jesst Vebbn was in charge. The Khagggun parted when they saw Jesst, but of course they eyed Kirlll with distaste bordering on loathing. And why shouldn't they? His presence was a harbinger of imminent death.

Jesst led him through the anteroom where the children were being processed. A single line had formed and, though Jesst appeared entirely oblivious, Kirlll registered like a blow to his body the fear and anguish on each and every face he passed. He could never get used to the so-called "recombinant experiments" the Gyrgon had ordered. These children, the sad consequence of Kundalan females being raped by battle-blooded Khagggun, were in any case mistakes.

"Poor things," Kirlll could not help but say. "They are born into misery."

"Typical Deirus. You have inverted the sentiment," Jesst said as they hurried on. "This program they are entering gives the miserable purpose. Look at them snivel and weep. Well, what can you expect from animals. Had they sufficient intelligence, they would stand proud and tall, knowing that they give their lives to further the higher science of the Gyrgon."

Kirlll bit his lip, contenting himself at staring murderously at the back of the Genomatekk's neck. At length, they passed through the large anteroom and into a narrow corridor lined on either side by tiny examination cubicles. These were slowly being filled by the hybrid children as they passed through processing. They were fairly easy to spot. Most of their V'ornn genes were expressed, overwhelming the Kundalan traits. But inside there were differences, though these differences varied widely. These were, of course, what interested the Gyrgon most.

Halfway down, Jesst stopped and parted a curtain.

"In here," he said. He hung back in the doorway as Kirlll entered, unable to bring himself any closer to the dying child.

Every twenty meters or so a Khagggun stood guard, as if these wretched children might prove a threat to the Genomatekks crisscrossing from cubicle to cubicle.

"What is the defect?" he asked in his clipped, clinical voice.

Kirlll stood over the child, a male of no more than four years, he judged. The child was very pale, his skin clammy, his breath shallow and irregular. His eyes, wide and staring, fixed on Kirlll, and terror coalesced in them, turning them dark and old beyond his years.

"Be calm," Kirlll told him. "I am here to help."

All the while, his expert hands were probing and palpating. He drew out a portable holoscanner and thumbed it on.

"Look at this," he told the child as he played it over his torso. "Hear that humming? That means it is making you better."

"Stop babbling," Jesst said impatiently, "and talk to me."

"He was born with two sets of hearts," Kirlll said as he studied the holoimage.

Now Jesst seemed interested. "Wouldn't that make him stronger?"

"One heart is Kundalan, the other is a V'ornn twinned heart. Apparently they are incompatible."

"That is a great pity," Jesst said. He crossed his arms over his chest and leaned against the doorframe. "Is there anything you can do for him?" In response to Kirlll's glance, he added, "I am not quite the ogre you believe me to be."

"The ogre spoke quite eloquently of animal pride."

"That was in the anteroom, in public. That is how I am expected to speak," Jesst said.

"You do not believe me."

When Kirlll did not reply, Jesst said, "It comes straight from the holotext. That much I am certain you know."

"I have read it," Kirlll said.

Jesst waited several moments before he said, "I know you do not approve of our program."

"I do not approve of causing or prolonging suffering, even in the name of Gyrgon high science." Kirlll watched as the child played with the holoscanner. "But what matter? The opinion of a Deirus carries no weight."

Jesst glanced over at the child. "You will have to perform an autopsy," he said softly.

Kirlll nodded, a jerk of his head. "Would that I could save him."

"I wish it too."

"Oh, I do not doubt it." Kirlll smiled benignly down at the child. "An enrollee with double hearts. Imagine the experiments."

"What is it," Jesst said, "that rankles you so?"

Kirlll turned and, with one hand still on the child, said, "He is an innocent, just as all of them here are innocents. They did not ask to be born, the circumstances of their life, their genetic composition, are not of their making. They were caused by bestial acts perpetrated by our own kind."

"Khagggun are not our own kind," Jesst said unexpectedly.

"Neither are Gyrgon, but we bow to their bidding all the same."

Jesst spread his hands. "Have we a choice?"

"*You* have a choice. You could ask to be reassigned."

"And risk having a Genomatekk with blood in his hearts take my place?"

Kirlll took a deep breath, let it slowly out. He shook his head then, turning back to the child, said, "I could use some help here."

The child was going into convulsions. There was no help for him, nothing in the vast Genomatekk arsenal could save him from the savage mistake of his conception. Somehow, sadly, that seemed appropriate,

Kirlll thought, as he directed Jesst to hold the child's arms and legs. He produced one of the small canisters he used on Terrettt and, holding open the child's fluttering eyelids, sprayed each eye in turn. Almost immediately, the convulsions subsided.

"What will happen now?" Jesst asked.

"He will sleep." Kirlll put away the canister, "and that sleep will become deeper and deeper until he is gone." He felt a curious sensation in his chest, a fizzing like a severed ion beam. "I will not leave him while he yet lives."

"We both will stay," Jesst said, surprising Kirlll once again. "But let us not keep vigil in silence."

"What would you speak of?"

"An inquiry has been raised about you."

Kirlll looked at him blankly.

"An internal inquiry, nothing dire, I am quite certain. These things crop up among Deirus from time to time." He shrugged. "I myself do not put much store in them, but nevertheless they must be dealt with in a timely manner or I am the one who will answer for the delay."

"What is the nature of this inquiry?"

Jesst, glancing at the dying child, said, "Or perhaps this is not the right time."

"I could use the distraction."

Jesst nodded. "The inquiry concerns the lovers you keep."

"What about them?"

"You know what about them. They are male."

"I am a law-abiding Deirus."

"Actually—" Jesst scratched the back of his neck—"the law, as it was drawn up by the Gyrgon Comradeship, states that same-sex fornication is forbidden." He smiled a porcelain smile. "But you already know this." There was the briefest pause. "Oh, I have no doubt of your usefulness to the Modality, Kirlll Qandda. No, indeed. But there are others . . ." Jesst broke off, seemingly at a loss as to how to proceed. "This is awkward for me."

"Imagine how I feel."

Jesst cleared his throat. "I want to make it clear that in my opinion the inquiry is off base, a total waste of time. And you are one of my most valued Deirus. Still, I must ask."

"Proceed."

"There seems in some quarters to be a certain suspicion concerning the SaTrryn Consortium."

"What is the nature of such suspicion?"

"And seeing as how you have been their Deirus—I mean, did you not preside over Hadinnn SaTrryn's death?"

"Sornnn SaTrryn asked me to do so, yes," Kirlll said.

"And that was not the first. Your involvement with them goes back, what, twenty years?"

"Twenty-seven."

Jesst nodded. "It's just that, well, officials are looking."

"For what?"

"An involvement with the, ah, the Kundalan Resistance."

Kirlll frowned. "What are you getting at?"

Jesst leaned in and lowered his voice. "Just this. If, let us say, the SaTrryn are involved with helping the enemy and if, let us say, you yourself are somehow involved."

Kirlll snorted. "This is quite a web you're weaving."

"Oh, not me. No, not at all." Jesst put a forefinger beside his nose. "But in certain quarters."

For the first time, Kirlll appeared shaken. "What quarters?"

"Very high up. More than that I am not at liberty to reveal." Jesst drew a little away. "Either way, it would not go well for you, do you see?"

"That is preposterous."

"Well, you and I perhaps know that. But as for the others."

"I am not saying . . . But if . . ." Kirlll seemed unable to meet the Genomatekk's eye. "What if I knew something? Information that could lead to the arrest of the traitor."

"That would absolve you of . . . well, of everything," Jesst said softly.

"Even my private life?"

"Even that."

"The child is crossing over," Kirlll said. He placed his finger on the side of the child's neck. The pulse was weak and erratic. It barely impacted his nerve endings. And then, in the wink of an eye, it was gone.

"He never had a chance," Jesst pointed out.

"That makes it worse, not better." The fizzing in Kirlll's chest had reached a crescendo.

Jesst cleared his throat.

"Not that I am saying I have direct knowledge of who the traitor is."
Kirlll Qandda still had hold of the child, and now he disengaged himself, a small but telling act of acceptance. "But it is possible that I have
recently heard something that would be of special interest to these
'others.' "

"You must tell me what you know," Jesst said urgently.

"I must think."

"I urge you not to take too long. The offer may be withdrawn at any
moment. And then."

"And then, what?"

Jesst looked into Kirlll's eyes. "I would be forced to continue the
inquiry into your private activities whether I wanted to or not."

"You are giving me no choice then."

"That is, regrettably for you, the case."

Kirlll felt that curious sensation in his chest slowly dissipating as he
took up his ion scalpel. He said a brief prayer for the child's departed
soul, a death song he had composed years ago more for his own benefit
than for the newly dead. Then he made the first incision, precisely
aligned and meaningful, like everything he did.

All the next day Tezziq put Riane through her paces, and so exacting
a taskmaster was she that Riane was exhausted by dinnertime. Immediately following, she took her bath and collapsed on her cushions.

She was summarily roused out of a dreamless slumber. Tezziq was
shaking her by the shoulder.

"He's coming," Tezziq whispered in her ear. "Baliiq is coming."

"Who?" Riane said drowsily. But she came fully awake when she saw
the figure in the doorway. He was standing with his powerful legs
spread, his brawny arms crossed over his chest. Riane sat up. "Don't
worry," she whispered. "I won't let him take you."

"It is not for me that he is here," Tezziq said breathlessly. "It is for
you."

"What?" Fear gripped Riane by the throat. "But I told you—"

"Yes." Tezziq held her close, felt her shiver. "I know."

"It must be some mistake. You have had but a few days to train me."
She looked into Tezziq's eyes. The thought of being subject to Makktuub's outsized lusts made her ill. "Surely that's not enough time."

"Baliiq is here. You must go." Tezziq pushed her gently off the cushions and onto the carpeted floor. "There is simply no alternative."

There is always an alternative, Mother had once told her, but her mind was so paralyzed she could think of nothing. She slid into the slipper-shoes the kapudaan had given her.

Dread was Riane's constant companion as she walked beside Baliiq. A feeling of unreality had invaded her, anesthetizing her, sapping her will. An image of what the kapudaan had done to Tezziq ran through her head, and she quailed. With an effort, she concentrated on Baliiq instead, trying to calm herself by studying him closely.

He was well muscled but, unlike the other guards Riane had seen, there was nothing thick or heavy about him. His hair was drawn back from his face, but instead of being wound on the top of his head, it hung in a long queue held at its end by a fillet of carved emperor carnelian. He moved with the same kind of liquid grace she had seen in the kuomeshals, as if he were simply an animated part of the landscape.

He said not a word to her as he led her down one tented corridor and up another, but often she felt the hot scrutiny of his gaze. Mostly, one passageway was indistinguishable from another until they came to one where the walls were strung with magnificent silk carpets, meant to be seen rather than walked upon. Their patterns, though varied, were united in their strict geometric nature. They all featured a central core of some sort, round or square, oblong or hexagonal, depending on the whim or the imagination of the artist-weaver, surrounded by bands that more or less spiraled outward in ever-increasing complexity until they reached the border.

The carpets became more ornate until she and Baliiq turned a corner and entered a corridor with plain whitewashed walls. At its far end was a spiral staircase fashioned from a deep lustrous bronze, worked into a filigree of vine stems and tiny starlike flowers. They ascended this, and soon found themselves outside on a vast terrace that overlooked the city. A walkway of carpets lay directly ahead of them.

Stars already throbbed in the vastness of the early-evening sky, scarred as it was by a pair of crescent moons so slender their green was almost white. A softly soughing wind carried the ubiquitous red dust and the rich, heady scents of roasting meat and brewing ba'du.

Riane saw Makktuub lounging on a densely patterned divan in the midst of a small, artfully arranged oasis of limoniq trees, potted and pruned into dwarves. The divan was covered in watered silk. To one side was a table laden with steamed and stuffed fruits, to the other was an ornately filigreed lyssomwood panel, the better, doubtless, to screen him from the ululating din of the streets and boulevards below.

The kapudaan stirred slightly as Baliiq brought her into his presence. With a flick of his fingers, he dismissed the albino. Riane was actually sorry to see Baliiq go. He had been a powerful presence but not a particularly forbidding one. He was not like the dull-eyed guards who lined the tents like cement bricks. There seemed something inside him waiting to emerge, a sense of tension, yes, but also a watchfulness, as if he were searching for the right time, the right place to reveal himself. But now that did not matter because he was gone and she was all alone on the terrace with Makktuub.

"So." Makktuub smiled from behind his dark, hooded eyes, but the smile, she felt, was thin and, for some reason, strained. "How have you fared with the oh-so-lovely Tezziq?"

"She is quite skilled in the ways of pleasure," Riane replied.

"And she is treating you well?" He was using one hand to lend emphasis to what he was saying. "She is keeping her jealousy in check? Is there anything for which you lack?"

"My freedom."

He sat up abruptly, and Riane tensed, sensing his strain breaking the surface. His eyes were deeply angry, and for a moment she was certain he was going to strike her as he rose off the divan. But instead, he stood watching her.

She tried to read his expression. There was a certain unease. It had been there a long time, like a ruin, something in the wilderness of the steppes, lost and almost forgotten. A pulse beat in his right temple, betraying a deeper anger. He wanted to say something, she could tell that, but he felt constrained. She could hear a sudden burst of shouts from the street below, the ululating prayers briefly interrupted, the altercation discordant after the unwinding music of the chants. Then it was over, and the prayer-songs began again as if the voices had never been interrupted.

"If you plan on taking me to bed," Riane said, "I will not comply. I want my freedom."

"Jiharre may heed your plea," he murmured, seeming now truly ill at ease, "but heaven itself knows when."

Astonished, she watched him hurry across the carpeted expanse and disappear down the spiral staircase into the palace. For a moment, she did not know what to do. The wind ruffled her hair, sounds arose from below, reciting tales of the city and its inhabitants. Inexorably, she was drawn to the near edge of the terrace. Beyond a waist-high parapet, she saw the nighttime sprawl of Agachire. Across the street, narrower than the avenue the palace fronted, she could see the parapet of another terrace, and across its expanse, the dim outline of another. Below, the street itself was clogged with foot traffic as well as slow-moving kuomeshal caravans. Females squatted, stirring fine-grained stews or stacking flat bread. Old men chanted, their heads together, their arms around each other's waists as they moved rhythmically back and forth. Lovers gazed into each other's eyes but did not touch. Instead, they fed each other dried fruits and sweetmeats from paper cones they had purchased from street vendors. Merchants argued with customers while children wove a wild and unpredictable pattern through it all. She was trying to calculate the odds of surviving a leap from the terrace when a figure emerged from behind the filigreed screen.

She felt her breath driven from her lungs. The figure was so startling, so out of place that she was rooted to the spot. Glittering in the spangled starlight, a Gyrgon stood, buried within his armor. The helm was high and angular, eared and horned and unvented, with a menacing ridged brow into which a row of alloy talons had been sunk. It projected a formidable appearance, this particular ion exomatrix. As it ought; it was a battle suit.

"I believe it is high time we got acquainted, Riane," the Gyrgon said, coming toward her. "My name is Nith Settt."

He held out a black-gloved hand, in the center of which sat something darkly familiar, and Riane's heart skipped a beat. *Dear Miina, no,* she thought.

"Please tell me," Nith Settt said softly and sibilantly as he glided toward her, "how you came to be in possession of this."

And it began to expand exponentially, Nith Settt holding it aloft for her to see, Nith Sahor's neural-net greatcoat.

Tettsie looked out at them, regal and commanding, and it seemed surely that the entirety of what she was, of what she had stood for existed in the muted colors and masterly brushstrokes that Marethyn had labored over for weeks.

"It's her completely," Sornnn said. "It's a marvelous accomplishment."

"I can't believe it," Marethyn said. "The painting was the point, and she never got to see it."

It might seem like a trivial, even a self-centered thing to say at the ending of a life as long as Tettsie's had been, but it was not. It was merely, finally, a way to make death—so deep a mystery—understandable. It also brought Tettsie's death down to a manageable size. It allowed Marethyn to go on with her daily life, it allowed her to sleep at night, though that slumber was often restless, interrupted by dreams she would rather not remember or interpret.

They stood in her closed and shuttered atelier, an embroidered indigo remembrance-cloth draped over the spot where Tettsie had died. According to custom, it would remain undisturbed for one month, after which it would be carefully wound into a tertium tube.

While Marethyn had gone about seeing to her grandmother's final arrangements, Sornnn, in his official capacity as Prime Factor, had been at Finial Hall, a cavernous, brooding space in a former Kundalan warehouse that had undergone a typically unlovely V'ornn transformation. He was adjudicating a protracted and acrimonious dispute he had inherited from the time when Wennn Stogggul had been the Prime Factor that concerned two Consortia, the Nwerrrn and the Fellanngg, over mineral rights on the western edge of the Borobodur forest. It was the sort of case, complicated and petty, that reaffirmed Sornnn's yearning for the brilliant uncluttered endless landscape of the Korrush.

"She was my mentor, my compass," Marethyn said. "What am I going to do without her?"

Sornnn took hold of her, turned her around to face him because he did not know what else to do. He felt helpless at the sight of her grief and vulnerability. "You have taken what she taught you," he said. "You are already your own mentor and compass."

"Do you really think so?"

He turned her around so she faced the painting again. "Look at her, Marethyn. This is your grandmother, but it is also your creation. What I see in there, the strength and pride and stubbornness and anger and loving kindness, comes from you."

And Marethyn was crying and laughing at the same time and whispering something Sornnn could not quite catch, which was all right because whatever was said was between her and Tettsie, as it should be, between granddaughter and grandmother who were mirror images, who had meant so much to each other.

Tettsie, who even in death knew what she wanted, had dictated instructions into a data-decagon she had long since given to Marethyn. Upon playing it back, they discovered these things: Tettsie wanted her ashes scattered over the deep pools outside the city walls where she and Marethyn had swum on hot summer afternoons. She asked that her house and its contents be sold, the proceeds delivered to a solicitor-Bashkir named Dobbro Mannx who had previously been instructed to hold the funds in a trust. Two items, alone, were to be retrieved and distributed thusly: To Marethyn, she bequeathed a red-jade box. To Petrre Aurrr, Sornnn SaTrryn's mother, she bequeathed a simple vera-dium necklace—her favorite—that held in its center a small but breathtakingly perfect Nieobian starwen. Cleverly, she also asked Marethyn to personally deliver the necklace to Petrre Aurrr.

"Sornnn, if I ask you to deliver the necklace, will you do it?"

"You could do it just as easily," he said. "She was your grandmother."

Marethyn held out the flat black case. "Yes. I am thinking of what Tettsie would want," she said, though he knew very well she was thinking of something else altogether.

Presently, he went, the case tucked underneath his arm, to his mother's residence.

Petrre Aurrr lived in a Kundalan confection, elaborate and airy, deep in the Eastern Quarter with a large atrium filled with dwarf clemett trees, bare and pale now, and delicately fringed evergreens that clattered softly in the knife-edged gusts of autumnal wind. It was just past sunset, the sky overhead streaked with orange and vermilion clouds, but at its very apex the heavens were a lustrous cobalt.

Sornnn's mother was a handsome woman, tall and stately. She wore robes the color of dried cor blood, a rich shade that suited her light eyes. She had the fine-boned hands of a sculptor, and a face that bore without apology the history of her life.

She looked at him, dumbfounded for an instant, when he appeared on her doorstep.

"May I come in?"

"Yes. Yes, of course."

The exchange, though brief, managed to reiterate the odd formality and awkwardness of their relationship.

The residence was decorated in a surprising and inventive admixture of cultures. Cool and crisply lined V'ornn furniture was covered with tactile and ornate Kundalan fabrics. Sornnn was rather surprised to see how well the meshing of the severe and the febrile worked, but as he drank it all in—the furniture, the carpets, chests, sideboards, shelves filled with mementos and curios, there was not one thing from his memory, from her previous life, from his family. And this was his mother's house.

He produced the flat black case. "I have—"

"May I get you a drink?" she said at the very same instant.

The brief silence somehow echoed Sornnn's anger and grief.

His mother stared into his eyes, ignoring the case. "Forgive me," she said, all at once. "An old friend has just died."

"I know, I—" He cleared his throat, which had turned dry as the Great Voorg. "Her granddaughter is an acquaintance." Those flat words, so devoid of emotion, seemed to him more stupid and spiteful than a mere falsehood. He patted the top of the case. "This is from your old friend."

With a bewildered look, his mother took the case and slowly, almost reverently, opened it.

"Ah," was all she could manage, and the tears began to flow down her cheeks. She went and sat down on a chair upholstered in the ornate Kundalan style, the open case on her lap. She stared out the sliding doors into the tree-filled atrium, idly fondling the necklace. "She loved that clemett tree. In Lonon, with the gimnopedes swarming, she would stand on her tiptoes to pick the ripest of the fruit. Then she would go into the kitchen and make the most delicious dessert. We would eat it for days, laughing over the dining room table. What fun we would have eating and talking! And now it's all . . . like grains of sand flowing through my fingers." She wiped her eyes. "No matter how hard I try, I can't seem to hold on to any of it."

"And not a single happy memory of your real family," he said with a bitter taste of the old familiar anger.

He was already at the front door, his hand on the ornate Kundalan latch, when his mother turned.

"Must you go? Already? I haven't given you anything to eat."

"It's better this way," he said with a strangled voice.

She stood, facing him. "I have many happy memories of you, Sornnn."

And that one line, so obviously a lie, loosed the cold rage he had vowed to keep at bay. "That seems odd," he said through gritted teeth, "considering how cold you became toward me."

She studied him for a long time. "Yes."

"Is that all you have to say." To his horror, he found that he was trembling.

"It couldn't be helped."

His anger flared full force. "What the N'Luuura do you mean, it couldn't be helped?"

She turned away.

"What did I do to disappoint you so?"

"Oh, Sornnn." Her voice held a desperate note of anguish. When she turned back her eyes glittered with tears. "If you believe nothing else, then I beg you to believe this: it had nothing to do with you."

"Then what was it?"

She shook her head. "Leave matters where they are. Believe me, you're better off—"

"That's right. Lies and silence. Why should I expect more from you?"

Her eyes went opaque, and for a moment he thought she hadn't heard or wouldn't respond. He felt like a child again, his chest tight with anger and longing and confusion. And he remembered the time he threw the Phareseian colorsphere across the chamber, turning his back on it, and on her. He wrenched the door open and went through it.

"All right, then," she said at last in a clear penetrating voice.

He paused, looked back because he could not help himself, because despite his anger she was his mother, and there was a part of him that had always loved her and needed her.

"Come back inside, Sornnn," she said softly.

He saw her in profile, her face suddenly weary but still achingly beautiful.

"Please."

He returned inside, closed the door behind him. His hearts were wrung out with emotion, and all at once he experienced a surge of panic and almost asked her to keep her secrets hidden. But, in the end, he kept silent.

"I was directed—ordered, actually—to act detached."

"I do not believe you," he said suspiciously.

"Sornnn, I cannot make you believe me, but if you continue to think that I am lying to you, we will never get anywhere."

He took a deep breath, and in a cold voice said, "So you were ordered to act coldly to me. By whom?"

She sighed. "By your father."

"Liar!" His scalp tingling, he strode back to the door, opening it.

"He was jealous, you see." She crossed the room after him, hurried on. "He didn't want to share you, with me or anyone else. At first I said no. He threatened me. I didn't care. I told him it was a hideous thing to do to you. I told him I wouldn't. Then he hit me, and hit me again, and kept on hitting me until . . ."

She turned away to stare out into the atrium again. "That clemett tree, now that all the leaves are gone, I can see I don't like its shape at all. It is in serious need of pruning."

"Is this . . . is it the truth—"

"I never wanted you to know. I prayed to Enlil."

"Now I need to hear all of it."

Her voice was no more than a strangled whisper. "He would have beaten me to death, you see. He had a need to control me, to put his boot on my neck and keep it there, pressing harder and harder." She was weeping again, soft silent tears rolling down her cheeks. "He needed to see what it would take to break me, I suppose. To strip me of my strength, my willfulness, my dreams of independence." She folded her hands over the necklace. "Well, clever thing, he found it." She turned her beautiful tormented tear-streaked face to him. "It was you."

Sornnn's brain buzzed, and his face burned. He thought of his mother and father together and apart, of the peculiar dynamics of their relationship, of the forces, intimate, exhilarating, crushing, that come to bear when male and female are linked in this way. In his own mind, his father had been a great and generous man, rare and unusual in his desire to embrace other cultures. That was how Sornnn saw himself, and he had simply assumed it had been the same with his father. But who knew what drove V'ornn to do what they did? Could he have misunderstood or missed completely his father's need to do what he did? He went, when he was able, and knelt beside her. All these years spent hating her. All that time wasted, how had she put it, like grains of sand running through her fingers.

He watched her as she went to a carved heartwood chest and opened it. When she came back to him, she had an object cradled between her hands. He knew what it was even before she gave it to him, lovingly preserved, her memories of him intact and glowing fiercely inside the Phareseian colorsphere.

"If you ever doubted that I loved you."

"Mother—"

"It's been a long time since you called me that."

She gazed into his face as he held his old toy, smiling sadly and joyfully, knowing as only a mother can that he was feeling again the heartsbeat of his childhood.

Night had stolen over the atrium, and all the trees were enameled in indigo. He sat in the brightly lit, high-ceilinged kitchen while his mother prepared a dessert from the last of the clemetts she had frozen at the end of Lonon. Together they ate it, talking of Tettsie first, then of even more intimate things, memories and misunderstandings Sornnn had thought untouchable even a week ago. By the time they had finished the delicious dessert, they had laughed not once but several times, Sornnn feeling an echo of Tettsie's hand on his arm and Petrre Aurrr touching the Nieobian starwen that nestled in the hollow of her throat.

Gossamer moonslight settled across the flat expanse of the terrace, turning the carpets night-blue and cream. The ululations of the faithful rose and fell with the wind. Nith Settt folded his arms across his horned and armored chest. "I will crush you like a tewrat unless you answer my questions."

Riane looked at him and tried to keep Annon's innate fear of Gyrgon in check. "You cannot get inside my mind as you can with your own kind."

"Not so easily, anyway." Nith Settt grinned evilly. "The more painful for you."

"Is there, in truth, no other thing you employ but coercion?"

"Fear is my middle name," Nith Settt said. "It was ever thus." He made an almost imperceptible motion, and Nith Sahor's greatcoat folded up upon itself. "Perhaps we need to start with an easier question," he continued briskly. "Why have you come all this distance to see Perrnodt?"

"I told Makktuub the truth. I wish to study under her."

"To become imari."

"Yes."

"I do not believe you. For one thing, you do not have an imari's subservient demeanor."

"Perrnodt will teach me."

"For another, how did you even know there was a dzuoko in the Korrush and where to find her?"

They had entered dangerous territory. "I heard about her from one of her former imari."

"Liar!"

He came closer, and she could scent him, through the spiced wind of Agachire, the odd commingling of clove oil and burnt musk.

"And I have the proof of it." Nith Settt began to circle her, the moonslight sliced and wafered by the polished surfaces of his alloy armor. It was the glow and spark of a living thing, a secret breath taken, a silent voice raised. "Here it is." He rattled the little package the greatcoat had become. "You arrive in the Korrush wearing a Gyrgon neural net—you, a Kundalan female." He shook the package in front of Riane's face. "Where did you steal this from, Resistance?"

"I am not Resistance," Riane said.

Nith Settt stood stock-still. "Do you know what happens when you lie to a Gyrgon?" He reached out with a gloved hand. "I *will* extract the truth from you." Lambent green arcs shot from fingertip to fingertip as hyperexcited ions were ramped up. "Even if I have to do it synapse by synapse, neuron by neuron."

Lethal fingertips very close to Riane's face, *A Gyrgon's touch is deadly*, how many times had Annon heard that when he was a child?

"I don't mind the process in the least. In fact, as a scientist I find it rather elucidating. But you, Resistance, you will never be the same again. Your brain will be fused and fried. You will become a drooling, shambling cipher with no will of your own. But you will remember everything. How does this future sound to you?"

Out of sight, children ran through the streets, shouting in mock battles. The prayer-chants wove like fishers' fine seines, waxing and waning on the whims of the wind. The moons' double scimitars, honed sharp by the clarity of the atmosphere, peeled back the darkness.

"What are Gyrgon doing in the Korrush?" Riane said at length. "It is my understanding that the V'ornn have no use for sea, steppe, or desert."

"Kundalan do not query V'ornn!"

"Why not indulge me in this? According to you, in a little while I won't be able to tell anyone anything."

Nith Settt grunted. "We conquer all races, each in its own way and in its own time. We are here in small numbers to serve as advisors to the Five Tribes in their internecine war with each other."

"To hear Makktuub tell it, the war will never end."

"Oh, it will end," Nith Settt said, "when all the Five Tribes are dead."

A cold trickle crawled down Riane's spine. "So that's how you're advising the kapudaan, by sowing continual seeds of dissension."

"They are religious fanatics. We are only giving them what they desire most. They are bloodthirsty, these Korrush denizens."

"Not nearly so bloodthirsty as you, I warrant."

"And I can almost taste your blood, Resistance." Nith Settt grinned evilly. "We are conducting an experiment in the power of religious belief. It is strong, indeed, among the tribes of this forsaken steppe. Their religion makes them stupid—stupid and blind. They believe that we have left them alone because they harvest spices, a commodity precious to us. They believe, because their religion makes them self-deluded, that we could not coerce them into harvesting the spices for us. So they happily trade with us and take our advice when we dispense it and do not realize that they are tewrats in a cage of our own devising."

"They will one day wake from this dream you have woven around them, and they will rise against you."

"Like the Kundalan have risen against us? Like the followers of the dead god Enlil have risen against us? We are Gyrgon! We are all-powerful!" Nith Settt raised his arms wide. "Look around you. These are a primitive, pathetic lot."

"Only by your warped standards."

The Gyrgon glowered. "Enough idle chatter. You will now tell me what I want to know."

"You will not believe me."

"If you lie, you will be punished. Proceed."

Riane took a deep breath. "I did not steal the greatcoat," she said. "I found it."

"You are correct. I do not believe you."

"The Gyrgon was dead."

"He was wrapped in his cloak."

"No, he was not."

Nith Settt cocked his head. "Did you know that each neural net carries the signature of its owner?"

Riane kept silent, but her mind was racing. The greatcoat had transported her and Eleana back from the Museum of False Memory, and it had transported her here into the Korrush. That could only mean one thing. Somehow, some way, through what numinous alchemy she could not imagine, Nith Sahor was still alive. And, to be sure, this needed to remain an absolute secret. It occurred to her, not without a good deal of irony, that Nith Sahor was now in the same position Annon had found himself in, alive but desperately trying to keep it secret from his legion of enemies, not the least being Nith Settt.

"This one belonged to a Gyrgon by the name of Nith Sahor," Nith Settt said.

"I noticed you used the past tense. So you know he's dead. This much you believe."

"Yes."

"He died in a ring of sysal trees just north of Axis Tyr. When I came upon him, he was surrounded by a pack of snow-lynx. Doubtless they had unwound the cloak the better to get at him."

"A sad and solitary death."

"In any event, I drove them off. I buried him and took the greatcoat. I thought it only fair to be recompensed for my labor."

"Not that the greatcoat is now of any use. Each neural net is genetically linked to its owner. When Nith Sahor died, it became inoperative." Nith Settt shook his head. "But there is something. You, a Kundalan female, buried a Gyrgon? Why didn't you simply let the snow-lynx rend him?"

"In our own particular way" Riane said, "we have come, to the difference between Kundalan and V'ornn."

Nith Settt grunted again. "We are strong. You are weak."

"If having reverence for life—all life—means we're weak—"

"It does."

"What, then, is left to say?"

"Much." The Gyrgon brandished his glowing glove in Riane's face. "You have not yet answered all my questions. I will know why you are seeking the dzuoko Perrnodt."

Riane could feel, like a scalpel slicing through her skin, the electromagnetic pulse from the ion arcs. It fizzed and buzzed and made her teeth ache.

The glove hovered briefly. "Last chance, Resistance." Nith Settt said. "Your world is about to be reduced to the size of your body, and believe me when I tell you that it will contain nothing but infinite pain."

Riane looked beyond the glove's obvious threat to the Gyrgon's menacing helm. "Has the ability to compromise fled you altogether?"

"Among us V'ornn there is a saying, 'Keep compromise at bay, and victory will be yours.' "

"Not here," Riane said, "and not tonight." She lifted her right hand to the nape of her neck, as if scratching an itch.

"What are you doing?" Ion fire erupted from Nith Settt's fingertips, blinding and deadly.

Riane pointed the cylinder Minnum had given her at Nith Settt and pressed the tiny gold firing disc. She was wholly unprepared for the result and, in her shock, nearly dropped the wand. The goron beam, a narrow opalescent column, rippled out from the tip of the wand. It was a tight-weave band, curling back on itself to make an endless loop, a stairway to everywhere and nowhere, an infinity-blade.

When the infinity-blade intercepted the Gyrgon's ion fire, there was neither a flash nor a thunderclap, nor anything else, for that matter, that the laws of physics dictated should occur when two opposing types of energy meet. Instead, it was like watching a raging fire being abruptly banked; the goron beam simply absorbed the hyperexcited ions.

Nith Settt reared back in shock.

Using her momentary advantage, Riane darted away from the Gyrgon, heading toward the near parapet. She knew she would have only one chance at this. She could hear the crackle and pop of the ion fire behind her and veered sharply to her right in the instant before the lambent energy reached her. She could feel an eerie coldness as it raced, flaming, by her. It struck the parapet, smashing a meterwide hole in it.

There was no time to consider consequences. Running at full tilt, Riane leapt, her legs, powerful and springy, propelling her forward. Her right foot came down squarely on the top of the parapet, and she pushed off it, launching herself into the air. At the very apex of her arc she tucked herself into a tight ball, the better to keep her momentum going. Then, with a bone-jarring lurch, she struck the floor of the neighboring terrace, rolling, sucking in air as she regained her feet. And resumed running.

All around her the torches and oil lamps of Agachire flickered and burned, sending a dim orange glow into the cool, crisp night, fingers of a great veined hand stretching into the vastness of the steppe.

She glanced back over her shoulder, saw Nith Settt spread his arms wide. Enveloped in cold blue ion fire, he levitated until he was about two meters in the air. Abruptly, the ion fire altered to a deeper hue, and he shot forward like a missile, spanning the space between terraces in no more than a heartsbeat or four.

He came on without settling to the terrace floor, moving faster than Riane could on her two legs. She picked up her pace, reached the far side of the terrace full out, and launched herself over the parapet at almost the same instant Nith Settt loosed another ion stream, which passed just above her head. Possibly this affected her concentration because she came up short, slamming into the front of the far terrace wall, hanging on to the leading edge of the parapet with her left hand while she transferred the infinity-blade to her teeth and reached up with her right hand.

Using both arms, she began to pull herself up, but at that instant another ion stream struck the parapet full on. Baked brickwork exploded, blinding her, and she felt her handhold disintegrate in a shower of shards. Cloaked by a welter of debris, she fell onto the back of a kuomeshal more or less in the middle of a passing caravan. All the breath went out of her, but she had the presence of mind to switch off the infinity-blade.

The entire caravan, panicked by the explosion and the stinging rain of shattered brickwork, kicked up their hooves and commenced a shambling gallop, ungainly but swift for all that. Everyone on the street was scattering, darting this way and that, overturning carts and small fires, rounds of bread rolling like wheels, screams and hoarse shouts replacing the music of the prayer-chants.

Using fingers and knees, Riane clung precariously to the small mountain of barrels lashed tightly between the animal's humps. Through the haze that hung in the night air she caught a brief glimpse of Nith Settt bent almost double over the parapet, looking this way and that, pulverizing brickwork in his fists, searching for her.

Choked in dust, her teeth rattling together, her nostrils filled with the strange pungent odor of the kuomeshals, Riane prayed to Miina that Nith Settt could not somehow use his technomancy to find her.

She heard the breathy singsong chiding of the caravan handlers running beside the animals, using their beat-sticks to keep them in a semblance of order as they attempted to calm them down. And, indeed, the entire caravan was slowing from its initial breakneck gallop down to a trot. From her makeshift perch, she could see the handlers' sweat-streaked faces as they continued to ply their beat-sticks to guide the kuomeshals, use their voices to soothe them.

They had entered another quarter of Agachire. The tents here were smaller, less ornate, though just as colorful. The torch-lined street wound this way and that, just barely avoiding the massed jumble of tents that arose helter-skelter on either side. The discordant clash of scimitars, the rhythmic beating of shields rose like a cruel winter wind, along with the rough-voiced bawdy songs endemic to warriors and thieves.

All at once, Riane became aware of a presence near her. One of the kuomeshal drivers was running alongside her. He was hooded and cloaked, like all the drivers, to keep the dust at bay. She drew the infinity-blade but did not activate it.

"Do not be afraid," the figure whispered hoarsely. "Come with me. I will take you to a safe place." He had not turned his head or altered his pace.

Riane said nothing, clinging tightly to the barrels.

"You must come now," he said, more urgently. "The kapudaan's guards are even now fanning out through the city to find you." He turned to her. "There is a group of them just ahead."

Now, by flickering torchlight, she could see a crescent of his face.

"Paddii!" The father of the baby whose life she had saved.

"Yes, yes," he said, reaching a powerful arm around her. "Come quickly! Come now!"

She let go of the barrels as he tugged her off. She swung her legs down, and he took off, holding her hand, dragging her along. Behind them, the caravan had been halted, and they could hear the harsh queries of the kapudaan's guards, the drivers' responses.

As she ran, Riane flexed her stiff fingers. Her legs were already getting a workout. Paddii led her down curving streets and crooked lanes, heading in a northerly direction, as best she could tell.

"How did you know?" she asked, when they had put sufficient distance between them and the guards.

"My cousin informed me. Baliiq, you know." He gave her a quick glance. "Are you all right? You were not mistreated?"

"Except for the Gyrgon—"

"Who?"

Riane shook her head. "Never mind." Was Nith Settt's presence here secret? If so, what did the Gazi Qhan make of the levitating figure on the terrace throwing cold firebolts? She had little time to contemplate this, for Paddii had ducked into a tent flap. Following him, Riane found herself inside a small space that might once have been used as a storehouse, but now seemed all but abandoned. A slight wind billowed the tent walls, and distant torchlight caused a ghostly aura to appear, bleaching the striped fabric.

"Here," Paddii said, thrusting a ball of clothes at her. "Best to change so you don't look like a daughter of the haanjhala." Without another word, he went out of the tent. She could see him standing guard, his back to her.

Quickly, she stripped off her filmy, filthy outfit and stepped into a pair of old, worn breeches, an oft-washed shirt, clean and smelling of strange herbs, a tanned-hide belt, wide and sturdy. There was also a pair of homely slipper-shoes, much scuffed and scarred, the color indeterminate, which she placed on her feet. She held in her hand the beautiful palace slippers Makktuub had given her.

"Leave them behind." Paddii gave her an appraising look as he reentered. "Your nose stud will be a bit of a problem, but for now it can't be helped."

As he led the way out of the tent, Riane said, "Where are we going?"

"To the place where Othnam and Mehmmer await you."

"This was all carefully planned, wasn't it?"

"From the moment they left the kapudaan's palace. We were only awaiting the signal from Baliiq. If Makktuub had not summoned you to the terrace, my cousin would have found some excuse to bring you there himself." He grinned hugely as he returned her dagger, which she had left in Othnam's safekeeping on the way into Agachire, and kissed her warmly on each cheek. "What, did you think Othnam would renege? He promised to deliver you to the dzuoko Perrnodt, and I swear by the Prophet Jiharre that is precisely what he will do."

14

Resurrection

Neither dead nor alive, the Ramahan sorceress Bartta, Giyan's twin sister, hung in the stasis-web of the sorcerous spell she had half conjured before the explosive fire had engulfed the *had-atta* and the small underground chamber in the Abbey of Floating White in which she had long ago secreted it. That she had been caught in the conflagration, completely unawares, was stuck in her mind like a pebble in a shoe. Each laborious thought brought to bear the pain of that failing.

In truth, Bartta could not think at all—at least, not in the way one customarily defines thinking. She hung in the stasis-web of her own incomplete manufacture without any sense of time or space.

To the extent that she thought, she existed. But that was all.

Until Giyan returned to Floating White and found her, where all the other Ramahan priestesses had failed. But then Giyan had an advantage.

While Konara Lyystra and Konara Inggres could feel only subtle unsettling hints, Giyan possessed the power to discover Bartta in her sorcerous stasis. So did Horolaggia. Giyan, for all her goodness and generosity of spirit, might have thought twice about freeing Bartta, for Bartta had spent the better part of the year now nearing its end torturing Riane both physically and psychologically. Once Bartta had discovered the existence of the Dar Sala-at, she had tried to brainwash her, in an attempt to use Riane to solidify and magnify her own power. This Giyan would never have tolerated, had she known of it, and though Bartta was her sister, she would never forgive her.

But Horolaggia had plans for the twins. And so, Giyan's first major order of business upon returning to the abbey after an almost eighteen-year absence was to direct her energies toward dismantling the stasis-web. This had to be done carefully for, though it was true that Bartta was trapped inside, it was the stasis-web itself that had saved her from death, wrapping its protective wings about her while the deadly fire that had raged through the chamber in which she had been torturing Riane destroyed the *had-atta*.

Toward this end, she took advantage of Konara Urdma's opportunistic but rather stupid nature. There was no point in introducing Cerrn-spore into Konara Urdma the way she had done with Konara Lyystra.

"Konara Bartta is still alive, you say?" Konara Urdma said uneasily.

The two of them stood now in the fire-blackened chamber. Konara Urdma had, of course, recognized Giyan, though it had been many years since Giyan had been summarily banished from the abbey with all the other Ramahan who possessed the Gift of Osoru. That Konara Urdma viewed Giyan with a mixture of awe and trepidation was of no consequence to Giyan. That Konara Urdma was assisting her, even though it was clear from how she held herself a little apart and ramrod stiff that the very thought of Bartta's return was a threat to her newfound power, gave Giyan a little thrill of pleasure. The very black thing inside her fed off fear, and as soon as it was practicable she meant to commence a course in the fine art of instilling fear in others. She would teach it, of course. Imagine, a daemon instructing Ramahan! The irony was positively exhilarating!

Giyan spread her arms, and the atmosphere inside the small close charred chamber turned gelid. Slowly, as if being coaxed out of dank shadows into the light of the flickering oil lamp, the stasis-web began to appear.

At first, it was nothing more than a crosshatch pattern trembling briefly in the corner of Konara Urdma's eye. She had seen it, or thought she'd seen it, but when she shifted her gaze to look, it wasn't there at all.

"I am not familiar with what you are doing. Is this an Osoru spell?" she asked Giyan. "I am firmly of the belief that Osoru is a dangerous form of sorcery."

"This is not Osoru," Giyan assured her. "I will not be bringing that back to the abbey." Giyan was not lying, for Horolaggia, like all daemons, had no natural access to Osoru. That was one reason he why he was expending so much energy in weaving the Malasocca. Giyan was fighting him every inch of the way with her impressive arsenal of Osoru spells. Also like all daemons, Horolaggia coveted those enchantments.

Often, he would grind his fangs with rage at the injustice of not being able to understand or hold in his head even a single Osoru spell. The Malasocca would change all that.

Now the pattern of the stasis-web here and there began to flicker, like the flame in the oil lamp. The shards turned into patches, which spread until the entirety of the cocoon had returned to light.

Konara Urdma gasped. "Is that truly Konara Bartta?"

Horolaggia, inside Giyan's mind, laughed silently. How satisfying this risk he had taken had become, and in such a short time! Oh, yes, he had been right to have seized the initiative, to move lightning quick while all the others hesitated, paralyzed by the promise of dire consequences. Miina was long vanished from this realm, and the Dragons were made powerless. As he predicted.

"Now come," Horolaggia commanded with Giyan's voice. "This is where I require your assistance."

As she strode forward, the scheming Konara Urdma at her side, she said, "As I have told you, because the stasis-web did not have time to fully form, undoing it is a delicate and complicated process. That is why two of us are needed. Now you must be careful and cleave to my instructions precisely. If you do not, if you deviate by even the slightest degree, Konara Bartta will not successfully emerge from it."

"You mean she could die?"

Giyan laughed silently at Konara Urdma's stupidity. "Very easily, yes."

She lifted her left hand, and a tiny spark spiraled out from her fingertips, arcing toward the point in the sorcerous cocoon where the outermost piece of the web was attached. The spark struck the point and, with an eerie creaky sigh, that small section of the web lifted.

"Ah, good, the web is come undone," Giyan said. "Now for the really difficult part." At her silent command a large oval basket appeared out of the gelid air. It was a color that made Konara Urdma's eyeballs ache when she looked at it for too long. Giyan handed it to her. "Now as I unwrap the web you will hold the basket beneath to catch the folds. You must not—and this is vital—you must not touch the folds, even inadvertently."

"What will happen if I touch the web?" Konara Urdma asked, accepting the basket.

"The web will be instantaneously poisoned and Konara Bartta will die stillborn inside it." Giyan pointed. "Now stand just there." And she nodded, raising both her hands again.

Something cracked inside Konara Urdma's inner ears, making her wince.

"Keep your position," Giyan admonished. "Steady your hands; they are trembling. Here comes the first layer."

Once, long ago, when her parents had taken her to the coast to see her long-lost uncle, Konara Urdma had seen fisherfolk hauling a sea-weedy net from the Sea of Blood. It was filled with flopping silvery fish. But in its center had been a dark squirmy thing with many tentacles that undulated and flicked, searching for something, it seemed, to wrap themselves around and crush.

The layer, as Giyan peeled it back from the rest of the cocoon, re-minded her of the squirmy tentacled thing that had haunted her dreams for as long as she remained on the coast. She had never been so happy to return to Stone Border. The thing oozed into the sorcerous basket she held with hands that still trembled despite Giyan's warning. And it did not lie there in the basket's shallow black bottom, but pulsed rhythmically like a living thing.

"Easy now," Giyan was saying. "Here comes the second layer."

Konara Urdma could see her concentrating mightily. Giyan had not exaggerated the complexity of her task. Konara Urdma's thoughts now turned to what she herself needed to do. She had despised Bartta even while she learned from her, despised her because Bartta had laughed at her dreams of ambition. Bartta had thought her weak, contemptible even. She had allowed Konara Urdma a modicum of power, then took enormous pleasure in periodically denying her that power, the better to illustrate their respective positions in the abbey hierarchy.

I don't even need to threaten you, Bartta had once told her gloatingly. *You haven't the imagination or ability to form an alliance against me. You're nothing more than a joke.*

Here came another layer, slithering with a cloacal glisten into the basket, and she adjusted her position slightly.

And now here she was as head of the Dea Cretan, and enjoying every moment of her triumph over Bartta, and what happens? Bartta's twin sister, once exiled, pops up out of nowhere, and already some of the younger konara are calling her Mother.

A third layer rippled downward into the basket.

Something had to be done, Konara Urdma knew that right away, but it wasn't until a moment ago that she could figure out what. How ironic that Giyan herself should provide the answer. She would dispose of Bartta by infecting the stasis-web, then she would throw the thing over Giyan and get rid of her, as well. But she had to be patient. Acting precipitously might arouse Giyan's suspicions. It had to look like an accident, a momentary slip on her part when the basket was heavy with the stasis-web, but while it was still attached to Bartta.

She waited until almost all the web was pulsing between her arms before she stumbled a little. Her right shoulder dipped down, the basket tipping with it, and the topmost layer of web slid against her forearm.

"Oh," she said as the thing slipped around her wrist. It seemed to her as if the web fairly bolted from the basket, whipping itself around her so quickly and completely that she had no chance to react or even to cry out. The last of it came off Bartta and wrapped itself around her. Not that she was aware of it; her consciousness was completely absorbed in the pain of her skin being dissolved layer by layer.

Giyan held the insensate, deformed body of her twin in her arms securely, if not lovingly. A brownish slime, interspersed with clots of a gelatinous whitish substance, covered Bartta from head to toe. That would pass now as Bartta began again to breathe the air around her.

Konara Urdma, locked inside her sorcerous cocoon, writhed and thrashed with increasing intensity. That, too, would pass.

Giyan smiled down and spoke softly, almost crooningly. "How does it feel to be eaten alive? Please, Konara Urdma, be so kind as to describe each sensation." She chuckled, a low evil sound. Horolaggia's sound. "I warned you, didn't I? I told you not to touch the web. But I knew you could not help yourself. Your desire to see Bartta dead was written all over your face. So I lied. But do not despair. You fulfilled your purpose. You see, the stasis-web is a very dangerous thing, especially when it is interrupted as this one was. The only way to get Bartta safely out was to give it a substitute. So I gave it you. The web is a living creature, as doubtless you can now attest. The fire wounded it because Bartta did not have enough time to complete it before the conflagration engulfed her. It has been in pain all this time, such terrible pain as you cannot imagine." She cocked her head at the thrashing cocoon. "But then again perhaps you very well *can* imagine." The brown goo was drying up, the white stuff shriveling into the tiniest beads, which then popped like air bubbles. Bartta's skin was reappearing, reddened as it tried to adjust to being out of the fluids in which she had been soaking, and scarred as was inevitable when the spell was not completed. This scar appeared on her right side. It slashed more or less diagonally from the dragged-down corner of her mouth, over her jaw, creasing the side of her neck. It was a coarse, ugly thing that no spell could reverse. *Well, she was already deformed,* Giyan thought. *What difference can another disfigurement make?*

Giyan shifted her sister to a more comfortable position. Horolaggia thought he'd have to do something about increasing this host's strength as soon as the Malasocca allowed. Giyan pressed her lips against Bartta's, pushed her tongue into her sister's mouth while the daemon-spore rolled off her furrowed tongue, attaching itself to the roof of Bartta's mouth and sinking in.

From a long way off, Horolaggia heard Myggorra's shout of triumph, and he said with Giyan's voice, "It is our time now, sister—mine and yours."

Every time Kurgan saw the Old V'ornn now, he was stitched with the thread of wariness. Knowing that the Old V'ornn was really Nith Batoxxx in disguise, knowing that Nith Batoxxx was either mad or . . . well, Kurgan did not know what. That was the problem, or part of it anyway. But when the Old V'ornn wished to see him he could not say no without his becoming suspicious. Arousing the Gyrgon's suspicions was the one thing Kurgan sought to avoid.

Kurgan could not believe how much he used to like the small artist's residence the Old V'ornn now owned, had liked in particular how the main rooms could be opened onto the lush garden he had as a boy helped the Old V'ornn to create. Now the place simply gave him the creeps. Much as he hated to admit it, he knew that when it came to Nith Batoxxx, to the horror he had seen reflected in the mirror, he needed help.

This particular evening, despite the chill, the villa's doors had been thrown wide. Red and blue leaves lay crinkled on the ground, swirled upward in occasional eddies by the wind. The gurgling of the pool in the hidden center of the garden could clearly be heard. A lone black-crow, perched on a bare branch, appeared to watch Kurgan as he crossed the threshold of the house and entered the garden.

"Over here." Despite the evidence of his age, the Old V'ornn's voice, strong and vibrant and somehow sinister, rose amid the foliage like the caw of another blackcrow.

Kurgan found the Old V'ornn on his knees, digging in the damp soil beside the pool with a crusty Kundalan spade. "Do you know anything about Indole al'Hul?" He held up a small mushroom with a flaring cap whose pinkish top was as pale as its gilled underside was dark.

Kurgan shrugged.

"*Indole al'Hul* means 'Mother of Terror' in one of the indigenous languages, I forget which." He rolled the slender stalk between his knobbed thumb and forefinger. "A rather fascinating little item." His coppery skin, pulled thin over veins and bones, glowed dully in the lozenges of light thrown by filigreed bronze oil lanterns he had lighted during the lees of the silvery autumnal afternoon. "When you consider what ingesting even a tiny amount does to the autonomous nervous system."

Kurgan hunkered down next to the Old V'ornn, who, he had discovered many years ago, was fond of his arcane lessons. "What will it do?" he said, returning with little effort to the role of dedicated student.

"It all depends. If you take it straight from the plant, it will shut the system down completely and finally," the Old V'ornn said. "Take it distilled and refined, and it causes a whole panoply of psychotropic effects."

"In other words, the victim loses his mind," Kurgan said, entering into the spirit of the lesson.

"In a manner of speaking." The Old V'ornn broke the delicate stem in two, watched the slow ooze of a pale yellow liquid. "That can be good, you know. This substance opens the mind up to the worlds around us, layers upon layers, unseen and unheard, but nonetheless quite real." His mischievous smile momentarily transformed him into a truant child. "Kundala, it seems, is a treasure trove of such chemical wonders. And the Ramahan know them all. Or at least they did." He stood up, dropped the mushroom, and brushed the dirt off his knees and hands. "The Ramahan were privy to many secrets, once upon a time."

Together, they wandered the garden's path until they came to the center. The Old V'ornn lifted a hand, indicating that they should sit on a bench beside the pool of purling black water that bubbled up from the bowels of the planet. Kurgan wrapped his cloak more tightly around him to keep out the increasing chill, but curiously the Old V'ornn appeared oblivious to the falling temperature.

When they had settled themselves, the Old V'ornn reached over and produced a dark bottle and two crystal goblets. "I have been waiting for the right moment," he said as he filled the goblets with fire-grade numaaadis. "A private moment." He handed Kurgan a goblet. "To toast your swift and unerring ascendancy to the post of regent of Kundala." The goblets rang as their rims touched. "Stogggul Kurgan, I salute you!"

Kurgan drank and waited for the other boot to fall. He knew the Old V'ornn well enough to suspect that he had not been asked here simply to be honored. They had not yet come to the heart of the matter. For there was always a heart to these interviews, as hidden as the pool at the center of this garden. This was the Old V'ornn's way. If Kurgan had been more self-aware, he would have known that it had become his way, as well.

"Do you find the fire-grade numaaadis to your liking?" the Old V'ornn asked.

"It is first tier," Kurgan said.

"A good year, no doubt. Go ahead. Drain your goblet. There is more to be drunk this night." That mischievous smile had reappeared.

But the moment Kurgan did so, the goblet slipped through his fingers, crashed to the stone path at his feet.

The Old V'ornn peered into Kurgan's face. "Regent, are you all right?"

Kurgan was already incapable of replying. The chill that had before crept through his flesh had now been dispelled by a powerful and not unpleasant heat that suffused him from his toes to the top of his skull. His head was expanding. Colors seemed to pulse to the soughing of the wind through the bare tree branches. The blackcrow appeared to be laughing at him. He tasted his own pulse as if it were food and drink he had just ingested.

"Even among the Ramadan, Indole al'Hul is a special mushroom." The Old V'ornn's voice boomed through the garden like thunder. "It was never particularly well-known or used. Hardly surprising, given its name. But, believe me, it does have its uses."

The Old V'ornn pulled Kurgan off the bench, but Kurgan's legs felt like liquid, and his knees refused to work. He half collapsed onto the path.

"And I was ever so careful refining and distilling it."

Kurgan felt nothing. He was too busy trying to keep all the colors of the garden from running together. This seemed to take more effort than he was able to give, and so with the able assistance of the Indole al'Hul elixir, he passed from a troubled state of consciousness into a deep and untroubled trance, where the drone of the Old V'ornn's voice was nothing more than the hiss and suck of an ocean's tide, a kind of static hanging in the background of his pulsing mind, a photonic communication just beyond hearing.

Beside him, the Old V'ornn, noting that Kurgan's eyes had rolled up into his head, metamorphosed into Nith Batoxxx. And yet, anyone familiar with Nith Batoxxx would say with utter certainty that this was not precisely Nith Batoxxx, for a dark and uncertain rim hovered about him, obliterating what the Ramahan would term the emanations of his essence. This penumbra, had anyone who knew him been present, would have hurt their eyes and made their throats close up, leaving them gasping. It was akin to a negative current, a darkness that flickered like cold flame, changing its shape from heartsbeat to heartsbeat.

"And so we have come, at last, to the heart of our current lesson." This voice, too, was different, subtly unlike that of either Nith Batoxxx or the Old V'ornn.

He put his long-fingered hand upon the crown of Kurgan's gleaming skull and his countenance briefly clouded over. "Is the Indole al'Hul doing its work? Even I, who have taken possession of you, Gyrgon, cannot know for certain."

Leaning over, he stared for a moment into the pool which, like the now shattered mirror in the regent's palace, reflected back at him that which Kurgan had clandestinely seen.

"One can learn so much about an individual through his birth-caul. But apparently not enough. It pains me now to admit that I was wrong about you."

He whistled an odd little tune, and the bright-eyed blackcrow spread its wings and swooped across the garden to perch upon his shoulder, where it commenced to hop, lunging its long yellow beak toward Kurgan's ear.

"No, no," the creature that had taken possession of Nith Batoxxx admonished. "Mustn't, mustn't."

After uttering a single shrill cry, the blackcrow settled down.

"Ah, Stogggul Kurgan, you already believe yourself different from other V'ornn." The creature inside Nith Batoxxx paused to observe the silently crackling penumbra that encircled him, and instantly suppressed it, knowing that he must not allow anyone to see his true self leaking out of his Gyrgon host body. "If you only knew how different!" He sighed as he stroked the blackcrow's glossy feathers. "But, given your volatile nature, it would be unwise to give you this knowledge."

He reached for a lantern. "And now it is time to see what the Indole al'Hul reveals about you."

Lifting the lantern, he examined the back of Kurgan's neck as if he were a primitive soothsayer. He fingered the skin between the two knobs at the top of Kurgan's spine.

"Nothing!" His head snapped up, his eyes blazing. "Is it possible that I am wrong again? And yet . . ."

His voice trailed off into the soughing of the wind. The blackcrow, sensing the gathering storm, was now in the highest branch of the tree, its wings folded tight against its sides. For a time, the thing inside Nith Batoxxx remained absolutely still. Then he gripped the edge of the pool, staring at it until its black water began to foam. In an instant, he plunged his head and shoulders into the roiling blackness of the water, opened his mouth—a mouth no V'ornn would ever recognize—and emitted a bellow of rage that was heard all the way to the sorcerous Portal of the Abyss.

When Jesst Vebbn entered the spice district it was nearing sunset, and the market was alive with a spray of shoppers dropping by on their way home to prepare the evening meal. As a consequence, the narrow aisles between the mounded displays were choked with Kundalan, house servants to wealthy Bashkir families.

Jesst was uncomfortable outside Harborside, uncomfortable, if truth be told, outside the thick-walled precincts of Receiving Spirit. Being so long in the service of Gyrgon, he supposed that he had acquired their aversion to the outdoors. But at Bronnn Pallln's insistence, their periodic rendezvous took place where they could pass for chance encounters or brief conversations between strangers.

Jesst had been treating the Bashkir's wife for years. Not that there was anything wrong with her. After her second visit he had realized that it was the attention she craved, attention Bronnn Pallln would not give her. Bronnn Pallln knew that she was healthy as a cor, knew further that she was doing no more than wasting Jesst's valuable time. Other Genomatekks had apparently not been so patient and forgiving. To show his appreciation, he paid Jesst an exorbitant amount of coins for each visit. Coins that Jesst would otherwise be unable to earn. And so, when Bronnn Pallln had come to Jesst, asking a favor, Jesst was not inclined to refuse him.

Bronnn Pallln adored cinnamon, and with fifteen different varieties being imported weekly from the Korrush, the cinnamon stalls were where Jesst found the Bashkir. Bronnn Pallln could have sent a servant, of course, but such was his fanaticism that he insisted on tasting and purchasing the cinnamon himself.

"Try this gowit," he said as Jesst came up. He held out his hand in the center of which was a small pinch of finely ground dark rose grains. "Go on," he insisted. "It is first-rate."

As Bronnn Pallln had taught him to do, Jesst took some between thumb and forefinger and placed it on the back of his tongue. Even this tiny amount was so strong it made his eyes water.

"Was I wrong?" Bronnn Pallln said.

Jesst had to admit that he was not wrong.

Bronnn Pallln nodded to the cinnamon vendor, held up three fingers, and the vendor began to fill a bag. "How goes our fishing expedition?" Bronnn Pallln said.

Jesst handed over a data-decagon. "This contains a transcript of the conversation I had with the SaTrryn Deirus, Kirlll Qandda. It has what you want."

Bronnn Pallln pocketed it with ill-disguised glee. "Excellent."

"There is something."

Bronnn Pallln raised his eyes heavenward and heaved a theatrical sigh. "There always is."

"You will have to deal with the regent's sister."

"Oratttony?"

"The other one. The pariah."

"Marethyn. Good N'Luuura, why?"

"It is all in the data-decagon."

"Kindly enlighten me now," Bronnn Pallln said in a tone that left no room for debate.

"According to the Deirus, Marethyn Stogggul knows the location of the Bashkir traitor's headquarters."

"Indeed." Bronnn Pallln thought a moment. "O, fortunate son that I am, it is the pariah." He laughed. "Considering how Kurgan Stogggul feels about her, I very much doubt he will mind the harsh treatment I have in store for her." He nodded. "You have done well."

As he prepared to move on, Jesst said, "I would like my payment."

Bronnn Pallln was counting his packages. "Patience is a virtue."

"It is a virtue of the poor. I have already pledged a down payment on a new residence."

Bronnn Pallln shrugged. "As it happens, that was unwise." He took possession of the bag of gowit cinnamon.

Jesst's face flushed with anger. "Our original agreement."

"The gimnopede is not yet caught."

"You have no intention of paying me anything, do you?"

Bronnn Pallln thought of Wennn Stogggul treating him with contempt; he thought about what it felt like to have power over others, and he discovered that he liked what he felt.

"Do not blame me for squandering away what you never had," he said.

"But we had a deal. You promised me payment if I delivered, and now I have. Is not a Bashkir's word sacred?"

"Only with other Bashkir," Bronnn Pallln pointed out as he took his leave.

15

Plots Most Sinister

Line-General Lokck Werrrent, the commander of the Khagggun forces for the Sudden Lakes quadrant, had set up his command center in Glistening Drum, a mountain town northeast of Joining the Valleys. Once, Glistening Drum had been a small village wholly in the service of the Abbey of Glistening Drum, the ruins of which could still be seen on a rubble-strewn promontory overlooking the town square. In the years after the Khagggun had razed the abbey, the village itself had oddly thrived, growing into a moderate-sized town, an agricultural hub that helped feed the burgeoning V'ornn population of Axis Tyr. It was here that most of the cor-milk cheese was crafted, owing to the verdant fields of first-quality ggley that covered the slopes of the mountainsides. Ggley was used in the fermentation process. It was a delicate herblike plant that thrived only in the local mountain terrain and was not suitable for export or long shipments.

Line-General Werrrent's decision to base his command center in Glistening Drum was quite deliberate. The town enjoyed a near-perfect central location he found both appealing and appropriate for his operations.

Nevertheless, he found that he needed to spend much of his time in Axis Tyr, especially since Kurgan Stogggul had succeeded his father as regent.

While he was in Axis Tyr on business, it fell to Wing-Adjutant Iin Wiiin to run the command center. Wiiin managed with a detached efficiency bordering on the pathological. No matter. Wing-Adjutant Wiiin had made himself indispensable, allowing the Line-General the latitude to take care of the ever more complex politics of war in the capital.

It was fortunate that Wing-Adjutant Wiiin enjoyed the confidence of his superior, for he was a thin, ropey-muscled individual who had been cursed with eyes placed too close together, a lipless mouth, and a complexion permanently scarred by a serious bout of Kraelian fireworm fever that somehow resisted all known genomic reconfiguring therapy. Even the lowest of Looorm found him repulsive. Though, so it was said, he loved nothing at all, it was clear to those he commanded that he liked overseeing a smoothly functioning hive of Khagggun. And while he did harbor other interests—for instance, he enjoyed hunting perwillon in the mountain caves—he seemed to those around him to live the dullest of lives. In fact, nothing could have been further from the truth, for Wiiin dearly loved the periodic clandestine meetings with the Line-General's Ramahan contact who provided the tactical information on current Resistance personnel and plans.

On this particular night, he was working late—for it could never be said, even by his bitterest enemies, that he was a shirker—when one of his Khagggun appeared with a message for the Line-General that had been left outside the command center. Werrrent had, a week before, gone south to Axis Tyr where, so far as Wiiin knew, he would remain for some time.

After dismissing the Khagggun, Wiiin opened the message. Almost immediately, he frowned. It was a curious thing, this message, handwritten in Kundalan, but containing in its upper right-hand corner the whorl of Line-General Lokck Werrrent's name in V'ornnish script. He read the message twice through, memorizing it. Then he held it to a flame until it charred into ash, which he ground to powder between his spatulate thumb and forefinger.

He rose, checked the time as he swung on the chest plate of his battle armor. Downstairs, he hurried across the open courtyard to the stables, where he signed out a cthauros and, mounting it, dug his heels into its flanks.

He rode due east for precisely three-quarters of a kilometer, whereupon he turned south and, as per the instructions in the message, rode until he had come to the northern edge of a lozenge-shaped copse of sysal trees. There, he reined in and waited.

The night was quite chill. A strong wind careened out of the northeast, bringing with it the bitter tang of Djenn Marre ice. He shivered a little inside his armor, thinking that it was going to be a long, cold winter. Two moons, pale green crescents, lent a ghostly light to the copse of thorned trees and the mountainous terrain all around.

"You are not Line-General Lokck Werrrent."

His saddle creaked as he turned, peering into the copse. "Who are you?" he said, half-drawing his shock-sword. "Show yourself or risk the consequences."

A young Kundalan female emerged from the shadows. She was garbed in the persimmon-colored robes of a Ramahan konara. She walked slowly, almost, Wiiin thought, painfully, with her arms folded across her ample belly.

He scabbarded his weapon. "Are you injured?" he inquired.

"I sent a message to Line-General Lokck Werrrent," the konara said. "Where is he?"

"I am Wing-Adjutant Iin Wiiin." He dismounted. "I speak for the Line-General in all matters, great and small."

"Are you privy to all the Line-General's secrets, Wing-Adjutant Iin Wiiin?"

"I do not understand your meaning."

"I know about the duscaant."

Wiiin stiffened. "What duscaant?"

The konara smiled a secret smile. "Come, come, Wing-Adjutant. Either you speak for the Line-General, or you do not."

"The duscaant the Line-General had secreted in the Abbey of Glistening Drum."

"No," the konara said slowly and distinctly. "The duscaant the Line-General had secreted in the Abbey of Warm Current."

"Ah, yes. I remember now. It was put there by Konara Yesttur."

"No. Konara Mossa hid it."

Wiiin nodded, obviously satisfied. "And you are?"

"Konara Eleana."

"Where is my regular contact?"

"Konara Bartta has met with an unfortunate accident."

"She is dead, yes. I meant her replacement, Konara Urdma."

"Ill." Eleana almost choked on the word. She had no idea who he was talking about.

He frowned. "This is unexpected."

You can say that again, Eleana thought. *What is going on at the abbey?* "Since Konara Bartta's death the abbey has been in turmoil."

"You have taken over Konara Urdma's, ah, duties."

"Only until she is recovered."

Wiiin frowned deeply. "She should never have been given this duty. She is often ill and does not meet her deadline."

"She was Konara Bartta's choice."

Wiiin took a breath. He disliked dealing with Ramahan; he could never quite allow himself to trust them fully. Still, these particular Ramahan, starting with Konara Mossa, had kept to their bargain, providing accurate intelligence they inveigled from Resistance members who were antagonistic to Kara, the new religion that had sprung up. "All right then. Let's get down to it. What do you have for me?"

"There is a Resistance cell camped fifty kilometers west of here." It was a blatant lie, but what else could she say?

"That's it? Surely Konara Urdma explained the parameters. We require *substantial* updates on Resistance movements in order to keep your abbey safe."

"Wing-Adjutant, I have for days now traveled far—"

"Yes, yes, all the way from Stone Border," he said impatiently. "What of it?"

She regarded him levelly out of dark eyes. "I am new at this. I am doing the best I can."

"Not good enough," Wing-Adjutant Wiiin said as he regained his saddle. "You have two weeks to gather the requisite intelligence. After that . . ." He shrugged. Wheeling his cthauros, he galloped back the way he had come.

Eleana stood still and silent, watching him as he passed over a moonslight-dappled rise and disappeared from view.

"Well done," Rekkk Hacilar said as he appeared from out of the depths of the sysal grove. The Teyj was on his shoulder.

They had been led here by the signature whorl of V'ornnish letters that appeared at the beginning of each scene the duscaant had recorded, for it had contained not only the date and time but the name of the Khagggun officer who had commissioned the espionage device: Line-General Lokck Werrrent. Rekkk had used his okummmon to fashion the raw-silk robes of a Ramahan konara for Eleana to use. Together, they had written, in Kundalan and V'ornn, the urgent message that had brought Wiiin here.

"Konara Urdma," Rekkk said. "Now we know the name of our traitor."

"Except that she hasn't shown up. I am getting an unpleasant feeling about the abbey." Eleana sighed and held her belly. "Stone Border is a long and arduous climb from here. I honestly do not know whether I can make it."

He put his arm around her and led her into the trees, where he sat her down with her back against a thick bole. As he gave her water from a skin, he said, "I cannot infiltrate the abbey on my own."

"If only Thigpen were here. Dear Thigpen! She would find a way to transport us."

He looked into the moons-struck darkness. "Don't worry. I will get us both there."

And I say there is a way to settle the dispute between the Nwerrrn and the Fellanngg Consortia," Bronnn Pallln said.

"I can just imagine," Dobbro Mannx chortled. "Have the regent declare both their claims null and void so your own Consortium can plunder the mineral-rich territory west of the Borobodur forest." Then the solicitor-Bashkir guffawed and lifted a fat forefinger. "No, wait, you would have to be Prime Factor to do that."

"But, if memory serves, the Pallln Consortium has a history of having the Stogggul ear." Line-General Lokck Werrrent glanced over at Bronnn Pallln. "Isn't that so?"

Pallln's expression was sour, despite the festivities of the dinner party at Mannx's opulent Eastern Quarter residence. These were fashionable affairs, held weekly with more or less the same personages, who would be treated to the marvelous cooking of the rotund Mannx's chef, after which, sated and half-drunk, they would retire to the library—or the garden, in warmer weather—for a small-wager game of warrnixx.

The Line-General was obliged to remind Bronnn Pallln several times before Pallln mumbled, "True enough."

"Then perhaps you would have no objection to a new member of the Great Caste making a small investment in—"

"Oho!" Mannx cried, "I do believe the Line-General has aspirations. Will you hang up your command to become a Bashkir?"

"I wish nothing of the sort," the Line-General said. "A taste is all I am looking for."

"Have a care, Line-General," said Glll Fullom, the patriarch, aged and revered, of his First Rank Consortium. "Your status as Great Caste is still covered with birth fluid. It would be prudent to wait."

Lokck Werrrent brooded in silence for a time, his thoughts like storm clouds boiling on the horizon. Since his fateful conversation with Star-Admiral Olnnn Rydddlin regarding the true purpose behind the promise to elevate Khagggun to Great Caste status he had his ear attuned for any signs that would prove Olnnn's suspicions justified.

"Just what is your meaning?" he said, perhaps a bit too testily. "That we Khagggun are not up to elevation?"

"Not at all." Glll Fullom seemed somewhat taken aback by the vehemence of the Line-General's reply. "I was simply delivering what I considered prudent advice."

A short, though slightly awkward silence ensued.

"Bronnn Pallln, in the matter of you and the regent," Mannx said brightly. He had a knack for keeping a party going. "I distinctly heard a 'but' hanging in the air like a rotten quilllon."

"No buts," Pallln said rather too defensively.

"If you will excuse an inquiring mind," Mannx said, "I must say I was rather surprised when Wennn Stogggul named Sornnn SaTrryn Prime Factor instead of you."

"What's the matter, don't you like Sornnn SaTrryn?" the Line-General said, still with a touch of peevishness. Sometimes the loose tongues of non-Khagggun got to him. "I have heard nothing but praise for the Prime Factor's abilities at mediation."

"There are some," Fullom said fruitily, "who believe the SaTrryn are already powerful enough without their scion being Prime Factor." He dipped his finger into a bit of stew left on his plate, stirred it around. "And there are others who believe that Sornnn SaTrryn's apparent love affair with the Korrush is a decadent and corrupting influence."

"Are you one of them?" the Line-General asked.

Fullom smiled and indelicately sucked stew off his fingertip.

Mannx spread his hands. "I mean to say, Bronnn Pallln, you deserved the office, didn't you? You have the seniority. You'd earned the right, hadn't you?"

"In fact," Pallln said, trying to shut out Mannx's words, which echoed his own thoughts, "I have a far better relationship with Kurgan Stogggul than I had with his father. In fact, Line-General, I have reached a certain understanding with the Star-Admiral himself."

"Is that so?" Werrrent said. He eyed Bronnn Pallln with his chron-osteel gaze. "Pray tell us more."

At once, Pallln regretted having opened his mouth. How could he have forgotten that Khaggun were insanely jealous of alliances?

"There is nothing to tell," he said.

"Oh, come now." Mannx looked around the table. "No one here believes that, *especially* not I."

Bronnn Pallln felt a murderous rage toward them for backing him into this damnable corner. "My conversations with the Star-Admiral are strictly private," he said curtly.

"Oho!" Mannx clapped his small, pudgy hands like a boy on his Ascension day. "So there *is* something afoot."

"What if there is?" Bronnn Pallln wondered what he was doing getting in deeper and deeper. But he was truly angry now, and he did not care. In fact, there was a terrifying elation in this kind of reckless behavior.

"We are all friends here." Mannx spread his hands over his portly belly. "If you are privy to the Star-Admiral's intent, I think you should tell us. In the strictest of confidence, of course." He laughed his infectious laugh. "My goodness, why else do we meet every week?"

"Of course!" the rest of them echoed in unison.

Bronnn Pallln waved them to silence. He looked around the table. He had their rapt attention, and that felt so good there was only one thing to do. "The Star-Admiral has been suspicious of Sornnn SaTrryn for some time," he said. "Now I have discovered that the SaTrryn scion is unfit to hold the post of Prime Factor." His hearts were racing; he had plunged all the way in.

The Line-General cracked his knuckles ominously. "What is this you say?"

"I have evidence that he is the traitor who is providing aid and Khagggun materiel to the Kundalan Resistance."

There ensued, not surprisingly, a stunned silence.

"The SaTrryn own the highest of reputations, and Sornnn SaTrryn is no exception," Line-General Werrrent declared. "This is the gravest of allegations. With the gravest of consequences."

Didn't Bronnn Pallln know that! But now the warrnixx-bones were cast, and he wondered briefly whether he had set his mind on this course before the evening had even begun. It would not surprise him in the least. He had been planning to petition the regent for an audience as early as the following morning. After all, he now had what Star-

Admiral Olnnn Rydddlin had asked him to obtain—Sornnn SaTrryn's head on a platter. Which grisly trophy would ensure his long-delayed ascension to the office of Prime Factor. But for tonight, at least, he could not help but boast among his friends and compatriots. And why shouldn't he boast about his accomplishment? He wanted to be Prime Factor more than anything in life. Wennn Stogggul had slammed that particular door in his face, but the new regent, through Olnnn Rydddlin, had opened it again.

"Please, Bronnn Pallln, do not let the Line-General's gruffness deter you," Fullom said. He was almost humming in delight. "It so happens that many Bashkir share the Star-Admiral's suspicions."

"I care nothing for the opinions of Bashkir." Line-General Werrrent shrugged his shoulders. "But if you have the evidence, this is something else again."

Bronnn Pallln was light-headed with triumph. All of a sudden Glll Fullom was defending him. Glll Fullom, who had never had a good word to say to him. A nexus of power had formed around him, a new and decidedly delirious experience that he was determined to prolong. Feeling as if his nerves were going to shatter at any moment, he produced the data-decagon Jesst had given him, which contained Kirlll Qandda's revelations concerning Sornnn SaTrryn. He placed it on the table.

The Line-General stared at it for a moment, then took out his data-reader and inserted the crystal.

"What is it?" Mannx cried. "What is the evidence?"

Line-General Werrrent passed the reader over and Mannx grabbed it avidly, scanned it quickly, then turned it over to Glll Fullom.

"It would be unwise to jump to conclusions," Werrrent said darkly, eyeing the transcript.

"I agree," Bronnn Pallln heard himself saying. "My first thought was to show it to the regent right away and let him proceed."

"I would advise caution in that matter," Fullom said softly. "This is, after all, Kurgan Stogggul we are speaking of. We all know what happened to his father."

"What is your meaning?" Line-General Werrrent said anxiously.

Fullom turned to him, addressing him directly. "I have it on good authority that Wennn Stogggul reneged on his solemn word to Star-

Admiral Kinnnus Morcha. Surely, Line-General, you already know that he ordered Kinnnus Morcha's assassination."

"You are speaking treason," Werrrent muttered.

"Not if it is the truth."

"But you have no proof," Werrrent said doggedly.

The old Bashkir shook his head. "You and I go back a long way, Line-General. We may disagree on this matter or that, but I know that you are a true patriot. So I trust that you will forgive me when I tell you that true patriots should not be blind."

"The Stogggul certainly have a history of being headstrong," Mannx said.

"Considering these allegations," Pallln said, "I think we would all be better served if I was the Prime Factor." He looked to Fullom, concerned that the old patriarch would have a negative reaction. But it was the Line-General who gave Pallln a significant look.

"As reprehensible as it looks," the Line-General said, "this evidence against Sornnn SaTrryn requires substantiation. Such as finding SaTrryn's headquarters."

"The trouble with a raid," Fullom said, "is that the SaTrryn own a number of warehouses. Which one is it in?"

"There I have the answer," Bronnn Pallln said. "Marethyn Stogggul has been there."

"But she is the regent's sister!" Mannx cried.

"We all know the family's contempt for her," the Line-General said, "and that includes the regent himself."

"Why should she tell you anything?" Fullom said.

After a moment's uncomfortable silence, Bronnn Pallln said, "Perhaps she wouldn't voluntarily."

They were all looking at Pallln again, and he felt a small shiver work its way down his spine. Addressing Line-General Werrrent, he said, "We will have to go after Marethyn Stogggul directly."

"The Stogggul Consortium is not one to trifle with," Werrrent offered. "It has many powerful friends and allies. If this intelligence proves incorrect or cannot be corroborated . . ." He stopped there, the implications of his words hanging ominously in the air.

"Timing is everything," Fullom mused. "The Line-General is right. We will get one chance—one only. We must make the most of it. He could order his Khagggun to pick Marethyn Stogggul up."

"To involve Khagggun at this stage would be imprudent," Werrrent cautioned.

Fullom crossed speckled hands over his bony chest. "Well then, Bronnn Pallln, it is up to you."

All his life, it seemed, Bronnn Pallln had been waiting for this moment. Now that it had come he felt no trepidation, no fear. His destiny had arrived, and he was going to seize it with both hands.

"I will take care of her myself," he said without hesitation. "Believe me when I tell you it will be a pleasure."

Not long after he attained the rank of Attack-Commandant, a rumor began to circulate concerning Accton Blled. The rumor, whose bones, like all things Khagggun, were picked clean by endless speculation, concerned the skull of a Corpius Segundian razor-raptor, and not just any razor-raptor, as those whispering the story were quick to point out, but a *korrrai*, the deadliest of the thirteen species. No one had ever seen this skull, mind you, but no matter. It was alleged to be in the possession of Accton Blled, having been severed from the powerful torso after the titanic struggle in which he finally slew it. Now, it was further whispered, he kept the eerily glowing memento by his cot and spoke to it each night before he slept, imparting to it secrets too terrible to relate to the living.

That this seemingly outlandish tale was passed around and taken with absolute gravity was a testament to the awe in which he was held by his compatriots.

Olnnn Rydddlin had, of course, heard this rumor. In point of fact, he had heard every variation of it, including the one that held that Blled had feasted on the *korrrai*'s raw and bloody flesh even as it convulsed in its death struggle. To him, the truth of such rumors was of no import. What was interesting was the fact that they existed at all.

He was still mulling this thought as he stepped off the Khagggun hoverpod onto one of the crumbling shanstone pathways that crisscrossed the inner courtyard of the Abbey of Warm Current. Several kilometers to the west was the somnolent, dust-blown village of Middle Seat.

"This is where they have been hiding out?"

"So the informant told us," Attack-Commander Blled said, "just before he, er, expired."

The two officers began to stride down the path.

"How long did it take him to die?" Olnnn inquired in the same tone
of voice a Bashkir would ask about the price of a metric ton of vana-
dium.

"The process was altogether efficient," Blled assured him.

"No time for fun?"

"I assumed the Star-Admiral wanted results quickly."

"You assumed correctly."

Armed and armored Khagggun, members of Blled's pack, stood at
varying intervals. The Attack-Commandant himself looked resplendent
in his armor. He had chosen burnt umber for his pack color, the light
burnished it with a rich glow.

"They were here, all right," Blled said, leading the way into the kitch-
ens and the sleep chambers. "And for quite some time."

He brought Olnnn into the Library. The Star-Admiral went over to
the shattered window.

"What happened here?"

"No idea. We found no traces of ion fire. In any case, the fugitives
are not here now."

Olnnn picked up a shard of colored glass, saw that it was actually
two or three that had been fused together by the high energy of whatever had been aimed at the window. He thought of the hole in the
laundry underneath the kashiggen Nimbus and wondered if there was
a connection in the source of the energy. Pocketing the glass, he walked
along the refectory table until he came to the books lying open on the
tabletop.

"Can you read this, Attack-Commandant?"

"No, sir."

"Any V'ornn in your pack read Kundalan?"

"Yes, sir."

Olnnn turned to glance at him. "Excellent. And what is his analysis?"

"He could not read these books, Star-Admiral. They are not written
in the common present-day Kundalan he knows."

"Was he of any help at all?"

"He said he thought these were books of spellcraft."

"Sorcery." Olnnn nodded. "All things considered, what do these books, open on the table, mean to you?"

"I would say the fugitives were looking for something," Blled answered without hesitation.

It was clear to Olnnn that Blled had been thinking about the question before Olnnn had even shown up.

"Something important, I warrant." He ran his finger down one page and up another. "I wonder what it was."

It was at that moment that he felt a tremor in his leg. His sorcerous leg, the one without skin and muscle and tendon. In the bones that Malistra had ensorceled when she had saved him from Giyan's spellcraft there began a motion not unlike bubbles rising to the surface of a pond. Olnnn, alarmed, clamped his fingers around his bare gleaming femur, and said nothing.

16

Crackle, Pop, Snap

Pierced by the fulkaan, Othnam, look at her."

Othnam nodded at his sister then, grinning, embraced Riane fully. "Out of the kapudaan's den." He nodded. "Truly, you are one of us now."

They were in among a small cluster of tents on the northern fringes of Agachire, and a little apart, so that the massed lights of the town seemed like a fire on the steppe. Unlike the section of Agachire the caravan had entered, there were no soldiers here, no rough talk or bawdy song. The night was alive with hymnal chanting and rhymed prayer. Just outside the tent was a ring of males, singing the prayer cycle, their heads together, their arms around each other's waists, moving rhythmically back and forth. She remembered just such a religious group on the street below the terrace and wondered briefly if it could be the same one.

For Riane was now among the Ghor, of whom, it seemed, Othnam and Mehmmer were a part. They were black-robed and swarthy-skinned, partially concealed behind white sinschals, embroidered with black runes.

Now, close-up, she could see that the ring was made up of males and females. As they moved back and forth in the prayer-cycle chant Riane could see a thin tanned-hide strap wound around each member's left arm midway between elbow and shoulder. These *ga'afarra*, like the close-weave scarves around their heads, contained the words of the Prophet Jiharre.

First, I must ask you to help me return to the palace and save Tezziq from her fate. I swore to help her. Whatever Makktuub may order her to do, I know that she is a good person, deserving of a life outside the accursed haanjhala."

Brother and sister exchanged glances. Then Othnam swore under his breath as he shook his head. Nevertheless, he spoke softly to Paddii, dispatching him to report their delay to the Ghor guarding Perrnodt. Paddii nodded and, with a quick prayer for their safety, left the tent.

"Expect our help," Mehmmer told Riane, "but not our empathy."

"The ajjan is your responsibility," Othnam warned. "We want nothing to do with her. Is this understood?"

"Perfectly," Riane said. "I would expect nothing more from you."

Mehmmer took a menacing step toward Riane. "We save her from the kapudaan's den, and this is how she rewards us."

She gripped her scimitar but before she could draw it her brother took her wrist and stayed her. "We have agreed to disagree on the subject of the ajjan," he said darkly. "But know this, Riane. Our beliefs are our beliefs. Do not expect us to change."

Riane was about to formulate another sharp retort when the image of Thigpen came to her. Not for the first time she wished the Rappa were with her. She missed Thigpen terribly. Right now her advice and wisdom would have been greatly appreciated. She tried to imagine what Thigpen would say to her. *Who are you, little dumpling, to judge these tribesfolk when they have just saved your life?* Besides, she was still withholding secrets from them. She had not told them that she had another compelling reason to infiltrate the kapudaan's palace as quickly as possible. It was imperative she regain possession of Nith Sahor's greatcoat before Nith Settt opened it again and discovered that it was not inactive. Then he would know that Nith Sahor had not died, after all.

"Thank you, Othnam, for your patience and your wisdom," Riane said in what she hoped was a conciliatory tone. "Thank you also for returning my dagger to me,"

Othnam inclined his upper body slightly. "When you gave it to me for safekeeping I could tell how much it meant to you. I thank you for honoring me in that fashion."

"Though we do not agree on every issue, we still have more in common than not."

Mehmmer jerked her head. "We had better go, if we are to help your ajjan friend."

They draped Riane in black Ghorvish robes and white sinschal, then took her out of the tent. The group of Ghor ceased their praying, turning to watch them, silent, wise-eyed. There was not a smile among them, but there was no animosity in their careful scrutiny of Riane. One of them, a bearded male with sunken cheeks and skin the color of Korrush dust, made a sign to Othnam, who halted them. Up close, Riane could see that he had eyes like Othnam's, a startling blue, flecked with emerald. Those eyes peered into hers now. He said his name was Mu-Awwul.

"So. You have come. Finally."

"I do not understand," Riane said. "Were you expecting me?"

"Othnam and Mehmmer explained to me how you killed the disguised sauromician. We have long suspected their infiltration to gain power in our region but until now we lacked concrete proof of their perfidy." Mu-Awwul's beard was long and curling, shot through with white, fine as gossamer. "There is something you must tell me, isn't there?"

"I came to the Korrush to find the dzuoko Perrnodt."

"This we already know."

"It is my hope that she will aid me in my search for the *Maasra*."

"Ah!" He rocked back and forth on his heels. "And why would you want the *Maasia*?" His extraordinary eyes held steady on Riane's face. It was as if he were seeing all of her at once.

"Someone important to me, someone I love, is being held prisoner. Only the Veil of a Thousand Tears can save her."

"Many Ghor have died because of the *Maasra*," Mu-Awwul said. "Many Jeni Cerii, for they also covet it greatly. Outlanders, as well, have ventured deep into the Korrush, expending their lives in their futile quest."

Riane felt her heart sink. "Are you saying that it doesn't exist?"

"It exists." Mu-Awwul nodded. "It has been handed down through time from one guardian to another."

"Where is this guardian? Where can I find the Veil?"

Mu-Awwul studied Riane. "What is it? You have not yet told me what you wish me to know." Mu-Awwul stroked his beard. "It is a secret. It is hidden but I know. Tell me, now."

Riane swallowed, glanced briefly at Mehmmer and Othnam.

"Is it that you do not trust them?" Mu-Awwul asked.

"I owe them my life."

The old Ghor lifted his sun-browned hands. They had the texture of the red soil of the Korrush itself. They were hands made capable by ropey veins and strong bones and a keen mind. He took Riane's face in his hands and bent her head toward him. "As I have foreseen, our prayers have been answered." He kissed the crown of Riane's head seven times. "The Prophet has sent us his greatest gift." He released Riane and addressed Othnam and Mehmmer. "It is just as I speculated when you told me that a Kundalan female appeared in your camp accompanied by your own docile lymmnal."

He said to Riane, "You are the messenger of Jiharre, Riane. The knowledge you have brought us has the potential to change the entire Korrush."

"If only we all have the courage to act on it," Othnam said.

"Enmity is the most difficult mind-set to break," Mehmmer said.

"The Prophet's tasks were difficult," Mu-Awwul said. "Why should he ask any less of his children?"

"Are you speaking only of the Ghor?"

There was a kind of collective gasp from the assembled, but the Mu-Awwul held up his hand for silence. "You are from Axis Tyr and are forgiven your ignorance." He pierced Riane with his penetrating gaze. "Jiharre worshiped Miina. The Sarakkon, too, worship Her through their own prophetess, Yahé. Every race on Kundala is related, Riane. No matter our differences we are united in this one thing."

He took her hands in his. The palms felt like sandpaper. "Your heart is pure, that much was never a secret. As I have said, many have died in the pursuit of the *Maasra*. The *Maasra* is like a living thing. It makes judgments, forms conclusions, takes action. If you are meant to find it, then you will. If you are not, then like all before you who were proved unworthy, you will die."

"If this dire warning was meant to dissuade me, it will not." Riane knew she was taking a chance by interrupting him. "Ten thousand pardons, wise one, but I am desperate. I must find the Veil before my beloved Giyan is lost to me forever. I beg you to help me."

"My advice is to continue with your search."

"I have been seeking Perrnodt. Nith Settt seeks her, as well."

Mu-Awwul nodded. "Perrnodt knows the sanctuary wherein the *Maasra* currently rests. Nith Settt seeks the *Maasra*. He wishes to resurrect Za Hara-at. Without the *Maasra* he will fail. How he knows this is a mystery to us."

Riane said gravely, "Mu-Awwul, I regret to tell you that this is not all the Gyrgon seek. Nith Settt told me that they have been in the Korrush for some time advising the kapudaan of the Five Tribes on how to wage war against one another. They have poisoned you each against the other. Even now, it seems clear to me, Agachire is preparing itself for all-out war against the Jeni Cerii. This is the Gyrgon's base mischief. They seek nothing less than your annihilation, observing with pleasure only a Gyrgon could know the mounting attrition as the killing escalates."

There was complete silence when Riane had finished, it was as if time had ground to a halt. Riane observed a number of emotions pass across the elder's lined and leathery face. No one moved; no one spoke. The air between them seemed to spark with the enormity of the revelation.

"Yes. Truly Jiharre's messenger." Mu-Awwul cupped the back of Riane's right hand in his, placed his other hand in the palm. Riane felt something pressed into her hand. Then he intoned several lines in a language Riane did not know.

She looked to Othnam who translated:

"In the Time before Time," he began, in the same odd singsong intonation Mu-Awwul had used, *"the Prophet Jiharre strode the mountains, searching for the hand of the Maker, and at length, he came upon this confluence of light and shadow, and he knew its worth, for it did not change come sunset, as moonrise lit it just as the sun had when it hung directly over his head. And in this way, Jiharre recognized the hand of the Maker and, gathering the confluence in the cupped palms of his hands, heard the prayer for unity forming in his head, and this most sacred of chants he passed on to the fruit of his loins, and they to theirs in the manner of all things sacred."*

Mu-Awwul waited until Othnam had finished translating before withdrawing his hand. Riane saw lying in the center of her palm a small polished stone of an irregular shape. It was dark green, veined with deep orange. In its center had been carved a bird, its wings spread wide.

"The fulkaan," Mehmmer said in tone of awe. "The companion of Jiharre."

"Also his messenger," Mu-Awwul said. "Power and *jjhani* flow from the image of the fulkaan."

Riane turned briefly to Othnam. *"Jjhani?"*

"It means . . ." Othnam screwed up his face.

"A kind of . . . spiritual harvest," Mehmmer broke in.

Riane nodded. "Thank you," she said to Mu-Awwul, and bowed her head. "I will treasure Jiharre's talisman."

"Treasure it, yes," Mu-Awwul said. "But use it, also."

"Use it? How?"

"When the time comes, you will know." He reached out, laid his thickly veined hands on Riane's a last time. "I thank you for the great gift you have given us. May you be guided by *azmiirha* always." Then he returned to the circle. The holy ones put their heads together, wrapped their arms around each other's waists, and resumed the prayer cycle.

Riane followed Othnam and Mehmmer as they hurried from the Ghor encampment, threading their way carefully through the jumble of narrow streets. On all sides of them, tents rose up, small and large. Twice, they spotted the kapudaan's guards and were forced to make anxious detours. Nevertheless, they covered the remaining half kilometer to the palace in good time and without incident.

As they crouched in the shadows across the street from the huge cluster of striped tents, Mehmmer said, "Now what?"

"We spent a lot of time figuring a way to get you out," Othnam said. "Getting you back in may prove even more difficult."

"Not necessarily," Riane told them. "Each midnight a holy man secretly comes to the provisions gate in the palace's west wall and is given entrance so that he may teach Makktuub the *Mokakaddir.*" She looked at them. "But of course you already know this since this holy man is a Ghor."

Othnam and Mehmmer exchanged worried glances. "You are mistaken, Riane. No Ghor teaches the kapudaan the sacred text."

"Are you certain?"

"Yes." Mehmmer nodded. "And, furthermore, no Ghor would enter the palace in secret and at night."

"Then he is someone dressed like a Ghor," Riane said. "Tezziq told me he was Ghor."

"The ajjan!"

"She would have no reason to lie to me," Riane pointed out.

Mehmmer grunted. "Since when does an ajjan need a reason to lie?"

Squinting up at the moons' positions in the sky, Othnam said, "We have only minutes to find this impostor and waylay him."

"This is nonsense," Mehmmer said sourly.

"What if it isn't?" Riane said.

Mehmmer nodded somewhat reluctantly. "If someone is, indeed, impersonating a Ghor I very much want to discover who in Agachire would blaspheme against Jiharre and the *Mokakaddir*, and why."

"It is obvious," Othnam said darkly. "To gain the ear of Makktuub."

"The accursed Gyrgon again? But a Gyrgon could not masquerade as a Ghor."

"He most certainly could," Riane said. "Gyrgon are shapeshifters."

Mehmmer screwed up her face. "What blasphemy is being whispered to our kapudaan in secret?"

They began to circle around to the western side of the palace. This obliged them to negotiate the edge of the bazaar, a warren of narrow, twisting alleyways and aisles between rolling carts and makeshift stands selling everything from dried fruits to cheap slipper-shoes to magnificent bejeweled necklaces to sober black *ga'afarra*.

Oddly, at this time of the night, the bazaar was jam-packed with buyers and sellers, barterers and thieves. Mehmmer explained that the market opened at sundown so that the deleterious effects of the burning day would not degrade the delicate spices. The air was as thick with heated bargaining as it was with the heavy scents of spices and roasting ba'du. Flickering torchlight reflected off the striped tent walls that rimmed the bazaar. In the constant crowd motion, shadows streaked the alleyways, moving as if by an unseen hand, writing profound and unfamiliar runes across glossy pyramids of spices, down sloping sides of rickety carts. There was, on the surface, an overriding sense of controlled chaos. But underneath, Riane could feel a tug of something darker, the keen sense of expectation that comes in the deeply anxious moments before war is declared.

The three of them made their way single file, slowly and carefully, as if negotiating a garden tangled with fishhook brambles. Othnam was leading, with Riane next and Mehmmer bringing up the rear. They were perhaps a third of the way across the perimeter of the bazaar when Othnam was brought up short. A hand sign from him made them duck back into the shadows of the tent walls. Up ahead, Riane could see a knot of four bare-chested palace guards standing watch, their beady eyes roaming the crowd, doubtless searching for Riane.

"This way," Othnam whispered as he led them down a side alley. They soon turned off it, twisting their way this way and that until Riane lost all sense of direction. And then all at once they turned a corner and by the light of flaring torches saw the west wall of the palace. Keeping to the shadows flung across the striped tent walls, they soon spied the provision gate. The sounds of the city drifted to them—the laughter of children at play, the soft chanting of prayer cycles, the crisp bargaining of merchants, the heated rumor mongering of a tribe on war footing.

"What if he doesn't come?" Mehmmer whispered.

"He will come," Riane said, though she had only Tezziq's word that he would.

Othnam was squinting at the western sky above the palace. "It is after midnight. We may have missed him."

"No," Mehmmer said. "We haven't."

They pressed deeper into the lengthening shadows as a small, bearded male dressed in black Ghorvish robes, his head swathed in the traditional white sinschal, turned a corner and headed toward them.

Riane slid down into deepest shadow, crouched and still, her head down, her face obscured. The false Ghor passed her and when she heard him being stopped by Mehmmer, she lifted her head.

"The way to the Giyossun district?" The false Ghor's voice was brittle and querulous with impatience. "You are on the wrong side of the city."

Mehmmer stood squarely in front of him, blocking his way. "Yes, but how do I—"

"I have no time for such foolishness, female," he said shortly.

"A thousand pardons," Mehmmer replied. "But I, also, am Ghor. I am new to Agachire and I ask only—"

"I have an appointment with the kapudaan himself."

The false Ghor tried to sidestep her, but she would not let him pass.

"Can you not spare a moment to help one of your kin?"

Riane rose and silently moved out into the street.

"You are trying my patience."

"But surely I do not need to remind you of the Prophet Jiharre's words—"

"Out of my way!"

The false Ghor was about to push Mehmmer, but some sense made him whirl. In that instant, Riane struck him a blow to the temple with the hilt of her dagger. His eyes rolled up, and he slumped to the ground, his arms outstretched.

"A disgusting creature," Othnam said as he stepped out of the shadows. "It was all I could do not to run him through with my push-dagger." He bent down and was reaching out toward the false Ghor when Riane gasped and pulled him back.

"Miina protect us all," she murmured.

Concern overran Mehmmer's face. "What is it?"

"Look there," Riane said, "at his left hand."

"He has six fingers!" Othnam exclaimed.

Mehmmer looked more closely. "And the sixth is pure black."

Black and ugly as death, Minnum had said of the sauromician's extra digit.

"It is a mark of Miina," Riane said. "He is a sauromician, long ago cast out of the Ramahan abbeys for his evil ways."

"And he has been whispering in Makktuub's ear, no doubt poisoning the kapudaan's mind." Mehmmer drew her slender-bladed scimitar. "We must kill him."

She sliced through the sauromician's throat. Blood fountained, then immediately congealed, turned black as his sixth finger. The wound to his throat closed, shrinking until it was no more than a pucker, a scar, before disappearing altogether.

Mehmmer stepped back, gasping as Othnam knelt, used his push-dagger to puncture the sauromician's heart. Again, blood spurted up, and again immediately congealed, the wound healing spontaneously.

"The sauromician is protected by a powerful spell of some sort," Riane said. "Keep away from him."

But Othnam would not listen. He reached out, touched the beard, which was as false as the sauromician's Ghorvish claim. He stripped it off, noting the sticky underside and, loosening Riane's sinschal, fastened it around her jaw. "There," he said. "At least this evil creature has provided us with something of value."

Mehmmer looked at them both. "We cannot simply leave him. He has seen my face and yours."

Riane knew Mehmmer was correct. If they simply walked away, the sauromician would surely come after them as soon as he regained consciousness. But without her own sorcery Riane had no chance to counteract the spell he had cast upon himself. She rubbed the side of her head. What was it Minnum had said about the sauromician? *You will know him by the stigmata the Great Goddess in Her wisdom has given him: on his left hand is a sixth finger, black and ugly as death.* As she thought about it, two phrases stood out, *in Her wisdom* and *black and ugly as death.* Why had Minnum chosen those particular words? He had told Riane that he was enjoined from teaching, but what if he been trying to give her clues as to how to handle a sauromician should she come upon one?

She stared down at the wrinkled, dark-skinned face, curved and deadly-looking as a knife blade. She looked at the left hand with its sixth digit, black as death.

. . . the Great Goddess in Her wisdom . . .

Unsheathing her dagger, Riane knelt beside the sauromician. The blade hovered over the hand then, remembering the spell, she put the dagger away. Taking hold of the sauromician's left wrist with one hand, she grasped the black digit in her other hand, snapped it quickly back. The bone snapped like a dry twig, the skin crackled like paper in a fire. With a *pop!* there emanated from the finger a foul stench like an open grave, making her gag.

The sauromician arched up and began to spasm, slamming his body again and again into the packed red dirt of the street. An eerie keening arose from somewhere deep inside him, setting Riane's teeth on edge. The body was suddenly, sickeningly flooded with a milky liquid oozing out of every orifice, every pore. Almost immediately, this liquid eva-nesced into a darkening steam, spawning an intense wave of heat that caused Riane to stumble backward into Othnam's arms.

"What in the name of Jiharre—!"

Mehmmer was mesmerized by the unholy disintegration as, in truth, they all were.

The body gave one final, terrifying thrash, the keening abruptly ceased, and the steam vanished, leaving, for only a moment, a skeleton, whose bones softened like clay oozing, liquefying and running into the dirt.

Bronnn Pallln had thought about the many ways he could approach Marethyn Stogggul. In fact, in the time since the fateful dinner party at Dobbro Mannx's residence, he had thought about nothing else. At night, he dreamed about her.

In the end, he decided to visit her when she was at her most vulnerable. And so it was that in the hour after she closed her atelier on Divination Street he found himself setting his private hoverpod down in a small clearing beside a series of deep pools several kilometers northeast of Axis Tyr. Marethyn, who had been kneeling beside one of the pools, looked up, and he immediately warmed to the fright in her eyes.

"Bronnn Pallln," she said, a catch in her voice, "what are you doing here?"

"Hunting." He took the sport ion pistol out of its holster and frowned. "You know, Kundala is famed for its large predators." He came toward her. "It is quite dangerous for a defenseless Tuskugggun like you to be out here on your own."

"Your concern is misplaced. I have been coming here without incident since I was a little girl."

She began to get to her feet, but a heavy hand on her shoulder kept her in place.

"Then you have been remarkably lucky." He brandished the ion pistol. "But you never know. There are reports of perwillon in the area."

"Perwillon inhabit caves," she said.

"Is that so?" His lips pursed. "And where did a Tuskugggun gain such knowledge?" He smirked down at her. "It wouldn't be from Sornnn SaTrryn, would it?"

"I . . . I do not know what you are talking about."

Bronnn Pallln gave her the same indulgent look she had seen the Genomatekks give Terrettt from time to time.

"You are an artist, are you not? I myself have no interest whatsoever in art; I cannot fathom the rationale for its existence, really. Why is it, I wonder, that you dedicate yourself to utter nonsense when you could be doing something useful like raising children."

"Why are you doing this? What do you want?"

He could feel her muscles bunching under the hand that kept her on her knees. "I am an exceedingly busy V'ornn, you know. And what am I busy at? you might ask. Tracking down the traitorous trail your Sornnn SaTrryn has made."

"He is not *my*—" She cried out as his finger dug into her shoulder.

"Do not interrupt or contradict me, Marethyn. This is the first lesson you must learn."

She did not answer, but he could see by the rapid rise and fall of her breasts how terrified he had made her. Thus confident, he continued.

"I came here today as a courtesy to warn you. Out of the loyal relationship I enjoy with your family and the high respect in which I hold your brother. Your involvement with Sornnn SaTrryn—and please do not bother to deny it—is a tragic mistake. You have put yourself in grave peril."

"What? How do you mean?"

"Firstly, Sornnn SaTrryn is not qualified to be Prime Factor. Quite apart from the obvious fact that he spends too much time in the Korrush and too little time at his duties here in Axis Tyr, he has a highhanded manner with the other Bashkir that is causing friction rather than reconciliation between the Consortia."

"What you are saying is absurd, poisoned. You hate him because you covet his position."

"Secondly," Bronnn Pallln went on relentlessly, "as I said, he is a traitor."

Marethyn laughed harshly. "You must think me an utter fool."

"If I thought that I would not be here now. I would let you be beheaded with your lover. But I will not." He tipped his head slightly. "Now listen to me carefully, Marethyn. I have evidence that he is the Bashkir who has been selling Khagggun weapons to the Kundalan Resistance. This is not so absurd now, is it, what with his deviant love affair with the Korrush." His fingers ground into muscle and bone, making her wince. "Now I say to you in all good faith that you must give him up before your brother is told of his perfidy. If you do not, well, you know Kurgan Stogggul better than I do. I will leave it up to your own imagination what he will do to you."

"I don't want to hear this."

"But you must. It is for your own good."

Tears came to Marethyn's eyes, and a sob seemed torn from her breast. "You know what this means."

"Yes. You love Sornnn SaTrryn, I can see, but he has played you false. The only possible explanation is that he has been planning to involve you as a cover for his traitorous actions."

"He never loved me," she wailed. "He was using me."

"Truly, I am sorry for this seeming harsh treatment, but given your history of being headstrong and stubborn what other course could I take?" Bronnn Pallln released her, took her tear-streaked face under her chin, and lifted it so that her eyes met his. "There is, however, a way out for you, if not for him."

"There is?"

Now he smiled, hearing the clear note of servility in her voice. Up until now, no one had succeeded in breaking Marethyn Stogggul. Studying her, he saw what her monstrous personality had for so long obscured. She was a beautiful, highly desirable Tuskugggun. Perhaps, when this was all over, he reflected, he would take her to bed, even marry her, get her with child, make a true Tuskugggun out of her. In fact, the more he thought about it, the better he liked the idea. What better way to cement his relationship with the Stogggul Consortium. Kurgan would have no choice but to respect the V'ornn who tamed his wayward sister, Marethyn.

He drew her up to stand beside him. "I have knowledge that Sornnn SaTrryn has taken you to his warehouse. The place of his Resistance activities."

"Is that what that chamber was? I was wondering why he had so many Kundalan artifacts." She began to cry again.

Foolish Tuskugggun, Bronnn Pallln thought. *Full of untenable emotion, therefore so easy to use and abuse.* He put his face close to hers. "You will take Line-General Lokck Werrrent there, Marethyn, and when Sornnn SaTrryn is arrested and charged with crimes against V'ornndom you will be safe from harm."

She looked deep into his eyes, her lips half-parted. "Do you swear this, Bronnn Pallln? I will not betray him otherwise."

Bronnn Pallln kissed her on one cheek, then the other. "Marethyn Stogggul, I swear on all that matters to me to protect you and keep you safe."

It's as obvious as that ugly scar on your face. The war will begin with the Jeni Cerii."

"Too obvious. It will come from another quarter. I say the Rasan Sul will be first to strike. They have been seeking ways to expand their spice explorations for years."

The two palace guards at the provisions gate were in the middle of this debate when Riane appeared before them. They were expecting the false Ghor, so waved her through. She had pulled her sinschal out over her forehead and had lowered her face, staring down at the tops of her stained and dusty slipper-shoes, but so engrossed were they in their feverish speculation she needn't have bothered.

Once inside, she kept her head down and quickly and silently made her way to the haanjhala, where she told one of the *saddda* guards that the kapudaan had asked for the first ajjan. When Tezziq was brought to her, Riane took her by the arm and hurried her away down the hallway.

By means of the special hand signs devised by Makktuub, Tezziq kept asking what she wanted. Riane, searching for a deserted chamber, ignored her. But as soon as she found what she was looking for, she pulled Tezziq into the tented chamber and half stripped off her false beard.

"Riane!" Tezziq's eyes opened wide. "You're alive!"

Riane embraced her. "Of course I'm alive."

"But I thought . . . well, Baliiq said that you had jumped from the terrace to your death. I did not believe him, but then the same story began to circulate through the palace. And now here you are."

"I made a promise," Riane said, holding her at arm's length. She pushed hair back from Tezziq's face. "And now I will take you with me out of here, but first I must retrieve something that was stolen from me."

"What?"

"Tell me, when you have been with Makktuub have you caught a glimpse of a tall figure in metallic armor?"

"The Gyrgon? Yes, I know of him. Makktuub speaks of him sometimes in the aftermath."

"Does he have quarters here in the palace?"

Tezziq nodded. "A chamber, small and spare as a beggar's, adjacent to the kapudaan's quarters."

"Take me there."

"No, I cannot!" Fear contorted Tezziq's beautiful face. "Please. Ask me anything else."

Riane gripped Tezziq's arm. "It is imperative that I retrieve what the Gyrgon stole from me."

"I have seen the cold fire come off him. I have seen the cruelty he is capable of." Tezziq shuddered, but she nodded and, taking Riane's hand in her own, began to lead them down a series of intersecting corridors. Each time they neared a guard, they shifted positions to give the impression that Tezziq was being guided by the Kapudaan's Ghorv-ish spiritual advisor. In this way, they traversed the distance between the haanjhala and Makktuub's quarters.

"Here it is," Tezziq said, shivering, as she brought them up short across from the tent flap. "Let me go in alone to see whether the crea-ture is there."

Riane watched her uneasily as she crept across the corridor, then, drawing herself up, swept into the tent. Riane heard only silence. A moment later, Tezziq stuck her head out and gave the all-clear sign.

The chamber smelled strongly of clove oil and burnt musk. It was at odds with virtually every other chamber in the palace—doubtless in all Agachire, for that matter. There were no cushions or carpets, no low chased-bronze tables, no decorations of any kind. In fact, the cham-ber was quite bare, save for one item, an alloy-clad container perhaps three meters long shaped like a compressed oval. There was a word etched into it in spiraled V'ornnish letters.

They stood still and silent, staring at the huge object.

"What does it say?" Tezziq whispered.

" 'K'yonnno,' " Riane said in a similar hushed tone. "It is the Gyrgon theory of Law and Chaos."

Tezziq wrinkled her brow. "I do not understand."

"The first rule of K'yonnno is Stasis and Harmony are synonymous. It is rumored that the Gyrgon mission is to find the key to immortality, which, if you think about it, is the ultimate stasis and, in their minds, at least, blissful harmony."

"But Jiharre teaches that for everything there is a time and a place and a purpose. Without the first two, the third cannot exist." She shud-dered. "I cannot imagine anything more horrible than life without pur-pose."

"I agree," Riane said, "which makes us so very different than the Gyrgon."

"So what is this?"

"I'm not sure," Riane said, approaching the huge object, "but if I had to guess, I'd say that it is where the Gyrgon sleeps."

She put her hands on the thick convex lid. It was smooth as crystal, so shiny she could see the rather startling reflection of the false Ghor she had become. She briefly touched the fulkaan stud in her nostril. Then, she found the catch and, depressing it, stood back. With a soft sigh, the lid lifted and she peered into the emptiness within. The interior appeared to be composed entirely of neural-net circuitry. A clutch of cables and flexible links attached to the net at different places lay curled, waiting for the Gyrgon to plug their free ends into his armored biosuit.

Riane peered more closely, for there, amid the serpentine clutter, was a small square black package. Nith Sahor's greatcoat.

She reached for it, but just as she did so, Tezziq clutched at her and mouthed the words, *Someone is coming!*

Riane clambered into the sleep casket, pulled a terrified Tezziq in with her and lowered the lid. Just in time, for voices burst into the chamber. The moment the lid had clicked into place, the neural net awoke, doubtless expecting to take Nith Settt into slumber. But there was plenty of room; the sleep casket was twice as deep as it had at first seemed.

Listening to the voices, Riane recognized Makktuub. By the neural net's banks of lights she could see Tezziq mouthing the name of the other speaker, Sawakaq, the minister who had originally brought her and Othnam and Mehmmer to the kapudaan.

"—should have begun twenty minutes ago," Makktuub was saying.

Riane scrambled to the foot of the sleep casket in order to better hear what was being said.

"The Ghor came through the provision gate on time. I checked with the guards," Sawakaq replied. "Then he disappeared."

"*Inside* the palace?" Makktuub's voice grew dark. "Another strange and unexplained incident to add to the rest that have occurred of late."

"Unsettling, to say the least," Sawakaq admitted. "I advise doubling the number of guards inside the palace."

"An excellent precaution, unless it is precisely what the Jeni Cerii are hoping we will do. No, instead, send a message to double our patrols along the Jeni Cerii border. If they seek to confuse us here in Agachire they will be sorely mistaken."

"And what of the Gyrgon?" Sawakaq said. "He was quite explicit about informing him about any changes in either our defensive or offensive battle plans."

"As you can see, minister, we are in his quarters. We came in good faith to keep him updated, but his movements are of his own design." Makktuub's voice became slightly more muffled, making it clear that he had moved back to the tent flap. "Find the Ghor, Sawakaq. Use whatever means at your disposal, but I want him brought to me forthwith."

"Yes, kapudaan."

Footsteps gliding away, then silence. Riane held her breath. She was very close to Tezziq, could feel her warmth, could see the inside of the sleep casket refracted in her glossy eyes. Tezziq's mouth was half-open as if she wanted to say something.

"Just a minute," Riane whispered and, raising her hands over her head, pushed the lid up. At first, she thought it was either locked or stuck, and she felt the sweat pop out along her hairline and under her arms. But possibly it was simply heavier pushing it from a crouched position than it had seemed lifting it when she was standing, because as she strained it began to move. Slowly, she rose from her squat, the lid swinging up, letting light into the interior.

Tezziq's eyes were half-closed, the pupils dark and dilated. Riane put an ear to her chest, could detect a shallow, ragged breath.

"N'Luuura, no!" she breathed.

The cables, alive as any creature, had inserted themselves into Tezziq at the insides of her elbows, the backs of her thighs, her navel.

Konara Inggres lit the prayer candle and the familiar scents of orange-sweet and mugwort wafted up to her. She studied the flame-bent wick, braided by the leyna, charred black at the tip. She studied the squat candle itself, the tallow mottled and beautifully translucent as ancient skin. She could recall fashioning candles similar to this one when she herself had been a novitiate, and found herself clinging to the sense of continuity the memory provided. On the scarred wooden table beside the candle was a well-used pewter dish with a wide flared lip in which were strewn the remnants of thick-sliced wrybread, the crusts yellow and glistening with half-melted cor butter. This homely sight was also of comfort to her, which was why she had come down to the refectory tonight. As a child, she had often sneaked into the refectory for this selfsame snack. Tonight a deep sense of panic gnawed at her. Her hermetic world—the one she had been born into, the one in which she had lived all her life—had suddenly been invaded, and the worst part was she did not know by whom or to what purpose.

"I thought I would find you here."

She started even though she knew the voice. Konara Lyystra came striding in, smiling widely. "Now that Mother has taken over and we are released from our punishment duties it seems I see you less and less."

"Other duties interfere," Konara Inggres said neutrally. She held herself still and steady as Konara Lyystra sat down across the long refectory table from her. The panic, held in temporary suspension by her will, burst like a blister, left her shaking. "There have been so many changes of late."

"I imagine you are referring to Konara Urdma's sudden death."

"Partially."

The wide smile never left Konara Lyystra's face. "An artery burst in her head, a congenital defect, no one could have known or suspected."

"There are other things." Konara Inggres said this warily.

"Could you be referring to Konara Bartta? We knew something was amiss when we entered the chamber in which she had secreted the *had-atta*. You yourself said—"

"I know what I said," Konara Inggres replied rather too sharply.

Konara Lyystra cocked her head. "It took someone of Mother's vast sorcerous skill to extract Konara Bartta from the stasis-web. But you knew. Your instinct was unerring."

Konara Inggres wrapped her arms around herself. It chilled her to the bone that Konara Lyystra's expression never changed. Nor had the slightly glazed look left her eyes. Ever since that night Giyan had arrived. What had happened in Konara Urdma's office when Konara Lyystra had gone to greet her? Konara Lyystra had not spoken of it, and as the days progressed, Konara Inggres became afraid to ask.

"You do not seem particularly pleased that she has returned," Konara Lyystra said, jolting Konara Inggres out of her brief reverie.

"I know very little about Giyan," Konara Inggres replied.

"I meant Konara Bartta."

That wide smile was unnerving, Konara Inggres thought, as if she knew a secret jest.

"I know how you feel about Konara Bartta. But I assure you that now that Mother is here everything will be all right."

It was positively sinister, that smile, Konara Inggres decided. And here was another thing that frightened her, her friend saying, *I know how you feel about Konara Bartta*, just as if they had never shared this antipathy. Which was why she had tried to avoid her, and when, like now, she could not, she was circumspect and wary.

"I am certain I will come to share your opinion," she lied.

Konara Lyystra took a crust of wrybread and popped it into her mouth without her smile narrowing one millimeter. "Excellent," she said. "We are all counting on it."

17

Chimaera

Just hours to midnight on this dank moonsless night in the ides of autumn, and the last dying leaf of summer had been ground to mulch beneath winter's oncoming heel. Out on the Sea of Blood, the lanterns on Courion's ship swung to and fro as the vessel passed through lashing wave crests and deep troughs. There were four such lanterns, ornately runed as a Sarakkon's head, one each on the high, arching prow and slender aft, two more midship, at port and starboard.

Courion had a striking and formidable appearance. He was, like most Sarakkon, tall and slender, well muscled and fit, his skin the deep color of pomegranates. He had a sleek, compelling face, with high cheekbones, dark intelligent eyes, and gently bowed lips that made him appear as if he were always slightly amused. Over his shaved, elongated skull was tattooed a bewildering array of runes that reappeared on bare arms that bulged from his sharkskin vest. He had a thick sable beard, curling and oiled, in which were threaded runes made of carved lapis lazuli and jade. His fingers were encircled with massive rings of star sapphire and ruby and lynx-eye. With each pitch and roll of the ship the ends of his wide, knotted belt, woven of cured sea grape, traversed a short arc. The pattern of knots was different for every Sarakkon Kurgan had seen. They bore great significance, but what they meant no V'ornn knew.

"Until tonight, we have not seen you since you attained the office of regent," Courion said. "Not even at the Kalllistotos."

Courion laughed, watching the line playing out from the tip of his fishing rod, fashioned from a searay's tail, which he had cured himself in a combination of mercury and sea salt in order to increase its strength while maintaining its flexibility. "How uninteresting is our free time without the magnificent entertainment of wagering against you."

"Knowing you, you only want to coerce me back into the ring."

"You fought well, acquitted yourself with a warrior's courage."

Kurgan had once made an imprudent wager with the Sarakkonian captain that he had promptly lost. In lieu of the payment he could not make, Courion had required him to fight in the Kalllistotos, garnering him a measure of respect from the Sarakkon no other V'ornn had attained. Save perhaps Nith Batoxxx.

"But I am regent now, and the regent of all Kundala has more to occupy him than the Kalllistotos."

"That is a very great pity."

"I still find time for combat practice." Kurgan felt the urgent need to keep talking in order to make certain his diaphragm kept all his three stomachs from rebelling. V'ornn did not take naturally to the sea.

"Good," Courion said. "A fit body is a virtue."

He could, of course, have met with Courion anywhere he chose, but he saw this fishing trip as a test of his own inner strength. Truth be told, he had been born without the desire to be like other V'ornn, and Nith Batoxxx, opportunistic as he was subversive, had nurtured this fortuitous aberration.

"I have an entire planet to oversee. Tedious work, for the most part, which surprises me somewhat."

"Why? Cogs and flywheels, the mechanics of anything is nothing but humdrum."

"You are right, of course," Kurgan acknowledged. "But I find compensation by being more closely in touch with the Gyrgon Comradeship."

"From what we have gleaned of you V'ornn, this is true of all regents." Courion gave several whiplike upward swipes with the tip of his searay rod.

Kurgan spread his legs a little more in order not to be tossed against the gleaming wooden taffrail. "Nith Batoxxx, in particular. You remember him. I met him on this very ship."

"We could hardly forget a Gyrgon." Courion pulled up hard on his rod; the tip had bent almost double. "Any Gyrgon."

Kurgan adopted a light, almost bantering tone. "Believe it or not, he is interested in something Kundalan. Seven Portals to a land of riches, so he claims."

"Oho! That is for us!" Courion cried. "We are all for riches!"

"I doubt he is telling me the whole truth. Do you know anything about these Portals?"

Courion shook his head. "Alas, no." He shrugged. "The only portals we know are on our ship."

"By the way, I never asked you. What was Nith Batoxxx doing on your ship?"

"Help us now," Courion said tersely as he hauled hard on his rod and began to reel in the line. "We seem to have hooked the monster of all Chimaera."

Of a sudden, as if to punctuate that remark, not three meters from the stern the sea began to boil. Kurgan saw something that turned his blood to ice. Something huge had leapt out of the water.

Its first breach gave him only a flash of a dark and sinuously glistening body that was almost all monstrous head. Then it was under again in a geyser of creamy foam, and Courion, braced against the taffrail, was reeling for all he was worth.

"Mother of Yahé, it's a black one!" Courion cried.

Members of his crew, who had been going about the business of keeping the ship on course, and others who had been off duty or be-lowdecks, came running and Kurgan heard them shouting excitedly to each other. Apparently a Chimaera of this size was rare enough, but a pitch-black one, to boot! They were agog. Just at that instant, the Chimaera leapt upward again and all of them—Kurgan included—got a good look at it. It was huge—perhaps half as long as the ship itself—with a long, tapering, forked tail, sharp as knife blades, and three wicked-looking cartilaginous dorsal fins rising off its back. In the flick-ering lanternlight, its absolute blackness was positively eerie, making it seem even larger and fiercer than it actually was. But by far its most hideous feature was its mouth, which, impossibly, appeared to take up the entire front third of the creature's muscular body. In midleap, it twisted itself, a hearts-stopping maneuver that slammed Courion into the rail. A cold red eye seemed to fix Courion in its mad gaze. Then, with a great fountaining that drenched Courion, Kurgan, and much of the crew, it plunged once again beneath the waves.

They all peered over the side. The wake the thing made in its frantic thrashing to free itself from the tormenting hook glowed phosphores-cent. And still Courion lifted the rod, reeled in more of the line, only to peel the line back out when the Chimaera made another dash away from the ship. Over the course of the next several hours it tried everything, including running under the ship, an attempt, Courion said, to get the keel to saw the line in two.

"That presupposes a will," Kurgan said. He was tired by this time; he could only imagine the exhaustion that Courion felt. "And a will presupposes a consciousness."

"You do not know this fish," Courion said tersely as he twisted the rod. "Mother of Yahé, he's running again."

"Why don't you let one of your crew spell you, at least for a little while?"

Courion shook his head. "Landing him will mean nothing, then. Until the hunt is played out and he is beside the ship, we must do this on our own."

Kurgan, watching Courion's bunched muscles, the sweat running off him, had to admire the Sarakkonian captain's courage and fortitude. Even a Khaggun would gain a measure of satisfaction observing his chronosteel-like tenacity.

It was after midnight by the time Courion at last got the best of the great Chimaera. It took one last, rather halfhearted run out to sea, then seemed to roll over, and Courion began his frantic reel-in, drawing it closer and closer to the stern of the ship where they stood, their muscles jumping with a surfeit of tension and fatigue. For almost an hour now, one of Courion's crew had stood by his side, a long pole with a bronze hook on one end held in a gnarled and swollen fist.

"Close," Courion said softly. "Very close now." He held his rod almost at the vertical as the spent Chimaera lolled nearer them.

Kurgan was watching it closely, feeling a stone lodged in one of his hearts at the size of its gargantuan maw, bristling with multiple sets of triangular, needle-sharp teeth, which occasionally snapped ineffectually at the air as it rolled this way and that.

"All right," Courion said to him. "When it is against the side of the ship we are going to give you the rod. Hold it in exactly the angle we designate and keep one hand on the reel so the line will not go slack." He glanced briefly at Kurgan. "This is most important because the line is the only thing keeping it in place." He grinned through his exhaustion. "Don't worry. You need hold it only long enough for me to gaff him."

A moment later, the beast banged against the hull and Courion's ship shuddered down to its keel. This close up, the Chimaera was so mammoth Kurgan had trouble processing the image. His mind kept wanting to shrink it down by half or more.

"This is the angle," Courion said, handing over the rod. "Yes, just like that." He made a small adjustment. "Brace your thighs against the rail, and for Yahé's sake keep your hand tight on the reel or we'll likely lose it."

Kurgan nodded and Courion took his guiding hand away. Kurgan could feel the tremorings of the creature as if they were seismic shocks transmitted up the taut line and down the searay rod. The Chimaera looked quiescent, more dead than alive to judge by the one red eye, clouded and still, that stared up into the night from the side of its long, tapering head. Translucent waves washed over it as the current bounced its body repeatedly against the hull, and still the eye remained fixed.

Next to him, Courion accepted the long gaff and, bending over the top rail, swung it down toward the Chimaera. With an expert motion, he fixed the hook in the upper corner of the beast's mouth, so that he could better maneuver it. Members of the crew had meanwhile been lowering a block and tackle on a heavy chain wrapped around a large hand-wound windlass, with which to winch the Chimaera out of the water. All that was left was for Courion to guide the beast onto the massive hook sunk into the block and tackle as it was lowered all the way to the foamy wave tops.

Kurgan took his assignment seriously. Knowing that he was out of his element he consigned himself to the expertise of the Sarakkonian captain, trusting that with each order obeyed he would learn something no V'ornn before him knew. In this vein he concentrated on keeping the angle of the rod just right, making sure the line stayed taut. His right hand was white as it tightly gripped the reel just as Courion had instructed. He was trembling a little, not out of fear but out of the sheer exhilaration at being in on the kill of this extraordinary hunt. His eyes burned a little in the biting salt wind, his nostrils flared at first scent of the Chimaera's blood, which leaked out of the side of its mouth where the barbed hook dug deep and where the barbed end of Courion's gaff further exacerbated the wound.

Courion had brought the Chimaera's head partway out of the water as the block and tackle was lowered the last several meters. He was now bent almost completely in half over the top rail. It was a delicate procedure considering the bulk of both fish and hook, and it had to be done just right. He hauled a little more on the gaff, straining to his limit as he pulled the Chimaera the few last centimeters above the waves.

At that instant, something quite extraordinary happened. Kurgan, who was concentrating on the beast, reeling in the line as Courion lifted it farther, saw it, but N'Luuura only knew whether anyone else had.

That great red eye, half-occluded and fixed, abruptly blinked and cleared. Kurgan's brain did not perhaps understand the significance of this but his body, already in full self-preservation mode, certainly did.

In a stupefying and cataclysmic display of canniness and strength, the Chimaera leapt clear out of the frothing water. As it did so, it torqued its body away from the ship, taking the gaff and Courion with it. Courion was lifted clean off his feet. His knees banged against the top rail and then, as the Chimaera started to fall back again into the water, he began to go over the side.

Though the beast's wicked move was accomplished in no more than a heartbeat, Kurgan saw it as if in slow motion. He saw its great red eye glaring as if in ferocious outrage. Was it looking at Courion or at him? Even later, in the besotted calmness of the aftermath, it was impossible to say, but he could not shake the disquieting conclusion that he had glimpsed a malign intelligence where he had least expected to find one. At the moment, however, he reacted without thinking. Letting go of the spinning rod, he grabbed Courion around the waist, pulling him back on board, anchoring him to the ship's deck as the gaff's hook tore free of the Chimaera's bloody mouth.

With little grunting sounds, Riane tried to pull Tezziq free of the Gyrgon umbilicals, but as soon as she did she was thrown back against the side of the casket by a painful shock wave. Riane shook her head to clear it. Tezziq looked glazed-eyed at her, tried to say something, failed.

"Stay calm," Riane said. "I will get you out of here."

Her gaze swept over the banks of readouts positioned strategically around the casket's neural net. Here, Annon's fluency in V'ornn was invaluable. She forced herself to read slowly and carefully, switching off the anxiety that urged her to get out of here before anyone else chanced by.

Decoding the Gyrgon sigils, she determined that each umbilical had a different purpose. In addition, each was attached to a different energy pod, so that even in an emergency situation they would continue to function. The cable snaking into Tezziq's navel provided nutrients, the ones inserted in the crook of her elbows contained a complex formula of electrolytes that restored the Gyrgon's often overtaxed neural grids, the umbilicals that had attached themselves behind her knees were pumping a powerful chemical cocktail that induced delta-level brain activity, in other words, deepest sleep. Beside each power node was a scale to calibrate accurately the amount of fluids being conducted through the cables. She could see that the normal dosage for a Gyrgon was more or less one-fifth of maximum.

She soon discovered that the only way to detach the umbilicals without trauma to Tezziq was to disengage their power sources from the neural net; as she had already learned, safeguard circuitry engaged the moment someone tried to remove them incorrectly or by force.

She could hear Tezziq sobbing a little, and she stopped what she was doing. "Are they hurting you?"

Tezziq's eyes moved wildly, their pupils dilated, and Riane began to worry about the effects the Gyrgon-manufactured chemicals might have on her system. She appeared to be dreaming with her eyes open, but was she dreaming Gyrgon dreams?

Riane kissed Tezziq's damp brow. "Hold on a little longer," she whispered. "I'll have you out of here in no time."

Returning to the power supplies, she saw that they were some kind of gel paks that pulsed with light. The first time she tried to disengage the first gel pak, a bolt of pain ran up her arm. She shook her hand to get the numbness out of it and tried again with the same result. This time it took longer to get the numbness out. She stared hard at the power supply, thinking. The pulse of light ran through it every thirty seconds. She tried touching the circuitry between the pulses and received no shock. So she began work, keeping counting silently to herself, lifting her fingers a second before the pulse appeared. In this way, she was able to disengage the first gel pak. Now she turned back to Tezziq, pulled the umbilicals from her elbows without incident. They left no entry at all, merely a welt of raw and reddened flesh.

Tezziq moaned a little, twitching, and Riane put a hand to her cheek before returning to the neural net. In the same manner she had handled the first power pak, she disengaged the second one. Out came the umbilicals from behind Tezziq's knees.

Two down, one to go, Riane thought.

But when she commenced to study the third power pak, she could see that it was different. The photon pulses rippled through it every five seconds. Not enough time for her to get the job done. She tried it anyway and lasted twenty seconds before the pain became too much and she had to take her hands away. She held them under her armpits, waiting for the numbness in her fingers to subside. While she waited she considered the photonic pulses, and when she felt the circulation returning she took out the infinity blade and, on a hunch, jammed it directly into the center of the gel pak. The unknown alloy pierced the skin of the power supply and the weapon absorbed the photonic pulses, drawing the energy out of the gel pak.

Behind her, Tezziq gave a little sigh and, as Riane removed the umbilical from her navel, she cried out as if in great pain. Her fingers gripped Riane's shoulders, her long nails digging into Riane's flesh.

A flash of anger caused Riane to stab the infinity blade into the nexus of the neural net. A welter of hyperexcited ions bubbled up, but as quickly as they exploded the infinity blade absorbed them, until there was no power left within the sleep casket. Riane felt a measure of satisfaction in the destruction.

She grabbed a gel pak, jamming it into her robes, gathered Tezziq into her arms, and lifted her out of the sleep casket. Tezziq moaned a little, and her eyes were rolling beneath her half-closed lids. Steadying herself, Riane unfurled Nith Sahor's greatcoat. Minnum had told her not to use sorcery in the Korrush save under Perrnodt's direction because it would likely draw the attention of the sauromicians. She did not know whether this warning might also apply to V'ornn technomancy, but she had no other choice. There was no way she could leave the palace the same way she entered it.

Throwing the greatcoat across her shoulders, she lifted its edge with her free hand, closing it over both her and Tezziq. She felt its sheltering embrace, the comfortable cavelike gloom that seemed to stretch on into infinity. Then, clutching Tezziq tightly to her, she thought of Othnam and Mehmmer and the powerful Gyrgon neural-net circuitry engaged, sweeping them away.

In the small hours, with the ship buoyed by a following wind, sailing peacefully back toward the port of Axis Tyr, Kurgan and Courion were belowdecks, comfortably ensconced in the captain's fan-shaped cabin. Runes were carved into every wooden surface, embossed on every metal surface, etched into every pane of glass along the bowed rear bulkhead. An embalmed searay, its stippled skin pale, shiny with lacquer, hung upon the concave wall over the bed. Its beautiful wings were stiff as shock-swords.

Courion had broken open a bottle of Sarakkonian brandy, a thick bitterish liquor Kurgan had never tasted before, for which he felt certain he could develop a strong and abiding liking. For a time they merely drank in a kind of companionable silence that was new for them both. Gradually, they began to speak of everything save Courion's brush with death.

Kurgan smelled the curious Sarakkonian spices that arose from their oils and unguents, their leathers and cloths, the deep orange wax with which they formed the molds of their indecipherable runes. He felt the gentle rolling of the deck beneath his feet and tried to attune his motions to that rhythm, to let it take him up in its arms, a V'ornn upon the ocean, an odd and disquieting thought because the V'ornn traditionally shunned oceans and deserts as being barren, empty of natural resources to plunder. And yet here he was, his hips moving as he had seen Sarakkon hips moving, timing his center of balance to the whims of the tide. He found that he very much liked the feeling of power it gave him, a kind of mastery over the sea no other V'ornn possessed.

At length, Courion said, "You acquitted yourself well. You saved us from the sea."

"Ironic, isn't it?" Kurgan took some brandy in his mouth, left it there until the soft tissue began to burn.

"The Chimaera is the subject of many legends. Therefore, it is both revered and feared by all Sarakkonian captains," Courion said. "Few would dare to fish for it; fewer still have landed one. As for the black variety, no captain has returned home to parade its carcass. To trifle with a Chimaera, many say, is to court disaster. A black one, especially, because they are exceedingly rare and, according to legend, intelligent."

Kurgan thought of that daemonic red eye staring at him with its malevolent intent clear and present. "You speak of the black Chimaera as if you had seen it before."

"Most Sarakkon have never seen one. Now we have encountered one twice. The first time, we were aboard the first ship we served on out of Celiocco on the southern continent."

"You were not a captain then."

"No. And not for years afterward." Courion stared into his drink as if searching for an answer to a long-held question. "We were just a raw mate. As such, we paid scant heed to the shoreside stories about the captain. As it happened, they were more or less right. He was a maniac. He would share nothing of our course even with his First. Two weeks out, we spied a mountainous black Chimaera just like this one and were ordered to give pursuit. The captain insisted on torturing it before going in for the kill. The sea was dark as midnight with its blood. He laughed at the Chimaera's pain, and at the last minute it turned and rammed the ship, stove in the hull below the waterline. The ship sank like a stone with all hands. We, alone, survived."

"How did you—?"

Courion shrugged. "We were extraordinarily fortunate."

"Now you and the black Chimaera."

"Linked as one? Our crew thinks so." Courion finished off his brandy in one swallow.

"And you?"

"We think it makes a fine midnight's tale."

There was a small silence. Kurgan looked at Courion, slightly tense now though he was stretched out in the lamplight. He thought of his Summoning when Nith Batoxxx had purportedly shown him his own fear—drowning off Courion's ship. Or was it drowning? *There is another thing here for you to fear,* Nith Batoxxx had said. *I find it interesting that you cannot yet identify it.*

The black Chimaera? But Kurgan had not yet known about it when the Summoning had occurred. Nith Batoxxx had said the construct had been created from Kurgan's own mind.

"You never answered my question about why Nith Batoxxx was on your ship."

"We think you should ask him."

Kurgan grunted. "Have you ever tried to ask a Gyrgon anything?"

Courion threw his head back, and his laughter bounced off the bulkheads.

Kurgan leaned forward, and said softly but distinctly, "I know."

Courion swung his legs around as he sat up. "What is it you know, regent?"

Kurgan came and sat down next to him. His nostrils flared at the spicy Sarakkonian scent. "Let us talk business for a moment. How can I obtain some salamuuun?"

"You know as well as we do. Take your leisure at a kashiggen."

"Yes, of course. But then there is the high price to pay and the artificial quota the Ashera set on it. Just between friends there must be another way."

Courion shrugged. "Why ask us? We are Sarakkon."

"Precisely!" Kurgan slapped his thigh. "And what would a Sarakkon know of this when no V'ornn save an Ashera has even an inkling?"

Courion sat silent and very still.

"Nith Batoxxx has an inordinate interest in salamuuun. Do not continue to deny it. I know it for a fact." Of course he did. Rada's illegal memory net had revealed as much.

Courion looked away. "It is not possible to discuss this."

"If Nith Batoxxx is planning on wresting control of the salamuuun trade from the Ashera, I would be most interested." Kurgan refilled his goblet. "But I will tell you this. If he is involving you in his dangerous scheme, I would be exceedingly wary."

"And why would that be?" Courion's voice was tightly throttled.

"To tell you the truth, I am beginning to suspect that he is mad."

Courion began to laugh.

"He exhibits manifestations of harboring two distinct personalities. You do not believe me? Sometimes his voice darkens and seems to be floating out of him. And his posture changes, one shoulder rising higher than the other. Have you not noticed this?"

The Sarakkonian captain drained his goblet. His expression had changed subtly. "These odd, quicksilver changes, we admit that we have wondered over them."

"They are getting worse, aren't they?" Kurgan put down his goblet. "Several days ago I caught him talking into a mirror, in a language I could not identify. That would be cause for alarm on its own. Then I got a look at what was reflected in the mirror."

The ship rocked a little in a freshening breeze, and then, its sails filled, it shot toward Harborside.

"What has five faces, two of them animal?" he asked.

Courion shook his head. "Were you drunk, regent?"

"I know what I saw. Five horrific faces, all vying to gain ascendancy at once. The deeply disturbing effect was of looking at living, breathing Chaos."

"We have heard that Gyrgon can take the form of many beings."

Kurgan shook his head. "No. This is another matter entirely." He ran his hands along his hairless skull. "This V'ornn. There is something different about him. More dangerous."

Courion shrugged.

"Look, what you do not seem to grasp is that it is a Gyrgon's perverse pleasure to give his word in trust *in order to break it*. They love playing with us as if we were toys."

"When it comes to other races, is that not an altogether V'ornnish trait?" A watch-change chime sounded, and Courion rose. "Time to go topside."

They clambered up the steep companionway at the end of the narrow corridor. At their backs a small squall had thrown itself over the stars. The night was thick and utterly black. Ahead of them, Axis Tyr lay in slumber, its sentinel lights glittering in a weblike tangle. Courion made his way to the high prow, and Kurgan followed him. The captain grasped the seaweed-encrusted hawser, adroitly balancing himself as he put one foot onto the butt end of the bowsprit. Above them, the great sails arched and cracked.

Courion shouted a series of clipped commands. Activity picked up immediately, the crew climbing into the rigging, preparing as they neared land, to furl the sails in stages.

"Gyrgon are dangerous enough," Kurgan said with some urgency, "without them being mad. I do not know what this one is capable of."

"Here is what we do not fathom," Courion said. "All this talk about the Gyrgon. And yet you belong to him."

"I belong to no one."

"You swore an oath of fealty to him on this very ship. You wear his okummmon."

"I will carve it out of my own flesh. When the time comes."

"Youthful folly!" Yet there was no derision in Courion's voice. *There is another thing here for you to fear.*

What could there be here to fear?

"I am deadly serious," Kurgan said.

Several nights ago, when he had gone to the Old V'ornn's villa something had happened.

He did not know what, except there seemed to be a small hole bored into his head, a void of memory toward the end of the evening that would not return no matter how hard he tried. This concerned him deeply. His hatred for Nith Batoxxx was now at a fever pitch. The thought that he was in some way being manipulated infuriated him.

Courion stirred. "For you, trust is such a fragile thing. Are we not correct, regent?"

"You are," Kurgan admitted. "We V'ornn find trust a disturbing and difficult concept to adhere to."

"We would give the world to be free of our bondage to the Gyrgon."

"Would you tell me why he is talking to you about salamuuun?"

The two of them were the still eye of the storm of activity that raged on all around them. No one came near them or even looked their way. A Sarakkonian crew was as completely disciplined as any Khagggun pack.

Courion said, "What is there but to trust you?" Leaning toward Kurgan, he said, "This salamuuun. Its chemical makeup has defied even the Gyrgon. Is that not correct?"

"Yes. Something in the compound destabilizes the basic complex molecule the moment anyone tries to analyze it."

"It happens that we have been refining a natural compound that achieves many of the same psychotropic effects as salamuuun." He pulled open an inner pocket of his leather vest and produced a yellow-white object that looked like a flower with severely erose petals. "This is *oqeyya*." He dropped it into Kurgan's hand. "It is a fungus that grows only in the caldera of Oppamonifex, the largest volcano in the Great Southern Arryx. Nith Batoxxx heard of it purely by accident sometime ago. He was in disguise in Blood Tide."

Kurgan knew the disguise—the Old V'ornn. But he said nothing of this to Courion as he gave him back the fungus.

"The *oqeyya* is dried for three weeks at high altitude. Then it is soaked in a thick mixture of herbs and carna oil. It is dried again, washed in seawater, and burnt. The green ash that remains has powerful psychotropic attributes."

"Is this *oqeyya* a viable substitute for salamuuun?" Kurgan's pulse was pounding as he imagined undercutting the Ashera Consortium. This new compound would ruin them.

"Not yet. There are one or two toxic side effects," Courion conceded. "But the Gyrgon has promised us that with his help it soon will be."

"Here is my advice. Never trust a Gyrgon. Especially not this one."

"What choice has he given us?"

Kurgan sat back, well pleased by the progress he had made this night. "Well, now, that is something for us both to determine."

A scattering of red dust bloomed along the road north as the ku- omeshals lumbered into the soft violet crush of twilight.

"It is time," Othnam said. "That you learn something of the Prophet Jiharre."

"*Koura,*" Mehmmer intoned. *It is written.*

Ahead, the Djenn Marre rose sharp as a serrated blade, seeming in the light peculiar to the steppe close enough to reach within a day's leisurely ride. Their snowcapped peaks, blindingly aglitter in the after-noon's silent fall into night, seemed for the moment immune even to Kundala's inexorable spin.

There was nothing leisurely in the kuomeshals' pace. Othnam and Mehmmer struck the hairy flanks of their mounts with short flexible sticks, and Riane did the same with hers in order to keep up with them. She had Tezziq's limp form draped over her thighs. Tezziq's head and feet jounced against the kuomeshal in time to its long loping stride. Riane had stripped off her ajjan's dress, clothing her in a spare Ghor robe and sinschal from Mehmmer's saddlebags. They were heading north to the rendezvous point, the place where the Ghor had taken Perrnodt. Nith Sahor's greatcoat was folded away beneath her robes. It would not have accommodated the four of them.

Othnam said, "Jiharre lived at the very top of the world, along the highest peaks of the Djenn Marre, where, we believe, Kundala meets heaven. His prophetic utterances frightened his family and the towns-folk, who were highly superstitious. They thought him a sorcerer, and shunned him. But their antipathy did not silence him. He was a prophet, and if his voice went against the grain, so be it. He did what he was called to do, what he fervently believed in, because without that you are nothing, life is nothing, might as well curl up, close your eyes, and wait for death to claim you."

Slowly, ice-blue shadows crept up from the mountain flanks, extinguishing the heart of the day's fire.

"Jiharre was exiled, cut off from his family and his friends, who turned their backs on him. They burned his clothes and his personal effects, grinding the ashes between the clawed roots of the mossarche tree, and poured boiling water on them so that they would forget him, so that his name might never again pass their lips. His people turned their backs on him because he dared to challenge their beliefs and biases, because he believed in something greater, a unifying force that ruled the Cosmos, and it was this force that spoke to him in holy visions, and these holy visions told him of the threat of a great evil to come, and what he was required to do. And so Jiharre went alone and unafraid into the wildness of the Korrush and founded Za Hara-at, Earth Five Meetings, a city of such power it stood guard against the ancient threat."

Behind them hunkered the striped jumble of lamplit Agachire, glittering on the steppe like a faceted jewel, packed zaggy streets smelling of spices and ba'du, dinners charring over crackling flames, chant-songs rising like perfumed offering smoke, the city preparing for the onset of darkness and war.

The three rode close together, hunched over to better protect themselves from the wind. Already Riane's legs ached from the unnatural position sitting between the humps, for the kuomeshal was larger and wider than any cthauros. She smacked the kuomeshal rhythmically with one hand while holding on to Tezziq with the other. Tezziq had not moved, had not regained consciousness, and this gnawed at Riane. The longer the ajjan remained unconscious, the more Riane worried about her.

"That's far enough," Riane said at length. "We have to look after Tezziq."

They heard her voice even over the wind, but failed to put up their beat-sticks. She dug her heels into her kuomeshal's sides so that it galloped ahead of them. Then she wheeled it abruptly around so that it stood in the path of their beasts.

They reined in.

"It is a mistake to stop," Othnam said. "For any reason."

"Especially for an ajjan," Mehmmer sneered.

"Go on without me, then."

Riane used the beat-stick to tap the crown of her kuomeshal's head, as Mehmmer had taught her to do, and it knelt, first on its forelegs, then on its two pairs of hind legs.

"You know we cannot do that." Othnam gazed down at her. "I fail to see the point."

"Why are you doing this?" Mehmmer snapped.

"Because she helped me." Riane poured some water from her skin over Tezziq's lips and cheeks. "Because she is my friend."

"She is *menne*, unclean, without faith," Mehmmer said. "She is no better than a kuomeshal."

"That is precisely how the V'ornn think of us," Riane said. "A lower form of life, fit only for drudge work and death."

"You should not be touching her," Othnam warned. "It is sacrilege."

"Why? I am not Ghor."

"You are the messenger of Jiharre," Mehmmer said.

"In your lore the Prophet Jiharre challenged the beliefs and biases of his own people. This you told me yourself. You said it yourself. If you cannot rid yourself of the enmity, then you are doomed to die in the Gyrgon's game."

"Perrnodt is your priority," Othnam said. "We will wait fifteen minutes, no more."

Hunched over the body, Riane whispered, "Tezziq, Tezziq. You must wake up now." She slapped the ajjan on both cheeks, and Tezziq's eyes fluttered open. "Ah, there, that's better," Riane said, smiling. "Here. More water."

As Tezziq drank, Riane said, "I am sorry. I should have protected you better than I did. I do not know what I would have done without your friendship." She gestured at the shadows that crept eastward across the undulating Korrush. "But here you are, outside the palace, free from your prison."

Looking slowly around her, Tezziq began to silently weep. "Ah, Riane, *wa tarabibi*, I have no words to thank you adequately." Then, abruptly, her head came up and she startled. "Who are those? Ghor?"

Her voice was thin and trembling. "They will kill me the first chance they get."

"They are Mehmmer and Othnam, brother and sister, and yes, they are Ghor, but they have pledged that you are safe with them."

Tezziq pressed herself into Riane's arms and shook her head. "No, no. You do not know the Ghor. They are fanatics. They will lie and cheat if it serves their purpose. This I have heard often from members of my own family before I was brought here."

Riane stroked the top of the ajjan's head. "They will not harm you, Tezziq. This I swear."

"I believe you, *wa tarabibi*," Tezziq whispered in her ear. "All the same, you would do well to keep a close eye on them."

"I will," Riane promised. She drew Tezziq up beside her, gave her a handful of dried fruit. "Eat this slowly while we ride. Do you think you are strong enough?"

"Strong enough to do whatever you ask of me," Tezziq said with a wan smile. Then, giving Othnam and Mehmmer a baleful glare, she climbed aboard the kuomeshal.

18

Trap

You are certain this is the place," Line-General Lokck Werrrent said. "So many of these Bashkir strongholds look alike."

Marethyn, standing in front of the looming facade of the warehouse, said, "This is the one."

Across the darkling scrim of the sky a Khagggun hoverpod hummed. There came the muted green flash of expelled ions as it banked south. Lights along Harborside were already on, the acid-bright aurora given off by the Kalllistotos floodlights hovered overhead, a vast bloodletting scar.

"Can you show me where?" the Line-General asked her. "Inside, I mean."

Marethyn nodded. Her hearts beat fast, and she conjured up images of Tettsie, of riding cthauros, of the red-and-gold woods in autumn. She was terrified and exhilarated. It was an effort to keep herself from trembling.

The Line-General used his ion cannon to defeat the lock. Then he gestured, and together they went into the interior. He was careful not to touch her or even to approach her too closely.

"I want to reiterate that you are not under suspicion," he said in his gruff but not unpleasant manner. "All that is required of you is the truth."

"You made that perfectly clear at the outset," Marethyn said, her face a perfect mask. "But I thank you for your kindness."

He grunted, switched on a portable photon torch. Echoes of their footfalls accompanied their progress down cramped aisles bordered on either side by neat stacks of crates, barrels, and boxes. The air was dense with dust and packing particles, which tickled the back of Marethyn's throat. She coughed into her hand, relieving some of the almost un-bearable tension.

Line-General Werrrent's photon torch picked out the Consortium crest stamped onto each box, barrel, and crate and he paused for a moment. "Again I will ask. You are certain this is the place?" he said sternly, as if to a small child whose grasp on the language was perhaps incomplete.

"Positive," she said in her most authoritative tone, and led him through the darkened interior up to the small, spare chamber in which she and Sornnn had made love. The door was closed and locked. It took Line-General Werrrent some moments to defeat this lock. With a contemptuous gesture, he kicked the door open.

He stared into the darkness for a moment, his hand in front of Marethyn's waist to keep her from going inside until he had a chance to look around. Using his photon torch, he quickly found the fusion lamps and powered them on. The chamber looked much the way she remembered it, the magnificent carpet, the shelves filled with Kundalan artifacts, the long boxes perched in one corner. There were no flowers in the vase, in fact, no vase at all on the small table.

"If I might ask," he said, "what were you doing here?" Seeing the blood rush to her cheeks, he added, "Come, come, my dear, I am a V'ornn of the Cosmos. I have heard it all."

"I am thinking of my brother," Marethyn said. "If he should find out that Sornnn SaTrryn and I—"

"You have my word that he shall remain ignorant of your private life. Are you saying—"

"It was late at night. We were both slightly drunk, I suppose. In any event, he swung me around and kissed me so hard I felt it all the way down to my toes. We . . . there wasn't anyplace else around. We happened to be standing right out front, and we were giggling a little, like children, and I guess we thought, well, why not?"

Line-General Werrrent nodded. "A little added piquancy, eh?"

By imagining the Line-General catching a sight of her naked, she made herself blush. "I really wouldn't want to say."

"I understand perfectly. You come here often, do you?"

"Oh, no. Just that once. I think we were embarrassed afterward. We are adults, after all."

"A wise decision." The Line-General began his reconnoiter. "Stay right here," he warned, "and be sure you touch nothing."

Crossing to the desk, he rummaged around, pulled open the drawers and emptied them, rummaged some more, all without finding anything. He took another look around, noticed the two long boxes, standing on end. Approaching them carefully, he stared at them for a long time.

"Khagggun alloy," he muttered.

"What does that mean?"

He ignored her, put one hand on the top box, set it carefully down on the dusty floor. Taking out his ion dagger, he pried open the lid. Marethyn took a couple of steps into the chamber to take a look over his shoulder. She saw, packed in a neat row, six new ion cannons.

Line-General Werrrent took one up, turned it over, peered at the serial number imprinted to the underside of the lower barrel. He did the same with each of them in turn. Then he opened the second box. He donned a communicator that wrapped around the back of his head. It had a thin armature that ended in a crystal ocellus four centimeters from his left eye. He opened a photonic channel and spoke a lot of gibberish, identifying himself by code, Marethyn surmised.

"I am in the sixth warehouse on—" He turned to Marethyn.

"Aquasius Street," she said weakly.

"Right. Aquasius Street." He turned back to the ion cannons. "Give me a readout on the war materiel stolen in the last six months. Serial numbers. Give me only ion cannons, handheld."

He waited a moment, then the readout appeared on the ocellus in front of his eye, magnified by the lens of the ocellus.

"Right. Get a pack in full battle armor over here right away." He rose, unwound the communicator from his skull. "This is Khagggun property, stolen two weeks ago," he said, apparently to Marethyn. Returning to the desk, he took out his shock-sword and sliced through it. He did this over and over until the desk lay in ruins.

"What . . . what are you looking for?" Marethyn asked. It was easy to sound frightened.

"A ledger of some kind, of transactions with the Resistance." He took a deep breath, looked around again. Then he swung his shock-sword in a horizontal arc and a line of the Korrush artifacts leapt off the lowest shelf and shattered on the floor. He used the toe of his boot to push aside the shards. Then he went to the next shelf up. He repeated the process again and again.

Marethyn saw the stone carving of the fulkaan fly into the air and smash open. She saw something bounce once, only to be hidden under the carving's powdery ruin, then the toe of Line-General Werrrent's boot flicked out and there it lay, an accusatory finger gleaming in the cool fusion lamplight, the incriminating data-decagon.

A re you certain this is necessary?" Konara Inggres tried to keep the apprehension out of her voice as Konara Lyystra led her to the door to what had been Konara Urdma's office.

"Mother wishes to see you," Konara Lyystra said with a firm hand on her elbow. "You aren't thinking of disobeying her, are you?"

"Of course not." Konara Inggres turned around, playing for time. "But can't you tell me why she wishes to see me? I mean, I have so much to do and so little time—"

"There is always time for Mother."

Konara Lyystra's lacquered smile was like a knife thrust in her belly. Where was her friend? she wondered for the thousandth time. What had been done to her?

"Lyystra, listen to me."

"Yes?"

Konara Inggres bit her tongue. Even her urgent tone could not wipe the placid expression off her friend's face. She could do ought but to give in to Konara Lyystra's gentle push. She opened the office door and, with an escalating sense of dread, walked into the office.

Giyan looked up as she came in. Konara Inggres could feel Konara Lyystra as close behind her as if she were a V'ornn Khagggun guarding a prisoner.

"Ah, Konara Inggres." With the warmest of smiles lighting her face, Giyan rose from behind the desk and hurried to greet her visitor. "So good of you to come." She took Konara Inggres' hand between her own. It was curiously cold and dry, like a marsh lizard's skin. "Sit down and we shall share icewine."

Konara Inggres perched on the edge of a chair while Konara Lyystra poured two goblets of icewine. When she had delivered them, Giyan dismissed her just as if she had been a rank acolyte.

Giyan handed Konara Inggres a goblet, then drew up another chair opposite her. She sat so close their knees fairly touched.

"So," Giyan said, "how are we coping with the recent changes at the abbey?"

She had the disconcerting habit of asking a question without the

proper inflection, so that it was often difficult to know whether she
was soliciting an answer or simply making a comment.

"All right . . . I guess."

"There is no shame in admitting the difficulties." Giyan leaned briefly
forward, patted her knee reassuringly. "My return. Konara Bartta's resurrection. Konara Urdma's untimely death. Any one of these changes
would be disconcerting. But all three taken at once." She clucked her
tongue against the roof of her mouth, an unfortunate sound like insects
rubbing their hind legs together.

"It has all been a little hard to fathom."

"Of course it has." Giyan patted her knee again. "I am glad you can
admit it. It is evidence that we are all Kundalan."

Was there a sarcastic gleam in Giyan's eyes, Konara Inggres wondered, or was she being paranoid?

"Konara Lyystra tells me that you have been a trifle, oh, how did she
put it again, cool, yes, that was it, *cool*."

"I don't think—"

"Oh, my dear, she is merely protective of you. And worried."

"Worried?"

"Certainly. The strain of the changes." Now Giyan's voice changed a
shade. "And of keeping your secrets."

"Secrets?" A thin coating of ice seemed to have formed in Konara
Inggres' belly.

"Konara Lyystra was candid enough to confide in me your dislike of
Konara Bartta, of the changes at work in the abbey curriculum."

Staring into those cold whistleflower-blue eyes, Konara Inggres could
do nothing but bite her lip in an agony of terror.

"Never you fear." Giyan winked at her. "The curriculum is about to
get a complete overhaul. I could not agree with you more. Disgraceful
what Konara Mossa and Bartta took it into their heads to do. I am about
to have a talk with my sister. I warrant it will not be a pleasant conversation, but she will soon see the error of her ways." Giyan's smile
seemed a meter wide. "I can be very persuasive when I set my mind to
it, let me tell you." She sighed. "And between you and me it was a
blessing that the Great Goddess Miina took Konara Urdma so precipitously. I would have had to strip her of her office, you see, and that
would have been more demoralizing to the abbey than the quick and
merciful death accorded her.

"So." She put her hands together. "Are there any questions you need answered?"

Konara Inggres shook her head. She was now in the grip of the fiercest terror she had ever known. It was all she could do to keep her teeth from chattering. She mumbled her good-byes as they rose. Her legs were stiff as tree trunks as she walked haltingly to the door, and when she passed beyond the threshold she broke out into a cold sweat.

That night Rada saw the regent's assigned Haaar-kyut saunter into Blood Tide. Though he was a First-Captain, he was dressed in a Third-Marshal's uniform. He pushed his way through the noisy throng and sat alone at a table. Rada waved away a waitress, went and took his order herself. When she returned with his goblet of mead, there was a data-decagon at the bottom.

He was very good, he did not make any sign that he knew her. His eyes did not follow her while she moved about the smoky room. And when she set the goblet of her best sweet mead in front of him he smiled up into her face.

She had heard some interesting gossip, and she had spent considerable time deciding what to put on the data-decagon and how exactly to phrase it. One item concerned the proliferation of laaga, the Sarakkon drug, among the youth of the city. Another the unrest building among the Khagggun who had not yet attained Great Caste status. There had even been an incident involving one of the Genomatekks who worked at Receiving Spirit who was attacked by a number of unidentified assailants. The hot rumor was they were Khagggun. Kurgan had asked her to find out what she could regarding the Portals, but there had been nothing to report. She had even asked a number of acquaintances and contacts without any success. At the last minute, she decided not to include her lack of success in this area. This was an interesting role for her to be playing, and, much to her surprise, she had warmed to it quickly. Besides the relief she felt at no longer having a debt to pay off, she experienced a little thrill of excitement at the level of clandestine service.

She watched from across the tavern as the Haaar-kyut drained his goblet and retrieved the data-decagon from his mouth. Then he paid his bill and left.

She went into the kitchen to make sure the orders were being filled properly. Steam rose from a multitude of black pots on the gigantic stove. A waft of pungent aromas tickled her nose. Passing behind her cooks, she took a sample from each bubbling pot, nodding approvingly after each taste. She paused behind one of her cooks and tapped him once on the back. He finished adding pepper to a stewpot, barked an order at his assistant, and, untying his apron, disappeared out the rear door.

Satisfied with her night's work, she returned to the riotous bedlam of the tavern proper just in time to watch a fight develop between a huge Mesagggun and a hulking Sarakkon with a skull full of hideous tattoos. She waited a moment before wading in to break it up. It was a pity, really. The V'ornn was bigger, but her money would have been on the Sarakkon.

19

Koura

High clouds streaked the vast sky, endless gossamer streamers caught up in the thermal currents. Others, thicker darker lower, crouched on the rim of the southern horizon, perhaps already ridding themselves of their turbulent moisture.

And so they continued their journey northward. Othnam had said that the Ghor were guarding Perrnodt at a sacred site of prayer and vigil some twenty kilometers north of Agachire. By Riane's estimation they were almost there, though the peculiar optical properties of the Korrush made such judgments notoriously inaccurate.

Up ahead, she could see a ring of thornbeam trees, gnarled and greyish black, their branches tasseled with fruit, their looping roots dug down deep in the barren soil to find water and nourishment. And she was reminded of the ring of thorned sysal trees within which, she had been told, Nith Sahor had lost his life. But if that were so, then where had he regained it? Another in an endless parade of Gyrgon enigmas.

Othnam raised his arm, slowing them as they approached the natural circle of thornbeams. And then he stopped altogether and the four of them sat side by side, silent, breathless.

At length, Riane said very softly, "What is it?"

"I do not know," Othnam said.

"There is no lymmnal," Mehmmer said, and her nostrils flared.

"No lookout. No Ghorvish brethren come to meet us."

Riane's stomach turned over as she saw brother and sister draw their scimitars and spur their kuomeshals on with their beat-sticks. She followed suit, and soon enough they were moving through the stand of trees.

Mehmmer gasped and Othnam muttered, "Ah, good Jiharre, no."

There, arrayed on the north side of the circle, four Ghor bodies had been strung up, hanging by their necks from the highest branches. At their feet, two lymmnal lay slaughtered and disemboweled.

"Paddii!" Riane cried.

The kuomeshals snorted and shook their great ugly heads, and it proved difficult to get them near the dangling bodies. Othnam started on the left, Mehmmer went to the center. Riane, for her part, urged her mount to the rightmost body and, swinging her dagger, cut Paddii down.

"All dead," Othnam said.

"Except Perrnodt." Mehmmer wheeled her kuomeshal around. "She has vanished."

Othnam had come up beside them. "Who perpetrated this outrage, Makktuub's guards?"

"No." Mehmmer shook her head. "Think, my brother. Think of the spy we executed not far from here."

"The Jeni Cerii have revenged themselves upon us. They murdered our brethren and have kidnapped Perrnodt."

"But where have they taken her?" Riane said, turning this way and that in the saddle.

Silence. Sun burning low in the sky, a copse of clouds, high and distant and still, baring the blank, uncaring face of the world. Somewhere it was raining, but here black carrion birds circled, effortlessly switching from thermal to thermal, patient as the Korrush itself.

While Tezziq watched with a closed face, Riane helped Othnam and Mehmmer dig a three-meter-wide depression in the reddish dirt. Then she and Othnam piled the bodies—Ghor and faithful lymmnal alike—in the center of the roughly circular depression while Mehmmer sang the death prayer in her clear strong voice. They would not have allowed Tezziq to help them even had she been inclined to, which clearly she wasn't. They did not allow her anywhere near the burial circle, but ordered her to stay with the kuomeshals. This she did without protest, turning her back, staring at the dark and brooding Djenn Marre, thinking perhaps of home, a place she had believed she would never see again.

Mehmmer continued singing the death chant, and Riane watched numbly as Othnam spread a line of a clear viscous substance on each of the bodies. Then, using a flint-box, he struck a spark and, at once, flames licked upward. He stepped back, joining Mehmmer in mid-stanza. Riane listened to the words rolling off their tongues and thought of Paddii joyfully holding his newborn, Paddii running beside the ku-omeshal on which she had found temporary shelter, Paddii giving her back her dagger, Paddii coming out here from Agachire to tell the Ghor guarding Perrnodt that she and Othnam and Mehmmer would be de-tained. Paddii had been killed because of her. Because of her desire to rescue Tezziq and Nith Sahor's secret. She knew she had done the right thing, but this could be no solace for Paddii or his family, and so she said a prayer of her own, a small thing, begging the forgiveness of the Goddess Miina. And she made herself believe that the flames heard the prayers for the spirits so recently departed even as they cleansed and consumed the husks of the chosen.

While the smoke wound its way toward the heavens, they spoke quickly and carefully, as if the very air they breathed was alive with malignant force.

"The situation has now changed," Othnam said. "We must return to get reinforcements."

"What about Perrnodt?" Riane said.

No one uttered a word.

Riane went over to the thornbeams under which the Ghor had been strung up. Pointing due west, she said, "What lies that way?"

Mehmmer shrugged. "Nothing but the wild."

"Unless you count the *in 'adim*, a series of low-lying washes."

"Dangerous, too," Mehmmer said. "The bottom looks dry, but often it's only a crust covering deep quicksand pits. No one goes there."

"What of Perrnodt?" Riane said. "Will they kill her? Take her back to their territory and imprison her? Hold her for ransom? Torture and rape her?"

"Who can know?" Mehmmer shook her head sadly. "We are not Jeni Cerii."

Riane looked directly at Tezziq, who still had her back to them.

"Tezziq," she said softly.

Tezziq turned around to face them.

"What will they do to her?"

"Why are you asking her?" Mehmmer said, alarmed.

"All she is intimate with," Othnam said, "is Makktuub's member."

"Tezziq," Riane said, ignoring them both, "do you know?"

"Even if I did"—Tezziq's eyes blazed at Mehmmer and Othnam—"Why should I tell you?"

"Because I am asking."

"This is nonsense," Othnam said.

"We are wasting precious time," Mehmmer said.

Riane walked slowly toward Tezziq. "Would you knowingly cause the death of another?"

At last, Tezziq's gaze fell upon Riane. "You know I would not."

"Perrnodt is not Ghor. But even if she were, it makes no difference."

"It makes a great deal of difference!"

"Why?"

"Because the Ghor—" Tezziq gave the brother and sister a quick glance as she lowered her voice. "They are evil, I have told you. The stories I have heard—"

"Are just that," Riane said. "It was Mehmmer and Othnam who helped me escape from Makktuub's palace."

"In exchange for what?"

"Nothing. They have asked me for nothing."

She turned to them, and said, "Is this true? Your motives were absolutely pure in helping Riane to escape from the haanjhala?"

Brother and sister exchanged a quick telling glance.

"Of course," Mehmmer said.

"No." Othnam took a step forward. "It is not, strictly speaking, the truth."

"Brother!"

"There!" Tezziq said triumphantly. "Didn't I tell you?"

"Let him speak," Riane said. To Othnam she said, "I once asked you why you were helping me. Was your answer a lie?"

"No. Neither was it the entire truth." Othnam sighed. "The whole truth is we wanted—"

"Makktuub had our parents executed," Mehmmer said quickly and angrily. "Because they stayed true to our faith, they would not compromise themselves, they would not comply with his order."

"Makktuub called it a misstep," Riane said.

"It is always thus. The executioner is free to couch the awful truth in euphemisms, while the poor victims are silenced." Othnam nodded. "In any event, it was a fatal decision."

"While we have pledged ourselves to be more pragmatic in order to keep the peace between Ghor and the kapudaan," Mehmmer said, "still we felt a desire to take our measure of revenge against him."

"To take you back from him," Mehmmer said, "simply because he desired you."

"In fact, I do not believe that it was Makktuub who wanted to imprison me," Riane said, thinking of how uncomfortable the kapudaan had been on the terrace. "It was the Gyrgon, Nith Settt. He had begun to question me about Perrnodt before I managed to escape. She seems to be the reason he was so interested in me."

"What about her?" Othnam began.

"We shall have to ask her," Riane said, "when we find her."

"*If* you find her," Tezziq said.

"As Othnam has said, we must make all haste back to the Ghor encampment to recruit reinforcements," Mehmmer said.

"If you do that, Perrnodt will surely die."

They all turned to their attention to Tezziq.

Riane found her tongue first. "What do you mean?"

"If we do not find her soon, they will kill her," Tezziq said.

Mehmmer snorted. "How could you possibly know such a thing?"

"I am Jeni Cerii," Tezziq said.

Mehmmer fell silent. Riane could see that Othnam was a little bit in shock.

"Tell us what you know, Tezziq," Riane said gently. "Please."

"The *in'adim*, that is where they will have taken her," she said.

"Why there particularly?"

Tezziq let out a slow controlled breath. "The Jeni Cerii use the *in'adim* as a place to hide, to stage raids against your tribe. If Perrnodt is still alive, that is where we will find her."

Toward sundown, Olnnn returned to the spice market. He was without armor. He had a small backpack strapped to his back. Ever since his meeting at Spice Jaxx's with Lokck Werrrent he had been haunted by something the Line-General had said. *You cannot imagine how many Resistance we have lost in this warren. They come here to disappear; it is a repository of the rotten, the subversive, and the disaffected.*

With furtive glances, a trio of Kundalan servants hurried by. A hunchback in tattered robes hovered near a cornice, watching the mounds of spices for his chance to cut and run. A Kundalan female with an evil and withered face eyed him warily as she took her purchases. A fat merchant, momentarily idle, did the same, wondering doubtless why the Star-Admiral was taking his leisure here. Which one of these vermin he needed to speak with—the rotten, the subversive, or the disaffected—was at the moment unclear to him. All he was certain of was that if he was ever going to find the fugitives, he needed to know where they were going. To do that he needed to know what they were looking for. He needed, therefore, to plumb the depths of the sewer running beneath Axis Tyr.

He could think of no better place to start than here.

Choosing an outside table at Spice Jaxx's, he ordered two tankards of warm ten-spice mead. He watched as sacks of fragrant gowit cinnamon were delivered to the merchant in the stall next door.

The trouble was he lacked the skills to talk to those outside the Khagggun Caste. To his credit he knew that. What was required was a guide. He wished he could ask Malistra for advice, or maybe a spell-casting to set him on the right path. But she was dead, and not even her Kundalan sorcery could bring her back. But thinking of her had put him in mind of another female. She was not Kundalan, but she was acquainted with many.

And here she came, bareheaded, diademed, glowering between her escort of two of Olnnn's own Khagggun.

"I trust you like ten-spice mead," he said when they had brought her to a halt before his table.

"I like it well enough," Rada said, sitting down at his invitation. She watched him dismiss the escorts. "Are you certain that you can trust me to be alone with you, Star-Admiral?"

"Let us not get off on the wrong foot," he said as amiably as he was able.

"Too late for that," she said shortly. "You had me marched out of Blood Tide like a common criminal."

"With your head bared you look like a common criminal. Or a Looorm."

"This is how I choose to look."

"Not when you are with me. Pretend you are a decent Tuskugggun. Raise your sifeyn."

She put her hands to her shoulders, slipped the gauzy cowl over her gleaming oiled skull.

He smiled. "Much better." He spoke to her as if she were a wayward child. "Now go ahead. Drink. I wish you to partake of my hospitality."

Rada engaged him with her eyes.

He shrugged. "As you wish."

"Nothing today is as I wish." She wore robes dark as a two-day bruise. Her beauty burst from this unlovely color like a cornflower rises from black dirt. "You have a harsh sense of hospitality, Star-Admiral."

"I am Khagggun. Everything about me is harsh." He shrugged. "What I know is war."

"And killing."

"War *is* killing."

"You might as well be speaking an alien language."

He smiled again. "Then we will not speak of war."

Rada took a sip of her mead. "That would please me."

Out in the market, the hunchback found his opening, swiped a handful of gowit cinnamon, and dashed off. Olnnn raised his hand and one of his Khagggun appeared from out of the teeming throng, caught the hunchback by the scruff of his filthy robes, dragging him back to the spice stall.

Rada, seeing what had happened, said, "Nothing is too insignificant for your attention."

"The law was broken. The criminal must be punished."

"Such a petty infraction. Such a poor criminal."

"Tell me," he said, "of what use is the law if it is not enforced absolutely?"

"Of what use is a Star-Admiral," she replied, "who applies the law blindly?"

He pushed his own tankard aside. "I require your assistance."

"So much for small talk."

He was doing his best to ignore her sarcasm, but he wondered whether he put up with it because of how beautiful she was. It was instructive seeing her away from the grim and grimy lamplight of her nighttime tavern. If not for her thorny mouth, he might admit that he was moved by her comeliness.

"I am in need of a guide," he persevered.

"Indeed. And what exactly do you need a guide for, Star-Admiral?"

"I am looking for a Kundalan sorceress."

She laughed.

He regarded her with an unhealthy mixture of lust and contempt. "As a Khagggun, I know I will never find one on my own. I know there are very few left on Kundala."

She pursed her lips as if deep in thought. "I believe we had something to do with that."

"We are blamed for all the Kundalan's ills," Olnnn said dismissively.

"Who else is to blame?"

"Why, the Kundalan themselves. They were well along on the slippery slope of corruption long before we arrived."

Rada finished her mead. "Why should I agree to be your guide?"

"I am ordering it."

"And if I should refuse?"

"Don't."

This was all he said, but his reply sent a chill down her spine. She well knew the stories about this new Star-Admiral, and was inclined to believe most of them. Her tough, bantering replies masked her stone-cold fear of him. It angered her that he could elicit such a shameful response in her. She felt the heel of his boot at the back of her neck, she tasted the dirt at her feet, and she nearly wept with the injustice of it.

She sought to cover her weakness with a straightforward question. "Tell me, Star-Admiral, what is it you wish to ask a sorceress?"

"I need her to read some passages in a couple of books."

She stared at him as a way of screwing up her courage.

"The fugitives are searching for something," he added. "I believe the only way to trap them is to find out what they are looking for."

"If we can find one."

"Don't tell me a sorceress has never walked into Blood Tide. You will find her."

His eyes were fever-bright, and again she felt herself grow frightened. She clasped her hands between her legs to stop them from trembling.

"What makes you think a sorceress will answer you truthfully?"

"You will tell me that, Rada."

They came quartering out of the northeast, Khagggun mounted on cthauros. There were five of them, not so many, Sornnn thought, but more than enough. The three First-Marshals had their ion cannons drawn.

Sornnn turned to the rather rotund figure of Bronnn Pallln. He had accepted Pallln's invitation to go night-hunting for claiwen, large, six-legged predators that could live as easily underwater as on land, whose natural habitat was the Great Phosphorus Swamp.

"Line-General Lokck Werrrent himself," Sornnn said. "What is this all about, Bronnn Pallln, do you know?"

Bronnn Pallln shrugged, acting stupider than he looked.

"Hold there!" Line-General Lokck Werrrent called. "Prepare to be questioned."

"Is this how you speak to the Prime Factor?" Sornnn called. "What mean you, Line-General, to intercept us in the dead of night?"

Line-General Lokck Werrrent reined in his cthauros as he came within six meters of Sornnn and Pallln.

"I might ask you what you are about in this wilderness at this late hour."

"Your concern for our safety is admirable, Line-General," Bronnn Pallln said rather jovially. "If you must know, we are hunting claiwen, though N'Luuura knows with all this clatter I doubt there's a beast within ten kilometers of here."

Line-General Lokck Werrrent did not respond. Instead, he held out his hand. In it was the data-decagon he had discovered in the secret warehouse chamber. "Here is evidence, hard and irrefutable." The Line-General held up the crystal so that its facets caught the moonlight. "A careful accounting of every theft of Khagggun war materiel for the past year and the subsequent sale of said war materiel to the Kundalan Resistance. These are the gravest offenses against V'ornndom, which demand the ultimate punishment. What say you in your defense, Bronnn Pallln?"

"Me?" Bronnn Pallln laughed, a high eerie sound with a note of disbelief. "But surely you mean Sornnn SaTrryn, Line-General."

"I mean you, sir."

"But the warehouse—"

"The stolen weaponry was found in a secret chamber in *your* warehouse, Bronnn Pallln, as was this ledger of your traitorous transactions."

"This . . . this must be . . . it has to be a mistake." Bronnn Pallln's eyes were as big around as plates. "Which warehouse, if you please?"

"The sixth one on Aquasius Street," the Line-General said.

"These days, save for temporary storage overruns, the warehouse is rarely visited by my Consortium."

"Which makes it a perfect venue for your traitorous activities," Line-General Werrrent said cannily.

"But . . . but Sornnn SaTrryn is the one with obvious leanings to the Korrush, while I have no such—"

"Do you take me for a fool, Bronnn Pallln? It would be sheer folly for a traitor to publicly announce his bias. Pending the regent's tribunal, you are now considered an enemy of the state." At his gesture, two of the Khagggun drew up, one on either side of Bronnn Pallln's cthauros. One leaned over, took the reins from his shaking hands.

"I gave you information." An increasing note of desperation had entered Bronnn Pallln's voice. "Marethyn Stogggul and Sornnn SaTrryn—" He turned suddenly. "You did this to me, Sornnn SaTrryn. You set me up."

"Come now," the Line-General said without a trace of sympathy. "Sornnn SaTrryn, will you please enlighten the traitor?"

"This is embarrassing, but Marethyn and I went a little crazy. We were drunk and—"

"Liar!" The blood rushed to Bronnn Pallln's face, and he became so agitated his cthauros began to snort and stamp, obliging the Khagggun on either side to hold on to him tightly.

The Line-General put his hand on the neck of Bronnn Pallln's mount, with one gesture calming the beast and silencing Bronnn Pallln.

"Please proceed," he said to Sornnn.

"We were in an exceedingly amorous mood," Sornnn said to Bronnn Pallln. "I apologize for breaking into your warehouse, but it was deserted and close at hand, and we did not think there would be any harm in—"

"This is the most outrageous lie."

"Marethyn Stogggul corroborates his story," Line-General Werrrent said blandly. "Who corroborates yours?"

"Talk to the Genomatekk, Jesst Vebbn. He will tell you that it was I who hired him to find out who the traitor was."

"We have already spoken to Genomatekk Vebbn," the Line-General said. "He came forward voluntarily and told us that you had asked him to fabricate false evidence against the Prime Factor."

"Why that slimy little—!" Bronnn Pallln roared even as he recalled how he had so cavalierly screwed Vebbn. "It is all a pack of lies! By N'Luuura's spiked gates, don't you see, they are plotting against me!"

"Oh, yes, of course," the Line-General said sardonically. "Sornnn SaTrryn, the regent's sister, Genomatekk Jesst Vebbn, they all bear you ill will and, to boot, are plotting with the Resistance." He shook his head. "Do you not hear how foolish you sound?" He gestured to his complement of Khagggun. "Take him away. I will catch up with you shortly. And if the prisoner continues his invective, do wire his mouth shut."

When they had gone, Line-General Werrrent said, "I apologize for his slander, Prime Factor."

"Not necessary," Sornnn said.

"Professional jealousy is a bitter tonic, eh, Prime Factor?"

"Truly poisonous," Sornnn agreed.

Line-General Werrrent shifted on his saddle. "I would ask you something."

Sornnn pulled his cthauros around.

"It is of a somewhat sensitive nature."

Sornnn was now greatly interested. "As you wish, Line-General."

"We are two patriots talking together in the fastness of the night."

"I understand completely, Line-General."

"Yes. I thought you would." Lokck Werrrent kept a tight rein on his mount. It had scented something crawling through the swamp and apparently wanted no part of it. "I am interested in your opinion concerning a matter of grave importance to . . . to the state." He lowered his voice. "Do you believe the regent, Kurgan Stogggul, wishes to continue with the program his father began to raise Khagggun to Great Caste status?"

Sornnn studied the other's blunt and brutal face. "You want me to be honest."

"Absolutely. Otherwise, I never would have asked."

"Wennn Stogggul felt no compunction in turning on his Star-Admiral," Sornnn said. "He was mad for power. From what I can see, his son Kurgan is no different. Except I believe Kurgan Stogggul to be far more intelligent."

The Line-General revealed none of his inner turmoil in his expression. "Please be so kind as to continue."

"Frankly, Line-General, I never could understand why the regent would add to the Khagggun's power. It made me wonder what he has planned for you."

Lokck Werrrent nodded formally. "I appreciate your candor."

"I fear for us." Sornnn turned his cthauros in the direction of Axis Tyr. "I fear for us all."

It was a mean place, the walls dark with scrawled epithets, the floor of packed dirt. The air was rancid with refuse and urine and indigence. Vermin crawled everywhere. Olnnn wrinkled his nose in distaste and shook Rada by her elbow.

"What joke is this?" he rumbled. "No sorceress would live here."

"If you touch me again," she said with a slight tremor, "I shall walk out of here, and you will not get what you want."

"You have no idea what I want."

She eyed him carefully. "If I were you, I would not make that wager, Star-Admiral."

They stood toe to toe for a moment in a kind of mental stalemate, fear and need weighing in equal measure while the scales tipped this way and that, buffeted by fierce emotion. At length, Olnnn chuckled.

"In truth, I have never met a Tuskugggun like you. I don't know whether to swat you or grab you by the waist and . . ." He stopped, recognizing that glare in her eyes. He put up his hands. "Yes, yes. I know you that well, at least."

As they recommenced their walk through the execrable warren of hovels deep beneath Devotion Street, he said, "Pity you were born female. I warrant you would have made a notable warrior."

"Pity I am V'ornn."

This response brought him up short. "What do you mean?"

She turned to him. "Had I been born Kundalan, I would be a warrior."

"Were you Kundalan," he replied dryly, "chances are you would be dead."

He heard the soft mewling of a small animal, the pad of tiny paws, but he did not turn around. From out of an open doorway arose a sudden gust of coughing and the sickly-sweet stench of disease.

"Remind me to have this festering sore razed."

"Yes, Star-Admiral," she said, matching his dry tone, "that is the answer."

"That is my answer, yes. I am Khagggun."

"And you are so proud of that!"

"Listen, you." He put his face in front of hers. "Many of my comrades have died to keep you and all you hold dear safe. How many? So many I have lost count. But when I sleep I see them. They come to me in my dreams and whisper their pride. It is their pride and their heroism that have kept us from being overrun by the Centophennni."

Their eyes locked. Something beyond hatred passed between them. So surprised was Olnnn that he drew back a pace.

"This way," Rada said, her voice slightly thickened in displaced emotion.

She took him into a chamber almost at the end of the corridor. Though bleak, it was less dank and noisome than the rest he had passed. Streetlight dribbled down a shaft and through a small window high up in a half-rotted wall. One lamp was lit, low and long-necked, of faithfully rubbed bronze. It was apparently filled with fragrant oil because the space was infused with a complex and spicy scent. By its glow Olnnn could see that the chamber was free of filth and litter. A single carpet was laid upon the floor of oversize stone squares. In the center of this carpet sat a figure, small, spare to the point of emaciation. It was also definitely male.

Olnnn regarded the figure with an ill-disguised disgust. "I am in need of a sorceress," he said. "Can you tell me where—"

"Rada," the figure said. "Why have you brought this killing engine here?"

"Forgive me, Sagiira. I had no choice."

"There is always choice, my child."

"Enough of this." Olnnn stepped forward. "There will be serious consequences if you do not produce the sorceress, old one."

"There are already serious consequences." Sagiira lifted an arm that seemed so utterly devoid of flesh it might have been mummified. "You have touched one of the sacred books of Miina." He held his head at such an angle Olnnn could not see the eyes in his skull-like face. "Tell me, killing engine, how does your leg feel?"

Olnnn automatically touched his ensorceled femur. "What do you mean?" But he knew. The fizzing sensation in his bare bones had not left him. And hadn't it begun just after he ran his finger down the page of one of the books that lay open on the refectory table in the Abbey of Warm Current?

"Why ask me?" Sagiira said. "When you already know?"

Olnnn glanced at Rada.

"I have done what you asked," she said softly. "Here is the only sorcerer I know."

"But he is male," he protested. "There are no male sorcerers."

Sagiira wagged his head. "What you do not know, killing engine."

"Do not call me that!" Olnnn snapped.

"You are what you are."

Olnnn scrabbled in his backpack, took out the book. As Sagiira shifted slightly to take it, lamplight played briefly over his face, and Olnnn saw that he was blind. It was as if his eyeballs had been plucked from his head.

"Were you born blind?" he could not help himself from asking.

"I had sight once." Sagiira ran his hands over the book. "That sense was taken away from me a long time ago." The open book lay in his meager lap. "Do you have any idea, killing engine, what it is like to lose your sight? No, of course you do not. You have no conception of what sight is or can be."

"Of course I understand."

"No. You are V'ornn." Sagiira's sticklike fingers paused on a page, tapped out a kind of rhythm. "In the time of long ago I could see the future. That was the major portion of my sorcery. Now I am blind in every way it means to be blind. Do you see?" He laughed, exposing brown teeth and inflamed gums. "I saw you coming, killing engine. I saw what you would do to us. I tried to stop them, but they would not listen. They threatened me, and foolishly I joined them, and for that great sin I was blinded." He cocked his head. "You do not understand a word I am saying, do you?" He shook his head. "The title of this book is *The Gathering of Signs*. But you knew that already, didn't you? Your bones told you. They are speaking to you, killing engine."

Olnnn stared at the sorcerer, wide-eyed. "How do you know that?"

"The spell lying in them came alive the moment you touched this book. Did I mention that it is sacred to Miina?"

"Yes you did, Sagiira," Rada said softly.

"Ah, ah!" He wagged his head. "Age creeps through me with the raking claws of a perwillon." He closed the book, hugged it to his sunken chest. "Once I could read this. I had it memorized. Now I am damaged—damaged beyond repair."

"There are fugitives I must find," Olnnn said, desperate to change the subject. "They were looking through this book, searching for something. What was it?"

"You must follow them north to find out," Sagiira said. "But these fugitives should not be your concern."

"One of them almost killed me. And because of her my leg—"

"Your leg is what should concern you," Sagiira said. "Or rather what lies beneath. The spell." His nose wrinkled. "I can smell it."

"What spell? The skcettta left a spell?"

"Not Giyan," Sagiira said softly. "The other sorceress."

"Malistra?"

The sorcerer nodded.

"I do not believe you," Olnnn said shortly.

"But you will." Oddly, Sagiira had turned his head toward Rada. "Because you cannot stop what Malistra has planned for you."

And, indeed, Olnnn could feel the fizzing in his bones building to a crescendo. All at once he cried out. Pain flooded the ensorceled leg, and he collapsed onto the stone floor.

"Here it comes, killing engine. Are you ready? No, I don't suppose you are."

Olnnn writhed in agony, rucking up the edge of the sorcerer's carpet. His eyes bulged in their sockets, and he gasped to breathe.

"No. Even a killing engine such as you is not prepared for *this*."

Olnnn felt something on his leg, or in it. Yes, that was it. Inside his femur a bulge was appearing. He watched in a kind of fascinated horror as a copper-colored serpent squeezed through the porous layers of his bare femur, its flat, wedge-shaped head coalescing as its body wound itself into a tight coil.

"Malistra!" he said in a hoarse whisper.

"She was powerful, all right," Sagiira said. "I think she fooled us all. Even her master."

Olnnn was in too much pain to try and make sense of the sorcerer's rambling. He had more pressing problems.

The serpent, coiling and uncoiling, glittered in the lamplight. All at once it began to hiss. Its obsidian eyes impaled Olnnn, and its forked tongue flicked out.

"Lisssten closssley, Olnnn. If you hear my voiccce, it meansss the ssspell I buried in the bonesss of your leg hasss been activated. You are doubtlesss with a female. Do you care for her? And ssshe for you? I hope so. Because now you are forever tied to her asss ssshe isss tied to you."

Out of the corner of his eye, Olnnn saw a look of horror etched clearly on Rada's face.

"You have never needed a female before. You do now," the serpent continued. "Only ssshe can eassse your pain. Eventually, you may forgo her company for asss much asss twelve Kundalan hoursss at a time. But that isss your limit."

"Why?" Olnnn cried. "Why are you doing this to me?"

"To protect you. You have a nemesssisss. A powerful nemesssisss who masssqueradesss asss your friend."

"Kurgan Stogggul," Olnnn said.

The serpent's forked tongue flicked out. "Given the opportunity, he will kill you. Sssooner rather than later. I sssaw thisss in my mind'sss eye while I wasss healing you, and I took thessse measssures." The serpent slithered along his bones. "There isss a very specccial power inssside Kurgan." The serpent reared its head, its forked tongue flicking past its lipless mouth. "I have given you the ability to kill him, but only if you can find it within yoursssself to change."

"What are you talking about?"

"All power corruptsss, Olnnn. If I learned anything in my lifetime it isss thisss. The bessst of intentttionsss are asss nothing to the corruptttion of the ssspirit power causssses. If you kill Kurgan, your power and pressstige will multiply a hundredfold. Asss you are now, it will corrupt you wholly. It will consssume you. The female will sssee that corruptttion doesss not dessstroy you."

"How can you know that I will not be corrupted along with him?" Rada cried.

The serpent's flat, triangular head turned in her direction, the eyes burning like cold flame. "What would you do with sssuch power, female?"

"Me? I—I have no idea."

The serpent's head shot forward. "Sssurely there are grudgesss to sssettle, enemiesss to be beheaded. You could have your pick of methodsss, sssavor the momentsss of—"

"What? No!" Rada recoiled. "You're evil. Pure evil."

"You sssee?" The serpent smiled, an unnatural expression for a reptile. "You do not covet sssuch power, you do not wisssh it. You will sssave him from himssself."

"What? I don't want any part of—"

Having delivered its message, the serpent was already coming apart at the seams. Copper scales pattered to the stone floor as the thing turned inside out. Immediately, it began to shrivel, darkening, breaking apart and curling like ashes in high heat. Within moments, it had vanished.

"This cannot be happening," Rada said, slightly stupefied. She turned to the sorcerer. "It must have been an hallucination."

Olnnn gripped his leg bones. "The pain is real enough." He was breathing hard.

"You would do well to listen to Malistra's words," Sagiira said. "Both of you."

"I want no part of this," Olnnn said.

"Nor I," said Rada.

"Foolish talk," Sagiira said. "You are caught in the spell. There is no alternative, no way out."

20

Twins

"This is an inferior host you have provided for me," Bartta said. Her hands, their backs still reddened from the aftermath of her ordeal, played over her own twisted, humped body, and her eyes blazed. "You have done this to me on purpose!" Myggorra, the archdaemon inside her cried. And gestured, rather theatrically. "Look at you—tall, golden-skinned, beautiful. Tell me you haven't given yourself the best of it."

"On the surface it may look that way," Giyan said with a small grimace, "but you cannot imagine how hard this host is fighting me: In this modern age it is difficult to believe that the Kundalan could have produced such a potent sorceress as this one."

Bartta sniffed. "You're just saying that."

Giyan's face was briefly distorted. "Would that I were, brother. It is taking almost all my energies just to keep her pinned in Otherwhere."

For Konara Inggres, tucked rather uncomfortably into a hidden niche behind the stone wall that housed the hearth, this curious conversation was freighted with strange cargo. When Giyan had said, *it was a blessing that the Great Goddess Miina took Konara Urdma*, all of Konara Inggres' fears had crystallized, because every Ramahan knew that Miina did not take the priestesses. When they died, one of the Five Sacred Dragons—which one it would be depended on the individual Ramahan—took them up in its mouth and deposited them into new bodies to be born again. From that instant onward, Konara Inggres had known that her suspicions had been correct. Giyan was not who she appeared to be, and neither was Bartta. But who were they? They spoke of hosts. What did that mean? And what did they want, why were they here?

When she had seen Bartta heading toward what had been Konara Urdma's office, she had been seized by a terrible premonition and, abandoning all thought of attending to her duties on the other side of the abbey, she had whipped around the corner. The service corridor, narrow and dingy, had thankfully been deserted, and she slipped into the small storage area, groped in utter darkness to the far wall, where she had depressed a camouflaged stud. A hidden door slid aside, and she had climbed in. Curled up in the cramped space, with her heart beating so hard she could feel it in her throat, she had put her eyes to the peepholes.

A brief but ferocious commotion snapped Konara Inggres out of her reverie. She put her eyes back to the peepholes in time to see Bartta's fingers around Giyan's throat. "With you so preoccupied I should have no trouble taking what should have been mine from the beginning."

Giyan bellowed from deep inside her, a horrifying, blood-congealing sound, and backhanded Bartta so hard she flew back across Konara Urdma's office, fetching up against a stone wall. "Watch your tongue," she cried. "Do not forget that it was I who decided to break the Law." She strode across the small chamber, catching the slightly stunned Bartta up by the front of her robes, shaking her like a leaf in a storm. "Mine was the risk and mine the reward." She spat into Bartta's face. "Besides, you were never a match for me, so do not entertain any vain-glorious ideas."

"What about the unholy war? When will it begin?" With Bartta's servile voice, Myggorra sought to deflect Horolaggia's towering rage.

"Ah, yes, the long-awaited war." Giyan, thus distracted, dropped her twin, walked slowly back to Konara Urdma's desk. "One Portal only is open, and that one just enough for us archdaemons to squeeze through with a few chosen others in altered form. All the Portals must be opened simultaneously for the invasion to begin in earnest."

"For that we need the Gatekeeper." Bartta rearranged the disarray of her robes. "And his identity is still another of Miina's mysteries."

Giyan's whistleflower-blue eyes glittered. "This is not a question for you to either ask or answer."

Bartta bristled. "Am I not deemed worthy?"

"All of us have a role to play," Giyan said simply. "This is the strength of the grand plan."

Bartta stamped her foot. "It is a way to keep me in line."

Giyan regarded her for a moment, then she rose and, laughing, clapped her sister on her round back. "It is always about you, isn't it?"

The laughter vanished without a trace. "That is why you obey me and not the other way around."

Konara Inggres tried to adjust her contorted body into a position marginally less painful. This clever little spy niche had been built by Konara Mossa in the days when she had reigned supreme at the Abbey of Floating White. To Konara Inggres' knowledge no one knew of it save herself and Konara Lyystra. They had stumbled upon it quite by accident and, climbing into its interior, it had been clear by signs of disuse that even Konara Bartta had not known of its existence.

Konara Inggres' attention was drawn back into the office by the sound of a knock on the door. When Giyan said, "Enter," Konara Lyystra appeared. She was glassy-eyed, and she moved with that peculiar stiffness Konara Inggres had noted with a mixture of dismay and apprehension.

"The mirrors," Konara Lyystra said, "have all been destroyed."

"Well, that is a relief," Giyan said. "Did you bring the recruit?"

"Yes, Mother."

In her tiny niche, Konara Inggres stiffened, her heart pounding painfully in her breast.

"I have brought Konara Tyyr."

Giyan nodded, but as Konara Lyystra turned to go, she said, "Konara Inggres may not be a candidate. If this proves true, she will, like Konara Urdma, have to be eliminated."

Konara Inggres jammed her fist into her mouth in order to stifle a scream.

"I believe I can bring her around," Konara Lyystra said.

"Do not allow your host's friendship with her to influence your judgment," Konara Bartta said. "All the konara must—"

Giyan held up a hand, and Bartta fell into a sullen silence.

"You have one week. No more," Giyan said to Konara Lyystra. "Is that understood?"

"Yes, Mother."

"Now. Bring in the recruit."

Konara Lyystra disappeared from view and Giyan drew forth from behind the desk a black serpentskin satchel, from which she took a small egg-shaped object. Then she did a very odd thing. She placed the object onto the center of her tongue. Just before it disappeared into her mouth Konara Inggres was certain she saw the egg-shaped object sprout ten short legs.

A moment later, the two konara appeared in the doorway. Konara Tyyr was white-faced and trembling, but she allowed Konara Lyystra to steer her in front of Giyan.

"Good evening, Konara Tyyr," Giyan said, smiling.

"Good evening, Mother."

"Has Konara Lyystra told you why you are here?"

"Yes, Mother."

"Then tell me."

"You must test me to see whether I am able to reach a higher state of consciousness."

"So that you may be closer to the Great Goddess Miina."

Konara Tyyr stared into Giyan's eyes.

"You do this of your own free will?"

"Yes, Mother."

Giyan nodded and briefly took Konara Tyyr's hands in her own. "You are ice-cold, my dear. We must warm you up." So saying, she grasped Konara Tyyr by the shoulders and kissed her hard on the lips.

Konara Inggres twisted around so she could see more clearly, so she could see Giyan's lips open, so she could see the passage of the ten-legged egg-shaped thing from Giyan's tongue to the other's mouth.

Immediately thereafter, Konara Tyyr's body began to thrash and convulse, obliging Giyan to hold on to her so tightly the marks of her fingers became weals. It was over so suddenly that for a moment Konara Inggres began to doubt what she had seen. Then the glassy-eyed expression she saw in Konara Lyystra reproduced itself on Konara Tyyr.

"You are arrived," Giyan said curiously.

And Konara Tyyr nodded. "I am free."

"Not quite yet," Giyan said softly, as Konara Lyystra guided Konara Tyyr to the door. "Have a care. Avoid excessive talk with the other Ramahan, and if you should see a mirror, destroy it rather than pass before it. Is this clear?"

"It is."

"Konara Lyystra will see to your full orientation."

Curled inside the spy niche, Konara Inggres was drenched in cold sweat. What profane ritual had she been witness to? she wondered.

Who was this Giyan? Clearly she was not simply the young Ramahan priestess who had been banished from the abbey over twenty years ago. In the interim, she had been the consort of the former regent of Axis Tyr before his death. Now she was a fugitive of the new V'ornn regime. But none of this explained her bizarre behavior.

"Now to work," Giyan was saying. "We must map out our changes for the Ramahan syllabus. Until we have trained our cadre of konara, you and I, dear Bartta, shall teach all classes, which we will hold in the main chapel under the eyes of the image of the Goddess Miina."

She chortled, a sound that all but froze Konara Inggres' blood. For it was a sound so harsh and evil it was difficult to believe that any Kundalan could ever utter it.

"And what shall we teach, do you think, Bartta? In Healing Arts we shall teach the power to instill fear. In Herbology, we shall instruct our charges to concoct poisons, tasteless, odorless, utterly undetectable. In Oracular History, we shall preach the wisdom of our father who art in hiding."

Konara Inggres was weeping. She could not make sense of any of this, but one thing she did know was that she was witnessing the beginning of the end of the Ramahan as Miina had conceived them. A despair such as she had never known now swept through her. She felt alone, terrified, witless. The presence of such evil here in Miina's sacred sanctum all but paralyzed her. Her sheer proximity to Giyan and Bartta seemed to be draining her ability to think clearly. She shivered, abruptly cold. It was as if the very life force was being drained out of her, and she grew even more terrified.

Her bloodless hands, pressed so hard against the intervening stone, began to tremble and she clamped her jaw shut lest the sound of her teeth rattling should alert Giyan and Bartta to her presence. She closed her eyes and recited to herself the seventh prayer.

O Great Goddess of the Five Moons
Who dwells in night's divine mystery
Hear me now, Your humble servant,
Who abides by Your Laws, who is guided by Your Word.
In death, let me be taken up by Your fierce Children.
Let me feel, O Goddess, their gentle kiss.

That I may live in hope
And do Your holy bidding to the end of days.

Her face was wet with tears. She felt like a lost, motherless child.

As they headed north, the waving grasslands gave grudging way to occasional outcroppings of rocks of an odd greenish grey hue. The terrain began a modest rise, and quite soon the rocks, which appeared more frequently, became boulders, then boulders that stood upon larger boulders, the Shoulders of Jiharre, as Othnam had called them. Thus were they forewarned that they were approaching the *in'adim*.

Othnam, who was in the lead, slowed his kuomeshal's pace from a brisk trot to a measured walk.

"We should dismount here," Tezziq said. "The kuomeshals do not like the *in'adim* and, in any event, on foot we will be able to approach with more flexibility and stealth."

Othnam and Mehmmer exchanged a quick glance.

"What if this is just a way for her to return to her people?" Mehmmer said pointedly.

"My sister is right," Othnam said. "Who knows what secrets of the kapudaan and the palace she might pass on to the Jeni Cerii."

"I am not a spy," Tezziq said. "I hold no love in my heart for Jasim, and I have no desire to return to his clutches."

"She wants to be free, nothing more," Riane said. "Freedom is surely a goal you as Ghor must understand."

Tezziq was shaking her head. "They do not believe me. I can see it on their faces."

Riane tapped her kuomeshal, who laboriously lowered itself to its knees. She and Tezziq dismounted. "At some point, I think you must take the leap of faith and accept that not all Jeni Cerii are your enemies."

"Surely you have family you long to see again," Mehmmer said, addressing Tezziq.

"I have lived almost my whole life in haanjhala, first Jasim's, then Makktuub's," Tezziq replied. "I had a sister and three brothers, but I cannot remember them. As for my parents—" She shrugged. "It was they who sold me to Jasim when I was eight. On the cusp of sleep, he poured into my ear many secrets. The haanjhala became my life. Why should I remember my parents or wish to see them again?"

"Tezziq and I are continuing on," Riane said to Othnam and Mehmmer's closed faces. "If you decide to return to your compound now, I will only be grateful for the help you have given me."

Sister and brother exchanged another of their charged glances.

"She is ajjan, and Jeni Cerii, to boot," Mehmmer said.

"We warned you," Othnam said. "She is your responsibility now."

"May Jiharre and the sacred fulkaan be ever with you, Riane," Mehmmer said by way of farewell.

Without another word, they wheeled their kuomeshals around and headed back toward Agachire.

The sky was white overhead, without perspective or limit. The ominous massif of the Djenn Marre appeared closer than ever, the mysterious font of the Great Rift dark with fulminating clouds. A sand-laced wind reached them, scouring from out of the Great Voorg to the southeast, obliging them to wrap their sinschals tighter around their faces.

"I will miss them," Riane said.

"Why? They are Ghor."

"And so should I hate and fear you as they do because you are ajjan and Jeni Cerii?"

Tezziq shook her head. "We are better off without them. They would never have willingly followed my lead."

Riane tied her kuomeshal's reins around an upright rock, took a waterskin and several other items out of the saddlebags, and they headed north up the steady incline toward the *in'adim*. It was not easy going, for the usually reliable footing of the Korrush had turned to sandy dune. Tezziq showed Riane how to walk with knees deeply bent, leaning into the slope, then leaning slightly backward on the downslope so as to maintain one's balance.

In this fashion, they proceeded for perhaps an hour. As they neared the crest of the highest dune they had so far encountered, Tezziq pressed the flat of her hand downward and, at the signal, they both dropped to their bellies, continuing their ascent in a crablike squirm. They paused just beneath the undulating crest of the dune, lifting their heads cautiously until they gained a view down into the *in'adim* itself.

Riane saw a series of large crescent-shaped gullies with slightly concave crusty bottoms across which expanse the wind from out of the Great Voorg sent skittering small snaking trails of sand. Of a semipermanent Jeni Cerii encampment there was no evidence. They crossed over the crest and, keeping to the dune's inner slope, continued heading northeast, following the sinuous spread of the *in'adim*.

"How far would they have taken Perrnodt?" Riane whispered.

"That depends on what they mean to do to her," Tezziq said over her shoulder. "But I would not think very far. Certainly they would keep her where they felt the safest, which would be here in the *in'adim*."

So far as Riane could see, the *in'adim* was nothing but sand. No rock, tree, blade of grass, not even a humble patch of lichen existed on the Shoulders of Jiharre. The sand itself, when she scooped up a handful, was coarse and rough as a rasp's crosshatched teeth, and was a brownish grey color not unlike that of dried Kundalan blood. Between slippage in the treacherous dune and the fact that visibility was limited by the extreme curves of the *in'adim*, their progress seemed painfully slow.

They came upon the first Jeni Cerii so quickly that Tezziq was obliged to push Riane onto her stomach. The two of them lay half-buried in the sand, their hearts thundering as they watched the Jeni Cerii warrior walking up from the basinlike bottom of the *in'adim*. He was heading directly toward them. Only a fortuitous hump in the side of the dune kept them out of his sight. But that would not last long.

Tezziq was thinking the same thing, for she put her lips to Riane's ear. "We must kill him quickly and silently. If he announces our presence to the others, all is lost."

Riane nodded. Tezziq was right, they had no choice. She withdrew her dagger and moved slightly in order to get herself into a more advantageous position. The Jeni Cerii was very close, and she steeled herself for what she had to do. She knew she would only have one chance, that she must kill him with the first swipe before he could raise his voice in alarm. Here he came. Her muscles tensed. She had decided to slit his throat; that way, even if her aim was off slightly, his throat would be so congested with blood he would not be able to make a sound.

Still, she wanted every advantage, so she waited until he was almost upon her before she sprang. Right now, the element of surprise was a weapon even more potent than her dagger. She drew her arm back, ready to spring, but at the last moment something froze her. A pulse beat in her temples, and her blood sang in her ears. She twisted backward, out of the Jeni Cerii's path and signed for Tezziq to do the same.

The ajjan, though curious, did as Riane ordered. The Jeni Cerii went past them, disappearing over the crest of the *in'adim*.

Riane scrambled back to where Tezziq lay.

"What happened?" Tezziq asked. "Why did you not kill him? He could have found us out. It was only the sheerest good fortune that he did not see us."

"Think so?" Riane turned and looked back down into the *in'adim*, pointing.

Tezziq tensed as she saw another Jeni Cerii heading up the dune.

"Do you see?" Riane whispered. "This one is coming from the same direction as the first one." She moved her arm, tracking the figure. "As he comes close, pay special attention to his feet."

"His feet? What—?" Then Tezziq saw it. "They are not touching the sand."

Sure enough, she had discovered the oddity that had at the last moment stayed Riane's hand.

"That is impossible."

"It would be," Riane said, "if this and the other one were really Jeni Cerii warriors."

Tezziq shook her head. "But they are Jeni Cerii warriors."

"No," Riane said, "they are holoimages." When she saw the bewildered look on Tezziq's face, she added, "They are a kind of projection, part of a Gyrgon's technomancy."

"Do you mean these things are not alive? But they look so real."

"That is the point," Riane said.

"But why are they here? What are they doing?"

"For one thing, they are meant to make us believe that Perrnodt was abducted by the Jeni Cerii." Riane was thinking furiously, one theory superseding another as she began to work out the trajectory of recent events.

"She wasn't?"

"No. I have been thinking about it. I have been wondering why Perrnodt never leaves her kashiggen. Why, if the Gyrgon Nith Settt wanted something from her, wouldn't he go to the kashiggen himself and get it from her? I think the only explanation is that for reasons I am not yet able to explain he could not get to her while she was inside the kashiggen."

"So he manufactured a situation where she would be forced out."

Riane nodded. "I believe Nith Settt realized that my escape meant the Ghor would hurry her from her sanctuary before it was surrounded."

"So the Gyrgon followed them, killed the Ghor and abducted her."

"That is what the holoimages mean."

Another was heading toward them, and Tezziq reached out her arm as if to make it pass through the image, but at the last moment Riane pulled her back.

"These holoimages cannot see, of course, but they are sentinels nonetheless. They can sense us if we come within about thirty centimeters of them. Khagggun—the V'ornn military caste—uses them as off-world scouts or in extremely hostile environments."

She glanced at Tezziq as they hunkered in the lee of the dune. "Where is the Jeni Cerii staging area?"

"Approximately five kilometers northeast of here. But you no longer believe they were involved in abducting Perrnodt."

"Exactly," Riane said. "That's why I think the Gyrgon will keep his distance from the staging area." She pointed. "All the holoimages came from the northwest. I think we should head in that direction."

"We will have to cross the in'adim basin," Tezziq pointed out.

"No problem," Riane said, unfurling Nith Sahor's greatcoat. But when she wrapped it around them, nothing happened. "That's very odd." She frowned, examining the inside of the flexible neural net. "It won't activate." She wondered what this failure meant and at once felt a chill in her belly. Was Nith Sahor dead? Is that why his greatcoat was inoperative? She prayed to Miina there was another explanation.

Folding the greatcoat away, she stared out over the innocent-looking basin. "Can you get us across?"

"I think so," Tezziq said.

Half-bent-over, they scrambled down the steep dune, sheets of sand cascading away from them. When they reached the edge of the basin floor, Tezziq grabbed a handful of sand and threw it out ahead of them. The sand sank into the basin.

"What is the quicksand like?" Riane asked.

"That depends on the currents," Tezziq replied. "It can be viscous, like honey, or watery, like gruel."

She scooped up another handful and threw it to the left. It, too, sank. But when she threw sand to the right, it remained.

"Fill your pockets," she instructed Riane. They heaped sand into every pocket in their robes.

"We must be careful, but we must not tarry," Tezziq warned, "for the *in'adim* is notorious for its sudden shifts, like currents in an ocean. What may feel solid one moment can liquefy the next. So, above all, we must keep going."

So saying, she stepped out onto the floor of the *in'adim*, placing her foot alongside the tiny mound of sand. Sprinkling more sand, she made her way forward. As Riane followed her, careful to place her feet in the imprints Tezziq made, she saw that they were not heading in a straight line. Rather, the solid ground took them on a circuitous route that often seemed to backtrack on itself. It was like being in a maze where the choice of routes had been rendered invisible.

At least, she thought, Tezziq kept them moving, though how much real progress they were making across the basin floor was difficult to determine. Each time they seemed to be pressing forward they would be stymied by a floating pond of quicksand they knew would pull them under if they stepped into it. What made Riane triply nervous was their obvious vulnerability out here in the flats of the *in'adim*. Not only was the barren waste without shelter, but there was nowhere to dodge a direct assault by a determined Gyrgon.

The light was changing as the afternoon waned. The flat, featureless sky had opened up into a bowl of beautiful blue porcelain banded by delicate ribbons of high cloud. Protected as they were by dunes on all sides, the air was still and limp, and a curious kind of enervating lassitude gripped Riane. Once or twice, she discovered to her horror that her eyelids had closed, and, following blindly, she had nearly stepped off the proscribed path made by Tezziq's footprints. High above, several birds, large, black, featureless at this extreme distance, effortlessly rode the thermal currents.

Instantly, like a bubble rising to the surface of a pond, another memory appeared out of Riane's enigmatic past. She was climbing a sheer cliff face, her clawed fingertips dug deep through snow and ice to the frozen rock face beneath. Above, a cloudless sky of purple-blue. Below, a dizzying vista of craggy rock, hard-packed snow veined with glittering ice. The wind rushing through the Djenn Marre moaned in conversation, and she spoke to it as if it were a living entity, as if it were an old friend. And still she climbed, the thin air sawing in and out of her lungs.

Her hands were numb as were her feet, but still she continued at a slow but inexorable pace. The sun with its purple spot hung in the sky, burning her skin. Ice and fire, all at once.

She heard it then, from somewhere far away, echoing through the crags, the song of songs, and her heart leapt with elation. She had found him, at long last. She stopped climbing, then, and waiting, hanging in space, kilometers from everywhere. It was just her and the Djenn Marre and the song of songs, coming closer and closer until, at last, she heard the steady beat of its enormous wings. She turned into the sun, squinting, and she saw its shadow approaching, and she opened her mouth to speak the words she had spent so many years learning to enunciate just right . . .

Riane, in the bowl of the *in'adim*, blinked and shook her head. What had triggered the memory? What did it mean? What had she been searching for amid the highest peaks of the Djenn Marre? What had she studied so long and arduously? She shook her head again. Like all the surfacing memories, this posed more questions than it answered. She had the sense of looking at a vast puzzle for which she only had a few tiles. Turning her mind away from this new mystery, she concentrated on helping Tezziq scatter sand, on putting one foot in front of another. But, somehow, she could not rid her mind of the Gyrgon, who had murdered the Ghor and made off with Perrnodt.

As if he had been conjured up by her thoughts, Nith Settt appeared on the far dune. Riane recognized the familiar high, angular helm with its finbat ears and evil-looking horns, the menacing row of alloy talons arching from the thick-ridged brow.

"I knew you would come, Riane," he said. "What I didn't expect was that you would drag this Jeni Cerii skcettta with you."

Riane pulled at Tezziq's robes. "We have to move. Now."

Nith Settt raised his arm, his black-gloved hand pointing toward them. Green ion fire sparked and stuttered.

In that instant, the patch of solid sand they were standing on disintegrated. Tezziq screamed, pitching forward. Riane leapt back, made a vain attempt to grab on to the ajjan. She landed on solid sand and stretched herself prone, reaching out for Tezziq. In the periphery of her vision, she saw Nith Settt crouched on his haunches, wrists resting easily on his knees, observing the drama.

"You stole something from me, Riane." His voice echoed over the flat expanse of the *in'adim*. "Now I will have it back."

Riane, wholly absorbed in trying to save Tezziq, could not even risk a glance in his direction let alone distract herself in useless conversation. Stretched out over the quicksand, she had managed to grasp a handful of Tezziq's robes.

"Let go of me," Tezziq cried. "The sand you're on may give way at any moment. Save yourself while you still can."

"Sound advice, Riane," Nith Settt called out. "Best to heed it quick as you can."

Riane ignored them both. She was busy hauling Tezziq toward her so that she could get a two-handed grip on her. This was not as easy as it sounded. The quicksand in this area seemed to have a viscous consistency that grabbed at any body in it, holding it fast. Riane felt her muscles bunch and strain. Tezziq was almost in range of her other hand when the basin floor shifted again, and Tezziq was pulled under.

"Give it up, Riane," Nith Settt said. "The ajjan is a lost cause."

Shut up, Riane thought. *Shut up.*

Wriggling herself farther out over the quicksand, she reached into the viscous muck. It was dark and oddly warm, and she thought of the legend that the *in'adim* had been made with the blood of the Prophet Jiharre. She was obliged to lean over so far that her cheek lay against the slowly shifting surface of the quicksand. Was it her imagination or could she smell the sweet-salt scent of blood? She renewed her grip on Tezziq and, using both hands now, hauled her back up. Tezziq's head and shoulders popped up above the surface, and the ajjan gasped and choked and spat up dark viscous fluid, almost as if she were vomiting blood.

"Can you move?" Riane asked her. "Just a little bit."

"A fool's effort," Nith Settt said. "Why do you even try?"

Tezziq was struggling forward with the greatest difficulty, and Riane could see the fear in her eyes.

"Just a little more, Tezziq. Please."

She squirmed forward herself, but as she did so, she felt a finger of sand give way beneath her.

"It's happening." Tezziq screamed. "There's no more time. Get back, Riane."

It appeared that the sand Riane was lying on was bifurcating, and it was anyone's guess whether either of the remaining tongues would be of sufficient mass to support her. The sand continued to crumble beneath her, and Tezziq twisted, trying to get away, but this only fired Riane's determination to hold on more firmly. She hauled with all her might.

"Impressive," Nith Settt said as he stood up.

Riane had forgotten all about him.

The Gyrgon gestured with his gloved hand. "Too bad it was all for nothing." An arrow of livid ion fire snaked out, catching Tezziq as she rose up on her knees. She arched back, her nails raking the air.

"No!" Riane cried, and lunged for her. But it was too late. Tezziq spun off the spit of sand, landing heavily in the quicksand. Her eyes were fixed and staring as she slowly spun, disappearing beneath the surface.

"*Wa tarabibi*," Riane whispered.

"Now that I have you to myself." Nith Settt's fingers curled upward, and another jet of ion fire spurted toward Riane.

"I applaud both your strength and your ingenuity, Riane," he said. "But the contest is done. I will not kill you as I did the ajjan. Not for some time, anyway. It seems to me that you are an altogether extraordinary Kundalan. Only when you have told me everything there is to know about you will I allow you the peace of death."

"You don't really believe that I will tell you anything, do you?"

"Oh, I *know* you will. Not that you will want to, no. But even an extraordinary Kundalan is only, after all, a Kundalan." The ball of ion fire was on the move, heading directly at Riane. "I know how to deal with your kind."

Riane ran. The ball of ion fire followed her. She changed directions; so did the ball. It was gaining on her. As she ran this way and that she could hear the Gyrgon laughing. Each desperate moment brought it closer to her. Its cold fire filled the sky. She could hear the evil sound of its energy-crackle as it split apart the very air around it.

"You cannot escape," Nith Settt shouted. "No matter what you do."

Riane changed tactics. Clearly, she could not outrun the ion fire. The only other alternative was to meet it head-on. From out of her sopping robes, she grabbed the gel pak she had disengaged from Nith Settt's sleep casket. Would it work? She had no way of knowing, but she had run out of alternatives. She turned and hurled it at the ball of ion fire. They met in midair. A white flash ensued, followed by a percussive burst that threw her onto her back. Gasping, she rolled over, digging in her robes for the infinity-blade. Gripping the wand tight in her hand, she rose, her heart thudding painfully in her breast. Her ears were ringing, and there were bright spots in front of her eyes. The ball of ion fire was gone, consumed in the midair ignition.

Dimly, she was aware of the Gyrgon with one arm thrown across his face. The blast had shaken even him, and that gave her heart as she launched herself at him. She held the wand in front of her, thumbing the gold disc as she crashed into him. Riane grimaced with the pain that branched up her arms and into her shoulders from the ion energy generated by Nith Settt's armored exomatrix. Frantically, she thumbed the wand's disc again. Nothing happened. The infinity-blade had not appeared.

The wand had only one charge remaining. There must be a way to activate—

Nith Settt's hands arced in toward her neck. Buried deep inside her, Annon recalled that their touch was supposed to kill, but she also retained a memory of something Eleusis Ashera had told Annon, that he had, in fact, survived a Gyrgon's touch. As Nith Settt's fingers closed around her throat she felt the pain of the ion surge overloading her nerve synapses. Bright colors sparked behind her eyes, and a curtain of blackness rippled through her as she passed in and out of consciousness.

And then she had the thought, and she thumbed the gold disc twice rhythmically in quick succession. The goron beam erupted, the helix-shaped infinity-blade unfurled, slicing through the ion fire, absorbing the hyperexcited ions, sucking them into itself.

With her last milliliter of strength, she swung the infinity-blade hard and fast, breathless at its power, and it turned the V'ornn-made alloy battle armor white as ice as it sliced through it. Nith Settt trembled and spasmed, an eerie sound emanating from him that echoed across the *in'adim*. The infinity-blade was devouring the Gyrgon-based energy with electrifying efficiency.

"Who are you?" Nith Settt whispered even as his helm cracked apart.

"I am she who is your death," Riane said through teeth clenched tight in pain and rage. "I am Revenge." She stared pitilessly down at his drawn and whitened skull, the embedded circuitry blackening, steaming even as she spoke. "I am the Dar Sala-at."

*A*nd now see what has happened.

The Gyrgon has been dispatched to whatever hellish clime he came from.

Watch your tongue, my dear. You know that clime, and it wasn't in the least hellish. The black Dragon, her scales opalescent in the sorcerous mist atop Heavenly Rushing, shook her beautiful head. *I was not, however, referring to the Gyrgon, who even I admit are better off dead.*

And look who sent him on his eternal journey! The great ruddy Dragon cried in his thunderous voice.

Yes, yes, the Dar Sala-at.

She has learned that they can be killed.

An important lesson, I admit. But at what cost, I wonder. What was Minnum thinking, giving her an infinity-blade? I told you sauromicians cannot be trusted.

You said they lie, and that is so, the red Dragon pointed out. *But trust is another matter entirely, isn't it?*

It sometimes astonishes me, Yig, the fascination you have with semantics.

He let out a blast of belching fire. *I am pleased, my dear, that after all these eons I still have the capacity to astonish you.*

I daresay, on occasion, you would astonish anyone. Even Miina Herself. But before you start your endless preening, please explain to me how the Dar Sala-at is to deal with the stirring of the sauromicians?

Evil luck, that, Yig admitted.

Evil, indeed. These sauromicians are a scourge. They have renounced Miina.

And the Ramahan have not?

The Ramahan will not turn on the Dar Sala-at.

Do not be so certain of that, Paow, now that Pyphoros and Horolaggia have gained a hoofhold.

The abbeys—what is left of them—have been rotten with evil for years, the black Dragon said. *This is simply the culmination. This is Ambat, the time of the Dar-Sala-at, the moment of Transformation. Either they will be destroyed utterly or there will be a complete reversal and they will be restored to their former sacred glory.*

Yig switched his great flame-studded tail. *Truly, how can this be Ambat? The Prophesy is not yet complete. All the players are not yet in place.*

But they soon will be, Paow. With Pyphoros' meddling the last is slouching toward consciousness, just as it was foretold.

Pyphoros! It is supremely troubling that he has been abroad, working his devious evil for more than a century.

Interesting the host he chose.

Interesting, yes. But hardly surprising, Yig said. *Pyphoros always flowed toward the power center. That was part and parcel of the Schism, wasn't it?*

Speak not of the Schism, Paow said shortly. *It is forbidden.*

Yig stamped his enormous taloned feet. *Too much these days is forbidden. I feel like Seelin, in chains of red jade—*

He broke off as Paow frowned or, more accurately, produced what was, in a Dragon, its approximate analog. Her arrow-point ears flattened against her glossy scales, and her nostrils flared. *Who comes?*

There could be heard, above the thunderous roar of the waterfall, the unmistakable sound of the beating of great wings. This was followed by a burst of living cobalt, as Eshir, the Dragon of air, descended through the thick, sorcerous mist to land beside her compatriots.

What news of our sister? The black Dragon asked nervously.

Seelin remains twenty thousand fathoms deep, Eshir said in her sweetly lilting voice. *The Keeper is so well protected he remains inviolate.*

Without Seelin, Yig said angrily, *the Transformation inherent in Ambat cannot take place.*

All this means, dearest, Paow said, *is that all the elements are not yet in place. I have told you, it is still early in the game.*

And all the circumstances are stacked against us, Yig muttered with ill-concealed impatience.

Paow put a black paw on his powerful foreleg. *Please, my dear, promise me that you will not interfere again.*

What? Eshir said. *What has happened?*

Go on, tell her, Yig grumbled. *She will find out sooner or later.*

Paow sighed. *Learning of Horolaggia's incursion into this realm, my darling mate took it into his scaly head to put Minnum into play.*

The sauromician?

The very one.

And because of him, Yig said, *the Dar Sala-at has slain the Gyrgon, Nith Settt.*

Now that is news! Eshir cried. *Pyphoros was getting too close to the Veil of a Thousand Tears.*

But the potential repercussions, Paow said. *In these dark days—*

These days have been made dark by the archdaemons, Yig said. *I am accused of being impetuous, but look at them! Horolaggia has basely broken the Primal Laws laid down before the beginning of Time, before the coming of Kundalan. Laws they know nothing about; Laws we Dragons must, in the absence of Miina, enforce. His transgression demands punishment, swift and certain.*

Oh, my dear, no! What do you propose? I will not allow you to expose yourself to more danger.

Am I not as brave as Seelin? Even while imprisoned, she managed to project herself into Kundala in order to help the Dar Sala-at.

This is her fate. She and the Dar Sala-at are joined.

As if she and I are not? Yig tossed his horned head, sending a geyser of flames arcing into the mist. *Dearest, do not worry so. Though circumstances grow darker with every day that passes, we shall yet prevail.*

From your mouth, Eshir said prayerfully, *to Miina's ear.*

Wherever in the Cosmos She may be, Paow whispered, twining her tail with her mate's. And as one, the three Dragons craned their serpentine necks up, looking past the curling opalescent plumes of mist to the vastness of other Realms, which remained a mystery even to them.

Book Three
RED-JADE GATE

Red jade is unique among all minerals for its capacity to conduct heat. Red-Jade Gate is a regulator, composed of a series of what might be termed canal locks to keep the hot emotions of anger, lust, and love in the proper balance . . .

—Utmost Source,
The Five Books of Miina

. . . O-Rhen Ka is the casting meant to open Red-Jade Gate. Keep the enemy in your line of sight; incant with extreme caution.

—The Book of Recantation

21

Crash

When she heard the signature hum of the Khagggun hoverpod, Eleana broke cover and began to run. She was carrying high and a sprint was no problem as long as she did not have to cover a great distance. The baby, pressing a little against her lungs, was tending to make her short of breath.

The lookout in the hoverpod saw her right away, and the craft changed course, dipping down to skim low over the terrain. The three Khagggun in the hoverpod were headed directly into the setting sun.

Eleana felt her breath hot in her throat, and she had to steel her nerves to continue to run when her instinct was to turn and face them. Still, this was Rekkk's plan and she had agreed to it and the moment she had revealed herself she was committed.

She hewed to the prescribed path, heading between two outcroppings of boulders. Beyond, there was a steep dropoff to a hedge-filled riverbank. She was more than fifteen kilometers from the Abbey of Warm Current and in no danger of leading the Khagggun back there.

Passing between the boulders, she felt a peculiar tingling in her spine, a rustle of fear, which she quickly brought under control. She trusted Rekkk; he had assured her that with so many boulders around to refract their ion beams they would not risk trying to shoot her from the fast-running hoverpod. She could hear the hoverpod's hum, louder now, as it drew nearer. As it rose a little to clear the tops of the boulders, she could hear the lookout communicating with the pilot.

She was past the rocks now and so was the hoverpod. The ground dropped away under her running feet so abruptly that her teeth clacked together. It was at this moment that Rekkk rose from his hiding spot on the far side of the easternmost boulder. He had fitted a stone, no larger, really, than a pebble, into the slot of the special okummmon that Nith Sahor had manufactured for him.

Rekkk, concentrating on what he wanted the pebble to become, aimed at a certain spot on the undercarriage of the hoverpod. The pebble—powered by Gyrgon technomancy—exploded out of the okummmon as if propelled by an ion launcher, tore through the air and, with a loud *ping!*, jammed itself into the hoverpod's left-hand spent-ion vent.

The craft immediately dipped to the left, and Eleana, on the alert for the noise, dropped as Rekkk had instructed her to do and rolled to her right. In this way, she was out of harm's way when the hoverpod's blunt left wing plowed into the ground. The bank was so steep that the hoverpod slewed violently, throwing its occupants off-balance. As they stumbled against the cockpit bulkhead, Rekkk was up and running, shock-sword out and humming as the hyperexcited ions arced between the twin blades.

The leading edges of his blades tore through the armor of the first Khagggun, severing an arm, plowing through several ribs. The Khagggun collapsed in a welter of blood, and Rekkk engaged the second Khagggun, flicking his weapon away and plunging his own through the Khagggun's hearts.

This aggressive attack proved a mistake, for Rekkk was fully extended, his shock-sword inside the dying Khagggun when the third slammed his thick-booted foot into the side of Rekkk's head. Rekkk grunted, staggered back, slipping on the slick bank and losing his grip on his shock-sword.

The third Khagggun pressed his advantage, vaulting over the side of the hoverpod, swinging a deadly ion mace over his head. Rekkk rolled, but the initial attack caught him a glancing blow on his shoulder. Inside the armor, his muscles went numb, and his fingers could not grip his own ion mace. He rolled back the other way, narrowly missing a massive second blow. The head of the ion mace bounced along the spongy bank, then whistled in the air as the Khagggun whirled it around for the death blow.

Rekkk desperately flexed his fingers, clumsily pulling his ion mace out of its sheath. But, in his prone position, it was the wrong weapon because he could not swing it with any force. He managed to struggle to his knees, but the blow from the Khagggun standing over him was already past its apex. The spiked sphere whistled through the air, blurred with the speed of its passage. And then the Khagggun reared back, his arms flying up, the ion mace whirling end over end out of his grip. Rekkk saw the point of a shock-sword—Eleana's shock-sword—protruding from his chest. She had struck him a fierce and mighty blow between the shoulder blades that had penetrated clear through him. He went to his knees, his arms flailing, and she pulled the blade free, sideswiping in a slow and deliberate fashion that took his head clean off his shoulders.

"N'Luuura take it," Rekkk gasped, "I taught you well."

Eleana grinned, fetched his shock-sword, and handed it to him as he regained his feet.

"You also taught me that a warrior must never lose hold of his weapon."

"I was concerned about you. And the baby." He grinned back at her. N'Luuura, it felt good to be on the move again. His bones had been getting soft with worry at the abbey.

Together, they wiped their blades on the thick mat of glossy green moss and hurled the two corpses from the hoverpod. Then they rolled all three down to the rushing water and pushed them in, where they spun away downriver.

They waited until the corpses had vanished around a bend, then they clambered back up the steep slope. Halfway up, Rekkk heard a tiny exclamation and turned in time to see Eleana sitting on the ground, her legs wide apart, her head between her knees.

"Eleana!" he cried, putting his arm around her.

"I'm all right," she said thinly. "I'm—" Then she coughed thickly and vomited.

Rekkk held her forehead while she retched miserably.

"I am so stupid," he murmured. "I should never have allowed you to run. The strain—"

"Oh, shut up and stop treating me like an invalid!" she snapped.

He handed her a water bladder, and she rinsed her mouth, then swallowed some water as best she could. She laid her head back in the crook of his shoulder.

"Ah, Rekkk, this baby thing is harder than I ever could have imagined."

"It's just new, that's all."

"No, no. You know it's more than that."

He smoothed the hair back from her face. "Eleana, what do you expect from yourself? You were born and raised into war—killing in order to survive, that's what you took in like mother's milk. But what you're beginning to learn now. Life isn't all mayhem and murder. It isn't all intrigue and betrayal. There are other moments." He put his hand gently on the curve of her belly. "Magnificent moments that will endure long after this war is over and done with."

She closed her eyes. "What if the baby comes . . . and Giyan is not here?"

"She will be."

"But what if?"

He kissed the top of her head. "Then we will deal with that, too."

"And Riane?"

"She is the Dar Sala-at," he said. "She will return from the Korrush stronger and more powerful." He put his knuckle beneath her chin and lifted her head. "It is written in your Prophesies, is it not?"

"So the Ramahan claim. But I have never seen these Prophesies, nor do I know anyone who has."

"Not even Giyan?"

"I do not know about Giyan."

"Then you must take it on faith that she has," he said softly. "You must take it on faith that the Prophesies exist and that they are true." He smiled down at her. "Even Nith Sahor believes in them."

She was far too distraught to pick up on his choice of tenses.

And then he laughed. "Imagine! A V'ornn trying to convince a member of the Resistance that the Kundalan Prophesies really exist! You see the absurdity of it."

She nodded. "But you are not like other V'ornn."

He squeezed her shoulders and she made a sign and he helped her to her feet.

"I'm all right now. Really." She pushed his hand away. "I want my baby to know his mother's strength." And she climbed the bank in swift sure strides, and they gained the lower wing of the hoverpod together.

Rekkk shook his head as he watched her, then he ducked down and removed the pebble from the left spent-ion vent and fired up the hoverpod. It was a little unnerving for Eleana to be in a Khaggun hoverpod—the Resistance had never captured one. Rekkk whistled and soon enough they spotted the red-blue-green blur of the Teyj. It sang a song when it saw them and landed on the edge of the cockpit, singing still.

"Hang on," Rekkk said, and Eleana gathered the Teyj to her, holding it against her just above the swell of her belly. The Teyj carefully folded its four wings and sang a soft unfamiliar song.

"Listen," she said, laughing. "I think it's singing to the baby."

Slowly, Rekkk manipulated the hoverpod, which shuddered and moaned as it disengaged its wing from the bank. Gaining the sky, Rekkk aimed it due north so as to avoid any major cities. The land fell swiftly away from them as they shot forward, the toylike trees becoming a long smear of green. They crossed a trailing spear of reddish light, saw the last shred of the sun sinking behind the western horizon, and then above them was the calm cobalt vault of the heavens. A cloudbank, curled low in the south like a dragon, hung motionless, its underside glowing pink and pristine for a moment before slowly fading to a smudgy grey.

Overhead, night rolled in. The wind had died, but the sky had turned frosty, stars aglitter, and Eleana pulled her cloak tighter about her shoulders and throat. She reached in a side pack she had provisioned before they left Warm Current and offered Rekkk some dried meat. He shook his head, and she gnawed on it without really tasting it. Her eyes watering and her cheeks grown numb, she hunkered down against an alloy bulkhead, took a handful of dried leeesta, and crumbled it in her palm. The Teyj ruffled its underwings and sat on the pillowy part of her thumb. It cocked an eye at her.

"Go on," she said. "You must be hungry even if Rekkk is not."

The Teyj ducked its scarlet-and-green-plumaged head and, using the tips of its sharp curved beak, devoured the small pieces of dried leeesta. Eleana hummed a little, comforted by its hunger. A small common normal act in her abnormal life. She reached out and stroked its tail. The Teyj ceased eating long enough to eye her again, the glossy black ball seeming to take all of her in. Then it went back to eating. Eleana, abruptly exhausted, put her head back against the bulkhead, closed her eyes, and drifted off to sleep.

She was roused by an insistent electronic sound, an arrhythmic beeping.

They were still going full out. Rekkk was using the photonic V'ornn navigational instruments to keep them on course in the darkness.

"What is it?" she asked as she gained her feet. The Teyj fluttered close by.

"It's a Khagggun pack code," Rekkk said. "Headquarters is trying to raise the crew of this hoverpod because they haven't checked in."

Eleana came fully awake, rubbed sleep out of her eyes. "I thought pack elements were only required to do so every fifty hours."

He grunted. "Apparently, the new Star-Admiral has increased the frequency for the pack elements looking for us."

The beeping continued unabated.

"Can't you disable it?" she asked.

"No. But, in any event, very soon now it will not matter."

"What do you mean?"

He glanced at her, his dark eyes grave. "If I were the watch commander and could not raise one of my pack elements, I would immediately dispatch a fully armed hoverpod to find out what happened."

"But they won't be able to find us. You'll see to that."

"Unfortunately, the device through which the codes are sent and received is an integral part of the craft, and I cannot disable it. It will pinpoint our precise location. They know where we are."

Eleana felt a cold dread creep through her. "Did you know this was going to happen?"

"Eventually, yes. I just thought we'd have more time."

She felt a shiver run down her spine. "How much time do we have?"

"Depends on how close the nearest hoverpod is." He shrugged. "An hour at most, I'd estimate."

She drew near him, and the Teyj fluttered into the crook of her arm. "What are we going to do?"

Rekkk was silent. He stared into the navigational interfaces. Eleana glanced behind them as if she could already sense their pursuers. The hoverpod flew on, fast as it could go.

In typical response, Olnnn wanted to kill Rada. In fact, he tried. Not once, but twice.

The first time, they were on their way back from the foul warren of hovels beneath Divination Street. They did not speak. There was nothing left to say.

A rumbling overtook them briefly as a hoverpod passed overhead, one of Olnnn's own newly instituted patrols. He heard a pair of Bashkir arguing stupidly over a business deal, another Bashkir, fat and soft and pampered by the tradition of his caste, laughing drunkenly with his

Looorm. A young Mesagggun walked hand in hand with a Tuskugggun, murmuring to one another. He looked darkly at a Kundalan servant scurrying along like a rodent eager to return to its hidey-hole.

And like a wyr-moth to a flame he hurried to meet his rage.

The alleyway in which they eventually found themselves was narrow and desolate. Sulphurous light spilled from the streetlamps. Dead leaves lay in thick drifts. All around them rose the nighttime roar of the city, the insistent susurrus of a million insects ceaselessly foraging.

There was the reek of violence in the air.

He watched Rada darkly as she walked in front of him. Tied to a Tuskugggun. The sheer unfairness of it made his blood boil. Without warning, he grabbed her around the wrist and whirled her to him so that he felt her hard breasts. He jammed his mouth down upon hers.

"Don't," she said. "I'll kill you," or something close to that.

Not that he heard or cared. He backed her against the damp and seeping wall and ground into her, and when she commenced to wriggle away, he slapped the side of her head so that it snapped back, then he tripped her, falling on her even as she fell, exulting in her hot and panting body beneath him.

She continued to squirm, and this exhibition of resistance, quite formidable for a Tuskugggun, made him even more determined.

He would have her and kill her and be done with it. All of it. Over in a few vicious moments. An eternity of violence encapsulated in the pulsing hearts of Axis Tyr.

He considered this just punishment, righteous retribution for her undisciplined mouth, for her effect on him. He used his thighs to spread her legs, used his clawed fingers to bare her breasts, burying his face between them until she bit his ear and drew blood, and he hit her again, this time with his balled fist.

She cried out in pain and the fire in his ensorceled bones rose up and gripped him. He faltered and slipped to his knees in front of her.

Her eyes found his, and she said, "Your violence will kill you. This is the lesson of that spell. How long will it take you to learn?"

He panted out his agony. "What I want," he rasped between gritted teeth, "is to be free of this accursed spell."

"Then let me kill you," she hissed. "It is the only way."

They lay like that, bitter enemies, locked in an intimate embrace they could neither tolerate nor avoid.

After a time, he began to laugh, and fell away from her. He watched her from glittering eyes as she rearranged her robes. The fire was slowly ebbing from his bones.

"Keep laughing," she said darkly. "You are an evil beast and one day I *will* kill you. You can make sure wager on it."

He marked her words, even though he had not meant to; somehow they heartened him.

The second time he tried to kill her was in broad daylight. Not that Olnnn cared a whit. He was Star-Admiral. Who was to gainsay his actions save the regent?

She was in his tent, and she said something, it did not matter what. It was her manner, her mocking tone, her flashing eyes that underscored her fearlessness. How could she not be afraid of him? He, whose ferocious temper gave even the most battle-hardened Admiral pause. Who was she? Only a Tuskugggun from whom he was used to eliciting fear and abject obedience.

With a guttural cry, Olnnn rose and, drawing a shock-sword from its alloy scabbard, thumbed it on. The tent filled with the humming of the hyperexcited ion flow arcing between the parallel blades. He came at her.

"Go on, kill me," she said. "Kill me now."

He meant to. He had murder in his hearts. But he could not. Already, the fire in his ensorceled bones was streaking through him, and he felt all the strength vanish from his sword arm. He dropped the shock-sword, stood with his shoulders slightly bowed.

"I cannot go on like this." His fists were clenched so hard his nails dug into his palms, drawing blood. "I have to murder something, or I will go mad."

She came up to him, then, and looked him in the eye. "It is hard for me to decide whether I hate or pity you more."

His bloody hand gripped her throat. In response, both her hands wrapped around his throat. Her thumbs sought the soft spot between the ridges of translucent cartilage.

"Let's make a pact," he growled. "We'll kill each other and murder this accursed spell together."

"I can smell you," she said.

"To march into battle is one thing," he rasped. "Even to be outnumbered, to face certain death at the hands of the Centophennni. But this is different." His eyes blazed. "My life has been warped by Kundalan sorcery until I can no longer recognize it."

"I can smell your cowardice."

He spat at her, and this made her smile.

"At least now I have an effect on you," she told him softly. "I am no longer a Tuskugggun nonentity, a wyr-maggot beneath your notice except to rape at will. I have engaged all your emotions, limited though they may be."

"I do not understand you." His head shook slowly from side to side. "I cannot live like this."

"Now you're getting it, Star-Admiral. That, apparently, was Malistra's point. You have to find another way."

"I am V'ornn. I am Khagggun. I know only one way to live."

"Then, as Sagiira told us, you will die. And if you die, so will I, because this spell has ensnared us both. But I will tell you this, Star-Admiral. I will make no double-suicide pact with you. I have no intention of dying anytime soon. If that means I have to keep you alive, by guile or by force, then that is precisely what I will do. I will change you, whether you like it or not."

I've picked them up on the scanner," Rekkk said. "Quartering in from the southeast."

There was no anxiety in his voice, no emotion at all. Eleana noted this with one part of her brain while with the other part she was preparing for war. She put one hand on her belly and wept inside that her baby should be caught in the same quagmire of violence that had ensnared her. This emotion did not stop her from rechecking her shock-sword.

"Are they gaining on us?"

"Just slightly," he said.

"Then we cannot outrun them."

"They are blessed with a following wind."

"Turn into it," she offered. "We can use it ourselves."

"I could do that. But it would take us kilometers to the west." He glanced at her. "The ion cannons should be in the locker just where you are standing."

She reached down, thumbed the electromagnetic latch as he directed, and drew out one of the blunt ugly weapons.

"You'll need to keep us very steady."

"When they get that close that could be a problem."

"Then the thing is useless."

"Prepare to use it, anyway."

She knew an order when she heard one, and since they had been on a heightened war footing ever since they had taken down the crew of this hoverpod, she obeyed. Crouched against the aft starboard bulkhead, she rested the triple barrel of the ion cannon on the top lip. She felt the deep vibration of the ion-fusion engines and knew right away how fruitless an exercise this would be. Still, she put her eye to the sighting mechanism. She could see nothing in the darkness, but quite soon, she knew, she would.

Even as she had that thought she felt the pitch of the engines alter. They were heading lower, and slowing. Well, that was something, she supposed. When the pursuing crew blew them out of the sky they would have a shorter distance to fall.

"I hope you know what you're doing," she said, as they continued their descent and deceleration.

"I want them to think I'm looking for a spot to land."

"What are you really doing?" she asked.

"Looking for a spot to land."

"Are you trying to make me laugh?"

"I don't know. Is it working?"

"I'll tell you when we get out of this."

She had turned the scope on the ion cannon up to its highest magnification, and now she thought she saw something, flickering like a low-magnitude star in a hazy sky. She had set the scope to detect spent-ion flux, and as soon as she got a computer lock in the scope's viewfinder she squeezed off her first round. At this extreme range, she did not expect to score a hit, and she didn't, but the salvo served notice that they were prepared to fight.

Behind her, Rekkk ducked as he banked the hoverpod, taking it between two rows of trees. Grey-brown branches whipped by, and the hoverpod began to buck. The trees were making it difficult for Eleana to regain a lock on the pursuing craft. The crew had not returned her fire, knowing the distance between them was still too great. Besides, from their point of view, there was no rush. They had sighted the renegade hoverpod; it was only a matter of time until they brought it down and killed or captured its occupants.

Rekkk took them low over a hill, through a shallow dell and across a small patch of open cor pastureland that stood between two tall stands of kuello-fir. Eleana recognized the hilly terrain. They were north of her birth territory and west across the Chuun River. She knew this area well, having hunted and been hunted by Khagggun across this thickly forested and rocky expanse.

They were skimming low now, meters from the rising terrain. Directly ahead of them rose the ragged mist-shrouded foothills of the Djenn Marre and Eleana's eyes grew wet at the sight of home.

Rekkk called for her to pilot the hoverpod, and she took over the controls, guided by his competent hands and his whispered voice.

"Keep us low as you can," he said and, behind her, began to remove the purple Haaar-kyut armor that had served him so faithfully since he had purloined it from the Khagggun barracks in Axis Tyr weeks ago.

Eleana was fighting a fierce downdraft that threatened to plow them into the steep side of a highland rock formation when Rekkk took over, swinging them briefly over to lift the left wing above a jagged outcropping, then leveling them off again.

A dull booming off to their right and rock and trees exploded in blue fire.

"They're within ion-cannon range," Rekkk said.

Eleana returned to her position against the aft starboard bulkhead, picked up her ion cannon. The pursuing hoverpod popped into her scope like a starburst, and she squeezed off a round, a near miss that nevertheless made the other craft veer sharply to the right.

Meanwhile, Rekkk was powering ion thrusters, so that they crested the near ridge with centimeters to spare. The hoverpod jounced as the undercarriage scraped an admonishing finger of the rock face. Above them, treetops exploded, raining down in a welter of shards burning with pale lambent fire.

The Teyj screamed shrilly, and Eleana dropped the ion cannon, spent the next couple of minutes flicking the burning debris out of the cockpit. It wasn't easy as the constant rolls Rekkk was putting them through tossed her from bulkhead to bulkhead.

All around them, the terrain was being ripped asunder, and even skimming as low as they were it was becoming increasingly difficult to outmaneuver the pursuing hoverpod.

"We're not going to make it," Eleana shouted.

"Have faith!" Rekkk shouted back.

At that moment, weapons fire struck the back edge of the right wing, searing through it. Eleana grabbed the fluttering Teyj with one hand, but was flung backward so violently she lost control of the ion cannon, which pitched over the side. She was scrambling for the weapons locker when the next blast struck them. The hoverpod seemed to scream, its nose rising almost to the vertical as Rekkk struggled to control it. The trailing edge of the left wing plowed a deep furrow into a small section of open field, then they struck the leading edge of a rock outcropping, and the alloy hull began to crumple.

Blinding waves of blue fire lit up the night, and Rekkk lifted Eleana, threw her over the steeply canted side of the hoverpod, jumped over himself. They sprinted into the burning trees, tucked low, one hand over their noses and mouths as they ran. Behind them, the hoverpod exploded in a blue-green fireball, the shock wave so great it spun them around, took them off their feet, tumbled them over roots, flattening fields of ferns. Then they were up and running again, the Teyj making for the swaying treetops. The pursuing hoverpod, ion cannons bristling, descended upon the flaming ridge, a full pack of Khaggun in armor the color of burnt umber disembarking at the double, led by Attack-Commandant Accton Blled.

The moment he hit the ground, Attack-Commandant Blled ordered three quarters of his pack to search for survivors. Under his exacting eye they paired up and fanned out, carving the immediate vicinity into segments.

As his Khagggun melted into the flaming woods that stretched up-ward along the high ridge, Blled directed the remainder of the pack to pick through the smoldering wreckage of the downed hoverpod. He held one Third-Captain back.

Drawing his shock-sword, he laid the double blade across the Khagggun's throat. "Third-Captain, did you not hear me say that I wanted these traitors alive?"

"I did, Attack-Commandant."

His pack was only weeks old. He had chosen them himself, but he had been given little time to gather his forces. He needed to be absolutely certain of every Khagggun.

"And yet," Blled said, "you fired the direct hit."

The Third-Captain licked his lips. "I was returning fire, sir, as I had been all along. I was aiming for the wing. It was not until I fired that I realized the hoverpod had already struck the ground."

"Is that an excuse?"

"No excuse is acceptable, sir," the Third-Captain barked.

"Just so," Blled said.

"Sir!"

His attention was diverted by a Second-Marshal, high-stepping through the cindered debris. "The heat was too intense to find mortal remains, but—" He was holding something in his right hand, blackened, still smoking.

Blled removed his shock-sword from the Khagggun's throat, took the item for a closer look. "A piece of battle armor." He ran a fingertip over the blistered surface. "Unmistakably."

"Purple." The Second-Marshal nodded. "The Rhynnnon Rekkk Hacilar was wearing a suit of stolen Haaar-kyut armor."

"No doubt," Blled said. "This is his." He handed it back. "If there are other pieces, find them and place them in the hoverpod."

"Yes, sir!" The Second-Marshal saluted and double-timed it back to the wreck.

Blled turned to the Khagggun, "It would seem as if the Rhynnnon is dead. But what of his Kundalan skcettta?"

"This was a very bad crash. It happened very quickly," the Khagggun said, knowing that boldness was now his only option. "The probabilities are they both burned to cinders. But if the skcettta somehow managed to survive, we will hunt her down."

"I do not deal in probabilities, Third-Captain. I am interested only in what is. But you are right about one thing: if the fugitives survived this crash, we will find them."

22

Dreams and Revelations

W *a tarabibi*, do not weep so."

Tezziq put her hand against Riane's feverish brow.

"You are injured, *wa tarabibi*," Tezziq whispered. "Lie back and rest. I will take care of you."

"But I cannot rest," Riane protested, though her head felt as if it were splitting asunder. "I must protect you."

"Against what?" Tezziq smiled and kissed Riane with lips cool as marble. "Nothing can harm me. Not while I am with you, *wa tarabibi*. You took me out of my silk-lined prison and set me free. What more could I ask of you?"

And then, to Riane's horror, the skin began to peel off Tezziq's face, dripping like candle wax onto Riane's chest, and Riane shivered deeply at the chill coursing through her, and she screamed, "Tezziq! Tezziq!" A skull grinning down at her. "Ah, Miina, no!"

And she started awake, the dream like awful tendrils snaking through her mind.

"Tezziq," she whispered, through dry lips. "*Wa tarabibi*."

"Sister!" Othnam called. "She is at last awake." And he bent down and gently guided Riane's lips to the waterskin.

When she had drunk her fill, Riane said, "You came back to help us. I knew you would."

"We could not leave you to your fate," he said with his typical quick grin. His teeth were very white against his darkly bronzed skin.

"The ajjan?" Mehmmer said as she squeezed in beside her.

"Dead," she whispered. "Sunk beneath the *in'adim*."

"The blood of Jiharre brooks no infidels."

"Jiharre's blood did not harm me," Riane said reasonably. "In any case, it wasn't the *in'adim*; Nith Settt killed her. She gave her life so that I might survive."

"Riane, you must eat," Mehmmer said sternly. "The battle with the technomage has depleted you badly."

"I have lost a good friend," Riane mourned. "I have no appetite."

"Forget your friend. She is beyond your help."

"I will replenish myself," she said softly, "if you will recite the prayer cycle for the dead."

All at once, her head was filled with Mehmmer's beautiful contralto, ululating the prayer for Tezziq's spirit.

"Where is the food?" she asked.

Othnam looked at her out of sad eyes. "There is Perrnodt to think of," he whispered. Mehmmer's ululations reverberated in her skull.

Riane sat up, groaned, and put her head in her hands. When she opened her eyes, Othnam and Mehmmer were gone. Had they ever been there? Riane could not stop the pounding in her head. She fell over sideways. Was it possible to have a dream within a dream? Had she been hallucinating Othnam and Mehmmer as well as Tezziq? Had the two Ghor tried to come to her rescue? Or had they never returned at all? But she was certain that they had come back.

There is Perrnodt to think of.

Perrnodt! She put the heels of both hands against the red sand, digging them in to keep herself from pitching over. She turned her head and saw the twisted remains of Nith Settt.

Crawling to the dead Gyrgon made her so dizzy she almost passed out. She sat very still and concentrated on breathing as deeply as she was able. Then she went on.

Dead, without his helm, he looked like a skeleton that had been badly burned in a fire of unknown origin. His armor was shredded, twisted into the shape of flower petals. The kind of flowers you conjure up in a dream. The veradium point in the crown of his skull shone dully in the morning sunlight. There was a rotten smell that began to make her sick.

She sorted through the remains. His flask had burst open in the conflagration, the water instantaneously evaporated, but she discovered in a rent alloy cylinder some food, warm and still smoking, that seemed edible enough. As she swallowed, she seemed to gain sustenance swiftly as if she were ingesting the flesh of her enemy, which infused her with supernal strength.

Her head was rapidly clearing. She rose and walked some distance away into the lee of a high dune. Part of it had been scooped out, no doubt by Nith Settt, to make a kind of cavelike shelter.

"Who are you?" she heard a female voice say from inside the cave. "Where is the Gyrgon?" The voice sounded oddly distant.

"I am Riane," she said.

Crouching, she cupped her hands to filter out the sun's glare and caught her first look at Perrnodt. She sat propped against the curved back wall of the cave. She looked to be more or less the same age as Giyan, with night-black hair, long and curling and wildly massed in a corona about her head. Though tall, she was whip-thin, and this, along with her very pale, very thin skin had the effect of making her appear fragile. Even with her pale eyes, her face was too severe to be beautiful, but this austerity lent her a kind of inner strength even in repose.

"The Gyrgon is dead," Riane said. "I have come a long way to find you."

Perrnodt scrambled forward. "I am imprisoned here. The Gyrgon erected some kind of ion field."

Riane tried to order her head to stop its throbbing. The low-angled morning sun only made matters worse. Right up against the barrier of the ion field, she looked it over carefully. She could see that it was composed of filaments of what appeared to be light particles that moved horizontally in sine waves across the mouth of the artificial cave.

Returning to the dead Gyrgon, she began to peel off his exomatrix in an attempt to discover whether, as in the case of the sleep chamber, there was any kind of energy source she could salvage. The pieces of the cracked exomatrix came away like the carapace of an armored beast. She carefully checked the concave inside of each one, but could find no evidence of a gel pak.

What then powered the exomatrix? Was it the energy field of the Gyrgon himself? If that was the case, she was out of luck. Or was she? She stared at Nith Settt for a long time, thinking. Then she placed her hands around the veradium point at the crown of his skull. Shielded from sunlight, it continued to emit a dim glow.

With a grunt, she took out her dagger and slammed it hiltfirst against the skull. The thing shattered like an eggshell and she extracted the veradium point. It was faceted like a crystal, and, like a crystal, it was

translucent. Holding it close to her face, she could see photonic filaments, similar to the ones embedded in the ion field, running through
it from top to bottom.

With it in her hand, she returned to the artificial cave entrance. The
end of the veradium point that had been embedded in Nith Settt's skull
was sharp as a quill point. She took this end and ran it down the ion
field, describing a vertical line. In its wake, the ion field wavered, and
she tentatively put her hand against it and folded it back. Quickly, she
ran the veradium point farther down the ion field. Then she stepped
through the rent sideways.

She heard a pop, felt a sudden, sharp pressure in her inner ears. But
she was through. She reached for Perrnodt, pulled her to safety.

They staggered into the deep shade in the lee of a dune and, almost
immediately, Perrnodt passed out. The headache Riane had awoken
with had returned with a vengeance. She knew that they both needed
food and drink. The Gyrgon's food was gone. Her kuomeshal, and its
supplies, was out of reach on the other side of the *in'adim*.

Wrapping herself once more in Nith Sahor's greatcoat, she closed
her eyes and pictured the spot where she had left the beast. Nothing
happened. She tried again. Still nothing. This was the second time it
had failed to work in and around the *in'adim*. Why? She shook her
head and immediately regretted it as the headache flared anew. She
could not worry about that now. She had the more pressing problem
of survival to consider.

She would have to brave the Jeni Cerii encampment.

She wondered if she dared leave Perrnodt here, alone and unprotected. But what choice did she have? They would soon both be dead
without nourishment. If only Mehmmer and Othnam had come back.
But they hadn't. She had to resign herself to the fact that they had
abandoned her at the last. They had helped her so much, and at such
a high cost, she could not bring herself to think ill of them.

She stood, walking into full sunlight so that she could judge the sun's
angle and the length of the shadow in the dune's lee. She judged that
she had about two hours to find the Jeni Cerii, steal the supplies they
needed, and get back here before Perrnodt was thrown into broiling
afternoon sunlight.

Brushing off the last of the sand from Perrnodt's halo of black hair,
she took her leave. Recalling her conversation with Tezziq, she headed

due north, closely paralleling the near side of the *in'adim*. She kept a wary eye out for Jeni Cerii patrols.

She passed across sandy scrubland, flat, featureless, ugly. Her Ghorvish robes had finally dried, but they were stiff with dirt, sweat, and silty muck from her nearly fatal swim in the *in'adim*. They felt as heavy as a velvet curtain and twice as hot. She began to sweat, and the more she sweated, the thirstier she became. She tried, as much as possible, to keep to shaded areas, but as the sun climbed toward its zenith, these cool spots evaporated to virtually nothing.

The sun burned her eyes, and she staggered. Her breath rasped in her throat. She sat down abruptly, her arms flailing, as the vision came upon her . . .

The Djenn Marre rises up all around her, the sharp purple ridges rimed with ice. Clear, crisp air, thin as a gossamer streamer of cloud, fills her lungs. The familiar chill even in full sunlight. She is skelling up a rock chimney, using precarious hand- and footholds. Far below, the chimney remakes itself in a new rockfall that has partially filled a tremendous crevasse. If she should fall . . . But that thought has never crossed her mind. She is a climber, as fearless as she is accomplished.

This is the first Riane, the one who existed before the spirit of Annon was put into her dying body. The Riane before the fall that had presumably caused her to lose her memory, before the duur fever that had racked her.

Riane the pure-blood Kundalan.

Now, as she looks up, she can see something perched on the very pinnacle of the rock chimney. From her current acute angle she cannot tell what it is. It looks, however, very big.

She continues her climb, the breath sawing through her half-open mouth. Disciplined, she pauses every few moments so as to conserve her energy. She sips water from a flask of some soft but durable substance she cannot name. The sky is utterly clear, an astonishing violet. Sunlight like a razor against her skin. She hangs in the deep shadow of an overhang and launches her head back, staring at whatever might be perched atop the chimney. She has watched it for weeks, this mysterious thing, wondering at that distance what it might be. Today she has decided to assuage her curiosity.

She is now almost three-quarters of the way up. Unlike other chimneys in her experience this one tapers very little or not at all. The rock is hard and clean. When she does not find adequate handholds, she uses a small, efficient metal implement—again, the name escapes her—to chip them into the rock face. The implement dangles from a braided cord around her right wrist. She made the cord herself, from the hide of a large animal she killed. She can see the animal, trace its outline with the delicate brush of memory, but its name dangles in the black abyss of forgetfulness.

The implement has a long, curved head, pointed at one end, wide-bladed at the other. She once buried the point of it in an attacker's eye. She can recall the feel of his callused hands on her shoulders, pushing her roughly down, his powerful knees spreading her legs. The matted hair of him, the smell of him, like the shining pelt, the stench of that animal she had killed. She had needed no one to come to her rescue. She had swung the implement in a short, powerful arc. Her attacker was too busy grunting to notice it until it pierced his eye. By then it was too late. It went right through into his brain. She had thrown him off even while he was still thrashing.

She is looking up now, into the violet sky, at the top of the chimney. Whatever is perched there seems at this distance to be floating. She is very close, but the shadows are so deep and sharp she still cannot make sense of the shape.

All at once, it detaches itself from the rock chimney and, soaring, spirals down toward her. It is so huge it blots out the sun. Chilled, she shivers.

And in fascination watches it come . . .

Riane, in the burning sand beside the *in'adim*, rolled over and moaned. Sand had attached itself to her lips, and she spat it out of her mouth. She immediately regretted the action because it cost her some vital fluid.

She stared up into the sky bleached white by the blaze of sun, and blinked. Another vision. Another shard of Riane's lost past. What did this one mean? What had been atop the rock chimney? What had she seen? Riane was left with the impression that this vision, above the others, was vastly important.

She was rolling this enigma around in her mind when she heard voices. She froze. The voices came from just beyond the low rise in front of her. She slithered on her belly up to the top of the rise. There in front of her were a pair of Jeni Cerii wrapped in blue-and-white-striped robes. They were armed with long, curved scimitars. Their heavily bearded faces were dark and shiny as oil-rubbed wood. Grained as well with the beat of the sun and the scouring of the wind. At their hips were waterskins and by the look of them they are full or almost so. Doubtless, they had food, as well.

Riane took her dagger in one hand, the dead infinity-blade in the other. Rising up into a squat, she made a sound. Instantly, the Jeni Cerii looked in her direction. They moved with astonishing speed. As they came they drew their scimitars. They did not seek to query her. And why should they? She had encroached on their territory. Their secret encampment was but a kilometer or two away. They did not care who she was; they wanted her silent and dead.

Riane threw the infinity-blade. It whirled, end over end, striking the lead Jeni Cerii square on his left knee. He went down, clutching his leg, and Riane feinted right, drawing the first swing of the second Jeni Cerii's scimitar. The air whistled at the wide blade's swift passage. Riane came in under the arc, jabbed out with the point of her dagger, piercing her assailant's side. He grunted, swiveled on his pivot foot and, ignoring the flow of blood, delivered a backhand swipe.

The flat of the scimitar struck the back of Riane's head, and she pitched forward. Immediately the Jeni Cerii was on top of her; she could feel his sticky blood. The blade of the scimitar came down, aimed for her neck, and she buried her dagger into the meat of his right fore-arm. He grimaced but made no sound, only leaned forward, keeping the scimitar on its downward trajectory.

She twisted the point inside him, dragged the blade through his muscle until she severed an artery. Blood fountained, and the Jeni Cerii's eyes rolled up into his skull. Using her hip, she flung him off her.

She was up and turning toward the Jeni Cerii she had immobilized when her right arm went numb and her dagger dropped from her nerveless fingers. It instantly sank into the sand. She saw the Jeni Cerii and the wound in her shoulder at the same moment. Limping forward, he head-butted her. She fell, half-stunned, and he grabbed the cowl of her Ghorvish robes, tossed her down the low rise. She landed in almost the same spot where the infinity-blade had fractured his kneecap. When she tried to regain her feet, he kicked her hard just below the ribs. Grinning, he limped over and delivered a lazy punch to the same spot.

Riane groaned, curling up into a ball. He struck the wound in her shoulder, and while she writhed in agony, he hefted his scimitar and studied the back of her neck, calculating the vectors of the killing blow.

Satisfied, he placed the slipper of his damaged leg on her side. Anchored by his good leg, he drew back the scimitar. Riane found that she could only move her top arm. She whipped it forward, her forearm smashing into his fractured knee.

The Jeni Cerii howled and collapsed on her. His weight bound her, hurting her hip. She was altogether numb between her legs. The blade of the scimitar lay between them, and she reached for it. He slapped her away and took possession of it, bearing down.

The pain in her hip was excruciating. It was at that moment that she realized she had fallen on the infinity-blade. Without thinking, she pulled it free, thumbed it on. The scimitar whistled at her, a blur of deadly motion.

Then, without warning, the infinity-blade awoke to life. Cutting through the oncoming scimitar it continued its relentless arc, slicing the Jeni Cerii in two.

Riane, lying half-insensate in a pool of blood, stared at the softly humming infinity-blade and wondered what had happened.

Giyan had a close and unique relationship with death. It seemed improbable that she should remember the feel of her own umbilical cord being wrapped around her neck at birth, that she could recall the murderous look on her mother's face as she prepared to kill her evil-omened twins. But she could.

Only the swift and timely intervention of her father had saved the infants' lives.

Another strand of the sorcerous web crept across her, and she screamed a silent scream. The strand was alive, as if it was made up of millions of tiny insects armed with barbed stingers.

Since childhood she had had a premonition that death, angry at being denied what was rightfully his, was never far from her side. Often, in dark corridors or lying in bed late at night, she would hear a whisper of the wind, the creak of an unseen door or floorboard, see the shadow-web of tree branches on the wall and know them for what they really were. Death stalked her in her dreams, as well, a handsome face, a compelling one not unlike that of Eleusis. It was as if in death Eleusis had melted into her in some elemental way. As if having been driven beyond the boundary of mortal flesh he had slipped easily into the role of death's-head.

The strand advanced millimeter by agonizing millimeter. She had sometime earlier come to the conclusion that it was going so slowly in order to maximize the pain it was causing her. Even so, she submitted without a struggle. And she had done so from the beginning. She had read enough about the Malasocca to know that the harder she struggled, the more agonizing the wrapping would become.

Now, trapped in her Osoru Avatar, enmeshed in the archdaemonic web of Horolaggia's design, she felt a welling of the slow assault of death. It was like a ringing in her ears, a knocking on the door to her soul, the swift *clip-clop* of approaching hooves. She could feel death's presence like the silent fall of ashes onto a gravestone.

The filament had begun at her right shin and ended at her left hip. A new one began, causing her to scream again into the anxious nothingness of Otherwhere.

She was not frightened of death, only frightened for her child. Bitter irony that the very sorcerous act that had saved Annon from his enemies had opened the Portal enough for Horolaggia to escape. If only her desperate love for her son had not caused her to cross the circle of the Nanthera. At the last moment, she had changed her mind. She could not bear the thought of losing him, of seeing his essence migrated into another body. She had wanted her Annon back. In a vain and foolish gesture, she had violated the circle of the Nanthera, had inadvertently broken the sorcerous lock on the Portal long enough for the archdaemon to slip through.

The sky had turned a sulphurous yellow, deep red above the darkling mountains closest to the Abyss. There, daemonic sigils rained down in a torrent from fulminating clouds.

All around her, hidden but heard, a vast and depthless lake in the mist, arose the moaning of the host of daemons incarcerated for eons in the Abyss.

The second filament completed its run, and a third appeared. There was no surcease.

The Ras-Shamra that was Giyan wept with the pain of integration with the archdaemon. He controlled her body, was inside it, working it like a puppet. But part of him was always here, spinning this agonizing web that slowly but surely was surrounding her in a cocoon.

When the spinning was done, when she was completely encased, she would die, and Horolaggia would claim her body as his permanent home.

Was there in truth nothing she could do? Stories she had read of the Malasocca hinted that this was so.

Another filament seared across her consciousness and it was all she could do not to cry out. The ground was wet with her blood. She felt the life force draining out of her.

The daemonic sigils continued their assault on the fabric of Otherwhere. An eruption began somewhere within the mountains. Lava and ash darkened the sky further. The stench of burning was everywhere.

The scar of chromium light struck the circular sea-green shanstone floor, the music picked up the beat, and the dancers responded instinctively. By day, the shanstone was dutifully polished to a reflective gloss, and each night lovingly scuffed to dullness. The dancers were moving in a kind of concentrated, frenzied, semireligious mass, a dervish of energy, an accident about to happen.

Three stories down, beneath desolate, starry Devotion Street, the music boomed. The quintet was V'ornn—Tuskugggun, of course, since they were the artists and musicians—but the music was an amalgam of gorgeous minor-key Kundalan melodies and tripartite dissonant V'ornnish harmonies. The trip-hammer tempos that gave it bones and brawn were strictly a product of youth, from one culture, the other, or both, it mattered not to either the quintet or the dancers.

Cthonne was jam-packed, youths not yet in their teens sandwiched together, sweaty, bug-eyed, grinning, put to the endurance test by the barrage of music, light, the intensity of the mass. Marethyn saw V'ornn, both Great Caste and Lesser Caste, and Kundalan, each with their own area of dancefloor, each with their own style of dancing, or possibly not because the longer she looked the more it seemed they had learned— or at least absorbed—from one another. For the serpentine line of demarcation was as fluid as the sands of the Great Voorg and, here and there, the two races danced side by side, or even for an instant mingled.

Marethyn was dismayed and delighted. When had this underground life sprung up, children climbing frantically into adulthood, breaking rules and regulations, flying in the face of V'ornn stratification, Gyrgon law? Rebels, just as she was.

"They look so blissful," Marethyn shouted in Sornnn's ear. "You would never believe they were enemies."

"They're not," he replied.

The chromium scar of light was joined by a cadmium oval so cool it risked sizzling like dry ice. A second drummer had joined the quintet, hooded and robed, playing not with traditional V'ornn titanium-alloy whisks but with thick-callused fingertips. The music took on a more sinuous beat, less industrial, more sonorous, with a texture like softly breaking waves. The hand-drummer began to sing, sinking into the syllables with the vigor of an ecstatic. The lyrics spoke of the pain of loss, the despair and the fierce joy of not belonging.

Sornnn, leaning in toward her, said, "Marethyn, tell me. How frightened were you with Bronnn Pallln and Line-General Lokck Werrrent?"

"Very frightened," she said.

The ghost of a smile on his face. "Only frightened?"

She looked at him. "No. Exhilarated, too."

"I am unsurprised. You played your part to perfection. You fooled them all—the Deirus, Pallln, Werrrent."

"I hope it was worth it."

"You know it was. We have neutralized a ruthless conniver in Bronnn Pallln and a dangerous enemy in Olnnn Rydddlin who, like many Bashkir, hates and fears me for my involvement in the Korrush." He looked at her. "Tell me about your fright."

She thought of the moment when she had run her finger along the dust in the warehouse and he had very gently and very romantically made certain that she would not do that again. Because it was not a SaTrryn warehouse, and he did not want anyone to know they had been there until the trap had been sprung. "Tell me how you managed to get those weapons inside Bronnn Pallln's warehouse."

He considered for a moment. "It was not difficult. Bronnn Pallln does not adequately compensate many in his employ, including the warehouse lading overseer. He was pleased to take the generous coin my representative offered him in exchange for an hour of his absence." He cocked his head. "Now, about your fright."

"What is this all about, Sornnn?"

"I want to know whether you would be too frightened ever to play out another such scenario."

"If the cause was just."

"Because you have a well-honed sense of self-preservation." He leaned in a little closer. "Your fear will protect you. It will keep your mind sharp in all situations."

Marethyn watched the ecstatic dancers because she was suddenly afraid not to. There was something both primitive and powerful in the strobing lights and the pulsing backbeat which seemed somehow synchronized with the rushing of the blood in her veins, pulling her away from everything, from the secret she now carried between her hearts. His secret. Because she knew this was about more than just Bronnn Pallln and Kurgan Stogggul, more than just about his life, important to her as it was. But she would not say anything about that now. Not unless he broached the subject first.

He had procured drinks from somewhere, had led them up to a balcony overlooking the cavernous space. The furious furnace heat of hundreds of moving bodies slapped them in the face. Incense was pearling, the air thick as stew. The oval of light accompanying the chromium scar had lowered to a liquid candied bronze.

They stood, leaning against the turned railing, looking down into the vast, writhing space so that Marethyn felt slightly giddy. Possibly it was the writhing beat, the primordial excitement of being here, a secret dance club where V'ornn and Kundalan existed side by side without enmity. She did not want to be afraid, so she put her head against his.

"My only regret," she said, "was that I abused my friendship with Kirlll Qandda. He is so kind to Terrettt, the only one in Receiving Spirit who is. Yes, I felt exhilaration, but I also am ashamed."

The youths seemed like one shining multilegged beast, a single-celled creature, amorphous and anonymous. Marethyn was aware of the slipstream of energy ripping through the club, aware, too, that she and Sornnn were observers, apart and, therefore, alone. And there arose in her breast a curious longing like a pain.

"Kirlll Qandda was bound to be squeezed. Think of it this way. The information you gave him may have saved his life."

Watching them like this, moving mindlessly, ecstatically, hypnotized by the backbeat, it suddenly dawned on her the risk they were all taking in congregating here. The complicity, the signature act of rebellion they shared, that had brought V'ornn and Kundalan together. Just as Eleusis Ashera had predicted when he had proposed the reconstruction of Za Hara-at, the city in the Korrush where V'ornn and Kundalan might live as equals. The project that had sown the seeds of his murder at the instigation of her own father.

"Still," he said, "if you are concerned about him, then by all means speak with him."

"What would I say?"

A youth in black and silver, coppery skull shiny with sweat, drifted across the balcony, moving somnolently into the reeflike shadows close to the wall. Marethyn's gaze was momentarily diverted from the dancers. The youth wedged his shoulder against the stone wall and lit a laaga stick. He sucked the pungent smoke deep into his lungs.

"If you speak with him, you cannot give anything away."

She nodded.

"Anyway." He took her hand. "Your actions had a greater effect. It is called liberation."

The lights had gone low, the music morphing into something looping and dreamy, a gentle respite, an oasis before the next sandstorm of music tore through the cavern. Sornnn was looking around as if he was expecting to locate someone in this controlled frenzy.

"There is something I want to tell you," he said in her ear. He was still looking about. "It's about my father."

They had not spoken about Sornnn's father since Tettsie's death, but under cover of night he had taken her to meet his mother, whom she adored within minutes. The two of them—Marethyn and Petrre Aurrr—had gone to the deep pools together, scattering Tettsie's ashes into the dark, chill water. Marethyn had yet to summon the strength to open the red-jade box her grandmother had left her. She simply could not bear to touch it; the wound was too raw yet. She needed time to settle into the notion that Tettsie was truly gone.

His lips fluttered against her ear as he spoke. "This is what I thought and held to be true. My father was a superb businessman, but he was removed from the V'ornn thusly: when he met the Korrush tribes, he fell in love with them, their customs, their culture, their view of life. Through them, he learned to love Kundala, and from that moment on he dedicated his life to trying to save it and its inhabitants. He was both a benefactor and a conduit for the Resistance. Now I am beginning to see him from a different perspective."

"Because of your mother."

"Yes, but there's something else," he said. "Tettsie helped me to stop looking at him with a child's adoring eyes. I see him now as he really was. And while I have little doubt that he harbored genuine feeling for the Korrush and its inhabitants, it seems to me that he was primarily motivated by the element of risk. Speaking to my mother, hearing her side of their relationship, many small unexplained quirks and incidents have come into focus." He leaned in, his lips up against the shell of her ear. "You see the logic of it, don't you, a V'ornn addicted to risk beats the independence out of his own wife because, in his own home, the place he comes to sleep at night, he has no tolerance for risk, the seeds of independence she will inevitably sow in his children." He pressed his forehead against the side of her skull and she put her hand to the back of his neck.

He said, "The greater the risk, the harder my father played for it. He simply could not stop himself. And it poisoned his relationship with my mother, in a very real sense destroyed his family, for without her we were surely the poorer."

He drew away for a moment and looked around, not nervous, and yet on a kind of alert, part of him roving the cavernous club in case there was a change, no matter how subtle, in the tenor of the night. The music beat urgently on.

"I think Tettsie knew this," he said. "I think it was what she was trying to tell me—what she wanted to warn me of. She did not want me pursuing you, drawing you into my secret world unless I was absolutely certain of how I felt about you. She did not want what happened to my mother to happen to you."

All at once, she felt the sudden return of her fear. "Sornnn—"

"Let me finish before I lose my nerve altogether." He took her hand. "I have loved you since the moment I first saw you, but if I could not trust you, there was no point in continuing. Do you see? Because of who and what you are. Because you are not like other Tuskugggun, because you are strong and want something more for yourself."

"You see me as strong, and so you imagine me fearless."

"You already know, or I think you do, why Olnnn Rydddlin has kept me in his sights. Shall I not go on?"

"Thank you. For loving me and for trusting me this much." She took hold of his hand. Gazed into his face, already feeling far away from here. "But I don't know. I want you to tell me everything. And yet this very thing makes me short of breath."

He leaned over and kissed her cheek. "You are an artist, Marethyn. Perhaps you should stay an artist."

She put her arms around his neck. "Take me home, Sornnn."

He kissed her then, long and hard with the music's throbbing pulse transmitted from his teeth to hers, and it seemed to last all the way back to her atelier.

In the rear, there was a loft, and above the loft arose a huge skylight. Years ago, when she had bought the atelier, Marethyn had installed a bed and some few furnishings she deemed essential, for she often worked long hours or was struck by inspiration at odd moments. So she often slept here, under the stars. She had always found this space private and romantic but never more so as when she shared it with Sornnn. In fact, on the occasions now when she slept here alone she felt bereft, and longed for him close and warm by her side, breathing soft and evenly, lulling her to sleep.

When, as now, returning from Cthonne, they made love, the space was transformed into a kind of temple, resplendent with glittering stars that appeared to belong just to them. Their passion seemed infinite, their capacity for pleasure expanding exponentially, and when they were finished and lay, drunk with lust and with each other, entangled and moist, Marethyn wept with a joy she could never have imagined.

And their whispered conversation.

"Sornnn."

"Yes."

"Beloved."

"*Wa tarabibi.*"

"Yes. *Wa tarabibi.*"

He laughed to hear her utter the Korrush phrase that was so resonant with meaning.

"Sornnn. I have never been so happy."

He raised himself on one elbow. "And I, *wa tarabibi.*"

They had not spoken again of that other thing, the thought of which made her lose her breath. He respected what she said, the only male ever to do so. And this made her love him all the more.

She held his face between her hands and gazed into his eyes. "And now I cannot sleep." Reluctantly, she let go of him. "I need to paint." As she lit the atelier's lamps, she said, "I will understand if you want to—"

"I will watch you," he said softly. "From here. Until dawn. Until you are finished."

Marethyn kissed him and, without bothering to put on a robe, went naked down to her easel and set out a fresh canvas. She found that she was in the kind of tightly controlled frenzy that presaged hours of intense work. Her hearts beat fast; her mind was on fire. She still felt him in her loins, still heard the insistent music of Cthonne in her inner ear, as if it had lodged there.

The instant she touched pigment to canvas she was engulfed again in Cthonne's sound, vibration, strobing light, a massed energy all attuned to the music's relentless beat, and she knew what it was she needed to re-create with bold strokes and nuances of color.

She listened to the beat remembered in her inner ear, letting it crash over her, become part of her, guide her brushstrokes, so that she was inside the energy stream, the great single-celled creature that pulsed and throbbed to the bone-jarring beat. All the while, she used her special artist's eye to decode the minutiae of detail into intent. She recalled a Kundalan female with her head thrown back, her long hair flying, a V'ornn male with metal eyes and a permanent sneer, dipping and swaying, a Kundalan couple dancing so close they could have been a single entity, a V'ornn couple with their backs to each other, mirroring each other's steps as if by telepathy, a host of others brought into clear and precise focus. And she sensed the strangeness of the palette laid out before her, the essential unease of it, detected these things like fugitive colors hidden beneath a topcoat of pigment.

She did not yet know everything that lay hidden here—this was the genesis, after all, for her seizure of controlled frenzy, the desire to parse out her memory of Cthonne, to depict it and in depicting it deconstruct it into discrete understandable segments—but one sentiment she was certain wasn't anywhere in Cthonne's packed space was a sense of certain defeat. Neither were the unending disappointment, nor betrayals, small and grand, failed hopes that appeared, to a greater or lesser degree, in almost every Kundalan she had met. There was a sense of serenity generated by the music and the energy that beat back the bleakness and despair that was everywhere else on Kundala. She saw it now. It was the promise of oneness, a surcease from the pain the Cosmos inflicted.

She thought of the youth in black and silver getting high on laaga and painted him, crammed in a corner, gaunt and bent as an old V'ornn. Here was the fright and the danger she herself felt so close to now. Living alongside the hope generated inside Cthonne was the sweaty hearts-palpitating pallor of desperation. These youths were on the edge, pushed to their limits by constant dread, a noxious and corrosive by-product of the century of enmity, hatred, brutal acts of war, bitter retaliations, racial slurs, unthinking violence.

And she thought of her original assessment. They were an accident waiting to happen. Possibly. But in the re-created scar of chromium light, she was painting a white-hot spotlight that pierced through flesh and bone to the very core of them, that would illuminate the deep vein of potential power that rippled beneath their brittle, honed, semisuicidal surface.

At firstlight, she broke off painting to make them some star-rose tea and breakfast. She could feel Sornnn's dark intense eyes following her and felt a delicious tingling all through her body. In the cupboard on a shelf by itself, she saw the still-unopened red-jade box Tettsie had left her. She held still, staring at it, her pigment-smeared fingers at her throat, clutching a carved crystal key held on a thin tertium chain. She could hear her own breath soughing in her inner ears. From the time that Tettsie's legacy was made known, she had never taken off this chain, had felt the small weight of the key burning in the valley between her breasts. Sornnn had never once commented upon it, but he liked to kiss it as he kissed and caressed the tops of her breasts. In this way, she realized that it had become part of her.

She felt abruptly, as if she had fallen into a dreamlike stupor. As if with someone else's hands, she reached up and brought the red-jade box down onto the shanstone counter. It seemed to burn her fingers with a cool steady fire.

Dimly, she heard Sornnn calling her name, asking if she was all right. She did not answer. Her fingers trembled as she took the key from around her neck and inserted it into the lock. She turned it and gasped as the box sprang open.

The interior was empty save for a small crystal, snugged into a satin cradle. It took her a moment to recognize it as a data-decagon. She held it in her hand, and before she could think about it inserted it into a data-port.

At once, Tettsie's face sprang to life on the small crystal screen. She was smiling her beautiful crinkled smile. Marethyn's eyes welled up with tears.

"Dearest Marethyn," Tettsie said. "I know you are grieving my death. I cannot stop that, nor would I even if I could. It is part of the natural process of letting go. But, while you grieve you must also celebrate my life."

This statement surprised Marethyn.

"Doubtless, it will surprise you to hear this, since you have been privy to all—well, mostly all—the hardships in my life. And they were grave, I grant you that. But believe me when I tell you that in time I was amply compensated. Now that I am dead I can admit how much it pained me to keep much of my life secret from you. This was not of my own volition; it was an absolute necessity. Ask Sornnn. He knows about such things. Intimately."

There was a brief pause, as if Tettsie had stopped the recording for a moment to gather her thoughts. Marethyn turned, saw that Sornnn had come silently down from the loft. He stood beside Tettsie's remembrance-cloth, watching her.

"You know," she said to him, the idea dawning on her. And she held out her hand. "Come here."

He stood beside her as Tettsie's legacy unspooled.

"I imagine he is there," her grandmother was saying. "Beside you. Holding your hand. He is a good V'ornn, and you possess the intelligence to decide whether or not he is for you. You may wonder how I know so much about him. This, also, is part of my secret life. Do you wish to hear this, darling? Think hard. If you wish me to continue, do nothing. Otherwise, pull the data-decagon now and see that it is completely and utterly destroyed."

A small silence ensued. Acutely slanting sunlight was flooding the atelier. Marethyn imagined she could hear the sun moving, a slow and deliberate creak as of aged bones, as it commenced its foreshortened arc across the sky. She gripped Sornnn's hand.

"So. You have decided," Tettsie said. "Good! Now you will hear everything."

Tettsie's face became more intent, and Marethyn realized that her grandmother was leaning forward.

"During most of my life with your grandfather I was desperately unhappy. For a time, I could only see myself in his image. Much to my horror, I found that I, like all Tuskugggun, had been brainwashed into believing a certain set of basic principles about myself as a female. Then as I told you, I rebelled. But eventually I discovered to my horror that my rebellion was only skin deep. Think how shocked I was, darling! And wounded. And in despair!

"And then, ten years ago, just after your grandfather died, I met someone. It was pure happenstance. We came across each other in the spice market, though we were there for totally different reasons. I had arrived at that place because I was lost and wanted to become more so. She was there on business.

"We began to talk. I suppose in those days I was wearing my despair like a sifeyn. She took me to Spice Jaxx's, where we had a drink. Well, the drink became two, then a meal, then tea. We spent all afternoon talking! What did we talk about? Everything, I suppose. But what was important was her vision of how a Tuskugggun could make the most of her life. How we, as Tuskugggun, could make a difference and in making a difference come to know—really know—who we were.

"It was she who told me how we Tuskugggun are defined by the males. How, through centuries of societal custom, we are taught to be and do and say what the males want us to be and do and say without even being conscious of it!

"And so, darling, my secret life began. And through this Tuskugggun I met Hadinnn SaTrryn, and then Sornnn. Well now, doubtless you are surprised again. I cannot say I blame you. I am certain that you thought you knew me through and through. We all believe that about our loved ones. But it simply isn't true. You never know it all, nor should you.

"I had planned to share this secret with you, my most beloved, when you and Sornnn were wed. If you are listening to this I am already gone. My health was fragile. I knew that. Please forgive me for not telling you. What would have been the point? There was nothing you could do, and you would only have worried."

Tettsie clucked her tongue against the roof of her mouth.

" 'How mysterious my Tettsie is!' I can hear you saying this to yourself. So now I will reveal the mystery. The way I broke free of my chains, the way I learned to live a full and rich life on my own terms was in joining this Tuskugggun and Hadinnn and Sornnn in aiding the Kundalan Resistance. They gave their skill and their cunning. I gave coins, which, thanks to your grandfather, I had in great abundance. I cannot tell you how deeply it pleased me to use his coins to aid the cause of freedom. It may sound simplistic, darling, but the slavery of the Kundalan is our slavery. Their freedom is our freedom. Once you see this, everything becomes so clear and well-defined.

"I realized quite belatedly that I was ashamed of being V'ornn. But better late than never! I found that I could neither condone nor forgive my own race's treatment of other species. I did not agree with its racial policy of world-rape. You see how deeply ingrained the brainwashing is. One does not even consider questioning what has over the millennia become the V'ornn way of life. I came to realize that my own personal despair was masking a greater truth: that I despised myself and my entire race. I did something about that. So can you. But only if you wish it.

"The bulk of my coins remain, as you know, in trust with Dobbro Mannx. Why did I do that, you might ask, instead of willing them to you? There are several reasons. The first is that I want them to go to the Resistance. The second is that having heard my secret, having come this far, you have a decision to make. I want you to continue my work. But it really doesn't matter what I want. Don't let an old Tuskugggun— and a dead one at that—influence your life. You are a highly gifted artist. You hardly need me to tell you that. And art can be enormously fulfilling, no question about it. But is it enough for you, Marethyn? I think I know you. Though I have already gone on record as saying no V'ornn really knows another completely I am old enough—and dead enough!—to indulge myself one last time in this manner.

"Sornnn is there with you now, isn't he? Yes, of course he is. But do not ask him his opinion, darling! When it comes to you, he has his own bias, as you are well aware! And he is a male. A most unusual male, admittedly, but still a male. This must be your decision. Yours alone. If you decide to go ahead, you will take this data-decagon to Dobbro Mannx. I have encrypted it for his data-port. It will give you access to the coins for the purpose already outlined. And Sornnn, well, Sornnn, you will introduce my beloved granddaughter to our mutual friend.

"Marethyn, if you decide to remain an artist, please be so kind as to give the data-decagon to Sornnn. He will decide how and when and by what clandestine means it will assist the Resistance."

Tettsie smiled, looking so much like the Tuskugggun who had taken the girl Marethyn to the deep pools in summer that Marethyn's hearts thudded with joy. "Marethyn, listen to me, I know this is an emotional moment for you. I also know that you tend to overthink decisions—especially ones you deem important. I beg you not to overthink this one. Listen to your hearts, your spirit, and do not be influenced by any V'ornn, including me. There are many ways to remember me. The painting you were doing of me is one such way. If this is your way, all the better for you. I beg you: do not do this for me, for any V'ornn but yourself. You cannot think your way to fulfillment; you must feel it. Come to think of it, it's instinctual, just like painting, so, really, for you it should not be difficult. Either way, I love you. You cannot know in how many ways you have brought me deep and abiding delight!

"Good-bye, my dearest child. I trust that your great and generous spirit will guide you onto the right path. Trust it as I do and you will not go wrong."

Tettsie's smiling image flickered and died.

Tears were streaming down Marethyn's face, and Sornnn put his arm around her, hugging her close. She felt his hearts beating in concert with hers. She heard her grandmother's voice like a prayer in her head. Over Sornnn's sun-warmed shoulder she saw the painting she had been creating. She studied it not with a critical eye for technique or color but to spark her memory of Cthonne. Something—some critical thing—kept drawing her back there.

Don't overthink your decision, Tettsie had warned her. *Use your artist's intuition.* What was the intuition telling her? She loved being an artist. It gave her a freedom and independence few Tuskugggun enjoyed. And yet, she had begun to recognize in herself a certain restlessness, an undeniable feeling that there must be more to life than what she had. And then Sornnn had come into her life, and she had love. But with him there was more than love. Together they had begun a secret life. Yes, it was true. In the clear light of Tettsie's legacy she could see that the moment she agreed to help Sornnn she had begun to be the V'ornn her grandmother hoped she would become. This decision had excited her, yes, but it had also frightened her deeply, which was why she had pushed it away. Because somewhere in the depths of her artist's spirit she had known there was more. She had known that he wanted to share this secret with her. At Cthonne, in the center of the frenzy, her fear had gotten the better of her, and she had pulled back.

Now the revelation had come from the mouth of her dead grandmother. She should have been shocked, stunned, upset. But she was none of those things. Instead, for the first time since she had become uneasy with her life, everything was clear, everything made sense.

Tettsie had been right. It had taken no thought at all. No decision she had ever made seemed so right. It was pure instinct.

She turned in Sornnn's arms and looked up into his face, and said, "Yes. I choose. I, Marethyn Stogggul. I choose yes."

"There can be no going back now, Marethyn."

"I do not want to go back. I do not know what I would do if I did."

She was frightened and exhilarated and very sure of what she was doing. These emotions produced from deep inside her a fleeting tremor in her hands, and she thought of Tettsie and growing old, and she knew that, like her grandmother, when her own time came she wanted to be proud of the life she had lived.

At last she understood why Sornnn had taken her to Cthonne the night before. Here existed a small but functioning model of Eleusis Ashera's dream where V'ornn and Kundalan lived side by side in peace and harmony.

Through her brushstrokes they were born again, all of them, and she saw them as Sornnn saw them, and knew that they, these youths, were also a bomb waiting to be detonated.

23

Take No Prisoners

Kurgan had reluctantly returned to his unutterably boring duties as regent. He found that as time went on he had lost all patience for the niceties of diplomacy and the arcane formalities of protocol. He barked at every V'ornn who crossed his path. He ground his teeth in frustration as he was slowly and inexorably buried beneath a mountain of minutiae.

Small wonder that he took as many breaks as he thought he could get away with, hanging over the balustrade of this balcony or that, sucking thick laaga smoke deep into his lungs. He liked the way it made him expand until he filled the entire palace. He opened his mouth and swallowed the structure whole. This brought a chuckle to his lips.

Often, he felt like killing something and, descending into the interrogation cells the Gyrgon had built beneath the palace, chose a prisoner at random and went to work on him with a lighthearted determination, whistling the hunting song the Old V'ornn had taught him when he was much younger.

The inevitable death, which would come suddenly and too soon, left him feeling emptier than before, and he would take his ire out on the first Haaar-kyut unfortunate enough to cross his path.

Possibly that was why, on this particular day, having grown weary of the drivel collecting around him, he did not visit the interrogation chambers. Instead, he smoked alone on one of the outer balconies that overlooked the crowded street.

He was thinking of Courion, wondering when he would hear from him, when he saw the young Kundalan female. He was certain it was the one he had seen before—from this very balcony, if he was not mistaken. The one he had forcibly taken that long-ago golden afternoon by the stream when Annon was still alive. Their last hunt.

He threw aside the butt of his laaga stick and called for a Haaar-kyut. The young Khagggun appeared instantly, and Kurgan pointed out the female before she could again vanish into the throng.

While the Haaar-kyut gave orders to have her fetched, Kurgan went in and read the latest data-decagon from Rada. He was beginning to wonder at the wisdom of his enlisting her. So far, the intelligence she had sent had been minor. On the other hand, he thought he should be happy at that. Then he came across the item about the Khagggun unrest. This was the second time she had mentioned it. Hadn't he ordered Olnnn Rydddlin to deal with any dissatisfaction among the lower-echelon Khagggun over the suspension of their Great Caste rights? What was the Star-Admiral up to? Certainly he hadn't yet captured Rekkk Hacilar and the Kundalan sorceress Giyan.

He banged a fist on the table so hard a pair of Haaar-kyut sprinted into the chamber, shock-swords drawn. He dismissed them with a back-hand wave.

Damn him to N'Luuura!

He turned at the sound of a voice. Expecting the Haaar-kyut guard with the Kundalan female, he turned, smiling, only to see the Star-Admiral striding out onto the terrace. The full force of his black mood blew like wind in a sail.

He took several strides around Olnnn Rydddlin and sniffed loudly. "What is this I smell? The stench of failure follows you like cor feces."

The Star-Admiral contrived to laugh, but Kurgan could tell that he had inserted a nettle, if only a small one, between the plates of Olnnn's gleaming blue-and-gold armor.

"I am pleased to see you in such a good mood, regent," Olnnn said. "I have, in fact, good news to report."

"You have brought the Rhynnnon's bloody head."

"No, regent."

"The sorceress skcettta Giyan, then?"

"No, regent."

"What, then, would please me?" Kurgan exploded.

"We have in custody the traitor who has been supplying the Resistance."

Kurgan paused, for a moment taken aback. "Really? And who might this traitor be?"

"The Bashkir Bronnn Pallln."

"Now that is interesting." Kurgan tapped his lips with a finger. "I wouldn't have thought . . . but then, why not? My father screwed him royally when he passed him over for Prime Factor. Of course he would have made a mess of the office; surprising he didn't make a mess of this as well."

"In the end, he did, regent."

Kurgan nodded. "And where is the traitor now? Down in one of my interrogation cells, no doubt?"

"No, regent. According to protocol, traitors against the V'ornn Modality are confined in Khagggun prison until they are bound over for the tribunal."

"I do not give a rotten clemett for protocol. I want Bronnn Pallln brought here. I want to interrogate the skcettta myself."

"But, regent. You can't—"

"I can't?" Kurgan shouted. "Since when does my Star-Admiral tell me what I can and cannot do?"

"Regent, I only mean . . . I am thinking of the high command. They will be displeased by this breach of—"

"Stop prattling, Star-Admiral." Kurgan's hand swept in an imperious arc. "Just do as I order."

"Yes, sir!"

"Now off with you. You have your duties to perform."

He grinned as Olnnn turned on his heel. He rubbed his hands together. At last some delicious action! "I cannot wait to begin."

Moments after the Star-Admiral left, the young Haaar-kyut returned with the Kundalan female. That should have pleased Kurgan, but it did not. On closer scrutiny, he saw that she was not the one he had taken down by the stream.

He cursed.

Annon was dead, and the female was lost to him.

He took her anyway, bent over like an animal, in a white-hot fury of motion and emotion. He used his fingernails to draw blood. She made no sound beneath him, not even a whimper, and this infuriated him all the more. His fingers were wound in her thick hair. Images of Courion and Nith Batoxxx danced in his head. He closed his eyes in an attempt to bring back that sun-dappled afternoon, the sight of the female that had so quickened his pulse.

He pretended with this imitation, bucking against her and grunting out his fantasy.

She was better than nothing. But still, when it was over, he had her thrown away like a loaf of stale wrybread because if it wasn't the real thing, he never wanted to see that face again.

The stench of death rose to bring the blackcrows in anxious flocks. Like all carrion birds, they were, despite their size, exceedingly skittish, bright gold eyes trying to look everywhere at once. With each small sound they rose in a blood-flecked cloud, only to settle again upon ridges of bleached bone and rotting flesh.

The leading edge of Attack-Commandant Blled's scouting party appeared, first one and then another, breaking cover, advancing in a semicrouch, covering the distance between the tree line and the perimeter of the mass grave silently and efficiently. Then Attack-Commandant Blled himself appeared, flanked by two more Khagggun.

"This is as far as they could have come," Attack-Commandant Blled said, checking a wrist readout. "If one or both of them are still alive." At his hand signal three Khagggun fanned out, beating the underbrush.

His communications officer began to receive a narrow-band photon burst. "There is still not one shred of evidence that anyone escaped the blast," he informed his superior. "And they have found more pieces of the Rhynnnon's armor at the wreck site, enough so they have more or less reconstructed the entire suit."

As his Khagggun had done, Attack-Commandant Blled walked all around the perimeter of the reeking pit. His Khagggun returned from their recon with negative results. Another hand signal and two Khagggun descended into the nauseating quagmire of the death pit. One of them began almost immediately to retch. His eyes tearing up, he fumbled his way back to the edge and began to climb out.

Attack-Commandant Blled said, "Get back in there, Third-Captain, and do your duty."

"With all due respect, sir," the Third-Captain said, "why are we wasting time looking for ghosts?"

At once, Attack-Commandant Blled went over and, with an almost nonchalant swipe of his shock-sword, severed the Third-Captain's head from his shoulders. The corpse danced a little jig before Attack-Commandant Blled kicked it on the shoulder, sending it toppling onto the oozing mound of Kundalan corpses.

"Any other questions need answering?"

Not one Khagggun said a word, but when Attack-Commandant Blled gave a hand sign another Third-Captain at once jumped into the pit.

The blackcrows screamed and lifted, so disturbing the Khagggun that they fired off several rounds from their handheld ion cannons before Attack-Commandant Blled ordered them to stand down. They ignored the unbelievable stench, the watering of their eyes, as they used their shock-swords to spear downward randomly into the morass. They held their breath as they picked their way through the pit. When they met at the far side they were gasping, and they scrambled up the slippery side of the grave, silently cursing N'Luuura as they at last regained firm ground. Their comrades gave them a wide berth, and there was a bit of good-natured ribbing at their expense.

Attack-Commandant Blled frowned, then nodded. "All right then."

And with a last look around he gestured, and they crept backward, reinfiltrating the forest whence they had emerged.

Silence returned to the pit of death, and the blackcrows once more settled, tearing ravenously at their own felled comrades along with the outsize, two-legged creatures on which they had been feasting for weeks.

One of the blackcrows, larger and more aggressive than the others, unearthed yet another layer of rotting dead. As others of its kind flocked to its discovery, it shrieked, slashing with its cruel beak until fear over-whelmed gluttony and they gave way, returning sullenly to the picked-over mounds, where they contented themselves with worrying the tough remnants of tendons off the ends of bones.

The blackcrow dug deeper, gorging itself on half-rotted flesh, all the while keeping its suspicious golden eyes upon its brethren to ensure that they maintained their distance. Doubtless it was this inattention that caused it to miss the sudden movement beneath it. The ion-dagger point pierced its breast, spitting the bird entirely in the instant before it could take flight. Its wings spread, trembling and quivering in spastic response, but the gold had fled its eyes; it was already dead.

Its brethren paused in their meal and fell upon it wholeheartedly when its huge black carcass came hurtling down among them.

Rekkk raised his head out of the center of the stinking quagmire, said, "N'Luuura take these blackcrows." He took a quick but thorough reconnaissance, then, reaching down, pulled Eleana, slithering, through the gelatinous muck. She was still clutching the hollow communicator sheath, used by Khagggun for photonic transmissions, that Rekkk had fashioned into breathing tubes for them.

"It worked," he said with some satisfaction. "They're gone."

Eleana led them to a small rill some three hundred meters northeast running swiftly through a gap in moss-covered rocks. There, they squatted and, as best they could, washed off the stench of death. Where the Teyj had gone they could not say. They were too exhausted to keep going. While Eleana foraged for edible mushrooms and ferns Rekkk searched out a suitable spot to spend what was left of the night. He found a cave, shallow but dry, in the shank of the massif that continued its rough, dizzying ascent all the way, it appeared, to Stone Border. Its only drawback was that it overlooked the death pit, which glowed eerily in the incandescent moonslight.

They dared not light a fire, so they ate the food Eleana brought back cold and raw. The taste was only marginally palatable, but at least the gnawing in their stomachs was somewhat assuaged. Rekkk volunteered to take the first watch, but as Eleana curled up against his back she felt wide awake.

"We are close to Stone Border," she said, "but the last few kilometers are the steepest."

Rekkk looked up into the heart of the massif. "There lies the Abbey of Floating White. And within it Konara Urdma, the traitor who is responsible for all those lost Resistance lives. We are the only ones who know her identity. We have to get to the abbey and neutralize her."

"Have you thought about how we'll gain entrance?"

He touched her swollen belly. "They will not refuse you, Eleana."

"You know, that just might work," she said. "Just as long as you don't frighten them to death."

24

The Collapse of Memory

Perrnodt's legs were already in sunlight when Riane returned to the dune. She took the dzuoko over her shoulder and carried her to the other side, where the shadows were already beginning to pool. She stretched her parallel to the dune so all of her was within the narrow band of shadow. As soon as she did so, Perrnodt's eyes fluttered open.

Riane collapsed to her knees, slowly gave Perrnodt some water, then drank some herself.

"Are you all right?" she asked. "You passed out almost as soon as I got you through the Gyrgon's ion field."

Perrnodt nodded and asked for more water.

Riane watched her drink. She was clothed in the blue-and-white-striped robes of one of the dead Jeni Cerii. It was blood stained and ripped where her dagger had punctured it on the side, but wearable. The same could not be said for the other robe, which had been shredded by the infinity-blade.

The weapon's abrupt resurgence had been much on her mind when she retrieved her dagger from its sandy grave, and all during the long and lonely walk back. When she had shed her filthy Ghorvish robes she had discovered the stone Mu-Awwul had given her engraved with the sign of the fulkaan. It had lain, forgotten, in the same pocket where she had placed the infinity-blade, and that had set her to wondering. She had placed the stone next to the infinity-blade. As it had drawn near she felt a kind of magnetic pull. When the stone touched the edge of the infinity-blade it began to pulse.

What was it that Mu-Awwul had told her when he had given her the stone? *Power and jjhani flow from the image of the fulkaan.*

At the time, she had imagined his words to be figurative. After all, he had given her a talisman of Jiharre, a symbol of good luck, of—in his word, *jjhani*—spiritual harvest. But now she saw that he had meant it quite literally. There was a power in the stone, strong enough to reactivate the infinity-blade. How this power could be compatible with the weapon was a complete mystery, one she meant to clear up with him as soon as she was able.

"I am feeling better," Perrnodt said, sighing. "But I am starving. I do not suppose you have food, as well?"

When Riane produced some dried meat from the satchel she had taken off the dead Jeni Cerii, Perrnodt said, "Judging by how you are dressed, you must have come across a Jeni Cerii raiding party."

As they ate, Riane told her of the Jeni Cerii camp. Then she recounted the recent history.

"I know you are Ramahan," Riane said. "I was told you know the location of the sanctuary where the *Maasra* is hidden."

Perrnodt eyed her suspiciously. "So much dangerous knowledge for one so young. And you have killed a sauromician and a Gyrgon, you say?"

"The remains of Nith Settt lie over there," Riane said, pointing. "The sauromician died near the kapudaan's palace in Agachire."

Perrnodt turned in that direction and sat very still. For a moment, nothing happened. Then Riane felt a kind of tremor as of the earth moving, but the earth was not moving. She saw Perrnodt's eyes roll up in her head and she knew what this tremor was. Perrnodt had parted the air. She was moving—or, rather, part of her was. She was not Thripping. This was something else altogether.

In a moment, the tremor had subsided, Perrnodt's eyes had returned to normal. "Yes," she said. "Nith Settt is, indeed, dead."

By the way she said this, Riane understood. "You believe I may be an agent of the Gyrgon."

"This Gyrgon—the one who was sent here—it is strange with him." She had a curious lilt to her voice, almost as if she were singing her words. "He knew of the *Maasra*'s existence. How? He wanted to get his hands on it. Why? Before this, the Gyrgon have never exhibited the slightest interest in the Prophesies or the lore of the Ramahan."

Riane, thinking of Nith Sahor, knew that to be not quite true. But then Nith Sahor was an anomaly among Gyrgon. All at once something struck her. She said, "The Veil of a Thousand Tears appears in Prophesy?"

"More than once," Perrnodt said. "It is written that the Dar Sala-at will claim the *Maasra*. It will be lost and rewon in bloody battle. In the process, the Dar Sala-at will be betrayed."

Riane felt her heart thudding in her breast. It was eerie hearing her own future spoken aloud as if it were already history. Did this mean that she no longer had free will? Which of her choices—because life, hers above all others, perhaps, was composed of crucial choices—would lead to this particular fate? Could she not find a way to keep the *Maasra* from being lost? Could she not maneuver so as to avoid this bloody war? What was the point of power, of being the Dar Sala-at, if her path was already set in stone?

And then another, more immediate, consequence hit her. *It is written in Prophesy that of the Dar Sala-at's allies one will love her, one will betray her, one will try to destroy her,* Giyan had warned her. Now Perrnodt had echoed that warning.

"What precisely are these Prophesies I keep hearing about? Is there a book, or a series of books that have been translated or interpreted by the Ramahan?"

Perrnodt produced a wan smile. "You have told me that you were trained at the Abbey of Floating White. But you are young yet, a novice. The Prophesies are for—"

"I am not simply a Ramahan novice," Riane said. "I am the Dar Sala-at."

Perrnodt neither exclaimed in wonder nor burst out laughing. She seemed to absorb this revelation with a degree of skepticism. Riane recalled Giyan telling her that even among the Ramahan there would be a fair amount of doubt because she was female, that there would be naysayers. She fervently hoped Perrnodt would not be among them.

"I must admit, that is quite a claim," Perrnodt said at last.

"It would explain how I was able to kill the sauromician and the Gyrgon, would it not?" Riane said cannily.

"Yes, that is a possible explanation," Perrnodt acknowledged. "On the other hand, you could simply be clever."

"In your time at the abbey did you ever know a novice clever enough to defeat such enemies?"

Perrnodt said nothing.

"One who could Thripp?"

"Actually, no." She smiled. "But I very much doubt you can, either."

"At the moment, you're right." Riane touched the mole beneath her right ear. "But take a look at this."

Perrnodt hesitated for an instant before leaning over. Riane turned her head to give her a better look. Perrnodt gave a tiny indrawn breath.

"You know what this is," Riane said. "My Gift was hidden for safe-keeping while I was in the Korrush."

"A wise decision." Two of Perrnodt's fingers were pressed against Riane's neck. "Who made it for you?"

"A sefiror named Minnum."

Perrnodt drew back as if stung. "Is that what that imp told you, that he was a sefiror?"

Riane nodded. "He's not?"

"He has taken a Venca word and—"

"I know what it means," Riane said. "Sefiror is one of a mystical community."

"Well. The novice knows a Venca word."

"I know more than a word," Riane said.

"It is impossible for a novice to have learned the Root Tongue," Perrnodt said in Venca.

"And yet I can speak Venca fluently," Riane replied in the same language.

Now Perrnodt did react. "Dear Miina!" she cried. "Everything you have told me is the truth. But the Dar Sala-at a female . . ." She shook her head. Still not quite believing it was so.

"You must tell me about Minnum," Riane said. "I believed him. I trusted him to lock away my Gift."

"First things first." Perrnodt beckoned. "Come just a bit closer."

When Riane had rearranged herself, Perrnodt put both hands on Riane. Riane felt a coolness seep through her. Perrnodt touched the false mole, and at once all her Osoru knowledge exploded in her mind like fireworks. She gasped, trembling a little with the delicate force of it.

"The power inside you—" Perrnodt sat back, shook her head. "One thing about Minnum, he does meticulous work."

"If he is not a sefiror—"

"Minnum is not a sefiror."

"What is he then? He said he was the last of his kind left alive."

Perrnodt laughed. "Would that it were so! But, alas, no. There are others of his kind secreted about. You yourself told me about one."

"I did?"

Perrnodt nodded. "Minnum is a sauromician."

"He is a male sorcerer," Riane said. "He was able to encapsulate my Gift, so I know he wasn't lying about that."

"But he was lying about almost everything else. Oh, do not blame him, my dear. He cannot help himself. His lying is a curse, part of his punishment."

"He told me Miina was punishing him for his sins."

"He did?" Perrnodt was clearly surprised. "Now that is interesting. I imagine it cost him a great deal to tell you that truth."

"And he told me to seek you out."

"Minnum did that?"

"He must have known that you would tell me the truth about him."

"That means he believes you are who you say you are."

"But he is not sefiror?"

"No. In every way imaginable sauromicians and sefiror are separate. For one thing, sauromicians are male while sefiror are both male and female. For another, the two employ an entirely different mode of sorcery. Sauromicians use a sorcery that is an offshoot—a corruption, really—of Kyofu. I say corruption because it is necromancy. This is impure. It involves killing and using the dead bodies as the basis for sorcery. They allowed other influences to create a kind of amalgam that they believe is more powerful than either Osoru or Kyofu."

"Is it more powerful?"

"I do not know. What I do know is that it is unholy. And being unholy, they cannot cleave to the power bourns that crisscross beneath the surface of Kundala. In fact, contact with the bourns will kill a sauromician. The sefiror, on the other hand, practice a sorcery that is based in part on the bourns. It is as pure as it is ancient. It is the twining of Osoru and Kyofu."

"It is called Qadi'ir."

"Yes. It is Eye Window. But there is another, more fundamental difference between sauromicians and sefiror," Perrnodt said. "Sefiror are Druuge." She looked hard at Riane. "Do you know of the Druuge, child?"

"Oh, yes. I have encountered them." And Riane told her how she had come upon a trio of the holy nomads in Middle Seat, how they had saved her from three aggressive Khagggun by chanting, by using her Third Eye to pull her into the Channel, as a lens to focus their sorcery—the magic of words.

"Great Goddess Miina!" Perrnodt breathed as she kissed the back of Riane's hand. "Now I see why Minnum believes. You truly are the Dar Sala-at."

Now Riane recognized the singsong lilt, she knew why Perrnodt was fluent in Venca.

"You are Druuge, Perrnodt!" she whispered fiercely. "You are Druuge!"

Pack-Commander Cooolm was in charge of the traitor Bronnn Pallln. The prisoner sat in two sets of ion chains, in the Khagggun thick-walled prison on Grey Vapor Street. It was not an assignment he found in the least palatable, but he could not work himself up into the requisite peak of ire. He knew his compatriots were off hunting down Kundalan Resistance cells while he was stuck herding a fat and traitorous Bashkir. He found he did not care.

He was no longer a young V'ornn in the full flower of his youth. He was battle-scarred; his once-vaunted viciousness melted into a weary indifference that only sporadically disgusted him. Lately, he had taken to frequenting a succession of Looorm in a bleak ggley-chain of nights whose sole purpose lay in the obliteration of memory. There were those comrades who believed Kundala was the end of the line, that the Gyrgon, having sunk into a haze of inaction and rueful reverie, would never give the order to leave. Pack-Commander Cooolm, having himself fallen into a similar stupor, provided no opinion on the hotly debated topic. However, he was aware enough to mark the increasing ferocity and repetition of this debate among the packs. One could almost call it an obsession. Better by far to keep these ruminations to himself, for if the rumors proved to be the case, he suspected that they had all fallen very far indeed from the moment, just over a hundred years ago, when they had first set their colonizing boots on Kundala.

He tuned out the prisoner's constant yabbering, looked upon him with contempt. Yet he received little pleasure in contemplating the excruciating pain of the forthcoming interrogation because he would have no hand in it. He was a mere guard, a lowly job a Third-Marshal could have handled. Not that he minded; he was tired from a lengthy evening excursion. Besides, he was Khagggun; his duty was to obey. His orders had come from Line-General Lokck Werrrent himself, and Cooolm was resigned to completing this wretched task without a hitch.

Doubtless, this was why he felt a sense of foreboding when he saw the fearsome Star-Admiral Olnnn Rydddlin approaching with his escort. Pack-Commander Cooolm ordered his Khagggun to attention. He barked at one of his pack to shut the prisoner up once and for all. He had had enough of his mewling protestations of innocence to last him a lifetime. Besides, he had no intention of allowing the Star-Admiral to be subjected to the foul cacophony.

Cooolm licked his lips. Why was the Star-Admiral here? Had he, Cooolm, done something wrong? He noticed that the Star-Admiral carried with him no bodyguard. Rather, and even more shockingly, he was accompanied by a Tuskugggun clad in a uniform sporting the Star-Admiral's own blue-and-gold colors!

"Pack-Commander, good day," the Star-Admiral said. "I am here to interrogate the prisoner myself."

Pack-Commander Cooolm, still staring openly at the Tuskugggun, was so taken aback that he was quite literally at a loss for words.

"You will allow me access at once," the Star-Admiral ordered, with a distinct edge to his voice. "And then you and your Khagggun will clear the area."

"Sir?"

"This interrogation is strictly classified."

"Yes, sir." Pack-Commander Cooolm snapped to attention. "At once, sir." At his hand signal, a member of his pack opened the door to Bronnn Pallln's cell. The Khagggun who had been in with the prisoner stepped out.

"Pack-Commander, your jaw is hanging open," the Star-Admiral said shortly. "Is there a problem? Do you require a Genomatekk?"

"No, sir. Not a bit," he yelped, deeply consternated. "But, sir. There is a Tuskugggun . . . I mean to say, she will be with you when you—"

"This is my staff-adjutant."

"I am not . . ." Cooolm gulped, but some perverse emotion caused him to persevere. "I am not familiar with that position, Star-Admiral."

"From now on see that you are better informed," Olnnn snapped, stepping smartly into the cell. "What is your name?" he added darkly.

"Pack-Commander Dorrt Cooolm, sir. Yes, sir. I will."

"Until further notice you are relieved of your command, Pack-Commander Dorrt Cooolm. Report to the western supply adjutant for immediate reassignment. Since you seem overly stressed, perhaps you will find transferring materiel more suited to your temperament."

"Yes, sir. Thank you, sir." Cooolm was now on the Star-Admiral's N'Luuura list. And in front of his entire pack. What must they think of him? He cursed his stupid mouth. Well, at least he hadn't been demoted. He bit his tongue so he would not further add to his misery. But, really, a Tuskugggun in Khagggun uniform. The sight made him want to vomit. Or murder the first Kundalan who crossed his path. And he could see from the look on every one of his pack that they were feeling precisely the same thing.

I know that look," Rada said to Olnnn as Cooolm and his pack of Khagggun moved out. "They have murder in their hearts."

"You had best get used to it. You will be seeing a lot of it in the days and weeks to come," he said. "Why worry about it? We Khagggun always have murder in our hearts; sometimes it seems to me we were all born that way. We are warriors. Think of it as an indispensable trait."

She laughed harshly.

He eyed her. "Come to think of it, though, we should get you armed and dangerous. I would not care to see you hurt in a brawl."

"I have broken up my share of brawls, Star-Admiral."

"Still. You are at my side. You require more appropriate garb."

She glanced over at the cowering Bronnn Pallln. "I had better take the gag out of his mouth."

"Why would you want to do that?"

She regarded him with some curiosity. "You did tell the Pack-Commander that you wanted to interrogate him."

"If you take the gag out of his mouth," Olnnn said, "he will only scream."

At this comment, Bronnn Pallln's already pale face turned ashen and, indeed, he began to scream behind his gag.

"That smell!" Rada pushed herself away from him. "Star-Admiral, he has soiled himself."

Without a word, Olnnn took Bronnn Pallln by the scruff of the neck and hustled him to the far end of the cell. When he saw Rada coming after him, he told her to stay at the door and make certain they remained undisturbed.

"What are you going to do?" she asked with no little suspicion.

"Just do as you are told," he barked at her.

Then he whirled and, with his back to her, hissed at Bronnn Pallln, "You bumbled everything, you Bashkir skcettta."

He hit Bronnn Pallln full in the face. The Bashkir stumbled back against the wall, his eyes fairly bugged out in abject terror. The Bashkir's knees abruptly buckled, and Olnnn was obliged to hold him on his feet.

"If becoming Great Caste means I have to be anything like you, then here and now I renounce it all."

The silent scream that clogged Bronnn Pallln's throat was cut short as Olnnn slammed the back of his head repeatedly against the wall. As blood spurted, he stepped briskly away, turning just in time to see Rada hustling toward him.

"I think the prisoner failed his first interrogation."

"You . . . you killed him. Murdered. Just like that." She was almost apoplectic. "How could you?"

He held her back from trying to help Bronnn Pallln, who with every progressively more labored beat of his hearts slid farther down the wall until all that was left was a wide smear of turquoise blood that dripped onto the top of his sweat-sheened head.

She made to strike him, and he stopped her. "First," he said, "in these matters you must learn not to gainsay me. Second, this Bashkir was a traitor to the V'ornn Modality. Evidence came to light that he was the leader of a conspiracy to sell arms to the Kundalan Resistance." Seeing the look of unrelieved hatred in her eyes, he began to shake her a little. "Third, and most importantly, he was in possession of knowledge that could compromise me with the regent."

"So you murdered him."

"I could not have him talking to the regent," he said at a low and savage pitch. "I induced this skcettta to find a way to ruin Sornnn SaTrryn, who is currently in the regent's favor. Somehow, he ended up implicating himself. Do you understand now? If the regent got his hands on him everything would have been put in jeopardy. *Everything*."

The stench of death hung heavy in the cell, enveloping them. Bronnn

Pallln seemed to stare at her out of bloodshot eyes with a mixture of accusation and shock.

She closed her eyes and, seeing him still, trembled a little. And Olnnn said in a gentle, almost tender tone, "You see, it is not so easy being a warrior."

25

How the Narbuck Is Born

The wind soughed fitfully through the Marre pines. All around them there were small stirrings. A trio of marc-beetles, large and black and glossy, marched across the needles no more than a meter from where they sat.

"Lying there still as death in that grave I was put in mind of my grandfather," she said. "Funny. I haven't thought of him in many years. It has been so long since I saw him, I can no longer remember what he looked like."

Wrapped tightly in her cloak, she settled more comfortably against him. "He used to take me for walks. I was very little. He'd put me on his shoulders. My legs dangled on his chest. His strong hands held me in place. He used to tickle the soles of my bare feet. Oh, Miina, help me to remember his face!"

"Tell me more about him," Rekkk said gently.

"I haven't forgotten his big square hands, ropey with veins," she said. "I can feel their strength now, as he grasped my ankles. He would take me to the deepest heart of the forest, where everyone else was afraid to go. Leaf-green and misty golden sunlight. Birds calling. Insects whirring by my face. And I was never frightened. Isn't that strange? But then, perhaps not. My grandfather, he made me feel safe." She sighed, overtaken by memory. "When we were deep inside the forest he would turn me in a slow circle, and say, 'I feel the world around me and this is good because then I remember the past fully and completely and I can see in my mind's eye how it was before.'"

Rekkk stirred. "Before we V'ornn came."

"Yes," she said very softly. "He always began the same way, used exactly the same words, as if it was a kind of ritual. As if it was his job to pass history on to me so that future generations who—"

Silence.

Rekkk looked out over the pitiless place of the dead. "Go on. It's all right."

Eleana could feel the baby breathing and Rekkk breathing as if they were all part of the same organism. "That future generations born and bred under V'ornn rule would remember what Kundala once was. And could be again."

He put his arms around her, and whispered, "Will you do something for me? I want to pretend that your grandfather is still alive, that just this once he has taken me into the depths of the forest with you, that he will tell me what it was like here once upon a time."

Eleana closed her eyes and willed herself to conjure up her grandfather, a big, sun-browned Kundalan who had lived his whole life out of doors. He had a large hooked nose, she recalled that clearly enough, and a generous mouth and laughing eyes, but somehow she could not put these parts together into a whole, and her heart ached. "He told me many tales of the Great Goddess Miina and the sorcerous creatures that once roamed the flanks of the Djenn Marre. But of all of Miina's creatures my favorite was the narbuck."

"What is a narbuck?"

"Ah, well." Her voice had turned dreamy. "Imagine a pure black cthauros, imagine him three times a cthauros' normal size, imagine he has six legs, white hooves, a long, curving neck, a proud head with expressive liquid eyes. Now imagine further that on the thick helmlike ridge of bone between those eyes rises a tapering spiral horn, straight as an arrow, white and glistening as moonlight, fully two meters long."

"Did these narbuck really exist?"

"Once upon a time," she whispered. "So my grandfather told me, and he never lied or even exaggerated. It would have gone against his idea of history, which was to him a holy thing."

"What did he tell you about them?"

Wind eddied in the cave mouth, stirred the long-branched kuello-firs. The shadows of the dancing boughs made it seem as if the dead, skeletal, half-eaten, were stirring.

"You don't want to tell a V'ornn?"

"No, Rekkk. You of all V'ornn should hear this." She shook her head. "It's just that, well, I'm realizing that I've never told anyone before."

He reached around her. "And now you will have your baby to tell.

So his past—the history of his world—will be as alive for him as his present will be."

She gazed out onto the stinking pit, a raw scar of the bitter present she fervently wished to keep from her son.

"As a V'ornn, I know the power and importance of the past only by its absence," Rekkk said. "The V'ornn have no past that is chronicled or fully remembered, no history of our homeworld survived. Radiation from the cataclysm that compelled our great leap into the Cosmos seeped into our core matrix. It took us some time to realize that our history was eroding, that every day we were losing more of it. Desperately, we tried to retrieve what was lost. To no avail. What remained were fragments which, we discovered, cannot be trusted. Once inside our data-matrix, the radiation evolved into a kind of virus, altering the matrix-code. Ever since that time we have been orphans, wanderers."

"Conquerors, despoilers. You take away from others what you yourselves have lost."

"I don't believe I ever thought of it quite that way," he said. "But I have no defense."

"The warrior lives within me still, I see."

"What did you imagine?"

"That motherhood would take . . . That having the baby would change me forever."

"Why worry about nothing? You are already changed from the Resistance leader Giyan and I contacted months ago."

She looked at him. "And you, Rekkk, you are changed most of all."

"V'ornn are not supposed to change."

"That is what I am saying."

He smiled a faraway smile and kissed her on the cheek. "Will you grant my request? I do so want to hear about the narbuck."

Turning, she grooved her back against his chest, returning to her contemplation of the moonslit night. Safe against his beating hearts, she marveled at this present which, even a few short months ago, she could never have imagined. "My grandfather loved the forests of the highlands where he was born and lived his whole life. Even as a boy no older than I am he preferred them to the company of other Kundalan. He would take the bow and arrows he'd fashioned himself and spend days alone in the forest, teaching himself the lore of the land.

He never thought about survival; the forest was his temple. He often told me he imagined that it had been made especially for him.

"Anyway, on the morning of his fifteenth birthday he was far to the north, hiking along a treacherous and enthralling ridge when he saw the narbuck. Not that he knew what it was. How could he? It had no horn. But it was big and so white as to seem colorless. It walked along the ridge on its six legs as delicately as if it were a dancer. And there was something about the animal, some aura or magnetism or what-have-you that he could not define but which, later on in life, when he told me the story, he knew was sacred.

"And of course he was right, for the narbuck is one of Miina's creatures, the original pair cast from The Pearl during the creation of Kundala itself."

"This narbuck he saw," Rekkk said thoughtfully. "Why did it have no horn?"

"I'm getting to that."

Rekkk looked over her head to the tops of the kuello-firs, where a crowned owl, its long brindled wings tucked tight around it, perched on the end of a swaying branch, staring at him, at the death pit, at everything at once, in that vaguely unsettling way owls have.

"So whatever this thing was—this holiness—took my grandfather by the heart and compelled him to follow the narbuck. That was not as easy as it sounds, for the ridge was partially composed of friable rock. Time and again my grandfather's boots went out from under him as small sheets of rock sheared off. But each time it happened, he learned something more about the nature of the ridge, which was a living thing, he would tell me.

"And my grandfather, he had no thought to stop or to turn back but only to go on, because it seemed very important to see where it was the narbuck would end up. He did not know where this conviction came from; he merely acquiesced to it, as a boy, floating in summertime, allows the current of a river to carry him where it will."

The crowned owl swiveled its head; something had caught its attention. Its huge pale eyes reflected the moonlight for just a moment, turning them eerily translucent.

"So now morning had melted into afternoon and afternoon had merged into twilight, and still he followed the narbuck over the monstrous snaking ridge. They had been climbing, mostly gradually, but even so, after all those hours, my grandfather was higher up in the Djenn Marre than he had ever been before. The weather had turned, and he could see dark clouds that earlier had lain sleeping far to the north, snugged behind the towering massif of the Djenn Marre, closer then, roiling in the newly gusting wind. And for the first time a spark of fear crossed my grandfather's mind at the thought of being caught out on this ridge in the coming storm.

"It was too late to turn back. All he could do is to follow the narbuck and pray to Miina that it would lead him to safety. That was the moment when he heard the first crack of thunder, booming across the plunging ravines on either side of the ridge. He felt the pressure plummeting, and he knew that the storm would be severe."

In an instant, the crowned owl's mighty wings unfurled, and it leapt off the branch, sailing silently through the night. Rekkk lost it for a moment as it dipped down, banking. Nothing but the wind soughing through the kuello-firs. Then it reappeared in a wholly different place, something struggling in its beak.

"Light was getting to be a problem, then the first of the rain hit him full in the face. The force of it, borne by the brunt of the swirling wind, nearly unseated him from his precarious perch, and he struggled a little, arms flailing. As he regained his balance, he noticed that the narbuck had stopped. It stood still, its head turned a little. It looked to my grandfather as if it was waiting.

"Clinging to the wet, slippery rock with boot soles and hands, he made his way toward the narbuck. Thunder boomed, louder this time, the sound displacing the air, making his eardrums hurt. As soon as he was a handbreadth away from the narbuck's flank it started up, its hooves *clip-clopping* across the friable rock without disturbing so much as a tiny shard. My grandfather saw this and decided to walk in the places the narbuck had trodden.

"The rain had picked up, and the wind as well. Thunder ripped through the clouds, which seemed no more than a meter or two above his head. And just when it appeared as if the storm would blow them both off the ridge, the narbuck led him off to the left, down a steep and narrow path, impossible to find, my grandfather would later swear to me, even in daylight.

"For twenty minutes or more they descended at a harrowing angle. My grandfather was like one blinded. In the pitch-darkness he put one hand on the narbuck's flank, allowing it to guide him. And then, all at once, they were off the ridge. My grandfather felt level ground beneath his boot soles, and he smelled wet rock, a ton of it rising steeply on both sides, and wind ripping down a narrow space, ruffling his hair, tingling his scalp. He felt the weight of the rock towers pressing in on both sides and he knew that they were passing through a gargantuan defile in the rock face."

The crowned owl, back in moonlight, had folded its wings, alighting on a branch significantly closer to the cave mouth. It seemed to stare right at Rekkk as it quickly broke the back of its dinner. Then, efficiently and fastidiously, it devoured the small mammal, bones, fur, and all.

"Just past the defile, my grandfather sensed the rock retreating. The rain pelted down and by the way the raging wind swirled, he believed they were in a large open bowl-like clearing. The narbuck had stopped, and this time there was a finality to the lack of movement that told my grandfather that the sacred animal had reached its destination. Thunder crashed, the boom hollowing out the bowl, defining the shape and size more clearly. It was vast, far bigger than my grandfather had imagined, and he found himself for a moment wondering how so large an open space could exist within the bosom of the mountain range.

"Then the narbuck snorted and raised its head, and my grandfather had the sense to back away. Not far but not so near, anyway. The thunder had become a constant thing, so deafening the ground trembled, and my grandfather clapped his hands over his ears, which did no good at all.

"And then, the clouds directly above them were lit up as if from the inside and for an instant the natural arena into which the narbuck had led him was revealed to him and all the breath went out of him for the size was beyond comprehension and my grandfather knew there could be but one explanation. He had been led into a holy place carved by Miina Herself into the Djenn Marre.

"And then there was no more time for thought because the blinding light, the arterial energy of the storm, lanced down and struck the narbuck between the eyes. The animal bellowed, louder than the thunder itself, as it was driven to its knees. It crouched there, quivering, altogether silent. It was no longer white, but black as deepest night, as if in that instant it had been cindered. My grandfather wondered if it was dead, and his heart began to shrivel at the thought so that he was compelled to run to its side, to stroke its wet and heated flank. And at his touch, its head came around on its long curving beautiful neck and he saw the horn, driven there by the lightning or possibly it was the bolt of lightning itself, made solid and manifest by the unseen hand of the Great Goddess.

"And for a moment my grandfather did not know whether he himself was alive or dead, whether he was really inside this numinous bowl or whether he was back on the ridge, mortally wounded by the storm, dreaming this fever dream as life slipped away. And then the most extraordinary thing on this most extraordinary of nights happened. The narbuck lowered its head so that the horn was tipped toward him. Rain curled down its tight-spiraled side; the edges appeared sharp as knife blades, they glittered as if embedded with faceted jewels. Nevertheless, because it was what the narbuck wanted, because he knows that it was why he was brought here, my grandfather reached out a trembling hand and grasped the horn. And in that instant he saw the shining magnificent face of Miina."

The crowned owl was gone, vanished into the night sometime while Rekkk's mind was reliving the creation of the narbuck. He watched the tips of the kuello-firs nodding in a kind of metronomic rhythm. His mind was alight with the story Eleana had just related, but it was also filled with the afterimage of the owl. He knew, because Giyan had told him, that the crowned owl was Miina's messenger. Often, it brought answers to difficult questions, but just as often it was the harbinger of violent death.

Rekkk said, "There has been no lightning on Kundala in all the time we have been here."

"And so the narbuck stopped being born."

"Why?"

"V'ornn destroy. It is in your blood. Miina would not allow you to kill the sacred narbuck."

"And yet this Great Goddess of yours allows us to murder Her children."

"You know why," Eleana said. "We were disobedient. The Ramahan usurped power, tried to gain control of The Pearl for their own selfish ends. For this blasphemy She has cast us into the pit, where we cannot get the stench of our own death out of our nostrils."

"What will end this cycle?" Rekkk asked. "How will the Kundalan find Her favor again?"

"You know that too," Eleana said. Her soft breath misted from between her lips. "Prophesy says the coming of the Dar Sala-at is the beginning of the Great Transformation."

Vapor hung off the trees branches, rose like smoke from the death pit. Rekkk wondered where the crowned owl had gone. Was it hunting in the shadows or had it returned to Miina's side?

"And what about me?" he said. "What will happen to the V'ornn if your Prophesy proves correct?"

"Who can say?" Eleana shrugged. "I doubt if even Lady Giyan knows."

Shadows lengthened, deepened in the waning of the afternoon. Riane was impatient to begin the next phase of her journey, but so near to the Jeni Cerii encampment she knew they dare not travel in daylight. Besides, their ordeals had left them depleted. So they sat at the base of the dune, ate and drank, regaining their strength.

"Giyan," Perrnodt said. "I have not heard her name in so long, but I think of her often. We knew each other briefly at the Abbey of Floating White, where you began your own training."

"Why were you living so far from the Great Voorg?"

"Not all Druuge spend their lives in the Great Voorg. But it is better if those who know of our existence believe that." Perrnodt sighed. "Our paths are written in Prophesy. Mine began by finding out the current state of the abbey's spiritual disrepair."

"I imagine you found it extensive."

"Frighteningly so."

"It has become worse." Riane gave her a look. "How did you end up here in the Korrush?"

Perrnodt smiled. "I did not end up here, as you put it. I was called. By the Great Goddess."

Riane drew her knees up to her breast. "Miina spoke to you?"

"Ah, no, child, not in so many words. But I felt Her here—" She pointed to the center of her forehead. "And here—" She placed her hand over her heart. "There was no question of not going."

"It was written. I know."

Perrnodt smiled.

"So you left the abbey and journeyed here."

"No. First I stayed in Axis Tyr for some time. Unexpectedly, I met someone. I broke my vows and bore him children." Her green-flecked eyes seemed to take in every iota of Riane's being. "The younger would be about your age now."

"You have not seen them?"

"That was the punishment for my transgressions. I abandoned them to come here. I had a vision. I was shown my path. I went unquestioningly."

Riane thought this very sad. "Are you a . . . do you have the Sight?"

"Why do you ask, child?"

"Because I have visions, too. And I want to know if I will eventually . . ." She broke off abruptly, bit her lip.

"You have heard that those with the Sight go mad."

"In the end, yes. That is what I have been told."

"That is not the entire truth. There are instances . . ." Perrnodt closed her eyes. "What I would not give to see Giyan again."

"Then you must take me to the sanctuary of the *Maasra*."

"Not yet, Dar Sala-at. You are not yet ready."

"But Giyan . . . Each moment the archdaemon's web spins more tightly around her. I have seen her. You cannot imagine how she suffers!"

"Ah, Dar Sala-at. Your great compassion is part of your makeup. But you cannot allow that great compassion to lead you to make foolish decisions. If I say that you are not yet ready to defeat Horolaggia, then you must trust that it is so."

Riane jumped up. "All I ever have is elders telling me what I cannot do!"

"Come, impatient youth, sit down next to me," Perrnodt said, smiling. "I will think of you as my own child. The child I have never seen and never will see. I understand at last why Miina called me here. Come, now. I will teach you all the things that you must know."

26

Higher Consciousness

Bronn Pallln's head, stuck on a Khagggun pike, crowned on the grounds of the regent's palace like the standard of a defeated race. Every time Kurgan saw it his teeth ground in fury. How had the traitor died so precipitously? How could Olnnn Rydddlin have been so careless?

And there was another thing he did not even consciously acknowledge. The sight of that severed head reminded him of his dream, recurring more frequently now, of what he thought of as the drowned female, white as ice, her long pale hair curling around her face like platinum and veradium serpents. *Help me!* she cried silently. *Please help me!*

Why had Olnnn Rydddlin been interrogating the prisoner himself instead of transporting him to the palace as Kurgan had ordered him to do?

Kurgan was so angry he had called for Line-General Lokck Werrrent. Though he was very much aware of the Line-General's relationship with Olnnn Rydddlin, Kurgan was absolutely certain of Werrrent's loyalty to the regent's office and the V'ornn Modality. That was not, however, how he began the conversation, for he had no intention of letting the Line-General know this was why he wanted to speak with him.

"We need an immediate redeployment," Kurgan said when Werrrent appeared before him. "Please send two packs to Za Hara-at. The Mesagggun and Bashkir architects require more security than they already have."

Werrrent was taken aback. "I beg your pardon, regent, but against what? A filthy backward tribe?"

"I do not know," Kurgan said as he tossed a data-crystal to the Line-General. But he recalled his sense of something stalking through the ruins when he and Sornnn SaTrryn had journeyed there some weeks ago. "Read the dispatch yourself, if you must. Someone or something is killing the V'ornn who venture too deep into the dig. This we must do if our architects are to get an idea of the city's layout." He paused a moment. "I know the Za Hara-at project is a private business arrangement between my Consortium and the SaTrryn. Nevertheless, I would consider it a personal favor if you would extend me the courtesy . . ."

"I understand." The Line-General nodded crisply. "I will do as you ask, regent."

"Excellent." Kurgan rubbed his hands together. "A suitable compensation will—"

"No compensation is necessary, regent, I assure you."

"Very well then. You have my thanks, Line-General."

As Werrrent turned to leave, Kurgan asked him to wait a moment. Werrrent turned back, waiting expectantly.

"As long as you are here," Kurgan said in a casual tone of voice, "please be good enough to enlighten me as to how Bronnn Palllin died in Khagggun custody."

It was a morning of fitful weather. Cold, damp, dreary. The sky, a dull, leaden color, seemed oppressively low. Occasionally, a fistful of rain clattered against the rooftops.

"I am afraid, regent, that I can add very little to the official incident report."

"Which I have already read," Kurgan said shortly. "Bronnn Pallln was overweight. He had a hearts condition."

"Then there is the matter of excessive fear."

"Excessive fear?"

"Yes, regent. I have seen it before in prisoners. It is true that your own fear can kill you."

"The back of Bronnn Pallln's head was caved in!"

Werrrent glanced out the window. "The Deirus did a remarkable restoration job, don't you agree?"

"I wanted to interrogate the traitor myself!" Kurgan thundered.

"I understand, regent."

"Do you? I wonder." Kurgan, hands clasped behind his back, stalked around the room, obliging the Line-General to keep turning in order to face him. "In hindsight, it seemed logical that Bronnn Pallln would be a traitor, passed over as he was for Prime Factor. But then I got to thinking. My father played Bronnn Pallln and his father for dupes; he skimmed a mountain of coin from the Pallln coffers and what did they do? They thanked him profusely for his sage advice and help." Kurgan snorted. "Does this seem the sort of Bashkir to be clever enough to engineer thefts from Khagggun warehouses?"

"He did not have to be clever, simply connected," Werrrent pointed out. "We have discovered during our time here that there is no dearth of clever Resistance members. They are fierce and courageous fighters even in the face of their desperate position. What they lack are resources, V'ornn connections." He shook his head. "N'Luuura take it if they ever evolve a charismatic leader."

"So then, from this discourse I take it you think Bronnn Pallln was guilty."

"We recovered a mountain of materiel from his warehouse—shockswords, ion cannons—virtually everything that was missing. He was our traitor, all right."

"Then we come back to the mystery of what the Star-Admiral thought he was doing."

"Perhaps only his job, regent. You have put him under severe pressure—"

"He told you that?"

"He may have, yes."

Kurgan came and stood very close to Lokck Werrrent. "These are perilous times. I hear things."

"What things, regent?"

"The Khagggun are unhappy with the suspension of the okummmon implants."

"I cannot deny that, regent. Their unrest grows every day."

Kurgan nodded. This confirmed Rada's reports. He knew Werrrent would not lie to him. "I gave the Star-Admiral explicit orders to keep the unrest under control."

"I believe it is under control, regent."

"But for how long? I told the Star-Admiral to deal with any unrest in no uncertain terms. We cannot afford a Khagggun riot. Has he done so?"

"I really cannot say. But speaking for the Khagggun under my own command—"

"Oh, I have no doubts about you, Line-General. None whatsoever. You have years of battle-hardened experience under your belt. Whereas the Star-Admiral, well, I don't think I have to tell you. He is young and fiery and oh so impetuous, yes?"

"There is nothing to fear from any Khagggun," Lokck Werrrent said, "so long as we are told the truth."

Kurgan nodded. "Then I am satisfied."

The Line-General knew a dismissal better than most V'ornn. He was halfway to the door when Kurgan said, "By the way."

Werrrent turned back. "Yes, regent."

"As a personal favor to me."

He bowed stiffly. "I serve the regent."

Kurgan came and said in a lowered tone of voice, "Keep an eye on him, would you? Nothing official, of course. Just between the two of us." He manufactured his warmest smile. "It is not that I distrust him, you understand. But the Star-Admiral's responsibilities are legion. I do not want him overwhelmed or forgetful of what he considers minor matters." He put his arm around Werrrent's broad shoulders. "I know I can trust you, Line-General. You two have a long history. I can be assured that you, of all the high command, will not hold his age against him. After all, you do not hold my youth against me." He nodded. "You see where I am heading, don't you? This is for the Star-Admiral's own benefit."

"As you wish, regent."

"As we both wish." Kurgan walked Lokck Werrrent to the door. "And if all goes well, I see a promotion at hand for you, Line-General. Yes, I most certainly do."

The V'ornn brain," Kirlll Qandda said to Marethyn, "is divided into nine main lobes." As he spoke, he pointed to the holoscan glowing with lambent light. "To wit, the dual forebrains, four transverse lobes, two in each side, here and here, and beneath these six, the sylviat, where the senses are decoded, the sinerea, the central lobe where cortasyne and other chemicals are manufactured, and the ativar, that is, the primitive brain."

Marethyn, having been summoned by Kirlll Qandda, stood beside him in his small cramped office-cubicle in Receiving Spirit. It was overstuffed with diagnostic and research implements, holoscreens, photon projectors and ion simulators of all kinds, and row upon row of datadecagons. She saw none of those things, however. Her mind was filled with the guilt she felt at having used him. Her guilt was all the greater with the realization that to save Sornnn she would do it all over again.

Kirlll's forefinger moved. "The ativar is partially embedded within the sylviat. As such, it is almost impossible to get at. It is the most convolute of all the lobes, and it is the least understood."

"Oh, Kirlll." Marethyn shook her head. "I feel like a first-year anatomy student."

The Deirus' face went pale. "My apologies, Marethyn Stogggul. My enthusiasm has overwhelmed my good sense."

"No, no. I am sure it's just . . . well, I am an artist not a scientist."

"The fault is entirely mine," he said abjectly. "I am most terribly sorry."

For the first time since she had walked into his office she realized that she had been avoiding his eyes. Now she looked into them and saw his own guilt, his belief that he had betrayed her secret tryst with Sornnn.

"I never cared for Bronnn Pallln, you know," she said softly. "I never trusted him at all."

He ducked his head. "When you are a Deirus . . . The pressure from all sides is unimaginable. Coercion is a way of life."

He stood there, staring at her like a whipped wyr-hound. She suppressed an urge to put her arm around him.

"Still. I should have resisted." He shook his head vehemently. "You are a good V'ornn. I understand that."

"Kirlll, I—" But no matter how bad she felt, she would not betray Sornnn's confidence. "Tell me about Terrettt, please."

He licked his lips and nodded, pointing to a photon-illuminated panel. "These are scans of Terrettt's brain." He switched to another holoscan, and then another and another. "As you can see, the ativar lobe is also most difficult even to map fully." He put up a final scan. "Until now. I have developed a method that isolates the ativar and allows a three-dimensional image to be taken of it." His forefinger described an arc that paralleled a dark grey shallow wedge. "We are looking now at that part of Terrettt's ativar never before seen. It is, in every way, anomalous."

"How would you know?" Marethyn asked. "You said before this was no way to scan it fully."

"But we have seen many, many ativar lobes during countless autop-

sies." He reached for a data-decagon. "Would you care to see the doc-
umentation? I have crystals of—"

"Perhaps some other time," Marethyn said. "Right now I want to
know what this discovery means for Terrettt."

"Why, it means *everything!*" Kirlll Qandda said with more animation
than she had ever seen in him. "I believe that I have discovered the
cause of your brother's mental aberration."

She peered more closely at the dark-grey shape. "It is a congenital
defect then."

"Well, that is possibly the most fascinating thing. I do not believe he
was born with this abnormally developed ativar."

Marethyn started, drawing away from the holoscan as if it had just
come alive. "But what other explanation is there?"

"I have done some preliminary tests. I wanted to complete them
before I summoned you." He slid a data-decagon into a communication
port, and a spiral of words and what appeared to be incomprehensible
mathematical equations bloomed on the holoscreen closest to her face.
"I cannot yet say with absolute certainty, but it is my hypothesis that
at a very early age a chemical cocktail was injected directly into Terrettt's ativar."

"What accusation is this?" Marethyn felt cold shock wash over her.
"What Genomatekk would do such a hideous thing?"

"None." Kirlll Qandda laced his long-fingered hands together. "No
Genomatekk would have had this knowledge so many years ago."

"Then who?"

Marethyn stared wide-eyed at him. All of a sudden, she felt the urge
to sit down and, as if divining her thoughts, he slid a chair behind her.

"Gyrgon." She whispered the word. "But why?"

"Why do Gyrgon do anything?" He shrugged. "It could only have
been an experiment."

"On a Stogggul?" She shook her head vehemently. "Impossible!"

"Nothing is impossible for Gyrgon," he said gently. "You know that
as well as I do."

Her hand curled into a fist. There were tears in her eyes. *Poor Terrett!*
"But what did they want with him? Have you any idea?"

"I have not yet completed analyzing the chemicals."

She jumped up. "But surely you must have, what did you call it?"

"An hypothesis. As it happens, I do." He wagged a bony forefinger. "But I doubt whether it will make you happy."

"I am thoroughly unhappy now," she said shortly. "What could possibly make me feel worse?"

He nodded. "As I said, the ativar is the least understood of all the lobes of the V'ornn brain. But, as it happens, it is a private study of mine. No V'ornn knows the precise function of the ativar. Some Genomatekk researchers have gone so far as to claim that it is vestigial, serving no modern-day function at all. I could not disagree more. My studies have shown that, among other things, the ativar once linked the V'ornn to, uh, how shall I say it, to a state of higher consciousness. But it is active and thus far from vestigial."

Marethyn's brow furrowed. "Higher consciousness?"

"Precisely. Think of it as a bridge from consciousness—the state you and I are in now—to something, well, 'other.' "

She shook her head. "I still do not understand."

"Higher consciousness," Kirlll Qandda said softly, "might be a dream state, something you and I experience as we arise from a deep sleep. Or again it might be an empathic state, or a telepathic one, or an ability to see the future. The Ramahan claim to achieve a higher state when they practice their sorcery. The point is, all these examples have one thing in common. They involve a disassociation from time and place, as well as a mysterious and ephemeral connection to another plane of existence."

Marethyn's hearts beat fast. "Madness."

"Well, yes. A lack of understanding of nonmainstream medical theory would of course lead Genomatekks to label these deeply disassociative states as madness."

She gripped the Kirlll's arms. "I want to see him. Now."

"I need to warn you—"

She felt a clutch in her throat. "He is not mad, then!"

Kirlll Qandda's expressive eyes caught hers. "Please listen carefully. This was a Gyrgon experiment and, unfortunately, not all of their experiments are successful."

She was shaking. "What are you saying?"

"The chemical cocktail appears to have been meant to alter the makeup of his ativar. But that is not the end of it. Because it was administered at such an early age I can only conclude that one of the goals was to increase the ativar's mass. In this, the Gyrgon were successful. Terrettt's ativar is larger and more highly developed than any we have in our database. Unhappily for him, something then seems to have gone wrong."

"What, exactly?" Her voice was harsh whisper.

"That is what we must find out," he said. "And we must do it without any outside interference." He paused to allow the full import of his words to sink in. "Do you understand me, Marethyn Stogggul?"

She nodded, already half in a daze. "I will tell no one."

"That's the spirit." Kirlll Qandda steered her toward the door. "I will take you now to see him."

Terrettt sat in his room, his chair facing the window, staring blindly at the Sea of Blood that lapped, dark and grey-green, at the pilings along the Promenade. All around him was a carpet of his latest paintings, sprouting like mushrooms from a forest floor. The stillness was palpable, rippling out from him to reach even into the darkest corners of his chamber. It seemed even to etch itself into the topographical map of Kundala's northern continent she had bought him months ago. Other than his paintings it was the only patch of color in the glaring white room.

The paintings rustled like kuello-firs as Marethyn moved them carefully out of the way, creating a narrow path for her and for Kirlll Qandda. It took her some time; often she stopped to study the paintings she held in her hands.

"They are becoming erratic," she said with a deep and abiding ache in her hearts.

"He is more and more fixated on these seven spots," the Deirus pointed out. "Once he embroidered them at the edges of his work, then they became more central, filling the sky or the sea. Now they are the dominant element."

"I have noticed the same thing," Marethyn said, scrutinizing the painting she held. "Ever since, I have been making a list of everything I can think of that is seven in number."

Kirlll Qandda chose two more at random and held them up. "It may mean nothing at all. That is to say, nothing that would have any meaning for us. He is often fixated on things."

"But it could be meaningful," Marethyn said. "And that is what I choose to believe."

Clutching her brother's paintings to her breast, she made her way to where he sat. He had given no indication that he had heard them or, indeed, that he was aware that he was no longer alone in the room.

Marethyn bent down and kissed him on his pale and damp forehead. "Terrettt, Terrettt!" she said softly but urgently. "It's your sister, Marethyn."

He said nothing; he did not move. In fact, he seemed scarcely to be breathing.

"Terrettt, how are you?"

Kneeling, she put one arm across his thin and bony shoulders. She could smell him, and though she had become somewhat inured to it, suddenly the mental state it bespoke made her weep.

He turned, his pale eyes studying her. It was as if the small, inconsolable sounds she made had woken him from his unnatural open-eyed slumber.

"Terrettt, I know what they did to you, the Gyrgon. I know you are not mad!"

"This cannot be wise—" Kirlll Qandda began, but stopped when she held up a hand.

"You are not mad, Terrettt." She delivered the sheaf of his most recent paintings, each covered by the seven colored whorls, into his lap. "Do you hear me?"

He nodded. At least she believed it to be a nod. She had to believe it, because what else was there for her when it came to him? She had never believed that he was mad, even when first the Genomatekks, then the Deirus had confronted her with all their so-called irrefutable evidence. Their mouths had said one thing, but her hearts had told her something altogether different. If anything, she had thought of him as a kind of prisoner, locked in a mysteriously malfunctioning brain. But she knew that deep inside him was a core that saw color and light, shape and composition, perspective and spatial relationships in the most extraordinary ways and was able to amalgamate them all into a fiercely imagined whole. Who, then, had the right to call him mad? No one!

Sucking back the drool from the corner of his mouth, he ran his fingertips over the rough surface of the top painting, but Marethyn scarcely noticed.

"Ah, Kirlll Qandda!" she cried, turning to the Deirus. "Thank you! You have given me back my brother!"

The Prophesies are written in no book," Perrnodt said between dae-monically difficult lessons in Osoru and Kyofu, the two different forms of sorcery. "You have encountered my kind before, so you know our traditional form of dress. You have seen that we cover the bottom half of our faces with the *saabaya*—a veil of purest undyed white mus-lin. The *saabaya* is covered with Venca script. These are the Prophesies, once handed down orally from one generation to another that are now lovingly and painstakingly inscribed on each new *saabaya* as it is made. We carry them with us wherever we go."

"But what are the origins of the Prophesies? Who made them?"

"The Dragons, Dar Sala-at. Miina's Five Sacred Dragons. They have second sight. The Prophesies are theirs."

Riane nodded. "I thought they might have come from Ramahan who became oracles."

"No. Those who have given in to that part of their Gift have all gone mad," Perrnodt said darkly.

Riane felt a sudden swift shudder pass through her.

"What is it, Dar Sala-at?"

"I think Giyan has oracular powers."

Riane rocked a little, and Perrnodt put an arm around her.

The seemingly endless Korrush day had swiftly, breathlessly fallen into the cavern of night, bringing with it an indigo chill. Stars burned in the velvet sky. Somewhere, far away, a lymmnal howled, and they were reminded of how dangerously close to the Jeni Cerii they were.

"All Kundala has fallen on evil times," Riane said. The V'ornn—"

"The V'ornn! They are only a symptom," Perrnodt spat. "It is our disease, Dar Sala-at. You have suffered in the Abbey of Floating White as I have. You know the pernicious nature of this disease. I believe absolutely that the V'ornn—this vicious pestilence, this accursed plague—was visited upon us by Miina. The Great Goddess in Her wis-dom knows that it takes extreme measures for the cure to be enacted. The evil must approach its zenith, the situation must become intoler-able for the Kundalan to cry out as one, for the Great Wheel to finally make its turn. For what else will save us but the wretchedness of our own despair? Only when we are faced with our own annihilation will we recognize the true evil of the path we have mistakenly taken. The trouble is the Kundalan capacity for self-delusion."

"What are you saying? That the cure is worse than the disease?"

"I am saying that they are two sides of the same coin. One cannot exist without the other. This is the Great Balance, the nature of the Cosmos. This pattern is repeated endlessly everywhere and everywhen. However, we need the Gift and the proper training to see it. This is what you must have if you are to prevail against your enemies. And believe me when I tell you that they are legion.

"The changes you must wring from us are of the most painful nature. Most will resist. Their faith will be sorely tested, and many will balk, even revolt against these changes because they are unknown and, therefore, too frightening. They will turn against you, join with your natural enemies, line up to eagerly slay you so that the life they know will not be shattered."

"I do not understand," Riane said. "The life they are living now is in bondage to the V'ornn. They are terrorized, tortured, killed at random and without warning."

"Everything you say, Dar Sala-at, is true. And yet, many will choose their current situation because it is all they know. They have grown used to the suffering. It is illogical; it does not make sense, and yet I can vouch for the truth of it because in my lifetime it has happened before. Do not make the mistake of believing that the V'ornn are the first threat to Kundala. There are histories here. Layer upon layer, buried in the red dust of the Korrush in Earth Five Meetings."

"Za Hara-at."

"Yes." Perrnodt's ripe eyes were shining. "Za Hara-at."

"I wish I had been alive when it was in full flower."

"Perhaps you were, in another lifetime." Perrnodt rubbed her palms together. "Now show me how you Thripp."

Riane closed her eyes, summoning the whorled mists of Otherwhere. She willed herself to spin and, spinning, project herself from the many layers of the Cosmos.

Nothing happened.

Her eyes popped open.

"You cannot Thripp, can you?"

Riane looked at the Druuge curiously. "How did you know?"

"Dar Sala-at, as I have been telling you, you have immense power within you. However, without the proper knowledge of how, where, and when to unleash it you will not long survive among your enemies." She opened her hands, palms up. "When Thripping was discovered among the Druuge eons ago it was used as a means of ethereal exploration. It was done in the abbeys and nowhere else. Even with the Gift, even with the mononculus to protect you from the radiation tides between Realms, you can only begin your Thrip in and around holy places. The location of abbeys is no haphazard. Each one was built above a nexus node of the power bourns that run deep in the mantle of Kundala. There are, of course, more nexus nodes than there are abbeys of sacred sites, but without being within a radius of thirty meters of one of these power nodes you cannot Thripp. Therefore, it becomes extremely important for you to be able to use your Third Eye to detect the bourns."

"But here where we are in the *in'adim* is a holy place. According to the Ghor, this is where the Prophet Jiharre was killed."

"That is an excellent point," Perrnodt said. "The explanation will not please you. You are correct. Beneath the *in'adim* lies a powerful bourn nexus. However, it is tangled and, therefore, inactive. This is one of the later examples of the slow creep of evil that infests Kundala. The planet is a living entity. The bourns are its arteries. If more tangles occur, the entire network of bourn will be in jeopardy of atrophying."

"What will happen then?" Riane asked with her heart in her throat.

"That is speculation," Perrnodt said. "But it seems likely that all sorcery will vanish with the bourns."

"We cannot allow that to occur."

"We trust in you, Dar Sala-at." Perrnodt arranged herself. "Shall we continue our lessons?"

Riane nodded. "When I was in the Abbey of Floating White, there were times when I felt the bourns humming."

"I daresay you did." Perrnodt took Riane's hands in her own. "Now I will teach you how to feel them all the time."

Mirror, Mirror

Konara Inggres could not sleep. Since she no longer felt safe roaming the backwaters of the abbey, she lay rigid on her cot, staring at the damp stone ceiling of her chamber. Every once in a while she emitted a small moan. Her mind was a seething labyrinth of dread. A litany of dire consequences crowded out coherent thought. Ever since she had painfully crawled out of the spy niche behind Konara Urdma's office she had been trying to make sense of everything she had seen and heard. In vain. Within every shadow she now saw the grinning face of evil. The stench of pure terror was upon her.

What had Giyan and Bartta become? What had Giyan done to Konara Lyystra and Konara Tyyr and why were mirrors so important to these evil infidels who had insidiously invaded the abbey?

At last, despite her attempts at prayer and meditation, the agitation that consumed her mind spilled over into her body, compelling her to sit up. She found herself drenched in cold sweat and, unable to find a calm place within herself, decided to take a shower. The smell of her own terror was making her sick to her stomach. Besides, while no mirrors were allowed in the Ramahan sleeping quarters—even those of the konara—there was a mirror in the baths.

When she arrived, the bath was lit only by the fitful glow of the lamps in the corridor. She went in and located the mirror. Standing before it, she looked at her reflection which, at first glance, appeared perfectly normal. But then as she had been able to do when she had entered the chamber where Bartta had secreted the *had-atta*, she began to discern something that wavered at the very corners of her consciousness, and she brought to bear that special sorcerous knowledge she had secretly acquired during her endless hours of research in the back rooms of the Library, the same knowledge that had allowed her to break Bartta's Spell of Binding on the *had-atta* chamber and to replace it without anyone being the wiser. Drawing upon certain texts, she had trained her Third Eye to pick up the ephemeral residue of sorcerous spells.

Now as she stared at her reflection she became aware of a flickering blackness, like dark flames fomenting in the edges of the mirror. Curious, she took hold of the mirror's frame and pulled it free. But there was nothing in it. The "mirror" remained on the wall.

She set the frame down and walked from side to side, looking at the reflective rectangle in order to get a better idea of what it was, for it was like no mirror she had ever seen or heard of. She conjured Transverse Guest, an Osoru spell meant to uncover the source of unknown castings. Extending a forefinger, she pressed it against the surface. The tip disappeared up to the first knuckle, and even though she pulled it out almost immediately, it retained the eerie sensation of having been dipped into ice water.

She peered more closely at the rectangle. Transverse Guest told her some things. For instance, she knew this was not an Osoru spell, but then again nor was it Kyofu. What, then, was it, and who had cast it? Konara Inggres was willing to bet that Giyan—or whatever had taken hold of Giyan's body—was responsible. The trouble was, these conclusions brought her no closer to an answer. She had only a rudimentary knowledge of corporeal possession, and whatever she did know was a by-product of her Osoru snooping in the Library's back rooms, an agglomeration of moments, brief and stolen so as not to arouse the suspicion of the other konara. She determined that she would have to return there with the express intent of finding out all she could on this little-known topic.

But first, she had to find herself a real mirror. All thoughts of a shower had vanished in the full bloom of purpose.

Carefully, she returned the frame to its place on the wall and was about to exit the baths when she heard furtive footfalls in the corridor heading her way. Just in time, she shrank furtively back into the shadows. Her heart was in her throat as she observed a group of young acolytes whisper by. At their head was a black-robed figure whose face was obscured by the edges of an enveloping cowl. She felt, as the cowled one passed, a certain chill run down her spine. Then she noticed something that paralyzed her with fear. One of the cowled figure's hands had a sixth finger. A *black* sixth finger, as if it had been seared in a furnace. From her studies of banned texts, she knew the cowled one must be a sauromician. She had thought them all long dead, scoured from life by Miina's vengeful hand, but now, evil upon evil, one was here skulking clandestinely around the bowels of the abbey.

The sauromician led the acolytes down the corridor and into a spare storeroom. There, he began to address them and Konara Inggres, her heart pounding in her chest, crept out to listen.

Terrifyingly, he spoke of Giyan as Mother, as the one who would reinvigorate the abbey, return the Ramahan to their rightful place as rulers of Kundala. The fact that the Ramahan had historically never served such a role seemed lost on these poor souls. But they did ask, timidly, to be sure, how Mother would save them from the tyranny of the V'ornn. The clever sauromician appeared prepared for just this question for, without skipping a beat, he answered in his dark and ominously furred voice that he would soon take them to see the Dar Sala-at. And when he did, they would swear to give their lives for the savior who was written in Prophesy.

Of course, these were basest of lies, Konara Inggres knew that. But the acolytes shared neither her experience nor her Gift, and so they were completely taken in. She backed away, her heart sick but knowing that for the moment at least she was powerless to stop the evil threading its way through the abbey. First things first.

Alone in the corridor, she wiped the sweat off her face with her sleeve, and on silent feet went in search of a mirror. This task, so simple on the face of it, proved quite impossible to achieve. The mirrors she knew of were either gone or had been replaced by the same sorcerous thing that she had discovered in the bath.

Her search at length led her deeper and deeper into the entrails of the abbey, until at length she came upon the excavation that Riane had worked on with the late Shima Vedda. It now lay deserted, ever since Bartta had thrown Shima Vedda down a cistern and killed her. The refectory that she and her crew had been in the process of restoring had been abandoned in favor of a newer one high up enough in the abbey to be lit by windows as well as lanterns. In truth, most Ramahan preferred the newer quarters, but Konara Inggres had wondered at the sudden change in design.

Now she came upon the old refectory just as Riane and Shima Vedda had left it that fateful evening when they had discovered the rent in the underfloor that opened up to the historic Kells below. Like every Ramahan, Konara Inggres was familiar with the legend of the Kells. When the Great Goddess Miina created the abbey, She placed at its heart a series of three sacred chambers known as the Kells from which She could observe unseen the holy work of Her disciples.

The rope ladder Riane had deployed in order to descend had been disposed of and the rent sealed over with a simple casting, the emanation from which drew Konara Inggres' attention even though it was beneath several heavy pieces of Shima Vedda's dusty and cobwebbed equipment. Leaning her shoulder into the effort, she moved the equipment away, stood panting a little, hands on hips, staring down at the spell, parsing it into its incantatory parts. With a whispered incantation and a wave of her hand, she dismissed the casting. Rummaging around, she discovered a small pile of wood and pitch-soaked reed torches. She lit one, tucked two more into the belt of her robe, and knelt over the rent in the floor, which was now quite a bit larger than it had been when Riane and Shima Vedda first come upon it, owing to the severe seismic activity of a month before.

Thrusting the flicking torch head down into the triangular chamber below, she discovered what seemed to be a citrine table just below her. By lowering herself with some care she was able to stand on this item, balance herself, then, with a shower of flaming sparks, jump the rest of the way to the black-basalt floor of the Kell.

As soon as she did so, she discovered that what she had been balancing on was no table at all, but a magnificent sculpture of the citrine serpent sacred to Miina. At least, she knew from her research that it had once been sacred to Miina. Nowadays, the acolytes were taught that the serpent was the Avatar of Pyphoros, that it was a symbol of lies and deceit and was thus anathema to the Great Goddess. She crouched beside the sinuous sculpture, ran her hand over the incised scales. Then, turning, she held the torch up and saw the niche in the wall where the citrine had been set Miina only knew how many centuries before. She was mystified. How it had moved from the wall to the floor she could not say, since upon a detailed examination of the niche she discovered neither a crowbar's mark nor the remnant of a sorcerous spell. In any event, there was no doubt in her mind that she had entered a holy place and, before she continued her search, she got down upon her knees in front of the citrine serpent, whose name was

Ghosh, and prayed for forgiveness and for the Goddess's blessed return.

She remained in this pose for some minutes after ending her prayer, immersed in silent meditation in order to gather her scattered wits and to try to banish the terror from her heart. Then she rose and continued downward, as Riane had done, pressing the bare mechanism she had discovered in the stone niche where Ghosh had resided. She rode the two-square-meter section of the stone floor downward into the Kell beneath. This one was a perfect square, enameled black. Besides the color, there were two notable items. One was a cenote, its heavy basalt cover lying to one side. The other consisted of a trio of carved animals, huge and lithe, with terrifying cats's heads and rippling pelts of gold strewn with jet-black spots. They had sleekly muscled bodies, powerful-looking jaws. Long, slender tails arched over their backs. Their mouths gaped open to show three rows of sharp teeth. Like the Ghosh in the Kell above, Konara Inggres could see where they had once been inset into the wall. Now they were arrayed around the well at the cardinal points of an equilateral triangle, as if waiting for something to emerge from the still, black water.

The cenote, in fact, gave Konara Inggres an idea. She searched her memory for the complete incantation, then, holding her hands out over the surface of the water, she cast First-Gate Correspondence. At first, nothing seemed to happen, and, seeing as how she had never before cast the Osoru spell, she did not quite know what to expect.

As she inclined her upper body over the well, she saw a whitish mist forming across the surface. At first, it was like the delicate skeins water spiders made as they skimmed over a pond, but soon enough, the mist coalesced into an opaque coating. She moved her hand in a counterclockwise motion over the mist, and it began to be drawn up, vanishing just before it reached her open palm. What remained, floating on the surface of the water, was a small copper-rimmed disc that shone in the torchlight. She plucked it off the water and turned it over, smiling into the image of her face reflected in the mirror.

Auraed in concentrated pools of bronze light, the creatures appeared to be moving in a slow formal ominous dance around the perimeter of a large oval. Headless and armless, they displayed every facet of their gleaming armor. And this armor of shimmering deeply colored alloy, browed, taloned, winged, and spiked, was wicked-looking.

"So," Olnnn said. "What do you think?"

"What can I think?" Rada replied. "I have never imagined myself in armor."

"If you are to be with me, then you must be armored, and you must learn how to wield a shock-sword."

"Have you come to a decision, Star-Admiral?" They turned as the armorer appeared. Like all V'ornn armorers she was a Tuskugggun, this one a small, unremarkable female named Leyytey, with dark eyes and an overserious demeanor. She pointed with a long, pale hand. The tips of her fingers were stained copper by her work. "This model is among my latest and would be perfect for your physique."

"The armor is not for me," Olnnn said. "It is for my new staff-adjutant."

"I am sorry, Star-Admiral, but he will have to come in. I cannot do a proper fitting otherwise."

"This is my staff-adjutant," Olnnn said, gesturing to Rada.

"Of course, Star-Admiral," Leyytey answered without missing a beat. She led them around the display. "In that event, may I suggest this one?" She indicated a suit of a dull bronze color. "I can easily modify it for a . . . smaller somatotype."

"See that it is done at once," Olnnn commanded. "And a shock-sword with your keenest killing blades."

As Leyytey passed behind Olnnn, Rada thought she saw a smirk briefly pass across the armorer's face, and she felt her cheeks flush with humiliation and anger at the knowledge that Leyytey must think her the Star-Admiral's latest conquest.

Rada spent some time watching Olnnn conduct business, delivered and dispatched by a fleet of hoverpods. It was the hoverpods that interested her. They were sleek and small. She wondered what their top speed might be. She ate a quick light breakfast from a leeesta stand next door to the armory. Across the teeming boulevard was the looming white facade of Receiving Spirit. Every once in a while just outside the entrance she saw a Gyrgon appear as if from a sorcerous mist and vanish just as mysteriously. They came and went with funereal gravity, and if it happened that some V'ornn was unfortunate enough to be within arms' length of one of them, they would stand very still until the Gyrgon was gone.

She heard Olnnn talking heatedly with one of his First-Captains.

They were discussing the regent. She was astonished by how much of the Star-Admiral's time was taken up with carrying out the orders—many of them petty—of the regent. She could see how much this angered Olnnn, and her conviction was borne out when she heard him curse mightily as the First-Captain turned smartly away. From what she had overheard it seemed possible to her that a rift had occurred between Kurgan Stogggul and Olnnn Rydddlin, and that interested her even more than the hoverpods.

When, an hour later, her equipage was ready, Olnnn instructed her in the method of putting on the armor. Then he took her directly to the Kalllistotos. The ring was deserted, as the slate of bouts was only at night.

"How does it feel?" he asked, as they climbed between the wires.

"A bit awkward," Rada told him, "but only when I try to change directions too quickly."

"You have good posture and muscle tone. And you are strong."

Leyytey had refashioned the armor in a glimmery blue-green, the Star-Admiral's color, and it sported the Star-Admiral's gold crest on shoulders and chest. At her side hung a shock-sword. Leyytey had asked her to hold many models in the two-handed grip Olnnn had shown her until the armorer was satisfied that she had one that was balanced just right for her height and weight. In the atelier, looking at herself in the armor, she had been overcome by a strange and slightly giddy feeling. She had always hated this armor as a symbol of male dominance and Khagggun arrogance. But now that she found herself inside it she felt infused with its power, and she had to fight against seeing herself as a leaf being borne aloft in a rising storm.

"Draw your shock-sword and hold it as I instructed you," Olnnn ordered, as they faced each other in the center of the ring.

The morning was cold and crisp, with none of the damp rawness of the previous few days. Everything sparkled as if it had been newly polished overnight. Heavily canted sunlight had just barely begun to creep across the Kalllistotos plaza. Rada felt dwarfed by the plaza's vast and chilly emptiness. She felt the maleness of the place—everything outsized and hulking and angular—and she imagined she could smell all the blood and pain that had been spilled in the ring.

"Defend yourself," Olnnn announced suddenly, sweeping his shock-sword toward her.

The first clang of alloy against alloy staggered her, and she almost dropped the weapon. Ribbons of pain veined her hands, and her forearms tingled unpleasantly.

"I do not know the first thing about this," she lied.

"Then you will have incentive to learn all the faster." Olnnn struck her blades again, not hard, not as if she were the enemy, but not a friendly tap, either. "As you can see, a shock-sword has two blades, parallel and in close proximity to one another. When you throw the safety off, an arc of hyperexcited ions flow back and forth, causing the blades to vibrate a thousand times a second. They can cut through anything. If you pierce an enemy just right, it will quite literally tear him to pieces. But the ion flow has its own rules and can be almost as dangerous to the one who wields it inexpertly." He droned on in this vein, telling her what she had already discovered.

She took her first swing at him, making sure she showed him her clumsiness. In the course of her life she had had cause now and again to take up a shock-sword and wield it. In fact, she had one stripped from a dead Khagggun in the Djenn Marre foothills that she had kept in a case beneath the floorboards of her office in Blood Tide. She had recently taken it home, secreting it where no one but she would find it. She had practiced with it daily, learning the hard way the trickiness of using it.

As Olnnn worked her around the ring, she allowed her clumsiness to vanish by stages, until by the third sweaty hour they engaged one another in a series of rapid-stroke attack-and-defense maneuvers.

"You are a quick study," Olnnn said, "for a Tuskugggun."

Despite the jibe, Rada could tell that he was as impressed as he was startled. For her own part, she could not despise him more. She was convinced that the creep on her flesh that had kept her awake ever since he had attacked her would never dissipate. Because of him she would never be the same. She had always been contemptuous of those weak-minded Tuskugggun who were dependent on males. Now it was she who was bound to one; and not simply a male, but a Khagggun, to boot! She wanted only to humiliate him as he had humiliated her. It felt to her now that the only way she could find sustenance was to feed on his abasement.

And it was this powerful prod that in the end drove her to abandon her caution and duel with him as an equal. Perhaps not physically as an equal, but she was possessed of a tenacious spirit and she had the element of surprise on her side.

The reddish oblate disc of the sun had risen high enough to seem as if it was spilling its blood into the ring as they came together this last time. She crossed his shock-sword at the base of the blades, then quickly disengaged and interlaced the tips with his, twisting sharply as she did so, then as his expression froze, sliced swiftly and decisively so that her blades ran down the entire length of his, interfering with the ion flow between his twinned blades. It was a dangerous maneuver, one that she had never tried before. If it was not performed correctly, the feedback from the dammed ion flow could severely damage her neural pathways.

With a deep-felt grunt she slammed her shock-sword home, the bases of their blades crossed, the guards clanging. She could feel the heat of his breath against her cheek, could see the surprise morph into humiliation in his expression. They were toe to toe, teeth gritted, the sparks from the dammed-up ion flow arcing in a kind of penumbra around them.

He grimaced with the pain she was causing him and did something with his wrists—it was too deft and quick for her to see what it was—and she was disarmed without being aware that she had let go of the hilt. Her shock-sword lay at her feet between them. He was wide-eyed and panting, and she willed herself not to look down, not to bend, not to go to one knee to retrieve her weapon.

"Had we been enemies, you would be dead now," he said, his voice hoarser than it ought to have been.

"But we *are* enemies."

He did not pull away, did not lay the edge of his blades against her throat, but stood with his legs wide apart, his knees slightly bent, staring at her as if she were the only object left in the world. She felt taken up by that gaze, as if she were held in a great hand, and she was terrified and immensely resentful. Terrified that she had suddenly, perilously exposed her secret self to him; resentful that he still seemed to have a mysterious power over her.

So when he reached out and touched her armored shoulder with his mailed hand she shrugged it off and turned away, baring her teeth at the few Mesagggun who had stopped on their way to their shift to observe the curious display. To her relief they started and hurried on their way, fearful of incurring an armored Khagggun's wrath.

"Rada."

She heard his voice from behind her. He spoke her name softly; nevertheless, it seemed to reverberate around the plaza as if mocking her. Yet it wasn't until he repeated her name that she turned and faced him.

He had retrieved her shock-sword. His own weapon was sheathed at his left hip. "Where did you—?"

She winced at the dreaded question. "I told you I was born a warrior."

"I did not believe you."

"Of course. I am Tuskugggun." She shrugged. "Well, perhaps after all it was luck."

He studied her, silent and inscrutable. At length, he held her shock-sword out to her hiltfirst. "This morning you earned the right to keep this," he said.

She wanted to spit in his face as he had spat in hers. But that would have made her just like him. Besides, she found to her dismay that her mouth was as dry as the Great Voorg. There was nothing for her to do but to hold out her hand. She felt the weight and the exquisite balance of the shock-sword as she took hold of it. She had waited a long time for this moment—all her life, it seemed. But never could she have imagined these circumstances.

"Star-Admiral," she said impulsively, "there is something that I—"

He waited, silently watching her.

She did not want to tell him all at once, did not want him to think this was an easy thing for her. "Recently, perhaps a week or so ago, the regent summoned me. He offered to make a deal. He was concerned that as regent he would lose touch with day-to-day life in Axis Tyr."

Olnnn's cruel mouth curled with the ghost of a smile. "What really concerns him are plots—plots he might not know about. After all, it was just such a plot that led to his father's demise."

Rada nodded. "In exchange for my being his eyes and ears in Axis Tyr, he agreed to repay the debt my mother ran up on Blood Tide."

Olnnn crossed his arms over his chest. "And did you accept Kurgan Stogggul's kind and generous offer?"

"What do you think? He is the regent."

His eyes narrowed warningly. "Why have you confessed this?"

"He took me by force that night. There was nothing I could do. Then."

"But now you are with me, and it is another story."

"It seems to me that the regent is no longer your friend."

"You have an inquisitive nature," he said shortly.

"I run a tavern." She shrugged. "It goes with the territory."

"You are in altogether different territory now," he said. "That nature may be an asset. Or it may get you killed." He cocked his head. "But I know you well enough to understand that such admonitions will not deter you. Say what you will."

"That night," she said, "the regent and I were interrupted by an urgent knocking on the door. I could see in the brief glimpse afforded me that the Gyrgon Nith Batoxxx was standing in the hallway just outside the bedchamber. The regent closed the door behind him but with my ear to it I could hear their conversation."

This made Olnnn laugh. It was a free and easy sound, and Rada recognized in it a kind of respect. "By all means, continue," he said.

"The conversation concerned the program to elevate Khagggun to Great Caste status."

Olnnn immediately looked around. As the hour had grown later, the Kalllistotos plaza had become infiltrated with the usual mob endemic to such areas of the city. Some were hurrying about their business, but others lounged against walls and pillars idly chatting and looking on. He nodded silently to her, and they climbed down and went swiftly to the nearby Promenade, where, she presumed, they would be mobile and he could keep them away from potential eavesdroppers.

Seabirds called through the morning chill. In the east, the morning's blush of rose could still be seen, flat and knifelike, just above the low grey cloud bank. An onshore breeze brought them the clean, bracing saline scent of the sea.

As they passed the ships at harbor, he said, "It is safe now to continue."

She told him what she had overheard, about how the Gyrgon were against the ascension, that they feared it would set a dangerous precedent for the other castes, that it was Kurgan Stogggul's idea to halt the process but that Nith Batoxxx wholeheartedly agreed. "Nith Batoxxx said that he would not tolerate any unrest among the other castes. He said that it was up to the regent to deal decisively with any sense of rebellion among the Khagggun."

"I knew it!" Olnnn smacked his fist into his hand. "That was my suspicion for weeks now. All I lacked was proof, and now I have it!"

It is assumed by many Ramahan—even some of the most senior kon-ara—that the power bourns running through the core of Kundala are all the same. This is not so."

Light winked out as another Korrush night arose from its dusty bed and the temperature began at once to cool. Perrnodt was sitting behind Riane, braiding her hair in the *mistefan*, the Druuge style. As she worked at this intricate task she continued with her lessons. She never stopped. While they walked northward, skirting the large Jeni Cerii encampment, while they ate, even during infrequent rest breaks while they occasionally relieved themselves, she continued. And there was no question of sleep. They kept walking and reviewing hard-won lessons. She showed Riane how to catch naps during the days as short as three minutes that were more refreshing than eight hours of the most tranquil slumber. In this way they were making good time, despite the cold that crept into the winter mornings, the intense chill that gripped them after the sun went down. Each shiver reminded Riane of the passing time. It was midwinter. Once the solstice arrived it would be too late to save Giyan from being permanently possessed by Horolaggia. If that happened, she would cease to exist. Horolaggia would have her skills, her memories, everything that she was, including her Gift.

"Are you listening to me?" Perrnodt said sharply. "There is no time for daydreaming. Every lesson I teach you is a vital one."

Riane nodded, apologizing.

"The bourns were laid down at Miina's direction by the Five Sacred Dragons," Perrnodt went on. "Since each Dragon represents one of the five elements—earth, air, fire, water, wood—the bourns exhibit the trait of whichever Dragon created it. For instance, the bourns deep beneath the Abbey of Floating White were laid by Paow, black Dragon of wood. She is the Dragon of Vision. By contrast, the bourns beneath Middle Palace in Axis Tyr were laid by Seelin, the green Dragon of water and of Transformation."

At once, Riane understood why it was Seelin whom Annon had seen when, briefly, the Door to the Storehouse had opened. "What about under the Abbey of Listening Bone," she said, "which is now the Gyr-gon Temple of Mnemonics?"

"Those bourns are unusual, even among Kundala's bourns. They were created together by the paired Dragons, Paow and Yig. Yig is the red Dragon of fire and of Power. Dragons may mate often but they pair only rarely, and then it is forever. Woe betide the fool who presumes to sunder a pair of Dragons."

"Why would anyone want to do that?" Riane asked.

"To break their power." Perrnodt sat back and cocked her head, sur-veying her handiwork. "Let me see. It has been some time since I tied the *mistefan*. Not a bad job of it."

She had divided Riane's hair into three thick streams of gold, inter-twining them tightly, the result being a wide braid that hung down Riane's back like a V'ornn shock-sword.

With night hard upon them, they rose and broke their meager camp. "Now where we are going," Perrnodt said, as they continued their jour-ney northward, "where the *Maasra* is hidden, is the most sacred place on Kundala." She pointed due north. "We go to Im-Thera. Or, more accurately, deep within the ruins of Za Hara-at."

As they walked, she made a tiny adjustment to Riane's *mistefan*. "The site was chosen for many reasons, chief among them being that the nexus beneath it is unique inasmuch as it is made up of bourns laid by all the Dragons. Which means that the five elements are interwoven in one spot. This being so, the power is immense. It is also exceedingly dangerous."

"Give me an example," Riane said.

"If mishandled, it has the potential to rip open the very fabric be-tween Realms. The chaos that would ensue from discrete Realms in-vading one another is incalculable. There are, for instance, forces within Realms which are inimical to others. The result of their meeting would be instantaneous annihilation for all the Realms involved in the rift, including ours."

Riane gave a little whistle of awe. Immense power. Perrnodt wasn't exaggerating.

"The *Maasra*, being semisentient, is able to tap into a small portion of this power," Perrnodt continued. "That is how, ultimately, it protects itself from those who covet it, those who would use it for their own gain or to further their ends."

"Then we need not fear others who would—"

She broke off at the telltale whisper of wind. A small furry ball came whizzing into view, and a familiar voice said, "Killing a Gyrgon and a sauromician! This is some mess you've managed to get yourself into, little dumpling."

"Thigpen!" Riane cried, stopping in her tracks. "How did you find me?"

"I cast the opals, how else?"

"I thought you weren't going to call me little dumpling anymore."

"I changed my mind," Thigpen said a little huffily. She shook something unseen off her orange-and-black-striped fur. "So long as you insist on being mischievous, I shall continue to call you little dumpling."

Riane grinned. "By Miina's grace, it's good to see you, old friend."

"Likewise, I'm sure."

Thigpen was up on her four hind legs, squinting hard. "And why, may I ask, have you disfigured your nose?"

Riane touched the ajjan stud. "The kapudaan of the Gazi Qhan had it done to me."

Thigpen sniffed. "Hardly a friendly gesture, if you ask me."

"It's a long story."

"A Rappa!" Perrnodt said, standing stock-still. "This is something of a surprise."

For an instant, they both fell silent. Riane was ashamed and quickly introduced the two of them.

"The Dar Sala-at's teacher," the Rappa said with palpable relief. "I have now gotten the best possible news!"

"Speaking of news," Riane said with no little apprehension, "what of Eleana and Rekkk?" Though she had locked away her vision of Rekkk's death fall, she had not forgotten it.

"There I am unfortunately in the dark," Thigpen confessed. "I had to leave them quite suddenly, and since that time I have been otherwise occupied."

"Well, that needs a bit of explaining."

"There was a disturbance." Thigpen's whiskers had begun to twitch, a sure sign of anxiety.

"What kind of a disturbance?"

Thigpen glanced at Perrnodt with a wary eye.

"It's all right. You can trust her, Thigpen. She is a Druuge."

"Really?" The Rappa's eyes opened wide. "She is not dressed like a Druuge."

"Why do you prevaricate?" Perrnodt said. "Your kind have been in the Great Voorg for centuries. They are Druuge companions."

Riane turned to Thigpen. "Why didn't you tell me?"

"I do not tell you everything," Thigpen said shortly. "My goodness, why would I want to overstuff your head with trivia when you already have so much to learn?"

"I would hardly call this trivia!"

"You will learn of the Druuge in your own time, little dumpling. It is not my place to speak of them."

"In this she is right," Perrnodt broke in. "But come. Let us return to the subject at hand. I have an unpleasant feeling it is urgent."

"In a moment," Riane said. "I have another question. It occurs to me that you must have known that Minnum could not be, as he claimed, a sefíror. Minnum is not Druuge. He is a sauromician."

"I see the teacher has been busy instructing her pupil," Thigpen said dryly.

"Never mind that. Why did you lie to me?"

Thigpen sighed. "We needed to find out what *Maasra* meant. For that, we had to find a dialectician, and to do that we had to—"

"Find someone who could cast Ephemeral Reconstitution," Riane said.

"Precisely." Thigpen nodded. "A sauromician. When you told me that you had stumbled across a sefíror I was delighted but dubious. It turned out that my suspicions were confirmed."

"But you did not give him away."

"If I had, would you have trusted him?"

Riane shook her head. "No."

Thigpen spread her forepaws. "Well, then."

"But *you* trusted him. A sauromician."

"I have seen Ephemeral Reconstitution cast before. In this, I knew he could not play us false without my knowing. And he did not."

"He lied about other things."

"That is self-evident. My only concern at the time was the conjuring of the spell." She bared her teeth. "If he had attempted to lie to us about that, I was prepared to deal with him." She stroked her whiskers with her forepaws. "Are you angry with me, little dumpling?"

"I am considering it," Riane said, only half-serious. "In the meantime, tell us about this disturbance."

Thigpen came down off her fours. "Before I do, I suggest we take a look at what is just up ahead."

Riane and Perrnodt turned. Long-winged carrion birds circled the sky just ahead of them. They hurried forward.

"I smell death," Perrnodt whispered.

A dark mound lay in their path not three hundred meters ahead. Riane could just make out the stiff-legged forms of a pair of kuomeshals, and her heart skipped a beat.

"Little dumpling, no!" Thigpen cried.

But Riane was already running toward the kuomeshals. They lay in a tangle, looking as if they had been felled with one titanic blow. Riane was brought up short at the sight of their heads. They looked as if they had exploded from the inside out.

"Sauromicians," Perrnodt said, coming up on one side of Riane.

"I knew it." The Rappa's whiskers twitched spastically. "Sauromicians are a vengeful lot. They always were." She put a forepaw on Riane's arm. "I am very much afraid you set this in motion when you killed one of them."

"We had no choice, Othnam, Mehmmer, and I."

"I am sure you didn't," Thigpen said gently. "However, no action is without its consequences."

They watched Riane as she pushed heavy legs away so she could get to the saddlebags.

"Dar Sala-at, Thigpen is right. If there are sauromicians around, it would be best if we steered clear of them."

"I know these bags," Riane said, becoming more frantic in her searching. "I know these kuomeshals." She leapt over the dead beasts. "They belong to my friends Othnam and Mehmmer."

"The Ghor brother and sister who befriended the Dar Sala-at during her time in Agachire," Perrnodt explained to Thigpen. Then they heard her cry out and ran after her.

They found her kneeling beside two bodies. One was male, the other female. Both were dressed in the black robes of the Ghor, though these robes looked as if they had been torn open by wild beasts. Ragged ribbons fluttered in the breeze. The bare torsos were black with blood.

The intestines had been removed. They curled about the corpses, slit open, pored over.

Riane remembered Minnum saying that sauromicians were necromancers. They divined things by killing and reading the entrails of the dead. "Othnam and Mehmmer," she whispered.

"The sauromicians have worked their black sorcery," Perrnodt said darkly.

"Killed very recently." Thigpen eyed the carrion birds overhead. "Else these two would be bare bones by now."

Perrnodt nodded, turned to Riane. "Did you ever tell these friends of yours that you are the Dar Sala-at?"

"Yes," Riane whispered. They had been with her when she had told Mu-Awwul who she was.

"Bad." Thigpen looked around worriedly. "Very bad, indeed, little dumpling."

"Now the sauromicians know, too," Perrnodt said.

Riane, horrified and deeply saddened, nevertheless drew on Annon's inflexible warrior's resolve. It was no time to be overwhelmed by emotion. The full force of the grief she carried would have to wait. She whispered through gritted teeth, "Perrnodt, do you know the Ghorvish prayer for the dead?"

"Dar Sala-at, I sympathize. But there is no time. It is more imperative than ever that we make haste out of this accursed wilderness. We are obviously deep inside sauromician territory."

Gently, Perrnodt and Thigpen raised Riane up, and they set off. They were careful not to let her look back. Overhead, the carrion birds circled lower.

Despite her resolve, Riane felt tears streaming down her face, now three of her Korrush friends were dead. *Because of me. If I had never come here. . . .*

"The disturbance, little dumpling," Thigpen said, unable to bear Riane's silent grief any longer. "It was in my birthplace." She meant deep inside the Ice Caves, where she and Riane had first encountered one another high up above Heavenly Rushing in the Djenn Marre.

Riane swallowed. Focusing on the friends here with her helped take her mind off those she had lost. And there was another thing. Thigpen's whiskers were twitching like crazy.

"There was a disturbance in First Cenote, the sacred pool near our birthing place," Thigpen said. "That is why I had to leave our friends so precipitously."

"How could you know about it?" Riane interrupted. "You were hundreds of kilometers away."

"I received a message. We are telepathic."

"Kind of you to finally mention it."

"Rappa telepathy extends only among our own kind," Thigpen said hastily.

Riane nodded. "All right. Continue."

"You remember First Cenote."

"Of course. There is a Prophesy among the Rappa that the Dar Sala-at will gaze into First Cenote and see the power of the Cosmos made manifest."

Thigpen nodded, amplifying for Perrnodt's benefit. "The Dar Sala-at told me she felt ill at ease when she neared it. At the time, I could not understand that because we always supposed that, like the pool at the base of Heavenly Rushing, First Cenote was a place sacred to Miina. However, when I asked her to look into it, she saw the image of Pyphoros, an occurrence that deeply disturbed her and puzzled me. At the time I said that something evil was at work."

"That's right." Riane nodded.

"I had no idea what it was, then subsequent events drove the mystery out of my mind. But when I was summoned back to First Cenote I knew immediately."

The Rappa's eyes were dark and hooded, and Riane realized with a start that they looked haunted.

"The reason there was a disturbance, the reason you saw what you saw," Thigpen whispered, "is that my brethren discovered that somehow Pyphoros has used First Cenote to escape from the Abyss."

Riane's heart was in her throat. She did not dare tell them that the Portal seal had been broken when Giyan had violated the sorcerous circle of the Nanthera in a futile attempt to get Annon back. To do so would have revealed that the essence of Annon lived on inside of her. And yet, in the next instant, Thigpen give her another shock.

"The truly frightening thing is that we have discovered that the rift in the seal of First Cenote is old," the Rappa said. "Perhaps a hundred years or more."

Riane's mind was racing. That meant there were rifts in two Portals. Giyan had performed the Nanthera less than a year ago.

"Ah, Great Goddess." Perrnodt's face was lined with worry. "Listen to me, Dar Sala-at. You said there was nothing to fear regarding the *Maasra* falling into evil hands. In fact, there is *much* to fear. You see, in the days when Za Hara-at was at its zenith, Pyphoros and his daemon army were locked away in the Abyss. There are secrets even now honeycombed within the bones of the ancient citadel that Pyphoros would give anything to possess. The Veil of a Thousand Tears is the key to all of them. Now that we know he has returned to this realm we can be absolutely certain he is scheming to get the Veil."

Riane thought about this for some time. At last, she said, "We shall simply have to make certain this never happens."

Perrnodt sighed. "I can guarantee there will be nothing simple about it."

"Do you mean to give up even before we have begun?"

Perrnodt called a halt to their trek. She ran her fingers through her hair seven times. With each pass, the wild mass became less curly. When, at length, her long hair streamed down her back instead of being a wispy halo around her head, she said calmly, "Sit behind me now, as I sat behind you. Now take my hair and divide it into thirds. I am going to teach you how to braid the *mistefan*."

As Thigpen looked on, as she felt Riane's hands grasping her hair, she said, "The *mistefan* is a powerful symbol among us, Dar Sala-at. It lets others know that we are prepared for battle."

Thigpen kept an eye out for sauromicians while Perrnodt instructed Riane. When they were done, the Druuge rose and pointed north.

"Let us now make all speed," she said. "Not three hundred meters ahead is the end of the dead space. We will be over a bourn nexus point, and we can Thrip to Za Hara-at."

28

Spinner of Webs

Kurgan watched the Tuskugggun crone at her spinning wheel. There was a concentration about her, an aura. She worked with thread painstakingly unraveled from a pile of stinking rags. This was her entire world.

This wreck of a building knelt atop the highest hill in Axis Tyr, the entire city laid out before it. Not three hundred meters away stood the soaring, fluted arabesques of the Temple of Mnemonics. The native Kundalan shanstone had been augmented by sheets of Gyrgon neural nets hung from the ramparts of the high walls. They fluttered like gargantuan banners in the early-morning haze, lending the structure a quasi-organic facade the original architects could never have imagined.

"What is she making?" he asked Courion in a hushed voice.

"We do not know. We sometimes wonder if she does."

A nasty looking wyr-hound lay by the hearth, watching them with distrustful eyes. Curved yellow fangs protruded upward from its lower jaw.

"Of course she is quite mad," Courion continued. "Who else would live in such close proximity to the Gyrgon?"

Kurgan glanced out the window. The empty street was guarded by small animals with fever-bright eyes and hollow rib cages. They cowered in the shadows of old Kundalan buildings ransacked at the beginning of the occupation. The cracked and stubbled faces stood deserted and forlorn, an archaeological site waiting to be discovered. There was about the area a massive, hollowed-out numbness that pressed down like deadweight. Some said this was a deliberate effect of the bannered neural nets.

Courion led the way past the crone.

He had contacted Kurgan at last. "After careful consideration of your warning regarding this Gyrgon, we believe we have come up with an answer to our mutual problem," he had said. "It is simply a question of how much risk you are willing to take."

"To get Nith Batoxxx off my back forever," Kurgan had replied, "I am willing to take any risk you propose."

Their shadows fell across the spinning wheel, but the Tuskugggun scarcely noticed. She was humming a plaintive tune in a clear, bright alto that belied her advanced age.

The rear of the cracked and half-razed residence consisted of two small rooms. One was clearly the Tuskugggun's bedroom, just a simple pallet and a couple of piles of clothes with not even a fusion lamp to be seen. It was as if her madness had driven her back into a dim prehistoric age. The other chamber was even smaller, a storeroom cluttered with useless junk. Webs clung in the corners. A ragged hole in the roof had been plugged with bits of scavenged wood and wool. A coating of dust thick as the crescent of his fingernail muffled their footsteps.

As he looked on, Courion slid aside a pile of rubbish. Beneath was a trapdoor flush with the filthy floorboards. Courion opened it and, beckoning the regent forward, disappeared from view.

Something made Kurgan look back into the main room. The spinning wheel was going, tapped rhythmically by the crone's long, veined fingers. She was looking at him without expression.

"What?" He jerked his chin. "Is there something you have to say to me?"

The crone continued her silent spinning.

Kurgan shrugged, stepped onto the topmost rung of a vertical wooden ladder, and climbed down into a confined space. Mold, borne on an insistent breath of air, tickled his nostrils. He turned into the breeze. Courion was lighting a torch. By its light, he saw that they were in a narrow tunnel. Its arched ceiling merged with the walls on either side. He put his hand out. The shanstone tiles were perfectly seamed one against the other.

"This will take us directly into the base of the temple's central core," Courion said.

Kurgan followed wordlessly. He was apprehensive, but he would be exiled to N'Luuura before he would admit it.

"How can you get us into the Temple of Mnemonics?" he had queried Courion when the Sarakkonian captain had outlined his plan.

"The *oqeyya*," Courion had replied. "Nith Batoxxx does not want to run the risk of carrying it himself. Accordingly, he provided us with a way to bring it to him in his laboratory. This way the risk is all ours."

Gyrgon were unpredictable enough, but Nith Batoxxx held deeper secrets that Kurgan was burning to know. He thought of the Old V'ornn's patient tutelage, of Nith Batoxxx's unnatural interest in him, especially now that he had become regent. What was the Gyrgon's ultimate purpose? He discounted anything Nith Batoxxx had told him or promised him. Obviously, these were all lies. He had no doubt that the truth lay hidden somewhere in the Gyrgon's laboratory. Courion knew that, too, which was why he had proposed this perilous raid.

The smell of damp stone. Somewhere water dripped, and there was a creaking, as of leather, old and stiff. The draft of air, gusting, whistled through a crevice and then, as if surprised by the sound, subsided.

They turned left, then right and, perhaps a hundred meters farther on, left again. Unlike most Kundalan structures the tunnel was featureless, and somehow this increased Kurgan's apprehension. He felt as if he were walking into a trap. He looked darkly at the back of Courion's head. What did he know of this Sarakkon, anyway? N'Luuura only knew where his real loyalties lay. Kurgan grasped the hilt of his triangular-bladed dagger and considered plunging it between the Sarakkon's shoulder blades. Trust was a difficult thing for most V'ornn; for him it was virtually impossible.

Each individual had his or her best interests at hearts. Once it became clear that one's own interests collided with theirs trust became illusory. As the Old V'ornn had beaten into him, trust no one, most especially those who would befriend you.

Wennn Stogggul had been paranoid. Kurgan had played upon his fears and caused his demise. He had promised himself that he would never become like his father. And yet he was affected by powerful genetic tides. Try as he might to blot it out, he heard his father's voice, a maniacal warning.

And yet the facts were these: this particular Sarakkon was as adventurous as Annon once had been. Brave as well, there was no denying that. And, perhaps most important of all, he was bound by the Sarakkon's strict code of honor. Kurgan had saved his life; he now owed Kurgan his loyalty.

Without warning, Courion turned to him and Kurgan drew his dagger partway out of its scabbard.

"Are you planning to cut us into ribbons, regent?" Courion said quietly. "Are we relying too much on our friendship? Should we never turn our back on you?"

They stood before a gigantic door made of a matte black metal he could not immediately identify. It was banded and studded with gold jade.

"You are not my friend," Kurgan said. "I have had but one friend, and he is dead."

"Pity."

"Dead at my conniving."

"You do not worry us, regent, if that is your meaning."

Kurgan came and stood very close to the Sarakkon. "We have shared some things, you and I, extraordinary things. But do not think for a moment—"

"And we shall share more, regent, even more extraordinary."

Kurgan stood looking into those depthless eyes, and the vision from his own mind Nith Batoxxx had shown him arose like a leviathan from the deep.

There is another thing here for you to fear.

What was it? What was here that he wasn't seeing?

Courion said, "Once we enter, do not talk or otherwise make a noise that could be overheard. This includes drawing your dagger. And remember. Step only where we step. The path that Nith Batoxxx has provided will take us safely through, but deviate from it only slightly, and we guarantee we will draw a cluster of Gyrgon, furious at our trespass."

Kurgan watched the Sarakkon turn a lever. A small door opened within the huge one, and they stepped through.

The tinkling of bells, the *tick-tock* of hyperexcited ions, the vibration of massive engines rumbling deep within the labyrinthine foundation. Courion had left the torch in the tunnel. They stood in pitch-blackness. Kurgan's fist was tight on the butt of his dagger. He fought the urge to draw it. The air was bristling with the sizzle of unknown experiments. He imagined a potent energy beam being pulsed from the maw of some newly imagined weapon.

Just ahead of him, Courion snapped on a handheld lumane that Nith Batoxxx must have given him. A narrow beam of highly concentrated light arose in front of them. Just enough collected at their feet for Kurgan to see by.

They set off.

Quite soon, Kurgan realized that the Temple of Mnemonics did not contain corridors like any normal structure. Whether this was a Kundalan design or a restructuring by the Gyrgon was impossible to say. They had walked only several paces before they dropped down a kind of shaft. All around them lights twinkled and stuttered. There appeared to be nothing solid beneath them, yet they descended at a steady rate of speed. Kurgan, somewhat startled, saw his reflection speeding past him, replicated again and again.

With a warning tilt of his head, Courion stepped out of the transparent shaft. Kurgan shadowed him, careful to step only where the Sarakkonian captain placed his high shagreen boots. This procedure was repeated three times. Once, they ascended, but for the most part they kept going down.

At last, the lumane beam revealed them to be in a large chamber. It was something of a relief after the enclosed spaces they had passed through. Kurgan was just thinking this when he saw that they had come to the edge. The floor simply dropped away at a ninety-degree angle. Courion briefly directed the lumane down, but even the powerful photon beam could not reach the bottom.

Then, before Kurgan's startled eyes, Courion stepped out into what surely must be naked space. He did not fall. He paused, beckoned to Kurgan. He placed one foot directly in front of the other, by which Kurgan deduced that he was walking along an exceeding narrow gangway. Kurgan followed him. There was no point in looking down, so he stared at the Sarakkon's intricate tattoos and made sure he was directly behind him.

In short order, they reached the other side. Ahead of them was a huge sphere. Courion walked to their right, around the curving side. At length, he came to a small circular hatch, which he fiddled open. He stepped through, and Kurgan followed.

Thirteen tear-shaped globes spinning in an oval orbit leaked cold purple-blue light onto a windowless lozenge-shaped chamber that, by its looks, could only be a Gyrgon laboratory. Oddly, the Kundalan murals on the walls had been left intact. Odder still, they were covered by a webwork of orangesweet vines.

"Nith Batoxxx's laboratory," Courion said. His voice sounded a little eerie inside the chamber.

"How did you know Nith Batoxxx would not be here?"

"This is the hour of salamuuun, a sacred time for him," Courion said. "He is scanning the Realms or whatever it is he does on his flights." He shook his head. "If we leave here within fifty minutes, we will not encounter him."

Kurgan took a look around. He could not believe it. He was in the center of the Gyrgon inner sanctum, the dark heart of the V'ornn Modality's dreams, and of its secrets. He was confronted by a multitude of holoscreens, massive databanks, tier upon tier of incomprehensible equipment.

He tried to take it all in. "Everything," he whispered. "Everything I ever wanted or aspired to is in this laboratory." He reached out, turning over one mysterious implement after another. "It is simply a matter of finding out where it is all hidden."

Courion was looking around the large egg-shaped chamber, whose virtually seamless skin crawled with rainbow colors.

Kurgan paused as he came upon a red veradium box. Opening it, he saw five birth cauls neatly arrayed. *What need would Nith Batoxxx have for these?* he wondered. He turned them over. On the inner surface of each one was etched the name of the V'ornn to whom the birth caul belonged. He went through three before the fourth caught him up short.

STOGGGUL TERRETT, he read.

Breathless, he turned over the last birth-caul and his hearts skipped a double-beat.

STOGGGUL KURGAN.

He was holding his own birth caul.

"Look! An opening of some kind."

At the sound of Courion's voice, Kurgan hastily put his birth caul back in the red veradium box and closed the lid. He turned. Courion was running his hand over the egg's pale skin. He hadn't seen what Kurgan had discovered.

The Sarakkon said, "Always when we came here Nith Batoxxx made certain it was sealed. He never went near it or even glanced at it. What do you think?"

Kurgan came over and stood beside him. He was still trying to work out why Nith Batoxxx would have his birth caul and that of his mad V'ornn brother. "A vault of some sort?"

Courion grinned. "What does one put in a vault?"

And Kurgan said, "Secrets."

Together, they peered at the round port. It had three shallow depressions in it.

"This V'ornn technology defeats us," Courion admitted.

He made way for Kurgan, who saw that the depressions were actually whorls. Kurgan searched through the Gyrgon's paraphernalia until he found what he wanted. Bringing the scanner back to the hatch, he ran it over the three depressions. Its photonic screen soon lit up with an enlargement of the whorls.

"There we go," Kurgan said in triumph.

Courion peered closer. "V'ornnish writing."

"Instructions."

Putting aside the scanner, he shook his head. "I do not trust this. Why put the correct sequence for opening the lock on the lock itself?"

Courion nodded. "Unless depressing the sequence as shown will backfire on the intruder."

"Killing him." Kurgan returned his gaze to the sequence. "Gyrgon possess a perverse sense of humor. What if we were to reverse the sequence?"

Courion licked his lips. "Are you willing to try?"

Without a word, Kurgan worked the depression in reverse order. A moment later, the hatch swung open, and a low illumination came on inside.

He laughed and, pushing the Sarakkon out of the way, ducked his head and stepped into the vault which, as it happened, was not a vault at all. Inside it held only a padded chair. Someone was strapped into it with his back to Kurgan.

"What is it?" he heard Courion say. "What treasure trove have you found?"

He reached out, spun the chair toward him.

"Oh, N'Luuura take it!" he cried, jumping back so hard he hit the back of his head on the edge of the chamber.

"What is it, regent?" Courion said from the laboratory.

He stared at the figure slumped in the chair. It was a Sarakkon. He studied the faintly curling lips, the pattern of tattoos across the Sarakkon's head, the runed cubes and balls of jade and lapis lazuli in his thick curling beard, the huge rings of star sapphire and ruby and lynx-eye on his fingers.

It was Courion, dead as a slaughtered water buttren.

Kurgan, uttering another curse, drew his dagger and emerged from the chamber.

There was Courion, alive as he had ever been. Except now he was laughing.

"Too late to be alarmed, Stogggul Kurgan."

Kurgan hurled the dagger at the Sarakkon captain, whose image was now rippling like a mirage. Nith Batoxxx caught the dagger in midflight with his mailed glove.

"Courion is dead," the Gyrgon said. "Pity, really. He was a rare specimen of his kind." He leered at Kurgan. "Still, you must admit he served his purpose admirably."

It so happened that Spice Jaxx's was open all the time. This suited its varied clientele, a fascinating mix found nowhere else in Axis Tyr, not even at Blood Tide. The merchants were, like their conical stacks of spices, night-blooming. Spice Jaxx's was their home away from home, a hushed, low-lit jewel box in the center of the spice market vibrating with the heady scents of cinnamon, pepper, and wer-mace that so moved them. Looorm took their leisure here in slow-paced languor, radiating like stars their artful, crystalline beauty. They drank as fashionably as they dressed, lifting tiny handleless cups of thick, rich ba'du imported by the SaTrryn as they gossiped among themselves. Even between bouts of energetic sex their gestures were small rituals of pleasure, artifice raised to a higher power called mystery. And then there were their high-paying customers, who came to fuel up on the good food and potent drink before and after their sweaty trysts. They also talked business, these wealthy Bashkir, with nothing more on their minds than the next great deal they had heard about or hoped to get wind of.

Every once in a while Kundalan drifters fell by for a hurried bite to eat, skittish as blackcrows, keeping a wary eye out for Khaggun patrols that never appeared. No V'ornn paid them much heed, certainly not the Deirus with whom they invariably shared space. No V'ornn, not even the Looorm, cared to be anywhere near the Deirus. But the Kundalan who arrived and departed like ghostly shadows had no such bias. There was even, on occasion, brief conversations between the two groups.

The Deirus were a naturally curious lot and, doubtless because of their own pariah status, they exhibited little of the xenophobia so prevalent in other V'ornn castes. Secrets were common currency to the Deirus. What they did, when they did it, and with whom remained sealed in granite vaults they carried within their hearts. The love they knew so intimately was evil. And yet they looked like every other V'ornn; they felt love as any V'ornn felt it. These were possibly the real reasons they were reviled.

Because they had learned to turn a blind face upon the world that feared and despised them, they could find it within themselves to have pity for the Kundalan.

It was to the shadowed space in the rear of Spice Jaxx's where the Deirus clustered that Sornnn now took Marethyn. They had spent an hour or so at Cthonne dancing with the ecstatic youths to the curious hybrid music the band played. The drummer, hooded and robed, had sat in again, his powerful hands beating a complex tattoo on the skins, driving the backbeat into every corner of the dancers' skulls.

They stood amid the Deirus and drank steaming ba'du, for which Marethyn was developing a serious love. Every so often as they spoke or gazed into each other's eyes they touched one another in the manner lovers know well. She was telling him about Kirlll Qandda's shocking revelations regarding Terrettt's condition, that tests had shown that Terrettt had been the subject of secret Gyrgon experiments on his ativar almost from birth.

"How could they have done such a thing?" she asked between sips of ba'du. "What would they have wanted from him? And why, particularly, Terrettt?"

"*Wa tarabibi*, this is the Gyrgon we're talking of," he said gently. "You may have to resign yourself to the fact that you will never know."

"I can never resign myself to such a thing," she said fiercely. "The Gyrgon destroyed my brother's life. Do you think I can just forget about what they have done?"

He signaled for another round of ba'du. "All right. What do you propose? March into the Temple of Mnemonics and demand an explanation?"

It was such an absurd notion that, despite the keen edge of her anger, she laughed. "No, of course not. I . . . well, I don't know yet. But give me some time. I will think of something."

Their ba'du was brought by a young Tuskugggun waitress of dark good looks whose skull gleamed with spiced oil. She placed the tiny cups in front of them without taking the empty ones away.

"Is everything to your satisfaction?" the waitress asked Sornnn in such an intimate tone that Marethyn felt herself bristle.

"A perfect drink in a perfect world," Sornnn replied.

Marethyn had no idea what he was talking about.

He downed his ba'du in one swallow, bade her do the same. When she had thrown the dark liquid down her throat she saw the beautiful waitress give Sornnn a brief nod. He took Marethyn's arm and, together with the waitress, they moved deeper into the shadows at the rear of Spice Jaxx's. Marethyn glanced back at the Deirus. They were talking with one another, oblivious. No one else was looking in their direction.

The waitress turned and disappeared through a door that lay hidden deep in the shadows. Sornnn and Marethyn followed her through.

She was waiting for them in a small chamber built of rough stone. Behind her was an equally rough staircase blasted out of bedrock. She had pushed her sifeyn off her skull, revealing a lovely diadem of tertium and veradium no waitress could afford.

"Marethyn," Sornnn said, lifting a hand toward the diademed Tuskugggun, "this is Rada TurPlyen. Rada, this is Marethyn Stogggul. She has agreed to take her grandmother's place in our organization."

Rada took Marethyn's soft artist's hand in her callused one. "This is such welcome news!"

And then it clicked into place. "You are the one Tettsie met here. The Tuskugggun who changed her life."

"A chance meeting so many years ago." Rada nodded. "And such a fateful one! But I rather think that your grandmother changed her own life. I was only a facilitator." She inclined her head toward Sornnn. "As were the SaTrryn."

"Rada is my connection to the Resistance," Sornnn said. "She has owned the Promenade tavern Blood Tide for some years. It was there she recorded the conversation between Olnnn Rydddlin and Bronnn Pallln that warned me of their plot against me. This was how, with your very capable help, I was able to defuse it."

"The ruse turned out to be an exceedingly clever one," Rada acknowledged. "Not only did it remove a cloud of suspicion from you, but the death of that snake Bronnn Pallln has put Olnnn Rydddlin in an increasingly untenable position with the regent." She shook her head. "But all this largesse has come at a heavy price. Almost everything we were able to steal from the Khagggun is now back in their hands."

Sornnn shrugged. "It could not be helped." Then he grinned at her. "On the other hand, I pity the Khagggun who uses any one of the ion cannons I spiked."

Rada laughed, clapping him on the back. "Well done, Sornnn!"

Marethyn felt another little stab of jealousy at the familiar manner in which Rada addressed him.

"How goes your balancing act?" Sornnn said.

Rada shrugged. "Too soon to tell."

"This is dangerous territory you have chosen to play in."

"I? I hardly had a choice in this. The regent made me an offer. If I had refused, I very much think I would never have walked out of the palace that night. And as for Olnnn Rydddlin, I had even less of a say. What strange luck has bound me in sorcery to him and to his sorcerous mistress, Malistra, I have yet to understand."

"In any event," Sornnn said, "we will miss your keen eyes and ears in Blood Tide."

She shrugged again. "I have left the running of the tavern to my sister Nestta, at least for the time being. She is smart and loyal. As for the data-decagons I weekly send the regent, they still contain a combination of truth we deem harmless and the disinformation you and my other contacts concoct. I make certain I am back at Blood Tide each week to place it in the regent's messenger's goblet."

Sornnn nodded, adding brief explanations here and there to bring Marethyn up to speed on Rada's triple role as spy for the regent, companion for the Star-Admiral, and continuing conduit for intelligence to the Resistance. Rada told them of the difficulties Olnnn was facing in keeping her new status from the regent's Haaar-kyut.

"Have you heard anything at all about these so-called Portals?" Rada asked. Sornnn had been one of the first contacts she had asked about them. "The regent's replies are becoming increasingly more filled with urgent questions about them."

"What Portals?" Marethyn asked.

Rada took out a laaga stick, lighted it. "It seems a particular Gyrgon, Nith Batoxxx, believes there are seven Kundalan Portals." She blew the aromatic smoke out through her nostrils. "What they lead to I have no idea. But the regent has informed me that he is most desirous to know their locations." She shrugged. "Anyway, who cares what the Gyrgon wants? I am pressing you, Sornnn, because I need to keep real intelligence flowing to the regent to mix in with the disinformation."

Sornnn shook his head. "Nothing so far. But it is hardly surprising. This sounds like something a Ramahan might know something about."

Rada nodded, took another hit off the laaga stick, and beckoned silently to them. She led them down the rough-hewn staircase. It was dark, but she did not once falter, proof that she was familiar with the route.

The staircase led to a subbasement in which a hole had been punched. A steep spiral of steps had been roughly hacked out of the bedrock. Without hesitation, Rada continued the descent, Sornnn after her. Marethyn brought up the rear.

It became increasingly cold and dank. Marethyn heard strange sounds echoing, deep and atonal. Then a brief drift of voices, as ephemeral as the smoke from Rada's half-open lips. Light flared below her, and she saw Rada and Sornnn standing on a floor of gleaming polished porphyry.

Wrought-bronze lanterns, filigree blackened with carbon and age, were set at intervals in triangular wall niches. They trailed off on either side for as far as she could see. Two youths were facing Sornnn and Rada, both more or less the same size. They watched her, silent and brooding, as she descended the last few treads. A Kundalan male and a female, armed with ion pistols and the haggard faces born of desperation. Rada took the laaga stick from between her lips and held it out. The female accepted it, inhaled deep into her lungs, and held it while she passed it to the male. He, also, took a big hit. They expelled the smoke together, slowly and luxuriously. He handed the laaga stick back to Rada.

The two of them continued to regard Marethyn as if deciding how they were going to kill her. The echoing sounds continued, and Marethyn had an intuition they were being watched from the shadows.

"This is Marethyn, Neyyore's granddaughter," Rada said, using Tettsie's real name. "She is taking her place." She introduced Majja, the female, and Basse, the male.

The two youths watched her sullenly, hip-sprung. They were all muscle and hard edges, hormones and attitude.

"In the mountains they have honored Neyyore," Rada said to Marethyn as if translating the youths' silence, "with fire and prayer. Miina has heard her name."

"Thank you." Marethyn ducked her head.

"Have you killed?"

Basse's question hung in the air like invective.

"Basse," Rada said quietly.

"No." He shook his head. One hand was on the grip of his ion pistol. "I want to know."

Majja said, "She doesn't look like she could kill a blood-flea."

"Have *you* killed?" It was a foolish question for Marethyn to have asked.

In a flash, Majja had drawn her ion pistol and jammed the muzzle into the side of Marethyn's neck. Rada and Sornnn each took a step away.

"Don't do that," Basse said, standing back so he could keep all of them in his field of vision. His ion pistol was half out of its holster.

"We are both female," Marethyn said to Majja. "Surely we both feel—"

"This isn't a game," Majja whispered fiercely.

"She thinks it's a game," Basse nodded.

"If you think it's a game," Majja said, "you are going to get yourself killed and possibly some of us with you."

"We won't have that," Basse said. "Do you understand?"

Marethyn nodded. She licked her lips. To think her life was in the volatile hands of these youths. How much laaga had they smoked? she wondered.

"Let's all lower our temperatures," Sornnn said. "Rada and I have brought you good news."

"We need good news." Majja put away her ion pistol and stepped back. "Three hours ago we found another mass grave."

"How big?" Rada asked.

"The biggest yet." Basse folded his arms across his chest. "More than three hundred."

"We are no longer able to stand our ground," Majja said.

Basse said, "We need more powerful weapons. Now."

"You know what happened," Sornnn said. "Our hoard had to be sacrificed for the greater good."

"There will be no greater good," Majja said heatedly, "unless we are better armed."

Sornnn shook his head. "These things take time."

Basse said, "The new Star-Admiral is relentless. Each day more of us die. Each day it is more and more difficult getting new recruits."

"These things take time," Majja sneered.

Basse said. "You V'ornn have the Cosmos, we have only Kundala. Can you understand that?"

"Please," Marethyn said. "We are here to help you."

The two youths exchanged a glance.

Majja put her hands on her hips and looked her square in the eye. "Let us see if you mean that, granddaughter of Neyyore."

"We know of a stash containing new-model ion cannons, proximity mines, ion-pulse projectors," Basse said. "The weapons are being convoyed in three armed grav-carriages from here in Avis Tyr to Line-General Lokck Werrrent's headquarters in Glistening Drum. It is scheduled to leave the Khagggun armory in three days' time. If we could lay an ambush—"

Sornnn was shaking his head. "It will be too well guarded."

Majja cocked her head. "But we have you, Rada. You are at the Star-Admiral's side. If you could give us the exact route . . ."

"I could never get it to you," Rada said. "Not with the Star-Admiral keeping such close track of my movements. I almost missed the rendezvous tonight."

"Find out what you can." Majja ran her hand down Marethyn's arm. "And give it to Neyyore's granddaughter. She will come with us."

"No," Sornnn said at once.

Marethyn, her hearts beating fast, said, "Sornnn, I promised to help."

"Not this way." He shook his head. "You will help the way Tettsie helped. You will provide us with the funding we need to—"

"We need the weapons!" Majja cried. "Now!"

"Otherwise," Basse said, "all the coins on Kundala will not avail us."

Marethyn nodded. "I will—"

"I forbid it!" Sornnn roared.

"You forbid it?" She turned to him. "You are the one who brought me into this."

"Not to go into battle. Not to be on the front lines."

"This is not for you to say," she said quietly. "These children are in battle every day. They are on the front lines. Why am I different? Why should I be protected?"

He took her in his arms. "Because I love you."

"And is there no one to love them? Or are their loved ones all dead by our hand?" She looked up into his face, placed her palm against his cheek. "Dearest Sornnn, I entered this of my own free will because this is what I wanted."

"Marethyn . . ." It was a kind of strangled cry.

She kissed him tenderly. "Now you must let me do what must be done."

29

The Dispossessed

Konara Inggres sat in one of the small chambers, windowless and airless, at the back of the Library and stared at the mirror she had conjured up. It was really quite beautiful, perfectly round, its frame of beaten copper incised with sigils that ran in a kind of sinuous dance all the way around its circumference. The reflection the mirror itself provided was extraordinarily clear and sharp, bright as a gimnopede's eye without even a hint of the wavering that was endemic to all Kundalan mirrors. In other circumstances, Konara Inggres would have been pleased with her accomplishment. As it was, however, the mirror's presence only seemed to increase her feeling of dread.

She had written a brief note to Konara Lyystra asking her to come to the Library, entrusting it to one of the acolytes for a sure and speedy delivery. Now, bathed in cold sweat, she had become terrified by the boldness of her design. She had never thought of herself as capable of being calculating and devious although, she supposed, learning to be politic might conceivably be cast in that mold. After overhearing the conversation between Giyan and Bartta she had no illusions concerning the risk to her body and spirit. But Konara Lyystra was her best friend. An evil daemon had invaded her, and if Konara Inggres could do something—anything!—to free her from its influence, she knew she had to try it.

The cubicle was at the very rear of the vast, two-story Library. Three of the four walls were covered from floor to ceiling with shelves. The seamless flow of books was interrupted only by the doorway and, above it, a decorative fanlight panel, now dark with dust and grime. It was into this shadowed recess that Konara Inggres had wedged her sorcerous mirror, having climbed up the rolling ammonwood ladder with which each of these cubicles was equipped. She sat at the rear of the compartment, facing the doorway, her eyes flicking upward now and again to find her own face staring back at her with a combination of shocked anticipation and acute anxiety.

She saw her friend striding confidently toward her across the polished agate floor of the Library and, all of a sudden, felt the need to urinate. Too late for that. Under the table, she crossed her legs. She had been here for hours, preparing herself for this very moment, but now that it was here she quailed inside. She concentrated on controlling her breathing and what she needed to say.

Konara Lyystra entered the cubicle. Difficult though it was, Konara Inggres stitched a natural-looking smile to her face, got up, and embraced her friend. As she did so, she looked up at the mirror and saw, to her horror, what was inhabiting Konara Lyystra's corpus.

It had the greasy-looking triangular head of a serpent and the body of a gigantic millipede. It was a Cerrn, the sorcerous mirror had revealed to her, a warrior-daemon one step up from a Tzelos. Even as her mind coldly registered this fact she could not have been more revolted. It was all she could do not to thrust the abomination away from her and run screaming from the cubicle. In fact, she wanted to turn away from the image, but she could not. Gripped by a horrific fascination, she continued to stare at the hideous thing, unsure of whether she was losing her mind. Inside, she wept, and prayed to Miina without understanding or insight as to how the Great Goddess could have abandoned her and all the Ramahan to this abysmal fate.

She ticked off the litany of crimes and heresies the abbey's ruling konara had been perpetrating against Miina for more than a century, and she knew the answer to her own question. Since the time of Mother there had been no strong and pious konara to wrest control from her power-mad successors. And with each one, the abbey had crawled further away from the sacred teachings of Miina.

Into her head slithered the doubts remembered from her recent debate with her best friend. What if Miina did not exist? What if she, Konara Inggres, and all Kundalan were alone in the darkness of this long night? She felt a wave of despair lap at her.

"You wished to see me," the creature posing as Konara Lyystra said to Konara Inggres, as they broke their embrace. "You said it was urgent."

"Urgent. Yes."

Konara Inggres gestured to a chair in which her friend seated herself while Konara Inggres returned to her accustomed seat behind the desk.

She put her elbows on the tabletop and laced her fingers together.

"I am eager to be able to spend more time with Konara Giyan."

"Mother."

"Yes." Konara Inggres nodded. "Mother." With each flick of her eyes, she saw reflected in the mirror the Cerrn squirming uncomfortably inside Konara Lyystra's body. Konara Inggres smiled to keep herself from screaming. "In her talk with me, Ko—Mother expressed a desire to see a modification in the curriculum. After careful consideration, I believe that she is right. As far as History of Sorcery is concerned, I was wondering whether you could advise me on how to redesign the syllabus."

Konara Lyystra smiled. "I would be delighted to help you all I can. But I think Mother will be the one to—"

"Of course she will approve the changes."

The Cerrn, dark and squirmy and repulsive, moved behind Konara Lyystra's eyes. "I believe she will be wanting to *make* the changes."

Konara Inggres sat back. "I see."

"Is that a problem in any way?"

"Not at all." Konara Inggres pursed her lips meditatively. "It's just that—"

"What?"

"Well, I hesitate even to bring this up."

"But why not?" Konara Lyystra's smiled broadened. "Are we not the best of friends? Do not the best of friends trust each other and share everything?"

"That's the way it has always been with us."

"Well, then. Nothing's changed, has it?"

Was that a dyspeptic note of paranoia Konara Inggres detected in her friend's voice or was it simply that she herself was balanced on a knife edge of suspense? She could not tell, but there was no point in dismissing the possibility.

She laughed softly, marveling at the naturalness of it. "Of course nothing has changed between us. Why should it?"

"I have become very close to Mother in such a short time. It occurred to me that you might have become a bit . . . well, you know . . ."

"Jealous?"

"Yes, that's the word," Konara Lyystra said a little too forthrightly. "Jealous."

"My goodness, no. It is a great honor for you, and it makes me proud that you are my friend."

Konara Lyystra beamed. "Yes, yes. That is as it should be."

In this way, Konara Inggres determined that there was a strict limit to the intelligence of the creature who had possessed her best friend. This knowledge added to a fundamental base. While she had been waiting for Konara Lyystra to arrive she had not been idle. Rather, she had been busy consulting the ancient ill-used books here, assiduously researching the subject of possession. For instance, she had discovered that possession of a Ramahan was possible only by a daemon, and possession by a daemon was only possible if one or more of the sorcerous Portals to the Abyss had been broken open.

There were several ways to go about a dispossession, as the ancient texts called the casting out of the daemon. This was not a simple procedure. The first step was to separate the daemon from the host body-mind network. The second, equally difficult feat, was then to kill or immobilize the daemon itself. There was, she had read, only a very short amount of time—perhaps as little as ten seconds—when the daemon, wrenched from its temporary home, was disoriented and thus assailable. The third step was perhaps the hardest, because when the daemon was inside its host it opened White Bone Gate. This was one of the fifteen Spirit Gates inside each individual. The opened gates allowed the body's natural energy to flow in a pattern unique to that individual. If there was a disruption in even one gate, an illness of the soul would result. White Bone Gate was the main bulwark against the infiltration of evil. If it was open or damaged, evil would inevitably enter to deform the spirit, and until that spiritual Gate was closed the host remained vulnerable to the incursion of evil. Konara Inggres had no doubt that this is what had happened to Bartta.

The Cerrn, the texts had revealed, made up in power for what it lacked in intelligence. It was a dangerous, even a formidable adversary for a konara trained in dispossession, let alone one like her who was struggling to absorb so much knowledge in a short amount of time. She could not afford to make a mistake, yet in the back of her mind was the thoroughly disquieting notion that her haste would almost ensure some kind of slip-up. She found that her palms were wet, and she rubbed them together underneath the table where Konara Lyystra could not observe her extreme anxiety.

She felt little filaments of terror shooting through her like painful sparks as she drew from a low shelf just behind and to one side of her a tray she had prepared some hours ago in the still-dark refectory.

As Konara Lyystra was about to stand up, she said, "Don't go. I took the liberty of preparing refreshments." She slid the tray onto the desktop and distributed the service. "A pot of cool sanguineaberry infusion and individual qwawd-blood puddings."

"Mmmm." Konara Lyystra's avid eyes were riveted on the array of puddings. "Looks absolutely scrumptious. You don't see those every day."

When she had read that many daemons loved qwawd blood, she had recalled a brace of the large birds hanging by their long necks in the refectory's cold room, waiting on the cooks to season and roast.

She poured the infusion into small ceramic cups and pushed a pudding in front of Konara Lyystra. Neither of these things would her friend have eaten on her own, but like many daemons the Cerrn suffered from an excess of greed, and she could see by the avid look on Konara Lyystra's face that she had, as it were, hit the peg square on its crown.

Without a word of thanks, Konara Lyystra popped an entire pudding into her mouth and nearly swallowed it whole. She washed the pudding down with her cupful of sanguineaberry infusion. While Konara Inggres was refilling her cup, Konara Lyystra reached for another qwawd-blood pudding. As she did so, her mouth fell open. Though she had steeled herself for the sight, Konara Inggres almost gagged as she saw the Cerrn's cilia rippling in its extreme greed across the top of the tongue. Immediately, she cast White-Bone Rushing Out, the dispossession spell she had learned earlier that morning but had, of course, never practiced.

For a moment, Konara Lyystra's body froze in midreach. Her eyes opened wide, and she began to blink very rapidly. So softly that at first Konara Inggres had to strain to hear, there emerged from her breast a sound not unlike the beating of insect wings.

The rest happened so quickly that Konara Inggres leapt back off her chair. First, Konara Lyystra's eyes began to bleed. Blood ran from her nose, drooled out of her mouth. Then, her head snapped back so that she was staring straight up at the vaulted ceiling, her jaws hinged open and, with a nauseating sound, the Cerrn was summarily ejected from its host.

For an instant, it lay stunned in a puddle of slimy gastric juices. It was smaller than Konara Inggres had imagined, and somehow mesmerizing in its altogether ghastly countenance. This last the text had covered but possibly not well enough, for Konara Inggres felt herself captive of her own morbid fascination and it was only when it began to stir, flopping and thrashing, that she reached for the shard of heartwood she had secreted on the shelf behind her.

But by this time the Cerrn had regained much of its senses and, recognizing its antagonist, rippled its multilegged body and shot through the intervening space toward Konara Inggres' face. Konara Inggres had barely time enough to impale it on the heartwood shard. Then she slammed it down onto the tabletop, sending teapot, cups, and disgusting qwawd-blood puddings flying in all directions. Using both her hands, she ground the stake all the way through the Cerrn while it twisted and beat itself in its death agonies.

At last it was still, and Konara Inggres, taking a deep breath, rushed around from behind the desk and knelt beside her friend where she had collapsed to the floor. Using the edge of her robes, Konara Inggres wiped the blood from Konara Lyystra's face and, for her efforts, was rewarded with her friend's eyes opening. They looked placid and calm with no trace of the squirmy darkness that had so recently haunted them.

Konara Inggres let out a laugh and, taking her friend's head in her lap, kissed her on the cheeks and forehead. "Ah, thank Miina!"

"Inggres," Konara Lyystra whispered in a thin, sere voice, "where am I? What has happened?"

Before Konara Inggres could reply, a shadow fell over them and they both looked to the figure looming in the doorway.

"Yes," Giyan said with a great deal of concern in her voice, "that is precisely what I want to know."

I told you to be careful, didn't I? I warned you there was something to fear in your relationship with the Sarakkon. I really must say I gave you every opportunity to prove your loyalty to me." Nith Batoxxx circled Kurgan, the triangular blade of the dagger slapping into his mailed palm. "And what happens?"

"How long?" Kurgan said tightly.

"You betray me the first chance you get."

"How long have you been Courion?"

All at once Nith Batoxxx strode toward him. "I am through playing games with you."

Kurgan neither cowered nor ran. He thought of the Tuskugggun crone, spinning her stupid wheel. Had she known? Is that why she had looked at him just before he had gone down the ladder? Or was she just, as Courion had said, mad? But, then, that hadn't really been Courion who had said that. It had been Nith Batoxxx.

"What has five faces," Kurgan said, "two of them animal?"

He grimaced in pain as the Gyrgon gripped him. The hyperexcited ions danced along his flesh, making him feel as if he were being dipped in fire.

Slowly, Nith Batoxxx turned him around until he was facing the egg-shaped chamber.

"This is a goron-wave chamber. Let me show you what happens to anyone who is put inside." He raised his free hand, and the circular hatch slammed closed. Another gesture brought down several holoscreens. He turned on the goron wave and when it had passed through the interior of the chamber, she opened the hatch and shoved Kurgan inside.

There, Kurgan was witness to the horrifying results. Courion's eyes were completely white, his teeth had turned to dust in his mouth and his tattoos had been burned all the way through his skull.

"And he was already dead," Nith Batoxxx said as he took Kurgan by the scruff of his neck and shoved him, stumbling, from the chamber. "Imagine what it will do to you."

Kurgan kept his mouth shut, knowing full well anything he said would infuriate the Gyrgon all the more.

"I am going to place you in there," Nith Batoxxx said, "and I am going to loose the goron wave a little at a time. I understand it is like having a million tiny mouths feed off you at the same time."

"Is this meant to frighten me?" Kurgan stood his ground. "I have been too well trained. I have no fear. Even you were unable to find any fear inside me. So you created your little fantasy with Courion."

"A test," Nith Batoxxx said. "Let us call it by its proper name. A test you failed."

"If failure means not having to be yoked to you, then it is well I failed."

Nith Batoxxx seized him so hard he rose into the air. "You swore an oath of fealty to me. Your word—"

"My word means nothing to the likes of you." Kurgan was spasming with the pain the Gyrgon was causing him. He could not imagine the goron-wave chamber being any worse than this. "You coerced that oath out of me. Did you really think I would abide by it?"

With a roar, Nith Batoxxx grabbed him by both hands. He almost passed out with the agony. There was no part of him that did not pulsate painfully with needles of hyperexcited ions. He could feel his hearts racing too fast; imagining his blood beginning to boil, he began to retch, but was quickly too weak even for that.

"I will not break," he whispered. "I will not bow down to you."

"Oh, yes, you will."

"I will die first."

"Then by all means." Nith Batoxxx grinned evilly at him. "You are Stogggul. I know your family rather well. You are all deceitful, lying skcettta."

"I owe all my deceit to the Old V'ornn." Kurgan tried to keep his voice steady. "I believe you know *him* rather well."

"What means this?"

"I think it is time we both stopped playing games," Kurgan said through chattering teeth. The Gyrgon's face, the goron-wave chamber, the entire laboratory was going in and out of focus. "I know who you are, who you become when you leave this temple and wander the streets of Axis Tyr. Show me the Old V'ornn." He knew, finally, that he was going to sob, so he laughed raggedly to cover it. "Show yourself! Come on, there's a good Gyrgon."

"You want me to reveal myself?" Nith Batoxxx thundered. "This is what you desire? So be it then!"

Kurgan gave a sharp yelp as the bronze skin and pulsing neural-net circuits at the crown of the Gyrgon's head peeled back in a surf of yellowish foam. This almost immediately evaporated into a mist, exuding the foul must of the grave. Instead of revealing bare skull, there appeared a black hole, from which snaked a scaled appendage, whiter than death. Then another appendage came questing and another until there were five in all.

These appendages shot straight up in concert. As they did so, they began to twine with one another. The rotten stench had by this time fully permeated the laboratory, and Kurgan felt once again the need to retch.

*   *   *

With the most serene of smiles on her face, Giyan made a vicious lunge for Konara Inggres, but Konara Inggres was prepared for this. She was already chanting, and in chanting, spinning, and spinning, Thripped out of the Library at the Abbey of Floating White into Otherwhere.

For a moment her mind was filled with the guilt of leaving her friend behind. But she knew that Giyan had given her no choice, and she shook her head to clear it. She was not yet such an accomplished Osoru sorceress, having trained herself in secret, that she understood the changes Horolaggia had wrought in this sorcerous realm. Nevertheless, the cacophony of wailing voices made her aware that all was not well here. And, unlike Riane, she had the advantage of years of book study, and therefore knew that somehow the veil between Realms had grown so thin it was in danger of rupturing. What damage daemons running amok in Otherwhere could perpetrate she could not imagine. She only knew that she could not allow it to occur.

She found herself on a vast plain running with blood. In the far distance she could make out the looming jagged length of the mountains within which, she could already sense, lay ominously beating the evil hearts of daemonic Avatars. Instinctively, she knew that she was no match for them, for she felt their power pulsing in waves that produced storm clouds, ruddy and fulminating, above the rock spires.

And so she kept her profile low, slouching in shadows, picking her way carefully across the newly blasted landscape. She had absolutely no experience with Thripping, and therefore felt dizzy and nauseous, not knowing that she needed a mononculus inside her to absorb the noxious radiation that existed in the netherspace between Realms. She simply put her feeling of weakness down to inexperience, assuming she would grow stronger with each Thrip.

Despite her temporary infirmity, she kept moving, wanting as soon as possible to find Giyan. It was not easy to think clearly, what with the growing din of the babbling voices and the fear of pursuit. She knew from her readings that the daemon in possession of Giyan could not Thrip; daemons could not employ Osoru sorcery. Similarly, it could no use Giyan's Osoru Avatar, for in order to possess a Ramahan it was quired to bind the sorceress's Avatar in Otherwhere. But she did that the archdaemons like Pyphoros had power over Avatars

He was wrenched from his incipient illness by the next pha⸢
was taking place in front of him. The twining appendages s
have reproduced. Now they were melding together, forming
of a huge and powerful-looking body. It appeared to be at on⸤
and animal in that its stance was a semicrouch, one should
than the other.

Then, from the core of this eerie headless trunk a hal⸤
emerged. It rapidly coalesced into a spinning orb. As the orb set⸢
the massive shoulders it spun more and more slowly, and Kurg⸤
now and again the hint of a face. But it was never the same face

The orb, coming to rest, resolved itself into a head unlike an
had ever seen, save once. Here before him was the thing with f
three Kundalan, two animal. His glimpse of it in the mirror l
too brief or perhaps too shocking for him to have kept a clear
of all the faces. But now he could see them clearly, and it se
him that each one was defined by a specific emotion. A long, s
face with black flashing eyes was animated by anger, another
fully sculpted, was lit by lust, a third, at once bloated and di
was the epitome of envy, a predator bird's imperious counten
diated pride, while a sleek catlike face watched him greedily.

Kurgan, for once in his life overwhelmed, struggled despite
to scramble away.

"The real me seems not much to your liking, regent, is tha⸢
say?"

The voice, deep and echoey, was the one he had heard sna
coming at times from Nith Batoxxx's mouth. It filled the enti
ratory like the bursting of a thunderstorm.

"What are you doing?" he cried. "What illusion are you castin⸤

The thing before him laughed. "Illusion? This world you li
the illusion. You V'ornn! You pass through space, you conquer
and races and think you are the emperors of the Cosmos. But y⸤
not the slightest conception of the multiplicity of the Cosm⸤
inhabit one tiny island in an ocean so vast it is beyond your
comprehension.

"Illusion?" The thing shook Kurgan like a rag doll. "You V'o⸤
more the illusion than I am. I am Pyphoros, Lord of archdaemon
I have at last returned to this realm from the prison accursed
confined me to eons ago."

own, and this was her fear now, that Giyan was possessed by an archdae-mon who would send its Avatar after her, even though it could only exist for a short time in this realm that had been created by Osoru sorcery.

She knew that she had a small window within which to operate. When she had conceived of the plan to dispossess Konara Lyystra of the daemon infesting her she knew there was a possibility of Giyan discovering what she was up to. Accordingly, she devised an escape route into Otherwhere—daring and dangerous inasmuch as she had never attempted to Thrip before. But she could think of no other way out of the dire straits unfolding in the abbey. She understood that she was not powerful enough to defeat the daemons already in residence. It was difficult enough to keep her Osoru abilities a secret from them and from the possessed Konara Lyystra. She knew she had to take action quickly or surely she would be found out and eliminated, as Giyan's possessor had so succinctly put it. In short, when she thought it through, she needed help. Sorcerous help on a powerful scale. And who better to provide that help than Giyan herself?

Now here she was slouching through Otherwhere, searching for Gi-yan's pinioned Avatar, with precious little time to consider her next move. She kept one eye ahead of her, the other on the fulminating clouds above the jagged peaks, knowing that it was there that she would first spot movement from the slumbering daemonic Avatars.

From what she had gathered from her clandestine reading of the forbidden Osoru texts, Otherwhere was a realm constructed on the bedrock of symbology, and as a sailor scans the horizon for a sail or a raised fist of land, so she looked for symbols. And, at length, she saw something, and headed for it as quickly as she dared.

As she approached, she saw that it was a gigantic inverted triangle, black as night, onto which was pinioned, head down, a great bird. And without being told, she recognized this bird from her readings as an Avatar known as Ras Shamra.

"Shima Giyan," she called softly, for shima was the level Giyan had attained before she had been banished from the abbey.

"Who calls me by my old title?"

And Konara Inggres gasped, for she was near enough now to see that the Avatar's eyes were blinded by blood that seeped from a thousand small cuts on her body.

"It is I, Shima Giyan, Leyna Inggres. Now Konara."

"Ah, ah, dear Inggres. I recall you as a little girl. I marked you as one with the Gift. Of course, I told no one."

Konara nodded her thanks. "Since you left, it seems that with each passing year the abbey is beset with more evil." She was grateful that Giyan was not wasting time asking her how she had managed to nurture her Gift in the hostile environment of the abbey.

"How much damage?" Giyan asked.

"You don't know?"

"I am cut off here. But quickly, tell me. Horolaggia cannot overhear us unless his Avatar appears."

Konara Inggres nodded. Her mouth was dry. "The daemon possessing you has taken over Floating White, and has brought Bartta back from her sorcerous limbo, only to be possessed by another daemon."

"This news is more evil than you know," Giyan said. "We are dealing with archdaemons. This means that Horolaggia is not the only one to have escaped the Abyss. He has somehow freed his brother Myggorra."

Konara Inggres gasped. "You are speaking of the offspring of Pyphoros!"

"Indeed. And in doing so they have violated the Primal Laws set down for mortals, creatures, sorcerers, goddesses, archdaemons, and daemons."

"Ah, Shima Giyan!" Konara Inggres cried all at once. "How can we be talking like this when you are held captive and in such agony? You have only to tell me how I can help you."

"You cannot," Giyan said. "At least not in the direct fashion you mean."

"How then? I know my power is no match for an archdaemon."

"That is true enough," Giyan said, "but we have yet to test your ingenuity against them. You must return to the abbey. In the most ancient section, below the commissary, are Miina's sacred chambers."

"The Kells, yes. I have seen them, Shima Giyan. It is there that I conjured the mirror in which I saw the Cerrn that had possessed my best friend, Konara Lyystra. I dispossessed it using White-Bone Rushing Out and killed it by impaling it on a heartwood stake."

"I congratulate you," Giyan said, "but know that White-Bone Rushing Out will work only with the low-level daemons like a Tzelos or a Cerrn. For those who have possessed me and my sister other measures must be taken."

"Tell me, Shima Giyan."

"The Veil of a Thousand Tears is being sought even now by . . . someone trusted by me. Her name is Riane. You must wait for her, for besides the death of the host, the Veil is the only thing that will dispossess an archdaemon. But I know that if you are here they must be aware of your Osoru Gift. You must wage a war of stealth against them. You must hide and keep yourself hidden even from those whom you have in the past trusted. I cannot stress this enough, no one inside the abbey can be trusted. You must assume that they are all compromised. All of them, do you understand?"

"Yes, Shima Giyan."

"This friend of yours."

"Konara Lyystra."

"For the time being you must forget her."

"But Shima Giyan."

The Ras Shamra shook its head. "No exceptions, Konara Inggres, none whatsoever. I understand your desire to help your friend. But you see the result. In casting White-Bone Rushing Out you gathered to you unwanted scrutiny. Now that you have identified yourself as their enemy they will not rest until they have destroyed you."

Konara Inggres forced down a rising panic. "But how will I wage this war of stealth you speak of in these dire circumstances?"

"By judiciously employing a weapon they cannot know is in your possession. Tell me, when you were in the Kells did you see Ghosh, the citrine serpent?"

"Yes, Shima Giyan. It was in the exact center of the Kell."

"It was not in its niche on the wall?" Giyan said sharply. "Are you certain?"

"Absolutely, Shima Giyan. I prostrated myself before it and prayed to Miina for guidance."

"And did guidance come?"

Konara Inggres thought a moment. "I suppose it did. Not long after, in the Kell just beneath, I discovered the cenote. Around it were arrayed in a perfect triangle three terrifying beasts carved of some stone I could not identify. They had pelts of gold leaf strewn with black spots. This cenote was where I cast the spell that conjured up the mirror." Seeing the Ras Shamra tremble, she hesitated a moment. "Is there something odd about what I have told you?"

"That Ghosh and the three Ja-Gaar are no longer where they have remained for centuries means there is sorcery more ancient even than the Ramahan at work. There is much to consider." Shaking the blood from its eyes, the Ras Shamra cast its glance as best it could toward the fulminating mountain range. "We have very little time left. Listen carefully to what I tell you. Return at once to the Kells. Pluck the right eye from Ghosh."

"But, Shina Giyan," Konara Inggres said, horrified. "The citrine serpent is sacred of Miina. I cannot deface—"

"You will do as I say!" the Ras-Shamra thundered with such utter authority that Konara Inggres could only bow her head.

"Yes, First Mother!"

"Why do you call me that?"

"The Prophesies, First Mother. They tell of the Ramahan sorceress who will be imprisoned in Otherwhere by the archdaemon. It is she who is destined to guide the Dar Sala-at. She is the First Mother."

"Be that as it may," the Ras Shamra said, "you will pluck the right eye from the citrine serpent. Do this by turning it three times left in its socket. You will then take it to the cenote where you conjured up the mirror and immerse it for thirty seconds, no more, no less. Do you understand?"

"Yes, First Mother."

"When you remove it—"

The sky seemed to be crying crimson tears, and the ground beneath Konara Inggres' feet trembled with ominous thunder.

The Ras Shamra did not have to tell Konara Inggres what this portended. "When you remove it," she hurried on, "place it wet upon the center of your forehead, in that spot between your eyes and above the bridge of your nose. Once you have immersed it, you must not allow it to dry. If you do, it will crack apart and fall to useless dust."

"Then what, First Mother?" Konara Inggres glanced nervously at the soot-black clouds rising swiftly from the mountain peaks. "What will happen when I place the eye against my forehead?"

"Go!" the Ras Shamra ordered. "Before he catches a glimpse of you!"

Konara Inggres closed her eyes. As she did so, she began to spin and, spinning, Thripped out of Otherwhere just as the clouds were rent asunder.

30

Za Hara-at

nd there it crouched, waiting on the edge of eternity. Darkling, windswept, subterranean. Half-devoured by time. Twilight at the rim of the Djenn Marre, in sight of the Great Rift.
Repository of ancient secrets, a labyrinth of blood-dark streets winding
out of light and time, entering another place. An almost forgotten city,
musty, deserted, guarded.

Za Hara-at.

Two kuomeshal stood side by side, heads down, drowsing. Coveys
of finbats fluttered in ragged streamers. A young Bey Das, skin dark as
pomegranate stew, long hair flying, dragged a kite behind him. He ran
in a straight line from the edge of the dig toward the ragged, flyblown
tents of Im-Thera. Tiny clouds of red dust floated in his wake. The kite
took flight in twilight's gusty arrival and the finbats veered away to
continue feeding. The kite dipped once, then soared heavenward, and
the boy made a brief ululating sound of triumph, only to be cut short
by his mother's angry cry of anxiety as she pulled him back to Im-
Thera.

In twilight, Za Hara-at was deserted. Though there was still plenty
of reflected light in the overwhelming sky, no Bey Das worked at the
dig after the sun slid behind the Djenn Marre. Light blazed from the
smallish encampment made up of Mesagggun and Bashkir architects
hired by the Stogggul and SaTrryn Consortia to begin the reconstruction
of Za Hara-at. The encampment was now completely surrounded by a
bristling of Khagggun armament. In the glare of artificial light, an ion
shield was being erected around the perimeter to keep out the unknown predator who stalked the crumbled avenues of Za Hara-at and
to keep in the terrified Bashkir who longed for Axis Tyr.

Into this unsettling twilight Thripped the three travelers. They arrived at the top of the main ramp that led down into the archaeological

remains of Za Hara-at. It was, Riane thought, like entering the skeleton of a great and fantastic beast, for she felt with her extraordinary Gift the life that pulsed in a place most believed had been dead and buried for centuries. The city was sitting on a network of bourn nexuses. She felt their separate vibrations like the sections of an orchestra tuning up.

"My kind have told countless stories of Za Hara-at," Thigpen said, her voice filled with awe. "But I am the first of my generation to see it."

"Once this was a thriving citadel," Perrnodt said, as they continued down the ramp. "And yet it was not the hub of ancient civilization, for it was designed and constructed for one reason. As a defense against an enemy so terrible that only such an engine of unimaginable power could save us."

"Too bad you could not have resurrected it to stop the V'ornn invasion."

"The engine was designed to facilitate the destruction of the one terrible enemy," Perrnodt said. "This is how such power is safeguarded."

They had reached the beaten-brass streets of Za Hara-at itself. Embedded in the streets were, here and there, runes carved from emperor carnelian and lapis lazuli. Riane knelt, ran her fingertips over the runes. They were Venca.

GATHER THE UNKOWING, she read.

"Perrnodt," she said quietly, "who built Za Hara-at?"

"We did. The Druuge." Perrnodt stared down a broad boulevard into the gathering darkness. "We needed help. The engine at the core of the citadel was too complex even for us to manage on our own. So we did something that was both necessary and foolish. We enlisted the daemons to assist us."

Riane stood. "I thought you told me that the daemons were imprisoned at that time."

"No. I said they were imprisoned at the height of Za Hara-at's power. They helped us build the engine and then, of course, they wanted control of it. That we could not allow. There was a fierce battle. Many on both sides were killed. Then Miina stepped in and imprisoned them in the Abyss. They never got to see the engine they had labored so hard to build."

"No wonder Pyphoros wants to return."

"He covets the terrible secrets buried here," Perrnodt said. "He will not rest until he gets them or is killed in the attempt."

Thigpen stirred uneasily as she glanced around. "Now that we know he has found his way into this realm we must be on our guard. Since we know that he cannot survive in his own form, we must look beneath the surface of those we may come across here. Any one of them could be possessed by the archdaemon."

"This way," Perrnodt said. She led them down the boulevard known as Gather the Unknowing, past the shells of gabled houses and columned temples. At length, it gave onto an octagonal plaza. Eight streets radiated out from its periphery.

"The Veil of a Thousand Tears is in a formidable lair," Perrnodt said. All around them rose double-storied structures whose purpose was impossible to imagine. "It is sealed inside a box of fire, which is surrounded by a coffin of water. In between is airless dark."

"How do we find it?" Riane asked.

"Not we, Dar Sala-at. You must do this alone. The Veil is semisentient. Go to the exact center of the plaza. Once you are there, it will sense you and guide you to it."

"Will it also tell me how to retrieve it?"

"No, and neither can I. That you must discover for yourself. I can tell you this much: keep track of the power bourns at all times."

"And when I do get it, what then? How do I use it to save Giyan?"

"You must find the way to free the Dragon's tears locked inside the Veil," Perrnodt said. "I regret that I do not have the requisite knowledge to tell you how to do so. You must trust yourself and the Veil. You must allow it to become a part of you. Once you merge with it, you will know the way."

Riane nodded. She did not want to leave her friends, but she had no choice. She looked Perrnodt in the eye, then she quickly knelt and ruffled Thigpen between her triangular ears.

"May Miina be at your side this night and always, little dumpling," the Rappa whispered.

Riane rose and walked to the center of the plaza. At once, she felt the bourn nexus point directly below her. The vibration slowly crept up from her feet through her legs into her torso. When it reached her brain, it spoke to her in the language of power bourns that Perrnodt had taught her. She turned forty-five degrees to her left and found herself facing one of the eight streets. As she headed toward it, she heard Perrnodt's voice calling through the failing twilight.

"Let the bourns guide you where they will, Dar Sala-at. Keep to the designated path and do not deviate."

Riane nodded. As she plunged into the thick gloom of the street, she lifted her open palm and conjured a small globe that hovered in the air just in front of her. It emitted a powerful beam of light that moved as she moved, illuminating the way ahead of her.

She continued on, cleaving to the path along the bourns. The evening collected around her like fragments of the past. Once, she looked up at the enormous bowl of the Korrush sky, and it seemed so distant it took her breath away. She reached a nexus and changed directions, following another bourn-line. All around her the citadel was breathing, churning the present into the past by the alchemy of its unique origin. Designed by Druuge, built by daemons to be an engine of unimaginable destruction. Lost now, dreaming of its lost zenith, endless, depthless. Deserted.

Except.

Riane, aware of a tiny tingle along her scalp, paused. Even though the power bourne urged her on, she turned to her right. She heard something, the creak of a board, the tiny discreet sound of a pebble dislodged, bouncing on beaten brass.

She saw something stir in an alleyway and took a step toward it. A step off the bourne.

Her sorcerous light illuminated a figure, impossibly tall, emaciated, pale as a corpse. Fillets of knucklebones ran through his elongated earlobes. He wore his hair long on the top, shaved on the sides. His face appeared devoid of any flesh whatsoever. It was as if the skin, yellow-white as tallow, had been pulled over bare bone, taut as a drum. His eyes, sunk deep into his skull, blazed pale as moonlight, the pupils tiny, black and pulsing. A runic scar, ruddy and livid, rose from the center of his forehead. His ebon robes fluttered like flags of death.

Sauromician!

Murmurous mouth like the blade of a knife.

He stepped back into the shadows of the alley and Riane felt a sudden compulsion to follow him. She took another step in his direction and shook her head. She felt like she was under water. That murmurous mouth. He had been casting a spell.

Keep to the designated path, Perrnodt had warned. *Do not deviate.*

Instinctively, she conjured Mounting Irons, and she was freed from the sauromician's spell. She peered into the alley, but he had vanished. She turned back, searching for the power-bourne, but it, too, had vanished.

She had lost her way and Za Hara-at had swallowed her whole.

Pyphoros was shaking Kurgan to the point of unconsciousness. The archdaemon had returned to Nith Batoxxx's body, but there was, at last, no longer any trace of Nith Batoxxx's personality. It had been entirely devoured.

Pyphoros, seeing Kurgan's eyes roll up, slapped his face hard to bring him back to full consciousness. "For your insolence and your treachery I should kill you on the spot. Part of me wants to, part of me would gain great pleasure in your death. But I have lavished too much time and energy on you. I have read the intestines of the dead and know that you have a greater role to play, a higher destiny than you know."

He brought Kurgan's face close to his own. "Know that I have come to love you as a father loves his child. But you are contrary and disobedient. You believe yourself able to outwit anyone, even me. So. You must be shown how wrong you are." His face was so close to Kurgan's that the regent was engulfed by the burnt sulphur of his breath. "You once made a blood oath to me that you have willfully violated. That cannot be tolerated. You are mine, Stogggul Kurgan. I chose you, and I made you mine. Now you will wear the mark that will always remind you of this truth."

He opened his mouth and a long thin black tongue emerged. It undulated like a serpent, quivering as it neared Kurgan's face. The regent tensed, tried to rear his head back, but Pyphoros held him in an inexorable grip.

"Is that fear I sense, Stogggul Kurgan?" Pyphoros crooned. "Fear at last?"

Kurgan glared at him.

"Good. I taught you better than that, didn't I? Yes. I taught you how to turn your heart to stone." The black tongue hovered over Kurgan's throat. "Now, once and for all, you will learn obedience."

The tip of the archdaemon's tongue opened like a tiny eye and a drop of a greenish liquid fell onto the hollow of his throat. Anyone else would certainly have screamed. Kurgan, silent, gritted his teeth. The eye opened again and another drop oozed out. Kurgan felt the pain reach all the way into the marrow of his bones, and this time he moaned.

"An archdaemon's saliva is to be avoided at all costs, so the Ramahan believe, because it causes pain beyond imagining." Pyphoros's face twisted into a monstrous grin. "Just two drops, regent. Imagine the damage a mouthful would do."

Kurgan lay trembling and sweating. At length, he touched the raw wound. The pain made him gasp anew.

"I have marked your flesh with my talisman, Stogggul Kurgan. Every time you see it you will know that our fates are entwined."

The archdaemon set him down none too gently. "While I have occupied this animated prison I have been active." Having delivered his punishment, he took on the pose of teacher, a role, Kurgan knew, he particularly relished. "At my connivance, the Comradeship is splintered beyond repair. Nith Sahor, the one Gyrgon able to heal the wounds, is dead. At Gyrgon direction, the Khagggun have annihilated your priests, outlawed the worship of your god, Enlil. Your Bashkir quarrel among themselves, your once mighty Khagggun grow restive and soft. And still you stay here, dreaming your salamuuun-induced dreams, sinking slowly but surely into the muck of time. Why haven't you gone?"

"I have as little respect for the Gyrgon as you do," Kurgan said. "Maybe even less."

Pyphoros struck him so hard he crashed sideways to the cool laboratory floor.

"If you do not respect your enemy, what chance do you have of defeating him?" He hauled Kurgan to his feet. "The same applies to an ally."

Kurgan wiped blood from his face. He tasted it in his mouth. He touched the slowly pulsing wound in the hollow of his throat. It had closed, leaving a small mark, dark as a Sarakkonian tattoo. "What is it you want from me?"

"Secrets. Information. Power. Ever since I returned to this realm I have been searching for the Dar Sala-at, the chosen of Miina, the great hero of Prophesy."

"Why?"

His balled fists shook with his rage. "It is so unfair! Imprisoned, all of us, by a Goddess who has lost Her mind!"

"You mean the Kundalan Goddess Miina? She exists?"

Pyphoros rounded on him. "If I wasn't in such a towering rage I would find your expression amusing. Of course she exists."

He peered at Kurgan. "But you comprehend something of this, don't you, Stogggul Kurgan? You are one of those special V'ornn who knows the truth when he hears it." His eyes seemed to writhe in their sockets. "To answer your question, I am searching for the Portals to the Abyss. I told you about them. All seven need to be opened before I can free the daemons from their eons-long prison. There is one—and only one—who can do this."

"The Dar Sala-at?"

"That would be convenient, wouldn't it?" Pyphoros shook his head. "No. It is foretold to be another. The Veil of a Thousand Tears will be able to identify him. That is why I will have the Veil at all costs. And it will be you, regent, who will help me obtain it."

Terrettt stared up into Marethyn's face and blinked away tears.

"He's crying," Marethyn whispered, bending over him.

"I have given him something new, something very different, formulated especially for his enlarged ativar." Kirlll Qandda sat on a small high stool in his patient's chamber at Receiving Spirit. "The crying is a good sign."

Outside the window, the Promenade, invaded by the storm, lay darkling and deserted. The turbulent Sea of Blood was stippled by silver rain. Ships, their sails tightly furled, their hatches battened down, rocked at anchor. The rain sluiced across their decks, gushed from their scuppers. Gusts of wind hurled fistfuls of it clattering against the thick shatterproof pane. The sound caused Terrettt to turn his head.

"It is rain, dearest," Marethyn said softly as she touched his cheek. "It is only the rain."

The walls were covered not only with the topographical map of the northern continent Marethyn had bought him but also with his latest paintings, which, more even than the earlier ones, were dominated by the seven whorled circles that looked to her like tiny whirlpools. She found them beautiful, hypnotic, almost haunting.

"Marethyn, there is something I have uncovered in my research into Terrettt's case," Kirlll Qandda said. And when Marethyn glanced at him, he went on. "I discovered that a Gyrgon was present when Terrettt was brought in for his infant's physical. Furthermore, I believe this same Gyrgon is the one who operated on Terrettt's ativar. His name is Nith Batoxxx. Do you know him?"

At once, the conversation between Sornnn and Rada at Spice Jaxx's sprang into her mind. The Gyrgon Nith Batoxxx desperately wanted to know the location of the seven Portals. But what had this to do with poor Terrettt? She shook her head. There was no use in involving the Deirus in her speculation.

Kirlll Qandda nodded. "I want you to continue what you were doing. Talk to your brother."

"Terrettt." She turned his face back until she was staring into his black eyes. She was filled to overflowing with her love for him, and this made her wonder if there was anyone to love Majja and Basse, the two Resistance fighters she had met. She was waiting for Rada to contact her so she could take them the route of the arms convoy. "Terrettt, it is me, Marethyn. Do you recognize me?"

For a moment, nothing happened, then she felt his head give a spastic nod.

"Oh, Terrettt!" Tears streamed down her face. She kissed his forehead, his cheeks. She was just about to draw back when she felt his hands on the back of her head, gentle as a spiderweb.

"Terrettt?"

Kirlll Qandda had hitched himself forward, an intense expression on his face as he silently urged her on.

"Terrettt, do you—?"

He opened his mouth and made a sound.

She cocked an ear. "What?"

The sound came again.

"He said 'Up'!" Marethyn breathed. "I'm sure. I heard it."

With the Deirus' help, she lifted him to a sitting position. He kept his arms around her. He did not want to let go, and this made her laugh again through her tears. When was the last time she had laughed in this room? Never. Never, never, never before.

His mouth was working again, and she said, "What is it, dearest? What do you want to say?"

"Mar."

Her eyes were shining.

"Mar-e-thyn."

"Yes, Terrettt! Marethyn!" she squealed. "Now can you say—"

"Mar-e-thyn. Can. You. See?"

She frowned. "See what, dearest?"

His face contorted. He was sweating with the effort to squeeze out the words.

"Can. You. See. What. Is. In. My. Mmmind."

Marethyn cocked her head. "How could I do that?"

"What. I. Have. To. Paint."

Now she frowned. "*Have* to? Darling, why do you *have* to paint anything?"

Kirlll Qandda had hopped off his stool and was now holding one of Terrettt's paintings off the wall. Now he returned and held it up in front of them. "Like this?" he said.

"Look," Terrettt said in his semigarbled way. "Look."

"What are we looking at, Terrettt?" Kirlll Qandda said.

Impatiently, his finger tapped each whirl. "Look," he said. "Look. Look. Look."

It happened by accident, really. Marethyn was sitting facing him. Directly behind him was the huge topographical map. Looking so intently at the painting, she was struck by how the colors conformed to those of the map. Then, with a start, she realized that the shapes more or less conformed also.

"Wait a minute!" She took the painting and went with it to the topo map. Terrettt swiveled around and started to make excited grunting sounds.

Kirlll Qandda came and stood beside her. "What is it?"

"Look," she said.

"Look!" Terrettt echoed with great enthusiasm. "Look, look, look!"

"The painting is a representation of the northern continent." She glanced quickly around. "All the recent paintings are!"

Handing off the painting to the Deirus, she took up one of Terrettt's brushes, dipped it in crimson pigment. Studying the painting, she made her first swirl on the map that corresponded to the first swirl Terrettt had drawn.

"It is in Axis Tyr," Marethyn said. "The Eastern Quarter."

"Yes!" Terrettt said in a kind of ecstasy. "Yes, yes, yes!"

"And here is another one in Stone Border." She made another swirl, and another. "And here, just north of the waterfall Heavenly Rushing."

She made four more swirls, following her brother's blueprint. These were in the heart of the Great Voorg, in the Great Rift in the Djenn Marre mountain range, and at the southern island of Suspended Skull, just off the coast in the Illuminated Sea. The last swirl she painted just outside the tiny, flyblown village of Im-Thera in the Korrush.

Red brush in her hand, she turned and stared at her brother. "What is so important about these places?" she asked. "Terrettt, what is in your mind? What do you want me to know?"

Terrettt tried to work his mouth, but only drool emerged.

Marethyn swung her gaze to the seven crimson swirls she had placed on the map and everything clicked in her mind. Looking at the map, Marethyn believed Terrettt, channeling some unknown force with his Gyrgon-heightened ativar, had located the locations of the seven Portals Nith Batoxxx was so desperate to find. But how was this possible? Had the Gyrgon engineered Terrettt to become some sort of homing beacon? She felt a profound chill at the thought of how Nith Batoxxx had manipulated him.

She felt him reaching out, and she took his hand. It was cold, and she saw the bloom of fear in his eyes.

Terrettt clutched her all the tighter. "There. Is. Something," he said. "Slow. In. The. Dark. Hanging. Feeding. Plotting."

"What?" she said, her hearts beating fast. "What is in the darkness?"

"Slow. In. The. Dark. Patient. Waiting."

"Waiting for what?" she asked.

"Slow. In. The. Dark. Waiting. For. The. Seven. To. Be. Opened. For. The. End. To. Come."

Riane, alone in the dark of Za Hara-at, wondered where the saurom-Rician was and when he would try to attack her again. She had walked in every direction without being able to find a trace of the power bourn. Now she felt a certain heat on her thigh. Digging into her robes, she discovered a warmth and drew out the stone given to her by Mu-Awwul, the chieftain of the Ghor. She saw that the image of the ful-kaan, the great bird of the Prophet Jiharre, was glowing orange. *Power and spiritual harvest flow from the image of the fulkaan,* he had told her. *Use it wisely.* She put the pad of her thumb over it and felt the quick deep throb of the power bourn.

She returned to it, grateful once more for Mu-Awwul's gift. It had

somehow repowered the infinity-blade, and now it had served as a beacon, guiding her back on her path. She hurried now, eager to get to her
destination and to leave the sauromician behind.

Her route took her ever deeper into the labyrinth of the dead city.
Often now she spotted breaks in the street, collapsed areas, either natural or made by the Bey Das. Wooden ladders with rungs wrapped in
rags led down to the underlayer. Everywhere torporous silence lay like
a fogbank. A cold wind soughed around corners, fled down the deserted
avenues. There was no sign of the sauromician.

Gradually, signs of the Bey Das archaeological team disappeared until, at length, she followed the bourn-line into a small and unprepos-
sessing plaza. Buildings seemed to crowd in on her from all sides. She
knelt, running her fingertips over the emperor carnelian and lapis runes
set into the cobbles. This was the Plaza of Virtuous Risk.

In the center was a triangular black-basalt plinth. This was interesting
because the dense stone, common enough around Axis Tyr, was unknown in the Korrush. She could not imagine what it would have taken
to bring it all the way here. As she approached, she saw that a huge
copper basin, verdigrised by time, had been set atop the plinth. Then,
as she walked around the plinth, her sorcerous lamp picked out the
runes that had been carved on each of the three sides. SEAT OF TRUTH,
SEAT OF DREAMS, SEAT OF DEEPEST KNOWLEDGE. These were the three
medial points around which the Kells in the Abbey of Floating White
were built. They corresponded to the crown of the head, the heart,
and the center of the forehead.

She moved closer, recalling what she had learned from Shima Vedda.
The first law of archaeology was the more time put into a structure, an
artifact, or a carving, the more important it is likely to be.

Standing upon the plinth, she peered down into the copper basin
and discovered that it was not a basin at all. It was a cenote like the
one in the abbey, filled with pitch-black water.

The Veil of a Thousand Tears is in a formidable lair, Perrnodt had told
her. *It is sealed inside a box of fire, which is surrounded by a coffin of
water. In between is airless dark.*

Riane was certain that she had come to the coffin of water.

31

Along Came a Ja-Gaar

Minnum stared bleakly at the sleety rain bouncing off the stone cistern in the center of the courtyard of the Museum of False Memory. He was sitting on a backless stone seat beneath the overhang of the loggia. The weather beat on the roof like a drum. He was wreathed in thought. Like a one-legged Kundalan, he had fallen into a reverie of how his life used to be, and he felt again that phantom tingle his power had brought him when he had been whole. He put his head in his hands. The sound of the sleet skittering across the courtyard was a malevolent whisper, mocking him. He held black thoughts in his head like a farrier holds a fistful of iron nails.

He could go on like this, lying to everyone including himself. Or he could screw up his courage and do what he should have done a long time ago.

He watched the sleety rain build up in the corners of his courtyard until it looked like cobwebs shining in the dusk. Interesting that he should think of this as his courtyard. That told him something. The question was whether or not he wanted to hear it.

At length, he rose and went inside and stood by the fire that blazed in the huge blackstone hearth. He held his palms out to the flames to warm them. Smoke curled up, and the fire snapped and sparked with an anticipatory energy. He sighed, shook his shaggy head from side to side. Curling a forefinger, he turned a long, sharp nail into the flesh of the inside of his arm. As the droplets of blood oozed out he took them on his fingertip and flicked them into the fire, which blazed up with a soft *Whoomp!* Briefly, the fire flickered, as if from a sudden draft, and for the blink of an eye turned blue-green. When it had returned to its natural hue, a figure stood in front of it.

The figure was cloaked from head to toe in a striped, beaded robe. Only eyes as pale as a winter sky showed. The bottom half of the face was covered in white muslin embroidered with script. Minnum squinted but could not tell whether the figure was male or female. Perhaps it did not matter. This was a Druuge, a member of the mysterious nomadic tribe that wandered the sandy wastes of the Great Voorg. Minnum believed that the Druuge were the original Ramahan, who broke away, deserting the abbeys before the corruption of power made its first insidious inroads. They were mystics and magicians of a level that terrified even him.

"Why have you summoned me?"

The Druuge spoke—no, Minnum thought, it was more of a singing.

"There are archdaemons about."

"Yes. Two Portals have suffered damage. Pyphoros—"

"Pyphoros has escaped?" Minnum could not help gaping. "I thought it was just Horolaggia who had managed to squeeze through."

The Druuge began to walk slowly around the exhibition space. "We knew the moment it happened."

Their extraordinary magic lay in their language. Yet another fact Minnum knew that he would not share with others. *So many secrets*, he thought. *Such terrible danger.*

"One should never underestimate an archdaemon," Minnum said, in an attempt to enhance his standing with the Druuge.

"One should never *misunderstand* an archdaemon," the Druuge corrected him. The beads on the robe swayed rhythmically.

Those pale eyes frightened Minnum. Unlike the old days, many things frightened him.

"If Pyphoros has returned to this realm," he said to the Druuge, "then he will want the Veil of a Thousand Tears."

"He wants more than that," the Druuge sang. "He wants all the secrets that lie hidden in Za Hara-at."

"But surely the Veil is—"

"The *Maasra*. What a sorry pass you have come to. You could not even remember its proper name." The Druuge was peering into a crystal case at the artifacts within. "Once you were fluent. Once you held the Power on the flat of your tongue. But now. Look how you have been brought low." The Druuge turned abruptly and took Minnum's hand in his. "When we gave you the job of curator, when we dispensed with the black finger Miina had given you as a stigma of your collective sin, we had a glimmer of hope for you."

The Druuge released Minnum's hand, went to another crystal case, beads clacking softly. "But what use is a curator with half a memory? Miina has taken from you all that made you what you once were. And now you know, sauromician-that-was, that power is sand sliding through your hands. You clasp your fingers together, make them into tight fists. Still the sand drains out."

"Do not remind me," Minnum said glumly. "I have toiled here in almost absolute isolation for many years. I have killed no one; I have refrained from divining through the dead. I have not practiced the dark arts of necromancy since I set foot in the museum."

"Is this an attempt to make me feel sorry for you, or are you simply feeling sorry for yourself?" the Druuge sang so that every stone vibrated to the sorcerous pitch.

"I gave the Dar Sala-at the infinity-blade. I did exactly what the red Dragon told me to do." Minnum tried not to look around him, in case the Druuge was reconstructing reality. "I have atoned, and still, as you say, the sand runs out."

The Druuge's silence seemed accusatory.

"I had the infinity-blade, and I chose not to use it."

The Druuge's pale eyes froze Minnum in his tracks. "Atoned, think you? And yet from your responses it seems clear you still covet power. The infinity-blade was meant for the Dar Sala-at. If you had tried to use it, you would have been struck lower than you are now."

"There is nothing lower than what I am now." He was shaking with repressed emotion. "You, holier than holy, cannot know what it is like to be among the damned." He threw his head back. "I want my old life back!" It was a howl of rage and pain.

"What you had can never be again." The Druuge paused before yet another case and peered within. "But should you desire it sufficiently, you can have a new life."

Minnum stared at the Druuge. Tears trembled in the corners of his eyes.

The Druuge fixed him in a truly terrifying gaze. "Once you were wise. You could be again. Miina in Her infinite wisdom has not deprived you of that possibility. But you must find your wisdom again in the very depths of your own spirit, where the wound Miina dealt you is deepest."

The Druuge said, "This is why you summoned me, sauromician-that-was."

Minnum's shoulders sagged. "I find that I . . . Over the years . . . It has been so long . . . I—"

"Tell me, are you happy here?"

"I do not want—"

"No." The Druuge's sun-browned hand came up. "Do not say what you do not want until you know for certain that it is not for you. You found this hallowed ground for a reason. In this museum of mysteries your new life begins. If you want it." The Druuge had returned to stand again before the fire. "Whether you think so or not, you are a born curator."

"What good is a curator who does not know the meaning of his exhibits?" he cried.

"Knowledge is benign until it is coveted by you or someone like you. When you or someone like you sees it as a means to an end it becomes a weapon."

The Druuge's song had turned abruptly dissonant, and Minnum clapped his hairy hands to his ears, fearing that the Druuge would bring the building down on him.

"You were witness to just such an act. You were there when The Pearl was taken."

"Yes."

"You stood by and did nothing."

"Yes."

"You joined the wicked. You became the wicked."

Minnum was shaking. His teeth chattered uncontrollably, and he prayed he would not wet his robes. He could not remember ever being so frightened.

"Think hard," the Druuge sang. "Try to remember where your wisdom resides. It waits for you. In pain. In the future."

"What more can I do than I have already done?" Minnum shouted in his fear. "Miina has chained me."

"It is not for you to say what the Great Goddess has done. In fact, She has given you the greatest gift. A chance to start over. What you do with this chance is entirely up to you."

Minnum took a step toward the Druuge. "I want—"

"What? Power? Revenge? Recompense for the injustices visited upon you?"

"You are baiting me."

"You want to ask me how long your punishment is going to last."

Minnum clamped his mouth shut in abject terror. That was exactly what he was going to ask.

"What do you want, sauromician-that-was? With me, you must tell the truth. If you do not, I will know, and it will be the end for you."

Minnum did not doubt the Druuge for an instant. His heart was beating fast. There was a blackcrow on a tree branch. He saw it with absolute clarity. His decision made, everything dropped away from him. There was a kind of relief in opening his heart.

He said, "I want not to be afraid."

The pale, terrifying eyes crinkled at their corners, and Minnum knew the Druuge was smiling.

"Well," the Druuge sang, "that is a start."

W hat is it he said to me? Oh yes, because you are an impetuous youth, he has ordered me to keep an eye on you." Line-General Lokck Werrrent grunted in disgust. "It is in your best interest for me to spy on you, Star-Admiral, as well as in the best interest of the Modality. The regent is certainly not lacking in nerve."

"He means to split us in two," Olnnn said. "He wants us to have at each other. That is is how he brought down his father and Star-Admiral Kinnnus Morcha. Egged on, they did his dirty work for him."

Werrrent and Olnnn stood beneath the striped awning of a noisy and jam-packed cafe. A stone's throw away sleety rain fell with a metallic clang and rattle in the enormous plaza. A burly Mesagggun engaged a Khagggun inside the brilliantly lit Kalllistotos ring. The upturned faces of the rapt crowd, jostling, shouting, unruly, glistened, ran with moisture. No one appeared to notice the foul weather, though occasionally one or the other of the combatants slipped on the increasingly slick surface of the ring.

They had already exchanged intelligence regarding Kurgan's desire to halt the implantation of okummmon in Khagggun.

"I will be blunt, Star-Admiral," Line-General Lokck Werrrent said under the noise.

A small smile played at the corners of Olnnn's cruel mouth. "As always, my good friend."

"I am not entirely comfortable."

Olnnn looked over his shoulder at Rada, clad in her blue-green armor, the Star-Admiral's golden crest on shoulders and chest. He was going to have trouble with this turn of events, that was clear enough. Well, there was no help for it but to take a hard line. That was the only way he was going to impose his will on others.

"Rada is my staff-adjutant. Where I go, she goes."

"But a Tuskugggun. This makes no sense, Star-Admiral. And if I may offer an opinion, it can only undermine your position of respect."

Olnnn clasped his hands behind his back, stared out at the match. The tide had turned. The burly Mesagggun was under an increasingly ferocious attack from the Khagggun. Blood was flowing freely, and the chants of the seething throng rose in volume.

Werrrent said, "I trust I need not remind you that when it comes to loyalty Khagggun have short memories. 'What have you done for me lately?' is the internal motto they live by. And why not? Each day they are asked to lay down their lives. It is not surprising that they need constant reminders of whom they owe allegiance to."

In the Kalllistotos ring, the Mesagggun's eyes were rolling up in his skull. The crowd howled, sensing the finish.

"They are like children, Star-Admiral. And like children their adoration can overnight turn to disgust." Werrrent was standing with his back ramrod straight. He was staring at the victorious Khagggun, arm thrust triumphantly up into the foul night. "It is hard being an idol. So difficult to live up to heightened expectations. And then there is this: at the first misstep, the idolaters turn murderous. Why? They despise you for having made fools of them."

"Do you consider Rada a misstep?" Olnnn asked.

"Come now, Star-Admiral, you know it is irrelevant what I think."

Olnnn smiled. "On the contrary, Lokck, as you think so do the others, high command, midechelons and lower ranks alike." He raised a hand. "Denying it would be a waste of both our time. And you will agree that neither of us has time to spare."

"The regent spoke of promoting me," Werrrent said.

Olnnn watched the silvery rain come down. "Is this your wish?"

"Not from him."

Olnnn smiled; he knew exactly what Werrrent meant. "There is currently a Deck-Admiral's position open."

"I was thinking more along the lines of Fleet-Admiral."

"A two-rank promotion. That would stir some talk." There were currently only two Fleet-Admirals on Kundala.

"Not as much as this new staff-adjutant of yours," Werrrent said dryly.

"She is here because I have ordered it," Olnnn snapped. "If that is insufficient—"

"It is entirely sufficient for me, Star-Admiral." He shrugged. "Still, talk centers on why she carries a shock-sword. Surely it is simply for show, and that has never been the Khagggun way."

Olnnn understood now what had to happen. If he could not count on Lokck Werrrent to accept Rada, then no Khagggun would, and he would indeed have made a fatal misstep.

He beckoned silently to her, and when she arrived at his side he said to Werrrent, "I will make you a wager, my staff-adjutant against a Khagggun of your choosing in the Kalllistotos ring with shock-swords. If she loses, she goes by the wayside and you gain the rank of Fleet-Admiral. But if she wins, she stays, you remain at your present rank, and your champion gets demoted." He grinned. "What do you say?"

"You are bluffing," Lokck Werrrent said.

"Pick your champion, then, Line-General."

Werrrent stood stock-still. Rada could see that he was debating the pros and cons of the wager. With so much at stake—a promotion that was obviously of great significance to him and a potential loss of face—she could tell that he did not want to take the wager. On the other hand, backing down would absolutely cause him humiliation. It seemed to her that Olnnn had overplayed his hand. He had backed the Line-General into a corner. In her years running Blood Tide she had always sought to find a reasonable way out for the antagonists who went at it inside her tavern, knowing that this was all they needed to settle their differences.

"Star-Admiral," she said before the Line-General could speak, "if I might—"

"Keep still, Staff-Adjutant," Olnnn said with a cutting glance at her. Didn't she know what was at stake here? "Speak only when you are spoken to."

"Now, hold on, Star-Admiral," Werrrent said. Anything to forestall the unpalatable choice he was being forced to make. "I would like to hear what she has to say."

Olnnn was glaring at her, but Werrrent, addressing her as if she were a child, said, "Go on, Staff-Adjutant with-no-name. Do not be afraid. I have known the Star-Admiral all his life. In these matters his growl is worse than his sword thrust."

"My name is Rada, Line-General. Staff-Adjutant Rada TurPlyen." She slowly drew her shock-sword from its scabbard. The two Khagggun watched her closely. Neither knew what she was about to say or do, which was her aim. Without saying a word, she had gotten them back on the same side. Now it was them versus her, far more familiar and comfortable ground for them.

"Line-General, the Star-Admiral trained me himself. Since you have known him all his life, you know what that means. I am good. I have excellent instincts, and I am fast. But I do not delude myself. I would be no match for any champion whose skills have been honed in battle." She reversed the shock-sword, laid the blades across her palm so that the hilt was toward him. "I surrender myself to you, Line-General."

But Olnnn had already stepped between them. "Rada, this is not possible. This wager is between the Line-General and myself. It is not for you to—"

Werrrent's hand on his shoulder stopped him in midsentence. "Star-Admiral, she is in armor, she is armed. She has the right."

Olnnn turned. "But Lokck."

"Either she is one of us, or she isn't."

Olnnn hesitated for just a moment, before he stood aside. "Take her blade, then," he said.

But Werrrent did not move. Instead, he said to Olnnn, "Thumb it on."

Olnnn looked at him. "I beg your pardon?"

"If she is Khagggun, she will hold the shock-sword with the blades active."

"She is not prepared. She has no idea."

Werrrent's steady gaze moved to Rada. "She has surrendered to me. It is my right to ask this of any warrior."

Rada thought Olnnn looked like he was in a daze. He nodded. She did not have to look at his face to know that he had been caught off guard.

Acutely aware of the Line-General's scrutiny, she held his gaze. Out of the periphery of her vision she saw Olnnn step up beside her. Once before she had held a shock-sword like this. She knew what was coming. Still, the jolt of agony as Olnnn thumbed on the ion flow took her breath away. She sucked in air. But she did not wince or cry out. The two Khagggun were watching her. She concentrated on breathing as the pain reached her hearts. The fire was so bad she thought it must shut down all her major organs. Her hands began to tremble.

"Line-General," Olnnn said softly.

Werrrent stood still and silent.

The tremor reached her forearms. Now she concentrated on breathing and not dropping the shock-sword. The pain raced up her spine, branched into the back of her neck, exploded in her brain. Her whole body was shaking.

From what seemed like far away, she heard Olnnn say, "N'Luuura take it, Lokck!"

The Line-General said, "Turn it off."

But when Olnnn moved to comply, he held up a hand. "No. She must do it herself."

"Lokck—"

"If she does," Werrrent went on inexorably, "I will not accept her surrender. She will remain your staff-adjutant." His eyes swung to Olnnn, "And you, Star-Admiral, will give me what I want."

Olnnn's gaze swung in her direction, he called her name, but she did not respond.

Already, she had twice fought off the blackness of unconsciousness. Her knees had turned to jelly; it was as if she had a tertium band around her chest squeezing all the breath out of her.

Olnnn called her name again.

She tightened her grip on the blades with one hand and almost passed out again. With her other hand, she fumbled with the button that would turn off the current of hyperexcited ions. Her fingers felt bloated to three times their size. She could feel nothing. In a moment she would begin to weep in pain and frustration, and everything would be for nought. At last, she maneuvered a knuckle into the button and the ion flow ceased.

Tears stood in the corners of her eyes. Olnnn was about to take her weapon from her when Lokck Werrrent intervened. He lifted the shock-sword from her numbed hand and slid it back into her scabbard.

He turned to Olnnn. "Star-Admiral, it seems to me Staff-Adjutant TurPlyen could use a stiff drink."

A waiter at the cafe cleared a table for them, and they sat, Rada between Olnnn Rydddlin and Lokck Werrrent. The entire staff was staring at her. She did not care. Werrrent ordered N'Luuura-Hounds—a shot of fire-grade numaaadis followed immediately by a goblet of mead.

After the potent drinks were downed, Rada felt her system coming slowly back to normal. She flexed her hands under the table out of sight of the males.

Lokck Werrrent wiped his lips. "Star-Admiral, let me say now that wagers between friends can only lead to discord. It was well that we found this one unnecessary." He did not mention Rada; he did not look at her. He had bought her a drink—a Khagggun drink—and this was enough.

Olnnn laughed. "I agree, Fleet-Admiral."

"Until the official ceremony I am still Line-General."

"In any case, now you can be a degree less jealous."

"I was never jealous."

"My father would have been if he had lived to see me be Star-Admiral at this age."

Lokck Werrrent cleared his throat. He knew what they were really talking about. Khagggun almost never spoke about such intimate matters as filial attachments. They were trained to think of their unit as their family. Loyalty, not sentiment, drove them. Which was why such moments were rare indeed.

"I am of the opinion that it is now the time of two armies."

Olnnn spread his hands.

"It is a fable." Werrrent's eyes cut to Rada for a moment. "Something tells me you should hear this too, Staff-Adjutant." He clasped both hands in front of him. "There were two brothers, as close as brothers could possibly be. Until the elder became regent and, locked inside his power, drew away from his younger brother. As the years went on, they spoke less and quarreled more. Over what? Petty matters, which before they would simply have laughed over. But now these petty matters vexed them most fiercely because they represented deeper irritations they could not express. They differed over matters of policy and protocol, the abuse of power, and, finally, the abandonment of law. And so the younger brother, estranged and full of righteous ardor, set about gathering an army of like-minded V'ornn. Hearing of his brother's treachery, the regent mobilized his own army and set a price on his brother's head."

"Is this true?" Olnnn said.

Werrrent pursed his lips. "Does it matter?"

Sheets of hard rain swept across the plaza, which had quickly emptied following the bloody conclusion of the last match.

"In the gloom just before dawn, the two armies came together," Werrrent continued. "They were evenly matched. Death was dealt by both sides, and decimation was the result. Worse. By day's end only a handful from each army remained, dazed, maimed, and bleeding, no longer remembering why they fought or who the enemy was.

"But the brothers knew. All that long day they had watched from their high outposts as V'ornn loyal to them had been slain, and now, at last, they approached one another, striding through the grisly mire of the battlefield. Their hearts were hardened, their minds were set. Power and the envy it gives rise to were the engines that propelled them both to strike. All through the night they did battle until the breath sawed through their open mouths, until their blood ran from a hundred wounds, until their legs trembled and they could no longer stand.

"And still they fought, until at last fatigue caused a misstep, and the younger brother dealt the regent a fatal blow."

The wind had picked up, the sleety rain coming in under the awning, which slapped noisily now like a blackcrow descending upon a corpse.

"A fine fable," Olnnn said. "The abuse of power was avenged."

"But we have not yet reached the end." Werrrent sat back. "The younger brother was so weakened by his wounds that he could not prevent one of his own V'ornn from stabbing him through the hearts. This V'ornn, a First-Captain, driven half-insane by the killing, rallied about him what was left of both armies and promptly installed himself as regent. The abuses of the slain regent were as nothing compared to what this V'ornn would perpetrate."

Olnnn took a breath. "Where were the Gyrgon?"

Werrrent blinked. "What?"

"How would the Gyrgon allow such a thing to happen?"

"It is a fable," Werrrent said.

"Of course it is."

"But it is also a warning."

Olnnn folded his arms across his chest. Werrrent rolled his empty glass around the tabletop. The two of them looked at each other, then away. A waiter passed by, a tray of food held high. Another began to clear a table. A V'ornn laughed at the back of the cafe, slamming the flat of his hand against his thigh. Two huge Mesagggun shouldered their way in, shook themselves like wyr-hounds, and sat down, stinking of oil and tar. In the plaza the rain speared down, drowning everything.

Olnnn fingered his okummmon. "N'Luuura take it," he growled, "we are like cor to the slaughter."

And Rada said, "Not if we slaughter the regent first."

When Konara Inggres returned to the Abbey of Floating White it was with a high degree of trepidation, not to say fear. She had no intention of running into the archdaemons in possession of Giyan's and Bartta's bodies, so she Thripped directly into the triangular Kell. Since they were sacred chambers, she felt safe, as if a small piece of the Great Goddess was still enshrined there.

She bent over, retching, and wondered if her sudden illness was a manifestation of her intense fear. The nausea soon passed, however.

Recalling the First Mother's instructions, she lit a reed torch. By its light, she saw that Ghosh, the carved citrine serpent, was not in the place she had last seen it. It had been moved back against the wall, as if someone had tried to return it to its original niche. She looked around, as if someone was waiting for her and would jump out of the dense shadows. Her heart beating fast, she thrust the flaming torch into every nook and cranny to assure herself that she was, in fact, alone in the Kell.

She found that she was sweating. Wiping her forehead with the sleeve of her robe, she placed the torch on a worked-bronze wall bracket and knelt before the beautiful and frightening countenance of the sacred serpent. As she studied the face she saw that the eyes were separate—whole cabochon citrines set into the cavities. Each eye was incised with iris and vertical pupil. With her hand nearly touching the right eye, she hesitated. The thing was so cleverly wrought it looked positively alive. Part of her was afraid the serpent would bite her. Then she remembered the First Mother's admonition for urgency, and she steeled herself.

Her fingertips transmitted the coolness of the semi-precious stone. Grasping the orb, she turned it left three times, and it plopped right into her hand. It was very heavy. It made her hand cold, and she began to tremble.

But she did not falter. Continuing to follow the First Mother's instructions, she took the torch and descended into the third and lowest Kell, the perfectly square chamber. The black-lacquered walls were reflected eerily by the flickering torchlight. She saw the three Ja-Gaar. They at least, along with the basalt cover to the cenote, were where she had last seen them.

Breathing a sigh of relief, she knelt beside the stone cenote and dipped the citrine eye into the still black water. She counted off the seconds to thirty. The cabochon lay in the palm of her hand. As she had not immersed it deeply, she could see it clearly. She blinked, at first uncertain of what she was seeing. The incised iris and pupil were gaining form and color. It was as if the black water was transforming the cabochon into Ghosh's eye.

She could see the iris turning a glimmering silver color and the vertical pupil inside a deep violet. The thirty seconds expired, and she pulled the orb out of the water. What had the First Mother instructed her to do next? Ah, yes, put the still-wet eye in the center of her forehead, precisely where she accessed her Third Eye.

She was about to do so when she became aware of a stirring of the water in the cenote. At first it was just the whisper of a ripple. She leaned over, peering into the cenote and saw, amid the utter blackness, a movement.

All at once, the water fountained up in a great froth, and Bartta leapt out, wide-eyed, ashen-faced, and grinning from ear to ear.

Konara Inggres screamed and toppled backward. As she did so, the citrine eye rolled across the black floor of the Kell. She moaned, scrabbling after it on all fours, but Bartta seized her from behind, pulled her down hard onto her stomach.

The breath went out of her as Bartta landed atop her. Bartta's mouth opened and a long, thin blue-black tongue flicked out, wrapping itself around Konara Inggres' hair. It lashed itself tight and pulled, jerking Konara Inggres' head back.

"You have disobeyed Mother," Bartta hissed in a voice clearly not her own. "You have lied. You have the Gift. You have Thripped." The tongue pulled back farther, and Konara Inggres arced like a bow and cried out. Pain lanced through her shoulders and neck. She saw spots before her eyes.

"Having been to Otherwhere you know the truth. You cannot be allowed to live. Nor is possession any longer a viable option. You are too much of a threat to us."

Bartta was making a sound. It was like the agitated susurrus of ten thousand famished stydil descending on a field of wrygrass. With a sickening start, Konara Inggres realized that the archdaemon inside Bartta was laughing.

"You sickening, weak-willed worm," Bartta croaked. "What right do you have to live your life in freedom when we have been trapped in loathsome misery for eons?"

Bartta gouged her painfully in the ribs with a long-nailed finger. "You Ramahan are too stupid for your own good. My father should have wiped you out wholesale instead of slowly eroding the nature of your religion. He is patient; I am not. Now that I am free of that hideous prison I want only to destroy that which put me there."

Konara Inggres said nothing. For one thing, stark terror had caused her to lose her tongue. For another, the pain was so intense that every nerve ending vibrated to the archdaemon's gouging. For still another, she was too busy keeping track of the skittering citrine eyeball as it caromed off the enamel-black walls of the Kell.

Bartta bent over her. "You assume I am going to kill you, but death is too easy an end for you. I am going to keep you alive. You will be my plaything. Torture will be your fate. Endless torture. Day after day, month after month, year after year I will return to you again and again and you will hang on the knife edge of agony. Pain will be your constant companion, an intimate that will become a part of you, until it takes you over wholly and you are defined by it."

Her fingers dug in deeper, making Konara Inggres cry out.

Eyes watering, Konara Inggres spotted Ghosh's eye, which had settled against one of the Ja-Gaar's forelegs. Blinking back tears of pain, she saw that it was still gleaming, still slick with the water from the cenote, and she remembered the First Mother's warning. Once the eye was immersed she could not allow it to dry out; otherwise, it would lose all its power.

"What are you doing? Trying to Thrip? I have fixed it so you cannot." Bartta jerked back on her hair with the archdaemon's powerful blue-black tongue. "You will pay attention to me!"

Konara Inggres tried to crawl toward the Ja-Gaar's foreleg. Bartta was a small female. Curiously, the possession had caused her to become even lighter. It had also made her far stronger. Konara Inggres made some headway before Bartta pulled her arm behind her back and began to twist it.

"I knew there would be fight in you!" Bartta hissed. "Well and good! I have thought of a way to subdue you." She lifted her head with its twisted expression. "Where are you? Show yourself!"

And obeying that command, Konara Lyystra descended into the Kell from the one directly above. Her gaze was steady, her expression fixed.

As Konara Inggres gasped, Bartta laughed, the archdaemon's mirth making her throat pulse like a wer-frog's.

"As you are about to discover, torture can take many forms," Bartta said with undisguised glee. "Here is your first taste." She fixed Konara Lyystra in her gaze, and said, "Take the needle I gave you and plunge it into the side of her neck."

"What have you done to her?" Konara Inggres cried. "I dispossessed her."

"That you did," Bartta cackled as Konara Lyystra moved toward them in an odd, jerky rhythm. "But Horolaggia and I captured her before she could escape us. We were stricken at what you had managed to do. You killed one of us. Murdered him in cold blood. But you left your friend behind, and we made her ours. Not in the same way. After what you did, we could not possess her again. So we did the next best thing. We exorcised her essence, stuffed it into a tiny black bottle inside her where she can never find it. Now she obeys us and only us."

"Lyystra," Konara Inggres called. "Lyystra, you must resist them. You must find yourself again."

Konara Lyystra kept coming on stiff legs, and Bartta—or the unholy thing inside her—was shaking with laughter.

"Go on, talk to her if you must," the archdaemon taunted. "For all the good it will do you."

"Lyystra, listen to me," Konara Inggres said. "Remember what I said about faith."

"Faith, faith, faith," Bartta scoffed, turning the word over as if it were a curiosity.

Konara Inggres contrived to ignore her. "If you doubt, then you are without shelter and comfort in the face of the storm. Without faith, the storm will take you over, Lyystra. You must not let that happen."

"Poor thing, she has no choice," Bartta hissed.

It was the archdaemon's imprudent words that galvanized Konara Inggres. It was clear that she could not gain the upper hand by sheer brute force. But sorcery was another matter altogether. She knew from her studies that daemons were cut off from Osoru. But could she overcome one with it, and an archdaemon to boot?

She shut out the pain, Bartta's mocking words, the fact that her best friend was advancing on her, grasping a needle loaded with Miina knew what noxious herbal concoction. She erased everything from her mind and opened her Third Eye.

"What are you doing?" Bartta croaked from seemingly far away. "I told you, you cannot Thrip your way out of this."

Konara Inggres conjured Net of Cognition. With it, she identified Lyystra's essence, even though the archdaemons had locked it away inside a sorcerous bottle. At once, she cast White Well, gathering the bottle to her.

"I said, what are you doing, stupid thing?" Bartta cried with a mighty jerk of her tongue on Konara Inggres' hair. When no answer was forthcoming, Bartta slammed her pointed chin into the back of Konara Inggres' head.

Konara Inggres' face hit the black-basalt floor, and, with a pain that reverberated through her, she felt her cheekbone crack. Still, she would not allow herself to be deterred. Conjuring Transverse Guest, she determined the sorcerous structure of the bottle and began to dismantle it.

Possibly it would not matter, though, for Konara Lyystra had reached her and, on Bartta's barked command, was kneeling beside her.

"The side of her neck!" Bartta cried. "Bury the needle deep where the banart can do its work quickly."

Despite herself, Konara Inggres began to thrash about. Her concentration slipped, and the archdaemon-made bottle began to remake itself. She stopped it, redoubling her efforts, and was rewarded with a thin streamer of warmth. Lyystra's essence was leaching back into her body.

Then she felt the first prick of the needle.

"Lyystra, have faith," she gasped. "Fight the evil inside you."

"I have no strength," Konara Lyystra said dully.

"Believe in Miina, and you will find the strength."

Konara Lyystra's eyes turned inward, an inner struggle that had already begun, working itself to the fore.

"Inggres? Is that you?" she said in a raspy whisper. The needle withdrew. "What has happened? My mind is . . . I cannot remember."

"Fetch the citrine ball that lies there by the creature's leg. Bring it to me."

At once the archdaemon's intense curiosity was piqued. "Why? What is it? What does it mean to you?"

"Shut up," Konara Inggres said through her haze of pain and was rewarded with another agonizing gouge.

Konara Lyystra had turned away. She was staring at the citrine ball.

"Lyystra, fetch it," Konara Inggres urged her. "Bring it here."

"Yes," Bartta hissed. "By all means fetch it. But bring it to me. I am your superior, girl. You will do as I say, or I will see to it that you are immediately expelled from the abbey."

"Lyystra, don't listen to her. She is possessed by an archdaemon. Everything she tells you is a lie!"

Konara Lyystra was on all fours, staring at both of them. Then she reached for Ghosh's eye, grabbed it, and turned back.

"I want it!" Bartta howled. "Give it to me!"

Konara Lyystra looked at it, saw that it was still wet, and began to wipe it on her robes.

"No!" Konara Inggres cried in terror. "Keep it wet. Lyystra, do you understand?"

Konara Lyystra looked at her out of bloodshot eyes. She nodded.

"Why?" Bartta screamed. "Why, why, why?"

"Inggres." Konara Lyystra's face was a mask of terror.

"Ignore the archdaemon," Konara Inggres said, "and bring it to me."

Konara Lyystra hesitated, just an arm's length away. "What if she is Bartta? If I disobey her, I will be exiled."

"Yes, you surely will, child." Bartta's cupped fingers beckoned. "All you need do to get back in my good graces is hand me the citrine ball."

"But she is not Bartta," Konara Inggres said. "The archdaemon has possessed her. You must believe that. Have faith."

Konara Lyystra nodded and gave her best friend Ghosh's water-slicked eye. As she did so, Bartta gave an impassioned scream. The long blue-black tongue erupted into view.

With a bloody hand, Konara Inggres pressed Ghosh's eye to the center of her forehead.

The blue-black tongue stabbed out and, like a sword, impaled Konara Lyystra through the throat. She screamed, blood fountained, and she began to gasp and gurgle.

Underneath Bartta, Ghosh's eye, bathed in the black, still water of the holy cenote, sank into Konara Inggres' forehead, pushing aside flesh, sinking into the bone of her skull. When it reached the outer sac of her brain a sorcerous light flared, falling upon the three carved Ja-Gaar, awakening them to life.

In this sorcerous light, Konara Inggres could see the chain-link leashes that bound the Ja-Gaar to her, against which they were now straining. She reached out, let go of the leashes, releasing the Ja-Gaar.

They were freed blinking into the smoking semidarkness. Their incandescent eyes fixed upon Bartta or—more accurately—that which lay like a canker inside her. Snarling, they launched themselves toward her like living missiles.

The archdaemon had just enough time to withdraw its wicked tongue before they were upon Bartta. The ferocity of their attack threw her completely off Konara Inggres. She rolled to the wall, her arms covering her face, her knees drawn up. This meant nothing to the Ja-Gaar, who began to maul Bartta savagely, ripping into her with fangs and claws as if in this primitive way they could extract the archdaemon wound like a great viper around her spinal column.

And perhaps they could, for there arose from Bartta's wide-open mouth a sound no Kundalan was ever meant to utter. It was a noise of such fearsome rage and pain as Konara Inggres had never before heard or could have imagined even in her worst nightmares.

But at that moment the archdaemon's bloodcurdling bellow was of only marginal interest to her. Ignoring her pain and the blood from her fractured cheek, she had crawled to where her best friend lay sprawled on the black-basalt floor.

"Lyystra," she whispered as she put her friend's head in her lap. In vain, she tried to stop the blood pulsing from the ragged wound in her throat. Holding her tight, she bent over and kissed her forehead. "I am here, as is the Great Goddess. We are both with you."

Konara Lyystra's face was appallingly ashen. Her body shivered and shook, and a raling came from her fatally congested chest. But at the sound of her friend's voice, her eyes opened, and she smiled.

"You were right. About everything." Her voice was so thick it emerged from her parted lips amid a welter of gurgling bubbles. "If I believe in Miina, will She save me from death?"

Konara Inggres forced a smile to her face. "You are not going to die."

"The archdaemon has done me grievous injury. There is no hope."

"Have hope. Have faith." She held her friend more closely.

"I do." Konara Lyystra looked up at her. All at once, her expression changed, and she gasped, a larger bubble forming between her lips. "I can see Her, Inggres. Oh, look! I can see the Great Goddess. She exists!"

In a corner of the Kell, the three Ja-Gaar were noisily and deliriously rending Bartta's body limb from limb.

Konara Inggres closed her eyes and began to pray.

The sacred Ja-Gaar had set up a howling. Miina only knew what it meant.

She looked upon Konara Lyystra, saw those bloodshot eyes staring past her, past the ceiling of the Kell. They were fixed on Miina or whatever it was she thought she had seen. A distant Realm. Darkness. Nothing.

Death.

She threw her head back and added her own long, mournful cry to the Ja-Gaar's bestial howls.

32

Light Floating on Water

The odd thing about where the cenote was located, Riane thought as she slipped into the pitch-black water, was that it had not been built directly on the bourn nexus that lay beneath this small plaza. In the chill, her mind worried at this oddity.

For a moment, she hung in the water. Finbats raced through the deserted plaza. Then, as if an invisible hand had reached up, she was pulled beneath the surface. The water was viscous and had a mind of its own. It wanted to pull her deeper. She fought against the pull. The utter blackness was oppressive. She kicked out, trying to regain the surface, but she could not even maintain her position. She was being sucked deeper. She pushed down a flash of panic and felt for the pulse of the power bourns, but there was not even the faintest trace of them.

The absence of light became overwhelming, and she reached out with her mind, repositioning the sorcerous lamp over the center of the cenote. She looked up and saw ten thousand tiny points of light dancing in the blackness. They were not random, she saw, but resolved themselves into spirals that descended into the cenote. She put her hand through a spiral, and it was as if the power bourn had speared her. That was why the cenote had been built slightly off the nexus. It held a rogue branch that was broken into spirals instead of running straight beneath Kundala's crust.

Linked now with the spiral bourn, she let it take her deeper, to the place where the water ended and she could breathe again.

The only problem was that she emerged into a vacuum.

It was hot inside the Khagggun enclosure, and staring at the tiers of data-decagons made Rada hotter. Sweat ran down the back of her neck, collected inside her armor. All around her, Khagggun moved at their precise, clipped pace, crisscrossing the enclosure with tight lips

and beady eyes. Behind her, Olnnn stood talking with two of his officers. The war against the Resistance was going well. Many were dead,
many more would be soon enough. Majja and Basse were right. The
time to be patient was over.

Without looking to the right or left, she walked to the tiers of data-
decagons. She knew where the one she wanted was because only the
previous day she had watched the Pack-Commander in charge of the
convoy put it there. She had been waiting for him, and had contrived
to walk by just behind him as the data-screen came on. It was fortunate
she did so because she had seen that the date the convoy was to leave
Axis Tyr had been pushed up a day.

She risked a glance over her shoulder. Olnnn was engrossed in discussion with his officers. The convoy was scheduled to leave in the
morning. It was now or never. Reaching out, she plucked the data-
decagon and slipped it into the reader slot. The screen bloomed to life,
and she concentrated fully. It took her a very short time to memorize
the route, but it seemed like an eternity.

She heard Olnnn call her name, and she felt a spasm between her
shoulder blades. Whipping the data-decagon out of the slot, she returned it to its tier. Then she turned on her heel and went to where he
was waiting. The conversation had broken up.

"What were you doing?" he asked.

"Reconfirming your schedule for the rest of the day."

He nodded. "I need you to run an errand for me." He walked with
her to an area of the enclosure where they had some privacy, and placed
a data-decagon in her palm. "Take this to Fleet-Admiral Lokck Werrrent. He is at the Western arsenal. Make certain you deliver this to
him and to no one else. Remain for his reply and bring it back to me
here. Is that clear?"

She nodded and went on her way, relieved to be out of there.

The data-decagon lay heavy and hot in the heart of her palm. If
Werrrent was currently at the Western arsenal, that must mean he was
overseeing the final preparations for the convoy. On her way to req-
uisition a hoverpod she contacted Marethyn, who was at Receiving
Spirit with her brother, Terrettt. Sornnn was with her. From the tone
of Marethyn's voice it sounded as if she had interrupted a serious conversation.

She signed out a hoverpod and as soon as she was aloft she put the data-decagon in the cockpit reader. She was anxious to know if Olnnn had any last-minute instructions for the convoy. In this she was to be disappointed. The data was encrypted.

The Veil is sealed inside a box of fire, which is surrounded by a coffin of water. In between is airless dark.

Riane hung in the vacuum. Her lungs were about to burst. She cast Earth Granary, the most potent healing spell, to create a bubble of air around her. But each time it began to form the vacuum collapsed it.

She was growing dizzy and dislocated. She could no longer distinguish up from down, the nothingness was endless, and her panic returned, splintering cohesive thought into a flock of birds that flew in every direction.

A throbbing commenced in her temples as her brain was deprived of air. There was a way out of the vacuum; she had only to find it. She knew she had to think the problem through, and she shackled the intense fear. What did she know? She had solved the first level by bringing light into pitch-darkness. But it was dark here, too. And airless. But her first instinct to create a bubble of air for herself had failed.

She started. Something had happened. What? Cold sweat broke out on her anew as she realized she had passed out for several seconds. She could not allow that to happen again, and she dug her fingernails into the palms of her hands, drawing blood. And pain. That was better. The pain would keep her awake and alert. What had she been thinking about before she passed out?

Laboriously, she went through the process again. She could sense her body straining for life. She so wanted to take a breath. A moment more and she would suck in the nothingness and die.

No air, no air.

Only one other chance and she took it. She conjured First-Gate Correspondence, transmogrifying the entire vacuum. Air flooded in and, with it, a kind of pale phosphorescence. She gasped, sucked in the air, felt her galloping pulse slowly subside.

She saw that she was floating in a donut-shaped space. Above her was the purling water. And directly ahead was a clear cube of fire. Within that, she knew, lay the Veil of a Thousand Tears.

*   *   *

Pyphoros began to arrange Courion's corpse, stretching it out fully on its back. They were still in Nith Batoxxx's laboratory deep in the heart of the Temple of Mnemonics. Kurgan was starting to feel the weight of the structure, the boundaries of the lab. He was certain the archdaemon had that in mind. He was sure the creature wanted him to feel as much a prisoner as Pyphoros himself felt. Kurgan had a dull headache, which had come on sometime after the sorcerous stone had been implanted in his skull. There must be some way to remove it, he was thinking. *Not in your world*, the archdaemon had said. What had he meant by that?

He watched as Pyphoros pulled the ion glove off his host body's right hand, leaning forward expectantly. This was the first time he had seen a Gyrgon's bare hand. The palm was an intricate mass of biocircuitry, as were the backs of the fingers. The characteristic ion sizzle was gone.

"Regent," Pyphoros said, "I believe it is time that you become acquainted with the high art of necromancy."

As Pyphoros extended the hand over the corpse a line of palest blue emerged from the tip of the middle finger. Despite the paleness of the color the light it emitted was so glaring that Kurgan instinctively put his hand up to shield his eyes.

"We open a fresh corpse and use our special skills to read the entrails."

The palest blue line descended toward Courion's abdomen and quickly slit it open from breastbone to pelvis. A gust of noxious gases issued forth. Courion's intestines bulged, gleaming evilly. The stench was overpowering. Not that Pyphoros seemed to mind. Kurgan's eyes were riveted on the intestines, which, guided by the blue rune, were spreading themselves out into what appeared to be a complex pattern.

"The dead hold secrets they never had in life."

The blue rune now became a fine line. He followed its slow and ominous movement as it described a serpentine path above the gleaming entrails. Here and there, the blue line opened the intestines, revealing dark and mysterious contents to the furiously intent Pyphoros. A kind of singsong humming was coming from him, not strictly speaking from his mouth, but from all of him at once.

"Here is the secret," Pyphoros said. "Running in stinking rivulets, in the blazing language of the dead." Abruptly, the palest blue line vanished, and the archdaemon looked at Kurgan. "Ah. This secret, regent, it is about you."

"Really?"

"You seem skeptical."

"Not at all."

Pyphoros laughed. "You really must learn how to be grateful, Stogggul Kurgan. This secret, if I decide not to tell you what it is, I guarantee that within hours you will be dead."

She's coming," Marethyn said. "The convoy date has been moved up. It is leaving tomorrow at sunrise."

Sornnn looked bleakly at her. He felt enmeshed in the revelatory information she had just given him. The genetic manipulation the Gyrgon had subjected Terrett to had somehow allowed him to locate the seven Portals Rada had told him Nith Batoxxx wanted. They had been arguing when the communication from Rada had come in. Sornnn had wanted her to go to Kurgan and tell him about the seven Portals. It seemed to him the perfect way for her to reconcile with him. Pride and, doubtless, the spectre of failure had made her balk. Not that he blamed her. He had had enough face-to-face experience with the new regent to know that Kurgan was both volatile and unforgiving. Still, he had pressed her. Not that Marethyn would ever admit it, but he suspected that her estrangement from Kurgan had had a serious and long-lasting effect on her.

"Our argument is moot," she said now. "I will be leaving the city before nightfall."

He took her elbow, steered her away from the sleeping Terrettt. They were alone in the room at Receiving Spirit. In the hallway, Genomatekks and Deirus could be seen hurrying past, silent and grim-faced. Once, the ion crackle heralded the presence of a Gyrgon, but they did not see him.

"Marethyn, this is crazy," he said. "I should be the one to go."

"You are Prime Factor," she pointed out with perfect logic. "You cannot risk being seen."

He had no answer for that.

"We have only a few minutes before Rada gets here." She slipped her hand into his, led him to the window. The sky was grey and angry-looking. Far out to sea, where the heavy clouds seemed to touch the horizon, it was teeming. The grip of midwinter had finally taken hold. The solstice was only days away. "I know you want to protect me, Sornnn. But try to see things from my point of view. That protection you're feeling is just another form of subjugation."

"I don't think it is."

"But the point is, darling, I do."

"Marethyn—"

"I want my life to count for something." Her eyes searched his. "This is how I will find out who I really am." She squeezed his hand and smiled. "I have no intention of being a martyr. I will come back to you, Sornnn. I swear it." A shadow passed across her, and she looked out the window. "Rada is here. I have to go."

She disengaged her fingers and kissed him hard on the lips. On her way out, she did not trust herself to look back. When she passed Terrettt's bed his eyes opened and he looked at her and spoke her name.

33

Sacrifice

I can feel him," Eleana said.

"He's kicking?" Rekkk asked.

"I don't know what the baby is doing," she said with a grimace, "but it hurts."

Rekkk put his arm around her and looked to the Teyj, who had gone on to reconnoiter. "We had better stop here and rest."

Eleana looked around at the rock-strewn mountain field they were crossing, its once lush summer grasses sere and shorn in brittle winter. "It is too exposed here." She heard the Teyj calling as it weaved and dipped in the air currents, and pointed toward the looming rock face. "The teyj has found a cave. We'll have plenty of shelter there against the heavy weather."

"You'll never make the climb."

"You should know never to say never to me, Rekkk." She grinned through her obvious pain. "You have as good as dared me."

And before he could stop her, she had set off, crossing the remainder of the field and starting up the slope that led to the first outcroppings of the mountainside. They were high in the Djenn Marre, at most a day from the Abbey of Floating White. Rekkk hurried after her, grabbing hold of the rock. The Teyj fluttered excitedly just over his shoulder. If they were going to get to the cave, he knew, they would have to do it before the wet weather settled in and made the rock face too treacherous to negotiate. Already, the following wind out of the south had picked up, turning the air leaden with incipient moisture.

These dark thoughts were abruptly terminated by Eleana's cry. He looked up so fast his neck cracked, and he scrambled quickly upward to find her clinging precariously with one hand while clutching her belly with the other.

"Eleana, what is it?"

But she only shook her head, her face scrunched up, and she put her head in the hollow of his shoulder as he took her in one strong arm and headed up the scree. The loose rock made it more difficult to make headway, but Rekkk persevered, using whatever was available to him— cracks, crevasses, the limbs of stunted trees, battered and twisted by the harsh weather—to continue their ascent. The breath came hotly to his lungs and his muscles felt as if they were on fire. Pain he had thought gone, associated with his wounds, returned to haunt him like a daemon. But he kept going though the way became steeper as he began to climb the true rock face, for he knew without question that their greatest danger was being caught on the vertical when the rain came.

He suppressed the urge to hurry, taking each step with care, testing hand- and footholds, while the wind gusted at his back and whistled in his ears. Once, he thought he heard something, and turned his head to look. But that action caused him to pause, and pausing was out of the question, so he saw nothing, and the moment the first slash of rain pattered against his legs he forgot all about the sound.

He looked directly above his head and tried to blot out Eleana's moans. He was terrified that she was going to have the baby right there without protection, and that he would be helpless to save it. He judged that they were perhaps two-thirds of the way to the top. He kept moving, the afternoon darkening radically, another spray of rain striking him like a blow. The temperature must have already dropped by a good ten degrees.

He kept moving, one leg, one arm at a time and his world came down to this crucial routine: search out a handhold, test it, haul them up, fight for a toehold, balance, then start all over again.

They were almost to the ledge where Eleana had spied the cave, but a great outcropping of rock intervened, overhanging his head. The way directly above was completely blocked. The rain had begun a more steady tattoo against the rock face. His entire back was drenched, and Eleana had commenced to shiver as well as spasm. In despair, he looked left and right, contemplating a lateral move, but no crack or crevasse immediately presented itself, and they had passed the last of the trees sometime ago.

"N'Luuura take it!" he cursed.

He heard the Teyj calling to him. It was banking and swooping, its four wings helping it to maintain its balance and altitude in the gusts. Rekkk saw where he was headed, a featureless block of rock just to his right. With the temperature dropping, the sleety rain was beginning to turn to snow. He squinted but could discern no handhold through the sharply reduced visibility. What was the Teyj thinking? A blast of wind almost dislodged him, and a host of flakes battered his face. His foot slipped on the wet rock, and Eleana groaned and he cursed. His fingers were rapidly growing numb.

The Teyj called to him once more, and he muttered, "To N'Luuura with it!" through gritted teeth as he reached over to his right. His fingertips felt along the rock and, at the very back of it, where it became part of the mountainside, he found the crevasse the Teyj with its keen eyesight and optimum vantage point had discovered. He curled his fingers into the crevasse, pulled, felt no give, and swung over. For a moment, he hung in space, feeling giddy with the height, then the toes of his boots caught a crack, and they were safe.

He allowed the Teyj to guide him the rest of the way, a surprisingly easy last hundred meters. Gaining the ledge, Rekkk gathered Eleana into both arms, ignoring the spasming of his overtaxed muscles, and ran for the mouth of the cave. The Teyj was already present as Rekkk laid Eleana gently onto the dry dirt floor.

He went into the cavern's interior, but this high up could find no dried branches or even twigs. He settled for a handful of desiccated bone shards, which he dropped beside Eleana. Placing one of the smallest shards in his okummmon, he conjured up fire in his mind and out of the okummmon's slot roared a jet of fire that lit the pile of bones.

The gale hammered full force at the mountainside, turning the night opaque, filling the cave mouth with a drifting of snow. The wind howled and moaned deep in the bowels of the cavern, and the Teyj violently ruffled its feathers in order to remain dry. Eleana shivered, moaning, bringing Rekkk's thoughts back to their present predicament.

"What is the matter with her?" Rekkk asked the Teyj. "Is the baby coming?"

The Teyj sang and Rekkk heard its voice in the serene center of his mind. It was the voice of Nith Sahor.

The baby will come when it comes. Eleana is ill.

"Why has it taken you so long to speak to me?"

My enemies have keenest ears. Rekkk. I am weak and vulnerable in this body. I could not take the risk of them overhearing.

Rekkk put the back of his hand against Eleana's forehead. "She is very hot."

Duur fever, Nith Sahor said in his mind. *It will get worse. It may not get better.*

Rekkk glanced up at the bird, hopping back and forth nervously on one foot then the other. "How do you know that?"

Because the disease is manufactured. By us. The Gyrgon.

"What? Why?"

It was an early attempt to subdue the Kundalan Resistance.

All at once Rekkk was full of rage. "Did you have anything to do—?"

Not personally. It was the brainchild of Nith Settt. I argued against it. All the same I am culpable.

"You must know its genetic makeup then," Rekkk cried. "Do something."

Would that I could. I have told you, in this guise I am severely limited.

"I can make almost anything with this okummmon you designed. Tell me what will cure her."

There is no cure I know of. We made certain of that.

"Ah, N'Luuura, if she dies . . ." Rekkk found that he was trembling.

Perhaps there is a way.

"Then N'Luuura take it, tell me what it is?" Rekkk shouted. "N'Luuura take it, why are you Gyrgon so enigmatic?"

We may seem so only because you have yet to learn our locutions. On the other hand, Rekkk, you know more than you think. You know that Eleusis Ashera learned to believe in Kundala, in the importance of Kundalan, and in their faith in Miina. You know that I, Nith Sahor, learned the same things. Now, Rekkk, you have a Kundalan lover, Kundalan friends to whom you are fiercely loyal.

Rekkk, holding Eleana in his arms, grazed her cheek with his lips. "How will any of this save Eleana and her baby?"

Tell me, Rekkk, would you die in order to save them?

"Of course. Yes."

Then perhaps that is the only way. The legend of the ultimate sacrifice runs at the very bedrock of Kundalan faith. It is the one weapon non-

Ramahan have in invoking enchantment. This much is certain: Gyrgon technomancy cannot save them. What is left save Kundalan sorcery?

As Attack-Commandant Blled crouched in the dense shadow of a rock outcropping, he could feel death at his shoulder, breathing softly and evenly. Not his death; the death of those he pursued. With darkness, the rain had changed to snow, heavy and wet and clinging, silencing the birds, bending the branches far below to its will.

Attack-Commandant Blled scooped a handful of snow and stuffed it into his mouth, he had not eaten since he had left his Khagggun in the dense forest near the death pit two days before. He gloried in the pain his stomachs were in; the sensation assured him that he was alive. From his vantage point, he could now and again make out through the swirls of snow the fitful glow of the fire emanating from the cave mouth on the ledge above him. The tingling sensation he had felt upon walking the perimeter of that pit had once again proved correct. He had picked up the fugitives' trail by being vigilant and patient. He had sent his Khagggun back to the crash site because he had too much respect for Rekkk Hacilar's almost uncanny ability to discern and thwart pursuit. Truth be told, there was another reason he had decided to continue on alone; he wanted the glory of their deaths all to himself.

As the storm howled around him he was immune to both the cold and the intense isolation it engendered. His inner eye gazed at the havoc and destruction it had been his pleasure to take part in on a dozen far-flung worlds. Like holographs lining a bookshelf he gazed lovingly on these scenes, milestones of his life, trophies of which he was inordinately proud. Nowhere present was any trace whatsoever of the Tuskugggun whom he had bedded or their offspring, unseen and unacknowledged. It could be said without fear of contradiction or exaggeration that his children, wherever they might be, were more dead than the corpses explored over and over again by his eidetic inner eye. It was not that he had forgotten them; for him they simply did not exist.

And as for the skull of the *korrrai*, it did not matter whether or not it was in his possession, whether or not he spoke to it. What mattered was that his compatriots believed these things completely with their hearts and with their spirits, for it was their conviction that conveyed upon him this almost supernatural power which nourished him in the cold and the dark of the raging storm.

Rekkk could hear the blood rushing through his veins even over the howling of the storm.

"What am I, Nith Sahor? Certainly I am no longer V'ornn."

Whatever you are, Rekkk, is for you and you alone to discover.

"One day, even if it is in another lifetime, I swear I will come to fully understand you." When he held out his arm the Teyj flew up and settled upon it. "Dear Teyj, take care of her." He put his hand on the crown of the bird's head. "I wish for you—"

I know what you wish for me, Rekkk. The song was like a caress in the center of his mind. *I wish the same for you.*

Rekkk lifted his arm, and the Teyj fluttered up. It settled between Eleana and the fire.

"This moment," Rekkk said. "You knew it would come, didn't you?"

I prayed that it could happen another way. This is a hard lesson to learn: even champions must die.

"I thought Gyrgon did not pray."

This Gyrgon does.

Rekkk nodded silently. Taking one last look at Eleana's pale and sweat-drenched face, he turned on his heel and went to the very lip of the cave mouth, and the snowstorm struck him a physical blow.

"Is this right?" he shouted. "Is this what I should be doing? Tell me! Give me a sign!"

The wind gusted and howled. His cloak was ripped from around his neck, spun off into the turbulent night. The snow engulfed him. He thought of all the wrongs he had committed, all the lives needlessly taken, all the cruelty and injustice he had meted out. He thought of the forgiveness with which his Kundalan lover and friends had blessed him.

And then he let go of everything: his guilt, prejudices, anger, impatience, frustration, uncertainty. His mind filled only with Eleana and her unborn baby, he spread his arms wide. "Here I am! I am Yours! Take me as You will! All I ask in return is that You spare Eleana and her child!"

And, tipped out over the ledge, he felt the storm's force gathering, the wind whirling like a vortex. Was that Miina's voice he heard, calling?

All at once he was taken off his feet. Sucked up into the maelstrom's bosom, he fell through the fusillade of snow.

34

Eleana's Choice

This close to the Veil Riane could hear it calling to her, although in point of fact she heard nothing at all. Rather, she felt the fluidic shifts in the place where she hovered suspended between water and fire. They radiated outward from the center of the cube of fire. She could feel the magnetic pull of the Veil, a kind of siren song, urging her to enter the fire and pluck out the Veil.

Still, she hung back.

There were lessons to be learned in every step she took here. Nothing was simple or as it appeared on the surface. This cube of fire, she was certain, was no different. Staring at the flickering flames, she reviewed what she had learned. She had survived the darkness of the water by bringing light into it, she had survived the vacuum by filling it with air. In retrospect, the pattern was clear. Both times, the solution involved the opposites.

Did that mean she needed to inject water into the fire in order to make the cube safe for her to retrieve the Veil? She reminded herself that in neither case had the application of opposites been straightforward or obvious. Otherwise, the bubble of air would have worked.

Something was bothering her. She moved closer to the fire, but still she did not feel any heat. She tried to peer more deeply at the flames, but it seemed impossible. Their centers were so bright they hurt her eyes, and she was forced to turn away.

There were any number of spells she could use in order to conjure water—Returning Current, Greater Mountain Stream—but she did not believe they were the answer. These flames were different; they would not respond to water. All at once, she had a clear and acute sense of danger. She did not think she would be given a second chance as she had here in the vacuum. If she guessed wrong, she was finished.

What was she to do?

And then she thought of Kunlung Mountain. It was an enchantment of sorts, though not a spell as either Ramahan or sauromician defined the term. The Druuge used it to reach a kind of equilibrium in the mind, the body, and the spirit. It was a high place, a consciousness of vista, hence all such enchantments have mountain in their names.

As she cast the spell, she felt herself rising through time and space until from the height of Kunlung Mountain she saw the entire view of the complex strongbox holding the Veil of a Thousand Tears. She peered down at the cenote filled with pitch-black water, the donut-shaped space in which she sat, cross-legged, dreaming the enchantment, and beyond, the cube of fire.

And that was how she saw it. The connection of all three vessels and the solution. She rose and, walking around the cube, discovered the pulse of the filament of bourn that passed through all three sections. Using it as a pathway, she used White Well to gather a rivulet of the pitch-black water above her and send it directly into the cube of fire.

Entering the cube, the rivulet of water circled the flames again and again, weaving a sphere of water to contain and then bank the fire. Only rose-colored embers remained.

And in their center, the Veil of a Thousand Tears.

It ran like a river, coiled like a serpent, rippled like a standard in the wind. It was a meter wide and perhaps three meters in length, although that was difficult to judge as its shape kept changing.

Riane reached in and took it.

It was translucent and felt like liquid, as if the tears of the Five Sacred Dragons had been sealed between gossamer-thin layers. She could feel each and every one of them pulsing as if with its own heart. And she thought she could hear the distant voices of the Dragons calling to her.

She also sensed the Veil as a living entity, just as Perrnodt had said. In her head flitted like fish about a reef not so much thoughts as emotions. The Veil knew who she was. It had almost immediately sent an unseen tendril into her heart and, embroidering its unique pattern there, had made its intentions known.

It knew of Giyan's plight, and in its unique language it began to paint pictures in Riane's mind, communicating to her just what she must do.

*   *   *

From his vantage point as he climbed the steep rock face, Attack-Commandant Blled saw Rekkk at the verge of the ledge that led to the cave in which his prey had taken shelter. And then the storm intensified, and the Rhynnnon vanished into a blizzard of snow. He never saw or even sensed Rekkk hurtle past him.

Blled held his position, at the ready. He waited for the storm to subside, for Rekkk to appear again. This close to his prey, he disliked losing sight of him. But when, after some time the storm did not abate, he continued his climb, knowing he could not last long out in it. He was thinking of the pleasure he would derive from dispatching the Rhynnnon himself, of watching the light go out of the traitor's eyes. He felt anticipation also at taking the measure of the Rhynnnon's companion, the Kundalan sorceress who had maimed Star-Admiral Olnnn Rydddlin. Other Khaggqun would have coveted the acclaim that would accrue to the one who brought back the pair's heads. Blled, however, was solely fixated on the pleasure he would derive from holding their still-pulsing hearts in his bare hand.

With these thoughts to warm him, he completed the almost vertical ascent in the most inclement weather. He had wanted to attain this before dawn and, hopefully, at the height of the storm, when he would be least expected and could therefore maximize the element of surprise.

Gaining the ledge, he lay on his side half-hidden in a snowdrift and cast his gaze about for the Rhynnnon. As far as he could tell, the ledge was clear; Rekkk Hacilar must have returned to the cave when the ferocity of the storm interfered with his reconnoiter.

He rolled through the drift. He could make out the cave mouth and, in a small lull in the tempest, a dark patch above and to the left. He made for that spot at a crouching run. It was perhaps a hundred meters from the cave mouth. Blowing on his fingers to keep them from stiffening, he made the climb up to the dark patch. It was a far easier ascent than the one he had just made.

As he grew closer, the dark patch resolved itself into an ear canal, one of those auxiliary tubes often found radiating from mountain caves. These invariably fed into the main cavern itself. He crawled into it and soon enough could make out the indistinct, fluttering sound of a voice. Drawing his ion mace, he headed down the canal, the voice growing more distinct with every moment.

*   *   *

Wake up. Eleana, wake up!
    The Teyj flew around her.
Eleana! Eleana!

The Teyj fluttered its upper wings against her cheek before settling onto her lap.

Eleana's fever dream was all at once filled with magnificent song, and she opened her eyes. The duur fever that had racked her had vanished as quickly as it had overtaken her. She gave a little gasp and clutched her belly.

"My baby!"

Fear not. He is fine, the Teyj sang. *He is blessedly untouched by the fever.*

Eleana blinked and looked around.

"Someone called me. It was like a symphony," she said, as if to herself. She said, "I'm thirsty."

She watched as the Teyj flew through the mouth of the cave into the snowstorm. Moments later, he had returned, fluttering in front of her face.

Open your mouth.

"What?"

You said you were thirsty. Open your mouth, Eleana.

Obediently, uncomprehendingly, she opened her mouth. To her utter astonishment, the Teyj poked its beak into her mouth. She gulped at the melted snow.

The Teyj drew back. *More?*

"Come here." She lifted her hand, and the Teyj settled on it. "Thank you."

You're welcome.

"I can't . . ." She shook her head. "You are speaking to me?"

Yes.

"Who are you?"

I think you know, Eleana, the Teyj sang. *I did not die in the ring of sysal trees.*

"Nith Sahor!" she cried in utter delight.

The Teyj ducked his head. *I instructed Thigpen to put me into the Teyj's body. For safekeeping from my enemies.*

She remembered that horrible night when they had been waiting for

Riane to get to the Storehouse Door in time. The night Nith Sahor's enemies had come for him. The night they had all thought he had been killed. In her mind's eye, she saw Nith Sahor, mortally wounded, nodding to Thigpen, saw Thigpen's paw touch the center of a small black object, saw it balloon like a sail, expanding outward until it hid them both. Now she knew what had happened.

She stroked the Teyj and kissed the fluffy crown of its head.

"Does Rekkk know?" she cried. "You must tell him, Nith Sahor. He will be so—"

Rekkk knew.

A chill ran through her, and she shook her head at the sorrowful tone of the Teyj's song. "What do you mean, Rekkk *knew.*"

The Teyj, growing agitated, fluffed its feathers. *There is no easy way to tell you this—*

"No!" Her hands flew to her mouth. "Oh, no!" Tears sprang to her eyes. "Please, please, please!"

He sacrificed himself to save you. There was no other way.

"Why?" she screamed. She was clawing her way to her feet. "Why was there no other way?"

Because you were dying. You—

"How could he make that choice? What made him think he had that kind of power?"

You would not have survived, Eleana. The baby would have died with you.

She stopped, trembling.

"Tell me this is a dream. Tell me I will wake up in a moment in the real cave, and Rekkk will be kneeling beside me."

The Teyj folded his four wings.

"Ah, Miina!" Eleana covered her face with her hands and began to sob. She dropped to her knees. "Cruel Goddess. Why have You done this to him? Punish those who torture and murder Your children. Kill all the V'ornn, Miina! But not him!"

Eleana, grieve for him, as I do. But do not despair. He prayed to Miina and, in the end, the Goddess heard him.

She lifted her head, stared at the Teyj.

He sacrificed himself so that you and your baby would live. This is his legacy, and it is meant for you.

"But I want him back!"

Her cry reverberated through the cavern and reached Attack-Commandant Accton Blled, crouched still as a dormant perwillon at the end of the canal. Slithering feetfirst into the cavern proper, he whirled his ion mace over his head.

The Teyj gave a warning screech and flew at him. Blled swung the ion mace with deadly accuracy, catching the bird on the wing. It went down in a heap of feathers.

That gave Eleana the time she needed to reach for her shock-sword and withdraw it.

"What have we here? The sorceress skcettta? You are younger than I had been led to believe. And pregnant at that!" Blled laughed at her. The ion mace made an ominous whirring as it spun faster and faster in a tight circle above his head. "Where is the Rhynnnon Rekkk Hacilar?"

Eleana rose, bracing her aching back against the wall. She clamped down hard on all the muscles in her abdomen. "You will have to go through me to get to him."

Blled laughed all the harder. "I see. This is what happens when Kha-gggun forsake their caste. They hide behind female robes." He shook his head, advancing on her. "By the look of you, you are in no condition to give me pause with either shock-sword or spell."

He swung the ion mace and she countered successfully, but the effort cost her. She quickly realized that the bout with duur fever had sapped a lot of her stamina. And because of the baby she had less than usual. But she was determined that he would not be born in a pool of his own blood; she vowed that Rekkk's sacrifice would not be in vain.

Blled came in low, the ion mace blurred in a wicked sideswipe. This time she barely got her blades in front of it. They rang like chimes. She felt awkward and sluggish. The parry staggered her more than it should have, and he swung a lazy, overhand blow. She flicked it away easily, but it was a setup. The ion mace whirred and swung out in an arc too wide to get inside her guard. Instead, the thick chain wrapped itself around her shock-sword's twin blades. At once he jerked the ion mace—and the shock-sword—toward him. But Rekkk had trained her too well, and she would not allow herself to be disarmed. His move brought her up against him, and he drove her to her knees with his fist. She uttered a little moan.

Blled, cursing mightily, rammed her, so that she struck the cavern wall with sickening force. Her head lolled, and she almost lost consciousness. Seeing this, he tried to wrench the shock-sword out of her fist. He almost succeeded, but she felt a painful spasm in her loins, a quick gush of fluids running down her thighs, and all her senses awoke to razor sharpness. The baby! It was coming!

With a strength born at the edge of survival she fought him. He cursed, and his concentration narrowed. Consequently, he did not see the Teyj flying toward him until it was too late. Its sharp bill punctured his cheek just at the edge of the lower occipital ridge. Blood spurted, and he lost vision in his left eye. Roaring, he lashed out. The Teyj tried to dip out of the way, but he grabbed two of its wings and ripped them from their sockets. The Teyj screamed. Blled, intent now on the creature, loosened his hold on his ion mace.

Eleana, breathing hard, slipped the blades from the chain and drove them tipsfirst clear through Blled's hearts. His eyes rolled over to fix on her before he toppled backward, drowned in his own blood.

She cast her eyes about for the Teyj, gathered it into her lap, and gave a little cry. She laced her fingers below her belly. "I feel him," she whispered as fluid gushed down her thighs. "Nith Sahor, the baby has dropped. He is coming."

Sweat rolled freely down her. Her thighs spread with a renewed spasm of pain. Pulling aside her robes, she could feel the slippery crown of his head.

"Nith Sahor," she called. "Can you believe it? He wants to come now!" She was laughing and crying at the same time. "Now? What is the matter with him? Oh, oh, it hurts!" Laughing and crying. Cradling the head. "I am going to have to give him some lessons in timing, don't you think?" She looked down at the broken-winged Teyj. "Oh, Nith Sahor, I am so afraid. Rekkk—I can't bear to think about him now. But if you die . . . N'Luuura take it, if you die I shall never forgive you!"

Eleana. I am here. A song whispered in the center of her mind.

She closed her eyes, tears dripping onto her breast. Thank you, Miina, she prayed.

I am dying . . .

"No, no, no, no!" It was a rising wail of despair.

I am sorry to disappoint you. I wanted to see your baby as much as Rekkk did, but I can remain in this state only so long. Still, it is . . . interesting to realize that I will be so missed.

"You can't die!" Eleana said fiercely. She moaned louder, widening her squat. The fire in her loins and low back felt like a terrible peristalsis. She gasped, trying as best she could to breathe between the contractions. "You have to help me. I cannot have the baby alone." Now she cradled his head and shoulders in her hands. There was fluid all over. The contractions were building to a crescendo. A moment more, and she held his head, shoulders, and torso. Weeping and laughing, the cavern echoing with her cries. The awful explosive pain that filled her belly made her desperate for it to be over as quickly as possible.

"He's coming," she gasped. "Oh, Nith Sahor, he's here." And she pulled the baby out and up into the light, slimy and dripping, indistinguishable from an animal. Cradling him against her shoulder she cut the umbilical and tied it off.

She turned the baby toward her. His face was pale. A quick clutch at her heart nearly unnerved her. Save for a tuft of black hair on the slick crown of his head, he looked almost entirely V'ornn.

"Nith Sahor," she cried, "he is so still and quiet!"

Eleana, bring him closer.

With a terrible fear driving her, she put the baby in her lap, next to the Teyj.

"Do you feel him?"

He breathes. But just barely.

"Ah, Miina!" she wailed. "No!"

He has both Kundalan and V'ornn hearts.

"Two sets of hearts," Eleana whispered. "That should be good."

In theory it is. But practically we have found that the V'ornn hearts often begin to overwhelm the Kundalan heart.

"In the body as on Kundala." She held the baby tighter. "Nith Sahor, make him breathe. Make him live."

Eleana, even if I weren't mortally wounded, in this guise I have access to very little technomancy.

"You must save my baby, Nith Sahor. You must!"

There is a way, Eleana, the Teyj sang. *But it is not without danger. It is not without drawbacks.*

"Anything!" she cried, nearly beside herself with grief. "Whatever it takes you must save him."

The Teyj scrambled painfully over the pale and nearly lifeless infant. *Eleana, you should know something—*

"Just do it!" she screamed.

The Teyj dipped its head, so that the tip of its bill touched a black object strapped to its leg. It was so small she had never noticed it before.

At once, the blackness inflated like a sail, engulfing the three of them. In an instant, they were sealed off from the world around them.

"I saw this before," Eleana breathed. "When Thigpen saved you from dying."

This is what I am telling you, Eleana.

"You mean you—"

It is the only way to save your baby. This is how both of us will live.

She gasped. "Oh, Miina! No, you can't—!"

Then your baby is doomed. As for me, I have had a long life. It does not matter if I die.

"But it does matter!" She was half-blinded by tears. "All life matters!"

Your baby's breath is giving out. Tell me what to do, Eleana. This is your choice.

"I cannot. You are asking me to play Goddess. It is not my place to decide who should live or die."

Didn't that decision come into play when you killed this Khagggun?

"That was different."

I assure you that for him it wasn't. He is dead. You killed him, Eleana. You made that choice instinctively. You must use your instinct again. Life or death, which will it be?

"But my baby? What will become of him with you inside him?"

Eleana, at this moment he has no brain function.

"Then he is dead already!" she screamed.

Not yet. Not quite yet. But the moment is passing. And then it will be too late. Choose now.

She threw her head back, clutched the infant and the Teyj to her breast. "I want my baby to live!"

All at once she could not breathe. It was as if the black sail had collapsed in on her, molding itself to her, to the contours of the baby. She tried to breathe but could not. She called out for Nith Sahor but she had no voice. She was in a dream. She looked down. Her last sight before she lost consciousness was of the Teyj. It was using its beak to pluck out its feathers. One by one it laid them across the dying infant until it was completely bald. Its skin was as black as the sail, as rectangular as the box that had been strapped to its leg. It no longer looked like a Teyj at all . . .

35

Nawatir

Rekkk fell through the fusillade of snow and wind, but he did not reach the ground. Instead, the whiteness thickened, deepened, and became opaque. The howling of the wind faded into a background wash, the snow whirled in concentric circles all around him, but he felt neither wind nor cold. As he watched, the snow seemed to congeal, grow solid, take form and shape. And within the form and shape a ruddy glow began to circulate, like a cyclone; the glow grew in size, the ruddy hue becoming more pronounced until it took on the vibrancy of rubies.

And then, out of this red, red mist, he saw the face—enormous, glowering, terrifying. He saw the teeth first, gigantic and sharp as knives, then the ruby-scaled snout with pulsing nostrils, the eyes with their vertical-crescent irises.

"N'Luuura take me!" he breathed. "What are you?"

I am Yig. Sacred Dragon of Fire.

"The Dar Sala-at has spoken of you. You are one of Miina's Five Sacred Dragons."

It is good that you know of me.

"What is this? I must already be dead."

"I assure you not."

"Then why have you saved me from dying? I have made a pledge."

It is you who have summoned me. Your warrior-prayer has brought down the fire from the skies.

"I was praying to Miina."

We are Avatars of the Great Goddess.

The face, initially so terrifying, now seemed so beautiful it brought tears to his eyes. "You heard my prayer."

You are Miina's child. Her priest. Her warrior.

He felt a shock wave arrow through him. "I thought that honor was reserved for the Dar Sala-at."

Yes.

What did that mean? he wondered. "But I am V'ornn."

You are Miina's child, Her priest, Her warrior.

"I do not understand."

The advent of the Nawatir is written in Prophesy.

He felt his insides began to congeal. "But you must take me. I have made my sacrifice. My faith. . . . I demonstrated . . . I pledged to give my life so that Eleana and her child might live."

Your faith is absolute, your pledge unshakable. These are attributes of a true priest and a true warrior. This is who you are.

"I wish Miina to hear me. I would not have them die. They are too precious to me."

Even though you have no conception of what that child could become?

"Without question."

Your faith is absolute, your pledge unshakable. Here is the proof of it.

"I am ready now to die."

The face of the Great Dragon showed many huge teeth. *Have my words fallen on deaf ears? It is not your moment to die, Nawatir. It is your moment to serve Miina. And to serve both Kundalan and V'ornn. There is a war coming. My brethren have tried to avoid it, but now even they see that it is inevitable. You are Nawatir. The protector of the Dar Sala-at. I charge you now with this office and bless you with Miina's grace.*

"If I am in truth this Nawatir you speak of, then I beg you guide me to Lady Giyan, your most devoted servant, that I may free her from her torment by the archdaemon Horolaggia."

Giyan is beloved of Miina, as is the Dar Sala-at, but her fate is her fate.

"She is also my beloved. I would not see her harmed."

You are the protector of the Dar Sala-at. It is not for you to question.

"If she dies—"

War breeds changes, Nawatir, and never a war so much as this one. Be forewarned. Everything—everything you know or have ever believed true— will change.

"My love for Giyan will never change. It will never die."

Without warning, Rekkk found himself being sucked into the gigantic image. Closer and closer he went. At the last instant, it opened its fiery mouth, and he entered a great and fathomless darkness. He felt an overpowering warmth suffuse him, ribbons of fire burned where blood had pumped through his veins. His mind buzzed with ten million voices all speaking at once. And then, abruptly, there was the utter stillness of death, or the state beyond death, and for just an instant Rekkk fretted that this was all a dream he was having on the point of death.

Then he felt his faith reignite the fire in his blood, and he was lifted up, transfixed and exalted in the very bosom of the Cosmos, and he felt the torrent of unimaginable life pulsing all around him. It was as if, for one moment, he had become a gravship falling though the star-studded multiverse, seeing and feeling everything. It was as if, for a moment in eternity, the Cosmos existed inside him.

Eleana cradled her baby, a beautiful boy. He was her baby, but he was also something more. She knew that, and yet she did not want to think about it. Not yet, anyway. The baby glistened and shone with viscous birth fluids as it howled its passage into a new life. She crooned to her child, and was about to wipe him down when a webwork of violet energy strands appeared as if from the underside of the black Gyrgon sphere that still enclosed them.

She started, her heart pounding hard in her breast, and sought to shield her baby. Then she realized that the energy lines were emanating from her baby, expanding upward into the black sphere. The baby quieted, and she watched, fascinated, as the birth fluids evaporated, and his skin took on a healthy pinkish glow. She watched the movement of his eyes, still blind to the outside world, and all at once she gave a startled cry. His pupils expanded and contracted, his head turned slightly as his eyes alit on her. His bow lips curled into a smile. He gurgled happily, and she held out her forefinger for him to grip.

Now the energy lines were multiplying, and she felt his heat, an oven in her arms, a fire. Did he have a fever? Was he ill? But, no. She saw him shimmer, his outline growing hazy and she shook her head, passed a hand across her eyes. Perhaps it was she who was ill, or more likely exhausted unto hallucination from her ordeal.

But when she looked again, her baby was no longer a newborn, but a child of six months. The web of energy lines had multiplied several times over. His mouth opened and closed, and she knew with a mother's intuition that he was trying to speak.

Dear Miina, she thought. *What is happening?*

But, of course, she knew. Nith Sahor, buried deep inside her son, had taken control. As the child shimmered again, his outline wavering, she wondered whether this was how Gyrgon passed through childhood. She hoped not. She could think of nothing sadder.

She was weeping now, for the years her son was losing, for all the experiences he was missing, and her tears made him blur before her eyes. Then, she felt him moving, touching her face, and in a beautiful, melodious voice, he said, "Oh, do not cry, Eleana. You who gave me life should feel only joy."

And she hugged him to her, a child of three years, or so she estimated, the minutes of his life speeding by so fast she could not keep track of them. And he threw his arms around her and kissed her, shimmering again, growing, maturing, spurred on by his Gyrgon technomancy. And he whispered in her ear the word she longed to hear.

"Mother."

Much to his surprise, Rekkk Hacilar, the Nawatir, found himself returned to the cave where he had left Eleana dying of duur fever. He had assumed that the red Dragon would take him to the Dar Sala-at, wherever she was in the wastes of the Korrush.

Passing a patch of ice, he saw himself clothed in deepest red, a cross-hatched tunic and trousers of an unknown, lustrous fabric, high, sueded boots, a thick belt from which hung two swords, their scabbards incised with Miina's sacred runes. Across his broad, square shoulders rode a hooded cloak that writhed and whipped as if of its own volition. Then, he peered closer into the impromptu mirror and, reaching out, pushed aside a crust of snowflakes. The face he saw reflected there made his V'ornn hearts pound in his chest. While he had retained his size and height, he no longer looked like a V'ornn. Rather, he had the coloring, the features of a Kundalan. Blond hair crowned his head, cheeks, and chin. He put his hand up, and wonderingly stroked his close-cropped beard. How odd, how luxuriant it felt to be growing these filaments called hair—and in such profusion! How pale his eyes, like the ice crowning the tops of the Djenn Marre! And his skull—it was no longer long and tapering, but as globular as any Kundalan's. Again and again, he traced with his fingertips the new contours of his face with its high cheekbones and generous lips. And, of course, he wondered what Giyan would think of him, and whether he would ever see her again.

Rekkk turned, hearing the sound of two voices talking. The female voice he recognized as Eleana's and he said a prayer of thanks to Miina. But the other voice, that of a young male, was unfamiliar to him. He was about to go and find out who was with Eleana when he sensed another presence.

It was then that he saw the huge, fearsome-looking animal coming out of the mist along the ledge. It was six-legged, black as pitch, with a tapering muzzle. Tufts of silken hair sprouted from the backs of its long legs, its elegant neck was a perfect arc, and its mane was thick, stiff as the bristles on a brush. Its huge golden eyes regarded him with uncanny intelligence. A long spiral horn, bluish white, coruscating, rose from its forehead.

"A narbuck," Rekkk whispered. "I thought you were a legend."

The narbuck stopped a pace in front of him. Then it lowered its muzzle into his hand.

"Stay," he said. "Will you stay?"

The narbuck snorted and shook its magnificent mane. He patted its flank, then he turned and went into the cavern. Rekkk Hacilar did not know what to do next, but it seemed that the Nawatir did.

Eleana saw him first and she put her arm protectively around her son. He was already a youth, and in many respects he resembled Kurgan, with his long, angular face with its cruel slash of a mouth. But instead of his father's night-black eyes, watchful as a snow-lynx's, he had Eleana's grey-green eyes, open and curious, and he had her rosy skin coloring, as well. He was holding a poultice against her lower belly. She was sitting with her back against the cavern wall. Her legs were drawn up by the fire. Her robes were blood-spattered.

"Who are you, stranger," Eleana said warily, "to come upon this cave?"

"Eleana, it is me. Rekkk."

"Rekkk is dead," she said dully. Her hand closed around the hilt of her shock-sword. "The Teyj told me. And, in any event, Rekkk was a V'ornn. Clearly, you are not."

"But it *is* me. I have been transformed."

Eleana thumbed on the shock-sword, but the youth beside her bade her put it down.

"Hear him out," he said in a melodious, golden voice. "Do not be in such a rush to judge."

"Who is this youth—?"

"If you are Rekkk Hacilar, which I very much doubt," Eleana said with an edge to her voice, "now is the moment to prove it." She had dropped the point of her weapon but she had not turned it off. The twin blades hummed ominously, the ion field between them resonating.

"We hid in that pit of death," he said, "buried in rotting corpses, breathing through reeds, in order to escape the Khagggun who were pursuing us."

Eleana's eyes opened wide, but still she did not relent. "And then, when we climbed out, what did we speak of?"

"You told me how your grandfather witnessed the birth of the nar-buck. How it was turned from white to black by the lightning bolt that came from the sky and buried itself in its forehead and remained there."

"Dear Miina! Rekkk!"

"There is a narbuck outside, Eleana. Whenever you want, I will take you out to meet it. It is a most magnificent creature."

"Rekkk, who are you? What have you become?"

"He has given himself into the arms of Miina," the strange Kundalan youth said, "and She has transformed him into the Nawatir, the holy protector of the Dar Sala-at."

Rekkk gave the youth a curious glance, then knelt in front of Eleana, took her pale hands in his. "Eleana! I thank Miina you survived."

"Ah, Rekkk!" She kissed his cheeks. "I thought you were dead."

"I would have been." He stroked her hair and hugged her to him. "I should have been." He shook his head. "It is a mystery. I would not let you and the baby die. I prayed to Miina to take me instead. I went to the ledge and stepped off, I fell into the storm but then I was taken up into the mouth of Yig, the red Dragon. He spoke to me, Eleana. He told me that it was not my time to die. He told me that Miina had heard my prayers, that She had chosen me to be the Nawatir."

"Rekkk." Her eyes were shining. "You were born for this. First, Nith Sahor's champion."

"Where is the Teyj?" For the first time, he glanced at the youth. "And you. I do not understand. You look so like Kurgan Stogggul and yet you have eyes just like—" He broke off, staring at Eleana.

She said, "You are not the only one to have experienced a miracle." She nodded. "That's right. My son."

"What? Had he lived your baby would have just been born." He gestured. "This male must be fifteen years."

"Thirteen, actually," the youth said. "Tomorrow I will be fifteen."

She told him how she and the Teyj had been attacked by the Khagggun who had been following them. How he had mortally wounded the Teyj and had brought on the baby's birth before she had managed to kill him. She pointed to where Sahor had dragged the corpse. "My baby was dying along with Nith Sahor," she said. "He used the same technomancy that had migrated him into the body of the Teyj to keep the baby alive."

She tapped Sahor's hearts and head. "He is in here."

Rekkk peered at him carefully. "But there are no neural implants, no circuitry whatsoever. And then there is *this*." He ruffled the tuft of black hair that arced in a wave from the top of Sahor's head.

"I am Sahor and something beyond," the youth said. "Though no longer Nith, I exist in here, in this body. I have altered it and it has altered me. I am neither V'ornn nor Kundalan. I am Other, and I am here for the rest of my life. This is only right, do you not agree, Nawatir." He produced a small black object, which he held in the palm of his hand. Tiny violet emanations crisscrossed its surface. "This taps into my Gyrgon DNA that had embedded itself into the Kundalan strand. It has greatly speeded up the aging mechanism. In seven days, when I reach the age of twenty, it will again tap into my DNA and my aging will return to that of a V'ornn." He put the black object away. "I have neither tertium circuits nor okummmon. Though I retain the Gyrgon neural-net strand in my DNA, I am forever cut off from the Comradeship. On the other hand, I sense that I have abilities I have not yet begun to explore. And I have a Kundalan mother. I believe I have gotten the better of the exchange." He grinned and gripped Rekkk's forearm. "It is good to see you back, Nawatir."

Rekkk regarded him gravely. "You knew. When you convinced me to seek Miina, you knew."

"Let us rather say I suspected." Sahor said. "My studies of Kundalan lore have served me in good stead. I have been thorough in my research.

In any event, I convinced you of nothing, Nawatir. I recognized the priestly devotion in you sometime ago. It was your faith and your faith alone that allowed you to be transformed."

The Veil of a Thousand Tears rippled around Riane, its fluid form fitting to the contours of her body. It painted for her a portrait of Za Hara-at. The ancient city was a gigantic engine, a complex instrument that had been used for fantastic feats of sorcery. This site had been chosen because every power bourn on Kundala intersected here. Each section of the city was built around a plaza, beneath which was at least one power-bourn intersection. Each section of the city was constructed for a different sorcerous purpose, each interlocked with its neighbors to create the whole, a grid that, when activated, was a source of almost incalculable sorcerous energy.

The Veil could be used for many things, depending on which Plaza of Za Hara-at it was in. In order to save Giyan, she must release the Dragon's thousand tears in the center of the Plaza of Perplexities.

She emerged from the cenote in the Plaza of Virtuous Risk into a biting wind. The finbats had vanished, but the sauromician she had glimpsed had returned.

He stepped from the shadows, chanting, and before she could defend herself he had impaled her on a forked spear of pale blue sorcerous energy. She saw that she was only an arm's length away from the bourn nexus that lay deep beneath the plaza. If she could maneuver herself over it she could draw from its power. But she could feel the spear shredding inside her, winding around her spinal column, and all at once she was paralyzed.

The sauromician, his black pupils throbbing, walked toward her. She could see that he was careful to avoid the power bourns.

"The Veil of a Thousand Tears," he said. "The ultimate prize." He thrust up his arm. "I will have it now!"

Pain began to crawl up Riane's spine as he tightened the spell upon her, and a terrible cold began to drain her of energy. At his murmured command, another forked spear streaked out toward the Veil.

"It is useless," Riane said. The paralysis was making talking difficult. "The Veil is semisentient. It will kill you if you try to take it from me."

"Oh, I am not an archdaemon. I have no intention of taking it from you, Dar Sala-at." He saw her reaction and laughed. The knucklebones through his ears shook. "Yes, I know who you are. Who else could have come into the Korrush and caused such havoc? Who but the Dar Sala-at could free the Veil from its hiding place?" He smiled, revealing abnormally long incisors. "I have been planning long and hard for this day. I know how to defeat the safeguards. I will take you and the Veil along with me." He cocked his head. "After a time, you will do as I tell you, and the Veil will do as you say. It is as simple as that."

"No, Talaasa," came another voice ringing across the plaza, "as it turns out it is not so simple at all."

Talaasa whirled, and Riane felt a slight lessening of the terrible cold that had flooded through her. She could turn her head enough to see the diminutive figure of Minnum approaching them.

The sauromician started to laugh. "What? You're not cowering in some ragged doorway? I thought the carrion birds had already feasted on your flesh."

"Mock me at your peril," Minnum said, coming on.

"Oh, do not concern yourself, Minnum. You are beneath my notice. You little pipsqueak. Where have you been hiding yourself? While I and my brethren toiled in onerous exile here in this wasteland you slipped away, turned tail, and ran into some hole in the ground. You hid from everything. Even your punishment."

"On the contrary. I found that there is no escape from Miina. No escape from the sins we committed."

"Sins!" Talaasa scoffed. "What word is that? We did what had to be done."

"Then you are still arrogant, still blind to the truth."

Talaasa spat. "Our 'sin,' if you could call it that, was that we failed in our mission. I intend to see that does not happen again."

"You are sadly mistaken."

"Our way is the only way." Talaasa shook with rage. "Idiot! You have only to look at what is left of the abbeys to see that they are dying without us. What the Ramahan need, what we and only we can provide them, is strong leadership. Don't you see how we were deluded by Mother? This sharing of power between males and females could never work, not for long, anyway. And why should it? Males are clearly superior in both strength and brainpower. The females were like a weight around our necks. They brought us down to their level. They emasculated us."

"You've had your say. Now back away," Minnum said. "Don't make me kill you."

"You know, Minnum, you were always laughable. But this newfound righteousness makes you pathetic."

Minnum gritted his teeth and cast a spell. Riane could feel it humming through the air. She could also feel Talaasa countering it.

"Is that the best you can do, little one?" He cast a cold-fire bolt, making Minnum jump back. "If you do not fear me yet, come closer. I will teach you." He cast a second bolt, which singed Minnum's hair. Minnum yelped and threw his arms wide. A thin orange spiral formed in the space between his hands, then abruptly fizzled out like a fire in a rainstorm.

"Oh, I think I am going to like this," Talaasa said, his eyes alight. He cast yet another bolt, this one straight at Minnum's chest. Minnum countered with a more potent spiral, which met the bolt halfway. The bolt was momentarily halted. The two concentrated on their duel. Talaasa gave a guttural cry. Sweat formed on Minnum's beetling brow and began to roll into his eyes. Gradually, the bolt crept toward Minnum as the spiral began to sag in its center.

Talaasa, sensing victory was near, redoubled his concentration. As he did so, Riane felt his grip on her relaxing a bit more. Now she was able to move slightly, and she wriggled, fighting against the bolt and the pain and numbing cold it was inflicting.

Centimeter by centimeter she contrived to twist herself toward the bourn nexus. But Minnum was sweating freely by then, and the bolt had almost cleaved the spiral in two. It was seconds away from piercing him through the heart. With one last surge, Riane crossed the nexus boundary and felt its vast power flood through her. Warmth broke the cold-fire bolt's grip, and Talaasa turned and screamed at her.

In that moment, Minnum gathered all his courage and sent his own cold-fire bolt hurtling at Talaasa. Seeing this, Riane began to conjure Reweaving the Veins, and Talaasa knew he had to counter it. She had distracted his attention long enough for the cold-fire bolt to smite him down.

As Talaasa went to his knees, the spell that had been holding her in the air vanished, and she was pitched along the cobbles of the plaza.

"Look out!" Minnum called, running toward her. "Roll the other way!"

Too late. She felt Talaasa's grip as he gathered her inside his long, spidery arms. She was still half-paralyzed and, out of the grip of the bourn nexus, shivering mightily.

"You're too close," Minnum shouted. "I cannot cast a spell without hurting you."

Out of the corner of her eye, she saw the black sixth digit on Talaasa's hand and lunged for it. He had been waiting for that. He slammed the side of her head against the cobbles.

Stars exploded behind her eyes and, above her, she could feel an itching along her flesh as the sauromician gathered another spell around them. She could feel it sliding over her skin like a birthing serpent, and she hauled on him, rolling him over, kicking him, rolling again, until she felt it.

He felt it too, the proximity to the bourn nexus, and he struggled against her, frantic to get away. But she had him, had the leverage, and she rolled him one last time through the boundary and into the bourn nexus.

Talaasa opened his mouth wide to scream, but he had already burst into flame, low and dense, a core without heat or light. Just a shimmer like fireflies on a lake at night, a smear of color that vanished all within the blink of an eye.

Then Minnum was at her side, hauling her up and brushing her off.

"Dear Miina," he said, breathless, "that was a close one!" He shook his head, his eyes alight. "The Veil of a Thousand Tears. It truly exists!"

"What are you doing here?" Riane waved her hand at him. "Never mind. There would be no reason to believe you, anyway."

"Have I lied to you? I don't recall—"

"Minnum," she said firmly, "I know you are a sauromician."

"Oh, dear, oh, dear!" he cried. "This will go ill with me, what with the sauromicians being deadly enemies of the Dar Sala-at."

"I already got a taste of that." She clapped him on the back. "Thank you for intervening. That was brave of you."

Minnum blushed and stammered his thanks. He seemed genuinely bewildered by his own bravery.

"Come on," Riane said breathlessly. "We need to get to the Plaza of Perplexities for the Veil to save Giyan."

36

Firefight

The leader of Majja and Basse's Resistance cell was a youth named Kasstna. He was no more than a year or two older than Basse, Marethyn guessed. He had the face of an animal, broad and flat, with diamond-shaped eyes. His shoulders and arms were massive, giving him a hulking, brooding appearance. In truth, she realized that he had no reason either to like her or to trust her. She was V'ornn; she was the enemy. And yet she had brought him and his cell vital information, intelligence that would go a long way to stemming the tide of death among them. Possibly he hated her for that. Though he readily took the intelligence she had passed on from Rada, it was clear that he did not trust her. He denigrated her every chance he got.

The cell had decamped in the middle of the night, in a metallic rain that sounded as if it was intent on shattering the trees. Marethyn, Majja, and Basse had, hours before, crept out of Axis Tyr using one of many Resistance tunnels that circumvented the city's well-guarded gates and rendezvoused with the cell. Marethyn was wearing a dark-colored tunic and trousers, high boots, a heavy traveling cloak to keep out the chill and damp. On her left hip was an ion pistol Sornnn had given her, riding low in its holster. Every once in a while, as she moved hunch-shouldered with the Kundalan freedom fighters, she touched the cold butt of the weapon both to assure herself of its power and keep him close to her.

The cell numbered twenty in all, riding powerful cthauros. No one spoke to her. But, then, no one spoke at all. During one of the short breaks, while they washed down cold tasteless concentrate with water, Majja showed her how to draw her ion pistol, aim it to track her prey, and fire. Basse, watching this demonstration, laughed silently, but afterward, he offered to share his laaga stick with her as well as with Majja. Her first instinct was to refuse, but then she thought better of it. She knew Basse was impressed by how expertly she rode. She did not have the hearts to tell Majja that she could shoot the tips off a gimnopede's tail feathers at fifty meters.

The three of them squatted under the canopy of a kuello-fir and listened to the sleet come down like an artillery barrage. They smoked silently. She looked into their eyes and wondered if they could possibly be as frightened as she was. Then she wondered if there was any fear left in them. They seemed like hollow shells, automatons mechanically putting one foot in front of the other, doing what had to be done. But in the silence of their own minds what were they thinking? She felt an urge to put her arms around them, to tell them that it was going to be all right. She wondered if they had ever been rocked to sleep. She sensed the cell around her, their collective breath a murmurous grace note. A scent arose from the bed of kuello needles, cutting sharply across the wind, and she realized the laaga had heightened her senses.

She saw Kasstna's outline appear. He made a curt gesture, and they were on their way again, riding swiftly upland. They had already left the city far behind. Roughly paralleling the convoy route, they nevertheless kept their lateral distance so as not to give away signs of their passage. Not surprisingly, the route's vulnerable points were few and far between. None was without disadvantages and dangers. Marethyn was impressed by how quickly Kasstna assessed them and decided on the one that would give their ambush the best chance of success.

The place he chose was a dry wash just west of Prosperous Reserve and south of Joining the Valleys. The Khaggun, true to their nature, were taking a route that skirted the villages and avoided entirely the most densely populated areas that lay between Avis Tyr and Glistening Drum. To do so, they had to pass through the dry wash. It had the advantage of giving the cell high ground from which they could attack the convoy on an equal level. There were two main drawbacks. It was only spottily forested, and there was a blind spot directly behind it, where the cliff face rose to a plateau higher than the one the Resistance fighters would be commanding.

A thorough reconnoiter of that plateau, however, convinced Kasstna that they had nothing to fear from the higher ground, and in the last hour before first light they set about preparing themselves to take control of the convoy. They were in possession of three medium-range ion cannons which, along with their sidearms and their ingenuity, would have to suffice.

He set two of the cell to watch their backs. The rest he deployed within the Marre pines. Marethyn did not get to see much of the preparations, which might have been the point because she was the first one he assigned to rearguard duty. She was sharing that responsibility with a swaggering, hollow-eyed male who, after coming over to sniff her like a wyr-hound, contrived to stay as far away from her as possible. She saw him through the predawn mist, smoking a laaga stick behind a cupped hand.

The sleet had stopped several hours earlier, which was just as well because the temperature had continued to plummet through the night. Now everything was layered with a thin, treacherous slick of black ice.

Firstlight broke. The convoy had left the Western arsenal. It would arrive in just over an hour. Marethyn found a stunted Marre pine, its canopy heavy with ice and, crouching, put her back against the rough-barked bole. Now and again, she caught a glimpse of Majja or Basse as they went about their assigned tasks. Once, she caught Kasstna glaring at her, and she returned his gaze unflinchingly. At last, he turned away, and she allowed the ghost of a smile to play around her mouth. Though her head had cleared, she could still taste the laaga. And she was thirsty.

She turned, cocking an ear. Away to the south, she thought she heard the telltale thrum of grav-carriage engines. The freedom fighters were readying themselves. The convoy was coming.

Though her fellow sentry appeared content to stay in one position, she was not. The cortasyne her body had been releasing ever since she had followed Majja and Basse out of Axis Tyr at last got the best of her. She jumped up and began a patrol. Her eyes scanned the higher plateau that ran behind the one the cell was on. Even though they had already checked it, this gave her something tangible to do.

She could hear the grav-carriages clearly now; they were less than a kilometer away and coming fast. The Khaggun would not want to spend more time than was necessary going through the dry wash.

In the hour or so since she had been assigned rearguard duty she had more or less memorized the terrain of the higher plateau. Now, as she scanned it once again, her eyes were caught by an anomaly. It wasn't very large. In fact, she had to stare at it for several minutes before she had satisfied herself it was really there.

She drew her ion pistol, and turned, briefly glancing over her shoulder, trying to locate Kasstna in the grey mist. But every member of the cell crouched hidden among the Marre pines, and, with the convoy almost upon them, she dared not approach their position. She decided, instead, to tell her companion.

The convoy's thrumming now filled the dry wash, echoing off the cliff faces. With one last look at the anomaly, she darted from tree to tree. Her companion hadn't moved. At least he had stopped smoking.

The first of the ion cannons erupted behind her as she reached him. He stood against the trunk of a Marre pine, staring at nothing. Marethyn tried to whisper to him, but the explosions swallowed her words. She touched him, and he fell over sideways. As he rolled over, she saw that the back of his neck had been severed by an ion dagger.

She did not stop to think how that might have happened. She grabbed the corpse's ion pistol and, sprinting from tree to tree, contrived to move nearer the anomaly. At the edge of the dry wash, the firefight had commenced in earnest. She could not spare the time to determine how the battle was going, but she now harbored the terrible suspicion that their ambush was known to the enemy.

She was now within range. From her crouching position she peered up to get a closer look at the anomaly when something struck her hard on the side of the head. She pitched over, her shoulder, then her head, hitting the ground. She sensed movement and saw the Khaggun who must have killed the other rear guard. Without thinking, she turned just in time to see a shock-sword cocked and ready to strike at her head. The Khaggun took one step toward her, slid on the black ice, and his shock-sword sank into the ground not three centimeters from her rib-cage.

For an instant all was silence around her. She stared up into the Khaggun's fierce, armored face. Reflected in it she saw her own death. Terror welled up inside her, and she raised her right arm without thinking and squeezed off a shot and blew his head off.

She rolled through a rain of blood, her hearts hammering in her chest. Her vision blurred. She was crying and vomiting and shaking uncontrollably. This was nothing like target practice. She had killed another being. Part of her wondered how that could be. How could she have taken a life? And she heard again Basse asking if she had killed, heard again Majja's mocking comment, *She doesn't look like she could kill a blood-flea.*

She got to her feet, forced herself to stop shaking. She could smell the Khagggun's death mingled with her own vomit. She wanted to run away and never look back. But she knew she could not. Then a premonitory shiver ran through her, and her blood ran cold. Looking back up the cliff side, she saw movement, and knew they were doomed.

She ran as fast as she dared into the midst of the firefight. The convoy hung in the air, its complement of Khagggun returning the Resistance fire. The Khagggun had already established a grav-bridge from the convoy to the cliff, and more were on the way. She found Kasstna, bloodied and on one knee, barking orders. She tried to tell him about the Khagggun creeping up on their rear, but he took one look at her disheveled state and assumed that she had lost her nerve. With a guttural growl, he shoved her away, and she ran, slipping and sliding on the black ice, dodging incoming ion-cannon fire, until she found Basse. Dead Resistance fighters lay in a tangle of limbs all around him.

He nodded grimly when he heard her news, and they went and got Majja. As they ran they saw Khagggun swarming along the grav-bridges, leaping onto the cliff, firing as they came on. Majja was using a couple of her dead compatriots as a kind of redoubt, and they had to pull her out of the fortification. The morning was ablaze with ion-cannon fire. More and more Khagggun were forcing their way over the grav-bridges. Together, they ran back to where Marethyn had last seen Kasstna, but when they arrived they found him and the rest of the cell dying or dead. They were the last ones left.

The ridge was teeming with Khagggun—those who had swung over from the convoy and the others who had been lying in wait. There seemed nowhere to go. The moment to retreat had passed, and surrender seemed the only viable option.

I remember my first kill," Olnnn said. "I was on Argggedus Three."

"I remember Argggedus Three well." Lokck Werrrent nodded. He looked resplendent in his new Fleet-Admiral's armor, emblazoned with the four-pointed star insignia of his new rank. "The place was a cesspit."

"I saw him, down through a stand of linm trees."

"I remember those trees. Nasty thorns that could shoot through a Khagggun's flesh."

Olnnn and Werrrent sat side by side in the Star-Admiral's hoverpod bristling with weaponry. Rada sat across from them. The lights of Axis Tyr raced by. The blur of a thousand faces. Sounds of the city broken off prematurely and trampled in the wake of their flight.

"He was crouched, this Argggedian, in a kind of natural arbor," Olnnn said. "He had been picking off our Khagggun all day. It took me three and a half hours to find him. And when I did I sighted him through the ion-cannon scope, pulled the trigger, and his head exploded. Just like that. One minute he was in the scope, glowing like a moon, the next, he was bloody meat. I didn't feel anything."

"You often don't," Werrrent nodded. "Not the first time, anyway."

Up front, in the cockpit, the pilot and First-Captain guard kept their eyes on the changing cityscape directly ahead.

Olnnn hunched forward. "Later that day, I engaged the enemy with the rest of my pack. Hand to hand. I looked the enemy in the eye and watched the life go out of him. It felt him quiver and jerk. Then it all made sense."

Rada listened to this conversation in silence. She could feel the tension coming off the two Khagggun in waves that made her skin itch beneath her armor. Olnnn had come up with a plan to murder the regent, or he and Lokck Werrrent had, she did not know which. Possibly it did not matter. She only knew that they were at the point of no return. That was why they spoke so earnestly about death, trying to parse it, to understand what was, essentially, unknowable. They were males, and they were Khagggun. They had to try or risk allowing the tension to get the better of them.

She was aware that Olnnn was speaking more rapidly than normal, as if he could not get the words out of his mouth fast enough. He sat with his left wrist on his knee. She saw that his fingers trembled just slightly, and by that alone she knew that he was afraid. He was a male and a warrior, and he was afraid. She had felt his courage, and now he was afraid, and this made her look at him in a different light. She thought that if she could not understand his anger, she could at last accept it.

The hoverpod was slowing. As it descended in a graceful arc Lokck Werrrent stood up. She saw that they were in a dark and deserted-looking part of the city. The nearest fusion lamp was out. A pair of wyr-hounds loped across the street. Werrrent gave Olnnn a significant look before stepping over the side. She turned, watching him walk in his stolid, methodical manner down the street. The wyr-hounds cringed, backing away with their teeth bared. As the hoverpod took off, she saw light glinting off Khagggun armor and weaponry.

They headed for the regent's palace.

Olnnn sat looking at her for some time.

"When are you going to tell me what you are planning?" she asked.

He came and sat next to her. She could feel his heat. It was almost as strong as the vibration of the hoverpod beneath her. He turned to her, and he kissed her hard on the lips.

With his hand at the back of her head, he whispered, "I know."

She looked at him quizzically, her hearts pounding.

"I know you memorized the route of the convoy. Lokck Werrrent and I created that route with special care. You see, there is only one place for a Resistance ambush, and we already have Khagggun hiding there."

"I have no idea what you are talking about."

He pressed her hand between his. "Your friends are walking into a trap, and there is nothing you can do about it."

She felt her hearts sink. She thought of Marethyn and wanted to weep.

"What I do not understand is why. Why would you betray your own kind to help *them?*"

"You who talk about the enemy like trophies would never understand."

"You are right." He nodded. "I will never understand treason."

"And what is it you and the Fleet-Admiral plan to perpetrate tonight?"

"It is not treason."

"Keep telling yourselves that."

"We are patriots. The regent must die. For the good of the Modality."

"Here is why I did what I did," she said. "It is because the V'ornn male has an infinite capacity for self-delusion. Any death can be rationalized. Many deaths discounted. The mechanism—"

He hit her hard across the face, and her head snapped back.

"Yes. Well." She would not put her hand to the rising welt. "That was to be expected."

He glared at her. "I thought you were different. I was even coming to grant you a modicum of respect."

"Here." She moved. "Let me spread my legs for you."

"And then you betray me."

"How typical of a male," she said. "This isn't about you."

"Why do you hate me so?"

Despite her predicament she felt a laugh escape her lips. "You really are a fool," she said.

He grabbed her then. "I know what I saw in your eyes in the Kal-llistotos ring."

"You saw nausea. My stomachs were upset."

With a grunt of disgust he released her. They were almost at the palace grounds. He lifted a finger. "No matter. It will all change in a heartsbeat. We are scheduled to meet with the regent out in the gardens. There, I will give him proof of your treachery, and he will love me for it."

"What use is that? If he incarcerates me or kills me, you will die."

"He will do neither," Olnnn said craftily. "Because as he is congratulating me for my success Werrrent's Khagggun will storm the gardens. They will kill his Haaar-kyut, and I will slit his throat."

The hoverpod was slowing again. Just below them, the grounds were brightly lit with fusion lamps, which cast the stands of close-cut sysal trees and hard-edged ornamental hedges in a harsh and feral light. A gimnopede nest, long abandoned and come undone, caught in the web-work of branches. The unexploded stumps of ancient sawn-down trees. They were the bare bones of what had once been the largest garden in Axis Tyr. What had been wild and magnificent was now diminished and rule-bound as Khagggun security procedures established clear-cut lines of sight from the palace outward. A rueful wind ruffled the shorn, browned wrygrass. The bow-backed stillness of defeat was everywhere. It was as if every mutilation and death perpetrated in the interrogation cells below the palace had its apotheosis there.

She could see a dozen armed Haaar-kyut stationed at strategic intervals throughout the garden. Kurgan Stogggul, arms crossed over his chest, was watching them descend. A Haaar-kyut stood next to him, whispering in his ear.

"As usual, one bodyguard," Olnnn said. "First target for Werrrent's best sharpshooter."

The hoverpod settled on the wrygrass, and Olnnn disarmed her, slipped a photon collar around her neck.

"You are my prisoner," he said in her ear. "Act like one."

"Who needs to act?" she said. Then, as they were about to alight. "Don't do this, Olnnn. Not yet. Remember the enchantment. Unless you are changed, you will not be able to kill Kurgan. You are still as duplicitous, as susceptible to corruption—"

He struck her a heavy blow on her cheek. "Shut up, skcettta," he said, pushing her out of the hoverpod. "I am not interested in a traitor's opinions."

Kurgan stood glaring at her as they approached.

"You made a fool of me," he said, and struck her with his balled fist. "What was it you were feeding me? Disinformation cooked up by the Resistance?" He struck her again so hard he drove her to her knees. Her head hung, lolling, and she wished for the plan to begin, wished for action. She vowed she would never be on her knees again.

Kurgan smiled at Olnnn. "Excellent work, Star-Admiral. My Haaar-kyut had begun to hear rumors about you and a Tuskugggun in armor. They had begun to doubt you, but I did not."

"Your faith in me is appreciated, regent," Olnnn said. "Many Kha-gggun—members of the high command included—are habitués of Blood Tide. Fire-grade numaaadis greases many wheels."

Kurgan nodded. "And mouths."

Without warning, the entire garden exploded into movement. Werrrent's sharpshooter took the regent's bodyguard down. The rest of the Haaar-kyut came under fire from Werrrent and his rapidly advancing pack. Olnnn drew his shock-sword and swung it at Kurgan. Kurgan stepped back, and Rada leapt for him from her kneeling position.

"Rada, no!" Olnnn shouted.

Her attack was so ferocious it forced Kurgan onto his back. She lunged for his dagger but he grabbed her forefinger, bent it back. She leaned forward with a forearm jammed against his throat. For a moment, they stared into one another's eyes. Then her finger snapped and a ripple of shock went through her. Kurgan pried her hand off the hilt of his dagger, drew it, and plunged it into her throat. She arched up, her arms flailing for him, and he plunged it into her again and again.

Olnnn, his teeth bared in a rictus of rage, hurled himself at Kurgan.

"I am meant to kill you," he cried. "It is my destiny!"

But then, to his stupefaction, the Haaar-kyut bodyguard Werrrent's sharpshooter had hit rose as if from the dead. As he did so, his outline wavered and rippled like water, revealing the form of the Gyrgon, Nith Batoxxx.

The Gyrgon pointed his left hand at Olnnn, but Olnnn kept coming on. He could feel the full force of Malistra's spell echoing through him like a howl. She had prepared him for this moment. He was a sorcerous assassin who could be stopped neither by ion fire nor by Gyrgon technomancy. He was invincible.

With his shock-sword centimeters from the regent's throat he was blasted back, taken off his feet. The sorcerous bones of his leg splintered and flew apart, and a cold such as he had never known fell upon him.

Pyphoros, in his Gyrgon host body, stood over him, his left hand outstretched.

"How does it feel," the archdaemon asked, "to have all the life force sucked out of you?"

Olnnn tried to reply, but he was mute. He could not understand what had happened. He had been bound for glory; Malistra had told him so. He was Star-Admiral. He had struck an alliance with the cleverest member of the high command. The power and the opportunity had been his, and he had seized it. Or had he? It all seemed an illusion now, the opportunity a trap, the glory leaking out of him with his blood. In an instant his life was over, and he had not even been granted an honorable death. He managed to turn himself slightly. He was lying beside Rada. Her eyes were staring and fixed. Her blood was still warm. His mind was filled with a vision of her in the Kalllistotos, her biceps tensed, her small breasts rising and falling, that look of absolute determination on her face. He thought that he had seen her then for the first time. Now, in a breath, she, too, was gone.

He felt inside him a kind of melting, as if his body, congealed in life, was now melting as death's furnace drew near. He rolled his bloodshot eyes and, looking down, saw, to his horror that the bones of his ensorceled leg were soft and yellow and sinuous. A head appeared at one end, a tail at the other, the serpent Malistra was glaring at him with tiny outraged eyes. Then the serpent broke apart, falling to ash, and he was flooded with a pain beyond all imagining.

A rhythmic rumble along the ground, the tromp of massed Khagggun boots. Harsh barked orders crisply carried out. Not his orders. Consciousness was fading and, with it, his life.

His arm felt as if it weighed a kiloton. He wanted desperately to touch her one last time, but her armor was in the way. The warmth of her flesh would have been such a comfort to him but all he could find was molded veradium, colored and polished to a high shine.

With his death and the dissipation of Malistra's spell, Pyphoros lost interest in him. All around them the chaos was slowly returning to order. After drawing the attacking force by initially falling back beneath their fire, the Haaar-kyut were reinforced by two packs that had been in hiding. They caught Werrrent's forces in a murderous cross fire.

"A massacre," Pyphoros said. "How exhilarating."

By this time, Kurgan had regained his feet. "It was well that the okummmon you created for the Khagggun high command allows you to secretly eavesdrop on their conversations."

"Their price for Great Caste status," Pyphoros said. "Nith Batoxxx believed that you cannot be too careful with V'ornn bred for war, and in this he was correct."

Kurgan noted the past tense. How long had the Nith Batoxxx personality been all but dead, he wondered.

First-Captain Kwenn trotted over and gave a concise report of the mopping-up action. All of the rogue Khagggun had been killed but their leader, Lokck Werrrent, was nowhere to be found. Kurgan ordered a wider search and put First-Captain Kwenn in charge. There was no point in alerting Kwenn—and by extension the rest of the Khagggun— that Werrrent could be tracked using his okummmon; that was sure to create a furor he did not want. He turned back to Pyphoros. "Look at me, drenched in blood."

"But not your blood, regent," Pyphoros observed. He gestured, and the bloodstains vanished.

Kurgan went and kicked the Star-Admiral's corpse. "You certainly took your time."

Pyphoros shrugged. "I did not anticipate the female's attack."

"I hope you will do better next time," Kurgan said.

The archdaemon laughed and cuffed him on the back of the head. "I have already done so. I can hear my beloved city singing. Za Hara-at has returned to life. At last, I know where the Veil of a Thousand

Tears is. Ready yourself, regent. Within moments we will be on our way." He spread his greatcoat around them. "First we must enlist SaTrryn Sornnn."

"The Prime Factor?" Kurgan frowned. He did not like the idea of any other V'ornn being informed of the Veil's existence. "Why do we need him?"

"He knows more about the buried city than anyone save the Bey Das who have been excavating there. In this accursed Gyrgon host body I cannot take the time to force information out of the Bey Das. SaTrryn Sornnn will readily do as you or I ask."

With her artist's eyes, Marethyn saw the last stages of the firefight as if it were a painting. Composition, textures, colors, and perspective resolved out of the clusters of sprinting Khagggun, firelight flickering, reflecting off their armor, bursts of green ion fire caught in the visors of their glittering helms, the lines of them advancing down off the cliff above them.

From their position hidden beneath a burning Marre pine, Basse aimed an ion cannon at the Khagggun busy slitting the throats of his mortally wounded compatriots.

"At least we'll take some of them with us," he said through gritted teeth.

Marethyn put a hand on the ion-cannon barrel. "Wait," she said. "I have a better way."

They dragged a dead First-Captain into the shelter of the Marre pine and Basse and Majja helped her strip the corpse of its armor. She put the helm on first and turned to them.

"What do you think?"

Basse nodded. Handed her the ion cannon while Majja helped her don the armor.

A few moments later, they emerged from the burning corona of the tree and hustled to the grav-bridge connected to the lead grav-carriage. Marethyn held the ion cannon at the backs of Basse and Majja, who appeared disarmed.

The Third-Marshal hanging back, guarding the grav-bridge, did not question his superior when Marethyn told him through the helm's comm system that she was bringing prisoners on board for interrogation. In fact, he leered at Majja, and said, "Yes, sir. Requesting my fair share of time with her, sir."

Marethyn contrived to ignore him, pushed the two Kundalan roughly onto the grav-bridge, her hearts fairly pounding out of her breast. They were halfway across when shouts broke out behind them. She turned to see the Pack-Commander breaking out of the firelight, gesturing at them.

"What is this?" he cried. "First-Captain, who authorized you to take Kundalan aboard the convoy?"

"Run!" Marethyn shouted as she tossed the ion cannon to Basse.

The three of them raced across the remaining span of the grav-bridge as ion fire broke out, whistling past them. Luckily, there was no blanket fire. The Khagggun had to be careful not to hit the grav-carriages themselves. Basse and Majja were on board when a well-aimed blast severed the grav-bridge and Marethyn felt herself falling. She held on as the section of the bridge she was on swung down, and she banged against the side of the grav-carriage.

She looked up. Basse was busy using the ion cannon on the three Khagggun who had remained on board, then he began to fire on the Khagggun crowding the ridge. Majja peered down at her and for a moment Marethyn, her hearts in her mouth, was terrified that Majja would choose not to see past her reflective visor. On the surface they were Kundalan Resistance and V'ornn Khagggun, bound in eternal enmity.

Then Majja reached down and grabbed her hand, hauled her up into the grav-carriage. As Basse continued to pepper fire into the Khagggun on board, they raced to the controls. Marethyn had driven enough hoverpods to figure out how to pilot the grav-carriage. She fired up the engines and pushed the throttle forward. With a deep and booming rumble, the convoy began to move. But, almost immediately, it began to heel over as they took a direct hit from the Khagggun on the ridge. She screamed to Basse as she struggled with the controls, and he returned the fire, his accurate shots killing some, making others scatter.

By that time, she had righted the grav-carriage. Basse continued his ferocious attack so that the return fire was sporadic and largely inaccurate. She had a little trouble maneuvering a convoy of three grav-carriages, but soon they had gained speed and altitude, leaving the carnage behind.

Basse, putting his ion cannon up at last, joined them in the cockpit.

"Where to?" Marethyn said. She had taken off her high, hard helm, and the wind and the sunlight had evaporated the sweat on her skull. She could not remember a landscape so sharply delineated or colors so vibrant. The world was singing to her.

He put a hand on her shoulder and pointed northwest. Marethyn, now firmly in control, banked them into the shadows of the looming Djenn Marre.

37

Night of a Thousand Tears

When the visitor's bell sounded in the Abbey of Floating White, it was Konara Inggres who answered its insistent call. The hour was deep in the night, but Konara Inggres was wide awake. She opened the door to three strangers riding on what appeared to be an enormous black cthauros. The gusty midwinter winds had snuffed out the gate lanterns. The strangers were backlit against a brilliant spangle of stars whose dancing light glittered off the silver-leaf domes crowning the nine slender minarets that rose from inside the bone-white stone walls. Down below, a wyr-hound started barking in the many-tiered village of Stone Border.

"How can I help you?" Konara Inggres asked, holding her lantern high.

"We are looking for Konara Urdma," said the beautiful young female with the grey-green eyes. She leaned to one side so she had a better view; she was sitting between her two companions. "You would not be Konara Urdma, would you?"

"No." Konara Inggres shook her head. "Konara Urdma is dead."

The three strangers exchanged a glance. "What happened?" the young female asked.

"Well, now, that depends on whom you ask. And the answer you get will depend on who you are." She took a step forward. "My name is Konara Inggres, will you tell me yours?"

Before they could answer, a gust of wind rattled the gates and the huge beast stamped one of its hooves. It turned its head, and she saw that it was not a cthauros at all but a narbuck.

"Merciful Goddess!" She went down on one knee. "My prayers have been answered." She rose and reverently touched the narbuck's damp muzzle, soft as velvet. Her hand briefly gripped its horn, and she sighed deeply. "We are delivered! Here is the Nawatir, riding a narbuck, one of Miina's sacred creatures not seen on Kundala in more than a hundred years." Konara Inggres was visibly shaking. "Then . . . which one of you is the Dar Sala-at?"

"Konara, the Dar Sala-at is elsewhere at the moment," the Nawatir said in a gentle and harmonious voice that stunned her as much as his appearance. "We three are her companions."

Konara Inggres' eyes were shining. "You have seen Miina, then. The Great Goddess has returned."

"Alas, no," he said. He was as terrifyingly tall, as broad-shouldered as any V'ornn she had glimpsed, but his face was that of a striking Kundalan with its ice-pale eyes, curling blond hair, and close-cropped beard. She especially liked his mouth, which was generously drawn and seemed somehow kind. "I am pledged to Her emissary, Yig."

"Merciful Goddess, you saw the red Dragon?" Despite the chill of night, Konara Inggres was sweating. Her world seemed to have completed the somersault that had begun when she had discovered that Giyan was possessed.

"It was Yig," Rekkk said, patting the narbuck's elegantly arched neck, "who provided me with my narbuck."

Konara Inggres made the sign of Miina. "One by one the Prophesies are coming true." She frowned. "But, Nawatir, your place is at the Dar Sala-at's side. Where, then, is she?"

"That is a long story," Rekkk said. "In the meanwhile, may we come in? Eleana has just given birth, and she is in need of rest and sustenance."

"Of course." As Konara Inggres ushered them through the gates her gaze lingered on the decidedly odd countenance of Sahor. *Another strange Kundalan*, she thought. He had the huge, watchful blue-green eyes and the guarded countenance of a sorcerer that was wholly at odds with the angular, almost cruel face. And she had never before encountered a Kundalan with only a tuft of hair at the crown of his skull. "But where is the newborn?"

"That is an even longer story," Eleana said. She was worried that the Ramahan would be suspicious of them. She tried not to look at Sahor as she said, "Do not be alarmed, my son is alive and in good health."

"Then all is as it should be," Konara Inggres said. "You could not have arrived at a more auspicious moment. I am in desperate need of allies."

"And why is that?" Rekkk asked as he dismounted from the narbuck.

"Come inside and you will see for yourselves."

They left the narbuck to wander the abbey's vast garden forecourt. Konara Inggres led them into an unlovely section of the abbey into which Ramahan were crowded. The chambers were in a state of total disarray, especially in the innermost one, where all the furniture had been shoved against the double doors leading deeper into the abbey. Sitting beside this barricade were three huge catlike creatures, their magnificent coats, golden with black spots, rippled. Their heads swiveled, and their small, triangular ears flattened back against their sleek heads. But they did not growl or bare their teeth.

"Ja-Gaar!" Sahor spoke for the first time.

"This is Sahor," Eleana said.

"I could not help noticing," Konara Inggres said as she took Eleana to lie down on a curved sofa she had not yet jammed against the doors. "A V'ornn with hair."

"He is special," Eleana said.

Flames leapt in well-stocked fireplaces. In one, a black-iron pot was suspended above the fire. After examining Eleana, Konara Inggres went to the hearth, ladling soup into a rough-hewn bowl. Then she ground up a combination of herbs, roots, and dried mushrooms and added them to the broth, which she brought over to Eleana and bade her sip slowly. Eleana did, watching the Ramahan behind her. They had a dazed and vacant look about them, as if a close family member had died suddenly and shockingly a handbreadth away. As in a firefight, time had telescoped for them. They youngest ones had tears on their cheeks. They kept their distance, slowing as they glided past. From the corners of their eyes they watched the newcomers as they did everything now, with a mixture of disbelief and apprehension.

"The abbey is at a crisis point," Konara Inggres said. She gestured. "Please, help yourselves. There is plenty." As an acolyte handed bowls to Rekkk and Sahor, she put her hands on her hips and told them in clear, concise terms how the possessed Giyan had shown up at the abbey.

At this startling piece of news, Rekkk and Eleana exchanged glances. Eleana saw the relief flood through him. Simply knowing where Giyan was, and that he was near to her again, gave him a renewed sense of purpose.

"This is good to hear," Rekkk said to Konara Inggres, confirming Eleana's thoughts. "We had lost track of her when she was possessed by the Malasocca."

"I am afraid I cannot share your opinion," Konara Inggres answered. "Giyan freed her twin sister, so that she could be possessed by Horolaggia's brother. Since then, the two of them have been infecting the Ramahan with daemons whose essence they have somehow smuggled through from the Abyss."

The Nawatir said, "Does the archdaemon inside her have the run of the place?"

"Not quite. Giyan—the real Giyan imprisoned in Otherwhere—told me how to bring the Ja-Gaar to life. They killed Konara Bartta, sending Horolaggia's brother back to the Abyss. They are keeping Horolaggia at bay, but only just. He seems to know that I will not let them loose on his host body as I did with Konara Bartta. Now the abbey has split into two factions," she concluded. "I lead one of them. The other—a far larger faction, I am afraid—follows the possessed Giyan. They claim that she has taken them to the Dar Sala-at."

"But that is absurd," Eleana said vehemently. "There is only one true Dar Sala-at."

Konara Inggres had begun to make a poultice for Eleana. "I have caught a glimpse of him and believe him to be a sauromician. I have done my reading. He has the black sixth finger."

The Nawatir wiped his lips. "In any event, the Dar Sala-at is female."

"That will make her work all the harder." Konara Inggres knelt, positioned the poultice beneath Eleana's robes. The Ramahan had begun to murmur among themselves. Possibly they were praying. Or weeping again. She rose. "There are those fixated on the well-established notion that the Dar Sala-at is a warrior and therefore must be male. Horolaggia is very cleverly playing upon that."

"All the more reason why we must help her all we can," Rekkk said. He told her how the Dar Sala-at was even now searching for the Veil of a Thousand Tears, which would dispossess the archdaemon Horolaggia and send him back to the Abyss without harming Giyan. "But our time has run out," he said. "The solstice comes at midnight, and there is still no sign that the Dar Sala-at has been successful. If we do not act immediately, it will be too late. Giyan will be doomed, and the archdaemon who possesses her will have access to all her memories and knowledge, including her Gift."

Konara Inggres gasped. "But that would mean that the archdaemon would be able to use Osoru."

"Precisely," the Nawatir said. "Giyan is my beloved. I will not let her die. If the Dar Sala-at cannot fight Horolaggia, then I must. Please. You must tell me where in the abbey he is."

"No!"

They all turned to look at Sahor, who had put his bowl aside. "Nawatir, as you said, it is almost solstice, and we have no margin for error. You love her too much; you will not be able to bluff him." The Ramahan were silent, their heads turned to stare at him. "I can."

"Impossible," Rekkk said. "I won't hear of it."

Sensing an impasse they could ill afford, Konara Inggres came and stood in front of Sahor. "You will have to gain the trust of the Ja-Gaar; you cannot go near the archdaemon without one." She stared him up and down. "Something tells me—what is it, I wonder, I see in those huge eyes? Are you the callow youth everyone sees, or are you far older and far more capable than any of us."

It was not a question she posed, and everyone in the little group around her knew it.

Nith Batoxxx is outside. Waiting." Kurgan pursed his lips. "Sornnn SaTrryn, you do not look well. Are you ill?"

"No, I—"

"Good. Because I need you at Za Hara-at. You know that dig better than any other V'ornn, even, I warrant, the Bashkir architects we have hired."

Sornnn's residence had about it the distracted air of transience. It was like a station that was now and again filled with the possessions of travelers but had nothing of its own. The soaring ceiling seemed therefore immense, the bare-walled rooms cavernous as a Nieobian cathedral. The two V'ornn looked lost within its reaches.

"Tell me again why we need to go to Za Hara-at in such a rush?" Sornnn said.

"Nith Batoxxx wishes it." The regent spread his hands. "And, after all, he has backed our project in the Comradeship. It is the least we can do."

"Yes, yes. Quite." Sornnn turned away, his thoughts turbulent with recent events. He was gathering maps and hastily jotted notes, paraphernalia he thought he might need. It was a good thing he made frequent trips to the Korrush and so had his things more or less permanently packed because at that moment his mind was far away from Axis Tyr. How could he have let Marethyn go off with a Resistance cell? How could he have stopped her? He shook his head. Would he even begin to understand the female of the species? Probably not, he admitted, but if anything happened to her . . . He could not afford to dwell on that black thought; otherwise he would be in despair.

"All right," he said. "I am ready."

Kurgan nodded and turned to the door. Just before he opened it, Sornnn said, "Regent, a moment."

Kurgan glanced back over his shoulder, a smile plastered to his face. He was in no mood for the SaTrryn's philosophical maunderings. "Some other time perhaps, Prime Factor. At the moment—"

Sornnn stood his ground. "You are going to want to hear this, regent, trust me."

"But Nith Batoxxx—"

"Especially before we go off on some mysterious mission with a Gyrgon."

Kurgan sighed and, nodding, came back to where Sornnn stood. "This had better be good."

Sornnn took a deep breath. "It's about your brother Terrettt."

"Oh, N'Luuura take it, nothing you could say about that mad V'ornn could possibly interest me. You are sorely trying my patience. Now come on."

"This thing is," Sornnn said patiently, "Terrettt isn't mad."

"Of course he is mad. Every Genomatekk who has scoped him—"

"The Genomatekks take their orders from the Gyrgon."

"We all do," Kurgan said shortly. "What is your point?"

"Marethyn found this out, through her own initiative and determination," Sornnn said. "That is my point."

"Why didn't she tell me herself?"

"I think you know why, regent." Sornnn remembered the glossary of key Bey Das phrases his father had complied, stuffed that, too, into his satchel.

"Kindly enlighten me."

"She is afraid."

"Please. I know my sister far better than you. She is afraid of nothing."

Was that a touch of pride in his voice, or was that wishful thinking on Sornnn's part? He said, "She is afraid that you will despise her no matter what she does."

Kurgan watched Sornnn carefully for a moment out of his night-black eyes. "She means something to you."

"So what? This discussion is about Terrettt."

"Not according to you."

Sornnn held up his hands. "You are right. The fact that you treat her with contempt is difficult for her to handle. I thought if she brought you this information herself it might effect a reconciliation."

"You are meddling in Stogggul affairs, Prime Factor."

"It will be the last time."

"That is reassuring."

Sornnn snapped his satchel closed. "Perhaps you would rather—"

"Let me hear what my sister discovered," Kurgan said firmly. "Initiative and determination are attributes I appreciate."

Sornnn glanced at the front door, then nodded. "Your brother Terrettt was the subject of a Gyrgon experiment," he said. In the silence that ensued he watched many emotions pass across the regent's countenance. "Still uninterested. Or shall I go on?"

Kurgan nodded numbly for him to continue.

"It seems that Terrettt has an overdeveloped ativar. That is the most primitive area of the V'ornn brain. It was deliberately enlarged. He was experimented upon since birth. Only the Gyrgon could do that."

The master of deceit knew the truth when he heard it. Kurgan's mouth felt dry and, thinking of Terrettt's birth-caul and his own secreted in Nith Batoxxx's laboratory, his skin began to crawl. "What . . . Does she know what the Gyrgon want with him?"

Sornnn had been set to tell the regent that Terrettt had somehow located the seven Portals Nith Batoxxx desperately wanted, but his well-honed instinct for survival stopped him. With V'ornn like Kurgan it was always best to hold the final card. "Not yet."

Kurgan ground his teeth in fury even as his mind raced back through time. He had been trained by a Gyrgon ever since he was very young, though Nith Batoxxx had chosen to hide that fact from him. Nith

Batoxxx had dosed him in the garden of the Old V'ornn's villa. He and his brother had been manipulated since birth, possibly—how could he know?—even before. And yet, it had not been the Gyrgon at all under whose spell he had fallen, but an alien creature's—the Kundalan arch-daemon Pyphoros. Oh, that was ten thousand times more humiliating! He cared nothing for Nith Batoxxx's fate; the Gyrgon deserved his living death. But as for Pyphoros . . . He touched the dark mark on his throat, and he found bubbling within him the burning desire to murder the perpetrator of this insidious web.

I do not like it here." Minnum shivered. "I do not like it at all."
  "Swallow your fears," Riane said. "The solstice approaches. There is but an hour until midnight. In order to save Giyan we must get to Perrnodt as quickly as possible." Just before, she had tried Thripping. But as in Axis Tyr, it was impossible to Thrip within the boundaries of Za Hara-at. Instead, they were obliged to retrace the power bourns back to where Perrnodt and Thigpen waited.
  A deathly glaze of darkness lay over the entire excavation site. All the buildings seemed connected, the city organic in some way that defied comprehension. Za Hara-at breathed, a soft rhythmic soughing of the wind. After so many eons buried it had not yet expelled its death rattle.
  Minnum kept glancing back over his shoulder. "There is something here. I can feel it."
  "More sauromicians?"
  "I do not know. No. I would not be able to feel them. They can mask themselves like spectres in the dead places between the power bourns. Something else. Something that frightens even them." He looked around wildly. "What if it's . . ." He wet his lips. "What if it is the archdaemon Pyphoros?"
  "Whatever it is you will protect me from it," Riane said, as they switched bourns. "Just as you protected me from Talaasa." She cocked an eye toward him. "I am told that I will have a protector sent from Miina. Perhaps you are my Nawatir."
  "Me?" Minnum laughed uneasily. "Please don't even think that, Dar Sala-at."
  "Tell me, Minnum, you are a sauromician and yet you speak of them as being separate from you."

He sighed. "I regret to say that you are correct. I wasn't entirely candid with you when we met at the museum. While I did, indeed, live here in the Korrush for some time, I left because of them, because I knew that after all this time of lying low they were beginning to talk of forming again."

"So you ran away."

"A shameful act. But what else could I have done?"

Riane, concentrating on tracing the bourns, said nothing. They were now in a plaza she could not remember crossing on her way to the cenote.

Minnum ran a paw through his tangle of hair. "Their dream, as Talaasa said, is to take over the abbeys and the spiritual direction of the Ramahan." He turned to her. "Dar Sala-at, hear me now. The sauromicians will fight you every centimeter of the way. You are anathema to them."

"But I am in Prophesy."

"That is precisely my point." Minnum paused. "They have become Prophesy deniers. Their contention is that the Prophesies are heretical, that they are nothing but lies meant to confuse the Ramahan and throw the abbeys into disarray. This, they say, has happened. That it *has* happened is a powerful argument on their side, and they know it. They have begun to gather followers, and more will join them, of that you can be sure.

"But there is another reason why I had to leave here. Once they made their decision, the sauromicians cut all ties with the Druuge and declared themselves enemies. I did not; I never cut my ties."

"Then why didn't you join the Druuge in the Great Voorg instead of fleeing to Axis Tyr?"

"Would that I had been able to. The Great Voorg is a sacred place. I am enjoined from going there."

All at once, Riane put a forefinger across her lips. The wind had died, but along the streets and avenues of Za Hara-at there came another sound. Minnum shivered. It was a howl, low and deep and agonized.

"What is it?" he whispered, despite Riane's admonishment to silence. "There is something here, I tell you." He looked around. "Something evil."

Was it Pyphoros? Riane's eyes were fixed dead ahead. "Whatever it is, it is between here and where we need to go."

"Is there time to make a detour?" Minnum asked.

"Right now I do not see that we have much of an alternative."

With the help of her Third Eye, Riane identified another route that began with a bourn-line that branched to the left. But as she ran toward it, she sensed the creature moving with her. Just to make sure, she went farther. The creature mirrored her, coming closer. They were out of options.

Go that way," Riane whispered to Minnum, pointing left to a perpendicular street.

"But you already—"

"Just do as I say!" Riane commanded.

She watched Minnum, shivering, walk hesitantly away. Her heart leapt. The thing in front of them did not move.

"Listen," she said. "We need help. For some reason, this thing is keyed to my movements, so you must get to Perrnodt and Thigpen and tell them what is happening. Tell them to meet me at the Plaza of Perplexities."

She described where the plaza was, and Minnum nodded.

"Now go on," she said. "Fast as you can!"

"Dar Sala-at—"

"Not now, Minnum." But she stopped. His eyes were magnified by tears.

"I am sorry that I cannot help you more—" He struck his forehead repeatedly with his balled fists. "All my sins, it seems, have come back to haunt me."

"Possibly that is why you are here now." Riane smiled. "Have faith."

He swallowed hard. Then he nodded and stood a little straighter. "I will find my way, Dar Sala-at. You can rely on me."

He loped down the street in his awkward manner. A moment later, he had vanished into the shifting shadows of Za Hara-at.

Riane returned her attention to the thing that crouched in wait for her somewhere along the bourn-lines ahead. Then she headed off toward the Plaza of Perplexities. She could feel the thing mirroring her movements, but for the moment it came no closer, for which she sighed in relief. The Veil guided her unerringly. But almost as soon as she came upon the plaza she felt the paving tremble beneath her feet and, turning, she saw that another cenote had appeared. Approaching it hesitantly, she saw that the cobbles around the plinth were seamless. It was as if the cenote had always been there. Mounting the plinth, she peered into the cenote. It was empty.

Now came a rising wind, localized and powerful, a brief funnel that set off her interior alarm. She had been in the center of such a wind funnel a number of times when she had used Nith Sahor's greatcoat. At the last instant, she leapt into the cenote, hanging against the inner wall with her hands gripping the edge of the flat lip.

In the plaza appeared a Gyrgon. He raised his hands and a host of fusion lamps ringed the plaza to light his way. Riane was astonished to see that he had with him Kurgan and another V'ornn. The sight of Annon's old childhood friend after so long stirred unpleasant memories of a fine mild day when they had together spied Eleana, and Kurgan had taken her by force, taken her despite Annon's attempts to dislodge him from—With a barely audible growl, Riane wrenched her mind away from the hateful moment. She peered hard at the third figure, trying to place him. It took her a moment of searching through Annon's memory, and then she had it. He was Sornnn SaTrryn.

What is a Gyrgon doing in Za Hara-at? she asked herself. And then she remembered what Perrnodt had told her, that until all seven Portals were open the archdaemons required a host body to remain in this realm for any length of time. She looked more closely at this Gyrgon. He was helmless and a kind of eerie inner flicker passed beneath the hairless skin of his skull, illuminating pulsing veins filled with a pale, yellow, bloodless substance. The pupils of his eyes pulsed, as well, expanding and contracting, and his mouth was working soundlessly like that of a puppet. And Riane, thinking, *What more perfect place to secret yourself if you were Pyphoros?* knew that she was at last confronting the archdaemon.

It was almost midnight. All she needed to do was hang, unseen, until they moved off to another section of Za Hara-at. It no longer mattered where Pyphoros looked; he would not find the Veil of a Thousand Tears.

Sornnn SaTrryn was consulting what appeared to be a map. "Where is it you want to go in Za Hara-at, Nith Batoxxx?"

"We need a cenote," the Gyrgon said, his voice thick and guttural with Pyphoros' daemonic energy. He pointed. "Just like that one."

Riane's heart skipped a beat. If they discovered her, she would never have time to save Giyan. Her intense anxiety and fear caused her to make her first mistake. She conjured Flowering Wand, a cloaking spell.

"What is that?" she heard the archdaemon possessing Nith Batoxxx scream. "I smell the whiff of sorcery!"

She heard the sound of boot soles slapping against the cobbles and knew they were headed her way. Cursing her own stupidity, she vaulted up over the lip of the cenote and crouched, using the cenote itself for cover.

"Who is that?" Pyphoros' angst-ridden voice rang through the dreaming plaza. "What foul sorceress goes there?"

Riane took out the infinity-blade wand. All she needed was one more charge and she could slice through the Gyrgon's armor. If she could kill the host body, Pyphoros would be sent back to the Abyss.

There was no shadow to warn her, and she had failed to conjure Net of Cognition to warn her of the archdaemon's proximity. Pyphoros stood atop the cenote, Nith Batoxxx's greatcoat swirling about him. As Riane looked up, he loosed a potent ion blast from the tips of his neural-net gloves, and Riane was sent head over heels backward. The wand went flying.

Another ion blast struck her and she sprawled on the cobbles, half-unconscious. The Gyrgon stalked after her. It was then that he saw what was wrapped around her.

"The Veil of a Thousand Tears!" he shrieked, eyes alight. "*You* are the Dar Sala-at? A *female*?" He began to laugh. "I am now just beginning to appreciate how mad Miina has become."

Riane shook her head, trying to clear it. Where was the infinity-blade wand? She saw the Gyrgon raise his arms and tried to move. But she could not even crawl. She braced herself for another ion blast, but instead she felt the tingle along her skin of a sorcerous spell, and all at once, she was lifted into the air and a cage of black and glittering strands formed around her. Each strand was growing what looked like needle-sharp thorns.

"I am sincerely in your debt, Dar Sala-at," Pyphoros said in a mocking tone. "I could not have found the Veil on my own, let alone retrieve it."

He wriggled his fingers, and the thorns began to grow inward toward Riane.

"I will have it now. That which is by rights mine."

Pyphoros worked the Gyrgon's mouth into the hideous rictus of a grin. "I know you are stubborn, Dar Sala-at. I know you will not willingly give it up. I do not care." He cocked his head. "Have you any idea how agonizing it is to be burned alive? No, how could you? But you will. Now."

The thorns began to drip an acrid, caustic fluid. Riane turned this way and that inside her sorcerous cage. Even so, a drop struck her bare arm, making her cry out. Her skin began to crisp in a neat circle the exact diameter of the drop of acid.

"What is this?" Sornnn said, as he and Kurgan came across the plaza. "What do you think you are doing?"

He started to lunge toward the Gyrgon, but Kurgan restrained him.

"Keep quiet," he hissed.

"I cannot keep quiet. He is torturing—"

"You will only get yourself killed," Kurgan said. "What is the point of that?"

More thorns popped out of the strands, growing, so many that Riane could not evade them. Wherever their oozing, viscous liquid struck, her skin began to burn. The pain was so intense that she was soon on the verge of passing out.

"It won't be long now, Dar Sala-at, before you are dead and the Veil is mine!" Pyphoros called.

Sahor held the Ja-Gaar on a short leash. It was not one he could see, but he felt it all the same. At first, Konara Inggres had balked. But then Sahor had said, "Fear is what I know best. Horolaggia is afraid of the Ja-Gaar. It is ingrained in all daemons. Trust me in this."

"Trust a V'ornn?" Konara Inggres shook her head. "Well, why not, when he knows more about daemonology than I do."

Sahor went down the dimly lighted corridor, moving slowly toward the heart of the abbey, where Horolaggia, controlling Giyan, had positioned himself. He was aware of a rustling around him and directed the Ja-Gaar to prowl this way and that. The beast was like a lantern held in the dark to keep nocturnal predators at bay. Wherever the Ja-

Gaar turned, the rustling fell back, momentarily stilled.

Konara Inggres had wanted to accompany him. She had argued that no one knew the layout of the abbey the way she did. But Sahor was adamant. He said that he did not want to have to worry about her safety while he was confronting the archdaemon. In the end, she had settled for providing him with a detailed map, which he instantly memorized.

He grimaced as his bones and muscles pulled apart and lengthened. He turned a corner and, despite the constant pain of his hyperkinetic growth, kept going. It was important to keep to a steady pace. The first lesson you learned about fear was that it was insidious. The second lesson was never to show it yourself. That was accomplished by never admitting to it. Once you did so it seeped into your face and betrayed you. Once your enemy could see your fear he could use it against you. You had no defense against your own fear.

An ocean of hormones raged through him.

The last thing he had seen before he left Konara Inggres' chambers was Eleana's face. She had struggled off the sofa, and he knew that if he left it a moment longer she would gather him into her embrace. So he turned and left.

Nevertheless, the image of her face stayed with him during the first nerve-racking moments of his journey into the hostile territory of the abbey. He knew he could not afford to have her arms around him because then he would fear for her, and he did not think that he could keep that fear under control. This wild emotion filled him with wonder. The transference into Eleana's baby had been unlike the transference into the Teyj. For one thing, the Teyj had been of his own design and manufacture; he had known precisely what to expect. With the exception of his diminished ability for technomancy, he had been who he always had been: Nith Sahor. For another, Eleana's baby was half-Kundalan. He had felt the differences right away, the heightening of emotions, the relaxing of Gyrgon's tertium-bound rules. And then there was Eleana herself. He had grown fond of her. Now he felt her woven into every strand of his DNA. He was no longer Nith; he never would be again. If he was still part Gyrgon, he was also now an equal part Kundalan. And he was all male rather than, as all Gyrgon were, male and female.

Eleana was his mother, and this was how he experienced her. To say that this was novel for him was an understatement. Gyrgon had no mothers—at least none they could remember. They were taken from the Breeders' wombs while still embryos because the attachments to the machinery of the Comradeship were so complex they had to commence before birth.

He had been trained as a scientist—all Gyrgon were, since science was at the root of their technomagic. But as his father had pointed out to him there had once been Gyrgon who had been artists, writers, painters, dreamers. Nith Sahor's own father had been among them. His father believed that all the great leaps of technomancy had come from the Gyrgon's artistic side, lost generations earlier. He had seen glimmers of these artistic traits in his own son.

Sahor had understood none of this until now.

Now he saw that there were things that ran deeper than science, that contrary to what he had grown up believing the Cosmos was an infinitely mysterious place for the simple reason that it was not ruled by science. Science was created by V'ornn in an attempt to explain the Cosmic mysteries. To be sure, some of them could be answered; otherwise, Gyrgon would never have created gravships and ion cannons. But those deeper mysteries for which they searched, questions that still confounded them, would remain forever beyond the realm of technomancy.

Miina knew the answers to those mysteries, he was convinced of that. Possibly the archdaemons did as well.

The corridor he had been following debouched onto a grassy courtyard. On the other side rose the temple facade behind which, Konara Inggres had said, Horolaggia was carefully plotting the demise of the Ramahan. He could sense all around him tiers of spectral faces, drawn in righteous anger. He could feel their enmity. An enmity the Ramahan Mother had toiled for centuries to keep from her charges. All her work had gone for nought. This was the lesson Nith Sahor had gleaned from his extensive readings of Kundalan lore. Even the most conscientious of mothers cannot protect her child from the vicissitudes of life. The best she can do is prepare her child to make his or her own decisions. And the only way to do that is to teach her child right from wrong. It was only now as Sahor that he understood that Gyrgon never had parents to teach them the difference.

The Ja-Gaar growled low in its throat, and it pulled him forward across the dark, sere grasses of solstice night toward the lair of the archdaemon. Sahor had no fear for himself, but his hearts beat fast in his chest for his mother. He longed to see her again. He realized that from the time of his birth until this moment he had never been apart from her. There was a hollow place inside him into which only she would fit. He blinked back tears without any understanding of what they were.

He was almost pulled off his feet as the Ja-Gaar strained against its leash. He went up the temple steps in its wake and passed through its mammoth portals. Clusters of low bronze oil lamps shed a ruddy illumination too fitful to penetrate the shadowed corners. A red-jade altar lay broken in two as if by a single rageful blow. The ceiling was swaddled in stifling darkness. The sense of desolation was palpable. The archdaemon Horolaggia had desecrated the temple.

The Ja-Gaar began to move in a circle, Sahor turning at its fulcrum. *If I die now it will be all right,* he thought. *I have penetrated to the very heart of the Kundalan mythos. I have ceased to be a member of the Comradeship. I have entered history, and all the mysteries that lie before me have become moot.*

"Who comes now into Mother's sanctum?"

Horolaggia appeared robed in Giyan's body. Sahor thought it astonishing how the possession had altered her. Possibly it was only now in the end stages that her exquisite face had been twisted by the archdaemon inside. She bore only a passing resemblance to the Ramahan priestess he had known, and he mourned for her.

"Who dares risk Mother's terrible wrath?" Horolaggia in Giyan's body stalked around the raised and shadowy periphery of the temple. "Surely not another Konara. Surely not a Ramahan at all." It was horrifying to see the grin he put on Giyan's face. "A boy? A *V'ornn* boy?"

Sahor ignored the archdaemon's words. He was concerned with his movement because Giyan now came down the marble stairs, her arms wide. Sahor loosed the leash a half meter, and at once the Ja-Gaar sprang forward.

Their movement caused the archdaemon to stop in his tracks. Giyan's whistleflower-blue eyes had turned whitish, as if she were very old or going blind.

"I am not Bartta," Horolaggia said. "I am beloved of many. You would not loose your Ja-Gaar on this flesh."

"I am V'ornn," Sahor said. "I care nothing for Kundalan, Giyan or otherwise. But you archdaemons are a threat to us. I *will* send you back to the Abyss by having the Ja-Gaar rend your host's flesh."

"What cruel injustice is my fate!" Horolaggia cried. "To be imprisoned for eons is terrible in itself, but to be misunderstood is, it seems to me, far worse."

"How many Ramahan have you killed since your escape? It is impossible to misunderstand murder."

"This from a representative of a race of murderers!" Horolaggia thundered. "How dare you seek to confine me to prison when it is you and your kind who should be locked away for all eternity!"

"I have no time to debate ethics with you," Sahor said. "It is minutes before the solstice, minutes before you take possession of Giyan forever. That I cannot allow." For this had been his plan all along. It was why he had convinced them to allow him and not the Nawatir to confront the archdaemon. For, in the end, he knew that Rekkk's undying love for Giyan would prevent him from saving them all by setting loose the Ja-Gaar.

And yet at the crucial moment of decision, he hesitated. He saw Eleana rising before him. What if this were she instead of Giyan? Could he allow the Ja-Gaar to rend her flesh into gobbets?

His indecision was his undoing. He had taken his keen eye off Giyan and now, from behind him, came the false Dar Sala-at, the sauromician Konara Inggres had glimpsed, to bind him and the Ja-Gaar in his venomous spell. His legs were paralyzed and the Ja-Gaar collapsed onto its side in a deep slumber from which no amount of tugging on its invisible chain could rouse it.

"Ah, yes, I can feel it!" Horolaggia cried in exultation. He jerked Giyan's head to the roiling darkness shrouding the ceiling. "Now approaches solstice! Now comes the end!"

The stench of her own burning flesh kept Riane from total unconsciousness. She was curled up in a ball, but still she was burning alive. She tried to reach out, but, imprisoned, she could not move. And then she remembered how she had freed Mother from her sorcerous prison, and she began to put the Venca letters into words, the words into phrases, the phrases into the Star of Evermore. It was very difficult. The pain caused her concentration to waver. She forgot words, forgot what she was doing. Her burning self revived her somewhat, and she forged on. And then she saw the Star of Evermore forming just above her head. Slowly it began to rotate. As it rotated, its points cut the strands of Riane's prison. As the strands were cut, the thorns shrank and vanished with small pops. Faster and faster the Star of Evermore spun, the air around her alive with its energy, and at last it cut through the first strand, and she fell to the cobbles, groaning in pain.

But already Pyphoros was striding toward her, his fingertips crackling with lambent blue ion energy.

"You cannot escape me, Dar Sala-at," he said. "Not now, not when I am so close to my goal." He was only two strides away, leaning forward. "The Veil belongs to me. I will have it."

Behind him, Sornnn had broken into a sprint. He had spied the wand, and now he scooped it up and cast it along the cobbles toward Riane. Riane, half-blind from the sorcerous acid, heard it skittering, and she rolled and reached for it. The wand hit the corner of a cobble raised slightly above the others. It came to an abrupt halt just out of her reach.

"What treachery is this?" Pyphoros turned and pointed and a bolt of ion fire struck Sornnn in the chest, taking him off his feet.

Pyphoros turned back.

Was Sornnn SaTrryn dead? She did not know. But his heroic act had given her a chance. She heaved herself over the cobbles. Her hand grasped the wand, she thumbed the gold button in the required rhythmic pattern, and the infinity-blade opened. It was pale and flickering, and her heart sank. Still, it was the only weapon she had, and she whirled with it. She aimed for his bare skull but he thwarted her, and she twisted the blade in midflight. Its edge bit into the Gyrgon's exomatrix. His glaring red-pupiled eyes looked half-mad, and she could see the archdaemon squirming behind them. He lifted his arm, protecting himself, and she swung again, penetrating to neural-net enhanced flesh. Thick yellow matter oozed, and Pyphoros bellowed.

Riane felt no triumph in this small victory, for the agony was cresting in every centimeter of her burned skin. Her bones felt as if they had turned to jelly.

She tried to concentrate on pushing the infinity-blade deeper, but the pain was overwhelming all her senses. Her eyes fluttered up, and Pyphoros redoubled his efforts. She staggered and almost lost her grip on the infinity-blade. She saw it flickering, or maybe it was her vision going in and out of focus, she no longer knew. Gritting her teeth, she put all her weight behind the infinity-blade, felt it sink another several centimeters into the Gyrgon.

Pyphoros screamed again. He was close enough to touch the Veil, but something was preventing him from getting near it. She thought she knew what it was. Her own life force.

She slid to her knees and heard laughter. It was Pyphoros, laughing at her because she was dying, because the Veil of a Thousand Tears would be his.

She could not allow that.

The infinity-blade was pale as death. A moment more and it would flicker out and Pyphoros would have his victory. She dug in her robe with a trembling, half-numb hand and drew out the fulkaan stone. It had reinvigorated the infinity-blade before, it should again.

But before she could bring it against the wand, Pyphoros grabbed hold of her hand.

"What is that?" he shrieked. "Give it to me!"

She felt a tremor from the stone, and a heat commenced where it lay in the center of her curled palm. And then she heard it again, that same howl, low and deep, that had so terrified Minnum.

Kurgan whirled. "What in the name of N'Luuura is that?"

The thing was on the move. It was coming.

At that moment, the infinity-blade flickered and died, and Riane felt the full crushing weight of the archdaemon's spell. Her consciousness followed the path of the infinity-blade, and she knew she was dying.

In the slow spiral downward, she returned again to the high tor of the Djenn Marre. The sun shone brilliant and white out of a sky so vividly blue it made her eyes ache. One cloud only wreathed the very top of the peak she was climbing. And then the cloud moved, coming toward her. Its outline resolved itself, and she saw that it was not a cloud at all but a great bird, black and white, as clouds often are. This giant avian opened its beak and uttered a howl, low and deep. With a great fluttering of its wings it turned itself, and with one taloned foot snatched her into the air, swinging her up onto its back . . .

The howl, deep and low, shattering the utter stillness of Za Hara-at, brought her back to consciousness. The bird came in low, sweeping over the ruins of the buildings surrounding the plaza. It headed straight for her, its startling violet eyes instantly assessing the scene.

Now she realized what it was, this bird. It was the fulkaan, the messenger and companion of the Prophet Jiharre. Riane—the original Riane who had lost her memory just before the essence of Annon had been migrated into her—had known Jiharre. She felt the burning of the stone in her palm. Now she knew why the fulkaan was keyed to her movements. It had been drawn by the stone into which its image had been graven.

Pyphoros ignored the fulkaan. He had his hands on the Veil. With Riane so close to death her life force was no longer strong enough to keep him from it. He was tugging at it, trying desperately to unwind it from her.

The fulkaan was swooping down very fast, its talons extended. At the last instant, Pyphoros threw back his head, opened his mouth. A jet of sorcerous flame struck the fulkaan. It screamed but still came on, and Pyphoros reached up, grabbed at it. Its wings beat frantically, and it began to veer away. Pyphoros lunged, ripping out one of its talons, which he flung away in disgust.

Though the fulkaan had failed to harm him, the brief respite gave Riane a chance to gather her strength.

But Pyphoros had drawn Nith Batoxxx's fingers into petrified claws, which renewed their pulling on the Veil with the archdaemon's own unnatural power. Riane had regained some strength, but not nearly enough. Slowly but surely the Veil began to unwind.

Riane brought her hands up, but they had no feeling. Pyphoros was going to get his heart's desire. His relentless tugging was unwinding it further. There was nothing more she could do.

And then she saw Kurgan coming up from behind Pyphoros. She saw the enmity in his eyes. At first, she mistook it for a hatred of her. His arm came up, and she saw the fulkaan's bloody talon. As he clutched it in his fist, she could appreciate just how huge it was. With an inarticulate cry, Kurgan plunged the talon into the Gyrgon's right eye. Pyphoros roared. Blood spurted out and, Riane saw, something else, squirming and dark, a glimpse of Pyphoros' real form.

Riane felt the release of the archdaemon's sorcerous grip on her, and she at once cast Earth Granary, feeling the strength flowing back into her life force, the barrier between the Veil and those who wished to misappropriate it.

Pyphoros was whirling this way and that in his pain, but she could already sense him, searching for her, wanting to return his ion grip on her. She saw the bloody eye, the essence of him squirming deep in the socket, and she cast Fly's-Eye, a Kyofu spell that caused a chaos of thoughts. It was a rather simple enchantment that Pyphoros would counter quickly, but she needed time now, as with each passing second her life force was returning.

She concentrated on his wounded eye, the one weakness in his sorcerous armor—the Gyrgon host body. She had been running through the passages of the two sacred books, *Utmost Source* and *The Book of Recantation*, the sources for Eye Window, the most potent form of sorcery. There was a spell called O-Rhen Ka. It opened Red-Jade Gate. It was an exceptionally dangerous spell because it unbalanced the emotional trine of anger, lust, and love. Madness, destruction, chaos were often the result.

Riane began the incantation, hesitated. She felt the grip of Pyphoros' spell returning and, fixing his wounded eye in her sight, she completed the incantation.

For a moment, nothing happened. The night seemed suspended on the back of an unnatural hush. Then, all at once, Pyphoros reared back. His hands clutched at his face, but it was too late. The eye socket sundered, his skull cracked open. As Riane ripped it away, Pyphoros came pouring out. The Gyrgon was dancing a kind of death jig. As the blood drained from him, so was Pyphoros' grip on life in this realm loosened. At that moment, the Gyrgon's life thread winked out. Pyphoros screamed as his essence poured out of the top of the shattered Gyrgon skull. He shot up into the darkness of the night in a knot of ebon mist. The fulkaan howled, his great beak snapping at it before he swerved away.

For a moment, Riane knelt dazed. Her stomach threatened to rise up into her throat, and felt an intense dizziness, the aftermath of casting O-Rhen Ka. It was then that she realized that she no longer had the Veil.

At first, she thought it was a dream. Then she looked up, blinking, and saw Kurgan, a vulpine grin on his face, the Veil in his arms.

"How sweet is fate, Dar Sala-at," he said, "that you have delivered to me my weapon against the Gyrgon."

For a moment, the two of them, old friends, baleful enemies, love and hate, loyalty and betrayal, were joined in an eerie symmetry neither understood.

"Give it to me," Riane said. "You have no idea—"

"Perhaps not," Kurgan said craftily. "But I mean to find out."

As Riane rose to confront him, he whipped out his dagger. "Come on," he hissed. "Killing you would be a bonus."

Riane lunged forward, but her dizziness put her off-balance. She saw the dagger rushing toward her. And then Kurgan's knees buckled, and he pitched forward onto the plaza paving, insensate. Riane saw Minnum standing just behind where the regent had been, his fist white where he had struck the regent a mighty blow to his side.

"I told you I wouldn't fail you," he said.

"Thank you," she whispered.

Riane gathered the Veil into her arms and sighed, as each and every one of the thousand tears seemed to speak to her at once. She made her way to the center of the plaza and, as it directed her, lifted the Veil above her head, wove it into the same knotlike pattern as that of the power-bourn intersection deep beneath her feet.

The Veil opened like the petals of the flower and out burst the thousand tears of the Sacred Dragons, fountaining up into the night, piercing time and space, becoming one with them. The tears were everywhere and nowhere. Silvery fish, they jumped and danced, slipping between worlds, dimensions, forming the complex skein of tiny incremental moments unseen and therefore unknown, moments that nevertheless exist, that become the real weight and force and power of history.

There was almost nothing left of the Ras Shamra. Horolaggia had bled her to the point of death. He had sewn her up tight in the Malasocca's sorcerous cocoon. Each filament pierced her flesh, bringing her renewed agony. The hour of winter solstice was arriving. Moment by precious moment, Giyan felt her life force leaching into the bloody ground of Otherwhere.

Her death was upon her and she wept, but not for herself. Death had no meaning for her. She wept for her child, Annon, removed from his life by her own hand. She wept for Riane, the unknown and untried vessel into which she had been forced to put him. For solstice was upon her, and that meant Riane had failed and, failing, was doubtless dead.

It was the cruelest fate that kept a mother from protecting her child.

She turned her reddened eyes, all but swollen shut, into the heavens of Otherwhere and waited for the white dragon avatar to swallow her whole, to rend her with its sorcerous teeth, to turn her into nourishment for its archdaemon.

But the white dragon did not appear, and then she noticed that the red fulminations behind the mountain range had vanished, as had the ceaseless cries of the multitude of daemons pressing at the barrier between Realms, for it was a fact that Otherwhere existed in that mysterious place between Realms.

Instead, a single tear appeared, shining silver. Then others joined it, and they all burst apart, again and again in a rainstorm that drenched her in blessed moisture. Wherever the tears struck—and they struck everywhere—the archdaemon's filaments were transmogrified into healing balm, until the Ras Shamra was restored.

The inverted triangle crumbled to dust, and with it Giyan's long imprisonment. Opening its long beak, the Avatar gave a shout of ecstasy that shook the very ground of Otherwhere. It soared high up into the tumultuous sky and, seeing that all was as it had ever been, it vanished.

38

Band of Outsiders

The oil lamps had lost their ruddy hue, and the suffocating darkness rushed out of the temple interior as if propelled by sunlight. The sauromician was burning. There was no fire, as such, and certainly no flames. Nevertheless, he burned, blackening where he stood, his face twisted in a rictus of death shock.

Suddenly, miraculously, Horolaggia was gone, vanished.

The Ja-Gaar, held at the very end of its leash, sprang forward as soon as it arose from the sauromician's spell. Sahor could not have stopped it even had he wanted to.

The Ja-Gaar leapt through the air, its muscles bunched, and bounded to where Giyan stood. There, it rubbed its sleek flank against her thigh. She reached down and put her hand into its open mouth and it growled, a soft, gurgly sound not unlike that of an infant feeding.

"You are back," Sahor said.

Giyan, as beautiful and radiant as she had ever been, came slowly toward him, the Ja-Gaar padding obediently at her side. Her eyes were their luminous whistleflower-blue.

She stood regarding Sahor for some time. "You look like your father. Almost. I know those eyes," she said. "Those are Eleana's eyes."

"I am her child," Sahor said. "But you know who I am."

She held out her hand, and he took it.

"You are no longer Nith," she said.

"I am neither V'ornn nor Kundalan. I am Other."

Her eyes were shining. "Yes." She turned, then, a certain tension coming into her frame. Sahor looked over his shoulder. The temple contained sixteen columns. She was staring at one as if it was alive.

"Come out," she said softly.

Rekkk stayed behind the column.

"Have you so soon lost your nerve, Nawatir?" Sahor called, not unkindly.

"I followed Sahor here," Rekkk said. His pulse was racing so fast that he could scarcely draw breath. Surely her powers as a great sorceress would enable her to recognize his spirit. But what if not? Worse, what if she could not love his altered countenance? His legs grew weak at the thought. "Something deprived me of the pleasure of killing the sauromician."

"The Veil of a Thousand Tears," she said, craning her neck for a glimpse of him. "Thank Miina."

"Then the Dar Sala-at was successful."

"She was." Giyan took a step toward him. "Nawatir, I need to see you."

"I am not—" All at once, gathering his courage, he appeared, blond, bearded his dark red cape swirling around him. His ice-blue eyes locked onto hers.

"You see, Giyan," Sahor said, "like me, he is not as he once was."

"Giyan—" Rekkk's hoarse voice was almost a heartrending cry.

"I see that Miina has taken you up in Her arms."

"The arms of Yig," he said.

She moved toward him. "To think," she whispered, trembling, "that you have encountered one of Her Sacred Dragons."

"I hardly know—" He stroked his beard, which still seemed odd to him. "The changes—"

She stopped in front of him. She could feel his tension, his uncertainty, his terror, and she reached out, her fingertips tracing with the delicacy and precision of the sightless the new ridges and rills, until she had absorbed every minute detail of his face.

"Inside still beat Rekkk's hearts. Inside still flowers Rekkk's love. This I know in the very depths of my spirit."

He held out his hand, and she took it.

"Take me in your arms, Nawatir. You are my beloved forever."

She had begun to weep, and Rekkk embraced her with great emotion. He held her tight and kissed her tenderly on her forehead, cheeks, and lips. Her hands traced the new contours of his face.

"Yes," she whispered. "Yes, yes, yes."

Rekkk felt as if at last his world was whole. "I thought I might never see you again."

"Did you lose faith, dearest?"

"On the contrary." He drew her scent into the very essence of his being. He was in an agony of longing for her, and he held her tight for a very long time. "I found it."

Riane opened her eyes. An intense warmth suffused her body, washing away all pain, even the memory of pain. She turned her head, saw Thigpen crouched tensely a short distance away from her. The Rappa was staring at her. Her whiskers were twitching incessantly.

"Little dumpling, are you all right?"

"Of course I am," Riane said. She rubbed her forehead, stared down at her arms and legs, which bore not the slightest trace of burns. She looked up. "Why are you crouched so far away?"

"It's that damned bird," Thigpen snorted. "He won't let me near you."

Riane turned to look. The fulkaan had placed himself near her as if he was her guardian. His predator's head was turned toward the Rappa. Riane laughed and rose on one elbow. "Come on now. He won't bite you."

Thigpen came hesitantly forward, and the fulkaan glanced at Riane, who nodded. A little ways away, she could see Perrnodt and Minnum tending to Sornnn SaTrryn while Kurgan looked on.

Noting the direction of her glance, Thigpen said, "The V'ornn Sornnn SaTrryn will be fine. The tears are healing him as they have healed you."

"And what of Giyan?" Riane said, sitting up suddenly as anxiety gripped her. "Is she alive or dead?"

"Have faith." Thigpen curled up against Riane's side. "The tears came before the stroke of solstice."

Riane could see Kurgan looking at her, and it gave her an eerie feeling. He could not know that the essence of his childhood friend and his family's enemy lurked inside Riane's body. And yet he recognized something in her, something he had not seen when they had encountered each other months earlier in the caverns below the regent's palace in Axis Tyr. She thought she saw in his eyes the desire to come over, to talk to her, but he did not. In any event, Perrnodt said something to him, and he turned his attention to her.

Thigpen's tail beat a brief tattoo. "At least we won't have daemons to worry about anymore."

Riane sighed. "I wish I could believe that."

"What do you mean?"

"They helped build this city. I think there is more to their story than we yet know."

The fulkaan stirred, his head swinging around, his piercing violet eyes taking in the two of them. He made a sound low in his throat, and Riane touched his wing tip.

Sensing the Rappa's unease, she stroked Thigpen's soft, thick fur. "This bird is a fulkaan. It seems I knew him in another time, another place."

She rose to her feet at the fulkaan's cry. Glancing around, she noted that Kurgan had suddenly vanished. In all the commotion, Thigpen had no idea what had happened to him and neither, it seemed, did anyone else. Shrugging, she trotted over to the cenote, Thigpen at her heels. The cenote, she noted, was now filled with water. The tears of the Dragons had collected there. She heard a distant calling, and she leaned in, immersing her hands. Immediately, the Veil began to reconstitute, weaving around her in the complex pattern of its own design.

But the cenote remained empty for only a matter of moments. All at once, water could be seen, glistening as it rose from some mysterious source far underground. Now the water was beginning to churn, and she steeled herself, alarmed that Pyphoros had somehow found a way back to this realm.

Her concern was misplaced, for now rising out of the cenote she saw Giyan, who was quickly followed by Eleana, a Kundalan warrior tall as a V'ornn, and another.

The Dar Sala-at ran into Giyan's arms, and they swung each other around.

"Thank you, Teyjattt," she whispered so only Riane could hear. "I owe you my life."

"No more than I owe you mine," Riane said. "How did you get here?"

"The cenotes form a sorcerous connecting network if you know how to navigate through them." She told Riane how they had been in the Abbey of Floating White, what had transpired there, and how, using the cenote in the black Kell, they had arrived at Za Hara-at. "Konara Inggres is now firmly in charge of the abbey," she concluded.

"We have nothing more to fear," Giyan told her. "When the tears of the Dragons sent Pyphoros and Horolaggia back to the Abyss, they destroyed the lesser daemons who had possessed the Ramahan and re-sealed the Portal I inadvertently cracked when I violated the Nanthera."

"The seal on the Portal at the bottom of First Cenote is also broken," Riane told her. "Pyphoros came through there long before you performed the Nanthera."

Giyan's expression clouded with concern for a moment. "As soon as we are fully recovered, we shall have to journey there to discover what created the rift in the first place."

With her arm around her child, she took Riane to meet the new Nawatir and Eleana's son. It took some time for Riane to grow accustomed to Rekkk Hacilar's new image. Though she thanked Rekkk and Sahor for their courage, she spoke to them a little distractedly. At the periphery of her vision was Eleana, her body strong and hard, her warrior's eyes watching shyly, angrily, warily. There hung between them the unpleasantness of their last parting, and something more that Riane could not bear to examine. How many times over the past weeks had she run their reunion dialogue in her mind? Always, it ended awkwardly and badly.

Only Minnum and Sornnn hung back. Neither felt they quite belonged in the company of the others. They had quickly gotten to know one another, and each was impressed with the other's knowledge of the Korrush and of Za Hara-at in particular. Sornnn said that he was considering staying on in Za Hara-at and wondered if Minnum would be interested in a job helping him explore the ancient citadel. When Minnum readily agreed to this excellent proposal, he felt this clinched his decision to remain at the dig.

In the morning, he would send a message to the Resistance asking for news of Marethyn. While it was true that he was anxious over her well-being, he also admired her ardor to perform on her own merits. And so his fear for her became a precious thing. A measure of the gravity of his love. He found that he liked to look at it from time to time to remind himself how radically his life had changed. He experienced it as a stillness inside him, as if she had placed her trust there, a gift, for him to discover after she was gone.

*   *   *

W hen Riane had introduced Giyan to Perrnodt there was an immediate spark that would have been of particular interest to her had she not had Eleana on her mind. She left them deeply engaged in sorcerous matters and approached Eleana, who was talking quietly with Sahor. Eleana had her arm circling his narrow waist. Sahor, intuitive almost to the point of telepathy, nodded to Riane, kissed his mother on the cheek, and sauntered off to try and communicate with the fulkaan. He had already become a lover of strange Kundalan creatures, seeing in them another key to Kundala's secrets that Nith Sahor had been searching for ever since he had landed on the planet.

For some time Riane and Eleana stood facing one another in silence.

"I am sorry for the way I left you," Riane began. "I never should have done that."

Eleana said, "I see the way you look at Sahor. I know you see Kurgan in his face. I beg you not to hate him."

"He has your eyes."

"He is not Kurgan. He never will be."

They walked a little farther away from the rest of the band of outsiders, as they now thought of themselves. In the east, the sky was lightening. There was a glow, faint but distinct in the intensely clear air of the Korrush, and it was possible to look at the Great Rift in the Djenn Marre and believe it was only kilometers away.

"I thought you hated me, that I had offended you."

"No," Riane said at once. "Never."

"Then why were you suddenly so cold?"

"I was . . . afraid."

Eleana looked at her. "Afraid of what?"

Riane could not say what she knew had to be said.

"We are not friends," Eleana said softly. "We were never *just* friends."

Riane felt her throat close up.

"Looking death in the face changes you. It changes who you are; it changes the entire tenor of life. What we have been through during the last weeks makes this absolutely clear to me." Eleana came closer. "No matter the consequences, we must not be afraid to say what is in our hearts." Her face had never been more beautiful nor more grave. "When we are apart I dream about you. When I see you I cannot cool my body down. I have never felt this way about anyone." She stopped, only a few paces away. "Say something. Please."

What could she say? Riane asked herself. *I love you* was so inadequate. Not to mention frightening in all its implications. She felt Annon's dagger—the one Eleana had given him—heavy on her hip. Unconsciously, she gripped its butt. She was not Annon anymore, and yet when she was with Eleana, when she saw that look in her eyes, she knew that Annon was still vibrantly alive.

Her obdurate silence was a mistake, however, because it caused Eleana to ask the question she most dreaded.

"Why did Lady Giyan give you Annon's dagger?"

"Because . . ." The words stuck in Riane's throat. All around them, it seemed that Za Hara-at was coming to life. A stirring, a sighing filled the air. It might have been the fluttery swoosh of finbat wings or the sweep of a gentle dawn breeze. But it also might be something ancient, sleeping for eons, coming, at last, awake. "Because you are right. Because we are not friends. Because we never were *just* friends."

APPENDIX I
Major Characters

KUNDALAN

Giyan—Bartta's twin sister, Ramahan mistress of Eleusis Ashera, mother of Annon Ashera

Bartta—Giyan's twin sister; Ramahan konara, head of the Dea Cretan

Riane—female orphan; the Dar Sala-at

Eleana—female from upcountry

Ramahan at the Abbey of Floating White:

Konara Urdma—head of the abbey

Konara Lyystra

Konara Inggres

Malistra—Kyofu sorceress

Thigpen—a Rappa, one of Miina's sorcerous creatures

Mother—high priestess of Miina

Courion—Sarakkon captain, friend of Kurgan Stogggul

Jerrlyn—head of the Fourth Agrarian Commune District (largest of seven)

Minnum—curator of Museum of False Memory

Cushsneil—Kundalan dialectician (deceased)

Majja—female Resistance fighter

Basse—male Resistance fighter

Kasstna—leader of Majja and Basse's Resistance cell

V'ORNN

Annon Ashera—eldest son of Eleusis Ashera

Kurgan Stogggul—eldest son of Wennn Stogggul

Marethyn Stogggul—Kurgan's younger sister

Terrettt—Kurgan's brother

Tettsie—Marethyn's maternal grandmother

Sornnn SaTrryn—prime factor, scion to Bashkir spice-trader family

Bronnn Pallln—Bashkir ally of Stogggul family, passed over for Prime Factor

Nith Sahor—a Gyrgon

Nith Batoxxx—a Gyrgon, see the Old V'ornn

Rekkk Hacilar—once Khagggun pack-commander, now Rhynnnon

Olnnn Rydddlin—once Rekkk Hacilar's first-captain, now star-admiral

The Old V'ornn—Kurgan's mentor; Nith Batoxxx's alter ego

Line-General Lokck Werrrent—Khagggun commander of the Land of Sudden Lakes corridor

Wing-Adjutant Mukc Wiiin—his adjutant

Glll Fullom—venerable Bashkir

Attack-Commandant Accton Blled

First-Captain Kwenn—Kurgan's Haaar-kyut

Dobbro Mannx—a solicitor-Bashkir of Tettsie's acquaintance

Petre Aurrr—Sornnn SaTrryn's mother

Rada—Tuskugggun owner of Blood Tide tavern

Jesst Vebbn—Genomatekk in charge of the 'recombinant experiments'

Kirlll Qandda—Deirus, Sornnn SaTrryn's friend

Nith Isstal, Nith Batoxxx's protégé

Nith Recctor—ally of Nith Sahor

Nith Settt—ally of Nith Batoxxx

Nith Nassam—ally of Nith Batoxxx

IN THE KORRUSH

The Five Tribes:

Jeni Cerii—warlords—territorial capital: Bandichire

Gazi Qhan—mystics—territorial capital: Agachire

Rasan Sul—spice merchants—territorial capital: Okkamchire

Bey Das—historians/archaeologists—many at Im-Thera, abutting main dig of Za Hara-at

Han Jad—artisans—territorial capital: Shelachire

Othnam—member of Ghor sect of Gazi Qhan

Mehmmer—Othnam's sister

Paddii—ally of Othnam's and Mehmmer's

Makktuub—kapudaan of Gazi Qhan

Jiharre—Prophet of the Gazi Qhan
Tezziq—Makktuub's first concubine
Mu-Awwul—Ghor elder
Perrnodt—Ramahan priestess

APPENDIX II
V'ornn Societal Makeup

The V'ornn are a strict caste society. Their castes are broken down thusly:

GREAT CASTE:
Gyrgon—technomages
Bashkir—merchant-traders
Genomatekk—physicians

LESSER CASTE:
Khagggun—military
Masagggun—engineers
Tuskugggun—females
Deirus—physicians relegated to taking care of the dead and the insane

In the V'ornn language, triple consonants have a distinct sound. With the execptions noted below, the first two letters are always pronounced as a W, thus:

Khagggun—Kow-gun

Tuskugggun—Tus—kew-gun

Mesagggun—Mes—ow—gun

Rekkk—Rawk

Wennn Stogggul—Woon Stow-gul

Kinnnus—Kew—nus

okummmon—ah-kow-mon

okuuut—ah-kowt

K'yonnno—Ka-yow-no

salamuuun—sala-moown

Olnnn—Owl-lin

Sornnn—Sore-win

Hadinnn—Had-ewn

Bronnn Pallln—Brown Pawln

Teyjattt—Tey-jawt

seigggon—sew-gon

skcettta—shew-tah

Looorm—Loo-orm

bannntor—bown-tor

Kannna—Kaw-na

Kefffir Gutttin—Kew-fear Gew-tin

Ourrros—Ow-ros

Jusssar—Jew-sar

Julll—Jew-el

Nefff—Newf

Batoxxx—Bat-owx

Boulllas—Bow-las (as in, to tie a bow)
Hellespennn—Helle-spawn
Argggedus—Ar-weeg-us

When a Y directly precedes the triple consonant, it is pronounced ew, as in *shrewd*, thus:
Rydddlin—Rewd-lin
Rhynnnon—Rew-non
Tynnn—Tewn
but:
K'yonnno—Ka-yow-no

Because the following word is not of the V'ornn language, the triple consonant does not follow the above rules, thus:
Centophennni—Chento-fenny

Triple vowels are pronounced twice, creating another syllable, thus:
Haaar-kyut—Ha-ar-key-ut
leeesta—lay-aysta
numaaadis—mu-ma-ah-dis
liiina—lee-eena
N'Luuura—Nu-Loo-oora

Normally, in V'ornn the *y* is pronounced *ea*, as in *tear*, thus:
Gyrgon—Gear-gon

Sa is pronounced *Say*, thus:
Sa Trryn—Say-Trean

Kha is pronounced *Ko*, while *Ka* is pronounced *Ka*, thus:
Khagggun—Kow-gun
Kannna—Kaw-na

Ch is always hard, thus:
Morcha—More-ka
Bach—Bahk

Skc is always soft, thus:
skcetta—shew-tah